"Jim B_____ world-b_____
_____iew

_____ bestselling author
_____r's Codex Alera novels

FURIES OF CALDERON

"Epic fantasy in the best way, inspired by Tolkien."
—Simon R. Green, *New York Times* bestselling author of
The Good, the Bad, and the Uncanny

"Filled with plot twists and white-knuckle suspense, this is a ripping good yarn that delivers terrific magic and nonstop action."
—Deborah Chester, national bestselling author of *The Crown*

"A fascinating world and magic system . . . the start of a promising series."
—*Locus*

PRINCEPS' FURY

"As is the case with Dresden, Mr. Butcher has the uncanny ability to make his Codex Alera Realm seem real; as he understands it is in the subtle details . . . an exciting fantasy thriller."
—*Midwest Book Review*

"Rousing . . . No less powerful than his intense battle scenes [are] Butcher's vivid characterizations."
—*Publishers Weekly* (starred review)

continued . . .

"A treat for action fans and series followers."　　—*Booklist*

"When it comes to versatility and rousing storytelling, Butcher is in a class by himself."　　—*Romantic Times* (top pick)

CAPTAIN'S FURY

"Sharp tactical plotting, hazardous cross-country travel, and a dash of sardonic humor mark Butcher's fourth Codex Alera novel...Butcher deftly deploys intrigue, conflicted loyalties, and hairbreadth action to excellent effect. Few writers balance military realism and cinematic swashbuckling with so much skill or wit."　　—*Publishers Weekly*

"The fourth Codex Alera novel further develops the world and characters of its predecessors and confirms Butcher's mastery of action-filled fiction."　　—*Booklist*

"I couldn't put this one down . . . great work."　　—*SFRevu*

CURSOR'S FURY

"Butcher deftly mixes military fantasy and political intrigue in the rollicking third Codex Alera book . . . Readers will cheer Tavi every step of the way."　　—*Publishers Weekly*

"The author of the Dresden Files modern fantasy series is equally familiar with old-style 'classic' fantasy, demonstrating his skill in complex plotting and vivid world-crafting to masterly effect."　　—*Library Journal*

"Plenty of military action and some interesting revelations about Tavi's past make this one of the best volumes yet in this entertaining series."　　—*Locus*

ACADEM'S FURY

"A fun romp of a book . . . The action is fast and furious."
—*SFRevu*

"Solid world-building, intriguing characters, and vivid action make this a solid addition to a marvelously entertaining series."
—*Publishers Weekly*

"High adventure with engaging characters and a satisfying conclusion."
—*Locus*

Praise for Jim Butcher's The Dresden Files

"What's not to like about this series? . . . I would, could, have, and will continue to recommend [it] for as long as my breath holds out. It takes the best elements of urban fantasy, mixes them with some good old-fashioned noir mystery, tosses in a dash of romance and a lot of high-octane action, shakes, stirs, and serves."
—*SF Site*

"Filled with sizzling magic and intrigue . . . will have fans rapidly turning the pages."
—*Booklist*

"Intense and wild . . . a skillful blend of urban fantasy and noir, sure to satisfy any fan and leave [him] begging for more."
—*The Green Man Review*

"A haunting, fantastical novel that begins almost as innocently as those of another famous literary wizard named Harry."
—*Publishers Weekly*

"Good fun for fans of dark fantasy mystery."
—*Locus*

FURIES OF CALDERON

BOOK ONE OF THE CODEX ALERA

JIM BUTCHER

ACE BOOKS, NEW YORK

THE BERKLEY PUBLISHING GROUP
Published by the Penguin Group
Penguin Group (USA) Inc.
375 Hudson Street, New York, New York 10014, USA
Penguin Group (Canada), 90 Eglinton Avenue East, Suite 700, Toronto, Ontario M4P 2Y3, Canada
(a division of Pearson Penguin Canada Inc.)
Penguin Books Ltd., 80 Strand, London WC2R 0RL, England
Penguin Group Ireland, 25 St. Stephen's Green, Dublin 2, Ireland (a division of Penguin Books Ltd.)
Penguin Group (Australia), 250 Camberwell Road, Camberwell, Victoria 3124, Australia
(a division of Pearson Australia Group Pty. Ltd.)
Penguin Books India Pvt. Ltd., 11 Community Centre, Panchsheel Park, New Delhi—110 017, India
Penguin Group (NZ), 67 Apollo Drive, Rosedale, North Shore 0632, New Zealand
(a division of Pearson New Zealand Ltd.)
Penguin Books (South Africa) (Pty.) Ltd., 24 Sturdee Avenue, Rosebank, Johannesburg 2196, South Africa

Penguin Books Ltd., Registered Offices: 80 Strand, London WC2R 0RL, England

This is a work of fiction. Names, characters, places, and incidents either are the product of the author's
imagination or are used fictitiously, and any resemblance to actual persons, living or dead, business
establishments, events, or locales is entirely coincidental. The publisher does not have any control
over and does not assume any responsibility for author or third-party websites or their content.

FURIES OF CALDERON

An Ace Book / published by arrangement with the author

PRINTING HISTORY
Ace hardcover edition / October 2004
Ace mass-market edition / July 2005
Ace premium edition / May 2010

Copyright © 2004 by Jim Butcher.
Map by Priscilla Spencer.
Excerpt from *Burning Alive* copyright © by Longshot LLC.
Cover art by Steve Stone.
Cover design by Rita Frangie.
Interior text design by Kristin del Rosario.

ISBN: 978-0-441-01268-8

ACE
Ace Books are published by The Berkley Publishing Group,
a division of Penguin Group (USA) Inc.,
375 Hudson Street, New York, New York 10014.
ACE and the "A" design are trademarks of Penguin Group (USA) Inc.

PRINTED IN THE UNITED STATES OF AMERICA

22   21   20   19   18   17   16

For my son, hero in training.
And in memory of my father, a hero in truth.

ACKNOWLEDGMENTS

I would like to thank Jennifer Jackson, for her excellent advice in reworking this book. Thanks to my wife and son, as always, and to the beta reading asylum. And a whole ton of thanks to all those insane men and women of the International Fantasy Gaming Society, with whom I have spent many a weekend slaying and being slain in return. Keep your foam swords dry, carry lots of water on course, and watch out for snakes and head shots.

But can anyone tell me why I have to keep carrying these whistles into games?

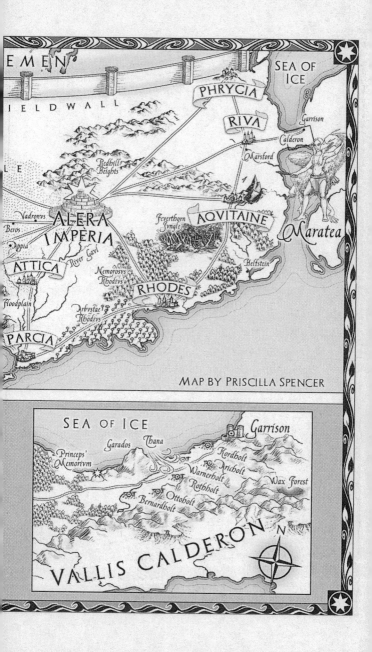

MAP BY PRISCILLA SPENCER

The course of history is determined not by battles, by sieges, or usurpations, but by the actions of the individual. The strongest city, the largest army is, at its most basic level, a collection of individuals. Their decisions, their passions, their foolishness, and their dreams shape the years to come. If there is any lesson to be learned from history, it is that all too often the fate of armies, of cities, of entire realms, rests upon the actions of one person. In that dire moment of uncertainty, that person's decision, good or bad, right or wrong, big or small, can unwittingly change the world.

But history can be quite the slattern. One never knows who that person is, where he might be, or what decision he might make.

It is almost enough to make me believe in Destiny.

—FROM THE WRITINGS OF GAIUS PRIMUS
FIRST LORD OF ALERA

"Please, Tavi," wheedled the girl in the predawn darkness outside the steadholt's kitchen. "Just this one little favor?"

"I don't know," said the boy. "There's so much work today."

She leaned in closer to him, and the boy felt her slender body mold against his, soft and flower-scented and delightful. She pressed her mouth to his cheek in a slow kiss and whispered in his ear, "I'd be very grateful."

"Well," the boy said. "I'm not sure if, um."

She kissed his cheek again and whispered, "Please."

His heart pounded more quickly, and his knees felt weak. "All right. I'll do it."

·◆◆◆◆· CHAPTER 1

Amara rode atop the swaying back of the towering old gargant bull, going over the plan in her head. The morning sun shone down on her, taking the chill out of the misty air and warming the dark wool of her skirts. Behind her, the axles of the cart squeaked and groaned beneath their loads. The slave collar she wore had begun to chafe her skin, and she made an irritated mental note to wear one for a few days in order to grow used to it, before the next mission.

Assuming she survived this one, of course.

A tremor of nervous fear ran down her spine and made her shoulders tighten. Amara took a deep breath and blew it out again, closing her eyes for a moment and blocking out every thought except for the sensations around her: sunlight on her face, swaying of the pungent gargant's long strides, creaking of the cart's axles.

"Nervous?" asked the man walking beside the gargant. A goad dangled from his hand, but he hadn't lifted it in the entire trip. He managed the beast with the lead straps alone, though his head barely came to the old bull's brown-furred thigh. He wore the plain clothes of a peddler: brown leggings, sturdy sandals, with a padded jacket over his shirt, dark green on homespun. A long cape, tattered green without embroidery, had been cast over one shoulder as the sun rose higher.

"No," Amara lied. She opened her eyes again, staring ahead.

Fidelias chuckled. "Liar. It's not a brainless plan. It might work."

Amara shot her teacher a wary glance. "But you have a suggestion?"

"In your graduation exercise?" Fidelias asked. "Crows, no. I wouldn't dream of it, *academ*. It would cheapen your performance."

Amara licked her lips. "But you think that there's something I should know?"

Fidelias gave her a perfectly guileless look. "I did have a few questions."

"Questions," Amara said. "We're going to be there in a few moments."

"I can ask them when we arrive, if you prefer."

"If you weren't my *patriserus*, I would find you an impossible man," Amara sighed.

"That's sweet of you to say," Fidelias replied. "You've come a long way since your first term at the Academy. You were so shocked when you found out that the Cursors did more than deliver missives."

"You love telling that story even though you know I hate it."

"No," Fidelias said with a grin. "I love telling that story *because* I know you hate it."

She looked down at him archly. "This is why the Cursor Legate keeps sending you *away* on missions, I think."

"It's a part of my charm," Fidelias agreed. "Now, then. My first concern—"

"Question," Amara corrected.

"Question," he allowed, "is with our cover story."

"What question? Armies need iron. You're an ore smuggler, and I'm your slave. You heard there was a market out this way, and you came to see what money could be made."

"Ah," said Fidelias. "And what do I tell them when they ask where I got the ore? It isn't just found by the roadside, you know."

"You're a Cursor Callidus. You're creative. I'm sure you'll think of something."

Fidelias chuckled. "You've learned delegating skills, at least. So, we approach this renegade Legion with our precious ore." He nodded back toward the squeaking cart. "What's to stop them from simply taking it?"

"You're the harbinger of a smuggling network, representing several interests in the business. Your trip is being watched, and if the results are good, others might be willing to bring supplies as well."

"That's what I don't understand," Fidelias said, his expression innocent. "If this is indeed a renegade Legion, as rumors say, under the command of one of the High Lords, in preparation for overthrowing the Crown— aren't they going to object to *any* word about them getting out? Good, bad, or indifferent?"

"Yes," Amara said. She glanced down at him. "Which works in our favor. You see, if you *don't* return from this little jaunt, word is going to spread all around Alera about this encampment."

"Inevitable, since word would get out anyway. One can hardly keep an entire Legion secret for long."

"It's our best shot," Amara said. "Can you think of anything better?"

"We sneak in close, furycraft ourselves into the camp, obtain evidence, and then run like the crows were after us."

"Oh," Amara said. "I considered it. I decided it was too brainless and predictable."

"It has the advantage of simplicity," Fidelias pointed out. "We recover the information, give solid evidence to the Crown, and let the First Lord launch a more comprehensive antisedition campaign."

"Yes, that's *simpler*. But once whoever is running this camp knows that they have been observed by the Cursors, they will *simply* disperse and move their operations elsewhere. The Crown will *simply* spend money and effort and lives to pin them down again—and even then, whoever is putting out the money to field their own army might *simply* get away."

Fidelias glanced up at her and let out a low whistle. "So you want to get in and out undetected, get word to the Crown and—then what?"

"Lead a few cohorts of Knights Aeris back down here and crush them where they lie," Amara said. "Take prisoners, have them testify against their backers, and wrap it all up right here."

"Ambitious," he commented. "Very ambitious. Very dangerous, too. If they catch on to us, they'll kill us. And it's reasonable to expect that they'll have Knights as well—and that they'll be on the lookout for a Cursor or two."

"That's why we don't get caught," Amara said. "We play the poor, greedy smuggler and his slave, haggle for all the money we can get from them, and leave."

"And keep the money." Fidelias frowned. "On general principle, I like any mission that involves a profit. But, Amara—there's a lot that could go wrong with this one."

"We are the First Lord's messengers, are we not? His eyes and ears?"

"Don't quote the Codex at me," Fidelias snapped, annoyed. "I was a Cursor before your mother and father had called their first furies. Don't think that because the First Lord has taken a shine to you that you know better than I do."

"You don't think it's worth the risk?"

"I think there's a lot you don't know," Fidelias said, and he looked very old for some reason. Uncertain. "Let me handle this, Amara. I'll go inside. You stay here, and I'll pick you up on the way out. There's no reason to risk both of us."

"No," she said. "In the first place, this is my mission to run. In the second, you will need your full attention to play your role. I'll be able to make observations—especially from up here." She slapped the gargant's broad back, and the bull snorted up a small whirlwind of trail dust in response. "I'll also be able to watch our backs. If I get the impression that they're onto us, we can get out of there."

Fidelias muttered, "I thought we'd just use this guise to pose as travelers. Get close and slip into the camp after dark."

"When no one else is coming in and when we're certain to arouse suspicion if we're seen?"

He blew out a breath. "All right," he said. "All right. We'll do it your way. But you're gambling yourself with the crows."

Amara's stomach fluttered again, and she pressed a hand to it, trying to will the fear away. It didn't leave. "No," she said. "I'm gambling both of us."

Though the gargant's plodding steps seemed slow, each covered many strides of a man. The great beast's thick-clawed feet ate the miles, though it stripped the bushes and trees of leaves along the way, adding to the layers of blubbery fat beneath its hide. If allowed, the humpbacked beast would wander into the richest forage and graze, but Fidelias handled it with a sure and calm hand, keeping the beast moving along the road, while he marched at the quickstep beside it.

A mile more, by Amara's estimation, and they had come within picket distance of the insurgent Legion's camp. She tried to remind herself of her role—that of a bored slave, sleepy and tired from days of travel—but it was all she could do to keep the mounting tension from rising in her shoulders and back. What if the Legion turned out to be nothing more than rumor, and her intelligence gathering mission, so carefully outlined and planned, turned out to be a costly waste of time? Would the First Lord think less of her? Would the other Cursors? It would be a paltry introduction into the ranks, indeed, if she stepped forth from the Academy and straight into a monumental blunder.

Her anxiety grew, like bands of iron stretching across her shoulders and back, and her head started to pound from the tension and the glare of the sun. Had they made a wrong turn? The old trail they followed seemed too well-worn to be an abandoned lumber track, but she could be wrong. Wouldn't they be seeing the smoke of a Legion's fires? Wouldn't they hear something, by now, if they were as close as she suspected?

Amara was on the verge of leaning down to call to Fidelias, to ask his advice, when a man in dark tunic and leggings and a gleaming breastplate and helmet melted into view beneath the shadows of a tree on the road no more than ten strides in front of them. He appeared without a warning of any kind, without a flicker of movement—furycrafting involved, then, and a fairly skilled woodworking at that. He was a giant of a man, nearly seven feet tall, and he bore a heavy blade at his side. He lifted one gloved hand and said, his tone bored, distant, "Halt."

Fidelias clucked to the gargant bull, slowing the beast to a stop after several steps. The wagon creaked and groaned, settling onto its wheels beneath the weight of the ore.

"Good morning to you, master," Fidelias called, his voice oozing nervous, obsequious good cheer. The senior Cursor doffed his hat and clutched it in his slightly trembling hands. "And how are you doing on this fine autumn morn?"

"You're on the wrong trail," said the dark giant. His tone was dull, almost sleepy, but he laid a hand on the hilt of his weapon. "This land is not friendly to travelers. Turn around."

"Yes, master, of course we will, master," Fidelias simpered. "I am but a humble peddler, transporting his cargo in the vain hope of finding a ready market. I have no desire for trouble, good master, only for the chance to attempt to recoup my losses on this most excellent but lamentably ill-timed bounty of—" Fidelias rolled his eyes skyward and dragged one foot through the dust of the trail. "Iron." He shot the giant a sly smile. "But, as you wish, good master. I'll be on my way."

The dark man stepped forward and said, "Hold, merchant."

Fidelias glanced back at him. "Master?" he asked. "Can I perhaps interest you in a purchase?"

The dark man shrugged. He stopped a few feet from Fidelias and asked, "How much ore?"

"Nearly a ton, good master. As you can see, my poor gargant is all but done in."

The man grunted, eyeing the beast, and swept his gaze up it, to Amara. "Who is this?"

"My slave, good master," Fidelias said. His voice took on a cringing, wheedling tone. "She's for sale, if you like the look of her, master. A hard worker, skilled at weaving and cooking—and more than capable of giving a man an unforgettable night's pleasure. At two lions, she's surely a bargain."

The man snorted. "Your hard worker rides while you walk, merchant. It would have been smarter for you to travel alone." He sniffed. "And she's as skinny as a boy. Take your beast and follow me."

"You wish to buy, master?"

The soldier gave him a look and said, "I didn't ask you, merchant. Follow me."

Fidelias stared at the soldier and then swallowed, an almost audible gulp. "Aye, aye, master. We'll be only a pace or three behind you. Come on old boy." He picked up the gargant's lead straps in shaking fingers and stirred the great beast into motion again.

The soldier grunted and turned to start walking back down the road. He let out a sharp whistle, and a dozen men armed with bows appeared from the shadows and brush on the sides of the trail, just as he had a moment before.

"Keep the men here until I return," the man said. "Stop anyone from coming past."

"Yes, sir," one of the men said. Amara focused on that one. The men all wore the same outfits: black tunics and breeches with surcoats of dark green and dark brown. The speaker, in addition, wore a black sash around his waist—as the first soldier had. Amara checked around, but none of the other men wore a sash—only those two. She made a mental note of it. Knights? Possibly. One of them had to have been a strong woodcrafter, to have hidden so many men so thoroughly.

Crows, she thought. *What if this rebel Legion turns out to have a full contingent of Knights to go with it? With that many men, that many powerful furycrafters, they could be a threat to any city in Alera.*

And, as a corollary, it would mean that the Legion had powerful backing. Any furycrafter strong enough to be a Knight could command virtually what price he wished for his services. They could not be casually bought by any disgruntled merchant set to convince his Lord or High Lord to lower taxes. Only the nobility could afford the cost of hiring a few Knights, let alone a contingent of them.

Amara shivered. If one of the High Lords was preparing

to turn against the First Lord, then there were dark days ahead indeed.

She looked down at Fidelias, and he glanced up at her, his face troubled. She thought she could see the reflection of her own thoughts and fears there in his eyes. She wanted to talk to Fidelias, to ask him for his thoughts on the matter, but she couldn't break her role now. Amara ground her teeth and dug her fingers into the pad of the gargant's riding saddle and tried to calm herself again, while the soldier led them to the camp.

Amara kept her eyes open as the gargant's plodding steps brought them around a bend in the trail and over a small hill, into the valley beyond and behind it. There, the camp spread out before them.

Great furies, she thought. *It looks like a city.*

Her mind took down details as she stared. The camp had been constructed along standard Legion lines: a stake-wall and ditch fortification built in a huge square, surrounding the soldier's encampment and stores. Tents of white fabric had been erected within, row after row of them, too many for easy counting, laid out in neat, precise rows. Two gates, opposite one another, led into the camp. The tents and lean-tos of the camp's followers spread out around it in ragged disarray, like flies buzzing around a sleeping beast.

People were everywhere.

On a practice field beside the camp, entire cohorts of men were drilling in formation combat and maneuvers, ordered about by bawling centurions or men in black sashes mounted on horseback. Elsewhere, archers riddled distant targets with their arrows, while furymasters drilled other recruits in the application of their basic warcraftings. Women moved among the camp, as well—washing clothes at a stream that passed by, mending uniforms, tending fires, or simply enjoying the morning sunlight. Amara saw a couple of women wearing sashes of black, on horseback, riding toward the practice field. Dogs wandered about the camp and set up a tinny racket of barking upon scenting the gargant as it came over the hill. To one side of the camp, not far from the stream, men and women had established what looked like a small market, vendors hawking wares from makeshift stalls and spreading them upon blankets on the ground.

"You're here between breakfast and lunch," said the soldier. "Or I'd offer you some food."

"Perhaps we'll take lunch with you, master," Fidelias said.

"Perhaps." The soldier stopped and looked up at Amara, studying her with quiet, hard eyes. "Get her down. I'll send out a groom or two to care for your beast."

"No," insisted Fidelias. "I'll be keeping my goods with me."

The soldier grunted. "There's horses at the camp, and they'll go mad if they smell this thing. It stays here."

"Then I stay here," insisted Fidelias.

"No."

"The slave then," he said. "She can stay here with the beast and keep him quiet. He'd spook if strange hands cared for him."

The soldier squinted at him, hard and suspicious. "What are you up to, old man?"

"Up to? I'm protecting my interests, master, as any merchant would."

"You are in our camp. Your interests are no longer an issue, are they?" The soldier put no particular emphasis on his words, but he laid one hand on the hilt of his sword.

Fidelias drew himself up, voice shocked and outraged. "You wouldn't dare."

The soldier smiled. His smile was hard.

Fidelias licked his lips. Then shot a glance up at Amara. She thought she saw something in it, some kind of warning, but he only said, "Girl. Get down."

Amara slid down off of the back of the beast, using the leather straps to help lower herself down its flanks. Fidelias clucked to it and jerked down on its straps, and the gargant settled lazily to earth with a contented rumble that shook the ground nearby. It leaned its great head over, tore up a mouthful of grass, and began chewing on it, huge eyes half-closed.

"Follow me," the soldier said. "You too, slave. If either of you gets more than three strides away from me, I'll kill you both. Do you understand?"

"I understand," said Fidelias.

"I understand, master," echoed Amara, keeping her eyes lowered. They followed the soldier then and crossed the stream at a shallow ford. The water was cold and flowed quickly over Amara's ankles. She shivered, goose-flesh racing up and down her legs and arms, but kept pace with Fidelias and the soldier.

Her mentor dropped back beside her and murmured, very low, "Did you see how many tents?"

She jerked her head in a nod. "Close."

"Well kept and neat, too. This isn't a gang of malcontent Steadholders. Professional military."

Amara nodded and whispered, "Serious money behind them. Is it enough for the First Lord to bring it to the Council?"

"An accusation without anyone to accuse?" Fidelias grimaced and shook his head. "No. We have to have something that incriminates someone behind it. Doesn't have to be ironclad, but we need something tangible."

"Do you recognize our escort?"

Fidelias shot her a look. "Why? Do you?"

Amara shook her head. "I'm not sure. Something about him seems familiar."

The other nodded. "They call him the Sword."

Amara felt her eyes widen. "Aldrick ex Gladius? Are you sure?"

"I've seen him in the capital, in the past. I saw his duel with Araris Valerian."

Amara glanced up at the man ahead of them, careful to keep her voice down. "He's supposed to be the greatest swordsman alive."

"Yes," said Fidelias. "He is." Then he cuffed her along the head and said, loud enough for Aldrick to hear, "Keep your lazy mouth shut. I'll feed you when I please and not a second before. Not another word."

They walked in silence, then, into the camp. Aldrick led them through the camp's gate and down the main path dividing the camp in half. He turned left and led them to what Amara knew would be, in an Aleran Legion's camp, the commander's tent. A large tent sat there, and two *legionares* stood outside it, breastplates gleaming, armed with spears in their hands and swords at their belts. Aldrik nodded to one of them and went inside. He appeared a moment later and said to Fidelias,

"You. Merchant. Come inside. The commander wants to speak to you."

Fidelias stepped forward, and Amara moved to follow him. Aldrick put a hand on Fidelias's chest and said, "Just you. Not the slave."

Fidelias blinked. "You expect me to just leave her out here, good master? It could be dangerous." He shot Amara a glance, which she did not miss. A warning. "To leave a pretty young girl in a camp full of soldiers."

Aldrick said, "You should have thought of that before you came here. They won't kill her. Get inside."

Fidelias looked back at her and licked his lips. Then he stepped forward into the tent. Aldrick looked at Amara for a moment, his eyes distant, cool. Then he stepped back inside. A moment later, he came back to the opening of the tent, dragging a girl with him. She was petite, even emaciated, and her clothes hung off of her like a scarecrow's. The collar around her neck, even on its smallest sizing, hung loosely. Her brown hair looked dry, brittle as hay, and she had dust on her skirts, though her feet were clean enough. Aldrick shoved the girl out unceremoniously and said, "Business." Then he tugged the flap of the tent closed and went back inside.

The girl tumbled to the ground, along with a woven basket, and landed with a soft cry in a tangle of basket and skirts and frizzy hair.

Amara knelt down beside the girl and asked, "Are you all right?"

"Oh, fine," the girl snapped. She rose shakily to her feet and kicked a puff of dust at the tent with her toe. "Bastard," she muttered. "Here I am trying to clean things up for him, and he throws me around like a sack of meal." Her eyes sparkled with defiance, and she turned to Amara. "I'm Odiana."

"Amara," she responded, feeling her mouth tug up at the corners. She glanced around her, licking her lips, and thought for a moment. She needed to see more of the camp. Try to find something she could take with her. "Odiana, is there any place to get a drink around here? We were traveling for hours, and I'm parched."

The girl tossed her frizzy hair over one shoulder and sniffed at the commander's tent. "What's your pleasure? There's some cheap beer, but it's mostly water. Optionally, we could get a drink of water. And if none of that suits you, I think there's some water."

"I'll have the water," Amara said.

"A dry wit," Odiana noted. She hooked the handle of the basket over the crook of her arm and said, "This way." Then she turned and walked with a kind of bristling, crackling energy through the camp, toward the opposite gate. Amara caught up with her, eyes flicking around. A troop of soldiers came jogging by, boots striking the ground in rhythm, and the two girls had to skip back, between two tents, to let them pass.

Odiana sniffed. "Soldiers. Crows take them all, I am sick to death of soldiers."

"Have you been here long?" Amara asked.

"Since just after the new year," the other said. "But there are rumors that we'll be leaving soon."

Amara's heart pounded. "Going where?"

Odiana looked at her with an amused smile. "You've not been around soldiers much, have you. It doesn't matter where you go. *This,*" she gestured broadly, at the camp, "never changes. It's the same, if you're down by the ocean or up at the Wall. And the men never change. The sky never changes, and the earth doesn't change enough to notice. This is it."

"But still. You get to go to new places. See new things."

"Only new stains on uniforms," said Odiana. The soldiers passed, and the girls stepped out onto the track again. "But I've heard further north and maybe east a ways."

"Toward Aquitaine?"

Odiana shrugged. "Is that what's that way?" She walked along and opened the basket as they neared the stream, rummaging around inside. "Here," she said. "Hold these." She thrust a pair of dirty plates into Amara's arms. "We can wash them while we're here. Crows, soldiers are so messy. But at least the *legionares* keep their tents clean." She fished out a bone and threw it toward a passing dog. Then an apple core, from which she took a judicious nibble before wrinkling up her nose and tossing it into the stream. Next came a piece of paper, which she hardly glanced at before flicking it aside.

Amara turned and stomped the paper flat with her foot, before the wind could catch it. Then she bent over and picked it up.

"What?" asked Odiana. "What are you doing?"

Amara picked up the paper. "Well. Um. It hardly seems like a good idea to just toss it on the ground if you're trying to clean up."

"If it isn't in the camp, no one will care," Odiana said. She tilted her head to one side, watching, as Amara unfolded the paper and studied the writing inside. "You can read?" the slave asked.

"Some," said Amara, distracted. She read the note, and her hands started shaking as she did.

Legion Commander, Second Legion,

You are hereby ordered to strike camp and make for the rendezvous point. You should arrive no later than the tenth full moon of the year, in preparation for winter. Maintain drilling until you march, and dispatch the men in the usual manner.

There was more, but Amara skipped over it, barely skimming, to see what was at the bottom.

Atticus Quentin, High Lord of Attica

Amara's breath caught in her throat, her heart racing. Her fears were true. Insurrection. Rebellion. *War.*

"What does it say?" asked Odiana. She shoved another plate into Amara's hands and said, "Here. Put these in the stream."

"It says . . ." Amara fumbled with the plates, moving to the water's edge and leaning down to drop them in. "It, uh. I can't really read it." She fumbled with the note, sliding it away, into one of her shoes, mind racing with the implications.

"You know," said Odiana, voice bright and cheerful, "I think you're lying. You don't often run into literate slaves. Who ask questions about troop movements. And who are also politically learned enough to realize the wider implications of one little note. That's the kind of thing you expect from, oh, I don't know." Her voice dropped, and she almost puffed, "One of the Cursori."

Amara stiffened and turned just in time to catch Odiana's bare heel in the chin. Pain flashed through her, dull and hot. The wasted-seeming girl had far more strength than Amara would have credited to her, and the blow stunned Amara and sent her tumbling back into the stream.

She stood up out of it, shaking water from her face and eyes and drawing in a breath to cry out to her furies—but water rushed down into her mouth and nose as she inhaled, and she began choking. Amara's heart raced with sudden panic, and she reached up to her face—only to find it coated to above the nose with a thin layer of water. She scraped at it with her fingers, but it didn't flow down, and she couldn't clear it away. She struggled and choked, but only more water rushed in, coating her like a layer of oil. She couldn't breathe. The world began to glaze over with darkness, and she grew dizzy.

The letter. She had to get the letter out, back to the First Lord. The proof he would need.

She made it to the bank before the water filling her lungs made her collapse. She writhed, smothering on dry land, and found herself staring at Odiana's bare, clean feet.

Amara looked up as the wasted slave girl stared down at her, a gentle smile on her face. "You needn't worry, love," the girl said. And she began to change. Her sunken cheeks filled out. The gangling limbs gained rondure, beauty. Hips and breasts began to curve in enticing lines, filling out the clothes she wore. Her hair grew a bit longer, lustrous, darker, and she shook it out with a little laugh, before kneeling down next to Amara.

Odiana reached out and stroked fingers through Amara's damp hair. "You needn't worry," she repeated. "We aren't going to kill you. We need you." Calmly, she removed a black sash from the basket, and tied it around her waist. "But you Cursori can be a slippery breed. We'll take no chances. Just go to sleep, Amara. It will be so much easier. And then I can send all the water back and let you breathe again."

Amara struggled and fought for simple breath, but none came. Darkness gathered, points of light appearing before her eyes. She clutched at Odiana, but her fingers had gone nerveless and weak.

The last thing she saw was the beautiful watercrafter leaning down to place a gentle kiss upon her forehead. "Sleep," she whispered. "Sleep."

And then Amara sank down, into the blackness.

⊶⊶ CHAPTER 2

Amara woke, buried to her armpits in the earth. Loose dirt had been piled over her arms and into her hair. Her face felt thick, heavy, and after a moment, she realized that her entire head had been liberally smeared with mud.

She struggled to gather her wits through a pounding headache, piecing together fragments of memories and perceptions until, with a dizzying rush of clarity, she remembered where she was and what had happened to her.

Her heart started to thud hard in her chest, and fear made her buried limbs feel cold.

She opened her eyes, and bits of dirt fell into them, so that she had to blink quickly. Tears formed to wash the dirt out. After a few moments, she was able to see.

She was in a tent. The commander's tent in the camp, she guessed. Light poured into it through a gap in the flap that served as a door, leaving the tent's interior described in terms of dimness, shadow, and dark.

"You awake yet?" croaked a voice from behind her. She turned her head, trying to look. She could barely see Fidelias out of the corner of her eye, but he was there, hanging in a cage of iron bars by straps around his shoulders and outstretched arms, leaving his feet dangling a good ten inches off of the floor. He had a swelling bruise on his face, and his lip had been split and was crusted with dry blood.

"Are you all right?" Amara whispered.

"Fine. Apart from being beaten, captured, and scheduled for torture and interrogation. You're the one who should be worried."

Amara swallowed. "Why me?"

"I think this can safely be considered a failing mark in your graduation exercise."

Amara felt her mouth curve into a smile, despite the circumstances. "We have to escape."

Fidelias tried to smile. The effort split his lip some more, and fresh blood welled. "Extra credit—but I'm afraid you won't get the chance to collect on it. These people know what they're doing."

Amara tried to move, but she couldn't struggle up out of the earth. She barely succeeded in freeing her arms enough to move them—and even so, they were thickly encrusted with dirt. "Cirrus," she whispered, sending her thoughts out, toward her fury. "Cirrus. Come pull me out."

Nothing happened.

She tried again. And again. Her wind fury never responded.

"The dirt," she said, finally, and closed her eyes. "Earth to counter air. Cirrus can't hear me."

"Yes," Fidelias confirmed. "Nor can Etan or Vamma hear me." He stretched his toes toward the ground, but could not reach. Then he banged his foot against the iron bars of his cage.

"Then we'll have to think our way out."

Fidelias closed his eyes and let out a slow breath. Then he said, gently, "We've *lost,* Amara. Checkmate."

The words hit Amara like hammers. Cold. Hard. Simple. She swallowed and felt more tears rising, but blinked them away with a flash of anger. No. She was a Cursor. Even if she was to die, she'd not give the enemies of the Crown the satisfaction of seeing her tears. She thought for a fleeting moment of her home, the small apartment back in the capital, of her family, not so far away, in Parcia by the sea. More tears threatened.

She took up her memories, one by one, and shut them away into a dark, quiet place in her mind. She put everything in there. Her dreams. Her hopes for the future. The friends she'd made at the Academy. Then she shut them away and opened her eyes again, clear of tears.

"What do they want?" she asked Fidelias.

Her teacher shook his head. "I'm not sure. This isn't a smart move for them. Even with these precautions, if something went wrong, a Cursor could slip away and be gone as long as he was still alive."

The flap of the tent flew open, and Odiana walked through it, smiling, her skirts swirling in the drifting dust the daylight revealed. "Well then," she said. "We'll just have to remedy that."

Aldrik came in behind her, his huge form blocking

out the light completely for a moment, and a pair of *legionares* followed him. Aldrick pointed at the cage, and the two went to it, slipped the hafts of their spears through rings at its base, and lifted it, between them, carrying it outside.

Fidelias shot Aldrick a hard look and then licked his lips, turning to Amara. "Don't be proud, girl," he told her, as the guards started carrying him out. "You haven't lost as long as you're alive."

Then he was gone.

"Where are you taking him?" Amara demanded. She swept her eyes from Odiana to Aldrick and tried not to let her voice shake.

Aldrick drew his sword and said, "The old man isn't necessary." He went outside the tent.

A moment later, there was a sound not unlike a knife sinking into a melon. Amara heard Fidelias let out a slow, breathless cry, as though he had tried to hold it in, keep from giving it a voice, and been unable to do so. Then there was a rustling thump, something heavy falling against the bars of the cage.

"Bury it," Aldrick said. Then he came back into the tent again, sword in hand.

The blade shone scarlet with blood.

Amara could only stare at the blade, at her teacher's blood. Something about it would not register on her mind. It simply would not accept the fact of Fidelias's death. The plan should have protected them. It should have gotten them close and away safely again. This wasn't how it was supposed to happen. It had never happened like that at the Academy.

She tried to stop the tears from coming, to push

Fidelias's face into the dark place in her mind with all the other things she cared about. They only flooded over her again, bursting free, and as they did, the tears came with them. Amara did not feel clever anymore, or dangerous, or well trained. She felt cold. And dirty. And tired. And very, very alone.

Odiana let out a soft sound of distress and came to Amara's side. She knelt down with a white kerchief in her hand and reached out to dab at Amara's tears. Her fingers were gentle, soft. "You're making clean spots, love," the woman said, her voice gentle.

Then she smiled as, with her other hand, she crushed fresh earth against Amara's eyes.

Amara let out a cry and thrust out a hand to defend herself, but she wasn't able to stop the water witch. She swept at her burning eyes with her dirt-crusted hands, but it did her little good. Her fear and sorrow turned itself into furious anger, and she started screaming. She screamed every imprecation she could at them, incoherent, and she sobbed into the earth, making muddy tears that burned her eyes. She thrashed her arms and struggled, useless against the grip of the ground she was buried in.

And in answer, there was only silence.

Amara's anger faded, taking with it whatever strength she had left. She shook with sobs that she tried to hold in, that she tried to keep hidden from them. She couldn't. Shame made her face burn, and she knew that she was trembling, from cold and from terror.

She started blinking her eyes again, slowly gaining back her vision—and as she did, she saw Odiana standing over her, just out of arm's reach, smiling, her dark eyes glittering. She took a step, and with one dainty, bare foot, she kicked more dust into Amara's eyes. Amara twisted and turned her head away, avoiding it, and shot the woman a hard glare. Odiana hissed and drew her foot back to kick again, but Aldrick's voice rumbled across the tent first.

"Love. That's enough."

The watercrafter flashed Amara a venomous look and retreated from her, to the back of Aldrick's stool, where she rested her hands on his shoulders in a slow caress, eyes on Amara the entire while. The warrior sat with his sword across his lap. He ran a cloth along its length and then tossed the rag onto the earth. It was stained with blood.

"I'll make this simple," Aldrick said. "I'm going to ask you questions. Answer them truthfully, and I'll let you live. Lie to me or refuse to answer, and you'll wind up like the old man." He looked up, his expression entirely without emotion, and focused on Amara. "Do you understand?"

Amara swallowed. She nodded her head, once.

"Good. You've been in the palace recently. The First Lord was so impressed with the way you handled yourself during the fires last winter, he asked you to visit him. You were taken to his personal chambers, and spoke with him. Is that true?"

She nodded again.

"How many guards are stationed in his inner chambers?"

Amara stared at the man, her eyes widening. "What?"

Aldrick looked up at her. He stared for a long and silent moment. "How many guards are stationed in the First Lord's inner chambers?"

Amara let out a shaking breath. "I can't tell you that. You know I can't."

Odiana's fingers tightened on Aldrick's shoulders. "She's lying, love. She just doesn't *want* to tell you."

Amara licked her lips, and then spat mud and dirt onto the floor. There was only one reason to be asking questions about the inner defenses of the palace. Someone wanted to take direct action against the First Lord. Someone wanted Gaius dead.

She swallowed and bowed her head. She had to stall them, somehow. Stall for time. For the opportunity to find a way to escape—or failing that, to kill herself before she could reveal the information.

She quailed at that thought. Could she do that? Was she strong enough? Before, she would always have thought she was. Before she had been taken, captured, imprisoned. Before she had listened to Fidelias die.

Don't be proud, girl. Fidelias's last words to her came back, and she felt her resolve weaken further. Had he been telling her to cooperate with them? Did he think the First Lord was already doomed?

And, she thought, should she? Should she go along with them? Offer to throw in? Should she cast aside what she had been taught, what she believed, for the sake of preserving her life? She couldn't attempt a ploy—not with Odiana there. The water witch would be able to sense whether or not she was sincere, damn her.

Everything was lost. She had led Fidelias to his death. Gambled his life and lost it. She had lost her own life as well. She might be able to redeem one of them, if she cast her lot with her captors.

Another surge of anger flooded through her. How

could she even be thinking such a thing? How could he have *died*? Why hadn't he seen it coming, warned her—

Amara lifted her head abruptly and blinked her eyes several times. Her anger evaporated. Why hadn't Fidelias warned her, indeed. The trap had been too well laid. They had been taken too cleanly. Which meant—

Which meant that Aldrick and Odiana had known that they were coming. And by logical extension . . .

She focused her eyes on the pair of them and swallowed, lifting her chin a bit. "I won't tell you," she said, and kept her voice calm. "I'll not tell you another thing."

"You'll die," said Aldrick, rising.

"I'll die," Amara agreed. "You and your water witch can go to the crows." She took a breath and then raised her voice, honed it to a dagger's edge. "And so can you, Fidelias."

She had a moment to take satisfaction in the flicker of surprise in Aldrick's eyes, the simple gasp that came from Odiana. Then she turned her eyes to the door and narrowed them, keeping her face set in a cold, hard mask.

Fidelias appeared in the doorway, his clothes still rumpled. He had washed the "bruise" off the side of his face, and was holding a clean white cloth to his bleeding lip. "I told you she'd see through it," he murmured.

"Do I get graded on it, *patriserus*?" Amara asked.

"A plus." Fidelias stared at her, and his mouth twisted into a grimace. "You will tell us what you know about the palace, Amara. It might get ugly before it's over, but you will. This is checkmate. You don't have to make it hard on yourself."

"Traitor," Amara said, dropping the word lightly.

Fidelias flinched. His grimace darkened to a scowl.

Odiana looked back and forth at the sudden silence and then offered, in a helpful tone, "Shall I fetch the branding irons, then?"

Fidelias turned to them and said, "I think we've been ham-handed enough, for the moment." He focused his eyes on Aldrick and said, "Give me a few moments alone to talk to her. Maybe I can get her to see common sense."

Aldrick regarded Fidelias with a steady gaze and then shrugged. "Very well," he said. "Love, would you?"

Odiana stepped around Aldrick's stool, eyes focused intently upon Fidelias. "Do you intend to assist her in any way or to attempt to prevent us from discovering what we wish to know?"

Fidelias's mouth quirked up at the corner, and he focused on the water witch. "Yes, I do. No, I don't. The sky is green. I am seventeen years old. My real name is Gundred." The woman's eyes widened, and Fidelias tilted his head to one side. "You can't tell if I'm lying, 'love'? I'm not some child. I've been deceiving crafters stronger than you since before you were born." His gaze flicked past Odiana to Aldrick. "It's in my best interest to get her to talk. In for a sheep, in for a gargant."

The swordsman smiled, a sudden show of white teeth. "Not going to offer me your word of honor?"

The Cursor's lip curled. "Would it matter if I did?"

"I'd have killed you had you tried," Aldrick said. "A quarter hour. No more." He rose, taking Odiana gently by one arm, and led her out of the tent. The water witch shot a glare at both Fidelias and Amara and then left.

Fidelias waited until they were gone, then turned to Amara and simply looked at her, saying nothing.

"Why?" she asked him. "*Patriserus*. Why would you do this to him?"

He stared at her, expression not changing. "I have served as a Cursor for forty years. I have no wife. No family. No home. I have given my life to protecting and defending the Crown. Carrying its messages. Discovering its enemies' secrets." He shook his head. "And I have watched it fall. For the past fifteen years, the house of Gaius has been dying. Everyone knows it. What I have done has only prolonged what is inevitable."

"He is a good First Lord. He is just. And as fair as anyone could want."

"This isn't about what's *right*, girl. It's about reality. And the reality is that Gaius's fairness and justice has made him a great many powerful enemies. The southern High Lords chafe at the taxes he lays upon them to maintain the Shieldwall and the Shield Legion."

"They always have," Amara interjected. "It doesn't change that the taxes are necessary. The Shieldwall protects them as well. Should the icemen come down from the north, they would perish with the rest of us."

"They do not see it that way," Fidelias said. "And they are willing to do something about it. The House of Gaius is weakened. He has no heir. He has named no successor. So they strike."

Amara spat, "Attica. Who else?"

"You don't need to know." Fidelias crouched down in front of her. "Amara. Think about this. Ever since the Princeps was killed, it has been in motion. The house of Gaius died along with Septimus. The royal line was never very fertile—and the death of his only child has been taken as a sign by many. His time is past."

"That doesn't make it *right*."

Fidelias snarled, "Get it out of your *head,* child." He spat on the ground, face twisted in fury. "The blood I've shed in the Crown's service. The men I've killed. Is that any more *right*? Are their deaths vindicated because I serve this First Lord or that one? I've killed. I've done worse, in the name of protecting the Crown. Gaius *will* fall. Nothing can stop that now."

"And you have cast yourself in the role of . . . what, Fidelias? The slive that rushes in to poison the wounded buck? The crow that soars down to peck at the eyes of helpless men not yet dead?"

He looked at her, eyes flat, and gave her a smile empty of mirth or joy or meaning. "It's easy to be righteous when you are young. I could continue to serve the Crown. Perhaps prolong the inevitable. But how many more would die? How many more would suffer? And it would change nothing but the timing. Children, like you, would come in my place—and have to make the decisions I am making."

Amara let her voice resonate with contempt. "Thank you, so much, for *protecting* me."

Fidelias's eyes flashed. "Make this easy on yourself, Amara. Tell us what we want to know."

"Go to the crows."

Fidelias said, without anger, "I've broken men and women stronger than you. Don't think that because you're my student, I won't do it to you." He knelt down to look her in the eyes. "Amara. I'm the same man you've known. We've shared so much together. Please." His hand reached for her grime-covered one. She didn't fight his grasp. "Think about this. You could throw in with us. We could help make Alera bright and peaceful again."

She returned his gaze, steady. Then said, very quietly, "I'm already doing that, *patriserus*. I thought you were, too."

His eyes hardened like ice, brittle, distant, and he stood up. Amara lurched forward, clutching at his boot. "Fidelias," she said, pleading. "Please. It isn't too late. We could escape, now. Bring word back to the Crown and end this threat. You don't have to turn away. Not from Gaius, And . . ." She swallowed and blinked back tears. "And not from me."

There was a pained silence.

"The die is cast," Fidelias said, finally. "I'm sorry you couldn't be shown reason." He turned, jerking his leg from her grasp, and walked out of the tent.

Amara stared after him for a moment, then looked down, to where she had palmed the knife Fidelias always kept in his boot, the one he didn't think she knew about. She shot a glance up to the tent, and as soon as the flap fell, she started attacking the dirt that pinned her. She heard voices talking outside, too quietly to be understood, and she dug furiously.

Dirt flew. She broke it up with the knife and then frantically dug it away with her hands, shoving it away, making as little noise as she possibly could—but even so, her gasps for breath grew louder, bit by bit, as she dug.

Finally, she was able to move, just a little, to shove enough loose earth forward to wriggle. She reached out an arm and dug the knife into the ground as hard as she could and used it as a piton to pull herself forward, up. A sense of elation rushed through her as she strained and wriggled and finally started snaking her way free of the confining earth. Her ears sang with a rush of blood and excitement.

"Aldrick," snapped the water witch, from outside the tent. "The *girl!*"

Amara stumbled to her feet and looked around wildly. She lurched across the tent to grasp the hilt of a sword lying across a table, a light gladius little longer than her own forearm, and spun, her body still clumsy from its imprisonment, just as a dark shape filled the entry flap to the tent. She lunged out at it, muscles snapping together to drive the point of the sword in a vicious stroke at the heart of the figure in the doorway—Aldrick.

Steel glittered. Her blade met another and was swept aside. She felt her point bite flesh, but not much or deeply. She knew she had missed.

Amara threw herself to one side, as Aldrick's blade rose in a swift counter, and was unable to escape a cut that flashed a sudden, hot agony across her upper left arm. The girl rolled beneath a table and came up on the far side from Aldrick.

The big man came into the tent and stalked her, pausing across the table. "Nice lunge," he commented. "You pinked me. No one's done that since Araris Valerian." He smiled then, that wolfish show of teeth. "But you aren't Araris Valerian."

Amara never even saw Aldrick's blade move. There was a hissing hum, and then the table fell into two separate pieces. The man started toward her, through them.

Amara threw the gladius at him and saw his sword rise up to parry it aside. She dove for the back of the tent, now holding only the little knife, and with a quick move slashed a hole in the canvas. She slipped through it and heard herself whimpering in fear as she began to run.

She flashed a glance behind her as Aldrick's sword opened the back side of the tent in a pair of strokes and he came through after her. "Guards!" the swordsman bellowed. "Close the gate!"

Amara saw the gate start to swing shut, and she slipped to one side, ran down a row of white tents, gathering up her skirts in one hand, cursing that she hadn't seen fit to disguise herself as a boy so that she could have worn breeches. She looked behind her. Aldrick still pursued, but she had left him behind, like a doe outstripping a big slive, and she flashed a fierce smile at him.

Caked dirt fell off of her as she ran for the nearest wall, and she prayed that she could get enough of it off of her to call to Cirrus. A stepladder rose up to the wall's defensive platform in front of her, and she took it in three long strides, barely touching it with her hand.

One of the *legionares,* a guard on the wall, turned toward her and blinked in shock at her. Amara made a ridge of her hand, let out a shout, and drove her hand into the man's throat, never slowing. He tumbled over backward, gagging and choking, and she ran past him, to the wall, and looked over.

Ten feet down to the ground level, and then another seven or eight feet of ditch lay beneath her. A crippling fall, if she didn't land correctly.

"Shoot!" someone shouted, and an arrow hissed toward her. Amara threw herself to the side, grasped the top of the wall with one hand, and vaulted it, throwing herself out into empty space.

"Cirrus!" she called—and felt the stirring of wind

around her, finally. Her fury pressed up against her, turned her body to a proper angle, and rushed down beneath her, so that she landed on a cloud of wind and blowing dust rather than on the hard ground of the ditch.

Amara gained her feet again and ran without looking back, stretching, covering the ground in leaps and bounds. She ran to the north and the east, away from the practice fields, away from the stream, away from where they had left the gargant and its supplies. The trees had been cut to make the walls of the encampment, and she had to run across nearly two hundred strides of broken stumps. Arrows fell around her, and one struck through a hanging fold of her skirts, nearly tripping her. She ran on, with the wind always at her back, Cirrus an invisible presence there.

Amara reached the shelter of the trees and paused, breathing hard, looking back over her shoulder.

The gates of the camp swung open, and two dozen men on horses, long spears gleaming, rode out and turned as a column, straight toward her. Aldrick rode at their head, dwarfing the riders nearest him.

Amara turned and ran on through the trees as fast as she could. The branches sighed and moaned around her, leaves whispering, shadows moving and changing ominously around her. The furies of this forest were not friendly to her—which made sense, given the presence of at least one powerful woodcrafter. She would never be able to hide from them in this forest, when the trees themselves would report her position.

"Cirrus," Amara gasped. "Up!"

The wind gathered beneath her and pushed her up

off the ground—but branches wove together above her, moving as swiftly as human hands joining together and presented her with a solid screen. Amara let out a cry and crashed against that living ceiling, then tumbled back to the ground. Cirrus softened her fall with an apologetic whisper against her ear.

Amara looked left and right, but the trees were joining branches everywhere—and the forest was growing darker as the roof of leaf and bough closed overhead. The beating of hooves came through the trees.

Amara struggled back to her feet, the cut on her arm pounding painfully. Then she started running again, as the horsemen closed in, behind her.

She couldn't have guessed how far she ran. Later, she only remembered the threatening shadows of the trees and a burning fire in her lungs and her limbs that even Cirrus's aid couldn't ease. Terror changed to simple excitement, and that transformed, by degrees, to a sort of exhausted lack of concern.

She ran until she suddenly found herself looking back—and into the eyes of a mounted *legionare,* not twenty feet away. The man shouted and cast his spear at her. She stumbled out of the path of the weapon and away from the horseman, into a sudden flood of sunshine. She looked ahead of her and found the ground sloping down for no more than three or four strides, and then ending in a sheer cliff that dropped off so abruptly that she could not see how far down it went or what was at the bottom.

The *legionare* drew his sword in a rasp of steel and called to his horse. The animal responded as an extension of the man's body and pounded toward her.

Amara turned without hesitation and threw herself off of the cliff.

She spread her arms and screamed, "Cirrus! Up!" The wind gathered beneath her in a rush, as her fury flew to obey, and she felt a sudden, fierce exultation as, with a screaming whistle of gale winds, she shot up, up into the autumn skies, her wake kicking up dust devils along the ridge that cast dirt up in the face of the unfortunate *legionare* and set his horse to rearing and kicking in confusion.

She flew on, up and away from the camp and paused after a time to look behind her. The cliff she'd leapt from looked like a toy from there, several miles behind her and one below. "Cirrus," she murmured, and held her hands before her. The fury gusted and swirled a part of itself into that space, quivering like the waves rising from a hot stone.

Amara shaped that air with her hands, bending the light, until she was peering back at the cliff through her spread hands as though she stood no more than a hundred yards away. She saw the hunting party emerge and Aldrick dismount. The *legionare* who had seen her described her escape, and Aldrick squinted up at the sky, sweeping his eyes left to right. Amara felt a chill as the man's gaze paused, directly upon her. He tilted his head to the man beside him, the woodcrafter Knight from before, and the man simply touched one of the trees.

Amara swallowed and swept her hands back toward the rebel Legion's camp.

Half a dozen forms rose up over the treetops, which swayed and danced beneath the winds, as though they had been the bushes in a holtwife's herb garden. They turned, and as one, they sped toward her. Sun glinted off of steel—armor and weapons, she knew.

"Knights Aeris," muttered Amara. She swallowed and let her hands fall. Normally, she would have been confident of her ability to outrun them. But now, wounded, and already exhausted in body and spirit, she was not so sure.

Amara turned and bade Cirrus to bear her north and east—and prayed that the sun would set before her foes caught up to her.

◇◇◇◇ CHAPTER 3

Tavi slipped out of his room, down the stairs, and through the silence of the last shreds of night before dawn. He entered the cavernous shadows of the great hall, noting a faint glow of light in the kitchens beside the great hall. Old Bitte rarely slept more than a few hours a night, and Tavi heard her moving through the kitchen, preparing it for the coming breakfast meal.

He unbolted the door and left the great hall for Bernardholt's courtyard. One of the steadholt's dogs lifted his head from the empty barrel he used as a kennel, and Tavi stooped to scratch the old hound's ears. The dog thumped his tail against the barrel's interior and laid his head back down to sleep. Tavi drew his cloak over his shoulders against the chill of the dying autumn night and opened the postern door to leave the safety of Bernardholt.

The door opened to reveal his uncle Bernard, leaning casually against the doorway, dressed in leathers and a heavy green cloak for a day in the wilderness beyond the steadholt's fields. He lifted an apple to his mouth and crunched into it. Bernard was a large man with broad shoulders and the heavy muscles of hard labor. His dark hair, cropped close in a Legion cut, showed a fleck or two of grey, though none such appeared in his close-trimmed beard. He wore a quiver of hunting arrows at his side, riding beside his Legion-issued sword, and he carried the stave to the lightest of his bows unstrung in his hand.

Tavi drew up short, with a flutter of apprehension. Then he spread his hands, silently conceding the victory to Bernard, and then offered his uncle a faint smile. "How did you know?"

Bernard returned the smile, though there was a wary cast to it. "Fade saw you drinking a lot of extra water last night, after you came in so late, and pointed it out to me. It's an old soldier's trick to get up early."

"Oh," Tavi said. "Yes, sir."

"I counted the flocks," Bernard said. "Looks like we might be a few heads short."

"Yes, sir," Tavi said. He licked his lips nervously. "I'm going to bring them in now."

"I was under the impression that you had done so last night. Since you marked down a full count on the tally slate."

Tavi's cheeks grew warm, and he felt glad for the

dimness. "Dodger led his ewes and their lambs out last night, when I was trying to bring the south flock in. I didn't want you to worry."

Bernard shook his head. "Tavi, you know that today is important. The other Steadholders will be arriving for the truthfind, and I don't need any distractions."

"I'm sorry, Uncle. Why don't you stay here, then? I can find Dodger and bring him back in."

"I don't like you wandering around the valley alone, Tavi."

"I'm going to have to eventually, uncle. Unless you planned on following me around for the rest of my life."

Bernard sighed. "Your aunt would murder me."

Tavi gritted his teeth. "I can do it by myself. I'll be careful and be back before noon."

"That's not really the point. You were supposed to bring them in last night," Bernard said. "What kept you from it?"

Tavi swallowed. "Um. I'd promised to do someone a favor. I didn't have time to get them both done before dark."

Bernard sighed. "Crows, Tavi. I really thought you had done a lot of growing up this season. That you were learning to handle responsibility."

Tavi felt suddenly sick to his stomach. "You're not going to gift me the sheep, are you?"

Bernard said, "I don't begrudge you getting your fair dues. I was glad—I am glad to help you get started with your own flock. But I'm not just going to throw them away. If you can't show me that you'll take care of them properly, I can't give them to you."

"It isn't like I'd be keeping them long."

"Perhaps not. It's the principle of the thing, lad. Nothing comes free."

"But *Uncle*," Tavi protested. "It's my *only* chance to make something of myself."

Bernard grunted. "Then you probably shouldn't have chosen to . . ." He frowned. "Tavi, what *did* you need to do that was more important than the flocks?"

Tavi's face grew warmer yet. "Um."

Bernard arched an eyebrow and said, "Oh, I see."

"See what?"

"There's a girl."

Tavi knelt and tightened the straps on his boots to hide his scowl and said, "Why would you say that?"

"You're a fifteen-year-old boy, Tavi. There's always a girl."

"No, there isn't," Tavi insisted.

Bernard mused over that for a moment and shrugged. "When you want to talk about it, let me know." He pushed himself off the wall with one shoulder and strung his bow with one leg and the pressure of an arm. "We'll discuss your gifting later. Where do you think we should pick up Dodger's trail?"

Tavi drew his leather sling from his pouch and put a couple of smooth stones into the pocket of his tunic. "Won't Brutus be able to find him?"

Bernard smiled. "I thought you said you could do this on your own."

Tavi frowned at his uncle and scrunched up his nose, thinking. "Cold's coming on, and they know it. They'll want evergreens for shelter and for food. But the gargants were turned out to forage on the southern slope of the valley, and they won't go anywhere near gargants if they can help it." Tavi nodded. "North. Dodger has taken them into the pine hollows over the causeway."

Bernard nodded in approval. "Good. Remember that furycrafting is no substitute for intelligence, Tavi."

"And intelligence is no substitute for a fury," Tavi muttered sourly. He kicked at the ground, scuffing up a small cloud of dust and dried, dead grasses.

Bernard laid a heavy hand on Tavi's shoulder, squeezed, and then started walking north, down the old lane worn by the passage of carts and draft animals and feet. "It's not as bad as you think, Tavi. Furies aren't everything."

"Says the man with two of them," Tavi said, following him. "Aunt Isana says you could challenge for full Citizenship if you wanted to."

Bernard shrugged. "If I wanted to, perhaps. But I didn't come into my furies until I was almost your age."

"But you were a slow bloomer," Tavi said. "I'm way past that. No one's ever been my age and furyless."

Bernard sighed. "You don't know that, Tavi. Relax, boy. It will come to you in time."

"That's what you've told me since I was ten. If I'd had furies of my own, I could have stopped Dodger and still . . ." He choked down his anger before he could blurt out the words.

Uncle Bernard glanced back at Tavi, smiling with only his eyes. "Come on, lad. Let's pick up the pace. I need to be back before the other Steadholders arrive."

Tavi nodded, and they broke into a mile-eating lope down the winding lane. The sky began to lighten as they passed the apple orchards, the beehives, and then the northern fields laid fallow for a season. The lane wound through a forest of mostly oak and maple, where most of the trees were so ancient that only the most meager grass and brush could grow beneath them. By the time the predawn pale blue had given way to the first tints of orange and yellow, they had reached the last stretch of woods before leaving the lands of Bernardholt. There the forest was not so old, and smaller trees and brush, some of it still living despite the lateness of the season, stood thick and heavy. Golden and scarlet leaves covered the dried skeletons of the smaller brush, and the naked, sleeping trees swayed in a chorus of gentle creaking.

And then something in his surroundings brought an odd kind of pressure to Tavi's senses. He stopped and let out a short, warning hiss of breath. From a full jog, Bernard abruptly dropped to a crouch, and Tavi instinctively followed suit.

Bernard looked silently back at Tavi, cocking an eyebrow in a silent question.

Tavi stayed on all fours and crawled up beside his uncle. He kept his voice to a whisper between panting breaths and said, "Up ahead, in that last stand of trees by the brook. There's usually a covey of quail there, but I saw them heading along the lane."

"You think something spooked them out," Bernard said. He murmured, "Cyprus," and flicked his right hand toward the trees beside him in a signal to the lesser of his two furies. Tavi looked up and saw a shape glide down from one of the trees—vaguely humanoid and no larger than a child. It turned pale green eyes toward Bernard for a moment, crouching down like an animal. Leaves and twigs seemed to writhe together to cover whatever shape lay beneath them. Cyprus tilted its head to one side, focusing on Bernard, and then made a sound like wind rustling through the leaves and vanished into the brush.

Tavi was winded from the run and struggled to slow his breathing. "What is it?" he whispered.

Bernard's eyes slipped out of focus for a moment before he answered. "You were right. Well done, boy. There's someone hiding near the footbridge. They've got a strong fury with them."

"Bandits?" Tavi whispered.

His uncle's eyes narrowed. "It's Kord."

Tavi frowned. "I thought the other Steadholders were supposed to be arriving later today. And why would they be hiding in the trees?"

Bernard grunted, rising. "Let's go find out."

Tavi followed his uncle on down the road. Bernard walked with quiet purpose toward the causeway, as if he had every intention of traveling past the hidden men. Then, without warning, he spun to his left, arrow in hand, drew back the bow and loosed a grey-feathered shaft at a clump of bushes and detritus a few paces from the near side of the small, stone footbridge that crossed a murmuring brook.

Tavi heard a scream, and the leaves and bushes thrashed wildly. A moment later a boy about Tavi's age emerged from the bushes, one hand clenched upon the seat of his breeches. He had a broad, strong build and a face that would be handsome if it had been less petulant. Bittan, of Kordholt, Kord's youngest son. "Bloody crows!" the boy howled. "Are you insane?"

"Bittan?" called Bernard in obviously feigned surprise. "Oh dear. I had no idea that was you back there."

From further down the trail, a second young man rose out of hiding—Kord's eldest son, Aric. He was leaner than his brother, taller, and several years older. He wore his hair pulled back into a tail, and pensive frown lines had already established themselves between his eyebrows. He watched Bernard warily and called, "Bittan? You all right?"

The boy screamed, furious, "No I'm not all right! I'm shot!"

Tavi peered at the other boy and muttered to his uncle, "You shot him?"

"Just grazed him."

Tavi grinned. "Maybe you hit him in the brain."

Bernard smiled a wolfish smile and said nothing.

From still further back in the brush, leaves crackled and dead wood snapped. A moment later, Steadholder Kord emerged from the bracken. He wasn't terribly tall, but his shoulders seemed too large for him, and his brawny arms looked unnaturally long. Kord wore a patched and faded grey tunic, badly in need of a thorough washing, and heavy gargant-hide leggings. He wore his symbol of office, the heavy chain of a Steadholder around his neck. The chain was smudged and looked greasy, but Tavi supposed that it made a better match for his unkempt greying hair and patchy beard.

Kord moved with an aggressive tension, and his eyes were cold with anger. "What the crows do you think you're doing, Bernard?"

Bernard waved a friendly hand at Kord, but Tavi noted that he held an arrow along with the bow in his other. "Little accident," he said. "I mistook your boy there for some kind of robber lurking by the road to attack travelers."

Kord's eyes narrowed. "Are you accusing me of something?"

"Of course not," Bernard drawled, his smile not touching his eyes. "This is just a misunderstanding. Thank the great furies no one got hurt." He paused for a moment, his smile vanishing before he said, quietly, "I'd hate to have someone get hurt on my land."

Kord snarled, a sound more bestial than human, and rolled forward a furious step. The ground under his feet rumbled and quivered, restless little hummocks rising and falling as though some kind of serpent slithered about just beneath the surface.

Bernard faced Kord without looking away, stirring, or changing his expression.

Kord growled again, and with a visible effort choked back his anger. "One of these days I'm going to get upset with you, Bernard."

"Don't say things like that, Kord," Tavi's uncle replied. "You'll frighten the boy."

Kord's eyes flicked to Tavi, and the boy felt suddenly uneasy under that intense and angry regard.

"He come into any furies yet, or are you finally going to admit what a useless little freak he is?"

The simple comment pierced Tavi like a thorn, and he opened his mouth to make a furious response.

Bernard settled his hand on Tavi's shoulder and said, "Don't worry about my nephew." He glanced at Bittan. "After all, you've got other concerns. Why don't you head on down to the steadholt? I'm sure Isana is getting something ready for you."

"Think we'll stay here awhile," Kord said. "Maybe eat a little breakfast."

"Suit yourself," Bernard said, and stared on down the lane. Tavi followed close behind them. Bernard ignored Kord until they had crossed the footbridge. "Oh," Bernard said, looking over his shoulder. "I forgot to mention that Warner already came in last night, Kord. His sons are on leave from the Legions so that they could visit their father."

"Bring them on," Bittan snapped. "We'll tear them apa—"

Kord delivered an openhanded blow to Bittan's face that knocked the boy to the ground. "Shut your mouth."

Bittan shook his head, dazed and scowling. He didn't answer Kord or look at his father as he stood up.

"Go on down," Bernard said. "I'm sure we can get everything worked out."

Kord didn't reply. He beckoned his sons with a curt gesture and started down the lane. They followed him, and Bittan cast a harsh, hateful glare at Tavi as he walked. "Freak."

Tavi clenched his hands into fists, but let the comment pass. Bernard nodded his approval, and they waited as Kord and his sons headed down the lane to Bernardholt.

As they watched, Tavi said, "They were there to attack Warner, weren't they, Uncle?"

"It's possible," Bernard said. "That's why your aunt asked Warner to come in last night. Kord is desperate."

"Why? It's Bittan that's been accused, not him."

"Rape is a Realm offense," Bernard answered. "Kord is the family head, and he shares responsibility for offenses against the Realm. If the truthfind shows that there needs to be a trial, and Bittan is judged guilty, Count Gram could remove Kord's claim to Kordholt."

"You think he'd kill to protect it?" Tavi asked.

"I think men who lust for power are capable of almost anything." He shook his head. "Kord sees power as something to satisfy his desires, instead of a tool to protect and serve the people beholden to him. It's a stupid attitude, and it will eventually get him killed—but until then it makes him dangerous."

"He scares me," Tavi said.

"He scares anyone with good sense, boy." Bernard passed his bow to Tavi and opened a pouch on his belt. He withdrew a small glass button from it and dropped it over the side of the footbridge and into the brook. "Rill," he said firmly. "I need to speak to Isana, please."

They waited there on the bridge for several moments before the sounds of the brook began to change. A column of water rose straight up out of the brook, taking on human form as it did so, until it had formed into a liquid sculpture of Tavi's aunt, Isana, a woman with the youthful form and features of a strong watercrafter, but the bearing and voice of a mature adult.

The sculpture peered around, eventually focusing on Bernard and Tavi. "Good morning, Bernard, Tavi." Her voice sounded tinny, as if it had come down to them through a long tube.

"Aunt Isana," Tavi said, bowing his head politely.

"Sis," Bernard drawled. "We just ran into Kord and his sons. They were waiting around in the brush near the north bridge."

Isana shook her head. "The fool can't be serious."

"I think he was," Bernard said. "I think he knows that with what Bittan did, Gram will get him this time."

Isana's mouth twisted into a wry smile. "I doubt

having a woman appointed the truthfinder for this crime has pleased him, either."

Bernard nodded. "You might want to make sure someone is close, just in case. They're coming down the lane to you now."

Isana's image in the water frowned. "When will you return?"

"Before noon, with luck. Before dinner, otherwise."

"Try to hurry. I'll keep things civil for as long as I can, but I'm not sure anyone but you can make Kord back down without shedding blood."

"I will. Be careful."

Isana nodded. "And you. Old Bitte says that Garados and his wife are brewing up a storm for us, by nightfall at the latest."

Tavi shot an uneasy glance to the northeast, where the towering mountain of Garados sat glowering down at the inhabitants of the Calderon Valley. Its upper slopes were already growing white with ice, and clouds obscured the topmost peaks, where the hostile fury of the towering mountain conspired with Lilvia, the fury of the cold gales blowing over the great Sea of Ice to the north. They would gather in clouds like herds of cattle, feed them to anger on the day's light, and drive them down over the inhabitants of the valley in a furystorm as the sun set.

"We'll be back long before then," Bernard assured her.

"Good. Oh, Tavi?"

"Yes, Aunt Isana?"

"Do you have any idea where Beritte would have acquired a fresh garland of hollybells?"

Tavi shot his uncle a guilty glance and blushed. "I guess she must have found them somewhere."

"I see. She isn't yet of marrying age, she's too irresponsible to care for a child, and she certainly is too young to wear hollybells. Do you think she'll be finding any more?"

"No, ma'am."

"Excellent," Isana said rather crisply. "We'll discuss the matter when you return."

Tavi winced.

Bernard held on to his chuckle until the water sculpture had lowered itself back into the brook, the contact with Isana ending as it did. "No girl, eh? I thought Fred was the one walking out with Beritte."

"He is." Tavi sighed. "She's probably wearing them for him. But she asked me to get them for her and . . . well it seemed a lot more important at the time."

Bernard nodded. "There's no shame in making a mistake, Tavi—provided you learn from it. I think you'd be smart to think of this as a lesson in priorities. So?"

Tavi frowned. "So what?"

Bernard kept smiling. "What have you learned this morning?"

Tavi glowered at the ground. "That women are trouble, sir."

Bernard's mouth opened in a sudden, merry roar of laughter. Tavi looked up at his uncle, and cast him a hopeful grin. Bernard's eyes shone with merriment. "Oh, lad. That's about half of the truth."

"What's the other half?"

"You want them, anyway," Bernard said. He shook his head, the smile lingering in his eyes, his mouth. "I did one or two stupid things to impress a girl in my day."

"Was it worth it?"

Bernard's smile faded, without giving the impression that he had become any less amused. It simply turned inward, as though what he was smiling at existed only within. Bernard never spoke of his dead wife, or their children, also gone. "Yes. Every bruise and every scrape."

Tavi sobered. "Do you think Bittan's guilty?"

"Likely," Bernard said. "But I could be wrong. Until we've had the chance to hear everyone speak, we have to keep an open mind. He won't be able to lie to your aunt."

"I can."

Bernard laughed. "You're quite a bit smarter than Bittan. And you've had a lifetime of practice."

Tavi smiled at his uncle. Then he said, "Sir, I really can find the flock. I can do it."

Bernard regarded Tavi for a moment. Then he nodded toward the causeway. "Prove it then, lad. Show me."

ᴐᴐᴐᴐ CHAPTER 4

Isana looked up from her scrying bowl with a faintly irritated frown. "That boy is going to get himself into more trouble than he can explain his way out of, one day." Wan autumn sunlight streamed through the windows of Bernardholt's main kitchen. The smell of bread baking in the wide ovens filled the room, along with the tang of the sauce sizzling on the roast turning over the coals. Isana's back hurt from a morning's work that had begun well before the sun rose, and there wasn't going to be a chance to rest any time in the immediate future.

Whenever she had a moment to spare from her preparations, she spent it focused on her scrying bowl, using Rill to keep a cautious eye upon the Kordholters and Warner's folk. Warner and his sons had added their efforts to that of Elder Frederic, master of the steadholt's gargants, as he and his brawny son, Younger Frederic, cleaned out the half-buried stables of the vast beasts of labor.

Kord and his youngest son lazed in the courtyard. The elder boy, Aric, had taken up an axe and had been splitting logs for the duration of the morning, burning off nervous energy with physical effort. The tension in the air throughout the morning was cloying, even to those without an ounce of watercraft in their bodies.

The hold women had fled the kitchen's heat to take their midday meal, a quick round of vegetable soup and yesterday's bread, together with a selection of cheeses they had thrown together then taken out into the steadholt's courtyard to eat. The weary autumn sun shone pleasantly down on the courtyard, the warmth of its flagstones sheltered from the cold north wind by Bernardholt's high stone walls. Isana did not join them. The tension building in the courtyard would have sickened her, and she wanted to save back her strength and self-discipline for as long as she could, in the event that she had to intervene.

So Isana ignored the rumble in her own belly and focused on her work, a portion of her thought reserved for her fury's perceptions.

"Aren't you going to eat, mistress Isana?" Beritte looked up from where she was carelessly slicing the skins from a mound of tubers, dropping the peeled roots into a basin of water. The girl's pretty face had been lightly touched with rouge, and her already alluring eyes with kohl. Isana had warned her mother that Beritte was entirely too young for such nonsense, but there she was, hollybells in her hair and her bodice laced with deliberate wickedness beneath her breasts—more eager to admire herself in every shiny surface she could find than to help prepare the evening's banquet. Isana had gone out of her way to find chores to occupy the girl's day. Beritte often enjoyed seeing young men compete with one another for her attention, and between her bodice and the sweet scent of the hollybells in her hair, she'd have them killing one another—and Isana had far too much on her mind to be bothered with any more mischief.

Isana glanced at the girl, eyeing her up and down, before she reached for the poker and thrust it back into the oven, into the coals where one of two tiny fire furies that regulated the oven wasn't doing its job. She raked the poker through them, stirring them, and saw the flames dance and quiver a bit more as the sleepy fury within stirred to greater life. "As soon as I have a moment to spare," she told the girl.

"Oh," Beritte said, somewhat wistfully. "I'm sure we'll be finished soon."

"Just peel, Beritte." Isana turned back to the counter and her bowl. The water within stirred and then quivered upward, resolving itself into a face—her own, but much younger. Isana smiled warmly down at the fury. Rill always remembered what Isana had looked like, the day they'd found one another, and always appeared in the same way as when Isana, then a gawky girl not quite Beritte's age, had gazed down into a quiet, lovely pool.

"Rill," Isana said, and touched the surface of the water. The liquid in the bowl curled over her finger and then swirled around quietly in response to her. "Rill," Isana said again. "Find Bernard." She pressed an image from her mind, down to the fury through the contact of her finger: her brother's sure, silent steps, his rumbling, quiet voice, and his broad hands. "Find Bernard," she said again.

The fury quivered and swirled the water about—then departed the bowl, passing through the air in a quiet wave Isana felt prickling along her skin, and then vanished, down through the earth.

Isana lifted her head and focused on Beritte more sharply. "Now then," she said. "What's going on, Beritte?"

"I'm sorry?" the girl asked. She flushed bright red and turned back to her peeling, knife flashing over the tuber, stripping dark skin from pale flesh. "I don't know what you mean, mistress."

Isana placed her hands on her hips. "I think you do," she said her tone crisp and severe. "Beritte, you can either tell me where you got the flowers now, or you can wait until I find out, later."

Isana felt Beritte's fluttering panic, dancing around on the edges of the girl's voice as she spoke. "Honestly, Mistress, I found them waiting for me at my door. I don't know who—"

"Yes you do," Isana said. "Hollybells don't just miraculously appear, and you know the law about harvesting them. If you make me find out on my own, by the great furies, I'll see to it that you suffer whatever is appropriate anyway."

Beritte shook her head, and one of the hollybells fell from her hair. "No, no, mistress." Isana could taste the way the lie made the girl inwardly cringe. "I never harvested any of them. Honestly, I—"

Isana's temper flared, and she snapped, "Oh, Beritte. You aren't old enough to be able to lie to me. I've a banquet to cook and a truthfind to prepare for, and I've not time to waste on a spoiled child who thinks that because she's grown breasts and hips that she knows better than her elders."

Beritte looked up at Isana, flushing darker with awkward humiliation and then snapped back with her own anger. "Jealous, mistress?"

Isana's temper abruptly flashed from a frustrated blaze to something cold, icy. For just a moment, she forgot everything else in the kitchen, all the events and disastrous possibilities that faced the steadholt that day, and focused her attention on the buxom girl. For only a moment, she lost control of her emotions and felt the old, bitter rage rise within her.

Every kettle in the kitchen abruptly boiled over, steam flushing out in a cloud that curved around Isana and flowed toward the girl, scalding water racing over the floor in a low wave toward her seat.

Isana felt Beritte's defiance transformed in an instant to terror, the girl's eyes widening as she stared at Isana's face. Beritte thrust her hands out as she stumbled out of her chair, the feeble wind sprites she had collected slowing the oncoming steam enough to allow her to flee. Beritte took a jumping step over the nearest arm of the onrushing water and ran toward the kitchen doors, sobbing.

Isana clenched her fists and closed her eyes, wrenching her mind from the girl, forcing herself to take deep breaths, to regain control of her emotions. The anger, the sheer, bitter rage howled inside her like a living thing trying to tear its way free of her. She could feel its claws scraping at her belly, her bones. She fought it down, forced it away from her thoughts, and as she did the steam settled and spread throughout the room, fogging the thick, rough glass of the windows. The kettles calmed. The water started pooling naturally over the floor.

Isana stood amidst the sweltering steam and the spilled water and closed her eyes, taking slow, deep breaths. She'd done it again. She'd let too much of the emotion she'd been feeling in another color her own thoughts, her own perceptions. Beritte's insecurity and defiant anger had glided into her and taken root in her own thoughts and feelings—and she had let it happen.

Isana lifted one slim hand and rubbed at her temples. The additional senses of a watercrafter felt like being able to hear another kind of sound—sound that rubbed against one's temples like eiderdown, until she almost felt that it was grating her skull raw, that blisters would rise on her face and scalp from the sheer friction of all the emotions she felt rubbing against her.

Still, there was little she could do about it now, but to control herself and to bear what came. One couldn't open one's eyes and later simply decide not to use them. She could dim the perceptions Rill's presence brought to her, but she could never shut them away altogether.

It was simply a fact a watercrafter of her power had to live with.

One of many, she thought. Isana crouched down, murmuring to the tiny furies in the spilled water on the floor, beckoning them until the separate puddles and droplets began running together in the center of the floor into a more coherent mass. Isana studied it, waiting for all the spare droplets to roll in from the far corners of the kitchen.

The reflection of her own face looked back at her, smooth and slender, and barely older than that of a girl's. She winced, thinking of the face Rill showed her every time the fury came. Perhaps it was not so different from her own.

She lifted her hand and traced her fingers over her cheek. She had a pretty face, still. Most of forty years, and she barely looked as though she had lived twenty of them. She might look as old as thirty, if she lived another four decades, but no older. There were no lines on her face, at the corners of her eyes, though faint shades of frost stirred in her auburn hair.

Isana rose and regarded the woman reflected in the water. Tall. Thin. Too thin, for a woman of her age, with scarcely any curve of hip or breast. She might have been mistaken for a gawky *child*. True, she may carry herself with more confidence, more strength than any child could muster, and true the faint grey touches in her hair may have granted her an age and dignity not strictly warranted by her appearance—and true, everyone in the whole of the Calderon Valley knew her by name or sight or reputation as one of the most formidable furycrafters in it. But that did nothing to change the simple and heartless fact that she looked like a boy in a dress. Like nothing any man would want to marry.

Isana closed her eyes for a moment, pained. Thirty-seven years old, and she was alone. No suitors, naturally. No garlands to wear, or dances to plan for, or flirtations to plot. That was all long past her, even with the apparent youth her watercrafting bestowed on her. The youth that kept her always a bit distant from the other women her age—women with husbands, families.

She opened her eyes and idly bade the spilled water to make itself useful and clean the floor. The puddle began sweeping over it obediently, gathering up bits of dust and debris as it did, and Isana went to open the door. Cold air poured in, sharp contrast to the steamy kitchen, and she closed her eyes, taking deep, bracing breaths.

She had to admit it. Beritte's words had stung her, not simply because she'd been feeling too many of the adolescent's intense emotions, but because they had rung true as well. Beritte had all the luscious curves and rondure that would draw any man in the Valley to her—and indeed, she had half a dozen of them dancing on her strings even now, including Tavi, though the boy tried to deny it. Beritte. Firm and ripe and able to bear strong children.

The way no one had thought Isana would ever be able to.

She pressed her lips together and opened her eyes. Enough. There was too much work to be about to let an old pain rise to the surface, now. Thunder rumbled over the Valley's floor, and Isana crossed to the northern window, opened it, and eyed the mountain peak to the north. Garados loomed in all of his surly majesty there, snow already gliding further down his shoulders and toward the valley floor, warning of the coming winter. Dark clouds gathered around his head, and as she watched, they flashed with dark green lightning, sending another rumbled warning across the Valley. Lilvia, then—Garados's wife, the storm fury, gathering up clouds for another assault on the people of the Valley. She would wait all day, gathering the warmth of the sun into her cloud-herds and then send them stampeding across the Valley in a rush of thunder and wind and, like as not at this time of the year, sleet and icy rain.

Isana pressed her lips together. Intolerable. If only a decently gifted windcrafter would settle down in the Valley, they might blunt the worst of Thara's storms before they ever reached the steadholts—but then, any windcrafter that strong would be serving as a Knight or one of the Cursors.

She walked to the sink and touched the spigot, alerting the furies inside that she desired water from the well. A moment later, it spilled out, cold and clear, and she filled a pair of pans before letting the furies stop the flow of it, then went around the kitchens and refilled the water in the pots that had boiled over. A moment later, she took the bread from the ovens, setting it out in its pans, and slipped the next round of pans into their places. She glanced around the kitchens once more, making sure that everything was in place. The puddle was finished with the floor, so she shooed it out the door to ease into the earth beside the threshold and sink back into the ground.

"Rill?" Isana called. "What's taking so long?"

The water bubbled and stirred in her scrying bowl

(which doubled as her mixing bowl most days), and then three little splashes announced Rill's presence. Isana crossed back to the bowl, drew her braid back over her shoulder, and regarded the surface of the water intently as the ripples stilled.

The fury showed her a dim view from what must have been a stagnant pool somewhere in the Pine Hollows. A murky shape that could have been Bernard paced across the image in the bowl and then was gone. Isana shook her head. Rill's images were not always entirely clear, but it seemed that Bernard and Tavi were still pursuing the missing flock.

She murmured a dismissal to Rill and set the bowl aside—and then noticed a sudden lack of sound from the courtyard. A breath later, the tension levels of Bernard-holt swelled into painful intensity.

Isana steeled herself against the perceptions and walked briskly out of the kitchen. She kept her breathing steady and held herself with rigid confidence. The hold-folk were pressed shoulder to shoulder, facing the center of the courtyard. They were silent, but for faint mutters and worried whispers.

"Kord," she murmured. Isana stepped forward, and the holdfolk made way for her, clearing a narrow path through the onlookers until she could see the scene in the center of the courtyard.

Two men stood facing one another in the courtyard, and the air between them practically thrummed with tension. Kord stood with his arms folded over his chest, the ground at his feet shifting and trembling. His greasy beard framed his smile sharply, and his eyes were bright and eager beneath his heavy brows.

Facing him stood Steadholder Warner, a tall man, slender as a post, with gangling arms and legs and a head that shone bald but for a fringe of wispy grey hair. Warner's narrow, chiseled face had flushed bright red in anger, and the air around him quivered and danced like heat rising off an oven.

"All I'm saying," Kord drawled, "is that if that little slut of yours can't keep her legs together and men out from between them, it's your problem, friend. Not mine."

"Shut your mouth," Warner snarled.

"Or what?" Kord asked, throwing a sneer into the words. "What are you going to do, Warner? Run and hide behind the skirts of a woman and whimper for Gram to come save you?"

"Why you . . ." Warner spat. He took a step forward, and the air in the courtyard grew detectably warmer.

Kord smiled, a flash of teeth and said, "Go ahead, Warner. Call it to *juris macto*. Let's settle this like men. Unless you'd rather humiliate your little whore by having her testify how she seduced my boy in front of every Steadholder in the Calderon Valley."

One of Warner's sons, a tall and lean young man with his hair shorn in Legion-fashion stepped up to his father and took his arm. "Pa, don't," he said. "You can't take him on in a fair fight." The other two took up a spot behind Warner, while Kord's sons mirrored them behind their own father.

Warner's daughter rushed to his side. Heddy's cobweb-fine hair rose and rippled in silken yellow waves in the heated air around her father. She threw a conscientious look around her, her face flaming scarlet with embarrassment. "Papa," she urged. "No, not like this. This isn't our way."

Kord snorted at the girl. "Bittan," he asked, glancing back at his son. "You stuck your wick in that skinny tramp? Might as well have gone after one of Warner's sheep."

Isana had to clench her fists and brace herself against the raw tide of emotions in the courtyard. From Heddy's panicky fear and humiliation to Warner's rage, to Kord's sly satisfaction and eagerness, every feeling washed over her, too intense to ignore. She forced them all away from her and took a breath. Kord's earth fury was a vicious beast, trained to kill. He used it to hunt and to slaughter his cattle. Any fury started taking on aspects of its partner, after a while, but even considering Kord himself, the earth fury was a bad one. A killer.

Isana swept a look around the courtyard. The holdfolk all stood well clear of the conflict. None of them wanted to involve themselves in a struggle between Steadholders. Crows take her brother! Where was he when she needed him?

The flood of intense anger from Warner grew more harsh—in only a moment more, he would give in to Kord's taunts and take the matter to *juris macto,* the Realm's legal form of duel. Kord would kill him, but Warner was too furious at the treatment of his daughter to consider that. Warner's sons, too, were flooding her with a growing torrent of anger, and Kord's youngest son burned with a barely disguised lust for violence.

Isana's heart fluttered with all the emotions, piling on top of her own fear. She pushed them all firmly away, struggling to master them—and stalked out into the courtyard, squarely between the two men, and put her hands on her hips. "Gentlemen," she said, letting her voice ring out. "You are interrupting lunch."

Warner took a step toward Kord, his eyes never leaving the other Steadholder. "You can't expect me to stand here and take this."

Kord sauntered forward a willing pace himself. "*Juris macto*," he said. "Just declare it, Warner, and we can settle this."

Isana spun to face Kord, meeting his eyes squarely. "Not in *my* courtyard you won't."

Bittan, behind Kord, let out a rough laugh and stepped forward, toward Isana. "Well, well," he said. "What we got here? Another little hold whore standing up for whore Heddy?"

"Bittan," Kord growled, in warning.

Isana narrowed her eyes at Bittan. The young man's confidence, arrogance, and a sickening rush of his lust whirled over her like a foul, greasy smoke. She watched him approach, arrogantly smiling as he eyed her, from her bare feet to her long braid. The idiot evidently did not know her by sight.

"Going bad early," Bittan commented. "But I bet you'd be good for a tumble." He reached out a hand to touch Isana's face.

Isana let him touch her for a moment, felt the desperate, arrogant need of the young man to prove himself in his own eyes. She reached up and seized his wrist and then said, voice cold, "Rill. Deal with this slive."

Bittan abruptly convulsed and threw himself backward onto the ground. He let out a strangled scream that cut off halfway through, as clear, foaming water burst from his mouth. He thrashed on the courtyard stones in a frantic tangle of flailing limbs. His eyes bulged, and he tried to scream again, nothing but water flooding from his mouth and nose.

Kord's other son rushed to his fallen brother, and Kord himself rolled forward a step with an angry snarl. "Bitch," he growled. The earth bulged beneath him, as though preparing to lash forward.

"Go ahead, Kord," Isana said, her voice icy. "But before you do, I should remind you that you are in Bernardholt, now. And you may *not* challenge me to the *juris macto*." She smiled at him, as sweet and venomous as she could manage. "I'm not a Steadholder."

"I can still kill you, Isana," Kord said.

"You could," Isana replied. "But then, I wouldn't be able to call Rill off of your boy there, would I?"

"And what if I could use one less mouth to feed?" Kord answered her, showing her his teeth.

"In that case," she said, "I hope you're ready to kill everyone here. Because you won't get away with cold murder, Steadholder Kord. I don't care how far we are from the First Lord's justice—kill me, and there won't be a place in the Realm where you can hide."

Isana promptly turned to Warner and snapped, "Wipe that smile off your face, Steadholder. What kind of behavior is this to show to my holders, and their *children*?" She stalked toward Warner with a scowl twisting her features. "I'll have your word that you won't engage in this idiocy again while you're a guest in my home."

"Isana," Warner protested, he and his sons still staring at Kord and his own brood, "that animal on the ground is the one who raped my daughter."

"Papa," Heddy sobbed, tugging at Warner's sleeve. "Papa, please."

"Your *word*, Warner," Isana snapped. "Or I'll rule against you in the truthfind right here and now."

Warner's gaze snapped to Isana, and she felt his sudden shock and surprise. "But Isana—"

"I don't *care*. You can't behave this way in my home, Warner, and my brother isn't here to knock sense into your fool head. Your word. No more of this duel nonsense. No more fighting in Bernardholt."

Warner stared at her for a moment. Isana felt the man's dismay, his anger, his helpless frustration. His gaze wavered and went to his daughter, and he softened, almost visibly. "All right," he said, quietly. "My word. For all of us. We'll start nothing."

Isana whirled back toward Kord, stalking toward the young man still choking on the ground, vomiting water. She brushed roughly past the older of Kord's sons (Aric was his name, she thought), and reached down to lay her hand on Bittan's forehead. The boy had gone beyond thought in his animal panic. There was no arrogance there, now, only a fear so intense that it made Isana's skin feel cold.

Kord sneered down at her. "I guess you're going to want my word as well."

"What would be the point," Isana snapped, keeping her voice low. "You're scum, Kord, and we both know it." Louder, she said, "Rill. Out." She stood away as Bittan spluttered and coughed, retching more water out, finally drawing in a gasping breath of air. She left him there, coughing on the ground, and turned to go.

The stone of the courtyard folded over one of her feet

with a simple and almost delicate finality. Her heart fluttered with her own fear as she felt Kord's cold anger on her back. She flicked her braid over her shoulder and shot him a look through narrowed eyes.

"This isn't over, Isana," Kord promised, his voice very quiet. "I won't stand for this."

Isana faced his dark stare, the cold and calculating hatred behind it, and borrowed from it, used it to steel herself against him, to return ice for ice. "You'd best hope it's over, Kord," she said. "Or you're going to think what happened to Bittan was a kindness." She flicked her eyes down to her foot and back up to him. "There's a space for you in the barn. I'll have some food sent down for lunch. We'll call you at dinner."

Kord remained still for a moment. Then he spat to one side, and nodded toward his sons. Aric collected the gasping Bittan, hauling him to his feet, and the three of them walked toward the wide doors of the roomy stone barn. Only as they left did the ground quiver beneath Isana's bare foot and let her go.

She closed her eyes, and the terror she'd been holding back, her own, flooded out and over her. She started shaking, but she shook her head to herself, firmly. Not in front of everyone. She opened her eyes and looked around at the courtyard full of people. "Well?" she asked them. "There is a lot of work to do before the feast come sundown. I can't do *everything* around here by myself. Get to it."

People moved, at her words, started talking again amongst themselves. Some of them shot her looks of mixed respect, admiration, and fear. Isana felt that last, like frozen cockleburs rolling over her skin. Her own folk, people she'd lived and worked with for years, afraid of her.

She lifted a hand as tears blurred at her eyes—but that was one of the first tricks a watercrafter learned. She willed them away from her eyes, and they simply did not fall. The confrontation, with its rampant tension and potential for murderous violence, had shaken her more than anything in years.

Isana drew in a careful breath and walked toward the kitchens. Her legs kept her steady, at least, though the weariness now crawling over her was nearly too much to bear. Her head ached with the efforts of the morning, with the pressure of all that watercrafting.

Fade came shuffling out of the smithy as she passed it. He moved with an odd little drag of one foot. Not a large man, he had been badly burned when he had been branded with a coward's mark, disfiguring the left half of his face—though that had been years ago. His hair, nearly black, had grown out long and curling to partially conceal it, and the scar tracing over his scalp, presumably a head wound also suffered in battle. The slave offered her a witless smile and a tin cup of water, holding it up to her along with a fairly clean cloth, far different from his own sweaty rags and burn-scarred leather apron.

"Thank you, Fade," Isana said. She accepted both and took a drink. "I need you to keep an eye on Kord. I want you to let me know if he or his sons leave the barn. All right?"

Fade nodded rapidly, his hair flopping. A bit of drool flicked off his half-open mouth. "Eye on Kord," he repeated. "Barn." He frowned, staring into space for a long moment and then pointed a finger at her. "Watch better."

She shook her head. "I'm too tired. Just tell me if they leave. All right?"

"Leave," Fade repeated. He mopped at his drool with one sleeve. "Tell."

"That's right," she said, and gave him a weary smile. "Thank you, Fade."

Fade made a hooting sound of pleasure and smiled. "Welcome."

"Fade, you'd better not go into the barn. The Kord-holters are there, and I get the feeling they'd not be kind to you."

"Ungh," the slave said. "Watch, barn, tell." He turned at once and shuffled off, quickly despite the drag of his foot.

Isana put Old Bitte in charge of the kitchens and returned to her room. She sat down on her bed, her hands folded on her lap. Her stomach fluttered nervously, but she forced herself to take deep breaths to stay calm. She had headed off the most immediate trouble, and Fade, despite his lack of skilled speech and his simple manner, was reliable. He would warn her if something else came up in the meantime.

She worried about Tavi—now more than any time she could remember. He was safe enough with Bernard to look after him, but her instincts would not relent. The pine hollows were the most dangerous stretch of land in the valley, but to her weary senses, the danger seemed deeper than that, and more threatening. There was something heavy and foreboding in the air of the valley, a gathering of forces that made the storm brewing over Garados look weak and tiny by comparison.

Isana laid down on her bed. "Please," she whispered, exhausted. "Great furies please keep him safe."

ᐂᐂᐂᐂ CHAPTER 5

Tavi picked up Dodger's trail within an hour, but from there it wasn't so easy. Tavi tailed the flock throughout the morning and into the early afternoon, stopping only to drink from an icy brook and to eat some cheese and salt mutton his uncle had brought with him. By then, Tavi knew that Dodger was living up to his name and leading them on a merry chase, looping back and forth through the barrens.

Though gloomy Garados grew ever taller and darker with storm clouds, Tavi ignored the glowering presence of the mountain and kept his focus on his work. Noon was well past when he finally caught up to the wily ram and his flock.

He heard the sheep before he saw them; one of the ewes let out plaintive bleats. He looked back over his shoulder, to where his uncle followed several dozen strides behind him, and waved a hand to let Bernard know he'd found them. He couldn't keep the grin off his face, and his uncle answered Tavi's smile with his own.

Dodger had led the flock into a dense thicket of brambles and thorns nearly as tall as Tavi himself and a hundred feet deep. Tavi spotted Dodger's curling horns and approached the old ram carefully, talking as he always did. Dodger snorted and pawed at the earth with his front hooves, shaking his curling horns threateningly. Tavi frowned at the ram and approached him more slowly. Dodger himself weighed better than a quarter ton, and the tough breed of mountain sheep the frontier folk of Alera favored, sheep big enough and strong enough to defend themselves against thanadents and worse, could become aggressive when threatened. Careless shepherds had been killed by their overexcited charges.

A sharp, sweet smell made Tavi stop in his tracks. He recognized the scent of slaughtered sheep, of offal and blood.

Something was very wrong.

Tavi approached more slowly, eyes carefully sweeping around. He found the first dead sheep, one of the lambs, several yards short of the brambles. He knelt down and studied the remains, searching for clues as to what had killed the animal.

It hadn't been slives. Slives could kill young sheep, even adults if they had numbers enough, but the poisonous lizards swarmed over corpses and ravaged them into strips of flesh and bared bones. The lamb was dead, but it only showed a single wound—a massive, clean cut that had nearly severed the lamb's head from its neck. A thanadent's talons might have been capable of inflicting such a wound, but when one of the great mountain beasts took a kill, it either devoured it on the spot or else dragged it off to a secluded lair to feed. Wolves—even the great wolves of the savage, barbarian infested wilds east of the Calderon Valley—could not have struck and killed so cleanly. And besides, any predator would have begun to devour the lamb. Beasts did not kill for sport.

The ground around the lamb was grossly disturbed. Tavi checked around quickly for tracks, but he found only the hoof-marks of the sheep and then some marks he was not familiar with, and could not even be sure were tracks. One partially disturbed track may have been the outline of a human heel, but it could as easily have been the result of a round stone being rolled out of its place.

Tavi rose, puzzled, and found two more corpses lying on the ground between the first lamb and Dodger's refuge in the thicket—another lamb and a ewe, both dead of similar massive, clean wounds. A powerful fury might have been capable of causing those wounds, but furies rarely attacked animals without being compelled to do so by their crafter. If an animal had not done the killings, only a man could have. He would need a viciously sharp blade—a long hunting knife or a sword, and might need fury-enhanced strength to help as well.

But the frontier valley rarely had visitors, and none of the holdfolk wandered through the pine barrens. Garados's looming presence made the land for miles about it seem heavy with apprehension, and it was nearly impossible to get a good night's sleep so near the old mountain.

Tavi looked up and frowned at Dodger, who remained in the entrance to the thicket, horns presented in warning, and Tavi suddenly felt afraid. What could have struck down those sheep that way? "Uncle?" Tavi called. His voice cracked a little. "Something is wrong."

Bernard approached, frowning, his eyes taking in Dodger and the flock, then the dead sheep upon the ground. Tavi watched his uncle take it in, and then Bernard's eyes widened. He rose and drew the short, heavy sword of the *legionare* from his belt. "Tavi. Come over to me."

"What?"

Bernard's voice took on a sharp edge of anger and command that Tavi had never heard in uncle before. "Now."

Tavi's heart began to pound in his chest, and he obeyed. "What about the flock?"

"Forget them," Bernard said, his voice crisp and cold. "We're leaving."

"But we'll lose the sheep. We can't just leave them here."

Bernard passed the sword to Tavi, scanning slowly around them, and fitted an arrow to the string of his bow. "Keep the point low. Put your other hand on the small of my back and leave it there."

Tavi's fear rose sharply, but he forced it away and obeyed his uncle. "What's wrong? Why are we leaving?"

"Because we want to get out of the barrens alive." Bernard started pacing silently away from the thicket, his face set in concentration.

"Alive? Uncle, what could—"

Bernard tensed abruptly and spun to one side, lifting his bow.

Tavi turned with him and saw a flash of motion beyond a small stand of young trees before them. "What is th—"

There was a hissing wail from their opposite side. Tavi whipped his head around, but his uncle was slower, spinning his entire body with his bow at arm's length, an arrow drawn back to his cheek. Tavi could do little but watch their attacker come.

It looked like a bird—if a bird could be eight feet tall and mounted on a pair of long, powerful legs, thicker and stronger-looking than a racing horse's, and tipped with wicked claws. Its head sat on the end of a long, powerful, flexible neck, and sported a hawk's beak, enlarged many times, sharp-looking and viciously hooked. Its feathers were colored in all dark browns and blacks, though its eyes were a brilliant shade of gold.

The bird bounded forward, taking a pair of steps and leaping into the air, both claws coming forward to rake while it beat at the air with ridiculously undersized wings. Tavi felt his uncle shove at him with his hip as he turned, and fell away and to one side, Bernard between him and the oncoming horror.

Bernard loosed his arrow without sighting. The arrow flew, struck at a poor angle, and glanced off the thing's feathers, skittering away in a blur of black and green fletching. The beast landed on Bernard, its claws raking, its vicious beak whipping forward and down toward him.

When hot droplets of his uncle's blood struck his face, Tavi began to scream.

The bird-thing's talons lashed out, raking and tearing. One of them ripped through Uncle Bernard's tough leather breeches at the thigh. Blood welled and flowed. Another talon tore through his hair, down toward his throat, but Bernard raised his arm, sliding the lethal claws away on the wood of the bow. The creature's vicious beak darted down at him, but again Bernard parried the attack away.

The great bird's beak darted to one side and snapped the heavy wood of the bow like a dry twig. It gave way with a sharp detonation as the heavy tension of the string was released.

Tavi raised the sword and started toward his uncle, screaming, but it didn't sound like his own voice. It was too high, too thin, and too terrified to be his voice. The bird's head swiveled toward him, golden eyes focusing on him with a terrible, mindless intensity.

"Brutus!" shouted Uncle Bernard, as the bird's attention focused on Tavi. "Take him!"

The earth at the bird's feet shuddered and then ripped itself upward, as Brutus came to Bernard's call.

A thin layer of soil peeled back away from raw stone. Brutus surged up from the earth like a hound emerging from boiling surf, head and shoulders of a great hunting dog made of soil and stone. The fury's eyes glowed green as emeralds and shone with a faintly luminous light. Brutus planted his front paws on the ground, hauling his pony-sized body forward, and stone jaws closed on the thigh of the attacking bird.

The bird let out a whistling teakettle scream, and its beak flashed down at the fury's head. The beak struck sparks from the stone, and one of the earthen hound's ears fell off, but Brutus didn't so much as flinch.

Tavi let out a shout and swung his uncle's sword with both hands. It struck at the base of the bird's neck, and Tavi felt the blow in his hand as the bird struggled and thrashed, a quivering sensation like that of a fish on a line. He drew back the sword and struck again. Dark blood splashed and stained the blade.

Tavi kept on swinging the sword, once dodging aside

from the bird's free talon. Again and again the heavy weapon bit into the bird's body or neck. Again and again, dark blood splashed up from the blade.

Brutus wrenched the bird to one side and threw it to the ground with bone-crushing force. Tavi screamed again, the blood roaring in his ears, and swung the sword at the bird's head like an axe. Tavi heard and felt the crunch of impact, and the bird collapsed, ceasing its thrashing and its teakettle screams.

Tavi trembled violently. There was dark blood on his clothes and on the sword in his hands and scattered over the bird's feathers and on the ground. Brutus still held the bird's thigh in his granite jaws. A stench wafted up from the body, foul and rotten. Tavi swallowed and felt his stomach roil. He turned away from the bird's body and toward his uncle, who lay prone on the ground.

"Uncle," Tavi said. He knelt down beside the man. There was blood on Bernard's clothes and on his hands. "Uncle Bernard."

Bernard turned his pale face up to Tavi, his features twisted in a grimace of pain. He had both hands clamped to his thigh, squeezing until his knuckles had turned white. "My leg," he said. "We've got to tie off my leg, boy, or I'm finished."

Tavi swallowed and nodded. He put down the sword and unfastened his belt. "What about Brutus?" he asked.

Bernard shook his head, a tight, small motion. "Not yet. Can't get anything through to him like this."

Tavi had to haul with both hands to move his uncle's leg enough to let him slip the belt around it, and doing so drew a grunt of pain from the big man. Tavi wrapped the belt as tightly as he could and then tied it off. Bernard let out another low sound of pain and removed his hands, slowly. Blood soaked his breeches, but no fresh scarlet appeared. The wound looked horrible. Muscles lay open, and Tavi thought he caught a glimpse of white bone beneath. His stomach heaved again, and he looked away.

"Crows," he breathed. He was still shaking, his heart still beating too quickly. "Uncle. Are you all right?"

"Hurting pretty good. Keep talking to me until it passes a little."

Tavi fretted at his lip. "All right. What was that thing?"

"Herdbane. They have them further south. Fever-thorn Jungle mostly. Never heard of one this far north before. Or that big."

"They kill for sport?"

"No. Too stupid to know when to stop. Once they scent blood, they tear apart anything that moves."

Tavi swallowed and nodded. "Are we in danger now?"

"Maybe. Herdbane hunt in pairs. Go look at the bird."

"What?"

"Look at the crow-eaten bird, boy," Bernard growled.

Tavi rose to his feet and went back over to the herd-bane. Its free leg twitched, the talons opening and clos-ing spasmodically. The smell of offal surrounded him, and Tavi held his breath, covering his nose and mouth with one hand.

Bernard grunted and sat up, though his head dropped for a moment as he did, and he had to brace his hands on the ground. "You killed it with the first blow, Tavi. You should have stepped back and let the thing die."

"But it was still fighting," Tavi said.

Bernard shook his head. "You'd laid its neck open. It

wasn't going to be fighting for long. Takes time to bleed to death, and until they do they can take you with them. Look at its neck. Right behind its head."

Tavi swallowed and walked around the corpse, and around Brutus as well, until he stood behind the bird's beak and looked as his uncle had directed him.

Something disturbed the feathers just behind the bird's head. He knelt down and reached out with tentative fingers to brush some of the feathers away and peer at whatever it was.

A circlet made out of a braid of several types of rough cloth and hide encompassed the bird's throat, denting in the muscle where it pressed. "There's some kind of collar on it," Tavi said.

"What's it made of?" Bernard rumbled.

"I don't know. Cloth and some leather in a braid. It doesn't look familiar."

"That's a Marat collar. We need to get out of the barrens, Tavi."

Tavi looked up, startled. "There aren't any Marat in the Calderon Valley, Uncle. The Legions keep them out. There hasn't been a Marat here since they had the big battle years and years ago."

Bernard nodded. "Before you were born. But two cohorts at Garrison doesn't necessarily keep them out if they aren't coming in numbers. There's a Marat warrior up here, and he isn't going to be happy that we killed his bird. Neither is its mate."

"Mate?"

"Marks on the top of her head. Mating scars. We killed the female."

Tavi swallowed. "Then I guess we should go."

Bernard nodded, the motion weary, unsteady. "Come here boy."

Tavi did, kneeling close to his uncle. One of the sheep let out a bleat, and Tavi frowned, looking up. The small flock milled around, and Dodger began to trot about, shoving them roughly back into a group with his horns.

"Brutus," Bernard said, his voice gruff and unsteady. He drew in a deep breath, expression becoming one of concentration. "Let go of the bird. Take us both back home."

The stone hound dropped the bird and turned toward Bernard. Brutus sank down into the earth again. Tavi felt the patch of ground he stood on begin to quiver and move. Then with a groan of tortured rock, a slab of stone perhaps five feet across rose up beneath them and began sliding southward, like a raft on a slow-moving river. The earth-raft drifted toward the entryway to the little clearing, slowly gathering speed.

Bernard muttered, "Just wake me up when we get back." Then he lay down and closed his eyes, his face and body going immediately slack again.

Tavi glanced at his uncle, frowning, and then back at the sheep. Dodger had them herded into the thicket again and had presented his horns—and not toward Tavi.

"Uncle Bernard," Tavi said, and he thought his voice sounded high-pitched and panicky. "Uncle Bernard. I think something is coming."

Tavi's uncle did not respond. Tavi looked around for his uncle's sword, but he had left it lying beside the herdbane's body, and it was now two dozen strides away. Tavi clenched his hands into frustrated fists. This was all his fault. If he hadn't shirked his duties to impress Benitte, he wouldn't have needed to come looking for Dodger and his uncle wouldn't have needed to follow him.

Tavi shivered. Suddenly, the possibility of death seemed very real, looming stark and close.

Shadows fell over the valley, and Tavi looked up to see racing clouds darken the sun, and he heard a distant rumble of thunder. Wind made the trees and scant brush begin to sway and stir, and the earth raft seemed to crawl. Though already up to the walking pace of a man, and still accelerating, Tavi found himself desperate to move faster and terrified that it might already be too late.

Tavi swallowed. If something came after them now, his uncle would not be able to help him. Tavi would have to handle it alone.

A high, whistling screech came from the trees to the west of them, up the slope.

Tavi jerked his head in that direction, but saw nothing. The screech repeated itself.

Another herdbane.

A second screech answered it, this time from the east of the earth-raft and from unnervingly close at hand. A third? Brush rattled perhaps fifty paces back in the trees. Then again, closer. Tavi thought he saw something moving toward them. Closing in.

"They're coming," he said, in a quiet voice.

Tavi swallowed. Though Brutus might eventually reach the pace of a running man and hold it for hours or days, he wouldn't get there in time to help them escape. Bernard had no chance at all of evading another herdbane as he lay unconscious, and Brutus's focus was all on bearing the pair of them back toward home.

Which meant that the only way his uncle could escape was if the herdbanes went looking somewhere else. If someone led them off in another direction.

Tavi took a deep breath, rolled off the earth-raft to one side of the trail, and lay completely still. If the herdbanes tracked movement, surely they would have more trouble with the wind rising and the trees and brush swaying in it. He would remain still for a while and then start making plenty of noise and motion, to draw the hunters away from their vulnerable prey.

Thunder rumbled again, and Tavi felt a tiny, cold raindrop splash on his cheek. He looked up and saw vast and dark clouds growing around the mountain. Another cold raindrop fell on him, and he felt a rush of fear that nearly forced him to empty his stomach. Furystorms could be deadly to anyone caught out in the open. Without the solid protection of the steadholt's walls or the protection of his own furies, he would be nearly helpless before the storm. Breathing fast and light, Tavi picked up several rocks that seemed a good size for throwing. Then he turned to the west and hurled the stone on the highest arch he could manage.

The stone flew in silence and struck on a tree trunk, making a sharp sound. Tavi pressed against the base of the tree and held still.

There was a whistle from the other side of the trail, and something moved through the brush, toward it. Tavi heard steps behind him, and then a great dark form flashed past him in near silence, a bound that took it across the rough trail Brutus's passage had made. Another herdbane, this one darker, larger than the first. It ran on its toes, though its talons rattled against fallen pine needles and its feathers brushed through the limbs of the evergreens. It went toward the spot where the stone had landed, vanishing back into the brush.

Tavi let out a breath. He threw another stone, farther away, back toward the clearing, rather than in the direction where Brutus was slowly bearing his uncle to safety. Then he crouched low and headed back toward the clearing himself, tossing a new stone every few paces. The wind kept rising, and more tiny, stinging droplets of near-frozen rain began to fall.

Tavi labored to keep his breathing as silent as he could and crept back to the clearing, quiet as a cat, creeping the last few paces on his belly, under the overhanging branches of one of the evergreens. The sheep were nowhere to be seen.

But the second herdbane was already there.

So was the Marat.

This herdbane stood at least a head taller than the first, and its feathers were darker, its eyes a browner shade of gold. It stood over the corpse of the bird Tavi had killed, one leg cocked up underneath its body, leaning its neck down to nuzzle its beak against its dead mate's feathers.

The Marat was the first Tavi had seen. He was tall, taller than anyone Tavi knew. He looked not unlike a man, but his shoulders were very broad, and his body heavy with flat, swift-looking muscle. He wore only a cloth around his hips, though that seemed mostly utilitarian, worn only to provide a belt to hang several pouches from, and from which depended something that looked like a dagger made of black glass. His hair was long and thick and looked sickly white in the dim grey light that shone through the rain clouds. He had tied dark feathers into his hair, here and there, and they lent him a savage aspect.

The Marat moved to the herdbane's body and knelt over it, reaching out to lay both wide, powerful-looking hands upon the beast. He let out a soft, keening sound, which was echoed by the male beside him, and both went still for a moment, bowing their heads.

Then the man snarled, splitting his lips apart, and his head turned this way and that, looking around him, white teeth bared. His eyes, Tavi saw, were precisely the same shade of gold as the herdbane's, inhuman and bright.

Tavi remained where he was, hardly daring to breathe. The Marat's features were not difficult to read. He was furious, and as the man turned his head in a slow circle around the clearing, Tavi saw that his teeth and his hands were stained with scarlet blood.

The Marat stood and held a hand to his mouth. He took a breath and blew, a wailing whistle flying from his lips, loud enough to make Tavi wince. He blew a short sequence, the notes higher and lower, long and short. Then he fell silent.

Tavi's brow furrowed into a frown, and he dropped his jaw a little, half-closing his eyes, and listened.

After a time, there came, half-mangled by the rising winds, a whistling answer. Tavi had no way of knowing what the answer said, but that there *was* an answer in itself was frightening enough. The whistling communication could mean only one thing: There were more than one of the barbarians here.

The Marat had returned to Calderon Valley.

Perhaps they were simply hunting, taking refuge from detection in the humanity-free area in the pine barrens around Garados. Or perhaps, Tavi's panicked thoughts ran, they were the advance scouts for a horde. But that seemed mad. A horde hadn't been seen in more than fifteen years—not since before Tavi was born, and while they had enjoyed a brief spate of victory, destroying the Crown Legion and slaying the Princeps Gaius, the Aleran Legions had crushed the horde only weeks later, dealing them such a deadly stroke that everyone had assumed that the Marat would never return.

Tavi swallowed. But they *had* returned. And if they meant to return in force, the Marat in the valley were probably advance scouts. If they were, they would never let one rather skinny and undersized boy who had seen them escape to warn others of their presence.

The Marat returned to glaring around the clearing. He seized several feathers and jerked them out of the dead herdbane, then reached up and tied them to strands of his hair. He made a whistling sound at the living herdbane, moving one hand in a gesture. The bird responded by moving in that direction in long, stalking steps, its eyes sweeping back and forth.

The Marat, meanwhile, dropped down to all fours. He sniffed at the blood on the fallen herdbane's claws and then, to Tavi's disgust, leaned down and ran his tongue along it. Then he closed his mouth with his eyes narrowed, tasting the blood as though it were a wine. The Marat opened his eyes again, remained low, on all fours, and began casting around the floor of the clearing like a dog after a scent. He paused at the fallen sword and picked it up, staring down at the weapon stained with the herdbane's blood. Then he lowered the blade to wipe it clean on the grass of the clearing and slipped it through his cloth-belt.

The wind continued to rise and changed directions at every breath. Tavi felt it brush against his back. He froze in place, sure that if he moved he would be immediately seen.

The Marat jerked his head up, abruptly turning to look directly at Tavi's hiding place. The boy swallowed, tensing in fear. The Marat let out another whistle and made a hand signal. The herdbane stalked toward Tavi's hiding place.

Just like a chicken after a bug, Tavi thought. *And I'm the bug.*

But a few steps later, the herdbane let out a shriek, turning to face south. The Marat followed the herdbane, golden eyes reading the signs of passage in the earth. He crouched down, nostrils flaring and looked up with a sudden, eager light in his eyes.

The Marat rose and began to stalk southward after Tavi's wounded uncle.

"No!" Tavi shouted. He threw himself to his feet and out of his hiding place, hurling one of his remaining stones at the Marat. His aim proved true. The rock struck the Marat high on the cheek, and blood welled from the gash.

The Marat stared at Tavi with those golden, bird-of-prey eyes and snarled something in a tongue Tavi could not understand. His intentions, though, were clear even before he drew the glass dagger from his belt. His eyes burned with anger.

The Marat let out a whistle, and the herdbane whirled toward him. Then he pointed at Tavi and let out that same whistling teakettle battle cry the dead bird had used.

Tavi turned and ran.

He had run from those larger and stronger than him

for the whole of his young life. Most games at the stead-holt involved chasing of one kind or another, and Tavi had learned how to make his small size and quickness work for him. He ran through the densest thickets of bracken he could find and slipped through mazes of thorns, windfalls, sinkholes, and young evergreens.

The wind grew stronger, filling the air with fallen pine needles and dust. Tavi ran west to lead them away from his uncle. The eerie wailing of the herdbane and its master raced after him, but fear gave his feet wings.

The boy's heart pounded like a smith's hammer, heavy and swift. He knew that he was alone, and that no one would come to help him. He had to rely on his own wits and experience, and should he falter or slow, the pursuing Marat and herdbane would have him. Sunset was drawing near, and the vast storm building over Garados had begun to spread over the Valley. Should the Marat, the storm, or the darkness catch him unprotected in the open, he would die.

Tavi ran for his life.

◦◦◦◦ CHAPTER 6

When twilight fell, Amara remained at liberty.

Her body ached to her bones. The first swift rush of flight had taken the strength from her, and the second, steadier flight would have been impossible without a fortunate breeze blowing north and east, in the direction she fled. She was able to use the prevailing currents of wind to assist Cirrus, and thus to conserve much of her own energy.

Amara kept low, at the tops of the trees almost, and although they swayed and danced at the passage of the miniature cyclone that kept her aloft, she was better off flying low, where the terrain might help hide her passage from the eyes of the Knights Aeris pursuing her.

The last, rust-colored light of sunset showed her a sparkle of water, a winding ribbon running through the rolling, wooded hills: the river Gaul. It taxed her remaining reserves to guide Cirrus to bring her in for a gentle landing and took even more of an effort to remain on her feet after the tension of flight left her. She felt like crawling into a hollow tree and sleeping for a week.

Instead, she reached down to her tattered dress, tore at the hem on one side, and from it withdrew a small disk of bright copper.

"River Gaul," she whispered, pushing whatever reserves she had left into the effort to speak to the water furies. "Know this coin, and hasten word to thy master." She dropped the coin, giving it a slight spin, and the image of the First Lord's profile spun and tumbled, alternating with the image of the sun in the bloody light.

Amara slumped down then, by the water, reaching out to cup her hands in it. Long runs were not as draining as an hour of flight—even on a good day for it. She had been fortunate. If the winds had been different, she would not have been able to escape to the Gaul.

She stared down at her faint reflection and shivered

for a moment. She thought of the water writhing its way up her hands, down her nose and throat, and her heart thudded with sickly fear. She struggled to force it away, but it wouldn't leave her. She could not make herself touch the water.

The water witch could have killed her. Amara could have died, right there. She hadn't. She had survived—but even so, it was all she could do to keep from cowering back on the bank.

She closed her eyes for a moment and tried to force the image of the woman's laughter out of her head. The men who had been chasing her presented no special fear. If she was captured by them, she would be killed with bright steel, perhaps brutalized—but all of that, she had prepared herself for.

She thought of the smile on Odiana's face as her water fury had smothered Amara, drowning her on dry land. There had been an almost childish, unrestrained glee in the woman's eyes.

Amara shuddered. Nothing had prepared her for that.

And yet she had to face that terror. She had to embrace it. Her duty required her to do no less.

She thrust her hands into the cold water of the river.

The young Cursor splashed water onto her face and made an abortive attempt to comb her hair with her fingers. Even though she wore it shorter than was customary, barely to her shoulders, and even though her hair was straight and fine, a tawny, brown-gold, still, a few hours in gale winds had tangled it into knots and made her look like a particularly shaggy mongrel dog.

She eyed her reflection again. Thin, harsh features, she thought, though with the proper cosmetics, she could whittle them down to merely severe. Listless hair, cobwebby and delicate—and currently as tousled as a haystack. Her face and arms, beneath the grime, were tanned as dark as her hair, giving her a monochromatic look in the water, like a statue carved of pale wood and then lightly stained. Her simple clothes were tattered, frayed at the edges from hours in the wind, and thickly stained with mud and spatters of dark brown that must have been blood around the slice in her blouse where her arm throbbed with dull pain.

The water stirred, and a furycrafted form rose out of it—but instead of the First Lord, a woman took shape. Gaius Caria, wife to Gaius Sextus, Alera's First Lord, seemed young, hardly older than Amara herself. She wore a splendid high-waisted gown, her hair coiffed into an intricate series of braids with a few artful curls falling to frame her face. The woman was beautiful, but more than that, she carried with her a sense of serenity, of purpose, of grace—and of power.

Amara abruptly felt like a gangling cow and dropped into a curtsey as best she could, hands taking the soiled skirts and holding to them. "Your Grace."

"Academ," murmured the woman in reply. "Not twenty days have passed since my husband gave you his coin, and already you interrupt his supper. I believe that is a new record. Fidelias, I am told, did not see fit to drag him from his meal or his bed until at least a month had gone by."

Amara felt her face flush with heat. "Yes, Your Grace. I apologize for the necessity."

The First Lady gave her an arch look, up and down the grimy length of her body. Amara felt her blush deepen, and she fought not to squirm. "No apology is necessary," Lady Caria said. "Though you might work on your timing in the future."

"Yes, Lady. Please, Your Grace. I need to speak to the First Lord."

Lady Caria shook her head. "Impossible," she said, her tone one of finality. "I'm afraid you'll have to speak to him later. Perhaps tomorrow."

"But, Lady—"

"He's swamped," the First Lady said, emphasizing each syllable. "If you feel the matter is an important one, Academ, then you may leave me a message and I will present it to him as soon as opportunity allows."

"Please forgive me, Lady, but I was told that if I ever used the coin, that the message was to be only for him."

"Mind your tongue, Academ," Caria said, her brows arched. "Remember to whom you speak."

"I have the orders from the First Lord himself, Your Grace. I only attempt to obey them."

"Admirable. But the First Lord is not a favorite professor you can simply visit yourself upon whenever you wish, Academ." She stressed the last word, very slightly. "And he has affairs of state to attend to."

Amara swallowed and said, "Your Grace, please. I will not be long in telling him. Let him judge if I am abusing the privilege. Please."

"No," Caria said. The sculpted figure looked over its shoulder. "You have taken enough of my time, Academ Amara." The First Lady's voice gained a note of tension, hurry. "If that is all . . ."

Amara licked her lips. If she could hold on a moment more, perhaps the First Lord would overhear the conversation. "Your Grace, before you go, may I give you a message to pass on to him?"

"Be quick."

"Yes, Your Grace. If you would only tell him that—"

Amara didn't get any farther than that before the watery form of the First Lady grimaced and shot her a cool glance, her features becoming remote and hard.

The water beside Lady Caria stirred, and a second furycrafted shape rose from it. This one was a man, tall, with shoulders that had once been broad, but were now slumped with age. He carried himself with a casual pride and a confidence that showed in every line of his body. The waterfigure did not appear in liquid translucence, as did Lady Caria's. It rose from the river in full color, and Amara thought, for just a moment, that the First Lord himself had somehow come, rather than sending a fury in his place. His hair was dark, streaked with silver-white strands, and his green eyes looked faded, weary, and confident.

"Here now," said the figure in a gentle, ringing bass. "What passes, my wife?" The figure of Gaius turned toward Amara, squinting. His features went completely still for a moment. Then he murmured, "Ah. I see. Greetings, Cursor."

Lady Caria shot her husband's image a glance at the use of that title, and then her remote gaze returned to Amara. "This one wished to speak with you, but I had informed her that you had a state dinner to attend."

"Your Majesty," Amara murmured, and curtseyed again.

Gaius let out a sigh and waved a hand, vaguely. "You go ahead, my wife. I'll be along shortly."

Lady Caria's chin lifted, tilting with a sharp little

motion. "Husband. There will be considerable consternation if we do not arrive together."

Gaius turned his face toward Lady Caria. "Then if it pleases you, wife, you may wait elsewhere for me."

The First Lady pressed her lips together, but gave a graceful, proper nod, before her image abruptly fell back into the water, creating a splash that drenched Amara to the waist. The girl let out a surprised cry, moving to wipe uselessly at her skirts. "Oh, my lord, please excuse me."

Gaius made a tsking sound and his image moved a hand. The water fled from the cloth of her skirts, simply pattered out onto the ground in a steady rain of orderly droplets that gathered into a small, muddy puddle and then flowed back down into the river, leaving her skirts, at least, quite clean.

"Please excuse the First Lady," Gaius murmured. "These last three years have not been kind to her."

Three years since she married you, my lord, Amara thought. But aloud, she said only, "Yes, Your Majesty."

The First Lord inhaled, then nodded, the expression brusque. He had shaved his beard since Amara had seen him last, and the lines of age, faint on the mostly youthful features, showed as dark shadows at the corners of his eyes and mouth. Gaius appeared to be a hale forty years of age—in fact, Amara knew that he was twice that. And that no silver had been showing in his hair when she arrived at the Royal Academy, five years before.

"Your report," Gaius said. "Let's hear it."

"Yes, milord. As you instructed, Fidelias and I attempted to infiltrate the suspected revolutionary camp. We were successful in getting inside." She felt her mouth go dry, and she swallowed. "But . . . But he . . ."

Gaius nodded, his expression grave. "But he betrayed you. He proved to be more interested in serving the cause of the insurrectionists than in remaining loyal to his lord."

Amara blinked up at him, startled. "Yes, milord. But how did you—"

Gaius shrugged. "I didn't. But I suspected. When you reach my age, Amara, people show themselves to you very clearly. They write their intentions and beliefs through their actions, their lies." He shook his head. "I saw the signs in Fidelias when he was only a little older than you. But that seed has picked a particularly vicious moment to bloom."

"You suspected?" Amara asked. "But you told me nothing?"

"Could you have kept it from him? Could you have played that kind of charade with *him*, who taught you, for the duration of the mission?"

Amara clenched her teeth rather than speak in anger. Gaius was right. She never would have been able to keep such knowledge from Fidelias. "Why did you send me?" Her words came out clipped, precise.

Gaius gave her a weary smile. "Because you are the fastest Cursor I have ever seen. Because you were a brilliant student at the Academy, resourceful, stubborn, and able to think on your feet. Because Fidelias liked you. And because I was sure of your loyalty."

"Bait," Amara said, her words still with hard edges, points. "You used me as bait. You knew he wouldn't be able to resist trying to bring me with him. Recruit me."

"Essentially correct."

"You would have sacrificed me."

"If you hadn't come back, I would know that you had failed in your mission, probably because of Fidelias. Either that, or you would have cast your lot with the insurgents. Either way, I would be sure of the color of Fidelias's cloak."

"Which was the point of the exercise."

"Hardly. I needed the intelligence, as well."

"So you risked my life to get it?"

Gaius nodded. "Yes, Cursor. You swore your life to the service of the Crown, did you not?"

Amara looked down, her face coloring, anger and confusion and disappointment piling up in her belly. "Yes, milord."

"Then report. I do have to be at dinner shortly."

Amara took a breath, and without looking up, she recounted the events of the day—what she and Fidelias had seen, what she knew about the insurgent Legion, and especially of the strength and estimated numbers of the Knights accompanying it.

She looked up at the end of her report. Gaius's face looked older, the lines deeper, somehow, as though her words to him had drained out a little more of his life, his youth, his strength.

"The note. The one you were allowed to read," Gaius began.

"A diversion, milord. I know. An attempt to cast suspicion elsewhere. I do not believe Lord Atticus to have a hand in this."

"Perhaps. But remember that the note was addressed to the commander of the *second* Legion." Gaius shook his head. "That would seem to indicate that more than one of the High Lords is conspiring against me. This may be the effort of one to ensure that the blame for the entire matter falls on the other."

"Assuming there are only two, milord."

Gaius's eyes wrinkled further, at the corners. "Yes. Assuming all of them aren't in it together, eh?" The brief smile faded. "And that they wished details of my inner chambers from you seems to indicate that they believe they could accomplish an assassination, and so take power directly."

"Surely not, milord. They could not kill you."

Gaius shrugged. "Not if I saw it coming. But the power to shake mountains does little good if the knife is already buried in one's throat." He grimaced. "One of the younger High Lords. It must be. Anyone of any age would simply use Time as his assassin. I am an old man."

"No, Your Majesty. You are—"

"An old man. An old man married to a willful and politically convenient child. An old man who rarely sleeps at night and who needs to be on time to dinner." He eyed Amara up and down and said, "Night is falling. Are you in condition to travel?"

"I believe so, milord."

Gaius nodded. "Events are stirring all over Alera. I can feel it in my bones, girl. The march of feet, the restless migration of beasts. Already the behemoths sing in the darkness off the western coast, and the wild furies of the north country are preparing a cold winter this year. A cold winter . . ." The First Lord drew in a breath and closed his eyes. "And voices speak loudly. Tension gathers in one place. The furies of earth and air and wood whisper everywhere that something dangerous is abroad and that the peace our land has enjoyed these past fifteen years nears its end. Metal furies hone the edges of swords and startle smiths at the forge. The rivers and the rains wait for when they shall run red with blood. And fire itself burns green of a night, or blue, rather than in scarlet and gold. Change is coming."

Amara swallowed. "Perhaps they are only coincidences, milord. They may not be—"

Gaius smiled again, but the expression was skeletal, wasted. "I'm not that old, Amara. Not yet. And I have work for you. Attend."

Amara nodded and focused on the image.

"Are you familiar with the significance of the Calderon Valley?"

Amara nodded once. "It lies just over the isthmus between Alera and the plains beyond. There is only one pass through the mountains, and it runs through the valley. If anyone wants to come into our lands afoot, they must come through Calderon Valley."

"Anyone meaning the Marat, of course," Gaius said. "What else do you know of the place?"

"What they taught at the Academy, milord. Very fertile land. Profitable. And it was where the Marat killed your son, milord."

"Yes. The Marat hordemaster. He killed the Princeps and set a chain of events into motion that will clutter the lecture halls and plague the students for a century to come. The House of Gaius has led Alera for nearly a thousand years, but when I am gone, that will be done. All that is left to me is to see to it that the power falls into responsible hands. And it would seem that someone seeks to make that choice in my stead."

"Do you know who, milord?"

"Suspicions," Gaius said. "But I dare not voice more than that, lest I accuse an innocent man and lose the support of the High Lords altogether, loyal and insurgent alike. You will go to the Calderon Valley, Amara. The Marat are on the move. I know it. I feel it."

"What do you wish me to do there, milord?"

"You will observe the movements of any Marat in the area," Gaius said. "And speak to the Steadholders there, to learn what passes."

Amara tilted her head to one side. "You suspect that the Marat and the recent insurgent activity are related, milord?"

"The Marat are easily made into tools, Amara. And I suspect that someone has forged a dagger of them to thrust at my heart." His eyes flashed, and the river rippled around the feet of the water image, in reaction to the emotion. "I may pass on my power to someone of worth, but while I live and breathe they will not take it from me."

"Yes, milord."

Gaius gave her a grim smile. "If you should stumble over some connection between the two, Amara, bring it to me. If I had a scrap of *proof* to lay before the High Lords, I could settle this without needless bloodshed."

"As you wish, milord. I will go there as swiftly as I am able."

"Tonight," Gaius said.

Amara shook her head. "I'm not sure I can do that, Majesty. I'm exhausted."

Gaius nodded. "I will speak to the south wind. It will help you get there more quickly."

Amara swallowed. "What am I to look for, milord?

Do you have any suspicions? If I know what to be on watch for . . ."

Gaius said, "No. I need your eyes open and unprejudiced. Get to the Valley. It is where events are centering. I want you representing my interests in them."

"Am I likely to face near-certain death again, milord?" Amara let just a hint of barb slide into the words.

Gaius tilted his head. "Almost certainly, Cursor. Do you wish me to send another in your place?"

Amara shook her head. "I wish for you to answer a question."

Gaius lifted his eyebrows. "What is your question?"

Amara looked steadily at Gaius's image. "How did you know, milord? How did you know I would remain true to the Crown?"

Gaius frowned, more lines appearing on his face. He remained silent for a long moment, before he said, "There are some people who will never understand what loyalty means. They could tell you what it was, of course, but they will never *know*. They will never see it from the inside. They couldn't imagine a world where something like that was real."

"Like Fidelias."

"Like Fidelias," Gaius agreed. "You're a rare person, though, Amara. You're just the opposite."

She frowned. "You mean, I know what loyalty is?"

"More than that. You live within it. You couldn't imagine a world in which you didn't. You could no more betray what you held dear than you could will your heart to stop beating. I am old, Amara. And people reveal themselves to me." He was quiet for a moment more, and said, "I never doubted your loyalty. Only your ability to survive the mission. And it appears that I may owe you an apology, on that count, Cursor Amara. Consider your graduation exercise a success."

Amara felt pride stir in her, an absurd feeling of pleasure that Gaius would praise her so. She felt her back straighten and her chin lift a little higher. "I am your eyes and ears to command, milord."

Gaius nodded, once, and behind Amara the wind began to rise, rustling over the trees like surf over sand, making them whisper and sigh in a vast, quiet chorus. "Go with the furies then, Cursor. For Alera."

"I *will* find what you need, Your Majesty. For Alera."

CHAPTER 7

Fidelias hated flying.

He sat on the litter, facing ahead, so that the wind sliced into his eyes and blew his hair straight back from his high forehead. On the seat facing him sat Aldrick the Sword, huge and relaxed as a newly fed lion. Odiana had curled up on Aldrick's lap to doze off hours before, and the water witch's dark hair danced and played in the wind, veiling the beauty of her features. Neither one evinced any signs of discomfort at the flight, physical or otherwise.

"I hate flying," Fidelias muttered. He lifted a hand to

shield his eyes from the wind, and leaned over the edge of the litter. A brilliant moon, looming large among a sea of stars, painted the landscape below in silver and black. Wooded hills rolled slowly beneath them, a solid darkness, broken here and there by silver-kissed clearings and winding, half-luminescent rivers.

Four of the Knights Aeris from the camp bore them through the air, one at each pole of the litter. They wore harnesses that fitted them to the litter, supporting the weight of the three people inside, while the Knights' weight, in turn, was borne by the powerful furies at their command. Another half dozen Knights Aeris flew in a loose ring around the litter, and moonlight glittered on the steel of their arms and armor.

"Captain," Fidelias called to the lead Knight. The man glanced back over his shoulder, murmured something, and drifted back through the air toward the litter.

"Sir?"

"Will it be much longer before we arrive in Aquitaine?"

"No, sir. We should be there before the hour is out."

Fidelias blinked. "That soon? I thought you said it would take us until dawn."

The Knight shook his head, eyes cooly scanning the sky ahead. "Fortune favors us, sir. The furies of the south are stirring and have brought us a strong wind to speed our way."

The former Cursor frowned. "That's highly unusual at this season, is it not, Captain?"

The man shrugged. "It's saved us hours of flight time and made it easier on everyone. We haven't even had to spell the men bearing the litter. Relax, sir. I'll have you in the High Lord's palace before the witching hour."

And with that, the soldier accelerated, moving to take position ahead of the litter again.

Fidelias frowned and resettled on his seat. He glanced over the side of the litter again, and his stomach jumped and fluttered with an irrational sensation of fear. He knew that he was as safe flying in the litter, escorted by Knights Aeris, as anywhere in the Realm, but some part of his mind simply would not casually accept the vast distance between himself and the ground below. Here, he was far from wood and earth, far from the furies he could call to his service, and that disturbed him. He had to rely upon the strength of the Knights with him rather than his own. And everyone other than himself had, in time, inevitably disappointed him.

He folded his arms and bowed his head against the wind, brooding. Gaius had used him from the very beginning. Used him with a purpose, to be sure, and never carelessly. He had been far too valuable a tool to waste through misuse or neglect. Indeed, at times, the precarious peace of the entire Realm had occasionally hinged upon his ability to accomplish on behalf of the Crown.

Fidelias felt his frown deepen. Gaius was old—the old wolf that led the pack—and it was nothing more than a matter of time before he was hauled down to his death. But despite that brutal, simple truth, Gaius continued to fight against the inevitable. He could have turned over power to a nominal heir a decade ago, but instead, he had held on, wily and desperate, and delayed matters for a decade by pitting the High Lords against one another in bids to see who could position his daughter or niece to marry the First Lord and give birth to the new Princeps.

Gaius (with Fidelias's aid, of course) had played the lords off of one another with merciless precision, until every High Lord of Alera spent years convinced that *his* candidate would surely be the one to wed Gaius. His eventual choice had pleased no one, not even High Lord Parcius, Caria's father, and even the most dense of the High Lords had realized, in time, that they had been played for fools.

The game had been well played, but in the end it had all been for nothing. The House of Gaius had never been a fertile one, and even if he had proved physically capable of producing an Heir (which Fidelias remained unsure about), the First Lady had not, as yet, shown herself to be with child, and palace rumor held that the First Lord seldom went to the same bed in which his wife slept.

Gaius was old. He was dying. The star of his House was falling from the heavens, and anyone who blindly clung to the hem of his robes would fall with him.

Like Amara.

Fidelias frowned, while something nagged at him, distracted him, burned in his belly. It was a pity, to be sure, that Amara had chosen a fool's crusade rather than making an intelligent decision. Surely, if he'd had more time, it may have proved possible to encourage her to see a more rational point of view. Now, instead, he would have to act directly against her, if she interfered again.

And he did not want to do that.

Fidelias shook his head. The girl had been his most promising student, and he had let her come to mean too much to him. He had destroyed some three score men and women in his years as a Cursor—some of them as powerful and idealistic as Amara. He had never hesitated to perform his duty, never let himself be distracted by anything so trivial as personal attachment. His love was for Alera.

And that was really the issue at hand. Fidelias served the Realm, not the First Lord. Gaius was doomed. Delay of the transfer of power from Gaius's hands to another could only cause strife and bloodshed among the High Lords who would wish to assume Gaius's station. It might even come to a war of succession, something unheard of since the dawn of Aleran civilization, but which was rumored to have been commonplace in the distant past. And should that happen, not only would the sons and daughters of Alera die pointlessly, fighting one another, but the division itself would be a signal fire to the enemies of the Realm—the savage Icemen, the bestial Marat, the ruthless Canim, and who knew what else in the unexplored wilds of the world. Above all else, such weakening of the Realm's unity had to be circumvented.

And that meant establishing a strong ruler, and swiftly. Already, the High Lords quietly defied the First Lord's authority. It would only be a matter of time before the High Lords and their cities disbanded the Realm into a cluster of city-nations. And if *that* happened, it would be simple for the enemies of mankind to quietly nibble away at those realms until nothing was left.

Fidelias grimaced, his belly burning more sharply. It had to be done, like a battlefield surgeon forced to remove a mangled limb. There was nothing that would make it less gruesome. The best one could hope for was to get it done as swiftly and cleanly as possible.

Which led to Aquitainus. He was the most ruthless, the most able, and perhaps the strongest of the High Lords.

Fidelias's stomach roiled.

He had betrayed Gaius, the Codex, the Cursors. Betrayed his student, Amara. He had turned his back on them, to support a man who might become the most ruthless and bloodthirsty dictator Alera had ever known. The furies knew, he had tried everything in his power to convince Gaius to take another path.

Fidelias had been forced to this.

It was necessary.

It had to be done.

His stomach burned as the glowing furylights of Aquitaine appeared on the horizon.

"Wake up," he murmured. "We're almost there."

Aldrick opened his eyes and focused on Fidelias. One hand absently caressed Odiana's dark wealth of hair, and she let out a pleased little whimper in her sleep, writhing in the man's lap with liquid sensuality, before settling into stillness again. The swordsman watched Fidelias, his expression unreadable.

"Deep thoughts, old man?" Aldrick asked.

"Some. How will Aquitaine react?"

The big man pursed his lips. "It depends."

"On what?"

"On what he is doing when we interrupt him with bad news."

"Is it all that bad?"

Aldrick smiled. "Just hope he's up drinking. He's usually in a pretty good mood. Tends to forget his anger by the time the hangover has worn off."

"It was an idiot's plan to begin with."

"Of course. It was his. He isn't a planner of deception or subterfuge. But I've never met a man who could lead

as strongly as he does. Or anyone with his raw power."
Aldrick continued stroking the sleeping water witch's
hair, his expression thoughtful. "Are you worried?"

"No," Fidelias lied. "I'm still too valuable to him."

"Perhaps, for now." Aldrick said. He smiled, a mirth-
less expression. "But I'll not be loaning you any money."

Fidelias clucked his teeth. "Direct action would have
been premature in any case. By escaping, the girl may
have done his Grace the biggest favor of his life."

"I don't doubt it," Aldrick murmured. "But somehow, I'm almost certain that he won't see it that way."

Fidelias studied the other man's face, but the swordsman's features revealed nothing. His grey eyes blinked
lazily, and his mouth curled into a smile, as though taking amusement in Fidelias's lack of ability to gauge him.
The Cursor frowned at the man, a mild expression, and
turned to watch the city of Aquitaine come into sight.

First came the lights. Firecrafters by the dozens maintained the lights along the city's streets, and they burned
with a gentle radiance through the mist-shrouded evening, all soft yellows, deep amber, pale crimson, until
the hill upon which the city was built seemed itself to
be one enormous, living flame, garbed in warmth and
flickering color. Upon the city's walls, and just beyond
them, lights burned with a cold, blue brilliance, casting the ground far around into stark illumination and
long black shadows, their harsh glare vigilant against any
would-be invaders.

As the litter glided down, and closer, Fidelias could
begin to make out shapes in the shifting lights. Statues
stood silent and lovely on the streets. Houses, all elegant
lines and high arches, contested with one another to

prove the most skillfully crafted, the most beautifully lit. Fountains sparkled and flickered, some of them illuminated from below, so that they burned violet or emerald in the darkness, pools of liquid flames. Trees rose up around houses and lined the streets, thriving and beautiful life that had been crafted as carefully as every other part of the city. They, too, wore veils of colored light, and their leaves, already changed into autumn's brilliant hues, shone in too many shades to count.

The sound of a bell tolling the late hour rose to the descending litter. Fidelias heard the trod of hooves upon paving stones somewhere below and raucous singing from a night club of some kind. Music came up from a garden party as the litter passed over it, strings supporting a sweet alto flute that pursued a gentle, haunting melody. The smell of wood smoke and spices still drifted on the evening breezes, along with the scent of late-blooming flowers and of rain on the wind.

To call Aquitaine beautiful was to call the ocean wet, Fidelias thought. Accurate enough, in its way, but wholly insufficient to the task.

They were challenged by a barking voice before they had come within a long bowshot of the High Lord's manor, a walled fortress surmounting the hill upon which the city stood. Fidelias watched as a man in the sable and scarlet surcoat of Aquitaine swept down from the air above. A dozen more hovered somewhere in the night sky above them, unseen—but the Cursor could feel the eddies of wind that their furies kicked up in keeping them aloft.

The challenger of the Knights Aeris guarding the High Lord's manor exchanged a pass phrase with the captain of Fidelias's own escort, though the exchange had the comfortable, routine air of a formality. Then the group swept on forward, down into the manor's courtyard, while more guards watched from the walls, along with leering statues wrought in the shapes of hunchbacked, gangly men. The moment Fidelias stepped from the litter, he felt the light, steady tremors of power in the earth that led back to each statue on the wall and found himself staring at the statues.

"Gargoyles?" he breathed. "All of them?"

Aldrick glanced at the statues and then to Fidelias and nodded once.

"How long have they been kept here?"

"As long as anyone remembers," Aldrick rumbled.

"Aquitaine is that strong . . ." Fidelias pursed his lips in thought. He did not agree with the principles of anyone who kept furies within such a restrictive confine—much less those who would trap them there for generations. But it certainly confirmed, had he been in any doubt, that Aquitaine's raw power was more than sufficient for the task at hand.

The Knights Aeris accompanying the litter departed toward a bunkhouse for food and drink, while the captain of Aquitaine's guard, a young man with an earnest expression and alert blue eyes, opened the door to the litter and extended a courteous hand to those within. Then he led them inside the manor proper.

Fidelias took casual note of the manor as he followed the young captain, marking the doors, the windows, the presence (or evident lack) of guards. It was an old habit, and one he would be foolish to surrender. He wanted to know the best way to leave any place he walked into. Aldrick walked beside him, casually carrying the still-sleeping Odiana as though she weighed no more than an armload of cloth, each footstep something solid, focused.

The young captain swung open a pair of double doors leading into a long feasting hall, complete with mountain-style fire pits built into the floors, already burning though the season had not yet grown truly cold. That dim, crimson light was the only illumination in the hall, and Fidelias took a moment to pause inside the doors and allow his eyes to adjust.

The hall stretched out, lined with a double row of smooth marble pillars. Curtains covered the walls, providing a bit of aesthetic warmth and the perfect cover for eavesdroppers, guards, or assassins. The tables had been taken down for the night, and the only furniture in the hall was a table and several chairs upon a dais at the far end. The shapes of people moved about there, and Fidelias could hear the gentle music of strings.

The captain led them all straight down the hall and toward the dais.

Upon a large chair covered in the fur of a grass lion from the Amaranth Vale sprawled a man—as tall as Aldrick, Fidelias judged, but more slender, and with the appearance of a young man in the prime of his youth. Aquitainus had high cheekbones and a narrow face, led by a strong jaw whose lines were softened by the tumble of dark golden hair that fell to his shoulders. He wore a simple scarlet blouse with black leather breeches and soft, black boots. A goblet dangled lazily in one hand, while the other held the end of a long strip of silken cloth that slowly unwound from the shapely girl dancing before him, gradually baring more and more of her skin. Aquitainus had eyes of pitch black, stark in that narrow face, and he watched the dancing slave with an almost feverish intensity.

Fidelias's eyes were drawn to the man standing behind and just a bit to one side of the High Lord's chair. In the dimness, details were difficult to make out. The man wasn't tall, perhaps only a few inches more than Fidelias himself, but was strongly built, his posture casually powerful, relaxed. He bore a sword at his hip—that much Fidelias could see—and a very slight bulge in his dark grey tunic perhaps revealed the presence of a hidden weapon. Fidelias met the silent man's eyes, briefly, and found the stranger's gaze to be opaque, assessing.

"If you value your head, Captain," Aquitainus murmured, without looking away from the girl, "it can wait until this dance is done." His voice, Fidelias noted, carried the faintest trace of a drunken slur.

"No, Your Grace," Fidelias said, stepping forward and past the captain, "it can't."

The High Lord's back stiffened, and he turned his head slowly toward Fidelias. The weight of the man's dark eyes fell onto the Cursor like a physical blow, and he drew in a sharp breath as he felt the stirring in the earth beneath them, a slow and sullen vibration, deep within the stone—a reflection of the High Lord's anger.

Fidelias assumed a casually confident stance and reacted as though Aquitainus had acknowledged him. He clasped a fist over his heart and bowed.

There was a long silence before Fidelias heard Aquitainus's reaction. The man let out a low and relaxed laugh that echoed throughout the nearly deserted hall. Fidelias straightened again, to face the High Lord, careful to keep his expression schooled into neutral respect.

"So," Aquitainus purred. "This is the infamous Fidelias Cursor Callidus."

"If it please Your Grace, Cursor no longer."

"You seem rather unconcerned with my pleasure," Aquitainus noted, with a droll roll of the hand still clasping the dancing girl's cloth. "I almost find it disrespectful."

"No disrespect was intended, Your Grace. There are grave matters that require your attention."

"Require . . . my . . . attention," murmured Aquitaine with an elegant arch of brow. "My. I don't think I've been spoken to in that fashion since just before my last tutor took that untimely fall."

"Your Grace will find me a good deal more agile."

"Rats are agile," sniffed Aquitaine. "The oaf's real problem was that he thought he knew everything."

"Ah," Fidelias said. "You will not face that difficulty with me."

Aquitaine's dark eyes shone. "Because you really do know everything?"

"No, Your Grace. Only everything of importance."

The High Lord narrowed his eyes. He remained silent for two score of Fidelias's quickening heartbeats, but the Cursor refused to let his nervousness show. He took slow and even breaths and remained silent, waiting.

Aquitaine snorted and drank off his remaining wine with an effortless flick of his wrist. He held the goblet out to one side, waited a beat, then released it. The blocky man beside him reached out a hand, snake swift, and caught it. The stranger walked to the table on the dais and refilled the goblet from a glass bottle.

"My sources told me that you had a reputation for insouciance, Fidelias," Aquitaine murmured. "But I had no idea that it would be so readily forthcoming."

"If it please Your Grace, perhaps we might table this discussion for the moment. Time may be of the essence."

The High Lord accepted the goblet of wine from the stranger, glancing at the pretty slave, now kneeling on the floor before him, head bowed. Aquitaine let out a wistful sigh. "I suppose," he said. "Very well, then. Report."

Fidelias glanced at the stranger, then at the slave, and then at the hanging curtains. "Perhaps a more private setting would be more appropriate, Your Grace."

Aquitaine shook his head. "You can speak freely here. Fidelias, may I present Count Calix of the Feverthorn Border, in service to His Grace, High Lord of Rhodes. He has shown himself to be a shrewd and capable advisor and a loyal supporter of our cause."

Fidelias shifted his attention to the blocky man beside the High Lord's seat. "The Feverthorn Border. Isn't that where that illegal slaving operation got broken up a few years ago?"

Count Calix spared the former Cursor a thin-lipped smile. When he spoke, his voice came out in a light, rich tenor completely at odds with the heavy power evident in his body. "I believe so, yes. I understand that both the Slavers Consortium and the Dianic League gave you commendations for valor above and beyond the call of duty."

Fidelias shrugged, watching the other man. "A token gesture. I never was able to turn up enough information to bring charges against the slave ring's leader." He paused for a moment, then added, "Whoever he was."

"A pity," said the Count. "I imagine you cost some-one a great deal of money."

"Most likely," Fidelius agreed.

"It could give a man good reason to hold a grudge."

Fidelius smiled. "I'm told those can be inimical to one's good health."

"Perhaps I'll put it to the test one day."

"Should you survive the experience, be sure to let me know what you learned."

Aquitaine watched the exchange, his dark eyes sparkling with mirth. "I hate to interrupt your fencing, gentlemen, but I have other interests this evening, and we have issues to discuss." He took another sip of wine and waved at the other chairs on the dais. "Sit down. You, too, Aldrick. Should I have someone carry Odiana to her chambers so that she can rest?"

"Thank you, sir," Aldrick rumbled. "I'll keep her with me and take care of her later, if it's all the same to you."

They settled down into chairs facing Aquitaine. The High Lord gestured, and the slave girl hurried to one side, returning with the traditional cloth and bowl of scented water. Then the girl settled at Fidelias's feet and unlaced his sandals. She removed the stockings, beneath, and with warm, gentle fingers began washing Fidelias's feet.

He frowned down at the slave, pensively, but at a second gesture from the High Lord, Fidelias uttered a concise report of the events at the camp of the renegade Legion. Aquitaine's expression darkened steadily throughout, until, at the end it had grown to a scowl.

"Let me test my understanding of what you are telling me, Fidelias," Aquitaine murmured. "Not only were you unable to attain intelligence regarding Gaius's chambers from this girl—in addition, she escaped from you and every one of my Knights."

Fidelias nodded. "My status has been compromised. And she has almost certainly reported to the Crown by now."

"The second Legion has already been disbanded into individual centuries," Aldrick supplied. The slave moved to kneel at his feet and to remove his sandals and stockings as well. The single, long piece of scarlet cloth wound around her had begun to slip and gape, displaying an unseemly amount of supple, smooth skin. Aldrick regarded her with casual admiration as he continued. "They will meet at the rendezvous as planned."

"Except for the Windwolves," Fidelias said. "I advised Aldrick to send them ahead to the staging area."

"What!?" snarled Aquitaine, rising. "That was not according to the plan."

The blocky Calix came to his feet as well, his eyes bright. "I warned you, Your Grace. If the mercenaries are not seen in Parcia over the winter, there will be nothing to link them to anyone but you. You have been betrayed."

Aquitaine's furious gaze settled on Fidelias. "Well, Cursor? Is what he says true?"

"If you consider adjusting to changing conditions in the field treachery, Your Grace," Fidelias said, "then you may name me traitor, if it pleases you."

"He twists your own words against you, Your Grace," Calix hissed. "He is using you. He is a Cursor, loyal to Gaius. If you keep listening to him, he will lead you to your death at Gaius's feet. Kill him before he poisons your thoughts any further. He, this murderous thug, and his mad whore—they all want nothing but your destruction."

Fidelias felt his lips tighten into a smile. He looked from Aquitaine to Calix—then to Aldrick, where the slave crouched at his feet, her lips parted, her eyes staring. Over Aldrick's lap, Odiana neither stirred nor spoke, but he could see her mouth turn up into a smile.

"Ah," Fidelias said, his own smile spreading wider. He folded one ankle over the other knee. "I see."

Aquitaine narrowed his eyes and stalked over to stand over Fidelias's chair. "You have interrupted a pleasant moment with the anniversary gift given me by my own dear wife. You have, it would seem, failed miserably in what you said you would do for me. Additionally, you have dispatched my troops in a fashion which could embarrass me acutely before the rest of the Lords Council, not to mention the Senate." He leaned down toward Fidelias and said, very gently, "I think it would be in your own best interest to give me a reason not to kill you in the next few seconds."

"Very well," Fidelias said. "If you will indulge me briefly, Your Grace, I may be able to let you decide for yourself whom you can trust."

"No!" sputtered Calix. "My lord, do not allow this deceitful slive to so use you."

Aquitaine smiled, but it was a cold, hard expression. His gaze swept to the Rhodisian Count, and Calix dropped silent at his glance. "My patience is wearing very thin. At the rate we're going, gentlemen, someone will be dead by the end of this conversation."

Heavy tension fell onto the room, thick as a winter blanket. Calix licked his lips, throwing a wide-eyed glare at Fidelias. Odiana made a soft sound and stirred artlessly on Aldrick's lap before settling again—leaving

Aldrick's right arm free to reach for his sword, Fidelias noted. The slave seemed to take notice of the tension as well and crawled a bit backward, until she was no longer between the High Lord and anyone else in the room.

Fidelias smiled. He folded his hands and rested them on his knee. "If it please Your Grace, I will need paper and pen."

"Paper and pen? What for?"

"Easier to show you, Your Grace. But if you remain unsatisfied after, I offer you my life as penance."

Aquitaine's teeth flashed. "My esteemed wife would say that your life is lost in either case, were she here."

"Were she here, Your Grace," Fidelias agreed. "May I proceed?"

Aquitaine stared down at Fidelias for a moment. Then he gestured toward the slave, who went scurrying, returning a moment later with parchment and pen. Aquitaine said, "Be quick. My patience is rapidly running out."

"Of course, Your Grace." Fidelias accepted the paper and pen, dipped the quill into the inkpot, and swiftly made a few notes on the paper, careful to let no one see what he was writing. No one spoke, and the scritching of the quill seemed loud in the hall, along with the crackle of the fire pits, and the impatient tapping of the High Lord's boot.

Fidelias blew on the letters, then folded the paper in half, and offered it to Aquitaine. Without looking away from the man, he said, "Your Grace, I advise you to accelerate your plans. Contact your forces and move at once."

Calix stepped forward at once, to Aquitaine's side. "Your Grace, I must disagree in the strongest terms.

Now is the time for caution. If we are discovered now, all will fall into ruin."

Aquitaine stared down at the letter, then lifted his eyes to Calix. "And you believe that by doing so you will protect my interests."

"And those of my Lord," Calix said. He lifted his chin, but the gesture meant little when the High Lord towered over him. "Think of who is advising you, Your Grace."

"*Ad hominem*," noted Aquitaine, "is a notoriously weak logical argument. And is usually used to distract the focus of a discussion—to move it from an indefensible point and to attack the opponent."

"Your Grace," Calix said, ducking his head. "Please, listen to reason. To act now would leave you at somewhat less than half your possible strength. Only a fool throws away an advantage like that."

Aquitaine lifted his eyebrows. "Only a fool. My."

Calix swallowed, "Your Grace, I only meant—"

"What you meant is of little concern, Count Calix. What you said, however, is another matter entirely."

"Your Grace, please. Do not be rash. Your plans have been well laid for so long. Do not let them fall apart now."

Aquitaine glanced down at the paper and asked, "And what do you propose, Your Excellency?"

Calix squared his shoulders. "Put simply, Your Grace—stick to the original plan. Send the Windwolves to winter in Rhodes. Gather your legions when the weather breaks in the spring and use them then. Bide. Wait. In patience there is wisdom."

"Who dares wins," murmured Aquitaine back. "I cannot help but wonder at how generous Rhodes seems to be, Calix. How he is willing to host the mercenaries, to have his name connected with them, when the matter is settled. How thoroughly he has instructed you to protect my interests."

"The High Lord is always most interested in supporting his allies, Your Grace."

Aquitaine snorted. "Of course he is. We are all so generous with one another. And forgiving. No, Calix. The Cursor—"

"Former Cursor, Your Grace," Fidelias put in.

"Former Cursor. Of course. The former Cursor here has done a very good job of predicting what you would tell me." Aquitaine consulted the paper he held. "I wonder why that is." He moved his eyes to Fidelias and arched his eyebrows.

Fidelias watched Calix and said, "Your Grace. I believe that Rhodes sent Calix here to you as a spy and eventually as an assassin—"

"Why you—" Calix snarled.

Fidelias overrode the other man, his voice iron. "Calix wishes you to wait so that there is time to remove you over the winter, Your Grace. The mercenaries will have several months to be tempted by bribes, meanwhile robbing you of their strength. Then, when the campaign begins, he will have key positions filled with people beholden to Rhodes. He can kill you in the confusion of battle, and therefore remove the threat you represent to him. Calix, here, was likely intended to be the assassin."

"I will *not* stand for this insult, Your Grace."

Aquitaine looked at Calix and said, "Yes. You will." To Fidelias, he said, "And your advice? What would you have me do?"

Fidelias shrugged. "South winds rose tonight where there should have been none. Only the First Lord could call them at this time of year. At a guess, he called the furies of the southern air to assist Amara or one of the other Cursors north—either to the capital or to the Valley itself."

"It could be coincidence," Aquitaine pointed out.

"I don't believe in coincidence, Your Grace," Fidelias said. "The First Lord is far from blind, and he has powers of furycrafting I can hardly begin to accurately assess. He has called the south winds. He is hastening someone north. Toward the Calderon Valley."

"Impossible," Aquitaine said. He rubbed at his jaw with the back of one hand. "But then, Gaius was always an impossible man."

"Your Grace," Calix said. "Surely you aren't seriously considering—"

Aquitaine lifted a hand. "I am, Your Excellency."

"Your *Grace*," Calix hissed. "This common born dog has called me a murderer to my face."

Aquitaine surveyed the scene for a moment. Then, quite deliberately, took three or four steps away from them and turned his back, as though to study a tapestry hanging on one wall.

"Your Grace," Calix said. "I demand your justice in this matter."

"I rather tend to believe Fidelias, Your Excellency." He sighed. "Work it out among yourselves. I will deal appropriately with whoever is left."

Fidelias smiled. "Your Excellency, please allow me to add that you stink like a sheep, that your mouth froths with idiocy and poison, and that your guts are as yellow as a springtime daffodil." He steepled his fingers, regarding Calix, and said, very soft and distinctly, "You . . . are . . . a . . . coward."

Calix's face flushed red, his eyes wild, and he moved, a sudden liquid blurring of his arms and hips. The sword at his side leapt free of its scabbard and toward Fidelias's throat.

As fast as Calix was, Aldrick moved faster. His arm alone whipped into motion, drawing the blade from his hip, across the limp form of the woman on his lap. Steel met steel in a ringing chime only inches from Fidelias's face. Aldrick slid to his feet, Odiana curling her legs beneath her as she lowered herself to the floor. The swordsman's face remained upon Calix's.

Calix eyed Aldrick and let out a sneer. "Mercenary. Do you think you can best an Aleran lord in battle?"

Aldrick kept his blade lightly pressed to Calix's and shrugged. "The only man who has ever matched me in battle was Araris Valerian himself." Teeth shone white in Aldrick's smile. "And you aren't Araris."

There was a rasp, and then steel glittered and blurred in the dim light of the hall. Fidelias watched, hardly able to keep up with the speed of the attacks and counters. In the space of a slow breath, their swords met a dozen times, chiming out, casting sparks from one another's blades. The swordsmen parted briefly, then clashed together again.

And the duel was over. Calix blinked, his eyes widening, and then lifted a hand to his throat as scarlet blood rushed from it. He tried to say something else, but was unable to make any sound.

Then the Rhodesian Count fell to the ground and lay unmoving, but for a few, faint tremors as his faltering heartbeat pumped the blood from his body.

Odiana looked up at Aquitaine with a small, dreamy smile, and asked, "Ought I save him, Your Grace?"

Aquitaine glanced back at Calix and shrugged. "There seems to be little point in it, dear."

"Yes, lord." Odiana turned adoring eyes to Aldrick and watched as the swordsman knelt down to wipe his blade clean of blood on Calix's cloak. The man clenched his fingers and let out a bubbling gasp. Aldrick ignored him.

Fidelias rose and went to Aquitaine's side. "Was that to your satisfaction, Your Grace?"

"Calix was useful," Aquitaine said. Then he glanced at Fidelias and asked, "How did you know?"

Fidelias tilted his head. "That he was planning to kill you? Were you able to sense it in him?"

Aquitaine nodded. "Once I knew to look for it. He fell apart as you described the role Rhodes had assigned him. We'll probably find a furybound dagger in his coat with my likeness and name etched into the steel."

Aldrick grunted, rolled the not-quite-dead Calix onto his back, and rummaged through his jacket. The telltale bulge Fidelias had seen earlier proved to be made by a small dagger with a compact hilt. Aldrick let out a hiss as he touched the knife and set it down hurriedly.

Fidelias asked, "Furybound?"

Aldrick nodded. "Nasty one. Strong. I think the knife should be destroyed."

"Do it," Aquitaine said. "Now, tonight. Odiana, go with him. I wish to speak to Fidelias alone."

The pair rested fists over their hearts and bowed their heads. Then Odiana slipped up to the swordsman's side and pressed to him until he circled her shoulders with one arm. The two left, without looking back.

On the floor, Calix let out his death rattle, and his eyes glazed over, mouth hanging slightly open.

"How did you know?" Aldrick repeated.

Fidelias glanced back at the dead Rhodesian Count and shrugged. "To be honest, Your Grace. I didn't know. I guessed."

Aquitaine half smiled. "Based upon what?"

"Too many years in this line of work. And I've met Rhodes. He wouldn't step an inch from his way to help someone else, and he'd cut off his own nose just to spite his face. Calix was being—"

"—too pleasant," Aquitaine murmured. "Indeed. Perhaps I should have seen it sooner."

"The important thing is that you acted promptly when you did see it, Your Grace."

"Fidelias," Aquitaine said. "I do not like you."

"You have no reason to."

"But I think I can respect you, after a fashion. And if it's to be a choice of who will put the knife in my back, I would rather it be you than Rhodes or one of his lackeys, I think."

Fidelias felt his mouth tug up at the corners. "Thank you."

"Make no mistake, man." Aquitaine turned to face him. "I prefer to work with someone to forcing them to my will. But I can do it. And I can kill you if you become a problem. You know this, yes?"

Fidelias nodded.

"Good," Aquitaine said. The High Lord covered his mouth with his hand and yawned. "It is late. And you are right about moving quickly, before the Crown has a chance to act. Get a few hours sleep. At dawn, you leave for the Calderon Valley."

Fidelias bowed his head again. "Your Grace—I don't have any chambers here, as yet."

Aquitaine waved a hand toward the slave. "You. Take him to your chambers for the night. Give him whatever he wants and see to it that he is awake by dawn."

The slave bowed her head, without speaking or looking up.

"Have you studied much history, Fidelias?"

"Only a bit, Your Grace."

"Fascinating. The course of a century of history can be set in a few short hours. A few precious days. Focal events, Fidelias—and those people who are a part of them become the ones to create tomorrow. I have sensed a distant stirring of forces from the direction of the Valley. Gaius is already arousing the furies of the Calderon, perhaps. History is stirring. Waiting to be nudged in one direction or the other."

"I don't know about history, Your Grace. I just want to do my job."

Aquitaine nodded, once. "Then do it. I will expect word from you." And without another word, the High Lord strode from the hall.

Fidelias watched him go and waited until the doors had closed behind him to turn to the slave girl. He offered her a hand, and she took it, her fingers warm and soft, her expression uncertain.

Fidelias straightened his posture, bent, and placed a formally polite kiss to the back of the slave's fingers. "Your Grace," he said. "High Lady Invidia. May I convey to you my heartfelt admiration."

The slave's expression flickered with shocked surprise. Then she threw back her head and laughed. Her features changed, subtle and significant, until the woman standing before him appeared to be several years older, her eyes holding a great deal more wisdom. Her eyes were grey, like ashes, and her hair had delicate feathers of frost all through it, though her features looked no older than a woman nearing her thirtieth year—all of the great Houses had that kind of skill at watercrafting (or nearly any other form of furycrafting one could name).

"How did you guess?" she asked. "Not even my lord husband saw through the disguise."

"Your hands," Fidelias replied. "When you washed my feet, your fingers were warm. No slave in her right mind would have been anything less than anxious in that room. She would have had chilly fingers. And no one but you, I judged, would have had the temerity or skill to attempt such a thing with His Grace."

High Lady Aquitaine's eyes shone. "A most astute assessment," she said. "Yes, I had been using Calix to find out more about what Rhodes was up to. And tonight was the night I thought I might get rid of him. I made sure that my husband was in a mood he would not enjoy being taken from and waited for the Rhodesian fool to shove his foot down his own throat. Though I must say, you seemed to pick up on what was happening and ensure that it carried through without any hints from me. And not the least bit of furycrafting to assist you."

"Logic is a fury all its own."

She smiled, but then her expression grew serious, intent. "The operation in the Valley. Will it succeed?"

"It might," Fidelias said. "If it does, it might accomplish what no amount of fighting or plotting could. He could win Alera without ever spilling Aleran blood."

"Not directly, in any case," said Lady Aquitaine. She sniffed. "Attis has few compunctions about blood. He is as subtle as a roaring volcano, but if his strength can be properly focused . . ."

Fidelias inclined his head. "Just so."

The woman studied him for a moment then took his hand. Her features shimmered and slid back into the mask of the slave girl she had worn before, the grey smoothing out of her hair, her eyes shading toward a dark, muddy brown, rather than grey. "In any case. I have my orders regarding you this night."

Fidelias hesitated, "Your Grace—"

Lady Aquitaine smiled. She touched her fingertips to his mouth and said, "Don't make me press the point. Come with me. I will see to it that you rest deeply in what time you have." She turned and started walking again. "You have far to go, come the dawn."

◦◦◦◦ CHAPTER 8

When twilight fell, Tavi knew that he was still in danger. He had not seen or heard either of his pursuers since he had slithered down an almost sheer rock cliff, using several frail saplings to slow what would have been a deadly plummet to a careening slide. It had been a perilous gamble, and Tavi had counted on the saplings' frailty to betray the heavy Marat warrior, killing or at least slowing him.

The plan had been only a partial success. The Marat looked once at the cliff and set off at a run to find a safe place to descend. It bought Tavi enough of a lead to attempt to lose his pursuer, and he thought that he had begun to widen his lead. The Marat were not like the Alerans—they had no ability at furycrafting, though they were reported to possess an uncanny understanding of all the beasts of the field. It meant that the Marat had no vast advantage—like Tavi, he had only his wits and skill to guide him.

The storm settled over the valley in a glowering veil as the light began to fade. Thunder growled forth, but there was no rise of wind, no fall of rain or sleet. The storm waited for night to fall in full, while Tavi kept a nervous eye on both the sky and the barrens around him. His legs ached and his chest burned, but he had avoided the Marat, and just before sundown he emerged from the barrens onto the causeway several miles west of the lane to Bernardholt. He found a deep patch of shade beside a windfall and crouched there, panting, allowing his tired muscles a brief rest.

Lightning flashed. He hadn't meant to move so far to the west. Instead of being nearly home again, Tavi would have an hour-long run just to reach the lane down to the steadholt. Thunder rumbled, this time so loud that it shook needles from the fallen pine beside him. There was a low, dull roar from the direction of Garados, and in a moment Tavi heard it growing nearer. The rain had finally begun. It came in a wave of half-frozen sleet, and Tavi barely had time to pull up his hood before a furious, frozen wind howled down from the north, driving rain and ice alike before it.

The storm devoured whatever meager scraps of daylight remained and drowned the valley in cold, miserable darkness, barring frequent flares of lightning skittering among the storm clouds. Though his cloak had been made to shed water, no fabric in Alera would have kept the rain and sleet of the furystorm out for long. His cloak grew cold and wet, clinging to him, and the bitter wind drove the chill straight through his garments and into his bones.

Tavi shivered hard. If he remained where he was, he would die from exposure to the storm in only hours—unless a bloodthirsty windmane beat the cold to the punch. And though Brutus had surely reached the steadholt with Bernard by now, he could not rely upon any of the holdfolk to rescue him. They knew better than to expose themselves to a furystorm.

Tavi peered at the windfall in the next lightning flash. There was a hollowed out space underneath, thick with pine needles—and it looked dry.

Tavi started crawling inside, and the next lightning flash showed him an image from a nightmare. The windfall already had occupants—half a dozen slives. The supple, dark-scaled lizards were nearly as long as Tavi was tall, and the nearest lay within arm's reach. The lizard thrashed restlessly, stirring from its torpor. It opened its jaws and let out a syrupy hiss, showing rows of needle-pointed teeth.

A thick yellow liquid coated the slive's front fangs.

Tavi had seen slive venom at work before. If the slive struck him, he would grow warm and sluggish, until he sank slowly down to the ground. And then the slives would drag him still alive into their lair. And eat him.

Tavi's first reaction was a terrified desire to spring away—but fast motion could trigger the surprised slive. Even if the slive missed, the filthy little scavengers would regard his flight as a sign that he was prey to be pursued and eaten. He could outrun them on open ground, but slives had a nasty tendency to remain on the trail of their prey, sometimes following for days, waiting for their target to sleep before moving in for the kill.

Fear and excitement made Tavi tremble, but he forced himself to remain calm. He withdrew as slowly and smoothly as he could. He had just gotten out of the slive's striking range when the beast hissed again and bolted out of its shelter and toward the boy.

Tavi let out a panicked scream, his light baritone cracking into a child's higher pitch as he did. He threw himself back from the slive's deadly bite, got his feet underneath him and started to run.

Then, to his complete surprise, he heard someone call out in an answering shout, one nearly drowned out by the rising winds.

Tavi snarled in frustration. The memory of the Marat warrior and his terrible partner came back to him in a flood of terror. Had they caught up to him?

The wind brought him another shout, the pitch too high to be the Marat. There was no mistaking the panic and fear in it. "Please! Someone help!"

Tavi bit his lip, looking down the causeway toward his home and safety—then facing the opposite way, toward the cry for help. He took a shaking breath and turned west, away from his home, and forced his tired legs into motion again, running along the pale stone of the causeway.

The lightning flashed again, a shuddering flame that swept from cloud to cloud, overhead, first green, then blue, then red, as though the furies of the skies had gone to battle against one another. Light bathed the rain-swept valley for nearly half a minute, while thunder shook the stones of the causeway and half-deafened him.

Shapes began to whirl down toward the ground through the tumult and rain, and raced and danced across the valley floor. The windmanes had followed the storm. Their luminous forms swirled and gusted effortlessly among the winds, pale green clouds, nebulous and vaguely human in shape, with long, reaching arms and skeletal faces. The windmanes screamed their hatred and hunger, their cries rising even above the bellowing thunder.

Tavi felt terror slow his legs, but he gritted his teeth and pressed on, until he could see that most of the windmanes in sight swirled around and around a central point, their pale, sharp-nailed hands reaching.

In the center of the ghostly cyclone, there stood a young woman Tavi had never seen before. She was tall and slender, not unlike his own Aunt Isana, but there the resemblance to his aunt ended. The woman had skin of dark, golden brown, like the traders from the southernmost cities of Alera. Her hair was straight and fine, whipped wildly about her by the wind, and was almost the same color as her skin, giving her something of the appearance of a golden statue. Her features were stark, striking, if not precisely lovely, with high cheekbones and a long, slender nose softened by a generous mouth.

Her face was set in a grimace of desperation and defiance. She wore a bloodstained cloth around her arm, and it looked as though she had torn her ragged, coarse skirts to make it. Her blouse was stained with grime and pressed against her by the rain, and a woven leather slave's collar circled her slender throat. As Tavi watched, one of the windmanes curled toward her in a graceful swoop.

The girl cried out, throwing one hand toward the windmane, and Tavi saw a pale blue stirring in the air—not as sharp or as well defined as the windmanes themselves, but flashing there momentarily nonetheless, the spectral outline of a long-legged horse, lashing out with its forelegs at the woman's attacker. The windmane screamed and fell back, and the woman's fury drove forward, though it moved more sluggishly than the manes, more slowly. Three more manes rushed the air fury's flanks, and the woman lifted her weight from a branch she had leaned upon, hobbling forward to swipe at the windmanes with desperate futility.

Tavi reacted without thinking. He lurched into a tottering run, clawing at his pouch as he did. His balance wavered in the darkness between thunderbolts, but only a breath later the clouds lit up again. Blue, red, and green lightning warred for domination of the skies.

One of the windmanes abruptly whipped around toward him and then surged at him through the frigid rain. Tavi clawed a smaller package from his pouch and tore it open. The windmane howled in a spine-tingling scream, spreading its claws wide.

Tavi grabbed at the crystals of salt within the packet

and hurled a portion of them at the windmane as it charged him.

Half a dozen crystals tore through the fury like lead weights through cheesecloth. The windmane let out an agonized scream, a note that sent terrified chills racing down Tavi's spine and into his belly. It curled in upon itself, green fire flaming up and over it as it began to tear, wherever the crystals had hit. In seconds, the mane tore apart into smaller fragments that dispersed and vanished into the gale—gone.

The others of its kind scattered out into a wide circle, letting out screeches of rage. The slave looked back at Tavi, her eyes wide with desperate hope. She clutched at her stick and hobbled toward him, the ragged shape of her fury once more becoming unseen, when the windmanes drew away.

"Salt?" she shouted, through the storm. "You have salt?"

Tavi managed to draw a ragged breath and to shout back, "Not much!" His heart thudded and lurched in his chest, and he hurried to the slave's side, casting a look out and around him at the pale phosphorescence of the windmanes, circling the pair at a wary distance. "Bloody crows!" he swore. "We can't stay out here. I've never seen so many in one storm."

The slave squinted out at the darkness, shivering, but her voice came to him clearly. "Can your furies shelter us at all?"

Tavi felt a sickly little rush in his belly. Of course they couldn't, as he didn't have any. "No."

"Then we've got to get to shelter. That mountain. There could be a cave—"

"No!" Tavi blurted. "Not that mountain. It doesn't like trespassers."

The girl pressed her hand against her head, panting. She looked exhausted. "Is there a choice?"

Tavi cudgeled his wits to work, to remember, but fear and exhaustion and cold made them as sluggish as a snow-covered slive. There was something he should remember, something that might help, if he could just think of what it was. "Yes!" he shouted, finally. "There's a place. It isn't far from here, if I can find it."

"How far?" asked the slave, eyeing the circling wind-manes, her words trembling as her body shook with cold.

"A mile. Maybe more."

"In the dark? In *this*?" She shot him an incredulous look. "We'll never make it."

"We're not spoiled for choice," Tavi called back, over the wind. "It's that or nothing."

"Can you find it?" the girl asked.

"I don't know. Can you walk that far?"

She looked hard at him for a moment, during another strobe of lightning, hazel eyes intent, hard. "Yes," she said, "give me some of the salt."

Tavi passed over half of the scant handful of crystals left to him, and the slave accepted them, closing her fingers over them tightly.

"Furies," she said. "We'll never get that far."

"Especially if we never get started," Tavi shouted and tugged at her arm. "Come on!" He turned to move away, but the girl abruptly leapt at him and shouldered him hard to one side. Tavi fell with a yelp, startled and confused.

He climbed back to his feet, cold and shivering, his voice sharp and high. "What are you doing?!?"

The slave slowly straightened, meeting his eyes. She looked tired, barely holding on to her wooden club. On the ground at her feet lay a dead slive. Its head had been neatly crushed.

Tavi looked from it to the slave and saw the dark blood staining the end of her club. "You saved me," he blurted.

Lightning flared again. In the cold and the gale, Tavi saw the slave smile, baring her teeth in defiance, even as she shivered. "Let's not let it go to waste. Get us out of this storm, and we'll be even."

He nodded and peered around. Lightning showed him the strip of the causeway, a dark, straight line, and Tavi took his bearings from it. Then he turned his back on the looming shape of Garados and started off into the darkness, fervently hoping that he could find the shelter before the windmanes recovered their courage and renewed their attack.

⊡⊡⊡⊡CHAPTER 9

Isana woke to the sound of feet pounding up the stairs to her room. The day had passed and night had fallen while she slept, and she could hear the anxious rattle of rain and sleet on the roof. She sat up, though it made her head pound to do it.

"Mistress Isana," gasped a breathless Beritte. She tripped in the darkness at the top of the stairs and stumbled to the floor with a gasp and an unladylike curse.

"Lamp," Isana mumbled, forcing out a familiar effort of will. The spark imp in the lamp flickered to life on its wick, giving the room a low golden glow. She pressed the heels of her hands to her temples, trying to sort out her rushing thoughts. Rain pounded, and she heard the wind gust into an angry howl. Lightning flickered outside, followed swiftly by an odd, bellowing thunder.

"The storm," Isana breathed. "It doesn't sound right."

Beritte gathered herself to her feet and bobbed in a hasty curtsey. Hollybells, the scarlet flowers just beginning to wilt, dropped petals to the floor. "It's horrible, mistress, horrible. Everyone's afraid. And the Steadholder. The Steadholder is here, and he's badly hurt. Mistress Bitte sent me to fetch you."

Isana jerked in a sharp breath. "Bernard." She pushed herself out of bed, rising to her feet. Her head throbbed with pain as she rose, and she had to rest a hand against the wall to keep herself from falling. Isana took a deep breath, trying to still herself against the rising panic inside her, to steel herself against the pain. Dimly, now, she could feel the fear and anger and anxiety of the rest of the people in the steadholt, rising up from the hall below. They would need strength and leadership now, more than ever.

"All right," she said, opening her eyes and forcing her features to smooth out. "Take me to him."

Beritte rushed out of Isana's room, and the woman

followed her with short, determined steps. As she stepped out into the hallway, the anxious fear flowing up from the room below began to press more firmly against her, almost like a cold, damp cloth that clung to her skin and began to seep inside her. She shivered, and at the top of the stairs paused for a moment, forcing the cold sensation away from her thoughts, until it no longer pressed so tightly against her. The fear would not simply go away, she knew, but for the moment it was enough that she distance herself from it, make herself functional again.

Isana then walked down the stairs, into Bernardholt's great hall. The room was fully a hundred feet long, half as wide, and made entirely of bedrock granite long ago raised from the earth. The living quarters above had been added on, wood beam and brick construction, but the hall itself was a single shaped piece of stone, wrought by long and exhausting hours of furycrafting from the bones of the earth. Storms, no matter how fierce, could not damage the great hall or anyone sheltered within it or the only other such building in the steadholt—the barn where precious livestock lived.

The hall was crowded with folk. All of the steadholt's residents were there, representing several large families. Most were gathered around one of the several trestle tables that had been set out earlier in the evening, and the food that had been in preparation since before dawn had been taken to the tables and laid out upon them. The mood of the room was anxious—even the children, who normally would have been screeching and playing games of chase as the storm gave them a virtual holiday, seemed subdued and quiet. The loudest voices in the hall were tense murmurs, and every time the thunder roared outside, folk would fall silent, looking toward the doors of the hall.

The hall was divided. Fires burned in the hearths at either end. At the far fire, the Steadholders had gathered at a small table. Beritte was leading her toward the other, where Bernard was laid. Between them, the holdfolk had gathered in separate groups, close together, with blankets laid by for sleeping on, should the storm last through the night. The talk was subdued—perhaps due to the confrontation earlier that day, Isana thought, and no one seemed to want to be too near either of the fireplaces.

Isana strode past Beritte and toward the nearer fire. Old Bitte, the steadholt's furycraft teacher, was crouched down beside where they had laid Bernard out on a pallet near the fire. She was an ancient, frail woman, whose long white braid hung to the small of her back. Her hands shook as a matter of course, and she couldn't walk far, but she was still confident, her eyes and her spirit undimmed by the years.

Bernard's face had the stark pallor of a corpse, and for a moment Isana felt her throat tighten with terror. But then his chest rose and fell in a slow, ragged breath, and she closed her eyes, steadying herself again. He was thickly covered with blankets of soft wool, except for his right leg, which was smeared with blood, pale, and uncovered. Bandages, also soaked in blood, had been wound around his thigh, but Isana could see that they would need changing shortly.

"Isana," Old Bitte croaked, her voice gently ragged with the roughness of her years. "I've done all I can for him, child. Needle and thread can only do so much."

"What happened?" Isana asked.

"We don't know," Bitte said, sitting back. "He has a terrible wound on his thigh. Perhaps a beast, though it could be a wound from an axe or a blade. It looks like he managed to put a tourniquet on it and to let it out once or twice. We may be able to save the leg—but he lost so much blood. He's unconscious, and I don't know if he'll wake up again."

"A bath," Isana said. "We need to draw him a bath."

Bitte nodded. "I've sent for one, and it should be here in a few moments."

Isana nodded, once. "And get Tavi over here. I want to hear what happened to my brother."

Bitte looked up at Isana, dark and keen eyes sad. "Tavi didn't come home with him, child."

"What?" Fear flooded her, swift and chill and horrible. She had to fight to push it aside, covering the effort by pulling tendrils that had escaped her braid back from her face. Calm. She was a leader in this steadholt. She had to appear calm, controlled. "Didn't come home with him?"

"No. He's not here."

"We've got to find him," Isana said. "This is a fury-storm. He'll be defenseless."

"Only that poor idiot Fade would go out into the storm at all, child," Bitte said in an even tone. "He went out to make sure the barn doors were sealed and was the one who found Bernard. The furies watch over fools and children, they say. Perhaps they will help Tavi as well." She leaned forward and said, lower, "Because no one here can do anything about it."

"No," Isana insisted. "We have to find him."

Several of the men of the steadholt struggled down

the stairs, carrying the big copper bathtub. They set it down on the floor nearby and then began, with the help of some of the children, to relay buckets of water to the tub from the spigot on the wall.

"Isana," Bitte said, her voice frank, almost cold, "you're exhausted. You're the only one I know who has a chance of bringing Bernard back, but I doubt you'll be able to do even that, much less find Tavi in this weather."

"It doesn't matter," Isana said. "The boy is my responsibility."

Old Bitte's hand, warm and surprisingly strong, gripped her wrist. "The boy is out there in that storm. He's found shelter by now, Isana. Or he's dead. You must focus on what you do now—or Bernard will be dead as well."

The fear, the anxiety pressed closer, in tune with the terror rising inside of her. Tavi. She shouldn't have let herself become so distracted with the preparations, shouldn't have let Tavi deceive her. He was her responsibility. The image of Tavi, caught in the storm, torn to shreds by the windmanes, flashed to the front of her thoughts, and she let out a quiet sound of frustration, helplessness.

She opened her eyes to find her hands shaking. Isana looked at Bitte and said, "I'll need help."

Old Bitte nodded, but her expression was nervous. "I've spoken to the hold women and they'll give you what they can. But it may not be enough. Without skilled watercrafting, there would be no chance at all of saving him, and even with it—"

"The hold women?" Isana snapped. "Why not Otto

and Roth? They're Steadholders. They owe it to Bernard. For that matter, why aren't they caring for him already?"

Old Bitte grimaced. "They won't, Isana. I already asked."

Isana stared at the old matron, startled. After a moment, she asked, "They *what*?"

Bitte looked down. "They won't help. None of them."

"In the name of all the furies, *why not*?"

The matron shook her head. "I'm not sure. The storm has everyone nervous—especially the Steadholders, worrying about their folk at home. And Kord has been working that for everything he can. I think he's hoping to stop the Meet."

"Kord? He's in from the barn?"

"Aye, child."

"Where's Warner?"

Bitte grimaced. "The old fool. Warner nearly flew at Kord. Warner's boys took him upstairs. That girl of his talked him into a hot bath, since they've not had a chance to bathe since arriving. Otherwise, they'd have been at one another's throats an hour ago."

"Bloody crows," Isana snarled, and rose to her feet. The men and children filling the tub blinked and took a cautious step back from her. She flicked a glance around the hall and then said, to Old Bitte, "Get him in the tub. They'll help my brother, or I'll shove those Steadholder chains down their cowardly throats." She turned on one heel and stalked across the hall toward the trestle table at the head of it, where several men had gathered—the other Steadholders.

Behind them at the fire were Kord's sons, the mostly silent Aric and his younger brother, the handsome—and accused—Bittan. Even as Isana crossed the hall, she saw Fade, his hair and tunic soaked with cold rain, his head ducked down, try to slip close to the far fire. He reached for the ladle standing in a pot of stew hung by the fire to stay warm.

Bittan scowled up at the slave from his seat immediately beside the fire. Fade moved a bit closer, his branded face twisted into a grotesque parody of a smile. He bobbed his head at Bittan nervously, picked up a bowl, and then reached for the ladle.

Bittan spat something to Aric and then said something harsh and sibilant to Fade. The slave's eyes widened, and he mumbled something in reply.

"Cowardly dog," Bittan spat, letting his voice rise. "Obey your betters. You stink, and I'm sitting here. Now get away from me."

Fade nodded and picked up the ladle, his motions hurried.

Aric spun the slave around by his shoulder and threw a short, sharp blow at his mouth. Fade let out a yelp and stumbled back from the fire, ducking his head repeatedly and shuffling off away from the young men.

Aric rolled his eyes and looked at Bittan, scowling. Then he folded his arms and leaned against the wall on the other side of the stone fireplace.

Bittan smirked and called after Fade, "Idiot coward. Don't come back." He bowed his head again, mouth tilted up at the corners in a cruel smile, contemplating his folded hands.

Thunder shook the air outside, and Isana braced herself against the accompanying flood of startled fear that flowed through the room. It washed over her a second later than she would have expected it, and she remained standing still, her eyes closed, until it had passed.

"That's crow fodder," snarled one of the men in the group around the table, the curse ringing out into the silence after the thunder had passed. Isana drew herself up short, assessing the Steadholders before she confronted them.

The speaker, Steadholder Aldo, continued, his hazel eyes fastened on Kord, his shaven jaw thrust out pugnaciously. "The holders of this valley have never stood idly by while one of the others needed help, and we're not going to do it now."

Kord tilted his grizzled head to one side, chewing on a bite of meat he had spit on his knife. "Aldo," he rumbled. "You're new to your chain, aren't you?"

Aldo stood over Kord, but the diminutive young man hardly topped the seated Steadholder by a head. "What's that got to do with it?"

"And you're not married," Kord said. "You don't have any children. Any family that you know what it's like to worry about."

"I don't have to have a family to know that you two," he spun and jabbed a finger at the other two men in the group, Steadholder's chains around both their necks, "should be on your feet and helping Bernard. Roth, what about when that thanadent was after your pigs, eh? Who hunted the thing down? And you, Otto—who tracked down your youngest when he went missing and brought him home safe? Bernard, that's who. How can you just sit there?"

Otto, a rounded man with a gentle face and thinning hair looked down. He took a breath and said, "It isn't that I don't want to help him, Aldo. Furies know. But Kord has a point."

Roth, a spare elderly man with a shock of white hair to go with his darker beard, took a pull from his mug and nodded. "Otto's right. There's more rain coming down than the valley usually sees in an entire autumn. If the valley floods, we will need every bit of strength we can save—to protect all of our lives." He frowned at Aldo, his expression drawing wrinkles to his brow that time had not. "And Steadholder Kord is also correct. You are the youngest here, Aldo. You should show more respect to your elders."

"When they whine like whimpering dogs? Should we do nothing because you *might* need your strength?" He turned and spat toward Kord. "Convenient for you. His death would end the Meet and you'd be off the hook with Count Gram."

"I'm only thinking of everyone's good, Aldo," Kord rumbled. The shaggy Steadholder split his lips into a yellow-toothed smile. "Say what you want of me, but the life of one man, no matter how fine, isn't worth endangering everyone in the valley."

"We've ridden out furystorms before!"

"But not like this," blurted Otto. Still, the man didn't look up. "This is . . . different. We haven't seen one this violent before. It makes me nervous."

Roth frowned and said, "I concur."

Aldo stared at them both, his hands clenching in frustration. "Fine," he said then, his tone low, hard. "Which one of you wants to be the one to tell Isana that we're going to sit on our hands and do nothing while her brother bleeds to death on the floor of his own hall?"

No one said anything.

Isana stared at the men, frowning, thinking hard. As she did, Kord passed his mug back to Aric, who refilled it and passed it back to him. Bittan, evidently recovered from his near-drowning, sat with his back against the wall, his head down, one hand half shielding his eyes as though his head hurt. Isana thought of his cruel treatment of Fade, and hoped that it did.

But something struck her odd about the Kordholders, about the way they had arranged themselves, or carried themselves, in the midst of the storm. It took her a moment to pick it out. They seemed more relaxed than the rest, less concerned about the battling furies outside the hall.

Carefully, she lowered her defenses, just by a bit, in the direction of Kord and his sons.

None of them were afraid.

She could feel nothing, with a casual reaching out of her senses, but a mild tension from Aric.

Thunder flashed again, and she knew she would never be able to raise her defenses again in time. She struggled to anyway—and again, the tide of terrified emotion came a beat later than she expected, enabling her to hold steady against it once more.

She found herself swaying on her feet, and then a hand gripped her arm, another her elbow. She looked up to find Fade standing beside her, holding her steady.

"Mistress," Fade said, ducking his scarred head in a clumsy little bow. The blood on his cut lip had begun to dry, blackening. "Mistress, Steadholder hurt."

"I know," Isana said. "I heard that you found him. Thank you, Fade."

"Mistress hurt?" The slave tilted his head to one side.

"Fine," Isana breathed. She looked around at the families, huddling together and listening to the fury of the storm outside. "Fade. Does this storm frighten you?"

Fade nodded his head, his expression absent, eyes focusing elsewhere.

"But you're not very afraid?"

"Tavi," Fade said. "Tavi."

Isana sighed. "If anyone can find him in this, it's Bernard. Brutus can protect him from the windmanes, and Cyprus will help him find Tavi. Tavi needs Bernard."

"Hurt," Fade said. "Hurt bad."

"Yes," Isana said, absently. "Stay near for a moment. I may need your help."

The slave grunted, without moving, though his distant expression left Isana uncertain that he had heard the command. She sighed and closed her eyes, reaching out to touch her fury.

"Rill," Isana whispered. She focused intently on an image of Bittan in her mind, picturing the young man as he sat against the wall. The water fury was a ripple along her spine, across her skin, as she focused her concentration—weary, but willing. "Rill. Show me."

Fade abruptly stepped away from her, mumbling, "Hungry." Isana watched him go, frustrated but unable to divert much attention from directing Rill. Fade edged toward the fire, looking at the Kordholders apprehensively, creeping toward the stewpot again, as though he expected to be driven away from it with another swift blow. Then he stepped out of her immediate view.

Isana sensed the fury's movement through the moisture-heavy air, brushing against her and then flowing outward. Isana felt the fury's motion almost as though it was her own arm reaching out toward the young Kordholder against the wall.

Rill touched on Bittan, and a jolt of vibrant fear lanced back to Isana through the fury's contact. She let out a gasp, her eyes widening, finally understanding what was happening in the room.

Bittan was working a firecrafting on the room, sending out a subtle apprehension to almost every person in it, heightening their fears and drawing their anxieties to the forefront of their thoughts. It was a subtle working— more subtle than she would have thought possible from the young man. He must have called his fury into the fire near him, which explained why he had claimed the space in front of it as his own.

With the realization, a wave of dizzying weariness passed over Isana. She lost her balance and stumbled forward, to her knees, lowering one hand to the floor to balance and lifting the other to her face.

"Isana?" Aldo's voice came to her clearly, and talk in the room dropped away to a near silence as the folk of Bernardholt turned their attention to her. "Isana, are you all right?"

Isana looked up to find Kord's sons looking straight at her, their expressions startled, guilty. Bittan hissed something to Aric. Aric's face hardened.

She looked up to tell Aldo about Bittan's firecrafting— and suddenly found that she couldn't push the air out of her lungs.

Isana lifted her head, eyes sweeping around in a sudden panic. She struggled to speak, but couldn't, her throat unable to expel a breath—or, she realized a moment later, to draw it in.

People crowded around her, then, Aldo leading the other Steadholders over to her with quick, fearful steps. The diminutive man picked her up and said, "Help me. Someone help!"

"What's wrong with her?" asked Roth. "Good furies, she's terrified."

Voices mingled and blended around her in a worried buzz. She struggled, reaching out for Rill, but the water fury only clouded around her, pressing close, in nervous reaction to Isana's own wild fear. As her helplessness increased, her mental defenses eroded, and the fear of those in the room flooded over more and more thickly as they pressed closer. She lost track of who was speaking and reeled in confusion.

"I don't know. She just fell. Did anyone else see?"

"Mistress?"

"Isana, oh great furies, she and her brother both—this is an evil day!"

Isana struggled to look around, pushing away Otto as he tried to open her mouth, to look down her throat and see if she was choking.

"Hold her!"

"Isana, calm down!"

"She's not breathing!"

Kord came over through the crowd, but Isana looked past the big Steadholder—to where his sons still sat by the fire, unnoticed. Bittan had looked up at her, and a cruel smile had twisted his handsome mouth. He clenched his fingers abruptly into a fist, and Isana felt an accompanying spike of blinding panic flash through her, driving away thought for a moment.

Beside Bittan sat Aric. Aric, Isana thought. A windcrafter. The quiet son of Kord wasn't looking at her, but he had his fingers bridged together and his expression was set in concentration.

Darkness swam in front of her eyes, and she struggled to mouth words to Aldo, who held her, his eyes wide with panic.

"Isana," he breathed. "Isana, I can't understand you."

Everything wavered, and Isana found herself laying on a table, the world spinning above her. Kord arrived, a sudden odor of stale sweat and roasted meat. He looked down at her and said, "I think she's panicked. Woman, calm down. Don't try to talk." He leaned over her, his eyes narrowing. "Don't," he muttered softly, eyes malicious and threatening. "Don't try to talk. Calm down and don't talk. Maybe it will go away."

Isana tried to push Kord away, but he was too big, too heavy, her arms too weak.

"All you have to do is nod," he whispered. "Just be a good girl and agree to let things go. It doesn't have to be this way."

She stared up at him, feeling her own helplessness and fear wash through her, felt herself losing control in the face of that terror. She knew that Bittan was making the fear worse, making her more afraid, but that bit of knowledge seemed to have no particular relevance before the wild, animal panic. If she did not give in to Kord, she was certain, he would stand by and let her die.

Fury flashed through her, then, a sudden fire that evaporated the fear. Isana raked her nails at Kord's eyes. He drew back from her before she could do more than leave a set of small, pink weals on his cheek, his eyes sparkling with anger.

Isana forced herself to sit up as her vision grew darker and darker. She pointed a finger, weakly, toward the fire.

Everyone turned to look—and Aldo's eyes widened in sudden comprehension.

"Bloody crows!" he snarled. "That bastard of Kord's is killing her!"

There was a general gasp. Confusion spread rapidly through the room, the heightened emotions already present making it flare up like a wildfire through dry grass. Everyone started crying out at once.

"What?" Otto looked back and forth. "Someone's what?"

Aldo turned and started shoving his way toward the fire. Then he yelped and fell forward, clutching at his foot where the stone floor had suddenly folded up and over it like a heavy cloth. The young Steadholder whirled and barked a word at the heavy wooden bench beside the table. The wood shuddered and then twisted, snapping with the brittle sound of old bones, sending splinters as long as daggers flying toward Kord.

The big Steadholder ducked toward Isana, away from the splinters, though one of them had opened his cheek in a sudden spilled sheet of scarlet blood. He lifted his fist and drove it toward her.

Isana rolled off the table and felt the big Steadholder's blow shatter the heavy oak like kindling. She crawled away from him on her hands and knees toward the fire and the man whose fury was smothering her.

She saw Fade at the fire, staring at all the confusion with a baffled expression, still half-bent over the pot, a ladle in one hand. He gabbled something and turned to flee, whimpering high in his throat. His feet stumbled over Bittan, as the young Kordholder stood to his feet, knocking the young man down. Fade let out a screech and fell to one side, steaming stew flying from both bowl and ladle.

It splashed all over Aric's frowning face, drawing a sudden scream of surprised agony from the slender windcrafter.

Isana drew in a shocked breath, even as she felt the wild confusion of emotion in the room vanish as suddenly as the shadow of a bird flying by overhead. People looked around for a moment, unbalanced by the sudden release from the firecrafting, backing toward the walls.

"Stop them!" Isana gasped. "Stop Kord!"

Kord let out a furious roar. "You barren bitch! I'll kill you!" The big man turned, and Isana could all but feel the stirring in the earth as he drew upon his fury for strength, lifted the broken trestle board of the table as though it did not weigh as much as a grown man, and swung it toward her. Aldo, his foot twisted and dragging, hauled himself to his feet and threw himself at Kord's legs. The smaller Steadholder hit the larger man low, dragging him off balance and sending the trestle plank sailing wide of Isana, cracking into the wall. Kord kicked Aldo away, as though he weighed no more than a puppy, and turned toward Isana once more.

Isana struggled to crawl away, calling Rill to her with desperate intensity. She heard a confusion of sounds around her, men cursing, a door banging open. The air suddenly shrieked, and a gale flung itself down the chimney and hurled a cloud of red-hot embers at Isana. She cried out, falling flat onto the earth, waiting for the pain to begin.

Instead, she felt them swirl up and past her, and Kord let out a sudden howl of dismay.

"There, Kord, you lying slive!" cackled Steadholder Warner, from atop the stairs. He stood naked and dripping with water, a towel wrapped around his waist, soap in his wispy hair and running down his skinny legs. His sons stood behind him, swords in hand. "It's about time someone taught you to respect a lady! Take them, boys!"

"Father," Aric called, through the confusion. Warner's sons leapt down the stairs. "Father, the door!"

"Wait!" Isana cried. She started to stand. "Wait, no! No bloodshed in my house!" A weight hit her from behind and pressed her ungently to the ground. She struggled and squirmed, to find Fade on top of her, firmly pressing her down.

"Fade!" she gasped. "Get off me!"

"Hurt Fade!" the slave gabbled, and hid his face against her back, sobbing, clinging to her like an overlarge child. "No hurt, no more hurt!"

Kord let out a bellow and caught the first of Warner's sons, as he threw himself at the big Steadholder. Kord grasped the young man by the wrist and belt and threw him across the room to crash hard into the wall. Kord rushed toward the doors to the hall, Aric and Bittan hard on his heels, and the folk of Bernardholt scattered from the Steadholder's path. He slammed into one of the doors and tore it from its hinges, letting in a howl of cold wind and half-frozen rain. He vanished into the night, his sons following.

"Let them go!" shouted Isana. So sharply did her voice ring out that Warner's other two sons drew up short, staring at her.

"Let them go," Isana repeated. She wriggled out from beneath Fade and looked around at the hall. Aldo lay gasping and hurt, and Warner's son slumped unmoving against the wall. At the other end of the hall, Old Bitte crouched over Bernard's pale and motionless form, an iron poker from the fire gripped determinedly in her withered fingers.

"Isana," protested Warner, coming down the stairs, still clasping his towel with one hand. "We can't just let them leave! We can't let animals like that go unstopped!"

Weariness and the pounding in her head met with the backwash of Isana's terror, of the panic at the sudden and vicious violence, and she began to shake. She bowed her head for a moment and willed Rill to keep the tears from her eyes.

"Let them go," she repeated. "We have our own wounded to attend to. The storm will kill them."

"But—"

"No," Isana said, firmly. She looked around at the other Steadholders. Roth was standing to his feet, slowly, and looked dazed. Otto was supporting the older man, and sweat shone on his mostly bald pate. "We have wounded to see to," Isana told the two men.

"What happened?" Otto stammered. "Why did they do that?"

Roth put a hand on Otto's shoulder. "They were firecrafting us. Isn't that it, Isana? Making us all more afraid, more worried than we needed to be."

Isana nodded, silently grateful to Roth, and aware that as a watercrafter, he would sense it. He smiled at her, briefly.

"But how," Otto said, his tone baffled. "How did they do it without one of us sensing it?"

"My guess is that Bittan built it up slowly," Isana said. "A little at a time. The way you can heat bathwater a little at a time, so that anyone inside doesn't notice."

Otto blinked. "I knew you could project emotions, but I didn't know you could do it that way."

"Most of the Citizenry who know firecrafting will do it to one degree or another, during their speeches," Isana said. "Nearly any Senator can do it without really thinking about it. Gram does it without knowing all the time."

"And while his son did it to us," Roth mused, "Kord fed us that nonsense about a possible flood—and we were worried enough to think that it sounded reasonable."

"Oh," Otto said. He coughed and flushed pink. "I see. You came down late, Isana, so you were able to notice it. But why didn't you just say something?"

"Because the other one was smothering her, dolt," growled Aldo, from where he lay. His voice carried the stress of the pain from his injured foot. "And you saw what Kord tried to do to her."

"I told you all," Warner said with a certain vicious satisfaction in his voice from his position on the stairs. "They're a bad lot all around."

"Warner," Isana said wearily. "Go get dressed."

The spare Steadholder looked down at himself and seemed to become aware of his nakedness for the first time. He flushed, then muttered something to excuse himself and hurried from the room.

Otto shook his head again. "I just can't believe someone would *do* that."

"Otto," muttered Aldo. "Use your head for something

besides a dressing mirror. Bernard is hurt, and so is Warner's son. Get them into a tub and craft them better."

Roth nodded decisively, visibly gathering himself together. "Of course. Steadholder Aldo," he inclined his head a bit, to the younger man, "was right all along. Isana, I offer you my full support in your crafting, as does Otto, here."

"I do?" Otto said. "Oh, I mean, yes, of course. Isana, how could we have been so stupid. Of course we'll help."

"Child," Bitte called from beside Bernard's still form, her voice high, sharp. "Isana, there's no more time."

Isana turned to look at Bitte. The old woman's face had gone pale.

"Your brother. He's gone."

CHAPTER 10

Tavi stumbled beneath the force of a sudden gust of wind. The girl caught his arm in one hand, keeping him upright, and with the other, she hurled a few scanty remnants of the salt crystals he'd given her a few hours before. There was a shriek from the faintly luminous form of the windmane behind the gust, and it withdrew.

"That's it," she called over the wind. "I'm out of salt!"

"Me, too!" Tavi answered her.

"Are we close?"

He squinted through the darkness and the rain, shivering and almost too cold to think. "I don't know," he said. "I can't see anything. We should be almost there."

She shielded her eyes from the stinging half-sleet with her hand. "Almost won't be good enough. They're coming back."

Tavi nodded and said, "Keep your eyes out for firelight." He gripped her hand tightly in his, before stumbling forward, through the darkness. Her fingers tightened on his own. The slave was stronger than she looked, and even though his hand had long since gone mostly numb from the cold and the sleet, her grip was painful, frightened. The wind and the deadly manes within it yowled, driving and cold and furious.

"They're coming," she hissed. "If we're going to get out of this, it has to be right now."

"It's close. It's got to be." Tavi squinted against the blinding rain, peering ahead of them as best he could. Then he saw it, a faint golden radiance flickering at the edge of his vision. In the storm, he had gotten turned around somehow, and he swerved abruptly to one side, hauling on the girl's wrist. "There! The fire! It's right there! We have to run for it."

Tavi drove his exhausted body forward, toward the distant light, and the ground began to slope upward, rising steadily toward it. The curtains of sleet and rain blinded him and veiled the light, so that it flickered like a guttering candle, but Tavi kept his eyes doggedly locked on his destination. Lightning snarled among the clouds in treacherous, blinding flashes, while the windmanes howled out their wrath overhead.

Tavi could hear the slave's labored, gasping breath even through the wind—she was evidently at the end of her endurance. Her footsteps staggered, as they grew closer to the glowing firelight. In the darkness, the windmanes screeched, and Tavi looked back to see one of them swooping down through the sleet, its face twisted into a grimace of hatred and hunger.

The girl's eyes widened as she saw Tavi's expression, and she began to spin about—but she was too late, her reaction too slow. She couldn't possibly turn to defend herself in time.

Tavi reached back and seized her wrist in both hands. With the weight of his whole body, he hauled her forward, past him, and sent her stumbling toward the light ahead. "Go!" he shouted. "Get inside!"

The windmane hit Tavi, and there was suddenly no air in his lungs, no warmth in his limbs. He felt his feet leave the ground, and he went tumbling, jouncing, and bounding down the slope and away from the shelter at its summit, blown like a leaf before the power of the storm. He rolled, arms and legs loose, struggling to keep from stopping too abruptly, to guide his fall down the hill and to its base. A grey stone appeared before his eyes in a flash of emerald lightning, and he felt himself scream as he flinched away from it.

He caught a flash of light reflected on water, on the ground, and aimed himself toward it through the half-dark, desperate and terrified. He came to a halt in the mud pooling at the bottom of the hill beneath a finger-width of freezing water, his arms sinking into it halfway to his elbows. He struggled and heaved them free of the muck, turning in time to see the windmane descend on him once more.

Tavi rolled to one side, the sludge slowing his movements, and felt the windmane's deadly chill settle around his mouth and nose, cutting off his air. He thrashed and flinched, but accomplished nothing. He could no more keep the fury from blocking his air than he could spread his arms and fly above the storm.

Tavi knew that he had only one chance, and that a slim one. He struggled to his feet, then leapt into the air and hurled himself sprawling in the muck. Cold, oozing mud and chilled water slithered over him, churned to the consistency of thick pudding by the storm. He wriggled down deeper, forcing his face into the mud, then rolled to his back, covering himself in it.

And suddenly, he could breathe again.

Tavi peered up at the windmane—but it wasn't facing him. The fury swirled and swooped around the point where it had first attacked him, its glowing, hungry eyes flicking back and forth. They never did settle on Tavi. The windmane screamed, and half a dozen of its fellows came looping down and around the area near where Tavi had fallen, spinning and spiraling, searching for him.

Tavi lifted a hand to brush mud from his eyes, a fierce grin stretching his lips. He'd been right. The earth. The earth that was the nemesis of furies of the air had covered him, hidden him from them. But it was bitterly, painfully cold. Tavi stared at the swirling windmanes and felt the chill settle into his bones. He was safe from the manes. But for how long?

The rain continued to pelt down, and muddy water

dribbled into Tavi's eyes. The rain would wash his coating of mud away in short order, assuming he didn't simply collapse to the ground and freeze. Moving as quietly as he could, he reached down and scooped more mud into his hand, dumping it onto his belly and chest, where the rain had begun to make headway.

Tavi peered through the storm and up the gentle slope of the mound, to where the light burned at its top, outlining an opening in a dark structure, otherwise invisible in the night. He saw no sign of the slave—which meant that she was either safe or dead. Either way, he had done everything he could for the young woman. He let out a hiss of frustration.

Instantly, three of the windmanes spun their glowing eyes toward him and flowed through the air, directly at his mouth.

A yelp started in his chest, but he stifled it from reaching his throat—instead, rolling away, through the mud for several paces, and got to his feet. Looking back, he saw the furies of the storm swirling around the spot where he had lain. They could not see him, perhaps, but they could surely hear him. Even in the din of the storm, they had heard his breath. He scarcely dared to breathe now and wondered if they would hear him moving.

Either way, he thought, the rain would expose him to them in a few moments. He had to get off of the open ground, to shelter. He had to try to slip past the furious windmanes.

Tavi would remember that walk for the remainder of his life, as the torment a starving mouse must feel when darting between the feet of giants to snatch at crumbs of food and then rush back to safety.

All around him, the windmanes swirled and howled. A young bounder buck came leaping out of the darkness across Tavi's tail, squealing and throwing his hindquarters wildly about. To the buck clung three of the windmanes, their claws raking, eyes blazing. As Tavi watched, the furies rode the bounder down to the ground, its horns passing harmlessly through them. The buck let out an awful scream, before one of the manes tore open its throat and two more flowed over its muzzle, cutting off its air. The bounder struggled in silence, thrashing and bucking as its blood flowed. The other windmanes nearby swirled closer, shrieking, clawed hands reaching.

The animal vanished into a luminescent mass of churning mist and vicious claws. Only moments later, the cloud dispersed into a dozen howling forms.

And all that remained of the bounder was a head, its eyes wide open and white with terror, beside a scattered pile of claw-rent meat and cracked, bloody bones.

Tavi's knees went weak, and for the space of several breaths, he couldn't remove his eyes from the gruesome spectacle. The lightning left him in the dark a moment later, leaving the sight of the poor buck's fate blazed across his vision. He opened his mouth to scream and found himself breathless, silent, as in the helpless terror of a nightmare.

Lightning split the sky again, and the fear took him and ate him in one bite. His trembling paralysis became a sudden surge of fragile, terrified strength, and he all but flew up the hill toward the promised safety of the light. He heard himself suck in a breath and scream, and the windmanes rose up around him in an angry chorus—but one without a director, without a tempo. They swooped and dove furiously around him, but none could see him. The protection of the earth held true, until Tavi had raced up the slope to its summit.

There, a simple dome of polished marble rose from the slope of the hill to the height of three men. Its open entryway glowed with a soft golden light, and above it, writ into the marble in gold was the seven-pointed star of the First Lord of Alera.

Tavi felt a section of earth as heavy as a feastday cake slough off of his back and heard the furies scream behind him. His own scream answered them, as the terrible wind raced toward him. He held his arms over his head and threw himself at the doorway.

And landed on hard, smooth stone, within a sudden and shocking silence.

Tavi jerked his eyes up and looked around, limbs quivering and shaking, his body frantically signaling his mind that he should get up, should keep running. Instead, he sat up, a twinge passing through his chilled muscles, and stared around him, panting and mute.

The beauty of the Princeps' Memorium would have taken his breath away, if all the running and screaming hadn't done it already.

Though outside the storm still raged, the lightning still flashed, the sleet and the thunder still hammered the earth, within the Memorium, those sounds came only as something very distant and wholly irrelevant. The earth might shake and the air fairly ignite with fury, but within the Memorium, there was only the slight ripple of water, the crackle of flame, and an almost meditative stillness broken by the sleepy chirp of a bird.

The interior of the dome was made not of marble, but

of crystal, the walls of it rising high and smooth to the ceiling twenty feet above. Light, from seven fires that burned without apparent fuel around the outside of the room, rose up through the crystal, bending, refracting, splitting into rainbows that swirled and danced with a slow grace and beauty within the crystal walls. The floor in the center of the dome was covered by a pool of water, perfectly still and as smooth as Amaranth glass. All around the pool grew rich foliage: bushes, grass, flowers, even small trees, arranged as neatly as though kept by a gardener.

Between each of the fires around the walls stood seven silent suits of armor, complete with scarlet capes, the bronze shields and the ivory-handled swords of the Royal Guard. The armor stood mute and empty upon nearly formless figures of dark stone, eternally vigilant, the slits in their helmets focused on their charge.

At the center of the pool rose a block of black basalt. Upon the block lay a pale shape, a statue of the purest white marble in the form of a young man. His eyes were closed, as though sleeping, and he lay with his hands folded upon his breast, the hilt of his sword beneath them. He wore a rich cloak that draped down over one shoulder, and beneath that, the breastplate of a soldier. At his feet lay a pale marble helm, complete with the high crest of the House of Gaius. His hair lay close-cropped to his head. His face was thin-featured, stark, handsome, and his expression peaceful, sleeping. Had the statue been a man of flesh, Tavi would have expected him to rise, don his helmet, and set about his business, but the Princeps Gaius had died long ago, before Tavi was born.

There was a motion at the edge of his vision, but he felt too tired to turn his head. The slave knelt down beside him, dripping and shivering. She touched his shoulder and drew her hand back to consider the soupy mud clinging to it. "Crows and furies. For a moment, I thought that a gargoyle had gotten in here."

He looked up at her suspiciously, but her eyes were dancing with weary mirth. "I didn't have time to wash up."

"I turned back to find you, but I couldn't see anything—and the windmanes closed on me. I had to run here."

"That was the idea," Tavi said, his tone apologetic. "I'm sorry, but it looked like you were about to collapse."

The slave's mouth quirked to one side. "Perhaps," she acknowledged. She scooped more of the mud off of him. "Very clever—and very brave. Are you hurt?"

Tavi shook his head, shivering uncontrollably. "Sore. Tired. And cold."

She nodded, her expression worried, and smoothed more muck from his forehead. "All the same, thank you."

He struggled to give her a small smile. "There's no reason to thank me. I'm Tavi of Bernardholt."

The girl's fingers went to the collar at her throat, and she frowned, lowering her eyes. "Amara."

"Where are you from, Amara?"

"Nowhere," the girl said. She looked up, sweeping her eyes around the inside of the magnificent chamber. "What is this place?"

"P-princeps' Memorium," Tavi stuttered, shivering. "This is the mound on the Field of Tears. The Princeps died here, fighting the Marat, before I was born."

Amara nodded, still frowning. She rubbed her hands together roughly and then laid her wrist over Tavi's forehead. "You're burning up."

Tavi closed his eyes and found them too heavy to open again. An odd prickling ran over his skin, slowly replacing the bitter, aching chill of the mud. "The First Lord himself made this place, they say. Made it in one day. When they buried everyone. The Crown Legion. The Marat didn't leave enough of the Princeps' body for a state funeral. They did it here, instead of taking him back to the capital."

The slave took his hand and urged him to his feet, though she, too, shook with cold. He let her, struggling to stand through the heavy, sweet lethargy in his limbs. He latched onto the words he was speaking, using them to hold on to consciousness. "Strong furies here. The Crown's furies. It was said they would have to be strong to keep the shades of all the soldiers at ease. Couldn't take them home. Too many dead bodies. Strong furies would protect us. Stone mound. Earth against air. Shelter."

"You were right," Amara said. She eased him back to the floor again, and he sank gratefully back against a wall. He could feel a distant heat, through the tingling in his body, something wonderful and soothing. She must have taken him over to one of the fires.

"All my fault," Tavi mumbled. "I didn't bring Dodger in. My uncle. The Marat are here."

There was a startled silence. Then she said, "What? Tavi, what are you talking about? What about the Marat?"

He struggled to say more, to answer the slave's question, to warn her. But the words became a jumble on his tongue and within his mind. He tried to force them out and found himself shaking too hard to get them out clearly. Amara said something to him, but it didn't make any sense, random sounds jumbled together. He felt her hands on him, then, scooping the half-frozen muck off of him and rubbing roughly at his limbs, but it felt very distant, somehow, very unimportant.

His head fell forward. It became a labor even to draw breath.

Blackness fell over him, dark and silent and complete.

ᴄᴄᴄᴄCHAPTER 11

Isana's heart twisted in her chest, and her throat tightened. "No," she whispered. "No. My brother isn't—he's not gone. He can't be."

Old Bitte looked down. "His heart. His breathing. They've both stopped. He just lost too much blood, child. He's gone."

Stunned silence fell on the hall.

"No," Isana said. She felt dizzy, stunned, and she had to close her eyes. "No. Bernard." The enormity of that simple finality, of death, fell on her like a mile of chains. Bernard was her only living family, and she had been close to him since before she could clearly remember. She could not picture a world without her brother in it. There had to be something she could do. Surely, something. She had been so close to securing the help she needed. If Kord and his sons hadn't been interfering, if they had only kept to themselves, there would have been two skilled watercrafters attending to Bernard before she was even awakened.

Let the crows take Kord and his murderous little family, Isana thought viciously. What right did he have to jeopardize the lives of others in order to protect his own position? Bernard could have been cared for. He could have *lived*.

She needed Bernard. The steadholt needed him. Tavi needed him.

Tavi. If anyone could find Tavi now, if anyone could help him, it was her brother. She had to have his help. She had to have him beside her. Without him, Tavi could be gone forever. He, too, could—

"No," Isana said aloud. She took a breath, steeling herself. She could not let Kord's viciousness kill her brother and Tavi all in one moment. She lifted her head and focused on Old Bitte. "No, this isn't over. Get him into the tub."

Bitte looked up at Isana, her expression startled. "What?"

"Get him into the tub," Isana said. She started rolling up her sleeves in brisk, short motions. "Otto, Roth, get over here and prepare your furies."

"Isana," Bitte hissed. "Child, you cannot do this."

"She can," said Otto, his voice quiet, his pate gleaming in the light of the fire. "It's been done before. When I was young, just taking my own chain, Harald the Younger's boy fell through the ice and into the mill pond. He was under for nearly thirty minutes before we could get him back up through it, and he lived."

"Lived," spat Bitte. "He sat in a chair drooling and never speaking again until fevers took him. Would you do that to Bernard as well?"

Roth grimaced and put a frail hand on Otto's shoulder. "She's right. Even if we bring his body back, his mind might not come along with it."

Isana stood and faced the two men. "I need him," she said. "Tavi is out in the storm. I have no time to discuss the matter. You were willing to help me a moment ago. Now do it or get out of my way."

"We'll help," Otto offered at once.

Roth let out a slow breath, his expression reluctant. "Aye," he agreed. "Furies willing, the attempt won't kill you."

"I'm touched by your enthusiasm." Isana stalked to the copper tub. Several of the holders, under Bitte's direction, lowered Bernard's limp form into the tub. The water stained pink, blood swirling languidly out from the wound in his thigh. "Get the bandage off," she instructed. "It won't matter now, one way or the other."

She knelt down by the head of the tub, reaching out to rest her fingers against Bernard's temples. "Rill," she whispered, reaching a hand down to touch the water, briefly. "Rill, I need you." She felt the water swirl, slowly, as Rill entered the tub. She could feel the fury's reluctance, its motions vague and unsure—no, not Rill's reluctance, but her own weariness. As tired as Isana was, doubtless Rill could not hear her clearly, could not respond to her as well as the fury usually might. In a moment more, that would not be an issue.

"Immi," Otto whispered. Isana felt the portly Stead-holder rest his hand on her shoulder, warm fingers tightening slightly in support. The waters stirred beneath her fingers anew, as the second fury entered the tub, a much smaller, more active presence than Rill's.

Roth put his hand on her opposite shoulder. "Almia." Once again, the water stirred with a stronger, more confident presence, the older Steadholder's fury carrying with it a sense of fluid strength.

Isana took a deep breath, focusing through her weariness and her fear and her anger. She pushed her wild concern for Tavi from her thoughts, her uncertainty that she could help her brother. She cleared everything away but her sense, through Rill, of the water in the tub and of the body it surrounded.

There was a certain feel to a body submerged in water, a kind of delicate vibration spreading out from the skin. Isana willed Rill to surround Bernard, so that she could feel for that fragile energy around him, the tremors of life. For a terrible moment, the waters were still and she could sense nothing.

Then Rill quivered in response to the barest traces of life in the wounded man. Isana felt her heart lurch in relief, and she murmured, "He's still here. But we have to hurry."

"Don't risk it, Isana," Roth said, his voice quiet. "He's too far gone."

"He's my brother," Isana said. She flattened her hands against either side of Bernard's thick neck. "You and Otto seal up the wound. I'll do the rest."

She felt Otto's hand tighten on her shoulder. Roth let out a quiet, resigned sigh.

"If you go in, you might not be able to get back out again. Even if you are successful in reviving him."

"I know." Isana closed her eyes, and leaned forward enough to plant a gentle kiss on her brother's head. "All right then," she said. "Here we go."

Isana let out her breath in a long, slow exhalation and poured her attention, her focus, her will forward into the water. The dull ache in her limbs faded away. The clenching tension in her back vanished. All the sensations of her body, from the too-cool skin beneath her fingers to the smooth stone beneath her knees and toes faded away to nothing. She felt only the water, the fading energy around Bernard, and the nebulous presence of the furies in the water with her.

Rill's presence pressed close to her, something like concern pressing against Isana's awareness. She touched Rill with her thoughts, giving the fury an image, a task. In response, Rill glided closer, into the same space Isana's awareness occupied. The sensation of the fury's presence overlapped with her own until she could no longer readily distinguish the two. Isana felt a brief surge of disorientation as she and the fury joined one another. Then, as always, Rill's perceptions began to flow into her in a slow rush of sounds, murky vision, and in surges of tangible, tactile emotion.

She looked up at the vague, pale shape of Bernard's body, at the even more blurred shape of her own, standing over him. Roth and Otto's furies hovered anxiously before her in the water, each visible to her, now, faint colors in a pair of cloudy forms.

She did not speak, but from here, it was a simple matter to send the words to Roth and Otto, through their furies. "Gather him up and seal closed the wound. I'll handle the rest."

The other two furies swirled off at once, gathering together the scarlet droplets of blood that had begun spreading into the bathwater, and shepherding them back to the gaping rent in Bernard's thigh.

Isana didn't wait for the furies to complete their task. She instead slipped closer to the fading aura around her brother, focusing upon it, and upon the much stronger thrum of life in the body touching Bernard—her own.

She knew that what she was to attempt was dangerous. The anima of life was never simple to touch or easy to manipulate. It was a force as potent and unpredictable as life itself—and as fragile. But dangerous or not, it had to be done. She had to try.

Isana reached out and made contact with that faint, fading quiver of life around Bernard. And then, touching upon that of her own body, above him, she gathered both together and melded them, blended them, drew upon the energy of her body to surround both of them, to an immediate, violent response.

Bernard's body convulsed in the water, a sudden thrash of motion that moved every muscle in him at once. His back contorted, and Isana felt more than saw his eyes fly wide open and unseeing. His heart contracted with a heavy, unsteady thumping sound, followed by another, and another. Isana felt a thrill of exhilaration fly through her and, with Rill, poured into Bernard through the wound in his leg, a rush of sudden confinement, a sense of herself stretching down hundreds of blood vessels, spreading through him, her awareness fracturing into a multitude of layers. She felt his weary heart, the bone-deep ache of his limbs, the terrifying cold of oncoming death. She felt his confusion, his frustration, his fear, the emotions pressing like a knife against her heart. She felt his body struggling against the injuries. Failing. Dying.

What she did next was not a process of logical thought, of stimulus and response, of procedure and reason. Her thoughts were too far divided, too many, too much to direct so clearly. Everything relied on her instinct, on her ability to release conscious will and to reach through him, sensing every part of the whole and then acting to restore it.

She felt it as a pressure building up against her, as steely chains of tension that closed in upon her myriad thoughts with a slow and steady inevitability, shutting them down, crushing them into stillness. She fought against that still- ness, fought to keep her awareness, her life, sparkling in every part of Bernard's wounded body. She threw herself into the struggle, straining against death, while around her, through her, within her, she felt every wavering, uncertain beat of his too-labored heart.

She held on to his life, as she felt Roth and Otto's furies send blood back into his battered body. She held on to him as the two watercrafters went to work upon the injury itself, closing the ragged wound and crafting the very fabric of his flesh together again. She held on, with all of her strength and in a horrible space between one heartbeat and the next realized that she could hold on no longer. She was losing him.

Through Rill she felt Roth's silent urging to withdraw, to flow back out of her brother and to her own body, to save herself. She refused, drawing more heavily on the energy of her body, feeding it to Bernard, to his laboring heart. She sent everything she could reach coursing into him and felt it flowing out of her, somewhere, felt herself growing weaker. She gave her brother all that she was: her love of him, her love for Tavi, terror at the prospect of his death, frustration, agony, fear, the joy of glowing memories, and the despair of the darkest moments of her life. She held back nothing.

Bernard quivered again and abruptly gasped in a breath of air that filled his lungs like cold fire. He coughed, and the horrible stillness abruptly fractured and fled as his lungs labored again and again and again.

Isana felt relief flood over her, as his body grew stronger, as the energy of him began to flow again, as the rhythm of his heart began to quicken and become regular, a hammer pulse that coursed throughout her awareness. She felt Rill dimly, as the fury moved through him, and felt her gentle confusion. Once again, Roth attempted to send something to her, through their furies, but she was too tired to understand it, too lost in relief and exhaustion to understand. She let her awareness drift, felt herself sinking down, into a darkness, into warmth that promised her rest from all of her anxiety and pain and weariness.

And then a dull fire pulsed in her. She thought that she remembered the sensation, from some time long before. Her descent slowed for a moment.

Again, the fire came. And again. And again.

Pain. I am feeling pain.

In a detached, remote, and unconcerned part of her awareness, she understood what was happening. Roth had been right. She had given too much of herself and had been unable to return to her own body. Too tired, too relaxed, too weak. She would die, back there beside the tub, her body simply slumping to the floor and empty of life.

The fire flared again, somewhere back up and away from the darkness.

The dead feel no pain, she thought. *Pain is for the living.*

She reached out toward it, toward that fire in the night. The delicious descent halted, though part of her screamed out against it. She reached back for the pain, but did not move, did not begin to rise again.

It is too late. I cannot go back.

She tried, regardless. She struggled against the stillness, the warmth. She struggled to live.

Sudden light flared like a newborn sun above her. Isana reached for it, embraced that distant fire with every part of her that still lived. It washed over her in a flood and became an instant, blazing torment, horrible and bright, an agony more searing than anything she had ever known. She felt a dizzying wrenching sensation and a sudden rush of confusion, of emptiness where Rill had been before, of more and more pain.

She went back into it, and gladly. The light, the agony, became all consuming, her limbs aching, her lungs burning with her ragged breath, her head pounding, and her mind screaming as raw sensation poured into it.

She heard shouts. Someone was screaming, and there was a heavy thump of impact. Then more screams. Fade, she thought.

"There," someone shouted. Otto? "Look! She's breathing!"

"Get a blanket," replied Roth's steady voice. "And another for Bernard."

"Broth for both, they'll need food."

"I know that. Someone get that idiot slave *out* of here before he hurts someone else."

The general cloud of pain over her began to resolve itself, by slow degrees, to a dull throb in her hand, and a sweet and oddly satisfying ache of exhaustion spread throughout her. She opened her eyes and turned her head to one side to see Bernard looking blearily around him. She fumbled her hand toward him and saw the fingers of it swollen and oddly shaped. She touched him, and the pain swept down on her, blinded her.

"Easy, Isana." Roth took her wrist and gently pressed her hand back down. "Easy. You need to rest."

"Tavi," Isana said. She struggled to force out the words, though they sounded blurry, even to her. "Find Tavi."

"Rest," Roth said. The old Steadholder looked down on her with gentle, compassionate eyes. "Rest. You've done too much already."

Bitte appeared beside Isana and assured her, "We'll get the Steadholder back on his feet by morning, child. He'll take care of everything. Rest now."

Isana shook her head. She couldn't rest. Not while the storm raged outside. Not while Tavi remained in it, helpless and fragile and alone. She started to sit up, but simply could not. She did not have the strength to do much more than lift her head. She fell back to the floor and felt a tear of frustration glide from one eye. That tear seemed to trigger others, and then she was weeping, silently, weeping until she could not see, could barely breathe.

She should have been more careful. She should have forbidden him to leave the steadholt this morning. She should have seen to her brother more swiftly, should have understood the Kordholders' plans before it had come to violence. She had fought as hard as she could.

She had tried. Furies knew, she had tried. But all of her efforts had been for nothing. Time had swept down on her, swift as a hungry crow.

Tavi was out there in the storm. Alone.

O furies and spirits of the departed. Please. Please let him come home safe.

◇◇◇◇ CHAPTER 12

Amara strove to ignore the exhaustion and the cold. Her limbs shook almost too hard to be controlled, and her entire body throbbed with weariness. More than anything, she wanted to collapse upon the floor and sleep— but if she did, it might cost the boy his life.

She had wiped the mud from his face and his throat as best she could, but it clung to him in a thin layer of slimy clay, grey-brown and mottled over paler skin. It made him look almost like a corpse, several days old. Amara slipped a hand beneath the boy's shirt, feeling for his heartbeat. Even in this weather, he wore only a light tunic and cloak for warmth, evidence of his hardy upbringing here on the savage frontier of the Realm. She shuddered, soaked and half-frozen, and glanced up yearningly toward the nearest of the funeral fires.

The boy's heartbeat thudded against her own mud-stained palm, quick and strong, but when she drew her hand out, she saw the mud dappled with bright scarlet. The boy was wounded, though it couldn't have been anything major—he'd have been dead already. Amara cursed under her breath and felt for his limbs. They were dangerously cold. While she struggled to force her weary mind to decide on a course of action, she began rubbing briskly, at once scraping more of the frigid mud off of him and attempting to restore warmth and circulation to his limbs. She called his name, several times, but though his eyelashes flickered, his eyes did not open, nor did he speak.

She took a quick look around the chamber. Amara shuddered to think of what the mud of the Field of Tears, where so many had fallen, might do to him if it got into his blood. She had to clean it off, and quickly.

She undressed him roughly. He was too limp and heavy, for all his slender appearance, to allow her weakened hands to be any more precise. His clothes tore in a few places before she got them off of him, and by the time she had, his lips had tinged with blue. Amara half carried, half dragged him over to the water and then down into it.

The water's warmth came as a pleasant shock to her senses. The pool's floor sloped down sharply until it was about hip deep, and even as she kept the boy's face out of the water, she sank gratefully into it and simply huddled there for a moment, until the rattle of her teeth chattering had begun to slow down.

Then she dragged him a few feet to one side, out of the mud-clouded water, and began to rub roughly over his skin, brushing the clay away until the boy was clean.

He had a shocking collection of bruises, scrapes,

abraded skin, and minor cuts. The bruises were fairly fresh, only a few hours old, she judged. His knees had several layers of skin peeled off, apparently a match to the ragged holes in his discarded trousers. His arms, legs, and flanks all showed patches of purple, slowly forming, as though he had been recently beaten, and a lattice of long, tiny cuts covered his skin. He had to have been running through thickets and thorns.

She cleared the mud from his face as best she could, using her already-torn skirts to clean him, and then dragged him back up, out of the water, and over to one of the fires.

As soon as she felt the air on her, she began to shiver again and realized that the water had not been nearly so warm as it had felt—she had simply been too cold, relatively, to feel the difference. She settled the boy in a heap on the floor, as near to the fire as she could manage, and huddled there for a moment, on her heels, her arms wrapped tight around her.

Her head nodded, and Amara let out a startled sound as she fell to her side. She wanted to simply surrender to the exhaustion, but she could not. Neither of them might wake up again. She felt her throat tighten on a whimper of protest, but she drove herself to her feet again, shivering nearly too hard to move, to think.

Her fingers felt like lead as she struggled from her own soaked clothing, thick and nerveless and unresponsive. She let the lighter clothing fall in a sopping heap to the marble floor and staggered to one of the stone sentries facing the bier. She clawed the red cape from its shoulders and wrapped it around her. Amara allowed herself a brief respite, leaning against the wall and shivering into the cape—but then drove herself along the wall to the next statue, and the one after, claiming both of those capes as well, then returning to the boy's side. With the last of her strength, she wrapped him in the scarlet cloaks, securing their warmth around him, near the fire.

Then, huddled into a ball beneath the scarlet fabric of the Royal Guard, she leaned her head back against the wall. It took nothing more than that for her to sleep.

She woke, warm and aching. The storm raged steadily, all howling winds and frozen rain. Amara pushed herself to her feet, her body weary, stiff from sleeping crouched down on her heels, and blessedly warm beneath the heavy fabric of the cape. She moved to look out of the doorway of the chamber. Night still reigned outside. Lightning flashed and danced without, but it and the accompanying thunder seemed more distant now, sound rumbling along well after the light. The forces of the furies of the air still battled, but the winter winds had pushed their rivals to the south, away from the valley, and much of the rain that fell outside now rattled and bounced against the cooling earth as true hailstones.

Gaius had to have known, Amara thought. He had to have been aware of the repercussions of calling the southern winds to bear her north to the valley. He had been crafting too long, and knew the forces that affected his Realm too well for it to have been an accident. Thus, clearly, the First Lord had intended the storm. But why?

Amara stared out at the bleak night, frowning. She would be trapped until the storm relented. *And so will be anyone else in the Valley, fool,* she thought. Her eyes widened. Gaius, with this act, had effectively called a halt to any activity within the Calderon Valley until the storm had relented.

But why? If speed had truly been of the essence, why rush her here, only to fence her off from acting? Unless Gaius felt that the opposition was already in motion. In that case, her arrival would put an effective freeze on their activities, perhaps giving her a chance to rest, regain her balance, before acting.

Amara frowned. Would the First Lord truly arrange such a deadly storm, a furycrafting of proportions she could scarcely visualize, merely to allow his agent to rest?

Amara shivered and wrapped the cloak around her a little more tightly. She could only deduce so much of Gaius's reasoning. He knew far more than most in Alera ever could—most would not even begin to grasp the scope of it. He was oftentimes a subtle ruler: Rarely did his actions have only one objective, only one set of consequences. What else did her ruler have in mind?

Amara grimaced. If Gaius had wanted her to know, surely he would have told her. Unless he trusted her competence to work out on her own what he intended. *Or unless he still doesn't trust you.*

She turned away from the doorway and padded silently back into the chamber, her thoughts in a whirl. She leaned against a wall beside one of the stone guardians, denuded of his cloak, and raked her fingers through her hair. She had to get moving. Surely, the enemies of the Crown would not be idle once the weather broke. She had to have a plan, at least, and get to work on it right away.

The first order of business, Fidelias would have said,

would be to gather intelligence. She had to establish what was going on in the Valley before she could effectively do anything about it, whether it be to act, to invoke her authority as a Cursor of the Crown to the local Count, or to report back to Gaius.

She swallowed. All she had to help her was the knife she'd stolen from Fidelias's boot and some clothing far too light for the weather it seemed she would be faced with. She looked back at the boy, curled on his side before the fire, shivering.

She also had him.

Amara moved to the boy's side and laid a hand on his forehead. He let out a soft groan. His skin was too hot, feverish, and his breathing had dried out his lips, cracked them. She frowned and went back to the water, cupping her hands together and carrying it back to the boy. She urged him to drink and tried to tip the water into his mouth. Most of it trickled through her fingers and splashed onto his chin and neck, but he managed to swallow a little. Amara repeated the process several times, until the boy seemed to relax a little, settling down again.

She studied him as she fetched another of the scarlet capes, folded it into a pad, and slipped it beneath his head. He was a beautiful child, in many ways, his features almost delicate. His hair curled around his head, dark, glossy ringlets. He had the long, thick lashes that so many men seemed to have and not care about, and his hands had long, slender fingers that seemed entirely oversized to the rest of him, promising considerable growth yet to come. His skin, where not marred with bruises or scratches, glowed with the ruddy clarity of youth that had somehow avoided awkward adolescence. She hadn't seen what color his eyes were, in the hectic events of the previous evening, but his voice had been clarion-clear in the storm, bell-sharp.

She frowned more seriously, studying the boy. He had almost certainly saved her life. But who was he? They were a considerable walk from any of the local stead-holts. She had chosen her landing site in order to avoid coming down within sight of any of the locals. So what had the boy been doing there, in the middle of nowhere, in that storm?

"Home," the boy murmured. Amara looked down at him, but he hadn't opened his eyes. His face twitched into a frown in his sleep. "I'm sorry, Aunt Isana. Uncle Bernard should be home. Tried to get him home safe."

Amara felt her eyes widen. Bernardholt was the largest steadholt in the Calderon Valley. Steadholder Bernard was the boy's uncle? She leaned closer and asked him, "What happened to your uncle, Tavi? Was he hurt?"

Tavi nodded, a dreamy motion. "Marat. The herd-bane. Brutus stopped it but not before it bit him."

Marat? The savages hadn't given the Realm any trouble since the incident on this very site, fifteen or sixteen years ago. Amara had felt skeptical when Gaius had voiced his concern about the Marat, but apparently one had come into the Calderon Valley and attacked an Aleran Stead-holder. But what did it mean? Could it have been one lone Marat warrior, a chance meeting in the wilderness?

No. Too coincidental for mere chance. Something larger was under way.

Amara clenched her hand on the fabric of the cape in frustration, wrinkling it. She needed more information.

"Tavi," she said. "What can you tell me of this Marat? Was he of the Herdbane tribe? Was he alone?"

"Had 'nother one," the boy mumbled. "Killed one, but he had 'nother one."

"A second beast?"

"Mmmhmm."

"Where is your uncle now?"

Tavi shook his head, and his expression twisted with pain. "Here. Was supposed to be home. Sent him home with Brutus, Brutus should have brought him back." Tears had started down his cheeks, and Amara swallowed upon seeing them.

She needed information, yes. But she couldn't torment an unconscious child for it. He needed rest. If he was the Steadholder's nephew, and the man had survived the attack, she could bring him home safely and almost certainly secure the Steadholder's enthusiastic cooperation.

"'M sorry," the boy said, broken and still weeping quiet tears. "I tried. Sorry."

"Shhhh," she said. She used an edge of the cloak to wipe the tears away. "Time to rest now. Lie down and rest, Tavi."

He subsided, and she frowned down at him, smoothing his hair back from his fevered forehead while he slept. If a lone Marat was in the Valley, perhaps the Steadholder had gone to hunt it down. But if so, then why would this boy be along? He had no particular skill at crafting, she judged, or he would have used it when the windmanes had been attacking them. He bore no weapons, no equipment. He couldn't have been hunting the Marat.

Amara inverted the idea. Had it hunted the folk of Bernardholt? Possible, particularly from the Herdbane tribe, if all that she heard of the Marat was true. They were a cold and calculating people, as ruthless and deadly as the animals that accepted them as one of their own.

But Marat didn't often take more than one beast as . . . what sufficed to describe the term? Mate? Companion? Blood-sibling? She shook her head with a shiver. The savages' ways were still alien to her, something fantastic from a tale rather than the businesslike reality she had learned from classes in the Academy.

Hordemasters took more than one beast, commonly, as a symbol of status. But what would a Marat hordemaster be doing in the Calderon Valley?

Invading.

Her own silent response to the thought gave her a little chill. Could the holders have run into the advance scouts of a Marat attack force?

The attack could hardly come at a more advantageous time for the enemy, Amara realized. The roads were slowly closing down for the winter season here among the northern cities. Many troops had been given winter furlough with their families, and folk of the countryside, in general, were winding down the frantic labor of harvest into the sedate pace of winter.

If the Marat attacked the Valley now, providing the forces stationed at Garrison were neutralized, they could wipe out every person in it and maraud through all the steadholts, practically all the way back to Riva itself. They might even, if they numbered enough, simply pour around the city and into Alera's interior. Amara shuddered to imagine what a horde might accomplish in that event. She had to contact the Count at Garrison—his name was Bram or Gram or something like that—and put him on the alert.

But what if the boy was lying about the Marat? Or mistaken? She grimaced. She knew the local Citizenry by name, at least, though the memorization of the Lords and Counts had been one of the more tedious chores at the Academy. She had no such knowledge of this Steadholder Bernard or of the folk of the Valley. By all accounts, they were a tough and independently minded folk, but she knew nothing about their reliability or lack of it.

She had to talk to this Bernard. If he had indeed seen a Marat hordemaster and been wounded by one of the great hunting birds of the outland plains, then she had to know it, secure his support (and hopefully some new clothes with it), and act.

She frowned. But she could expect the opposition to be moving as well. Fidelias had lead her into a trap she had escaped by the smallest of margins. She had been pursued for several hours and escaped the Knights Aeris sent after her through skill and good fortune. Did she suppose that Fidelias would not continue the pursuit?

In all probability, she realized, his business lay here, in the Calderon Valley. That had to be one of the reasons Gaius sent her here. Fidelias was her *patriserus*. *Or had been,* she thought, with a bitter taste in her mouth. She knew him, perhaps better than anyone else alive. She had seen through his deception at the renegade camp, though only barely.

What would Fidelias do?

He would judge her by her previous actions, of course. He would expect her to arrive in the valley and promptly to make contact with the Steadholders, coordinating information and after suitable data had been gathered, to take action against whatever was happening, whether it meant falling into a defense within one of the strongest steadholts or mobilizing the men of the Valley and the troops of Garrison to meet it.

And what would he do to stop it?

He'd find me. Kill me. And sow confusion among the holders until his plan could begin.

A slow chill went through her. She considered the situation again, but it was perfectly typical of Fidelias. He preferred simple approaches, direct solutions. Keep lies simple, he had always told her, keep plans simple. Leave them open to modification, and use your eyes, your head, more than any plan.

Word of a Cursor in the Valley would spread among the holders like wildfire. She might as well paint a circle over her heart and wait for an arrow to soar into its center. A slow chill crawled through her. He *would* kill her, now. Fidelias had given her a chance, and she had made him suffer for it. He would not allow himself to make the same mistake again. Her teacher would kill her, without a moment's hesitation, if she got in his way again.

"That's what I'm here to do," she whispered. She started shivering again.

Though she tried to tell herself that it was not fear coloring her decision, she felt it, tickling at her belly, racing with cold spider-fingers up and down her spine. She could not allow herself the luxury of openly invoking her authority and revealing herself to Fidelias. To do so would be to invite her own death, swift and certain. She had to remain quiet, as covert as possible. A runaway slave would be a far less unusual occurrence here at the frontier than an emissary of the Crown warning of possible invasion. She couldn't allow her identity to be known until she knew who she could trust, who could give her information that would let her act decisively. To do any less would be to invite her own death, and possibly disaster upon the Valley.

She looked down at the boy, her thoughts still in a tangle. He hadn't needed to come and help her the previous evening, but he had. The boy had courage, even if he lacked some more life-preserving common sense, and she had little choice but to be glad that he did. That said something of him, and in turn of the folk who had raised him. In his sleep, in his fever, he had spoken not to a mother or a father, but to his aunt, whose name apparently was Isana. An orphan?

Amara mused, and as she did, her belly rumbled. She rose to her feet and padded among the trees planted around the pool. As she expected, she found more than a few fruit-bearing trees among them. Gaius never acted with a single consequence in mind, when he could manage several at once. In creating this Memorium for his fallen son, he had raised a spectacular tribute to the Princeps' memory, reminded the High Lords exactly what power he commanded, and provided a place of refuge for himself (or for his agents) all at the same time.

She picked fruit from the trees and ate, studying the area around her. Amara went to the statues. They had been armed with genuine shields and with weapons, the short, vicious blades of the Royal Guard, meant to be used in close quarters, to incapacitate or kill in a single blow. She slid one from its sheath and tested it. Its edge proved to be keen, and she returned it to its resting place. Food, shelter, and arms. Gaius was a paranoid old fox, and she was glad for it.

Her arm twinged as she slid the sword back, and she glanced at the dirtied bandage on it. She retrieved the knife from her discarded skirts and cut a fresh bandage from them. She dried it, first, near one of the fires, before cutting the old one off, cleaning the wound with fresh water, and applying fresh wrappings. Something else tugged at her attention, but she pushed it firmly away. There was work to be done.

Amara moved quickly then, making sure the boy was sleeping peacefully. She gathered fruit onto one of the shields, using it as a platter, and rested it near him. She washed their clothing in the pool and used branches from the small trees to dry them over one of the other fires. She called upon the weary Cirrus to stand guard around the Memorium and to warn her should anyone approach. And when those chores were done, she found a smooth stone among the soil of the plants and used it to hone the edge of her knife.

That was when the tears took her. When the memories of years of instruction, conversation, of life shared with the man who had been her teacher came rolling back over her. She had loved him, in her own way, loved the danger of her work, loved the experiences he shared with her, loved the life to which she had been called. He had known how much being a Cursor meant to Amara. He had known, and he had done everything to help her with her studies, with graduating from the Academy.

He did everything except tell you the truth. Amara felt the tears rising, and she let them come. It hurt. It hurt to think that he had turned against the Realm, that he had, in that single act of treachery, endangered all that she had struggled to achieve, to fight to protect. He had declared his life's purpose as a Cursor to be empty, meaningless, and by extension, hers as well. His actions, not his words, said that it all had been a hollow, vicious lie.

No matter what happened to Amara, she would stop him. Whatever he had planned, however he had justified it, Fidelias was a traitor. That cold fact struck her through the heart, again and again. The knife whispered it, as the stone glided along the blade's edge, the steel wetted with her own tears. *Traitor. Traitor.* She would stop him. She *had* to stop him.

Amara did not let herself make a sound. She buried the sobs in her belly, until her throat ached with the pain of holding them back. She blinked the tears from her eyes and honed the edge of the little knife, until it gleamed in the light from the fire.

◌◌◌◌ CHAPTER 13

Before noon of the next day, the Knights Aeris brought Fidelias, together with Aldrick the Sword and the mad Odiana, down into the western end of the Calderon Valley. Grey clouds hung low and glowering overhead, though their threat was an empty one. The storm that had preceded them during the previous night had already headed off to the south, where distant thunder could only barely be heard. They were attired warmly against the near-winter cold of the Valley, and breath steamed before every mouth.

Fidelias stepped from the litter with a grimace and demanded of the Captain of the contingent of Knights, "You are *certain* that no one has arrived?"

The man murmured something into the air, then tilted his head to one side, his eyes abstracted, listening. He nodded a moment later and said, "Livus reports that there are still Marat scouts moving here and there. None of our observers saw anyone new coming into the Valley."

"That wasn't the question," Fidelias said. He heard the sharp edge in his own voice. "The last thing we need is an envoy of the Crown rousing Garrison or bringing in reinforcements from Riva."

The Captain shook his head. "The storm last night was long and extremely violent. No one could remain out in it and live. I suppose it's possible that someone skilled could have come in under it, if they could have gotten to cover quickly enough—"

"She could." Fidelias cut off a reply with a wave of his hand. "The crows take Gaius and everyone with him. He always loved to show off. Even when creating distractions."

"Someone's a grumpy boy this morning," Odiana murmured to Aldrick. The big swordsman debarked the litter and turned to lift the shapely woman lightly from it to the ground. The water witch gave Fidelias a smirk that fairly smoldered with sensuality and pressed herself against Aldrick's side, beneath the curve of his arm. "One would think that he hadn't gotten enough sleep last night, love."

"Peace," Aldrick rumbled, the thick fingers of one huge hand sliding over her mouth, a casual motion. The woman's eyes closed, and she let out a happy sigh.

Fidelias ignored the barb from the woman and said to the Captain, "This is no time to get sloppy. Give the girl's description to our men in Riva. If she comes through, stop her. Quietly. The same if any of the other Cursors I've described to you show themselves."

The Captain nodded. "And what do I tell the men here?"

"The same. If you see someone unfamiliar in the air, kill them. It shouldn't take me long to make contact with our source. Then we move."

The Captain nodded. "We were fortunate to have the wind last night, sir. We were able to bring in more men than we thought would be available."

"Fortunate." Fidelias laughed and tried to ignore the tension burning in his stomach. "That wind brought the storm and with it one of the Crown's own, Captain. I would not be so certain it was such a blessing."

The Captain saluted stiffly and took a step back. He murmured something else to the air, then beckoned with a hand to the Knights supporting the poles of the litter. The men rose in a sudden column of rising wind and soared into the air and through the concealing under-belly of the clouds above within a few moments.

Aldrick waited until they were well gone to say, lacon-ically, "You may have been a little hard on them. If the

Crown wanted to craft someone into the Valley, nothing they could have done would have stopped him."

"You don't know Gaius," Fidelias replied. "He is neither all-knowing nor infallible. We should have moved last night."

"We'd have arrived amidst the storm," the swordsman pointed out. "It could have killed us."

"Yes, the nasty storm," Odiana murmured. "And then, too, ex-Cursor, you would not have been given enough time to enjoy the pretty slave child." The last few words of the sentence dripped with a kind of gloating glee. The woman smiled, her eyes sparkling, as Aldrick absently covered her mouth with his hand again. She bit at his fingers, letting out a soft growl, and the swordsman let her, a smile touching his mouth.

Fidelias stared hard at the water witch. She knew. He couldn't be sure how much she knew, about Aquitaine's wife and the aftermath of the dismal little scene the previous evening, but he could see knowledge glittering in her eyes.

His belly burned a bit more as he considered the possible consequences, should Aquitaine learn of his wife's liaison with Fidelias. Aquitaine seemed the type to overlook the forest for the trees, at times, but he would surely have little patience with anyone who would risk humiliating him by lying with his wife. The few bites of biscuit Fidelias had managed to get down during the flight threatened to come hurtling up again. He kept the tension off of his face and thought that he would have to do something about the water witch: She was fast becoming a liability.

Fidelias gave her a flat, neutral little smile and said, "I think we should focus on the task at hand."

"Seems pretty straightforward," Aldrick commented. "Get on the horses. Ride to the meeting point. Talk to the savage. Ride out again."

Fidelias glanced around and then murmured for Vamma to fetch the horses. The earth fury moved beneath his right foot, a stirring in the ground of acknowledgment, and vanished. "I don't anticipate that the ride will be a problem. The savage might."

Aldrick shrugged. "He won't be a problem."

The former Cursor began tugging on his riding gloves. "You think your sword will alter anything for him?"

"It can alter all sorts of things."

Fidelias smiled. "He's Marat. He isn't human. They don't think the same way we do."

Aldrick squinted at him, almost frowning.

"He won't be intimidated by you. He regards your sword as something dangerous—you'll just be the soft, weak thing holding it."

Aldrick's expression didn't change.

Fidelias sighed. "Look, Aldrick. The Marat don't have the same notion of individuality that we do. Their whole culture is based around totems. Their tribes are built upon commonality of totem animals. If a man has a powerful totem, then he is a formidable man. But if the man has to hide behind his totem, instead of fighting beside it, then it makes him somewhat contemptible. They've called us the Dead Tribe. They regard armor and weaponry as our totem—dead earth. We hide behind our dead totems rather than going into battle beside them. Do you see?"

"No," Aldrick stated. He slipped Odiana from his side and started to draw on his gloves, unconcerned. "That doesn't make any sense."

"Not to you," Fidelias said. "It makes perfect sense to a Marat."

"Savages," Aldrick commented. Odiana turned to the packs and drew his scabbarded sword from it. He held out his hand, without looking, and she slipped the weapon into it, then watched as the swordsman buckled it on. "What happens if he doesn't cooperate?"

"Leave that to me," Fidelias said.

Aldrick raised his eyebrows.

"I mean it. Keep your weapon at your side unless everything goes to the crows."

"And if it does?"

"Kill everything that isn't you, me, or the witch."

Aldrick smiled.

"What do I do?" Odiana asked. Her duty to Aldrick done, she wandered a few paces away, drawing the toe of her shoe through the mud, lifting her heavier, warmer skirts enough to be able to study the buckles.

"Just keep an eye on the Marat. If you feel them get angry, warn us."

Odiana frowned and looked up at Fidelias. She placed a hand on the shapely curve of one hip and said, "If Aldrick gets to kill someone, I should get to as well. It's only fair."

"Perhaps," Fidelias said.

"I didn't get to kill anyone last night. It's my turn."

"We'll see."

Odiana stamped her foot on the ground and folded her arms, scowling. "Aldrick!"

The big man went to her, taking off his cape and

absently slipping it over her shoulders. The fabric could have wrapped around her twice. "Quiet, love. You know I'll let you have what you want."

She smiled up at him, winsome. "Truly?"

"Don't I always." He bent to the woman and kissed her, one arm pressing her against him. Her full lips parted willingly to his mouth, her body arching against his, and she reached up a hand to rake her nails through his hair, evidently delighted.

Fidelias rubbed at the bridge of his nose, where tension had begun to gather into a headache, and walked a short distance away. The horses arrived a moment later, nudged into a calm walk by Vamma and subtly guided over the ground. Fidelias called to the other two, who broke from their embrace only reluctantly, and the three saddled and mounted without further discussion.

As he had predicted, the ride passed uneventfully. Etan bounded along before them through the trees, the wood fury taking the form of a large, silent squirrel, always just far enough into the shadows to be seen only in faint outline. Fidelias followed the bounding, flickering shape of his fury without the need for conscious effort; he had been using Etan to track for him and guide him since he was barely more than a boy.

They crossed the Crown causeway and rode north and east through barren woodland filled with ragged pine trees, brambles, and thorns, toward the glowering shape of mountain rising up several miles before them. The mountain, Fidelias remembered, as well as the pine barrens around it, had a bad reputation for being hostile to humans. Little wonder the Marat had wanted a meeting near to what would be a safe area for his kind.

Fidelias flexed his right foot in the stirrup as he rode, frowning. The boot didn't fit correctly without his knife in it. He felt a faint and bitter smile stretch his lips. The girl had been brighter than he'd given her credit for. She'd seen an opportunity and exploited it ruthlessly, just as she'd been taught to do. As her *patriserus,* he felt an undeniable stirring of pride in her accomplishment.

But as a professional, there was only a cold, tense frustration. She should have become an asset to his effort, and instead she had become a dangerously unknown factor in the play of events. If she was in the valley, there was no limit to how much havoc she could potentially wreak with his plans—and even if she wasn't, the distraction of guarding against the possibility was nothing trivial in itself.

How would he disrupt the plan in motion, were he in her place?

Fidelias considered it. No. That would be the wrong approach. He preferred short, brutal solutions to such matters, the less complicated the better. Too much could go wrong with finesse in a situation like this.

Amara thought in a far less linear manner. The simplest solution would be to get to the nearest Steadholder, declare her status, and dragoon everyone she could lay her hands on into spreading word through the valley that some sort of mischief was abroad. In that event, he'd have several dozen woodcrafty holders roaming about the valley, and one of them would almost certainly see something and know it for what it was.

If she did that, identifying herself and her location, matters would be simpler. A swift stroke would remove her from the equation, and he could then muddy the waters until it was too late for the holders to stop matters from proceeding.

Amara would realize the danger of such a course, naturally. She would need to be more circumspect than that. Less linear. She would be improvising as she went along, while he would by necessity play the hunter, beating the bushes to force her to move and then acting swiftly to cut off anything she might attempt.

Fidelias smiled at the irony: It seemed they would both be playing to their strong suits. Well enough, then. The girl was talented, but inexperienced. She wouldn't be the first person he had outmaneuvered and destroyed. She wouldn't be the last.

A flicker of motion from Etan warned Fidelias that the three riders were not alone in the grey shadows of the woods. He drew his mount to a stop at once, lifting his hand to signal the others to do the same. There was silence there among the dimness of the evergreens, broken only by the breathing of the three horses, the drip of rainwater from the trees to the forest floor, and the soft sigh of cold northern wind.

Fidelias's mount threw back its head and let out a short, shrill sound of fear. The other two horses picked up on it, heads lifted high and eyes wide and white. Odiana's mount threw its head about and danced to one side, nervous and spooky. Fidelias reached out to Vamma at once, and the earth fury acted upon his will, spreading to the beasts around him the soothing calm of the deep earth. Fidelias felt the earth fury's influence expand like a slow wave, until it rippled over the horses, stealing away the restless agitation and letting their riders bring the beasts once more under control.

"Something watches," the water witch hissed. She drew her mount close to Aldrick's side, her dark eyes glittering and agate-hard. "They are hungry."

Aldrick pursed his lips, then put one hand on his sword. He didn't otherwise straighten from the relaxed slouch he had maintained during the whole ride.

"Easy," Fidelias murmured, putting a hand on his horse's neck. "Let's move forward. There's a clearing just ahead. Let's give ourselves some open space around us."

They eased the horses forward into a clearing, and though the mounts were under control, they still tossed their heads restlessly, eyes and ears flicking about for some sign of whatever enemy they had scented.

Fidelias led them to the center of the clearing, though it scarcely gave them thirty feet on any side. The shadows fell thick through the trees, the wan grey light creating pools of shifting, fluid dimness between branch and bough.

He scanned the edges of the clearing until he spotted the vague outline of Etan's form, the squirrel-like shape flickering around the edges of a patch of dimness. Then he nudged his horse forward a step and addressed it directly. "Show yourself. Come out to speak beneath the sun and the sky."

For a moment, nothing happened. Then a shape within that dimness resolved itself into the form of a Marat and stepped forward into the clearing. He stood tall and relaxed, his pale hair worn in a long braid across his scalp and down the nape of his neck. Dark, wiry feathers had been worked into the braid. His wore a buckskin belt and loincloth about his hips and nothing more. He bore a hook-shaped knife in his right hand, gleaming like dark glass.

At his side paced a herdbane, one of the tall predator birds of the plains beyond. It more than matched the Marat in height, though its neck and legs were so thickly built with muscle as to seem stumpy and clumsy. Fidelias knew that they were not. The bird's beak gleamed in tandem with the Marat's knife, and the terrible, raking claws upon its feet scratched through the bed of damp pine needles covering the forest floor and tore at the earth beneath.

"You are not Atsurak," Fidelias said. He kept his voice measured, clear, his speech almost rhythmic. "I seek him."

"You seek Atsurak, Cho-vin of the Herdbane Tribe," the Marat said, his own guttural voice in the same cadence. "I stand between you."

"You must stand elsewhere."

"That I will not do. You must go back."

Fidelias shook his head. "That I will not do."

"Then there will be blood," the Marat said. His knife twitched, and the herdbane beside him let out a low, whistling hiss.

From behind Fidelias, Odiana murmured, "Ware. He is not alone."

Fidelias followed Etan's flickering, unseen guidance. "To our left and right, at right angles," he murmured back to Aldrick.

"Aren't you going to talk?" Aldrick asked, his voice a lazy drawl.

Fidelias reached up a hand to scratch at his neck, squinting at the Marat. "These three evidently disagree with their Cho-vin. Their chief. They aren't interested in talking."

Odiana let out a breathy, "Oh, goodie."

The former Cursor gripped the hilt of the knife that hung at the back of his neck and whipped his arm forward and down. There was a flicker of grey light on steel, and then the spikelike throwing knife buried itself in the herdbane, its handle protruding from the bird's head, just where its beak met its skull. The herdbane let out a scream and leapt into the air in a great spasm. It fell to the forest floor, screaming still, thrashing viciously in its agony.

From the left and right came a sudden shriek of sound, the war cries of the birds and their masters, one savage paired with a bird rushing the group from either side. Fidelias felt, more than saw, Aldrick slip to the ground and turn to face one pair, but he heard quite clearly the rasp of the man's sword being drawn. Odiana murmured something under her breath, a soft, cooing sound.

The lead Marat rushed to the fallen herdbane's side for a moment and then, with a decisive motion, ripped the hook-shaped knife over the bird's throat. The herdbane let out a final, weak whistle and then shuddered to stillness on the ground as its blood stained the earth. Then the Marat turned toward Fidelias with his face set in a flat, murderous rage and flung himself at the former Cursor.

Fidelias barked a command to Vamma and flicked his hand in his attacker's direction. The ground beneath the Marat bucked in response, throwing him to one side, sending him sprawling. Fidelias took the opportunity to dismount from his increasingly agitated horse and to draw the dagger from the sheath at his hip. The Marat regained its balance and rushed him, aiming to move past his opponent, raking the horrible knife along Fidelias's belly in passing, disemboweling him.

Fidelias was familiar with the technique and countered by facing the Marat squarely, meeting his rush with one boot abruptly thrust out at the Marat's knee. He felt his foot connect hard, and something snapped in the Marat's leg. The Marat let out a squall and fell, whipping its knife at Fidelias's thigh as it did. The Aleran pushed away from the Marat's body in the same motion, pulling his leg clear a finger's width ahead of the knife, then turned to face his opponent.

The Marat attempted to rise to his feet, only to have his knee buckle. He fell into the pine needles. Fidelias turned and walked toward the nearest tree, glancing back at the others as he did.

Aldrick stood at the edge of the clearing, facing out, his blade gripped and held parallel to the ground, his arm extended straight out to his side, an almost dance-like pose. Behind the swordsman lay a herdbane, its head missing, its body flopping and clawing wildly, evidently unaware of its own impending death. The Marat that had rushed Aldrick knelt on the forest floor, its head lowered and swaying, its hands pressing at its belly and stained with blood.

On the other side of the clearing, Odiana sat on her horse, humming quietly to herself. The ground in front of her had, it had seemed, quite abruptly transformed into bog. Neither Marat nor herdbane could be seen, but the silt and mud before her stirred vaguely, as though something thrashed unseen beneath its surface.

The water witch noticed him looking at her and commented, her tone warm, "I love the way the ground smells after a rain."

Fidelias didn't answer her. He reached up, instead, using his knife to make a deep cut, scoring a branch on the nearest tree. He broke it off and, as the others turned to watch him, put his knife away, took the heavy branch in both hands, and, from out of the lamed Marat's knife reach, methodically clubbed him to death.

"That's one way to do it," Aldrick commented. "If you don't mind spattering blood everywhere."

Fidelias tossed the branch down to one side. "You got blood everywhere," he pointed out.

Aldrick walked back to the clearing's center. He took a handkerchief from his pocket and used it to fastidiously clean his blade. "But mine's in a pattern. It's aesthetically pleasing. You should have had me do it for you."

"Dead's dead," Fidelias said. "I can do my own chores." He glanced at Odiana and said, "Happy now?"

The water witch, still atop her horse, smiled at him, and let out a little sigh. "Do you think we shall have more rain?"

Fidelias shook his head and called out, "Atsurak. You saw what they intended." He had the satisfaction of seeing Aldrick tense and half-turn to one side, and even Odiana caught her breath in her throat. The former Cursor smiled and took up his horse's reins, laying a hand on the beast's neck and stroking it.

From the trees came a gravelly voice, a satisfied-sounding, "Hah." Then there was the sound of motion through the brush, and a fourth Marat appeared. This man had eyes of glittering, brilliant gold, a match for those of the sleek, swift-looking bird beside him. He wore his knife at his belt, rather than in his hand—and he also carried a sword, bound with a rawhide thong about its hilt and blade and slung over one shoulder. He had a half dozen grass plaits bound over his limbs, and his face had been rawly abraded, bruised. The Marat stopped several paces from the trio and held up his hands, open, palms toward them.

Fidelias mirrored the gesture and stepped forward. "What I did was necessary."

Atsurak looked down, at the dead man only a few paces away, whose skull Fidelias had crushed. "It was necessary," the man agreed, his voice quiet. "But a waste. Had they met me openly, I would have killed only one." The Marat squinted at Odiana, staring at the woman with a silent, hawklike intensity, before turning an equally intent regard to Aldrick. "Deadlanders. They fight well."

"Time is pressing," Fidelias responded. "Is everything in readiness?"

"I am the Cho-vin of my tribe. They will follow me."

Fidelias nodded and turned to his horse. "Then we go."

"Wait," Atsurak said, lifting a hand. "There is a problem."

Fidelias paused and looked at the Marat chieftain.

"During the last sun, I hunted humans not far from this place."

"Impossible," Fidelias said. "No one goes here."

The Marat took the sword from his shoulder, and with a pair of casual motions, unbound the thong from the weapon. He flicked it forward, so that its point drove into the ground a pace ahead and to one side of Fidelias.

"I hunted humans," Atsurak said, as though Fidelias hadn't spoken. "Two males, old and young. The old commanded a spirit of the earth. My *chala*, the mate to this one," he put his hand on the herdbane's feathered back, "was slain. Wounded the old one. I hunted them, but the young one was swift and led me from his trail."

Aldrick stepped forward and took up the sword from the ground. He used the same cloth he had cleaned his own weapon with to brush the mud from the blade. "Legion-issue," he reported, his eyes distant. "Design from a few years ago. Well cared for. The wrappings are worn smooth." He took off a glove and touched his skin to the blade, his eyes closing. "Someone with a measure of experience used this, Del. I think he's a Legion scout. Or was one."

Fidelias drew in a sharp breath. "Atsurak. These two you hunted. They are dead?"

Atsurak shrugged. "The old one's blood flowed like a stream. His spirit carried him away, but he was already pouring out into the earth. The young one ran well and was fortunate."

Fidelias spat a sudden, acid taste out of his mouth and clenched his jaw. "I understand."

"I have come to look at this valley. And I have seen. I have seen that the Deadlanders wait to fight. That they are strong and watch carefully."

Fidelias shook his head. "You were unfortunate, Atsurak, nothing more. The attack will be a victory for your people."

"I question your judgment. The Marat have come. Many tribes have come. But though they have no love for your people, they have little for me. They will follow me to a victory—but not to a slaughter."

"All is in readiness. Your people will sweep clean the valley of your fathers and mothers, and my lord will see to it that it is returned to you. So he has pledged."

Atsurak's lip curled into something like a sneer. "Your Cho-vin. Cho-vin of the Aquitaine. Do you bear his totem as bond?"

Fidelias nodded, once.

"I will see it."

Fidelias stepped back to his horse and opened one of the saddlebags. From it, he drew Aquaitaine's dagger, its hilt elaborately worked with gold and with the seal of the House of Aquitaine. He held it up, so that the savage could see the weapon. "Satisfied?"

Atsurak extended his hand.

Fidelias narrowed his eyes. "This was not a part of our agreement."

The Marat's eyes flashed with something hot, vicious. He said, in a very soft voice, "Nor was the death of my *chala*. Already, there is bad blood between your people and mine. Now there is more. You will give me your Cho-vin's totem as bond. And then I will fulfill my end of the bargain."

Fidelias frowned. And then he flicked the knife, still in its scabbard, to the Marat in an underhand throw. Atsurak caught it without looking, nodded, and turned to walk back into the woods. A few paces past the first branches, he and the stalking bird beside him vanished.

Aldrick stared after the savage chieftain for a moment and then at Fidelias. "I want to know what in the name of all the furies you think you are *doing*."

Fidelias glared at the man, then turned back to his mount and secured the saddlebags again. "You heard him. Something's got the Marat spooked. Without the dagger, he wasn't staying."

Aldrick's expression darkened. "That's a signet weapon. It can be traced back to Aquitaine. He's a Marat hordemaster. He's going to be fighting in the front of the bloody battle—"

Fidelias grated his teeth and spoke in a slow, patient tone. "Yes, Aldrick. It can. Yes, Aldrick, he will. Thus, we had best be damned sure that the attack succeeds." Fidelias slapped the saddlebags back over the horse. "After the Valley has been taken, it won't matter what plunder the Marat have. Events will be in motion by then, and it will all fall into politics."

Aldrick gripped Fidelias by the shoulder and spun the smaller man to face him. The swordsman's eyes were hard. "If it doesn't, there's evidence. If it gets back to the Senate, they'll bring charges against him, Fidelias. *Treason.*"

The former Cursor glanced down at Aldrick's hand, then up the length of the swordsman's arm to his face. He met his eyes in silence for several seconds, before saying, "You're a brilliant fighter, Aldrick. You could kill me, right here, and we both know it. But I've been playing the game for a long time. And we both know that you can't do it before I have a chance to react. You'll be less of a swordsman without your hand. Without your feet." He let the words hang in the air for a moment, and the ground shifted, very slightly, beneath the pair of them, as Vamma stirred through the earth. Fidelias let his voice drop to something quiet, cool. He used the same tone when ordering a man to dig his own grave. "Make up your mind. Dance or stand down."

Silence stretched between them.

The swordsman looked away first, his stance shifting back into his usual, relaxed slouch. He picked up the weapon the Marat had left and stood facing the other way for a moment.

Fidelias let out a slow, silent breath and waited for the too-quick pulse in his throat to slow down again. Then he turned and mounted his horse, folding his hands over the pommel to hide their trembling. "It's a necessary risk. We'll take precautions."

Aldrick nodded, his expression unhappy, resolved. "What precautions?"

Fidelias jerked his chin toward the sword. "We start with finding these two who have actually seen the Marat in the Valley. If that belonged to a retired scout, he might work out what's going on."

Odiana nudged her horse over to Aldrick's, took the reins, and led the mount over to the man, her eyes on Fidelias, her expression pensive. The swordsman mounted and slipped the captured sword away, into a strap behind the saddle. "So we find them. Then what?"

Fidelias turned his horse and started riding out of the clearing, aiming their path in a gentle circle around the outside of the mountain, toward the causeway, where he was most likely to find the signs of anyone passing from the mountain and toward the nearest steadhold. "We find out what they know."

Odiana asked, "And if they know too much?"

Fidelias glanced at his riding gloves and flicked a drying spot of blood from one of them. "We make sure they stay quiet."

CHAPTER 14

"And that's what happened," Tavi said. "It all started with that one little lie. And all I wanted to do was to get those sheep back. Show my uncle that I could handle things without anyone's help. That I was independent and responsible." He picked up a rind from one of the bright orange fruits and threw it back into the plants at the water's edge, scowling, his thoughts in a turmoil.

"You don't have any furies at all?" the slave repeated, her voice still stunned. "None?"

Tavi hunched his shoulders against her tone and gathered the scarlet cloak closer around him, as though the fabric might ward off the sensation of isolation her words brought him. His voice came out harsher than he'd meant it to, defensive. "That's right. So? I'm still a good herder. I'm the best apprentice in the Valley. Furies or not."

"Oh," Amara said quickly. "No, I didn't mean to—"

"No one means to," Tavi said. "But they all do. They look at me like . . . like I'm crippled. Even though I can run. Like I'm blind, even though I can see. It doesn't matter *what* I do, or how well I do it, everyone looks at me the same way." He shot her a glance and said, "Like you are, right now."

Amara frowned and rose, her torn skirts and her appropriated cloak swaying about her ankles. "I'm sorry," she said. "Tavi it's . . . unusual, I know. I've never heard of anyone with that problem before. But you're also young. It's possible that you just haven't grown into it yet. I mean, you're what? Twelve? Thirteen?"

"Fifteen," Tavi mumbled. He rested his chin on his knees and sighed.

Amara winced. "I see. And you're worried about your service in the Legions."

"What service?" Tavi said. "I don't have any furies. What are the Legions going to do with me? I won't be able to send signals, like the aircrafters, hold the lines with the earthcrafters, or attack with the firecrafters. I won't be able to heal anyone with the watercrafters. I can't forge a sword, or wield one like a metalcrafter. I can't scout and hide, or shoot like a woodcrafter. And I'm small. I'm not even good for handing a spear and fighting in the ranks. What are they going to do with me?"

"No one will be able to question your courage, Tavi. You showed me that last night."

"Courage." Tavi sighed. "As near as I can figure it, all courage gets you is more of a beating than if you'd run away."

"Sometimes that's important," she pointed out.

"Taking a beating?"

"Not running away."

He frowned and said nothing. The slave remained silent for several moments, before she settled down beside him, wrapping the scarlet cloak around her. They listened to the rain outside for a few moments. When

Amara spoke, her words took Tavi off guard. "What would you do, if you had a choice?"

"What?" Tavi quirked his head and looked up at her.

"If you could choose anything to do with your life. Anywhere to go," Amara said. "What would you do? Where would you go?"

"The Academy," he said, at once, "I'd go there. You don't have to be a crafter, there. You just have to be smart, and I am. I can read, and write, and do figures. My aunt taught me."

She lifted her brows. "The Academy?"

"It isn't just for Knights you know," Tavi said. "They train legates there, and architects, and engineers. Counselors, musicians, artists. You don't have to be a skilled crafter to design buildings or argue law."

Amara nodded. "Or you could be a Cursor."

Tavi wrinkled up his nose and snorted. "And spend my life delivering mail? How exciting could *that* be?"

The slave nodded, her expression sober. "Good point."

Tavi swallowed against a sudden tightness in his throat. "Out here, on the steadholt, crafting keeps you alive. Literally. Back in the cities, it isn't as important. You can still be someone other than a freak. You can make your own life for yourself. The Academy is the only place in Alera where you can do that."

"Sounds like you've thought about this a lot," Amara said quietly.

"My uncle saw it once, when his Legion was on review for the First Lord. He told me about it. And I've talked to soldiers on their way up to Garrison. Traders. Last spring, Uncle promised me that if I showed him enough responsibility, he'd give me a few sheep of my own. I figured out that if I took care of them and sold them next year, and saved up all of my pay from the Legions, that I could put together enough money for a semester at the Academy."

"One semester?" Amara asked. "What then?"

Tavi shrugged. "I don't know. Try to find some way to stay. I might be able to get someone to be a patron or . . . I don't know. Something."

She turned to look at him for a moment and said, "You're very brave, Tavi."

"My uncle will never give me the sheep, after this. If he's not dead." The tightness in his throat choked him, and he bowed his head. He could feel tears filling his closed eyes.

"I'm sure he's all right," the slave said.

Tavi nodded, but he couldn't speak. The anguish he'd been trying to keep stuffed down inside rose up in him, and the tears fell onto his cheeks. Uncle Bernard couldn't be dead. He just couldn't. How would Tavi ever be able to live with that?

How would he ever face his aunt?

Tavi lifted his fist and shoved angrily at the tears staining his cheeks.

"At least you're alive," Amara pointed out, her voice quiet. She put a hand on his shoulder. "That's nothing to take lightly, given what you went through yesterday. You survived."

"I get the feeling that when I get back home, I'm going to wish I hadn't," Tavi said, his voice choking, wry. He blinked away the tears and summoned up a smile for the young woman.

She returned it. "Can I ask you something?"

He shrugged. "Sure."

"Why endanger what you'd been working toward? Why did you agree to help this Beritte if you knew it could cause problems for you?"

"I didn't think it would," Tavi said, his voice plaintive. "I mean, I thought I could have done it all. It wasn't until nearly the end of the day that I realized I was going to have to pick between getting all the sheep in and those hollybells, and I'd promised her."

"Ah," said the slave, but her expression remained dubious.

Tavi felt his cheeks color again, and he looked down. "All right," he sighed. "She kissed me, and my brains melted and dribbled out my ears."

"Now that I can believe," Amara said. She stretched her foot toward the water, flicking idly at its surface with her toes.

"What about you?" Tavi asked.

She tilted her head to one side. "What do you mean?"

He shrugged and looked up at her again, uncertain. "I've been doing all the talking. You haven't said a thing about yourself. Slaves don't usually wander around this far from the road. Or a steadholt. All alone. I figured that, uh, you must have run away."

"No," the young woman said, firmly. "But I did get lost in the storm. I was on my way to Garrison, to deliver a message for my master."

Tavi squinted up at her. "He just sent you out like that? A woman? Alone?"

"I don't question his orders, Tavi. I just obey them."

Tavi frowned, but nodded. "Well, okay, I guess. But,

do you think you could come along with me? Maybe talk to my uncle? He could make sure you got to Garrison safely. Get you a hot meal, some warmer clothes."

The slave's eyes wrinkled at the corners. "That's a very polite way to take someone prisoner, Tavi."

He flushed. "I'm sorry. Especially since you probably saved my life and all. But if you are a runaway, and I don't do something about it, the law could come back to hurt my uncle." He pushed his hair back from his eyes. "And I've done enough to mess things up already."

"I understand," she said. "I'll come with you."

"Thank you." He glanced up at the doorway. "Sounds like the rain's stopped. Do you think it's safe to go?"

The slave frowned and looked outside for a moment. "I doubt it's going to get any safer if we wait. We should get back to your steadholt, before the storm gets bad again."

"You think it will?"

Amara nodded, the motion confident. "It has that feel to it."

"All right. Are you going to be all right, walking?" He glanced at her and down at her foot. Her ankle was swollen around a purpling bruise.

Amara grimaced. "It's just my ankle, not the rest of the foot. It hurts, but if I'm careful I should be all right."

Tavi blew out a breath and pushed himself to his feet. All the cuts and injuries twinged and ached, muscle protesting. He had to brace his hand on the wall for a moment, until he got his balance back. "Okay, then. I guess it isn't going to get any easier."

"I guess not." Amara let out a small, pained sound as

she got to her feet as well. "Well. We make a fine pair of traveling companions. Lead the way."

Tavi headed out of the Memorium and into the chill of the northern wind blowing down from the mountains in the north and the Sea of Ice beyond. Though Tavi had kept the scarlet cloak from the Memorium, the wind was still almost enough to make him turn back inside and seek shelter. Frozen blades of grass crunched beneath his feet, and his breath came out in a steamy haze before his mouth, swiftly torn apart by the winds. There could be no more argument on the subject: Winter had arrived in full force upon the Calderon Valley, and the first snow could not be far behind.

He glanced at the slave behind him. Amara's expression seemed remote, distracted, and she walked with a definite limp, bare feet pale against the icy grass. Tavi winced and said, "We should stop before long, to get your feet warmed up. We could strip one of the cloaks, at least try to wrap them."

"The wrappings would freeze," she said, after a moment's silence. "The air will keep them warm better than cloth. Just keep going. Once we get to your stead-holt, we can warm them up."

Tavi frowned, more at the way her attention seemed fixed on things elsewhere than at what she had to say. He resolved to keep a close eye on her: Frozen feet were nothing to scoff at, and if she was used to life in the city, she might not realize how dangerous it could be on the frontier, or how quickly frostbite could claim her limbs or her life. He stepped up the pace a little, and Amara kept up with him.

They reached the causeway and started down it, but

had walked for no more than an hour when Tavi felt the ground begin to rumble, a tremor so faint that he had to stop and place his spread fingers against the flagstones in order to detect it. "Hold on," he said. "I think some-one's coming."

Amara's expression sharpened almost at once, and Tavi saw her draw the cloak a little more closely against her, her hands beneath it and out of sight. Her eyes flick-ered around them. "Can you tell who?"

Tavi chewed on his lip. "Feels kind of like Brutus. My uncle's fury. Maybe it's him."

The slave swallowed and said, "I feel it now. Earth fury coming."

In only a moment more, Bernard appeared from around a curve in the road. The flagstones themselves rippled up into a wave beneath his feet, which he kept planted and still, his brow furrowed in concentration, so that the earth moved him forward in one slow undula-tion, like a leaf borne upon an ocean wave. He wore his winter hunting clothes, heavy and warm, his cloak one of thanadent-hide, layered with gleaming black feather-fur and proof against the coldest nights. He bore his heaviest bow in his hand, an arrow already strung to it, and his eyes, though sunken and surrounded by darker patches of skin, gleamed alertly.

The Steadholder came down the road as swiftly as a man could run, his pace only slowing as he neared the two travelers, the earth slowly subsiding beneath his feet until he stood upon the causeway, walking the final few paces to them.

"Uncle!" Tavi cried, and threw himself at the man, wrapping his arms as far around him as they could go. "Thank the furies. I was so afraid that you'd been hurt."

Bernard laid a hand on Tavi's shoulder, and the young man thought he felt his uncle relax, just a little. Then he gently, firmly pushed Tavi back and away from him.

Tavi blinked up at him, his stomach twisting in sudden uncertainty. "Uncle? Are you all right?"

"No," Bernard rumbled, his voice quiet. He kept his eyes on Tavi, steadily. "I was hurt. So were others, because I was out chasing sheep with you."

"But Uncle," Tavi began.

Bernard waved a hand, his voice hard if not angry. "You didn't mean it. I know. But because of your mischief some of my folk came to grief. Your aunt nearly died. We're going home."

"Yes, sir," Tavi said quietly.

"I'm sorry to do it, but you can forget about those sheep, Tavi. It appears that there are some things you aren't swift to learn after all."

"But what about—" Tavi began.

"Peace," the big man growled, a warning anger in the tone, and Tavi cringed, feeling the tears well in his eyes. "It's done." Bernard lifted his glower from Tavi and asked, "Who the crows are you?"

Tavi heard the rustle of cloth as the slave dipped into a curtsey. "My name is Amara, sir. I was carrying a message for my master, from Riva to Garrison. I became lost in the storm. The boy found me. He saved my life, sir."

Tavi felt a brief flash of gratitude toward the slave and looked up at his uncle, hopefully.

"You were out in that? Fortune favors fools and

children," Bernard said. He grunted and asked, "You're a runaway, are you?"

"No, sir."

"We'll see," Bernard said. "Come with me, lass. Don't run. If I have to track you down, I'll get irritable."

"Yes, sir."

Bernard nodded and then frowned at Tavi again, his voice hardening. "When we get home, boy, you're to go to your room and stay there until I decide what to do with you. Understand?"

Tavi blinked up at his uncle, shocked. He had never reacted like this before. Even when he'd given Tavi a whipping, there had never been the sense of raw, scantily controlled anger in his voice. Bernard was always in control of himself, always calm, always relaxed. Looking up at his uncle, Tavi felt acutely aware of the sheer size of the man, of the hard, angry glitter to his eyes, of the strength of his huge hands. He didn't dare speak, but he tried to plead with his uncle, silently, letting his expression show how sorry he was, how much he wanted things to be right again. He knew, dimly, that he was crying but he didn't care.

Bernard's face remained hard as granite, and as unforgiving. "Do you understand, boy?"

Tavi's hopes crumbled before that gaze, wilted away before the heat of his uncle's anger.

"I understand, sir," he whispered.

Bernard turned away and started walking down the causeway again, back toward home. "Hurry up," he said, without looking back. "I've wasted enough time on this nonsense."

Tavi stared after him, shocked, numb. His uncle

hadn't been this angry the day before, when he'd caught Tavi leaving. What had made this happen? What could drive his uncle to that kind of fury?

The answer came at once. Someone he cared about had been harmed—his sister Isana. Had she truly almost died? Oh, furies, how bad was it?

He had lost something, Tavi knew, something more than sheep or status as a skilled apprentice. He had lost his uncle's respect—something that he had only just begun to realize that he had possessed. Bernard had never treated him like the others, not really—never shown him pity for his lack of furycraft, never assumed Tavi's incompetence. There had been, especially over the past few months, a kind of comradeship Tavi hadn't known with anyone else, a quiet and unobtrusive bond between near-equals, rather than his uncle speaking down to a child. It was something that had been built slowly over the past several years, as he served as his uncle's apprentice.

And it was gone. Tavi had never really realized it was there, and it was gone.

So were the sheep.

So was his chance at the future, of escaping this valley, escaping his own status as a furyless freak, an unwanted bastard child of the Legion camps.

Tears blinded him, though he fought to keep them silent. He couldn't see his uncle, though Bernard's impatient snarl came to him clearly. "Tavi."

He didn't hear Amara start walking until he had stumbled forward, after his uncle. He put one foot in front of the other, blindly, the ache inside him as sharp and more painful than any of the wounds he had received the day before.

Tavi walked without looking up. It didn't matter where his feet were taking him.

He wasn't going anywhere.

⬦⬦⬦⬦ CHAPTER 15

For Amara, the walk back to Bernardholt proved to be a long and arduous exercise in ignoring pain. Despite her words to Tavi earlier that morning, her ankle, injured during the wild landing beneath last night's storm, had stiffened and burned hideously, barely supporting her weight at all. Similarly, the cut Aldrick ex Gladius had dealt her back in the renegade camp throbbed and ached. She could barely ignore one injury without the other occupying her full attention, but even so, she had enough presence of mind to feel pain on behalf of the boy trudging along in front of her.

The reaction of his uncle had not been unkind, she thought at first. Many men would simply have commenced with beating the boy, and only after would they have had anything to say about why the beating had been delivered, if at all. But the longer she walked, the more clear it became just how deeply injured the boy had been by his uncle's words—or perhaps the lack of them. He was used to being treated kindly, and with some measure of respect. The quiet, cool distance that the Steadholder

had shown was new to Tavi, and it had hurt him badly—
dashing his hopes for making a future for himself at the
Academy and driving home the notion that without
furycrafting of his own, he was nothing more than a
helpless child, a danger to himself and others.

And here, on the wild frontiers of the realm of humanity, where life or death hinged on the daily struggle
against hostile furies and beasts, perhaps it was true.

Amara shook her head and focused on the stones of
the causeway beneath her feet. Though she felt some
empathy for the boy, she could not allow his plight to
distract her from her task, namely, to discover what was
happening within the Valley and then to take whatever
action she thought best to see to it that the Realm was
protected. She already had some facts to piece together,
and her attention was best spent on them.

The Marat had returned to the Calderon Valley,
something that had not happened in nearly seventeen
years. The Marat warrior Tavi and his uncle had confronted could well have been an advance scout for an
attacking horde.

But the growing light of day made that possibility
seem increasingly remote, bringing inconsistencies to
light. If they had truly encountered a Marat, why had
the boy's uncle showed virtually no relief upon finding
his missing nephew? For that matter, how had the Steadholder been on his feet again at all? If the wounds were as
serious as the boy had described, it would have taken an
extremely talented watercrafter to have had Bernard on
his feet again, and Amara didn't think that anyone that
skilled would live far from one of the major cities of the
Realm. Surely, the injury must have been less than the

boy described—and if that was true, then perhaps the incident with the Marat had been likewise exaggerated.

Put into the context of fiction, Tavi's tale of his adventures the previous day made a great deal more sense. The boy, crushed with feelings of inadequacy, could have made up the tales in order to make himself feel more important. It was a far more plausible explanation of what he had told her.

Amara frowned. It was a more plausible explanation, but the boy's courage and resourcefulness could not be denied. Not only had he survived the violent furystorm of the evening before, but he had also rescued her—at considerable danger to himself—when he could have taken himself to safety without risk. Such courage, conviction, and sacrifice rarely went hand in hand with falsehood.

In the end, Amara decided that she had very little information to work with, until she had spoken to the uncle as well—and he seemed to be in no mood for any kind of discussion. She would have to learn more. If the Marat were preparing to attack again, defending against them would require a major mobilization, at the end of the year and at fantastic expense to both the High Lord of Riva and the Crown's treasury. There would be resistance to such news—and if she went to the local Count with nothing more than the word of a shepherd boy to go on, she would doubtless hear endless repetitions of the tale of the boy who cried thanadent. She would need the testimony of one of the Count's trusted landowners, one of the Steadholders, to get more than a token response.

The best reaction she could hope for in such a case would be for the Count to dispatch scouts of his own to find the enemy, and even if they managed to return from such a deadly encounter, it might be with a Marat horde on their heels. The Marat could swallow the valley in one assault and ravage the lands around Riva, while its High Lord, held captive by the onrush of winter, could do little but watch his lands be destroyed.

Ideally, with Bernard's testimony, she might get the Count to mount a more active defense from Garrison, and to send to Riva for reinforcements. Perhaps even manage a preemptive strike, something that might disperse the wave of an oncoming horde before it broke upon the Realm's shores.

On the other hand, if there was no imminent invasion and the Crown's agent roused the local Legions and incurred vast expenditure on Riva, it would be a major embarrassment before the other High Lords, and the Senate. Gaius's reputation might not survive the subsequent attacks, further agitating the already restless High Lords with what could be tragic results.

Amara swallowed. Gaius had assigned her to represent his interests in the Valley. Her decisions would be his. And while he would bear the moral and ethical responsibility for her actions here, the High Lords might demand legal retribution against her for the misuse of Crown authority—and Gaius would be compelled to grant it. Imprisonment, blinding, and crucifixion were some of the gentler sentences she could expect from such a trial.

The Crown's reputation, the possible security of the Realm, and her own life rode upon her decisions. Best she make them carefully.

She needed more information.

They came to Bernardholt some time just after the sun reached its peak.

Amara was struck at once by the solidity of the place. She had been born and raised in a steadholt, and she knew the signs of a strong holding—and one in a heightened state of alert. The steadholt's central buildings had walls higher than some military encampments, reaching nearly twice the height of a man and made of seamless, dark grey stone, laboriously raised from the ground by a powerful earthcrafter. The gates, heavy oak bound with steel, were half-closed, and a grizzled holder wearing an old sword stood on the wall above them, squinting laconically out over the distance.

Outbuildings stood not far from the walls, all of them one-story affairs, including what looked like a forge, vast gargant burrow, a combination barn and stables, and several animal pens. The granary, she knew, would be within the central enclosure, along with the kitchens, the living areas, and several smaller holding pens for animals, usually used only in emergencies. A pair of gargants, tended by a tall, handsome young man with wind-ruddy cheeks and black hair, stood in harness, waiting patiently while he threw several long, heavy ropes into a sack and secured it to one side of the harness.

"Frederic," Bernard called, as they drew closer. "What are you doing with the team?"

The young man, already tall and strong for a boy not yet old enough to depart for the Legions, tugged at a forelock with one hand and ducked his head to the Steadholder. "Taking them down to the south field to pull out that big stone, sir."

"Can you handle the fury in that one?"

"Thumper and me can, yes sir." The boy started to turn away. "Hullo, Tavi. Glad you're back in one piece."

Amara looked at the shepherd boy, but Tavi barely lifted his gaze to the other young man. He waved a hand, the motion vague.

Bernard grunted. "There's another storm in the air. I want you back in two hours, Fred, whether the stone's moved or not. I have no intentions of more people getting hurt."

Frederic nodded and turned back to his work, as Bernard strode on to the gates, nodded to the watchmen over them, and slipped into the steadbolt proper. Once inside, Bernard said, "Tavi."

The boy, without waiting to hear anything else, paced toward the side of the great hall and flung himself up the wooden staircase built along the outside of the building and into a door on the upper story, where Amara knew living quarters would commonly be situated.

Bernard watched the young man vanish inside with a grimace on his face. Then he let out a heavy sigh and glanced back at her. "You, come with me."

"Yes, sir," Amara said, and sketched a small curtsey. It was then that her ankle chose to give out on her altogether, and she wavered to one side with a little yelp.

Bernard's hand shot out and gripped her shoulder, through the scarlet cloak, steadying her—and closing tightly over the painful cut on her upper arm. She let out an involuntary gasp of pain, and her balance swam.

The big Steadholder stepped forward and simply picked her up as though she weighed no more than a child. "Crows, girl," he muttered with a scowl. "If you were hurt, you should have said something."

Amara swallowed, as a pang of relief from her beleaguered body warred with a nervous anxiety at the Steadholder's sudden proximity. Like Aldrick, he was an enormous man, but he exuded none of the sense of placid, patient danger that surrounded the swordsman. His strength was something different—warm and reassuring and alive, and he smelled of leather and hay. Amara struggled to say something, but wound up remaining awkwardly silent as the Steadholder carried her into the great hall and then into the kitchens behind it, where warm air and the smells of baking bread wrapped around her like a blanket.

He carried her over to a table near the fire and promptly sat her down upon it.

"Sir, really," she said. "I'm all right."

Bernard snorted. "The crows you are, girl." He turned and drew up a stool to the table and sat down on it, taking her foot quite gently between his hands. His touch was warm, confident, and again she felt soothed, as though some of that confidence had transferred into her by the touch. "Cold," he said. "Not as bad as it could be. You used crafting to keep your feet warm?"

She blinked at him and nodded mutely.

"No substitute for a good pair of socks." He frowned over her foot, fingers moving smoothly. "Hurt there?"

She shook her head.

"There?" Pain flashed through the whole of her leg, and she couldn't keep the grimace from her face. She nodded.

"Not broken. Sprain. We need to get your feet warmed up." He rose and walked to a shelf, withdrawing a small copper tub. He touched a finger to the spigot above the washbasin and held his hand beneath it until the water streaming out steamed and turned his skin red with its heat. Then he started filling the tub.

Amara cleared her throat and said, "You are the Steadholder, sir?"

Bernard nodded.

"Then you should not be doing this, sir. Washing my feet, I mean."

Bernard snorted. "We don't hold much with that city nonsense out here, girl."

"I see, sir. As you wish, of course. But may I ask you another question?"

"If you like."

"The boy, Tavi. He told me that you were attacked by a Marat warrior and one of their war birds. Is that true?"

Bernard grunted, his expression darkening. He tapped the spigot again rather sharply, and the water cut off with an apologetic little hiccup. "Tavi likes to tell stories."

She tilted her head to one side. "But did it happen?"

He placed the tub on the stool he'd sat upon a moment before and took her foot and part of her calf in hand. For a moment, Amara was acutely conscious of the sensation of his skin upon hers, the way the cloak and her skirts had fallen to reveal her leg nearly to the knee. She felt her face heat, but if the Steadholder took note of it, he gave no sign. He slipped her injured foot into the water, then motioned for her to put the other there as well. Her cold-numbed feet tingled unpleasantly, and steam curled up from the tub.

"How did you hurt your leg?" he asked her.

"I slipped and fell," she replied. She repeated to him

her story, about carrying a message to Garrison on behalf of her master, adding in a fall just before Tavi found her.

The Steadholder's expression darkened. "We'll have to send him word. You're not in any shape to continue traveling for another day or two. Wait until your feet have warmed up. Then dry them off and have a seat." He turned toward a larder, opened it, and withdrew a homespun sack full of tubers. He dropped that, a large bowl, and a small knife on the table. "Everyone under my roof works, lass. Once you warm up, peel these. I'll be back directly to see about your arm."

She lifted a hand, resting it over the bandage on her opposite arm. "You're just going to leave me here?"

"With that ankle you won't be going far. And there's another storm rising. The closest shelter, other than this hall, is the Princeps' Memorium, and it looks like you've already cleaned that place out." He nodded toward the scarlet cloak. "I'd be thinking about what I was going to say to Count Gram about that, if I were you. Safeguarding the Memorium is his responsibility. I doubt he's going to be terribly happy with you. Or your master, whoever he is." Bernard turned and started to leave through the doors to the hall.

"Sir," Amara blurted. "You didn't tell me if it was true or not. What Tavi said about the Marat."

"You're right," he said. "I didn't." Then he left.

Amara stared after the man for a moment in frustration. She looked from the doorway he'd vanished through, down to her feet in the steaming basin, and then back up again. Sensation was returning to her feet in an uncomfortable ripple of sharp pinpricks. She shook her head and waited for the feeling in her feet to return to something closer to normal.

A maddening man, she thought. Confidence bordering upon arrogance. She would not be so poorly treated in any court in the Realm.

Which was the point, of course. This was not one of the cities. Here, on the steadholt, his word was literal law, on nearly any matter one could name—including the disposition and nondebilitating punishment of a runaway slave. Were she a slave in fact, rather than in fiction, he could have done nearly anything to her, and as long as he returned her in one piece, and capable of fulfilling her duties, the law would support him as though he were a Citizen. Instead of caring for her and leaving her in a warm room with her feet in a hot bath, he could have as easily stabled her with the animals or put her to any of a number of other uses.

Her cheeks flushed again. The man had affected her, and he shouldn't have. She had seen him riding an earthwave—he *was* an earthcrafter, after all. Some of them could affect the temperaments of animals and the base natures of human beings, as well, draw out raw, primal impulses that otherwise would never surface. That would explain it.

But then, and more to the point, he had been very gentle with her, when he held her. He needn't have done so much as let her onto his land, and he had all but forcibly pressed hospitality onto her. Despite his threats and words, he hadn't locked her in a cellar or shown anything but concern and kindness.

Amara stirred her feet in the water, frowning. The Steadholder was clearly a man who commanded some measure of respect in his people. His steadholt was solid and obviously prosperous. The holdfolk she had seen had been clean and well fed. His reaction to the boy had been severe, in its own fashion, but restrained by the standards of most of the Realm. Had the man wanted her, he could simply have taken her, and not bothered with crafting her into a frenzy.

The contrast of his strength, physical and otherwise, against several demonstrations of gentleness was a surprising one. Though she had no doubts that he could be a hard man when called upon, she sensed a genuine kindness in his manner and an obvious love for the boy.

Amara drew her feet from the tub and patted them dry with the towel, then lowered herself from the table and perched gingerly on another stool. She reached for the paring knife and one of the tubers and started skinning the peel off of it, dropping the peel in a smooth spiral into the tub of water she'd just used and depositing the flesh of the root into the bowl the Steadholder had left her. The task was soothing, in its own way, repetitive, comforting.

She had been through a lot in the past few hours. Her world had been shaken, and she'd faced death at close quarters more than once. That might explain the sudden vibrance of her emotions, of her pure physical reaction to the Steadholder. He was, after all, an imposing and not unattractive man, she supposed. She might have had the same reaction to anyone in such proximity to her. Soldiers reacted that way often, when death was so near at hand, seizing at any opportunity to live life more richly, more fully. That must have been it, Amara decided.

But that got her no closer to accomplishing her

mission. She blew out a frustrated breath. Bernard had neither confirmed nor denied the encounter with the Marat. Any mention of it, in fact, seemed to have made him increasingly evasive. Much more so, she thought, than was reasonable for the situation.

She frowned over that thought. The Steadholder was hiding something.

What?

Why?

What she wouldn't have given, at that moment, to be a watercrafter, to have been able to sense more about him—or to have had more experience in reading people's expressions and body language.

She had to know more. She had to know if she had a credible witness to bring before the local Count or not. She had to know if the First Lord's fears were viable.

Bernard came back a few moments later, carrying another bowl under one arm. The Steadholder lifted his eyebrows, his expression surprised. Then he scowled at her, coming over to stand by the table.

"Sir?" she asked. "Did I do something wrong?"

"Crows, girl," Bernard said. "I thought you'd still be warming your feet up."

"You wanted me to peel these, sir."

"Yes, but—" He made an irritated noise. "Never mind. Sit back, let me see your feet again. And your arm, while we're at it."

Amara settled back on her stool, and the Steadholder knelt down on the floor in front of her, setting the bowl to one side. He lifted her feet, grunted something, and then reached into the bowl, drawing out a small jar of some kind of pungent-smelling ointment. "You've got some cuts, from the hills," he said. "Doubt you even felt them, as cold as your feet were. This should help keep them clean and numb some of the pain, when you start getting the feeling back."

He smoothed on the ointment with broad, gentle fingertips, on both feet. Then he drew out a roll of white cloth and a pair of shears. He wrapped her feet carefully in the cloth and finally drew from the bowl a pair of slippers with flexible leather soles and a pair of grey woolen socks. She began to protest, but he shot her a glare and put both socks and slippers on her. "Big feet, for a woman," he commented. "Had some old slippers that should do for a while."

She studied him quietly, during the process. "Thank you. How badly off are they?"

He shrugged. "They look like they'll be all right to me, but I'm no watercrafter. I'll ask my sister to take a look at them when she's feeling better."

Amara tilted her head to one side. "Is she ill?"

Bernard grunted and stood up. "Move that cloak back and roll up your sleeve. Let me have a look at that arm."

Amara moved the cloak back from her shoulder. She tried to roll the sleeve of her blouse up, but the injury was high on her arm, and the cloth bunched too much to allow it. She tried anyway, and the sleeve pinched in on the wound. Pain flashed through her arm again, and she sucked in a shaky breath.

Bernard said, "That's no good. We'll have to get you another shirt." He lifted the shears and, carefully, started snipping the bloodied sleeve away, a little above the first cut in the fabric. He frowned at it and then at the scarlet cloth of the bandage. The frown only deepened when he unwound the bandage and found the cloth clotted to the wound. He shook his head, fetched fresh water and cloth, and began to soak the bandage and to pull gently at it.

"How did you hurt your arm?"

Amara used her other hand to brush at her hair, pulling it back from her face. "I fell, yesterday. I cut it."

Bernard made a quiet sound and said nothing more until he had soaked the cloth and teased it gently off of the cut without tearing it open. He frowned, and with the cloth and water and soap, cleaned it gently. It burned, and Amara felt her eyes tear up again. She thought she would break down crying, simply from the exhaustion and the constant, relentless pain. She closed her eyes tightly, while he continued the slow, patient work.

There was a rap at the kitchen door, and a nervous voice, belonging to the boy he'd called Frederic, said, "Sir? They're asking for you outside."

"I'll be there in a moment."

Frederic coughed. "But, sir—"

The Steadholder said, voice hardening slightly, "Fred. In a moment."

"Yes, sir," the boy said. The door closed again.

Bernard continued with the wound and murmured, "This should have had stitches. Or someone to craft it closed. You fell?"

"I fell," Amara repeated.

"Apparently you fell along the blade of a sharp sword," the Steadholder commented.

He rinsed and dressed the wound once more, his hands gentle, but even so her arm throbbed and ached horribly. More than anything, Amara wanted to go somewhere dark and quiet and curl into a ball. But she shook her head and said, "Sir, please. Is the boy's story true? Were you really attacked by the Marat?"

Bernard took in a deep breath. He walked away and then came back to her and draped a soft, gentle weight over her shoulders—a blanket. "You're asking a lot of questions, girl. Not sure I like that. And I don't know if you're being honest with me."

"I am, sir." She looked up at him and tried to smile.

His mouth crooked up at one corner. He glanced at her before turning away to pick up a towel, hanging from a peg near the basin. "I've got a problem with your story. No one would send a slave that was hurt as badly as you out to run a message. That's insane."

Amara flushed. "He didn't . . . exactly know." That much was true, at least. "I didn't want to miss the opportunity."

"No," Bernard said. "Girl, you don't look much like most slaves I've seen. Particularly pretty young women in service to a man."

She felt her face heat still more. "What do you mean, sir?"

He didn't turn toward her. "The way you hold yourself. The way you blushed when I touched your leg." He glanced back and said, "Very few people disguise themselves as a slave, for fear they won't be able to get back out of it again. One has to be either foolish or desperate."

"You think I'm lying to you."

"I *know* you're lying," the Steadholder said, without malice. "It just remains to be seen if you're foolish or desperate. Maybe you need my help, or maybe you just need to be locked in a cellar until the authorities can collect you. I've got people to look after. I don't know you. I can't trust you."

"But if—"

"This discussion," he said, "is over. Now shut your mouth, before you pass out."

She felt him move closer and looked up just as he lifted her up again, keeping her unwounded arm against his chest. She didn't mean to, but she found herself laying her head against his shoulder and closing her eyes. She was just too tired, and it hurt too much. She hadn't slept since . . . had it been two days ago?

". . . going to be in here fixing dinner," Bernard was saying, "so we'll move you to a cot by the fire in the great hall. Everyone will be in here tonight, because of the storm."

She heard herself make a small sound of acknowledgment, but the ordeal of having her wounds cleaned, coupled with her exhaustion, left her in no condition to do more. She leaned against him and soaked in his warmth, his strength, drowsing.

She didn't stir until he began lowering her onto the cot. The door to the hall opened, somewhere behind him and out of her sight. Footsteps came toward them, but she couldn't see who they belonged to and couldn't work up the energy to care. Frederic's nervous voice said, "Sir, there's some travelers asking for shelter from the storm."

"That's right, Steadholder," said Fidelias, his voice even, pleasant, using a relaxed Rivan accent as though he were a native. "I hope the three of us won't be an inconvenience."

◻◻◻◻ CHAPTER 16

Isana woke to the sounds of wind groaning over the valley and the hollow clanging of the storm chimes hanging outside.

She frowned and rubbed at her eyes, struggling to orient herself. Her last memories were of being carried to her bed, after tending to Bernard. She must have slept for hours. She didn't feel thirsty, which was no surprise; Rill often tended to such matters on her own initiative. But her stomach growled and roiled with an almost painful need for food, and her body ached as though she'd not moved for days.

Frowning, Isana pushed aside the purely physical sensations, until she reached something deeper, more detached. And once she had isolated that feeling, she focused on it, closing her eyes to shut out the miscellaneous emotional noise she always felt around her.

Something was wrong.

Something was very wrong.

It was a quiet, nauseating feeling deep down, something that made her think of funerals and sickbeds and the smell of burnt hair. It felt familiar, and it took her a moment to track back through her memory, to realize when she had found such a sensation within her before.

Isana's heart lurched in sudden panic. She threw off the covers and rose, drawing a robe on over the shift she'd slept in. Her hair hung down past her waist, loose and tangled, but she left it so. She belted the robe and stepped toward her door. Her balance swayed, and she had to lean against the door for a moment, closing her eyes, until she regained her balance.

She opened the door to find her brother moving quietly out of his room across the hall. "Bernard," she cried, and went to him, gripping him in a sudden, tight embrace. He felt warm and solid and strong in her arms. "Oh, thank all the furies. You're all right." She lifted her eyes to his and asked, anguish making the words tight, "Is Tavi—"

"He's all right," Bernard said. "A little banged up, not terribly happy, but he'll be fine."

Isana felt sudden tears blur her eyes, and she pressed her face against her brother's chest and hugged him again. "Oh. Oh, Bernard. Thank you."

He hugged her back and said, voice gruff, "Nothing I did. He'd already taken care of himself and was on the way home."

"What happened?"

Bernard was silent for a moment, and she could feel the discomfort in him. "I'm not sure," he said finally. "I remember setting out with him yesterday, but beyond that . . . nothing. I woke up in bed about an hour before sunrise."

Isana forced the tears back and stepped back from him, nodding. "Crafting trauma. Memory loss. Like when Frederic broke his legs."

Bernard made a growling sound. "I don't like it. If what Tavi says is true—"

She tilted her head to one side. "What does Tavi say?"

She listened as Bernard recounted Tavi's story to her, and she could only shake her head. "That boy." She closed her eyes. "I don't know whether to hug him or scream at him."

"But if we were attacked by one of the Marat—sis, this could be very bad. We'd have to take word of it to Gram."

Isana bit her lip. "I think you should. Bernard, I've got a bad feeling. Something's wrong."

He frowned down at her. "What do you mean, wrong?"

She shook her head and knew that the frustration she felt showed in her voice. "Bad. Wrong. I can't explain it." She took a deep breath and told him very quietly, "I've only felt like this once before."

Bernard's face went pale. He was silent for a long minute before he said, "I don't remember any Marat, 'Sana. I can't take word of it to Gram. His truthfinder would know."

"Then Tavi will have to do it," Isana said.

"He's a child. You know how Gram is. He'll never take Tavi seriously."

Isana turned and paced a few steps, back and forth. "He'll have to. We'll make him."

Bernard shook his head. "No one *makes* Gram do anything." He shifted his weight a bit, so that more of his body fell between Isana and the door to his room.

"This isn't anything to trifle with, or to let Gram's stiff neck—" Isana frowned and leaned to look past her brother. Without changing expression, he moved a bit more to block her view with his body. Isana let out an impatient breath and shouldered her brother a bit to one side, looking past him.

"Bernard," she said. "Why is there a girl in your bed?"

Her brother coughed and flushed. "Isana, when you say it that way—"

She turned to blink up at him. "*Bernard*. Why is there a *girl* in your *bed*?"

He grimaced. "That's Amara. The slave Tavi helped. I was going to lay her down on a cot by the fire, but she panicked. Begged me not to let her sleep down there. Whispering like she was afraid of something. So I told her I wouldn't, and she just passed out." He glanced back toward his room. "I brought her up here."

"To your bed."

"Isana! Where else was I supposed to take her?"

"Just tell me you don't think she's actually a lost slave who Tavi happened to rescue."

"No," he said. "I don't. Her story didn't add up. It sounded all right at first, but I cleaned out her cuts and didn't give her anything for the pain. She got tired fast. Nearly collapsed."

"She's hurt?"

"Nothing to kill her, so long as she doesn't take fever. But yes. Her feet got cut up on rocks, and she's got what looks like a blade wound on her arm. Says she got them falling down."

"Clumsy girl," Isana said. She shook her head. "Sounds like she's someone. Maybe an agent of one of the Lords?"

"Who knows. She seemed decent enough. I suppose she could be what she says."

A quiet and desperate fear curled through her. Isana felt her hands start to shake, and her knees. "And she just happened to arrive that close to him?"

He sighed and shook his head. "I didn't like that part,

either. And there's more. Strangers, downstairs. Three of them. They're asking for shelter until the storm blows over."

"And they just happened to show up today." Isana swallowed. "It's happening, isn't it."

"We knew it might."

She swore softly. "Furies, Bernard. Crows and bloody furies."

His voice sounded pained. "Isana—"

She held up her hand toward him. "No, Bernard. No. There's too much to do. How is Tavi?"

He pressed his lips together for a moment, but said, "Not good. I was hard on him. Guess I was upset at not knowing what was going on. Worried."

"We have to find out what's going on. We must know whether or not he's in any danger."

"All right. What do you want me to do?"

"Get downstairs, to those strangers. Be polite with them. Get them some food. Get their shoes off."

"Their shoes—?"

Isana snapped, "Have someone wash their feet, city-style. Just do it." She closed her eyes, thinking. "I'll talk to Tavi. And this Amara. Make sure they aren't hurt worse than you thought."

"She's exhausted," he pointed out. "Looks like she's been run into the ground."

"She shouldn't be up to telling much of a lie, then," Isana said. "I'll be downstairs to talk to the strangers in a bit. Do you know how the storm is shaping up?"

He nodded. "Not as bad as last night, but not pretty. Everyone should be all right if they're indoors, but I've called everyone into the hall, just to be safe."

"Good," Isana said. "The more people there, the better. Don't leave them alone, Bernard. Don't let them out of your sight. All right?"

"I won't," he promised. "What about Tavi? He should know."

She shook her head. "No. Now more than ever, no. He doesn't need that on his head."

Bernard looked unhappy with her words, but did not gainsay them. He turned toward the stairs, but hesitated, looking into his bedroom, at the girl who lay on the bed. "Isana . . . the girl is barely more than a child. She's exhausted. She had a chance to do wrong, and she didn't. Tavi says she saved his life. You should let her rest."

"I don't want anyone to be hurt," Isana said. "Go on."

His expression hardened. "I mean it."

"All right."

He nodded to her and vanished silently down the stairs again.

Isana went back into her bedroom and took up her bone-handled brush. She took it with her, gathering her hair over one shoulder, and knocked at Tavi's door. There was no response. She knocked again and said, "Tavi, it's me. May I come in?"

Silence. Then the doorknob turned and the door opened a fraction. She opened the door the rest of the way and walked into the room.

Tavi's room was dark, with no lights lit. Of course, he couldn't use the furylamps, she reminded herself, and he'd been inside since Bernard had come home earlier that day. With the windows shuttered and the storm gathering outside, the place held a surprisingly deep collection of shadows. She could just see him settling back down onto his bed, no more than a dim outline across the room.

She began to brush at her hair, giving him a chance to speak. He remained silent, and after several moments she asked, "How are you feeling, Tavi?"

"Why don't you tell me?" he said, his tone sullen. "I don't know any watercrafting, so how am I supposed to know?"

Isana sighed. "Tavi, that's not fair. You know that I don't have a choice about what I sense from others."

"Plenty of things aren't fair," he shot back.

"You're upset about what your uncle told you."

"I worked all year to get those sheep he promised. And this . . ." He shook his head, his voice tightening with anguish, frustration that pressed against Isana like the heat from an old fire.

"You made some bad choices, Tavi. But that doesn't mean that—"

"Choices," Tavi spat the word bitterly. "As though I ever had that many to make. It isn't like I'm going to have to worry about that again, now."

She tugged the brush at a tangle in her hair. "You're just upset. So was your uncle. This isn't anything to get worked up about, Tavi. I'm sure that when everyone's calmed down—"

The sudden surge of frustration and pain from Tavi hit her like a tangible wind. The brush tumbled from her fingers and to the floor. She caught her breath, though the intensity of the boy's emotions nearly robbed her of balance. "Tavi . . . are you all right?"

He whispered, "It's nothing to get worked up about."

"I don't understand why these sheep are so important to you."

"No," he said. "You wouldn't. I want to be by myself."

Isana pressed her lips together and bent carefully to recover her brush. "But I need to talk to you about what happened. There are some things—"

Anger, real, vibrant rage rushed across the room along with the other sensations pouring from him. "I am *finished* talking about what happened," Tavi said. "I want to be alone. Please leave."

"Tavi—"

His dim shape rolled over on the bed, turning his back to the door. Isana felt her own emotions begin to drift dangerously toward what the boy felt, his feelings beginning to bleed into hers. She drew a breath, steeling herself against them and said, "All right. But we aren't through talking. Later."

He didn't answer.

Isana retreated from the room. She had hardly shut the door when she heard the latch slide shut on the inside and lock it closed. She had to take several steps down the hall before she emerged from the deluge of the boy's emotions. She couldn't understand it: Why was Tavi so upset over what had happened?

More to the point, what didn't she know about the events of the day before? Could they have any bearing on the arrival of so many strangers to the Valley at once?

She shook her head and leaned against the wall for a moment. Tavi had a powerful personality, a formidable force of will that lent his passions an extra weight, somehow, and forced her to struggle more sharply to keep them separate from her own. Not that it was surprising that she should feel him more keenly than anyone else, in any case. She loved him too much, had been near him too long.

To say nothing of the other reasons.

Isana shook her head firmly. Regardless of how drained she felt from last night's crafting, there was no time to waste. She should have remembered her purpose when speaking to the boy: to learn what she could of the previous day's events that Bernard could not remember.

She turned toward her brother's room and took a deep breath. Then she paced inside, determined.

Bernard had left the lamp burning on a low flame, and the room's interior was lit by soft, golden light. Bernard lived simply: He had, ever since Cassea and the girls had died. He had removed all of her things, packing them in a pair of trunks stowed underneath his bed. He lived out of a single trunk, now, as he had in the Legions. His weapons and gear were stowed on racks on one wall, across from the bare writing desk, all the records for the steadholt stowed neatly in its drawers.

The girl slept in Bernard's bed. She was tall, with lean features that seemed particularly drawn in the light, dark circles like bruises beneath her eyes. Her skin glowed golden, almost same shade as her hair. She was beautiful. A braid of leather circled her throat.

Isana frowned at her. Her brother had gotten down the extra blankets and piled them over the girl—though she had evidently stirred enough that her feet had slipped from beneath them. Isana stepped forward absently to cover her feet again and saw that they had been bandaged and covered in slippers of soft calfskin.

Isana stared down at the slippers for a moment. Pale white, stitched neatly, with delicate beadwork tracing a design over the tops. She recognized it at once: She had done it herself, perhaps ten years before. The slippers had been a birthday gift for Cassea. They had been in the chest beneath the bed for more than a decade.

Isana stepped back from the bed. She wanted to speak to the girl—but her brother had warned her against disturbing her. She had hoped for years that he would find someone else, after he'd lost Cassea and the girls, but he never had. Bernard had continually kept a quiet distance between himself and anyone else, and those who lived in the Valley, those who remembered his wife and daughters, had simply given him the solitude he wished.

If her brother had found it in himself again to reach out to someone else—and from his words to her and the way he had treated the girl, it seemed that he had— could she so readily act against him?

Isana stepped forward and laid her hand across the girl's forehead. Even before she had reached out through Rill, she felt the mild fever in her. She shivered and slowly extended her senses out, through the fury, and into the sleeping slave.

Bernard had not been mistaken. The girl bore several injuries, from painful cuts upon her legs to a painfully swollen ankle to a sharp, vicious cut along her upper arm. Her body had been pushed to exhaustion, and even in sleep, Isana could feel that the girl was gripped by a terrible worry and fear. She murmured softly to Rill and felt the fury course gently through the girl, mending closed the smaller cuts and easing the swelling and pain.

The effort left Isana's head light, and she drew her hand back and concentrated on remaining on her feet.

When she looked down again, the girl had opened her exhausted eyes and was staring up at her. "You," she whispered. "You're the watercrafter that healed the Steadholder."

Isana nodded and said, "You should rest. I just want to ask you one question."

The girl swallowed and nodded. She let her eyes fall closed.

"Have you come for the boy?" Isana asked. "Are you here to take him?"

"No," the girl said, and Isana felt the simple truth in her words as clearly as the tone of a silver bell. There was a purity to the way she spoke, a sense of sincerity that reassured Isana, let her shoulders unknot, if only a little.

"All right," Isana said. She adjusted the blankets over the girl, covering her feet once more. "Sleep. I'll bring you some food in a little while."

The girl did not reply, motionless on the bed, and Isana withdrew from the room, to the top of the stairs. She could hear voices, below, as the holdfolk gathered into the hall. Outside, thunder rumbled, low and ominous, from the north. The events of the night before, the Kordholders' attack on her, came rushing back in memory, and she shivered.

Then she straightened and walked down the stairs, to deal with the other strangers who had come to Bernardholt.

CHAPTER 17

Fidelias waited until the big Steadholder had padded up the stairs and out of his sight, carrying someone wrapped in a blanket. The former Cursor glanced around the hall. For the moment, at least, he and his companions had been left alone. He turned to Odiana and Aldrick with a frown.

Aldrick stood staring after the Steadholder and murmured, "Well, I wonder what that was all about."

"Fairly obvious," Fidelias said. He glanced at Odiana.

"Fear," she whispered, and shivered as she leaned closer to Aldrick. "The most delicious fear. Recognition."

"Amara." Fidelias nodded. "She's here. That was her."

Aldrick lifted his eyebrows. "But he never turned around. You never saw her face."

Fidelias gave Aldrick an even look and suppressed a surge of irritation. "Aldrick, please. Do you expect her to hang a sign on the door that she's here? It all fits. Three sets of tracks—the boy's, the Steadholder's, and hers. She was limping. That's why he was carrying her."

Aldrick sighed. "All right then. I'll go up and kill those two, and we can be about it." He turned away and lifted a hand to his sword.

"*Aldrick*," Fidelias hissed. He seized the swordsman's

arm at the biceps and reached down into the earth to borrow from his fury's strength. He stopped the larger man cold.

Aldrick glanced down at Fidelias's arm and relaxed. "That was the point, wasn't it?" the swordsman said. "Fidelias, we *have* to stop them from reporting to Gram. Without the element of surprise, this entire campaign could be for *nothing*. We came here to find the Steadholder and the boy who had seen our friend Atsurak, and kill them. Oh, and the agent of the crows-eaten *Crown* if we happen to run across her, which we have."

"Love," Odiana said. "We still don't know where this boy is, do we? If you go and kill the ugly little girl right now, won't the Steadholder object? And then you'd have to kill him as well. And anyone else upstairs. And all these people here . . ." She licked her lips, her eyes bright, and said to Fidelias, "Why shouldn't we do this again?"

"Remember where you are," Fidelias said. "This is the most dangerous area of the Realm. Powerful furies, dangerous beasts. This isn't one of the old plantations of the Amaranth Vale. It breeds strong crafters. Did you see the way that boy handled those gargants out front? And he calmed our mounts when they got nervous— that wasn't me. And he did it without so much as stopping to make an effort. A *boy*. Think about it."

Aldrick shrugged. "They don't go armed. They're Steadholders, not warriors. We could kill them all."

"Probably," Fidelias said. "But what if that retired Legionnaire Steadholder is a strong crafter to boot? What if some of the other holders here are that strong? Odds are some of them would escape—and since we don't know who the boy we're looking for *is* we'd never know if we got him."

"What about that boy out front?" Odiana asked. "That lovely strong tall one with the gargants."

"His feet are too big," Fidelias said. "The rain all but obliterated the tracks, but the ones from earlier today are clearer. We're looking for a smallish boy, not growing a beard yet—or possibly a girl. Atsurak probably wouldn't know the difference at that age, if a girl had been wearing breeches. The Marat don't make the same distinctions we do."

"He had big hands, too," Odiana mused, and leaned against Aldrick, her eyes heavy, drowsy. "May I have him, love?"

Aldrick leaned down and absently kissed her hair. "You'd only kill him, and then he'd be no good to you."

"Get the idea out of your heads," Fidelias said, his tone firm. "We have an objective. Find the boy. The storm is rolling in behind us, and everyone will be gathering into the hall. As soon as we find him, we'll take him, the Steadholder, and the Cursor and leave."

Aldrick grunted assent. "And what if we don't? What if he's already gone off to Garrison to warn the local Count?"

Fidelias grimaced and looked around. "I grew up on a steadholt, and you'd never keep something like that a secret. If that's what has happened, we'll hear about it when everyone gathers in."

"But what if—"

"We've borrowed trouble enough," Fidelias sighed. He shook his head and slapped Aldrick's arm gently, releasing him. "If the boy has already left, the storm will be as dangerous to him as anyone. We'll catch him, and the result will be the same." His eyes glittered. "But Aldrick. Why don't you take Odiana out to make sure the horses are all right? I'll handle things in here, and if there's killing to be done, I'll let you know who and where."

Aldrick frowned down at him. "You sure about this? In here by yourself—what if you need help?"

"I won't," Fidelias assured him. "Go on to the stables. Make it clear that you're looking for a bit of privacy. I'm sure they'll let a couple of newlywed travelers have it."

Aldrick arched his brows. "Newlywed?"

The water witch's eyes smoldered. Odiana flashed a smile to Fidelias, then turned to Aldrick with a sway of her hips and took one of his hands in hers. She kissed his fingers as she walked backward, toward the doors to the hall. "I'll explain it to you, love. Let's go find the stables. There will be hay there. Would you like to see the hay in my hair?"

Aldrick's eyes narrowed, and he let out a low and not unpleased sound. "Ah." He started out, keeping hold of Odiana's hands. "I knew there was a reason I liked working with you, old man."

"Just be listening," Fidelias warned quietly.

The witch nodded and replied, "Keep a cup in your hands, and drink in the cup. I'll hear." Then she and the swordsman vanished toward the stone stables.

No sooner had they left than Fidelias heard a heavy tread on the stairs leading down into the hall, and the Steadholder appeared again, his face set in something between a frown and a scowl. He looked around and said, "Sorry about that. Just had to take care of someone hurt."

"Ah," said Fidelias, studying the man. He stepped with the faintest trace of hesitation on his left side, as though it pained him slightly to do so. If he had been wounded, as Atsurak had indicated, then the wound had been crafted shut—which meant that a reasonably powerful watercrafter resided in the steadholt as well. "Nothing too bad, I hope."

The man shook his head and said, "Nothing we can't handle." He extended a hand to several seats by the fire. "Sit down, sit down. Let me get you a cup of something hot."

Fidelias murmured a thanks and settled down by the fire with the large man. "Steadholder . . . Bernard, I assume?"

"Just Bernard, sir."

"Please. Just Del."

The Steadholder half-smiled. "Del. So what brings you out to Garrison this late in the year, Del?"

"Business," Fidelias replied. "I represent a group of investors who fronted several prospectors money to locate gems in the wilderness over the summer. They should be coming back in, with the weather turning worse, and we'll see what they've found."

Bernard nodded. "I thought you had a couple more with you. Where did your friends go?"

Fidelias gave him a warm grin and a wink. "Ah yes. My guardsman is a newlywed, and I let him bring his wife with him. They went out to check on the horses."

The Steadholder gave Fidelias a polite smile. "To be young again, eh?"

Fidelias agreed, "My days of creeping off to stables with blushing maids are long past."

"The storm's coming in. I want to have everyone here in the hall, just to be safe."

Fidelias nodded. "I'm sure they'll be along in a little while."

The Steadholder nodded. "See to it that they are. I'll have no one harmed while under my roof."

Fidelias detected a slight edge to the words, one the Steadholder himself probably wasn't aware of. His instincts twinged, a low and subtle alarm lending an edge of tension to him, but he nodded and smiled and said, "Of course."

"If you'll excuse me, then. I need to make the rounds and make sure everything's secured before the storm comes down."

"Of course. Again, thank you for your hospitality. If I can be of any assistance to you, let me know."

Bernard grunted and rose, his expression preoccupied. Fidelias watched the man carefully, but could read little of him through his body language. Tense, to be sure, but wouldn't any Steadholder be, when facing a threat to his holders? He carried his leg stiffly, still, as he moved out of the hall and into the courtyard, and just before he left, the big man glanced over his shoulder, toward a staircase in the far corner of the hall.

Fidelias watched him and waited until the Steadholder had left the hall to glance at the staircase himself. Interesting.

A moment later, a pretty young girl brought a steaming mug out to Fidelias's seat by the fire, presenting it to him with a slight curtsey. "Sir."

He smiled at her and accepted the mug. "Thank you, young lady. But please, call me Del."

She smiled at him, a winsome expression. "My name is Beritte, sir—Del."

"A lovely name for a lovely girl." He sipped at the drink, a tea he vaguely recognized. "Mmmm, wonderful. I suppose you've had an interesting few days here, with the storm and all that's happened."

She nodded, folding her hands in front of her and inhaling just enough to let her bodice round out her young breasts. "Between all the excitement yesterday and then last night, it's been one thing after another. Though I suppose it isn't anything compared to the life of a gem merchant, sir."

His eyebrows lifted, and he said, letting a small smile touch his mouth, "I don't remember mentioning that to you, Beritte. I thought I was alone with the Steadholder."

Her cheeks colored bright scarlet. "Oh, sir—I'm sorry. I've a little windcrafting you see and . . ."

"And you listened in?" he suggested.

"We so seldom have visitors to Bernardholt, sir," the girl said. She looked up, her eyes direct. "I'm ever so interested in new, exciting people."

Who are wealthy gem merchants, Fidelias thought wryly. "Completely understandable. Though honestly, from the things I've heard . . ." He leaned closer to her, looking left and right. "Was the Steadholder really hurt yesterday?"

The girl knelt down beside the chair, leaning toward him just enough to let him see the curve of her bosom should he look down. "Yes, and it was terrible. He was so pale that when Fade—Fade's our idiot, sir, the poor man—first dragged him in here, I thought the Steadholder was dead. And then Kord and his sons went mad, and the Steadholders all set to fighting one another with their furies." Her eyes gleamed. "I've never seen anything like it. Perhaps later, after dinner, you'd like to hear more about it."

Fidelias nodded, meeting her eyes. "That sounds very exciting, Beritte. And the boy? Was he hurt as well?"

The girl blinked at him for a moment, expression confused, and then asked, blankly, "Tavi, sir? Is that who you mean?"

"I'd only heard there was a boy hurt as well."

"Oh . . . I suppose you mean Tavi, then, but he's no one. And even though he's the Steadholder's nephew, we don't really like to talk about him very much, sir. He and simple Fade."

"The boy's an idiot as well?"

"Oh, he's clever enough, I suppose—just as Fade is handy enough with a smith's hammer. But he's never going to be much more than Fade is." She leaned closer to him, so that her breasts pressed against his arm, and whispered importantly, "He's furyless, sir."

"Entirely?" Fidelias tilted his head, holding his cup where he could be sure his voice would strike the drink within it squarely. "I've never heard of such a thing. Do you think I could meet him?"

Beritte shrugged. "If you really want to. He went up to his room, when the Steadholder brought him and that slave home. I suppose he'll be down for dinner."

Fidelias nodded toward the stairs the Steadholder had glanced at. "Upstairs there? Do you know if the slave is up there as well?"

Beritte frowned at him. "I suppose. They'll be down

for dinner, I expect. I'm cooking tonight, and I'm a very good cook, sir. I'd love to hear what you think of—"

A new voice interrupted the girl, confident and smooth. "Beritte, that will be quite enough from you. You've chores in the kitchen. Attend to them."

The girl flushed an angry and embarrassed pink, rose to give Fidelias a swift curtsey, and then fled the hall, back toward the kitchens.

Fidelias lifted his eyes to see a tall, girlish figure wearing a dressing gown. Long, dark hair spilled over her shoulders, down to her waist, Her face was youthful, with a pleasingly full mouth. She carried herself with quiet confidence, and he noted the threads of silver in her hair. This would be the watercrafter, then.

At once, Fidelias drew in his emotions, carefully controlling them, veiling them from her perceptions, even as he rose to bow to her. "Lady Steadholder?"

She regarded him with a cool expression, her own features every bit as masked as he knew his own were. "I am the Steadholder's sister, Isana. Welcome to Bernardholt, sir."

"A pleasure. I hope I did not steal away the girl for too long."

"As do I," Isana said. "She has a tendency to talk when she should listen."

"There are many like her across the Realm," he murmured.

"May I inquire as to your business in Bernardholt, sir?"

The question was innocuous enough, but Fidelias sensed the trap in it. He kept tight rein on his feelings and said, blithely, "We seek shelter from the coming storm, lady, and are passing through on our way to Garrison."

"I see." She glanced after the girl and said, "I hope you have no plans to make away with any of our young people, sir."

Fidelias let out a low laugh. "Naturally not, lady."

Her eyes moved back to his and remained there, steady, for several long beats. He regarded her in reply with a blank, pleasant smile.

"But where are my manners?" the woman said. "A moment, sir." She crossed to the fire and took from a shelf near it a pan, some clean cloths. She filled the pan from the pipe that passed through the rear of the fireplace, the water steaming, and moved back to him. She knelt in front of him, setting the pan aside, and began unlacing his boots.

Fidelias frowned. Though the gesture would have been common enough in a city, it was rarely observed in the steadholts, particularly those this far from civilization. "Really, lady, this isn't necessary."

She looked up at him, and he thought he caught a glimmer of triumph in her eyes. "Oh, but it is. I insist, sir. It is to our very great honor that we treat our guests with courtesy and hospitality."

"You're already doing enough," he said.

She tugged his boot off and tossed it to one side. The other soon joined it. "Nonsense. My brother would be horrified if I did not treat you with all the honor you deserve."

Fidelias settled back with his tea, frowning, but unable to voice any particular protest against the ritual. As she washed his feet, people began to trickle into the hall by threes and fours and fives; families, mostly, he noted. The steadholt was a prosperous one. Though the seats around the fire were given a respectful space, the rest of the large hall was soon filled with motion and sound and quietly festive talk—the mark of a folk who knew that they were safe, while outside the thunder rolled, the wind was rising, and the storm chimes were clanging away in steady rhythm.

Isana finished and said, "I'll just have these brushed clean, sir, and send them right back to you." She rose, taking his boots in hand. "I'm afraid we can offer only clean blankets and a place beside the fire this night. We'll have our dinner together and then turn in for the night."

Fidelias glanced at the stairs and then back to the watercrafter. Simple enough, then. Once everyone was sleeping, even the suspicious watercrafter, it would be an easy enough matter to slit three throats in the darkness and slip away before morning light. "Everyone together at dinner." He smiled at her and said, "That sounds per—"

The doors to the hall abruptly slammed open, and Aldrick stormed in, letting in the howling wind. Rain and sleet pounded down around his broad shoulders and across the threshold with him. Odiana clung to his side. Both looked disheveled, straw littering their hair and clothing. Aldrick cut through the crowded hall and came straight to Fidelias, the holders scattering out of his way, like sheep before a running horse.

"Fidelias," Aldrick breathed, keeping his voice low. "Someone has let our horses out. They know."

Fidelias let out a curse and looked toward the water-crafter—only to see her holding her skirts with one hand while she dashed up the far staircase, his boots in her other.

"Bloody crows," he breathed, rising, feet cold upon the floor. "I'll get the horses and the Steadholder. The boy and Amara are up those stairs." He turned to Aldrick, feeling for the knife hidden in his tunic, and said, "Kill them."

⬦⬦⬦⬦ CHAPTER 18

Tavi eventually came to the conclusion that he was sulking.

It wasn't easily reached, of course. It took nearly ten minutes of staring at the wall in smoldering anger after his aunt's departure before it occurred to Tavi that she did not look at all well. That, in turn, led to worrying about her, and after that it became impossible to sustain a good, sullen rage. The anger slowly faded and left him feeling tired, sore, and hungry.

Tavi sat up on his bed and swung his legs over the side. He kicked his feet, frowning, while he thought about the events of the past day, and what they meant to him.

He had neglected his responsibilities and told a lie. And now he suffered for it—and so did the people who cared about him. His uncle had been wounded badly in his defense, and now Aunt Isana looked as though the efforts of healing his uncle's leg had damaged her health. Such things were not unheard of. And even though Bernard tried to hide it, his uncle walked with a very slight limp. It was just possible that he would keep it, that the injury had done permanent damage to his leg.

Tavi rested his chin in his hands and closed his eyes, feeling foolish, selfish, childish. He had been so focused on getting the sheep—his sheep—back, on keeping his uncle's respect, that he had forgotten to behave in a manner that was worthy of it. He had exposed himself and others to great risk, all for the sake of his dream—the Academy.

If he had gotten to the Academy as a result of his ill-considered choices, would it have been worth it? Could he really have made a better life for himself, knowing what he had traded away to get it?

"You are an idiot, Tavi," he mumbled to himself. "A true, shining example of idiocy."

Matters could be much worse for him—much worse for his family, as well. He shuddered at the thought of his uncle, dead on the ground, or his aunt laying beside a healing tub with her eyes empty, her body still breathing but already dead. Though things had not played out the way he had wished them to, they could have been more disastrous.

Though he ached in every muscle and his head felt light and feverish, he went to the door. He would find his aunt and uncle, apologize to them, and offer to make amends. He had no idea what he would do, but he knew that he had to at least try. They deserved that much.

He had to earn the respect he wanted, not through

daring or cleverness, but simply through hard work and reliability, just as his uncle and aunt had.

Tavi was about to open the door when there came a swift, soft rapping at his window.

He blinked, looking back across the dimness of his room. Outside, the wind was rising, and he had already put up the storm shutters. Perhaps one of the more mischievous wind furies had rattled the shutters.

The knock came again. Three quick knocks, two slow, three quick, two slow.

Tavi went to the window and unfastened the latch to the storm shutters.

They sprang open, all but knocking him down, and let in a torrent of cold, misty wind. Tavi drew back several steps, as someone slipped into the room, lithe and nearly silent.

Amara made a soft, quiet sound and slipped entirely into the room, then turned and shut the window and the shutters behind her. She was wearing what looked like a pair of his uncle's trousers, belted about her slender waist with a heavy leather cord. His tunic and shirt billowed on her, as did the heavily padded jacket and cloak, but she had secured them with more strips of leather, so that she was quite evidently functional in them. She wore pale slippers on her feet and what looked like several layers of socks under them. In one hand, she held a bundle that included an old leather pack of Bernard's, his hunting bow, a handful of arrows, and the sword they'd recovered from the Princeps' Memorium.

"Tavi," she said. "Get dressed in warm clothes. Bring extra socks, some blankets, food if you have any up here. We're leaving."

"Leaving?" Tavi stammered.

"Keep your voice down," the slave hissed.

Tavi blinked and mumbled, "Sorry."

"Don't apologize. *Hurry.* We don't have much time."

"We can't leave," Tavi protested. "The storm's coming in."

"It won't be as bad as the last one," Amara said. "And we can take more salt with us. You have a smokehouse here, yes? Salt for the meat?"

"Of course, but—"

Amara crossed to his trunks, swung the first open, and started digging.

"Hey!" Tavi protested.

She threw a pair of heavy trousers into his face, followed by three of his thickest shirts. She followed that with his jacket from its peg on the wall and then his second-best cloak.

"Get those on," Amara said.

"No," Tavi said, firmly. "I'm not leaving. I just got back. People got hurt trying to come and find me. I'm not going to make them go through that again. You can't expect me to put the people of my own steadholt in danger so that I can go running off with a fugitive slave!"

Amara went to the door and checked the latch, making sure it was shut. "Tavi, we don't have time. If you want to live, come with me. Right now."

Tavi blinked at her, so startled that he dropped the clothes he had been holding. "Wh-what?"

"If you don't leave with me, right now, you aren't going to live through the night."

"What are you talking about?"

"Get dressed," she said.

"No," he snapped. "Not until I know what's happening."

Her eyes narrowed, and for the first time he'd been near her, Tavi felt a sliver of fear quiver through him. "Tavi. If you don't get dressed and come with me, I will knock you out, wrap you in a blanket, and take you with me."

Tavi licked his lips. "N-no you won't," he said. "You couldn't carry me down through the hall, and you won't be able to carry me out the window, either—or on the ground. Not with your ankle hurt."

Amara blinked at him and then ground her teeth. "Too clever," she muttered. "This steadholt, maybe every one in the Valley, is in danger. I think you and I can help them. Tavi, get dressed. *Please.* I'll explain while you do."

Tavi swallowed, staring at the young woman. The steadholt in danger? What was she talking about? The last thing he needed was to go chasing off again, to prove to everyone who mattered that he couldn't be trusted.

But Amara had saved his life. And if she was telling the truth . . .

"All right. Talk." He stooped down to recover his clothes and started shrugging into the shirts.

Amara nodded and came closer, holding the clothes for him, helping him into them. "First of all, I'm not a slave. I'm a Cursor. And I've been sent to this valley at the command of the First Lord himself."

Tavi blinked up at her and then stuffed his arms into the sleeves. "To deliver mail?"

Amara sighed. "No. That's just one of the things we do, Tavi. I am the agent of the First Lord. He thinks this valley may be in danger, and he sent me to do something about it."

"But you're a girl!"

She frowned at him and jerked the next shirt down over his ears roughly. "I'm a Cursor. And I think the First Lord is right."

"But what does this have to do with me? With Bernardholt?"

"You've seen the danger, Tavi. I need to take you to Garrison. You have to tell the Count there what you saw."

A cold feeling chilled Tavi, and he blinked up at her. "The Marat," he breathed. "The Marat are coming. Aren't they? Like when they killed the Princeps."

"I think so," Amara said.

"My uncle saw them, he's the one that should go. The Count would never believe that—"

"He can't," Amara said. "Crafting trauma, when he was healed. He doesn't remember any of it."

"How do you know that?" Tavi demanded.

"Because I listened. I faked passing out, and I listened in on all the talk up here. Your uncle doesn't remember, and your aunt is suspicious of me. There's no time to explain it to them—we have to leave here, and right now."

Tavi tugged the heavy tunic on over the shirts, his hands moving more slowly now. "Why?"

"Because downstairs are some men who are here to kill you, me, and anyone who has seen the Marat."

"But why would another Aleran do that?"

"We *really* don't have time for that. They're the enemy. They want to unseat the First Lord, and they want the Marat to wipe out the steadholts in the Valley so that the Realm perceives the First Lord as weak and ineffective."

Tavi stared at her. "Wipe out the Valley? But that would mean . . ."

She regarded him, her face drawn. "Unless we take warning to the Count, unless the forces at Garrison are ready to meet them, the Marat will kill everyone. This steadholt and all the rest as well."

"Crows," Tavi whispered. "Oh, crows and furies."

"You're the only one who has seen them. The only one who I can use to convince the Count to rouse Garrison." Amara stalked back over to the window, opened it again, then turned to Tavi and extended her hand. "Are you with me?"

They used a sheet from Tavi's bed, tied to its leg, to drop from his window to the courtyard below. The wind whistled from the north, bringing with it the stinging chill of true winter. Amara went down first, then beckoned to Tavi, who tossed down a bundle thrown hurriedly together into the blankets from his bed. Amara caught it, and then the boy swallowed, and slithered down the sheet to the stones of the courtyard.

Amara led them across the courtyard in silence. No one was in evidence, though the light and noise from the hall could be heard through its thick doors. The gate door was open, and they slid through it and out into the outbuildings. Full dark was getting close, and shadows lay dim and thick over the cold ground.

Tavi led them past the stables and over to the smokehouse. The building shared a wall with the smithy, where both could use the same chimney for a fire. The sharp smell of smoke and meat hung around the smokehouse in a permanent cloud.

"Get the salt," Amara murmured to him. "Just take the sack, if there's one at hand, or a bucket. I'll keep watch here. And hurry."

Tavi slipped inside, where the fading twilight held little sway, and fumbled through the dark, to the shelf at the back of the smoke room. He stopped to take down a pair of hams that had been hanging, and dropped them into his makeshift bag. The salt, all rough crystals, filled a large homespun sack. Tavi tried to lift it and grunted with effort. Then he put it back down, took one of his blankets, and tore off a couple of large sections. He piled heavy salt crystals into them, and twisted them shut, tying them with several lengths of leather cord kept on hand for hanging the meats.

He had just picked them up and was heading back for the door when he heard a squealing sound outside the smokehouse. There was a hiss of breath and a pair of heavy thumps. Tavi hurried outside, his eyes wide, his heart pounding in his chest.

There, Amara knelt with one knee on the chest of a fallen man, a knife gripped in her hand and pressed to his throat.

"Stop," Tavi hissed. "Get off of him!"

"He snuck up on me," Amara said. She didn't move the knife.

"That's Fade. He's no danger to anyone."

"He wouldn't answer me."

"You scared him," Tavi said and shoved at her shoulder. Amara shot him a look, but didn't fall. She took the knife from Fade's throat and rose back and away from the fallen slave.

Tavi leaned down and took Fade's hand, hauling the man to his feet. He wore heavy clothes against the gathering cold, including a woolen cap with flaps that hung down to his shoulders and dangled like the ears of a gangly puppy and secondhand gloves missing several fingers. The whole side of the slave's face was slack with fear, and he stared at Amara with wide eyes, backing up from her until his shoulders touched Tavi's chest. "Tavi," Fade said. "Tavi. Inside. Storm coming."

"I know, Fade," Tavi said. "But we have to go."

"There's no time for this," Amara said, shooting a glance behind her. "If one of them sees us—"

"Tavi stay," Fade insisted.

"I can't. Me and Amara have to get to Count Gram and warn him that the Marat are coming. She's a Cursor, and we have to go before some bad men try to stop us."

Fade turned to blink his head slowly at Tavi. His face twisted in confusion, and he asked, "Tavi going? Tonight?"

"Yes. I have salt."

Amara hissed, "Let's go then. No time."

Fade frowned, almost scowled. "Fade, too."

"No, Fade," Tavi said. "You have to stay here."

"Going."

"We have to travel light," Amara said. "The slave stays."

Fade threw back his head and let out a howl like a wounded dog.

Tavi choked and lurched toward the man, covering his mouth with one hand. "Quiet! Fade, they'll hear us!"

Fade ceased howling but looked at Tavi, his expression steady.

Tavi looked from Fade to Amara. The Cursor rolled her eyes and gestured at him to hurry. Tavi grimaced. "All right. You can go. But we have to leave right now."

Fade's mouth broke into a witless smile behind Tavi's hand, and he started chortling. He held up a hand to them, dashed inside the smithy, and emerged a few heart-beats later bearing a battered old rucksack on his back and muttering excited, nonsense phrases to himself.

Amara shook her head and asked Tavi, "He's an idiot?"

"He's a good man," Tavi said, defensively. "He's strong and he works hard. He won't get in the way."

"He'd better not," Amara said. She slipped the knife away into her belt and threw her bundle at Fade. "I'm hurt, he's not. He carries mine."

Fade dropped it and scraped a bow to Amara as he picked up the bundle of blankets and appropriated gear. He lifted that one to his other shoulder.

Amara turned to lead them away from Bernardholt, but Tavi put his hand on her shoulder. "These men. Won't they catch us if we're on foot?"

"I'm not good with horses. You're no earthcrafter. Is the slave?"

Tavi glanced at Fade and grimaced. "No. I mean, he knows a little metal. And he makes shoes for the horses, but I don't think that he's an earthcrafter."

"Better we walk then," she said. "One of the men after us is, and he can make the horses do what he wants to."

"On horseback, they'll be faster."

"That's why we'd better get going. Hopefully they'll be here until morning."

"Meet me at the stable," Tavi said, and hurried off toward it in the growing dark. Amara hissed at him, but Tavi ignored her, moving to the stable doors and inside.

He was familiar with the animals of Bemardholt. The sheep milled sleepily in their pen, and the cattle took up the rest of the room on the same side. On the other, the hulking gargants lay blowing lustily in their sleep in their burrow—and behind them, Tavi heard the noise of restless, nervous horses.

He slipped silently down through the stable, before he heard a sound in the loft, above him, the storage space between the rafters and the peak of the roof. He froze in place, listening.

A tinny voice said, from the loft, "Between all the excitement yesterday and then last night, it's been one thing after another. Though I suppose it isn't anything compared to the life of a gem merchant, sir."

Tavi blinked. The voice was Beritte's, but it came as though through a long pipe, distant and blurred. It took him a moment to realize that it sounded the same as when his aunt spoke to him through Rill.

A woman's voice, strange to Tavi and near to hand, murmured with a sort of languid laziness, "There you see, love? He has a drink now, and we're able to pay attention. Sometimes it's nice to hurry."

A strange man's voice answered with a low growl. "All this hurrying. When we kill them and finish the mission, I'm going to lock you in a room in irons for a week."

The woman purred, "You're so romantic, my love."

"Quiet. I want to hear what he's saying."

They fell into silence while tinny voices came down to Tavi on the floor. He swallowed and moved very quietly, forward, past the spot in the loft the voices came from, and down to the stalls where the strangers' horses had been put.

Though their gear had been removed, the horses still wore their bridles, and the saddles had been stood on end on the floor beside them, ready to be thrown on and cinched, rather than resting on the pegs on the other side of the stables and their blankets drying on the ground.

Tavi crept into the first stall and let the horse smell him, keeping a hand on the animal's shoulder as he moved to its saddle and knelt beside it. He drew the knife from his belt and, quietly as he could, started cutting through the leather of the saddle's girth. Though the leather was thick, his knife was sharp, and he cut through it completely in only a moment.

Tavi repeated the gesture twice more, leaving the stall doors open and cutting the other two saddles to uselessness. Then he went back, gathering up the horses' reins, keeping his motions as slow as possible, and led them out of their stalls and back down the stables toward the doors out.

As he passed the spot in the loft where the strangers lay, Tavi's throat tightened and his heart hammered in his chest. People, people he had never seen and did not know were there to kill him for reasons he could not fully understand. It was all too strange, almost unreal—and yet the fear in him, something instinctive and all too certain, was very real indeed, like a trickle of cold water gliding slowly down his spine.

He had led the horses past the loft when one of the beasts snorted and tossed its head. Tavi froze in place, panic nearly sending him running.

"Fear," hissed the woman's voice, suddenly. "Below us, the *horses*."

Tavi jerked on the reins and let out a loud whistle. The horses snorted, breaking into an uncertain trot.

Tavi let go of the reins to dash ahead to the stable doors and throw them open. As the horses went through, Tavi let out a scream that warbled into a high-pitched shriek, and the horses burst out into a run.

There was a roar from behind him, and Tavi glanced over his shoulder in time to see a man, even bigger than his uncle, come crashing down from the loft, a naked sword held in his fist. He looked around him, wildly, and Tavi turned and fled into the darkness.

Someone seized his arm and he almost screamed. Amara clapped cold fingers over his mouth and dragged him into a run, north and east, toward the causeway. Tavi glanced around behind him and saw Fade shuffling along under the weight of his burdens, but no one else seemed to be following them.

"Good," Amara hissed. He saw the flash of her teeth in the growing dark. "Well done, Tavi."

Tavi shot her a grin and one to Fade as well.

And that was when the scream came to them, from behind the walls of the steadholt proper, clear and desperate and terrified.

"Tavi," Isana screamed. "Tavi, run! Run!"

⟨⟩⟨⟩ CHAPTER 19

Tavi ran.

His muscles were sore and the myriad scratches felt horrible, sending curling ribbons of pain through his skin, but he was able to run. For a while, Amara ran beside him in silence, hardly limping at all—but after a quarter mile, her motion became uneven, and on her exhales she started letting out whimpers of sound. Tavi dropped his pace a bit to run beside her.

"No," she gasped. "You have to keep going. Even if I don't get to the Count, you have to."

"But your leg—"

"I'm not important, Tavi," Amara said. "Run."

"We need to head east," Tavi said, staying beside her. "We'll have to find a place to cross the Rillwater, but there's thick and twisty woods on the other side. In the dark, we could lose them there."

"One of the men behind us," she panted. "Wood-crafter. Strong one."

"Not there," Tavi said. "The only one who has ever gotten along with those furies is my uncle, and it took him years. He showed me how to get through them."

Amara slowed and nodded, as they neared the top of a hill. "All right. You, come here." She beckoned to Fade, who shuffled to her obediently. She took the bundle from him and took out his uncle's bow and the arrows with it. She braced the bow against her leg and leaned hard on it, bending it enough to string it, then took it in hand and picked up the arrows. "I want you two to get into the woods. Keep going through them."

Tavi swallowed. "What are you going to do?"

Amara took the sword from the bundle and slipped it through her makeshift belt. "I'm going to try to slow them here. I'll be able to see them coming here as well as anywhere."

"But you're standing out here in the open. They'll just shoot you."

She smiled, grimly. "I think there will be a bad wind for it. Leave me some of the salt. Once that storm hits, we should be free to start evading them a little more securely."

"We'll stay here and help," Tavi said.

The Cursor shook her head. "No. You two get moving. Just in case things don't go well. I'll find you by morning."

"But—"

"Tavi," Amara said. She turned to him, frowning gently. "I can't protect you and still fight here. These men are powerful crafters. You can't do anything to help me."

The words hit him like a physical blow, and he felt a surge of frustration, helpless anger, that raced through him and for a moment washed away the aches of his body. "I can't do anything."

"Wrong," Amara said. "They'll be using earth and woodcrafting to track you—not me. I'll be able to ambush them, and if I get lucky I might stop them altogether. Get moving and keep their attention on you."

"Won't their earthcrafter feel you?" Tavi asked. "And if they're using wood, too, you can't climb a tree to get off the ground."

Amara glanced to the north. "When that storm gets here, the furies in it . . ." She shook her head. "But I can take advantage of things now. Cirrus."

She closed her eyes for a moment, and the wind began to rise around her. It made the loose clothing on her billow and flap, though Tavi, standing only a few feet away, felt nothing. Amara spread her arms slightly, and the wind gusted her completely off the ground for a moment— and then settled into a whirlwind that threw up dust and debris and specks of ice in a cloud around her legs to the knee. She hovered there, momentarily, then opened her eyes and drifted left and right, experimentally.

Tavi stared at her, stunned. He had never seen such a display of windcrafting. "You can fly."

Amara smiled at him, and even in the dimness her face seemed bright. "This? This is nothing. Maybe after all this is over, I can show you what real flying is." She nodded. "Those storm furies you have here are bad ones, and there's not much time before they get here. But this will keep Fidel—the enemy from sensing me."

"All right," Tavi said, uncertainly. "You'll be sure to find us?"

Amara's smile faded. "I'll try. But if I haven't in a few hours, then keep going yourself. Can you get to Garrison?"

"Sure," Tavi said. "I mean. I think I will. And Uncle will be coming. He can find us anywhere in the Valley."

"I hope you're right," Amara said. "He seems a good man." She turned her back on Tavi and Fade, frowning, facing back the way that they had come. She set an arrow to the bow. "Get to Garrison. Warn the Count."

Tavi nodded, then dug into his bag and got out one of the bags of salt. He threw it down, not far from Amara, but not too close to the fury holding her in the air, either. She glanced back and down at the salt and then at Tavi. "Thank you."

"Good luck."

Fade tugged at Tavi's sleeve. "Tavi," he said. "Go."

"Yeah. Come on." Tavi turned and started down the hill, picking up to a jog again. Fade kept pace with him, the slave seemingly tireless and uncomplaining. They left Amara behind on the hilltop, and the darkness of settling evening swallowed her from sight. Tavi took his bearings from the slope of the hill, a pair of boulders he and Frederic had once teased, and before another quarter hour had passed, they had found the edges of the wood and slipped into shadows of the pines and aspen and beneath the long fingers of the barren oak.

Tavi slowed his pace to a walk then, breathing in swift pants. He held a hand to his side, where a slow, throbbing pain was starting to rise. "I haven't ever done this much running all together," he told Fade. "Getting cramps."

"Legions, run. March. Train." Fade said. The slave looked behind them, and the shadows fell over the coward's brand on his marred face. His eyes glittered. "Tavi in the Legions, run lots."

Tavi had never heard so many words from the slave all together, and he tilted his head to one side. "Fade? Were you in the Legions?"

Fade's expression barely moved, but Tavi thought he detected a sense of deep, slow pain there, nonetheless. "Fade. Coward. Ran."

"Ran from what?"

Fade turned away from Tavi and started walking deeper into the woods, making his way east. Tavi looked after him for a moment and then followed him. They made good time for a while, though Tavi tried to get Fade to talk with several other small questions, he did not respond to them. As they moved, the wind continued to rise, and it made the woods whisper and creak and groan. Tavi saw movement around him, in the branches and the hollows of the trees—the furies of the wood, restless as the animals before the coming storm, skittering back and forth and watching silently from the shadows. They did not frighten Tavi—he was as used to them as to the animals of the steadholt. But his hand stayed close to the knife at his belt, just in case.

Soon, the sound of running water came to them through the trees, and Tavi hurried forward, taking the lead from Fade. They came out on the banks of the Rillwater, a small and swift river that rushed through the Calderon Valley from just east of Garados and raced off into the mountains south of the Valley.

"All right," Tavi said. "We need to find the ford Uncle marked. So long as we start from there, I can find our way through the woods and out the other side. Otherwise, the furies there will twist us around and we'll get lost. Uncle said that when he was young, a couple of people got lost in the twisty woods and never came out again. He found them starved to death less than a bowshot from the causeway, but they'd never found it."

Fade nodded, watching Tavi.

"I can get us through, but we have to start with the path Uncle made." He chewed on his lip, looking up and down the river. "And with this storm coming, too. Here." He dug into his makeshift pack and passed the second sack of salt back to Fade. "Hold on to that, in case we need it. Don't drop it."

"Don't drop it," Fade repeated, nodded solemnly.

Tavi turned and started upstream. "This way, I think." They made their way along the stream, and night settled over them entirely. Tavi could barely see to walk, and Fade stumbled and muttered behind him.

"Here," Tavi said, finally. "Here's where we cross. See that white rock? Uncle had Brutus set it there so it would be easier to find." Tavi slipped down the bare, chill earth of the bank to the stream.

Fade let out a yelp.

"Fade?" Tavi turned around in time to see someone moving toward him in the dark. Something hit his face, hard, and he felt his legs go loose and relax. He fell back, into the swift, shallow, chilling flow of the Rillwater, blinking and trying to focus his eyes. He tasted blood in his mouth.

Bittan of Kordholt leaned down enough to drag him up by the front of his shirt and hit him again, another hot flash of pain. Tavi yelped and tried to throw up his arms to protect himself, but the larger boy's fists landed with a cool, sadistic precision, again and again.

"Enough," Kord's voice rumbled. "Get out of the damn water, Bittan. Unless you want to get drowned again."

Tavi looked up, blearily. He could see Kord hulking on the bank, his lank and greasy hair swinging as he turned his head to look at the stream. A form lay on the ground before him, motionless: Fade.

Bittan hauled Tavi out of the water and threw him at the bank, an ugly smile twisting his handsome face. "Climb out yourself, freak."

Tavi climbed out of the water, shivering, even as the wind began to shriek and howl overhead. The storm, he thought numbly. The storm was on them. Tavi moved to Fade and found the slave still breathing, though he didn't move. He could see blood gleaming on Fade's scarred face.

Bittan followed Tavi up from the stream and kicked him, knocking him forward and back to the ground. "Looks like you were right, Pa."

Kord grunted. "Figured they'd send word to Gram about that little fracas the other night. Didn't figure they'd send the freak and the idiot, though."

Aric's voice came to them quietly. Tavi looked up to see the tall, slender man, a dark shadow a bit separated from the other two. "The boy's smart, Pa. He can write. You have to write to file legal charges."

"Doesn't add up," Kord said. "Maybe they would send him in good weather, but not with this storm coming."

"Unless Bernard's dead, Pa," Bittan said, spiteful. "Maybe that bitch died trying to save him. He looked like a dead man."

Kord turned to Tavi and nudged the boy with his boot. "Well, freak?"

Tavi thought furiously. There had to be a way to stall for enough time for Amara to catch up to them, or for his uncle to find them—but what were they talking about? A fracas the other night? Had something happened when his uncle came home wounded? That had to have been it. Had they tried to kill Bernard? Is that why they would be concerned with someone filing legal charges with Count Gram?

Kord nudged him again and said, "Talk, boy. Or I'll bury you right now."

Tavi swallowed. "If I tell you, will you let us go?"

"Us?" Kord asked, warily.

Aric said, "He means the idiot, Pa."

Kord grunted. "Depends on what you say, freak. And if I believe you."

Tavi nodded and said, without looking up, "A Marat warrior injured Uncle. He got hurt protecting me, and I got away. One of the First Lord's Cursors came to Bernardholt, and now I'm trying to get to Count Gram to warn him that the Marat are coming and that he has to rouse the garrison and prepare to fight."

There was a moment's stunned silence, and then Kord guffawed, a quiet, hoarse sound. Tavi felt a hand grip his hair, and Kord said, "Even a freak should be smarter than to think something like that would fool me."

"B-but," Tavi stammered, his heart hammering with a sudden panicked terror. "It's the truth! I swear to all the furies it's the truth!"

Kord dragged him down the bank and said, "I'm tired of your lying mouth, freak." Then he shoved Tavi's head into the freezing water and bore down with all of his strength.

‑‑‑‑CHAPTER 20

Amara tried to still the frantic pounding of her heart and to slow her breathing. Cirrus swirled and spun beneath her feet, though to her the air beneath her felt almost as solid as the ground itself. Even so, the wind fury's best efforts moved her ever so slightly from side to side, up and down, and would make shooting impossible if she wasn't calm and focused.

The pain of her injured ankle and arm, though lessened by Isana's ministrations, was by no means absent. She tested the pull of the bow and felt it in her arm, her left, in which she held the heavy wooden weapon. She would not be able to hold it drawn for long—not surprising, since it was probably made with the thews of the enormous Steadholder in mind.

Shaking and unable to aim for long, she would have to wait until the enemy was close before she shot—and she would have to take down the swordsman, first. She would never defeat him with the blade she carried. His experience and furycrafting would make him a living weapon, unstoppable to someone not equally gifted.

If she had time, Fidelias would be her next target. Cirrus could defeat even her old teacher's formidable woodcrafting-enhanced archery. His earthcrafting, however, would give him strength she could not hope to match. It would be all he needed to shatter her defense and defeat her, in an absence of other factors. Even with Cirrus lending speed to her strikes, she was only marginally his equal with a blade.

The sword was for the water witch, though it would suit Amara equally well to shoot the woman. Though she was not, in open battle, the threat the other two were, she was dangerous nonetheless. Even though Amara would have the freedom of concentration to smother the woman, she could not likely accomplish it before if the witch could cross the distance between them—and if she managed to touch her, Amara was done for. Of the three, she was the only one Amara could reliably overcome with the blade.

Poor options, she thought. A poor plan. She was unlikely to be able to shoot a second arrow, even presuming the first arrow managed to strike down Aldrick ex Gladius, a man who had faced some of the most skilled warriors alive—Araris himself!—and defeated them, or at least lived to tell the tale. But if they were allowed to catch up to the boy, even if they came close, he was certain to be killed—and the boy was the only one whose testimony could convince the Count at Garrison to mobilize and raise the alarm.

Amara stood facing the darkness behind the already departed boy and the slave with him and realized that it was very probable that she was about to die. Painfully. Her heart raced with a frantic terror.

She bent down to pick up a pair of arrows from the ground. She slipped one through her belt and set one to the bow. She checked the hilt of the sword with one hand, reasonably sure that she could draw it forth without slicing her own leg off or cutting the belt that kept the clothes she'd stolen from flapping like a banner.

She looked to the north and could feel the storm furies out there, up by the ominous form of a mountain whose tip held the last purple light of sunset upon it, like some balefully glowering eye. The clouds moved down, swallowing the mountain's head as they did, and Amara could feel the freezing fury of the coming storm, a true winter howler. Once it arrived, presuming it didn't kill the boy, it would make pursuit of him impossible. She didn't have to win. She only had to slow down those behind them.

So long as she provided a delay, death was an acceptable outcome.

Her hands shook.

Then she waited.

She couldn't feel the earthcrafting move past beneath her, but she saw it—a barely perceptible wave in the earth, a ripple of motion that flowed through the ground, briefly unsettling it as a wave does water. The wave flashed by and moved on behind her. Her feet hadn't come within a handsbreadth of the ground as it went past. It couldn't have detected her.

She took a slow breath and blew on the fingers of the hand that would hold the string, the arrow. Then she lifted the bow, ignoring the twinge in her arm, and willed herself forward and a bit down the slope ahead of her, so that she would present no profile against the purpling sky or the storm-lighted clouds.

She saw motion against the dark earth and remained as still as she could, willing Cirrus to hold her steady. Another pulse went by in the earth, this one stronger, nearer. Fidelias had crafted such a search before, and she knew how effectively he could use it to find someone not wise enough to get his feet off of the ground.

The shape came closer, though she could not tell who it was, or how many there might be. She drew the bow as tight as she comfortably could, held with the strung arrow pointing at the ground. The motion came closer, and she could hear footsteps, make out the shape of a large man, the glint of metal in the darkness. The swordsman.

She took a breath, held it, then drew, aimed, and loosed, all in a single motion. The bow thrummed, and the arrow hissed through the darkness.

The shape froze, one hand lifting toward her, even as the arrow leapt across the yards between them. She heard the wooden shaft shatter, an abrupt crack of sound. She reached for the other arrow at her belt, but the man in the darkness hissed in a quiet voice, and something caught her wrist in a sudden, crushing grip.

Amara looked down to find the arrow's shaft wrapped around her wrist and just winding about the belt, so that her hand was fastened to her middle. She spun, gathering momentum to throw the bow at her assailant, thus freeing her left hand to make an awkward draw of the sword. But even as she turned, the bow in her hands abruptly warped and slithered around her arm, more swift and lithe than a serpent. It wasn't long enough to wrap about her torso as well, but once about her arm it hardened, straightening her limb, until her hand was held well out and away from the sword at her waist.

Amara turned her head to see the man rushing her, and she flung herself straight up, over his head, Cirrus assisting her. She flipped in midair and managed to bring her heel down onto her attacker.

She missed her target, the nape of his neck, and her scything kick landed on his shoulder instead. Cirrus stopped her feet from touching the earth, but even as she regained her balance, a hand, brutally strong, wrapped around her ankle, swung her in an arc overhead, and brought her crashing down onto the frigid ground.

Amara struggled, but the impact had stunned and slowed her. Before she could escape, the man had pinned her, full weight of his body on hers. One hand had closed around her throat and twisted her head aside, to near the breaking point, as easily as though she had been a weak kitten.

"Where is he?" Bernard snarled. "If you've hurt that boy, I'll kill you."

Amara stopped her struggling and willed Cirrus away, so that she lay quietly beneath the enraged Steadholder. She could see the dark-haired giant out of the corner of her eye, dressed only lightly against the weather, bearing a woodsman's axe, which had been let fall before he seized her. She had to struggle to breathe, to speak. "No. I didn't hurt him. I stayed back to stop the men after him. He and the slave went on ahead."

The granite grip on her head eased, marginally. "Men after him. What men?"

"The strangers. The ones who came in when you carried me into the hall. They'll be after us, I'm sure of it. Please, sir. There's no time."

The Steadholder growled. He kept her pinned with one hand and with the other drew the sword from her belt and tossed it aside. Then he patted at her waist, until he found the knife she'd stolen from Fidelias inside her tunic, and roughly tugged aside her layers of clothing to remove it as well. Only then did he let his grip on her jaw and throat ease. "I don't know who you are, girl," he said. "But until I do, you're going to stay right here." Even as he spoke, the earth curled up around her elbows and knees, turf and roots twisting into place, locking her limbs to the ground.

"No," Amara protested. "Steadholder, my name is Amara. I'm one of the Crown's Cursors. The First Lord himself sent me here, to this valley."

Bernard stood up, away from her, and rummaged in a pouch at his side. He took something from it, then something else. "Now you're not a slave, eh? No. My nephew's out in this mess somewhere, and it's your fault he is."

"It's because I led him from the steadholt that he isn't dead already!"

"So you say," Bernard said. She heard water gurgle from a flask into a cup or a bowl. "Where is he now?"

Amara tested the bonds of earth, uselessly. "I told you. He and Fade went on ahead of me. He said something about a river and a twisty wood."

"Fade went with him? And these men chasing him? Who are they?"

"A traitor Cursor, Aldrick ex Gladius, and a water witch of considerable skill. They're trying to kill anyone who saw the Marat moving in the Valley. I think because they want a Marat surprise attack to succeed."

"Crows," Bernard spat. Then he said, raising his voice a bit, "Isana? Did you hear?"

A voice, tinny and faint, echoed up from somewhere near at hand. "Yes. Tavi and Fade will be at the Rillwater ford. We must get there immediately."

"I'll meet you," Bernard rumbled. "What about the girl?"

Isana's voice came a moment later, as though she spoke under a great strain. "She means no harm to Tavi. I'm sure of that. Beyond that I don't know. Hurry, Bernard."

"I will," Bernard said. Then he stepped back into her vision and drank away whatever was in the cup. "This man after you, with the swordsman. Why did you expect him instead of me?"

Amara swallowed. "He's an earth and woodcrafter. Very experienced. He can find the boy." She lifted her head, looking at him intently. "Let me up. I'm the only chance you have to help Tavi."

He scowled. "Why do you say that?"

"Because you don't know these people," Amara said. "I do. I can anticipate him, what he's going to do next. I know his strengths, his weaknesses. And you can't defeat his swordsman alone."

Bernard stared down at her for the space of a breath, then shook his head irritably. "All right," he said. "Prove it. Anticipate him. Tell me where he is."

Amara closed her eyes, trying to remember the geography of the region. "He knew I would expect him to follow, directly. That's his strength. But he didn't follow. He anticipated me, and he's moving around, to get ahead of the boy. Check the causeway, the furies in the cobblestones. He'll have made for the road and be using those furies to help him get ahead of the boy, so that he can cut him off." She opened her eyes and watched the Steadholder's face.

Bernard growled something quietly, and she felt a slow, silent shudder in the earth. There was silence for a moment, while the big man knelt and put a bare hand on the ground, closing his eyes with his head tilted to one side, as though listening to a distant music.

Finally, he let out a breath. "You're right," he said. "Or seem to be. Someone's earthwaving through the road itself, and fast. Horses, I think."

"It's him." Amara said. "Let me up."

Bernard opened his eyes and rose decisively. He recovered his axe, gestured at the earth, and Amara abruptly found her limbs free, the bow and the arrow returning to their original shapes, unwinding from her arm. She clambered to her feet again and recovered the sword and knife from the ground.

"Are you going to help me?" he asked.

Amara faced him and let out a shaking breath. "Sir. I swear it to you. I'll help you protect your nephew."

Bernard's teeth flashed, sudden in the darkness. "Good thing you're not going after these people with wood from their own trees."

She slipped the sword through her belt. "I hope your shoulder doesn't hurt too much."

His smile widened. "I'll make it. How's your ankle?"

"Slowing me," she confessed.

"Then get your fury to lift you again," he said. He drew a piece of cord from his pouch, ran it through the back of his belt, and tied it closed in a loop. He tossed the loop to her and said, "Keep your body behind mine and stay low. The wood will make my passage clear, but don't go waving your head around, or a branch might take it off."

Amara barely had time to breathe her agreement before the ground itself rumbled, and the Steadholder took off at a bounding run, the earth impelling him forward with every step. She turned and ran to keep up with him, but even in her best condition she would have been hard pressed to hold the pace. She managed to take several steps to keep close to him, one hand clinging to the loop of leather cord, then leapt in the air, calling to Cirrus as she did.

The presence of her fury solidified beneath her feet, and she flowed over the ground after the Steadholder, tugged forward by the cord. If he noticed her weight dragging at him, it did not show, and the man moved through the night with perfect confidence and near-perfect silence, as though even the withered grass beneath his feet conspired to cushion the impact and lessen the noise of his passing.

Before she had gotten her breath back, they had passed into the woods, and Amara had to duck her head to keep branches from slashing at her face. She hunched down in the Steadholder's shadow, once jerking her feet up as he leapt a fallen tree that Cirrus hadn't quite managed to carry her feet over.

"Got them!" he said, in a moment more. "At the ford. Fade's on the ground, Tavi's partly in the water and . . ." He snarled. "And Kord is there."

"Kord?" Amara demanded.

"Steadholder. Criminal. He'll hurt them."

"We don't have time for this!"

"So sorry it's inconvenient, Cursor," Bernard snapped. "I can't feel your friends. They've left the road."

"He must be concealing his own passage," Amara said. "He never passes up a surprise attack. It won't be long before he gets to the boy."

"Then we have to defeat Kord and his sons first. I'll take Kord, he's the old one. The other two are up to you."

"Crafters?"

"Air and fire—"

"Fire?" Amara blurted.

"But cowards. The taller one is more dangerous. Hit them hard and fast. Over the next rise."

Amara nodded and said, "I will. Cirrus!" The Cursor gathered the air beneath her and with a rush of

swirling winds swept herself from the ground, through the stark branches of the barren trees and into the air above them.

◇◇◇◇ CHAPTER 21

The waters of the little river were ice-cold, swift. Tavi's mouth went numb the moment Kord pushed his head into the water, and his ears tingled and burned with sensation. Tavi struggled, but the Steadholder's grip was too strong, fingers tangled tightly in Tavi's hair. His greasy Steadholder's chain thumped against Tavi's shoulders. Kord pressed down brutally, and Tavi felt his face mash up against the rocks at the bottom of the river.

And then that inexorable pressure vanished. Tavi felt himself hauled back, by the hair, and thrown through the air to land upon the ground many feet away. He came down upon something warm and living, that proved to be a dazed Fade. Tavi lifted his head, blinking water from his eyes, toward Kord, but someone moved between them, blocking his view.

"Uncle!" Tavi said.

Bernard said, "Get Fade up and get him out of here, Tavi."

Tavi scrambled to his feet, hauling Fade up with him, and swallowed. "What are we going to do?"

"Get clear. I'll handle things here," Bernard said. Then he turned his back to Tavi, keeping himself between Kord and his nephew. "This time, Kord, you've gone too far."

"Three of us," Kord growled, as his sons took up a position on either side of him. "And one of you. Plus the fool and the freak, of course. I'd say that you're the one who has his neck stuck out, Bernard."

The ground in front of Kord rumbled, shifting, and the thing that hauled itself up out of the earth, its hide and limbs all of stone, looked like nothing that Tavi had ever seen. It had the long body of a slive, but its tail curled up over its back, held in the air like a club. Its mouth was hideously elongated and filled with flint-sharp jags of teeth. As Tavi watched, it twisted its head to one side, opened its jaws, and let out a granite-deep, rumbling growl.

Beside Kord, Bittan took the cover from a ceramic firepot. Red flames licked up from it as he did, and they curled into the shape of a reared serpent, hovering and ready to strike, flaming eyes bright. The tall and slender Aric, on Kord's other side, steepled his fingers together and wind and bits of bracken swirled around him, casting back his cloak in a shape vaguely like great wings.

"Don't do this, Kord," Bernard said. The ground beside him stirred, and then Brutus thrust his way up out of the soil, until the rocky hound's broad head rested beneath Bernard's hand, emerald eyes focused on the Kordholters. Brutus gave his great shoulders a shake, sending earth and small stones skittering down off of his flanks in a miniature avalanche. Tavi saw Bittan blanch and take a small step back. "You're digging yourself deeper into your own grave."

"Trying to take *my* land," Kord spat, "from me and *my* family. What gives you the right?"

Bernard let out his breath in a sigh, glancing upward for a moment. "Don't play righteous with me, slaver. The storm's almost here, Kord. Last chance. If you back down, right now, you get to live to face Gram's justice instead of mine."

Kord's eyes flashed. "I'm a Citizen, Bernard. You can't just kill a Citizen."

"That's on your lands," Bernard said. "We're on mine."

Kord's face went white. "You self-righteous bastard," he hissed. He threw his hands forward and screamed, "I'll feed you to the crows!"

The stone beast before him lurched forward across the stony ground, lizard-quick. Even as it did, something lashed out from Aric, the blurred shape vaguely reminiscent of a bird of prey as it sped toward Bernard. Bittan hurled his firepot down into the nearest brush, and even damp, the wood went up in a sudden blaze, the flame-serpent within it swelling to twenty times its previous size in the space of a long breath.

Bernard moved quickly. He threw his hand toward Aric's attacking fury, scattering a fistful of salt crystals through the air. A whistling shriek went up from the air before him, even as Brutus lunged forward, clashing against Kord's fury with a shockingly loud crunch of impact. Both furies blended into a mound of stone that sank into the earth, where the surface of the ground twitched and bulged, where the Steadholders' furies battled out of sight beneath it.

Kord let out a bellow and came for Bernard. Tavi's uncle hefted his axe and swiped it at the other Steadholder.

Kord threw himself back and to one side, and Bernard followed him, lifting the axe for another strike.

Tavi saw Aric draw a knife from his belt and head for Bernard's back. "Uncle!" he shouted. "Behind you!"

And then a column of wind so furious and strong that it almost seemed a solid mass hammered down into Aric's back, throwing him hard against the earth. The young man let out a choked cry and began to rise, but from the dark sky above, Amara dropped onto his back, her stolen clothes flapping wildly in the sudden wind. Aric had time to let out a strangled shout, and the winds gathered around the pair of them in a sudden shriek of sound. Tavi saw Amara's arm lock beneath Aric's chin, and then the pair of them were rolling around on the ground, Aric struggling to dislodge the girl from his back.

Tavi turned in time to see Kord strike his uncle's arm, knocking the axe from his hand. The weapon tumbled end over end and vanished into the water of the river. Bernard didn't waste a moment, but threw his balled fist into Kord's ribs, a blow that lifted the other man from the ground and sent him tumbling. Bernard pursued him, but Kord rose up again with fury-born fortitude, and the two met in a close grapple, the earth quivering and shaking beneath them.

Light and heat fell on Tavi from one side, and he turned to see Bittan standing before a blazing column of brush. "Well, well," Bittan glowered. "Looks like that leaves me to take care of you." Bittan raised his arms with an ecstatic cry, and brought them down again. The flames leapt up into a pillar that fell, swift and bright and horrible, toward Tavi and Fade.

Tavi let out a yelp and dragged the slave to one side

with him. Flame washed against the earth like water, sparks and smoke billowing out from it, heat rushing through the night. Tavi smelled burnt hair, and, regaining his feet, tugged Fade with him toward the water of the river. "Fade," he gasped. "Fade, come on. Come *on*."

Bittan's laughter rang out harsh in the ruddy light. The fallen column of fire danced and writhed over the ground like an enormous serpent, snaking its way between Tavi and the dubious shelter of the river's chilly waters. The fire leapt from bush to bush and tree to tree behind Bittan, growing, its crackling growl increasing to a sullen roar.

"Bittan!" Tavi shouted. "It's getting away from you! You'll kill us all!"

"I don't think you're in a position to lecture me on furycrafting, freak!" Bittan called. He turned to the burning brush beside him, scooped up a handful of blazing material, and hurled it at Tavi. Tavi threw up his cloak against it, softening the impact of the burning brush, but little licks of fire clung to the cloth. He beat at them frantically.

"I just can't decide," Bittan yelled, his voice jeering. "Whether you should smother or burn!"

Fade, the unmarred side of his face swollen and already purple with bruising, finally began to support most of his own weight, blinking his eyes around him in confusion. He pawed at Tavi's cloak, making little mewling sounds, his eyes sweeping around them, around the flames.

"I have an idea," Bittan said. "How about I fry the simpleton first! Then I can move on to you, freak." He gestured with a hand, and from within the flames, that same serpent-shape coalesced. It writhed for a moment, curling—and then shot toward Fade's chest like a streak of sunlight.

Fade let out a yelp and, with more speed than Tavi would have credited to the slave, he leapt aside, blundering into Tavi. The slave's momentum carried them both toward the fiery barrier between them and the water, tumbling over one another. Fade's back rolled against the ground as they went through the fire, and the slave let out a shriek of pain, clutching tightly to Tavi. The boy struggled to free himself, they both toppled into the Rillwater.

"No!" Bittan shouted. He strode unharmed through the fires and down to the water's edge. He lifted his arms again and sent another tendril of flame racing toward them. Tavi threw himself back against Fade, knocking them both under the water's surface. Fire splashed across the top of the water, a distant roar and a violent light above them.

Tavi stayed under the water's surface for as long as he could, but he could hold his breath for no more than a few seconds. He hadn't had a chance to get a proper breath before diving, and the water was simply too cold. He struggled further away from the near shore and Bittan's raging fury, before he broke the surface, coughing and spluttering. He hauled Fade along with him, more or less by main strength, afraid that the panicked slave might drown himself before realizing that the water wasn't deep enough.

Bittan stood at the very edge of the water and let out a shout of frustration. The flames behind him leapt skyward as he did. "You gutless, crow-eaten little freak! I'll burn you and that gibbering fool to cinders!"

Tavi clutched at the floor of the river beneath him and seized up a stone the size of his fist. "You leave him alone!" he shouted, and flung the stone at Bittan.

It flashed across the intervening space and struck the bigger boy in the mouth. Bittan flinched back, letting out a yowl, and tumbled backward to the ground.

"Uncle!" Tavi shouted. "Uncle, we're in the water!"

Through a roil of smoke, Tavi saw his uncle draw back a fist and ram it hard into Kord's throat. The other Steadholder stumbled back with a choked shout, but didn't lose his grip on Bernard's tunic, dragging him down with him and out of Tavi's sight.

Not far away, Amara rose away from an unmoving Aric, wincing and holding one forearm, where blood wetted her sleeve. Aric's knife, it seemed, had scored on her, even if it hadn't kept her from throttling him. She looked around and shouted, through the smoke, "Tavi! Get out of the water! Don't stop in there, get out!"

"What?" Tavi shouted. "Why?"

He had no warning at all. Wet, supple arms abruptly twined around his throat, and a throaty, feminine voice purred, in his ear, "Because bad things can happen to pretty little boys who fall into the river." Tavi started to turn, to struggle, but he was hauled beneath the river's surface with breathless speed, and the arms at his throat tightened. Tavi tried to plant his feet on the river's bed, to force his head up above the water, but somehow his feet never found purchase, as though the river's bed had been coated with slime wherever his feet touched, so that they forever slipped and slid aside.

"Poor pretty," the voice at his ear murmured, perfectly clear. He could feel the press of a strong but shapely body against his back. "It isn't your fault that you saw what wasn't to be seen. It's a shame to kill a pretty one, but if you'll just lay quietly and take a deep breath it will be over soon, and you'll still be pretty when they put you in a box. I promise."

Tavi struggled and writhed, but it was useless against the soft, subtle strength of that grip. He could have wrestled her all day and never gained the upper hand, he knew: She was a watercrafter, like his aunt, and a strong one at that, and the waters of the river itself were being used against him.

Tavi stopped struggling, which made his assailant let out a soft, approving murmur. Cold lips pressed against his ear. He was starting to grow dizzy, but his mind raced furiously. If she was a watercrafter like his aunt, then she would have the same problems Aunt Isana did. For all the advantages watercrafters enjoyed, they had to put up with more than almost any other craft, the disruption that their extra senses picked up from other people—emotions, impressions, feelings.

Tavi focused for a moment on his own helpless, fluttering fear, terror that made his heart race, stole the dregs of air remaining in his lungs ever more quickly away from him, brought him that much closer to drowning. He dwelt on that terror, let it build in him, and added to it the frustrations of the day, the despair and fury and hopelessness he had felt upon returning to Bernard-holt. Every emotion built on the next, and he fed them all with a frantic fury, until he could scarcely remember what his plan had been to begin with.

"What are you doing?" hissed the woman that held him, threads of uncertainty lacing through the throaty assurance of her voice. "Stop it. *Stop* it. You're too *loud*. I *hate* for it to be too loud!"

Tavi struggled uselessly against her, panic now overwhelming him in fact as well, blind and numbing fear blending in with all the other emotions. The woman let out a shriek and curled away from him, releasing him and wrapping her arms around her own head.

Tavi choked, his lungs expelling whatever was left in them as he struggled toward the surface. He only just managed to get his head out of water, to take a single deep, gasping breath, before the water itself bubbled up around him, sudden and enveloping, and dragged him back under.

"Clever boy," hissed the woman, and Tavi could see her now in the reflected light from the fires on the bank, a beautiful woman of dark hair and eyes, body lushly curved and inviting. "Very clever. So passionate. Now I can't hold you while you go. I wanted to do that much for you. But some people are never grateful." Water pressed about him, as strong and as heavy as leather bonds, pressure that shoved his limbs together, wrapped him up like a parcel of bread. Terrified, he struggled to hold on to that last breath for as long as he could.

The woman remained before him, eyes narrowed spitefully. "Foolish. I was going to give you the raptures. Now I think I'll just break that pretty neck." She flipped a wrist, the gesture dainty, but the water around Tavi suddenly slewed around his head and began twisting his jaw slowly to one side. Tavi struggled against it, but the water seemed just a little bit stronger than he. The pressure on his neck swiftly built and became painful. The woman came closer, eyes round and bright, watching.

She didn't see the sudden motion in the water behind her, but Tavi saw his aunt Isana's hand come out of the murk. One hand seized the woman by the hair, and the other raked abruptly across her eyes. Pink tinged the water, and the woman let out a sudden, piteous shriek. Isana appeared more fully, thrusting both hands toward the woman, palms out, and she suddenly flew through the water, and then up and out of it, as though hauled away by a giant hand.

As soon as the woman sailed up and out of the Rillwater, the pressure on Tavi's neck eased, and he found himself able to move his limbs. Isana moved to him, and together they broke the surface of the river, Tavi gasping and choking.

"*My* river," Isana snarled after the departed water witch. Isana called to Fade, who lunged through the water to Tavi. The slave drew one of Tavi's arms around his shoulders, holding the boy up and out of the water.

Tavi stared at his aunt's hand, where the nails seemed to have grown to twice their usual length, like shining-edged claws. Isana took note of his glance and gave her hand a shake, as though relaxing muscles cramped from sewing. Once, twice, and the nails appeared as they always had, practically short and neatly groomed—but stained with spots of blood. Tavi shivered.

"Get him to the far shore," Isana instructed. "There are two more out here, and matters aren't settled between Kord and Bernard as yet. Tavi, get through the woods. When the storm comes, you'll be safe for a time."

Bittan, bloody-mouthed, appeared on the shore. "You barren witch!" he howled at Isana. He gestured, and fire leapt toward them.

Isana rolled her eyes and flipped a hand toward Bittan. A wave rose to meet the flames, drowning them and continued forward to clutch at the young man's feet, washing them out from under him. He went down with a yelp, spluttering, and scrambled back away from the shore.

"Get through the woods," Isana continued. "Get to Aldoholt, by the lake. I'll have word to him by then, and he'll either get you to Gram or get Gram to you. He'll protect you until then. Do you understand, Tavi?"

"Yes, ma'am," Tavi gasped. "But—"

She leaned into him and pressed a kiss against his forehead. "I'm sorry, Tavi, so sorry. There's no time for questions now. You must trust me. I love you."

"I love you, too," Tavi said.

Isana turned her head, and the fires spreading on shore reflected in her eyes. "It's spreading. And the storm is nearly here. I have to call down Nereus, or Lilvia will whip those fires until they devour the Valley." She looked back to them and said, "Tavi, get away from the river. As far away as you can. Head uphill. Take Fade with you, and keep a close eye on him—I don't know what made you bring him along." She shot a glance past Tavi to the slave, who offered a witless smile to Isana and ducked his head.

She shook hers in response, kissed Tavi's head again, and said, "Go, quickly." And with that, she turned and vanished down into the waters of the river again.

Tavi swallowed and tried to help Fade, as the slave moved out of the river to the far side and up onto the shore. Tavi looked back as he moved out of the water.

Kord lay on the ground, curled onto his side, weakly struggling to get back to his feet. Bernard, his face bruised and his tunic torn, stood with Amara at the white rock of the ford, their backs to Tavi, facing the woods.

From the smoke and the shadows of the trees there limped a man, middle-aged, barefoot, and of innocuous height. He swept his eyes around the fire-lit stream and then focused on the two people standing at the ford, then past them. Tavi felt the man's eyes touch on him like cold, smooth stones, calmly weighing him, assessing him, dismissing him. The man lifted a hand, and Tavi heard the tree nearest him buck and tremble, and he turned in time to see it pitch forward toward him.

Bernard's head whipped around, and he raised a fist. As swiftly as the first, a second tree uprooted itself and toppled, landing hard against the first, so that the two fell against one another, each supporting the other from falling, while Tavi and Fade stood trembling in the arched space beneath them.

"Impressive," the man said. He focused on Bernard, and abruptly a wave of earth lashed out toward Tavi's uncle. Bernard planted his feet on the ground, teeth bared in a grimace, and a second wave rose in front of him, gathered momentum toward the stranger's attack. Bernard's efforts were evidently not enough. The ripple in the rock tore through his own efforts and ripped apart the ground he and Amara stood upon, sending them both toppling.

Tavi cried out, for even as his uncle fell, the stranger drew from beneath his cloak a short and heavily curved bow. He set an arrow to the string and drew with a cool precision. The shaft leapt across the stream, toward Tavi.

From the ground, Amara cried out and slashed her

hand at the air. The arrow flicked itself abruptly aside and rattled into the woods behind Tavi.

The man let out a short, frustrated noise and said, "Pointless. Kill them."

From behind him stepped the man Tavi had seen earlier, sword again in hand, quietly lethal intent in his eyes. The swordsman glided forward, toward Amara and his uncle, the blade catching the scarlet light of the fires raging around.

Kord had regained mobility and hauled himself to one side. He roused Aric with a few kicks and started to fall back into the woods, letting his son scramble after him as he tried to regain his senses. But even as Kord left, there was a rattle in the blazing brush, and Bittan backed out of the middle of a blaze, blinded and choking on the smoke. He waved a hand before his face and found himself standing a few scant feet from the swordsman, between the man and Bernard.

Tavi never even saw the swordsman's arm move. There was a hissing sound, and Bittan let out a surprised choke, and fell to his knees. The swordsman moved past the boy. Tavi saw scarlet puddling around Bittan's knees, and the boy fell limply over onto his side.

Tavi felt his gorge rise in his belly. Fade let out a hiss of breath and clutched at Tavi's arm.

"Bittan," Aric choked. "No."

For a moment, that tableau held, the boy on the ground in a pool of his own blood, scarlet firelight all around, the swordsman, blade extended to his side, moving with patient grace toward the people standing between him and Tavi.

Then everything happened at once.

Kord let out a bellow of raw and indiscriminate rage. The earth rippled around him and lashed out toward the swordsman.

Amara came to her feet, her blade in hand. She threw herself forward even as the swordsman's blade descended toward Bernard, intercepting it. The earth heaved and threw them both to one side, locked together in a close-quarters struggle.

The innocuous looking man extended his hands toward the far side of the river, and the trees groaned in response, the air filling with the twist and crackle of branches, of movement.

And the storm arrived.

One moment, there was relative stillness—and the next, a wall of fury and sound and power thundered down over them, engulfed Tavi's senses, blinded him, and whipped the surface of the river to icy foam. The flames Bittan had started buckled for a moment beneath the wind's onslaught, and then, as though the storm had sensed their potential, they blossomed and bloomed, spreading and growing with a speed as terrifying as it was amazing. To Tavi, it almost seemed as though faces gibbered and shrieked in the wind around those flames, calling them, encouraging them.

Fade let out a squeal, cowering down against the winds, and Tavi abruptly remembered his aunt's commands. He seized the slave by the arm, though still terrified for those behind him at the ford, and dragged him into the twisting woods, along the paths he knew, even in the semidarkness, away from the river.

They struggled forward together, holding one another in the screaming, frigid gale, Tavi filled with a sense of gratitude that there was another living human being there to touch. He was unsure for how long they struggled away, their path winding forward and then slowly uphill, before he heard the flood waters.

They rushed forward, nearly silent, preceded only by a whispering sigh and the groans of a thousand trees stirred in their ancient earthy beds. To the top of a hill, Tavi and Fade struggled, and he turned back to see, dimly through the ferocity of the storm, the dancing of the trees, that some pent-up tide had been loosed from up the stream of the Rillwater. The little river had exceeded itself and flooded its banks, and those cold, silent waters began to swallow Bittan's fires as swiftly as they had spread. The waters rose, and in that screaming cyclone of the furystorm, Tavi was uncertain how anyone, even his aunt, could survive such an onslaught of the elements. Terror rushed through him, pounded through his veins with his blood.

Darkness swallowed the land as the silent waters of the flooding river swallowed errant flame, and in moments the werelightning of the furystorm flashed, green and eerie, to show Tavi which way to go. In silence, he turned back to his path and stumbled forward, leading Fade. Twice, windmanes swept toward them, but Tavi's salt crystals, though partly dissolved from their time in the water, drove them away.

They made their way from the twisting wood an endless time later. Fade let out a sudden yelp and threw himself against Tavi with a sob of fear, forcing the boy down, the slave's heavy body atop him.

Tavi wriggled and struggled to get out from under Fade, but only managed to free his head enough to crane his neck over the man and to see what had frightened him.

Around them stood a silent half-circle of Marat warriors, unmistakable with their pale braids and powerful bodies clad, even in this vicious weather, only in a brief cloth at the hips. Each of them stood very tall and more broad in the shoulders than Tavi could easily believe, with dark, serious eyes the same shade as the chipped stone tipping their broad-hafted spears.

Without expression, the tallest of the Marat stepped closer. He put his foot on Tavi's shoulder and rested the tip of his spear against the hollow of Tavi's throat.

◇◇◇◇ CHAPTER 22

Fidelias twisted himself up and out of the chilling waters of the angry river, frozen fingers clutching hard against the branch of the tree he had crafted within his reach. He felt numb, and his heart labored painfully against the shock of the cold water. The cold beckoned him with a slow, seductive caress, encouraging him to simply sink into the waters, relax, let his troubles slip away into the darkness.

Instead, he secured a hold on the next higher branch and hauled his body up out of the water. He huddled there for a few moments, shaking, struggling to gather his wits about him again, while the furystorm raged around him, winds hauling at his sodden clothes.

The one good thing about the flood, he decided, about the freezing water, was that he could no longer feel the cuts on his feet. He'd done his best to ignore them while recovering the horses, but the rocks and brush had been merciless to his skin. The woman, the watercrafter, had been onto them from the beginning, he decided. Clever, getting his shoes like that. She'd been planning on the boy running, and on hampering pursuit.

Fidelias leaned against the trunk and waited for the waters to subside. They did, in rapid order, proving more than anything else that the flood had been a deliberate crafting rather than a natural event. He shook his head. Odiana should have given them warning—but perhaps she had been overmatched. The locals were no amateurs at their furycrafting and had lived with the local furies for years. They would know them, be able to use them more effectively than even a crafter of Fidelias's own level of skill. The Steadholder, for example—he had been formidable. In a direct, fair confrontation, Fidelias was uncertain whether or not he could simply overcome the man. Best then, to ensure that any future contact with the fellow discounted the possibility of a fair fight.

But then, that was in general Fidelias's policy.

Once the waters had receded back down into the river's original bed, Fidelias slipped down from the tree, grimacing as he got back to the ground. The pitch of the winds had only increased since the storm had rolled over them, and surviving in it had to be his first priority. He knelt by the trunk of the tree, resting a hand lightly on the sodden ground, reaching out for Vamma.

The fury responded to him at once, vanishing into the deep earth for several moments before rising back up toward him. Fidelias cupped his hands, and Vamma returned, providing what it had been sent to retrieve—a handful of salt crystals and a flint.

Fidelias pocketed the flint and swept the salt into a pouch, keeping a few pieces in hand. Then he rose, noting how slowly his body responded, and shook his head, shivering. The cold could kill him, if he didn't get warmed up, and quickly. Rising, he dispatched Etan to look for signs of his companions, and Vamma to search through the surrounding earth, for signs of movement. If the locals, either the Bernardholters or those they had been fighting, were still at hand, they might feel few compunctions about finishing the job the watercrafter had started.

Fidelias had to hurl salt at a swooping windmane, while he waited for his furies to return to him. It didn't take long. Etan appeared within a few moments and led him forward, through the blinding storm, down along the path of the river.

Several hundred yards downstream, Fidelias found Aldrick. The swordsman lay on the ground, unmoving, his fingers still locked around the hilt of his sword, buried to its hilts in the trunk of a tree. He had apparently managed to keep the flood from sweeping him away entirely, but had not taken into account the threat the elements represented. Fidelias checked the pulse at the man's throat and found it there, still strong, if slow. His lips were blue. The cold. If the swordsman was not warmed, and quickly, he would die.

Fidelias debated allowing it to happen for a moment. Odiana remained an unknown quantity, and as long as she had Aldrick with her, she would be difficult to move against. Without the swordsman, Fidelias could remove her at leisure, and if Fidelias was fortunate, perhaps Aldrick's death would unhinge her entirely.

Fidelias grimaced and shook his head. Aldrick could be arrogant, insubordinate, but his loyalty to Aquitaine was unquestioned, and he was a valuable resource. Besides which, Fidelias liked working with the man. He was a professional and understood the priorities of operating in the field. Fidelias, as his commander, owed him a certain amount of loyalty, protection. Convenient as it might be to him, in the long term, he could not allow the swordsman to come to grief.

Fidelias took a moment to draw strength from the earth, pouring into him in a sudden flood. He jerked the sword from the tree's trunk, and peeled Aldrick's hand from its hilt. Then he picked up the man and slung him over one shoulder. His balance wavered dangerously, and he took a moment to breathe, to steady himself, before taking up the naked sword and turning, with Aldrick, to march away from the river, up out of the flood-saturated ground of the river's course.

Vamma shaped out a shelter from a rocky hillside, and Fidelias ducked into it and out of the storm. Etan provided ample kindling and wood, and Fidelias managed to coax a pile of shavings into flame using the flint and Aldrick's sword. By slow degrees, he built up the fire, until the inside of the furycrafted shelter began to grow warm, even cozy.

He leaned back against the wall, his eyes closed, and dispatched Vamma and Etan again. As tired as he was, there was still a job to do. Fidelias remained silent for a moment, letting his furies gather information about those who still moved in the wild storm outside.

When he opened his eyes again, Aldrick was awake and watching him.

"You found me," the swordsman said.

"Yes."

"Blade isn't much good against a river."

"Mmmm."

Aldrick sat up and rubbed at the back of his neck with one hand, wincing, gathering himself back together with the resilience of his craft—and of comparative youth, Fidelias thought. He wasn't young anymore. "Where's Odiana?"

"I don't know yet," Fidelias said. "The storm offers considerable danger. I've found two moving groups, so far, and I think there's at least one more that I can't pinpoint."

"Which one is Odiana in?"

Fidelias shrugged. "One is heading to the northeast, and one to the southeast. I thought I felt something more directly east of here, but I can't be certain."

"Northeast isn't anything," Aldrick said. "Maybe one of the steadholts. Southeast of here, there isn't even that. Turns into the Wax Forest and the plains beyond it."

"And east is Garrison," Fidelias said. "I know."

"She's been taken, or she'd have stayed close to me."

"Yes."

Aldrick rose. "We have to find out which group she's in."

Fidelias shook his head. "No, we don't."

The swordsman narrowed his eyes. "Then how are we supposed to find her?"

"We don't," Fidelias said. "Not until the mission is finished."

Aldrick went silent for several seconds. The fire popped and crackled. Then he said, "I'm going to pretend I didn't hear you say that, old man."

Fidelias looked up at him and said, "Aquitaine assigned you to this personally, didn't he?"

Aldrick nodded, once.

"You've been his right hand through most of this. You know all the details. You're the one who has handled the money, the logistics. Yes?"

"What's your point?"

"What do you think is going to happen if the mission fails, hmm? If Aquitaine is in danger of exposure? Do you think he's just going to give you a wink and a nod and ask you not to mention it where anyone could overhear? Or do you think he's going to make sure that no one ever finds your body, much less what you know about what he is planning."

Aldrick stared steadily at Fidelias, then tightened his jaw and looked away.

Fidelias nodded. "We finish the mission. We stop whoever is going to the local count, send in the Windwolves, and turn the Marat loose. After that, we'll find the girl."

"To the crows with the mission," Aldrick spat. "I'm going to find her."

"Oh?" Fidelias asked. "And how are you going to manage that? You have many skills, Aldrick, but you're no tracker. You're in strange country, with strange furies and hostile locals. At best, you'll wander around lost like an idiot. At worst, the locals will kill you, or the

Marat will when they attack. And then who will find the girl?"

Aldrick snarled, pacing back and forth within the confines of the shelter. "Crows take you," he snarled. "All of you."

"Assuming the girl is alive," Fidelias said. "She is quite capable. If she has been taken, I am sure she is well able to survive on her own. Give her that much credit. In two days, at the most, we'll go after her."

"Two days," Aldrick said. He bowed his head and growled, "Then let's get started. Now. We stop the messengers to the Count and then we get her."

"Sit down. Rest. We've lost the horses in the flood. We can wait until the storm is out, at least."

Aldrick stepped across the space between them and hauled Fidelias to his feet, eyes narrowed. "No, old man. We go now. You find us salt, and we go out into that storm and get this over with. Then you take me to Odiana."

Fidelias swallowed and kept his expression careful, neutral. "And then?"

"Then I kill anyone that gets between me and her," Aldrick said.

"It would be safer for us if we—"

"I couldn't care less about safe," Aldrick said. "Time's wasting."

Fidelias looked out of the shelter at the storm. His body ached in its joints, groaned at the abuse that had already been heaped on it. His feet throbbed where they were cut, steady, slow pain. He looked back to Aldrick. The swordsman's eyes glittered, cold and hard.

"All right," Fidelias said. "Let's find them."

CHAPTER 23

Amara had never been so cold.

She swam in it, drifted in it, a pure and frozen darkness as black and as silent as the void itself. Memories, images, danced and floated around her. She saw herself struggling against the swordsman. She saw Bernard, on his feet and coming toward them. And then the cold, sudden and black and terrifying.

The river, she thought. *Isana must have flooded the river.*

A band of fire settled around her wrist, but she noted it as nothing more than a passing sensation. There was just the darkness and the cold—the burning, horrible purity of the cold, pressing into her, through her skin.

Sensations blurred, melted together, and she felt the sound of splashing water, saw the cold wind rippling across her soaked skin. She heard someone, a voice speaking to her, but the words didn't make any sense and ran too closely together for her to understand. She tried to ask whoever was speaking to slow down, but her mouth didn't seem to be listening to her. Sounds came out, but they were too cracked and rasping to have been anything she meant to say.

Sound lessened, and the cold lessened with it. No

more wind? She felt a hard surface beneath her and lay there upon it, abruptly and overwhelmingly tired. She closed her eyes and tried to sleep, but someone kept shaking her just as she was about to get some rest, waking her up. Light came, and an ugly, unpleasant tingling in her limbs. It hurt, and she felt tears come to her eyes, simple frustration. Hadn't she done enough? Hadn't she given enough? She'd already given her life. Must she sacrifice her rest as well?

Coherence returned in a rush, and with it pain so sharp and rending that she lost her breath and her voice in the same gasp. Her body, curled into a ball, had tightened into a series of cramping convulsions, as though doing everything in its power to close itself off from the cold that had filled her. She heard herself making sounds, grunting noises, guttural and helpless, but she could no more stop making them than she could force herself to straighten her body.

She lay on stone, that much she knew, in the clothes she'd stolen from Bernardholt—but they were soaked through with water, and crystals of ice were forming on the outermost layer of cloth. There were sloped walls of rough stone around her that had stopped the howling winds. A cave, then. And a fire, that provided light, and the warmth that had brought tingling pain flooding back into her body.

She was freezing, she knew, and knew as well that she had to move, to get out of the clothes and closer to the fire, lest she sink back into that stillness and never emerge from it.

She tried.

She couldn't.

Fear filled her then. Not the rush of excitement or the lightning of sudden terror, but slow, cool, logical fear. She had to move to live. She could not move. Hence, she could not live.

The helpless simplicity of it was what stung, what made it real. She wanted to move, to uncurl her body, to creep closer to the fire—simple things, things she could do at any other time. But for lack of that ability now, she would die. Tears made her vision blur, but they were halfhearted, too empty of the fire of life to warm her.

Something came between her and the fire, a shape, and she felt a hand, huge and warm—blessedly warm—settle on her forehead.

"We've got to get those clothes off you," Bernard rumbled, his voice gentle. He moved closer to her, and she felt him lift her like a child. She tried to speak to him, to help him, but she could only curl and shudder and make helpless grunting sounds.

"I know," he rumbled. "Just relax." He had to struggle to get the shirts off, though not much—they were so large on her. The clothes came away like layers of frozen mud, until she wore only her underclothes. Her limbs seemed shrunken and wrinkled to her. Her fingers were swollen.

Bernard laid her down again, close to the fire, and its heat flowed over her, easing the cramped tension in her muscles, slowly lessening the pain that had come with it. Her breathing began to be something she could control, and she slowed her breaths, though she still shivered.

"Here," Bernard said. "I got it wet, but I've been drying it out since we got the fire going." He lifted her, and a moment later settled a shirt, a little damp but warm with the heat of the fire, over her. He didn't bother to slip the sleeves on, just wrapped her in it like a blanket, and she huddled under it, grateful.

Amara opened her eyes and looked up at him. She lay curled on her side. He sat on his legs, holding his own hands out to the fire, and was naked above the waist. Firelight played over the dark hairs on his chest, over the heavy muscle of his frame, and made soft lines of several old scars. Blood had dried in a line on his lip, where a blow from the other Steadholder had apparently split it, and his cheek had already darkened with a bruise, reflected by others on his ribs and belly.

"Y-you came after me," she said, moments later. "You pulled me out of the water."

He looked over at her, then back at the fire. He nodded once. "It was the least I could do. You stopped that man."

"Only for a few seconds," she said. "I couldn't have stood up to him for long. He's a swordsman. A good one. If the river hadn't flooded when it did—"

Bernard waved his hand and shook his head. "Not that one. The one who shot the arrow at Tavi. You saved my nephew's life." He looked down at her and said, quietly, "Thank you."

She felt her cheeks color, and she looked down. "Oh. You're welcome." After a moment she said, "Aren't you cold?"

"Some," he admitted. He nodded toward where several articles of clothing were spread on stones near the fire. "Brutus is trying to spread some heat into the stones beneath them, but he doesn't really understand heat too well. They'll dry in a while."

"Brutus?" Amara asked.

"My fury. The hound you saw."

"Oh," she said. "Here. Let me." Amara closed her eyes and murmured to Cirrus. The air around the fire stirred sluggishly, and then the smoke and shimmering waves of warmth tilted, moved toward the clothing. Amara opened her eyes to inspect Cirrus's work, and nodded. "They should dry a little faster, now."

"Thank you," Bernard said. He folded his arms, suppressing a shiver of his own. "You knew the men after Tavi."

"There was another, too. A watercrafter. Your sister threw her out of the river."

Bernard snorted, a smile touching his face. "She would. I never saw that one."

"I know them," Amara said. She told him, in brief, about Fidelias and the mercenaries and her fears for the Valley.

"Politics." Bernard spat into the fire. "I took a steadholt out here because I didn't want anything to do with the High Lords. Or the First Lord, either."

"I'm sorry," Amara said. "Is everyone all right?"

Bernard shook his head. "I don't know. After that fight, I can't push Brutus too hard. He's mostly making sure that other earthcrafter can't find us. I tried to look, but I haven't been able to locate anyone."

"I'm sure Tavi's well," Amara said. "He's a resourceful child."

Bernard nodded. "He's clever. Fast. But that might not be enough in this storm."

"He had salt," Amara said. "He took it before he left."

"That's good to know, at least."

"And he wasn't alone. He had that slave with him."

Bernard grimaced. "Fade. I don't know why my sister puts up with him."

"Do you own many slaves?"

Bernard shook his head. "I used to buy them sometimes, give them the chance to earn their freedom. Lot of the families on the steadholt started that way."

"But you didn't give Fade that chance?"

He frowned. "Of course I did. He was the first slave I bought, back when I raised Bernardholt. But he spends the money on things before he saves up to his price. Or does something stupid and has to pay for repairs. I stopped having the patience to deal with him years ago. Isana does it all now. All his clothes get ruined, and he won't stop wearing that old collar. Nice enough fellow, I suppose, and he's a fairly good tinker and smith. But he's got the brains of a brick."

Amara nodded. Then she sat up. The effort of it left her gasping and dizzy.

Bernard's hand steadied her, warm on her shoulder. "Easy. You should rest. Going into water like that can kill you."

"I can't," Amara said. "I have to get moving. To find Tavi, or at least try to warn the Count at Garrison."

"You aren't going anywhere tonight," Bernard said. He nodded toward the darkness at one side of the cavern they huddled in, where Amara could distantly hear the howl of wind. "That storm came down and it's worse than I thought it would be. No one's moving tonight."

She looked at him, frowning.

"Lay down," he told her. "Rest. No sense in making yourself more tired."

"What about you?"

He shrugged. "I'll be fine." His hand pushed gently on her shoulder. "Rest. We'll go as soon as the storm breaks."

Amara stopped struggling against the warmth easing into her with a sigh of relief and let his hand push her down. His fingers tightened slightly, and she felt the strength of them through her skin. She shivered, feeling at once a sense of reassurance and a sudden spasm of raw, physical need that curled in her belly and lingered there, making her heart speed up again, her breathing quicken.

She looked up and saw in his face that he'd seen her reaction. She felt her cheeks color again, but she didn't look away.

"You're shivering," he said, quiet. His hand didn't move.

She swallowed and said, "I'm cold." She became acutely aware of her bare legs, brazenly on display, and curled them up toward the shirt (his shirt) that he had draped over her.

He moved then, his hand sliding from her shoulder. He stretched out on his side, his chest against her shoulders, so that she lay between him and the fire. "Lay back against me," he said, quiet. "Just until you get warm."

She shivered again and did, feeling the strength of him, the warmth of him. She had an urge to roll onto her other side, to press her face into the hollow of his shoulder and throat, to feel his skin against hers, to share that closeness, that warmth, and the thought of it made her shiver again. She licked her lips.

"Are you all right?" he asked.

"I'm . . ." She swallowed. "Still cold."

He moved. His arm lifted, then draped across her,

careful, strong, drawing her back a bit more firmly against him. "Better?"

"Better," she whispered. She turned, hips and shoulders, so that she could see his face. Her mouth lay a breath from his. "Thank you. For saving me."

Whatever he'd been about to say died on his lips, and his eyes focused on hers, then on her mouth. After a moment of aching silence, he said, "You should go to sleep."

She swallowed, her eyes on his, and shook her head. She leaned toward him then, and her mouth touched on his, his lips just a little rough, soft, warm. She could smell him, his scent like leather and fresh wind, and she felt herself arch into the kiss, slow and sweet. He kissed her back, gently, but she could feel the faint traces of heat in it, feel the way his mouth pushed hungrily at hers, and it made her heart race even more swiftly.

He ended the kiss, lifting his mouth away from hers, his eyes closed. He swallowed, throat working, and she felt his arm tighten on her for a moment. Then he opened his eyes and said, "You need to sleep."

"But—"

"You're half frozen, and you're afraid," Bernard said, quiet. "I'm not going to take advantage of that."

Her face colored, and she looked away from him. "No. I mean—"

He laid his hand on her head and pressed gently down. His other arm shifted, moved beneath her head, so that her cheek rested against it instead of her own. "Just rest," he said, quietly. "Sleep."

"Are you sure?" she asked. Despite herself, her eyes blinked closed and refused to open again.

"I'm sure, Amara," he said, voice a low rumble she felt against him as much as heard. "Sleep. I'll watch."

"I'm sorry," she said. "I didn't mean to—"

She felt him lean down to her and press his mouth against her damp hair. "Hush. We can talk about it later, if you want to. Rest."

Her cheeks still warm, Amara leaned back against his warmth and sighed. Sleep took her before she remembered drawing that breath in again.

The light woke her. She still lay by the fire, but the cloaks that had been drying now lay over her, keeping her warm, but for her back, which felt as though it had just begun to cool. Bernard wasn't in sight, and the fire had burned low, but grey light shone from one side of the small cave.

Amara rose, wrapping the cloaks about herself, and walked toward the mouth of the cave. She found Bernard there, still shirtless, staring out at a landscape shining in the predawn light, ice coating every surface, every branch of every tree. Sleet-ice mixed with snow lay over the ground, softening everything with white, making sounds seem closer, granting the land the strange half-glowing light of winter. Amara stopped for a moment, just to stare at the land and then at Bernard. His expression was hard, alarmed.

"Steadholder?" she asked.

He lifted a finger to his lips, eyes focused elsewhere, head tilted to one side, as though listening. Then his eyes snapped abruptly to the south, at the still-shadowed trees that stood in silent, glinting stillness.

"There," he said.

Amara frowned at him, but stepped closer, wrapping

the cloaks a little more tightly about herself against the cold outside. Winter had come in force, with the storm. She glanced at Bernard and then at the trees he stared at so intently.

She heard it before she saw anything, a low swelling sound that began to gather, to grow closer. It took her a moment to identify the sound, to sort it out into something she could recognize.

Crows. The cawing of crows. The cawing of thousands of crows.

Even as she started to shiver, they appeared, black shapes against the predawn sky, from the direction Bernard faced, flying low over the trees. Hundreds of them, thousands, flooded through the air like a living shadow, blackening the sky, flying north and east over the Calderon Valley, moving with an uncanny certainty, with a purpose.

"Crows," she whispered.

"They know," Bernard said. "Oh, furies. They always know."

"Know what?" Amara breathed.

"Where to find the dead." He let out an unsteady breath. "They smell a battle."

Amara felt her eyes widen. "They're flying toward Garrison?"

"I have to find Tavi and Isana. Get back to the steadholt," Bernard said.

She turned to him and took his arm. "No," she said. "I need your help."

He shook his head. "My responsibility is for my holders. I have to get back to them."

"Listen to me," she said. "Bernard, I need your help.

I don't know this valley. I don't know the dangers. I'm afraid to take to the air in daylight, and even if I got to your Count alone, he might not listen to me. I need someone he knows with me. I have to get him to react to this as strongly as possible if there's to be any chance of protecting the Valley."

Bernard shook his head. "This has nothing to do with me."

"Is it going to have anything to do with you when a Marat horde comes down on Bernardholt?" Amara demanded. "Do you think you and the people there will be able to fight them?"

He looked at her, uncertain.

She pressed him. "Bernard. Steadholder Bernard. Your duty is to your people. And the only way to protect them is to warn Garrison, to rouse the Legions. You can help me do that."

"I don't know," Bernard said. "Gram's a stubborn old goat. I can't tell him I've seen the Marat in the Valley. I don't remember it. His watercrafter will tell him that."

"But you can tell him what you *have* seen," Amara said. "You can tell him that you support me. If I have your support, he'll have to take my credentials as a Cursor seriously. He has the authority to bring Legion strength to Garrison, to protect the Valley."

Bernard swallowed. "But Tavi. He doesn't have anyone else to look after him. And my sister. I'm not sure she came through last night all right."

"Are either of them going to be all right if the Marat exterminate everyone in the Calderon Valley?"

Bernard looked away, back to the crows that still

streamed overhead. He growled, "You think someone's watching the air?"

"There's a full century of Knights stationed at Garrison," Amara said. "With a pair of infantry cohorts to cover them, they could stand off a dozen hordes. I think whoever has arranged this has a plan to assault them and destroy them before the Marat come."

"The mercenaries," Bernard said.

"Yes."

"Then there might be more people trying to stop us from reaching Garrison. Professional killers."

Amara nodded, silent, watching his face.

Bernard closed his eyes. "Tavi." He was quiet for a moment before he opened them. "Isana. I'll be leaving them alone in this mess."

She said, quietly, "I know. What I'm asking you is terrible."

"No," he said. "No. It's duty. I'll help you."

She squeezed his arm. "Thank you."

He looked at her and said, "Don't thank me. I'm not doing it for you." But he covered her hand with his and squeezed quietly.

She swallowed and said, "Bernard. Last night. What you said. You were right. I'm afraid."

"So am I," he said. He released her hand and turned to go into the cave. "Let's get dressed, get moving. We've got a long way to go."

CHAPTER 24

Isana heard a woman's voice say, "Wake up. Wake up." Someone slapped her face, sudden and sharp. Isana let out a surprised sound and lifted her arms in an effort to protect her face. That same voice continued, just as before, "Wake up. Wake up," and slapped her at measured intervals until Isana curled away from the blows, rolling to get her hands and knees beneath her, and to lift her head.

Isana felt hot. Sweltering. Her skin had soaked with sweat, and her clothes clung to her, likewise damp. Light was in her eyes, and it took her a moment to realize that she was on a dirt floor, that there was fire all around her, fire in a circle perhaps twenty feet across, a ring of coals and tinder that smoldered and smoked. Her throat and lungs burned with thirst, with the smoke, and she coughed until she almost retched.

She covered her mouth with her shaking hand, tried to filter out some of the smoke and dust in the air as she breathed. Someone helped her sit up, hands brisk, strong.

"Thank you," she rasped. Isana looked up to see the woman she'd seen in the Rillwater, strangling Tavi. She was beautiful, dark of hair and eye, curved as sweetly as any man could desire. Her hair hung in damp, sweaty curls, though, and her face had been smudged with soot. The skin, in rows that reached across her eyes, was bright pink, shiny and new. A small smile curved her full mouth.

Isana hissed out a breath in surprise, backing away from the woman, looking around her, at the fires, a low ceiling, smooth, round stone walls not far beyond the ring of coals. There was a door leading out, and Isana tried to stand and move toward it, only to find that her legs would not obey her properly. She stumbled and fell heavily onto her side, near enough to the coals that her skin heated painfully. She pushed herself back from the fire.

The woman helped, dragging Isana back with a cool efficiency.

"Nasty, nasty," the woman said. "You must be careful, or you'll burn." She sat back from Isana, tilting her head to one side and studying her. "My name is Odiana," she said then. "And you and I are prisoners together."

"Prisoners," Isana whispered. Her voice came out in a croak, and she had to cough painfully. "Prisoners where? What's wrong with my legs?"

"Kordholt, I think they called it," Odiana said. "You're experiencing crafting sickness. When Kord found you by the banks of the flood, your head was broken. They made me mend it."

"You?" Isana asked. "But you were trying to hurt Tavi."

"The pretty boy?" Odiana asked. "I wasn't hurting him. I was killing him. There's a difference." She sniffed and said, "It wasn't anything personal."

"Tavi," Isana said, coughing again. "Is Tavi all right?"

"How should I know?" Odiana said, her tone faintly

impatient. "You tore my eyes out, woman. The next thing I saw was that ugly brute."

"Then you're not—" Isana shook her head. "Kord took you prisoner?"

She nodded, once. "He found me after the flood. I had just put my eyes back together." Odiana smiled. "I've never managed my nails like that before. You'll have to show me how it's done."

Isana stared at the woman for a moment, then said, "We have to get out of here."

"Yes," Odiana agreed, looking at the door. "But that seems unlikely for the moment. He's a slaver, isn't he, this Kord?"

"He is."

The dark haired woman's eyes glinted. "I thought as much."

The thirst in her throat abruptly became too much for Isana to ignore, and she murmured, "Rill, I need water."

Odiana let out an impatient sigh. "No," she said. "Don't be an idiot. He's ringed us in fire. Dried us out. Your fury cannot hear you, and even if it could, you'd not be able to dampen a washcloth."

Isana shivered, and for the first time since she'd found Rill, she felt no quivering response to her call, no reassuring presence of the water fury. Isana swallowed, eyes shifting around the interior of the building. Meat hung from hooks on some of the walls, and smoke lingered in the air. A smokehouse then, at Kord's steadholt.

She was a prisoner at Kord's steadholt.

The thought chilled her, sent a quiver creeping along her scalp, to the roots of her hair.

Odiana watched her in silence and then nodded,

slowly. "He doesn't intend for us to ever leave this place, you know. I felt that in him before he brought us here."

"I'm thirsty," Isana said. "Hot enough to kill us in here. I have to get a drink."

"They left us two tiny cups of water," Odiana said, nodding to the far side of the circle.

Isana looked until she saw the pair of wooden cups and pulled herself to them. The first she picked up was light, empty. She dropped it to one side, her throat on fire, and tried the second.

It was empty as well.

"You were asleep," Odiana said, calmly. "So I drank it."

Isana stared at the woman in disbelief. "This heat could kill us," she told her, struggling to keep an even tone.

The woman smiled at her, a lazy, languid smile. "Well it won't kill me. I've drunk enough for two."

Isana clenched her teeth together. "It makes the most sense anyway. Use it. Call your fury and send for help."

"We're far from any help, holdgirl."

Isana pressed her lips together. "Then when one of them comes in—"

Odiana shook her head slowly and spoke in a cool, passionless, practical tone. "Do you think they've never done this before? This is what slavers *do,* holdgirl. They left enough to keep us alive. Not enough to allow one of us full use of her fury. I'd try, it wouldn't work, and they'd punish both of us."

"So that's it?" Isana said. "We don't even try?"

Odiana closed her eyes for a moment, looking down. Then she said, very quietly, "We're only going to get one chance, holdgirl."

"I'm not a gi—"

"You're a *child*," Odiana hissed. "Do you know how many slaves are raped within a day or so of capture?"

The thought made Isana feel cold again. "No."

"Do you know what happens to the ones who resist?"

Isana shook her head.

Odiana smiled. "Take it from me. You only get to resist once. And after that, they make sure that you never want to try it again."

Isana stared at the woman for a long moment. Then she said, "How long were you a slave?"

Odiana brushed her hair back away from her face with one hand and said, voice cool, "When I was eleven, our Steadholder sold my father's debt to a group of slavers. They took all of us. They killed my father and my oldest brother, and the baby. They took my mother, my sisters, me. And my youngest brother. He was pretty." Her eyes grew distant, and she focused them on the far wall. Fire glowed in them, reflection. "I was too young. I hadn't begun my cycle, or come into my furycrafting. But I did that night. When they took me. Passed me around the fire like a flask of wine. It woke up, and I could feel *everything* they felt, holdgirl. All of their lust and their hate and fear and hunger. It washed through me. *Into* me." She began to rock back and forth on her heels. "I don't know how you came into yours, watercrafter. When you first started feeling other folk. But you must thank all the furies of Carna that it wasn't like my awakening." The smile crept back to her lips. "It's enough to drive one mad."

Isana swallowed and said, "I'm sorry. But Odiana, if we can work together—"

"We can get killed together," Odiana said, her voice becoming edged again. "Listen to me, holdgirl, and I'll tell you what happens. I've done it before."

"All right," Isana said, quietly.

"There are two kinds of slavers," Odiana said. "The ones in it for professional reasons, and the ones who take it personally. Professionals work for the Consortium. They don't allow anyone to damage or use their merchandise, unless it's as discipline. If they like you, they'll invite you to their tent and give you nice food and talk and charm you. It's the same as a rape, only it takes longer and you get a good meal and a soft bed afterward."

"That's not Kord."

"No, it isn't. He's the other kind. Like the ones who took my family. For him, it's knowing he's beating someone. Knowing he's breaking someone. He doesn't want to deliver a high-quality product, ready to work or pleasure. He wants us broken into pieces. He wants us to be animals." She smiled and said, "When he takes us, that's just part of the process that he enjoys a bit more than the others."

Isana's stomach quailed. "Takes us," she whispered. "He's—"

The other woman nodded. "If he wanted to kill you you'd already be dead. He has other plans for you." She sneered. "And I saw some of the other women he keeps at this place. Rabbits. Sheep. He likes them helpless. Not fighting back." She shivered and stretched, her back arching sinuously, her eyes closing for a moment. She moved one hand to the throat of her blouse, tugging at it, pulling buttons open, the sweaty cloth clinging to her.

"Are you all right?" Isana asked.

Odiana licked her lips and said, "I don't have much time. Listen to me. For him, the game is breaking you, and to do that he has to make you afraid. If you aren't afraid, he has no power over you. If you're quiet and reserved, you aren't what he wants. Do you understand?"

"Y-yes," Isana said. "But we can't just stay here—"

"We survive for as long as you don't break," Odiana said. "To him I'm nothing but a pretty whore to be used. You he wants broken. As long as you remain in control of yourself, he doesn't get what he wants."

"What happens if I do break?"

"He kills you," she said. "And he kills me because I saw you, and he hides the bodies. But it won't be an issue."

"Why not?"

"It won't," Odiana says. "One way or another. Hold out for a day. That's all. Because I promise neither of us will draw breath for half an hour if you break. That's why I drank both cups."

Isana fought to take a breath, and her head spun. "Why you drank both cups?"

"Have you ever tasted aphrodin, holdgirl?"

She stared at Odiana. "No," she said. "Never."

Odiana licked her lips, smiling. "Then it would have unnerved you. Wanting when you knew you shouldn't want. At least I know what it's like." She stretched again, unbuttoning her blouse lower, showing the soft curves of her breasts. She adjusted the fall of her skirt so that it bared one strong, smooth thigh, and ran a fingertip along it. "Let's review our stratagem. I'm going to make them happy. And you're going to not care. There, that's simple."

Isana felt her insides twist, felt sickened as she stared at the other woman. "You're going to—" She couldn't finish. It was too horrible.

Odiana let her lips curve into a smile. "The act isn't unpleasant you know. In and of itself. It's rather nice. And I won't be thinking about them." The smile grew a bit wider, and the whites showed around her eyes. "I'll be thinking of the pieces. The pieces left when my lord catches up to them. He will see to his duty, and then he will come for me. And there will be pieces." She shivered and let out a soft gasp. "And there. I'm happy already."

Isana stared at the woman, revolted, and shook her head. This could not be happening. It simply could not be happening. She, with her brother, had worked the whole of their adult lives to make the Calderon Valley a place safe for families, for civilization—for Tavi to grow up. This wasn't a part of the world she had worked to build. This wasn't a part of what she dreamed.

Tears welled in her eyes, and she fought to restrain them, to hold back the precious moisture before it fell. Without thinking, she reached for Rill's help and did not find it. Tears trickled over her cheeks.

She hurt. Deep inside. She felt horribly, utterly alone, with only a madwoman for company. Isana reached out for Rill again, desperate, and felt nothing. Again she tried, and again, refusing to accept that her fury was beyond her reach.

She didn't hear the footsteps until they were immediately outside the smokehouse. Someone shoved the door open. The hulking, ugly shape of Kord and those of a dozen other men stood silhouetted by the light of the circle of coals.

CHAPTER 25

Being captured, Tavi thought, was a twofold evil. It was both uncomfortable *and* boring.

The Marat hadn't spoken, not to the Alerans nor to one another. Four had simply held spear tips to Tavi's and Fade's throats, while the other two trussed their arms and legs with lengths of tough, braided cord. They took Tavi's knife and pouch away and searched then confiscated Fade's battered old pack. Then the two who had tied them simply flung them over one of their broad shoulders and loped off into the storm.

After half an hour of jouncing against the Marat warrior's shoulder, Tavi's stomach felt as though he'd been belly diving from the tallest tree along the Rillwater. The Marat who carried him ran with a pure and predatory grace, moving along the land at a mile-eating lope. He leapt over a streambed, and once a low row of brush, evidently entirely unencumbered by the weight of his prisoner.

Tavi tried to keep track of which way they were headed, but the darkness and the storm and his awkward position (mostly upside down) made it impossible. The rain turned into pelting, stinging sleet, blinding him almost entirely. The winds continued to rise and grow colder, and Tavi could see the windmanes moving in the storm, wild and restless. None of them came near the Marat war band.

Tavi tried to mark where he was by the lay of the ground rolling by under his nose, but the storm began coating it in a layer of plain, monotonous white. He had no way of getting his bearings by the kind of rock or earth beneath him, no way to guide himself by the stars, no way to orient himself upon the lay of the land. Though he tried for an hour more, he gave it up as pointless.

That left him with only the fear to think about.

The Marat had taken him and Fade. While they appeared, outwardly, much like Alerans, they were not truly human and had never shown a desire to be so, and instead remained the primitive savages who ate fallen foes and mated with beasts. Though they lacked fury-crafting of their own, they made up for it in raw athletic ability, courage that was more madness than virtue, and vast numbers that dwelt on the unknown stretches of the wilderness that began on the eastern side of the last Legion fortification, Garrison.

When the Marat horde had rushed into the Valley, killing the Princeps and annihilating his Legion to a man, they had been driven out only through heavy reinforcements from the rest of Alera and hard, vicious fighting. Now they were back, presumably to strike in secret—and Tavi had seen them and knew of their plans.

What would they do to him?

He swallowed and tried to tell himself that the pounding of his heart was the result of the battering he was taking on his captor's shoulder, rather than from the quiet terror that had taken up residence in him and slowly grew with every loping stride.

An endless time later, the Marat came to a gradual halt. He growled something in a guttural, swift-sounding tongue and took Tavi from his shoulder, lowering the boy to the ground and stepping firmly on Tavi's hair with one naked, mud-stained foot. He put his hands to his mouth and let out a low, grunting cough, a sound that it did not seem possible for a human-sized chest to make.

An answering cough rumbled from the trees, and then the ground shook as huge, heavy shapes, dark in the storm and night, stepped toward them. Tavi recognized the smell before he could make out the exact shape of the creatures: gargants.

The Marat who had carried Tavi, evidently the leader of the group, slapped the nearest gargant on the shoulder, and the great beast knelt down with ponderous gentility, teeth idly working over several pounds of cud. The Marat again spoke to the others and then picked Tavi up. Tavi looked around and saw a second Marat lifting Fade.

The Marat carried him under one arm as he put a foot in the joint of the gargant's foreleg and half jumped up to the great beast's sloped back, where he settled onto some sort of riding saddle consisting of a heavy mat woven of the same coarse cords as the ones that bound Tavi, made out of gargant-hair.

He tossed Tavi belly-down over the mat and whipped a few more cords around the boy, as casually as any muleteer packing his charges. Tavi looked up at the Marat. He had broad, rather ugly features, and his eyes were dark, dark brown. Though he was not as tall as Tavi's uncle, his shoulders and chest would make Bernard seem positively skinny, and slabs of heavy muscle moved beneath his pale skin. His coarse, colorless hair had been gathered back into a braid. He looked down at Tavi, as he settled onto the gargant, and the beast began to rise, without any apparent signal from its rider. The Marat smiled, and his teeth were broad and white and square. He rumbled something in that same language, and the other Marat let out rough, coughing laughs, as they mounted their own gargants.

The great beasts rose and set out at a swift pace in a single file, their huge strides eating up ground faster than Tavi could run, steady and tireless as the stars in the sky. Tavi could just make out Fade's shape, tied on the gargant behind them. He grimaced and wished he could at least be with the slave. Surely Fade was terrified—he always was.

They rode for a length of time Tavi could hardly guess at, considering that he had been tied facedown, and he saw little more than one leg of the gargant and the snowy white ground rolling by beneath him. A sudden, low whistle broke the monotony. Tavi glanced toward the source of the sound and then up at his captor. The Marat shifted his weight slightly backward, and the gargant slowed its steps by degrees, coming to a ponderous halt.

The Marat did not bother to have the gargant kneel, but swung from a braided cord, knotted every foot or so, down from the saddle, and gave a low whistle in answer.

From the darkness emerged another Marat, broad of shoulder and deep of chest, panting, as though from a run. His expression seemed, to Tavi, to be sickened, even afraid. He said something in the guttural Marat tongue, and Tavi's captor put a hand on the younger Marat's shoulder, making him repeat himself.

Once he had, Tavi's captor gave a short whistle, and another Marat from down the row of gargants swung down from his saddle, carrying what Tavi recognized as a torch and a firebox of Aleran manufacture. The Marat knelt, holding the torch up with his thighs, and with a stone struck sparks from the firebox and lit the torch. He passed it over to Tavi's captor, who kept his hand on the young Marat's shoulder and nodded to him.

Tavi watched as the younger Marat led his captor to a vague form in the snow. Tavi could see little of it, other than that the snow over it had been stained with red. The Marat took a few paces more. Then a few more. More lumps in the snow became evident.

Tavi's stomach twisted with a slow shock of understanding. They were people. The Marat were looking at people on the ground, people dead so recently that their blood still stained the newly fallen snow. Tavi looked up and thought he saw light from the Marat's torch reflected from water not far away. The lake, then.

Aldoholt.

Tavi watched the Marat walk a quick circle, the light of his torch at one point catching the sloped walls of the steadholt proper. Bodies lay in a line leading from the steadholt gates, one by one, as though the holders had made a last-moment effort to run, only to be dragged down, one at a time, and savaged into the snow.

Tavi swallowed. Without doubt, the holders were all dead. People he had met, people he had laughed with, apologized to—people he knew, ravaged and torn to shreds. His belly writhed, and he got sick, trying to lean far enough over the side to sick up onto the ground instead of the gargant's saddle.

The Marat leader came back, though he had passed the torch to the younger one. In each of his hands he held a vague, lumpy shape, which Tavi identified only as the Marat got close to the gargant.

The Marat leader held the shapes up in the light of the torch, letting out another low whistle to his men. Firelight fell on the severed heads of what looked like a direwolf and a herdbane, their eyes glassy. The residents of the steadholt, it seemed, had not died alone, and Tavi felt a helpless little rush of vengeful satisfaction. He spat toward the lead Marat.

The lead Marat looked up at him, head tilted to one side, then turned to the younger one and drew a line across his throat. The younger dropped the torch's flame into the snow, quenching it. The Marat leader dropped the heads and then swarmed up the knotted cord back onto the saddle. He turned to Tavi and stared at him for a moment, then leaned over and touched a spot on the saddle that Tavi hadn't been able to avoid staining when he got sick.

The Marat lifted his fingertips to his nose, wrinkled it, and looked from Tavi to the silent, bloody forms in the snow. He nodded, his expression grim, then took a leather flask from a tie on the saddle, turned to Tavi, and unceremoniously shoved one end of the flask into his mouth, squeezing water out of it in a rush.

Tavi spluttered and spat, and the Marat withdrew the flask, nodding. Then he tied the flask to the saddle and let out another low whistle. The line of gargants moved out into the night, and the spare Marat swung up behind another rider further down the file.

Tavi looked back to find his captor studying him, frowning. The Marat looked past him, back toward the steadholt, his broad, ugly features unsettled, perhaps disturbed. Then he looked back to Tavi again.

Tavi puffed out a breath to blow the hair out of his eyes and demanded, his voice shaking, "What are you looking at?"

The Marat's eyebrows went up, and once again that broad-toothed smile briefly took over his face. His voice came out in a basso rumble. "I look at you, valleyboy."

Tavi blinked at him. "You speak Aleran?"

"Some," said the Marat. "We call your language the trading tongue. Trade with your people sometimes. Trade with one another. The clans each have their own tongue. To one another, we speak trade. Speak Aleran."

"Where are you taking us?" Tavi asked.

"To the horto," the Marat said.

"What's a horto?"

"Your people have no word."

Tavi shook his head. "I don't understand."

"Your people never do," he said, without malice. "They never try."

"What do you mean?"

"What I say." The Marat turned back to the trail in front of them, idly ducking under a low-hanging branch. The gargant swayed a bit to one side, even as its rider did, and the branch passed the Marat by no more than the width of a finger.

"I'm Tavi," he told the Marat.

"No," the Marat said. "You are Aleran, valleyboy."

"No, I mean my name is Tavi. It's what I am called."

"Being called something does not make you that thing, valleyboy. I am called Doroga."

"Doroga." Tavi frowned. "What are you going to do to us?"

"Do to you?" The Marat frowned. "Best not to think about it for now."

"But—"

"Valleyboy. Be quiet." Doroga flicked a look back at Tavi, eyes dark with menace, and Tavi quailed before it, shivering. Doroga grunted and nodded. "Tomorrow is tomorrow," he said, turning his face away. "For tonight, you are in my keeping. Tonight you will go nowhere. Rest."

After that, he fell silent. Tavi stared at him for a while and then spent a while more working his wrists at the cords, trying to loosen them so that he could at least try to escape. But the cords only tightened, cutting into his wrists, making them ache and throb. Tavi gave up on the effort after an endless amount of squirming.

The sleet, Tavi noted, had changed into a heavy, wet snow, and he was able to lift his head enough to look around him a little. He couldn't identify where they were, though dim shapes far off in the shadows nagged at his memory. Somewhere past the lake and Aldoholt, he supposed, though they couldn't be heading anywhere but to Garrison. It was the only way into or out of the Valley at that end.

Wasn't it?

His back and legs were soaked and chill, but only a while after he noticed that, Doroga glanced back at him, drew an Aleran-weave blanket from his saddlebags, and tossed it over Tavi, head and all.

Tavi laid his head down on the saddle-mat and noted idly that the material used in its construction was braided gargant hair. It held his heat well, once the blanket had gone over him, and he began to warm up.

That, coupled with the smooth, steady strides of the beast, were too much for Tavi in his exhausted state. He dozed off, sometime deep in the night.

Tavi woke wrapped in blankets. He sat up, blinking, and looked around him.

He was in a tent of one kind or another. It was made of long, curving poles placed in a circle and leaning on one another at the top, and over that was spread some kind of hide covering. He could hear wind outside, through a hole in the roof of the tent, and pale winter sunlight peeked through it as well. He rubbed at his face and saw Fade sitting on the floor nearby, his legs crossed, his hands folded in his lap, a frown on his face.

"Fade," Tavi said. "Are you well?"

The slave looked up at Tavi, his eyes vacant for a moment, and then he nodded. "Trouble, Tavi," Fade said, his tone serious. "Trouble."

"I know," Tavi said. "Don't worry. We'll figure a way out of this."

Fade nodded, eyes watching Tavi expectantly.

"Well not right this minute," Tavi said, after a flustered moment. "You could at least try to help me come up with something, Fade."

Fade stared vacantly for a moment and then frowned. "Marat eat Alerans."

Tavi swallowed. "I know, I know. But if they were going to eat us, they wouldn't have given us blankets and a place to sleep. Right?"

"Maybe they like hot dinner," Fade said, darkly. "Raw dinner."

Tavi stared at him for a minute. "That's enough help, Fade," he said. "Get up. Maybe nobody's looking and we can make a run for it."

They both stood up, and Tavi had just crept to the tent's flap to peek out, when the flap swung out, letting a flood of pale sunlight in along with a slender Marat youth dressed in a long leather tunic. His hair had been pulled into a braid identical to Doroga's, though his body was far more slender, and his features far finer, sharper. The youth's eyes were an opalescent swirl of colors, rather than the dark brown of Doroga's. His eyes widened upon seeing them, as though surprised, and a chipped dagger of some dark stone seemed to leap into his hands and swept at Tavi's face.

Tavi leapt back, fast enough to save his eyes, but not quickly enough to avoid a swift, hot pain, high on his cheek. Tavi let out a yelp, as Fade whimpered and jerked frantically at Tavi's shirt, dragging him back and unceremoniously to the floor behind himself.

The Marat blinked at them, startled, and then demanded something in the guttural Marat speech, his voice high and, Tavi thought, perhaps nervous.

"I'm sorry," Tavi said. "Um. I don't understand you." From the floor, he showed the Marat his open hands and tried to smile, though he supposed it looked rather sickly. "Fade, you're standing on my sleeve."

The young Marat scowled, half lowering the knife, and demanded something else, this time in a different-sounding tongue. He looked from Tavi to Fade, face twisting into revulsion as he studied Fade's scars.

Tavi shook his head, glancing at Fade, who moved his foot and warily helped Tavi to his feet, watching the young Marat with his eyes wide.

The tent flap opened again, and Doroga entered. He stopped for a moment staring at Tavi's face. The burly Marat growled something in a tone that Tavi recognized extremely well—though he normally heard it from his uncle after something had gotten complicated.

The youth spun to face Doroga, hands sweeping behind his back and hiding the knife. Doroga scowled and rumbled something that made color flush the youth's cheeks. The youth snapped something back, to which Doroga replied with an unmistakable negative slash of his hand, together with the word, "*Gnah.*"

The youth thrust up his chin defiantly, snapped something in terse terms, and darted out of the tent, past Doroga's reach, moving as quickly as a frightened squirrel.

Doroga lifted a hand and rubbed at the side of his face with it, then faced Tavi and Fade. The Marat studied them both with his dark eyes and grunted. "My apologies for the behavior of my whelp, Kitai. I am called Doroga. I am the headman of the *Sabot-ha*. Of the Gargant Clan. You are Alerans and my prisoners. You are the enemy of the Marat, and we will partake of your strength."

Fade whimpered in his throat and clutched at Tavi's arm hard enough to make it go numb.

"You mean," Tavi asked, after a moment's silence, "that you're going to eat us?"

"I do not wish to," Doroga said, "but such is the decree of Clanchief Atsurak." He paused for a moment, eyes focused on Tavi, and said, "Unless this judgment is contested by our laws, you will give your strength to our people. Do you understand?"

Tavi didn't. He shook his head.

Doroga nodded. "Listen to me, valleyboy. We-the-Marat prepare to move against the Alerans of the bridge valley. Our law calls you enemy. No one speaks otherwise. So long as you are enemy of the Marat, you will be our enemy, and we will hunt you and take you." He leaned forward, speaking slowly. "So long as no one speaks otherwise."

Tavi blinked, slowly. "Wait," he said. "What if someone says that I'm not an enemy?"

Doroga smiled, showing his teeth again. "Then," he said, "we must hold trial before The One, and discover who is correct."

"What if I say we're not your enemy?"

Doroga nodded and stepped back out of the tent. "You understand enough. Come outside, valleyboy. Come out before The One."

◇◇◇◇ CHAPTER 26

Tavi glanced back at Fade and then followed Doroga out of the tent and into the blinding light of the first day of winter. Sunlight poured through crystalline skies to blaze over the snow that covered the ground in an almost perfect layer of white. It took Tavi's eyes long seconds to adjust and for him to squint around him as he emerged from the tent, Fade clutching at his arm.

They stood among hundreds of Marat.

Marat men, most of them as heavily built as Doroga, sat at cooking fires or watched casually, hands near the hafts of spears or on chipped-stone daggers or furyforged Aleran blades. Like Doroga, they wore only a brief loincloth, despite the weather, and evinced no signs of discomfort, though some of them wore cloaks of hide and fur that seemed more ornamental or martial than made with the intention of keeping their owners warm or dry. Children ran here and there, dressed in the same long leather tunic Doroga's whelp had worn, and watched the strangers with obvious interest.

To Tavi's astonishment, the women wore nothing more than the men, and lean, muscular legs, naked, strong shoulders and arms, and other things a proper Aleran boy was not supposed to see (but wanted to anyway) abounded. Tavi felt his face flush, and he shielded his eyes furiously, trying to pretend it was still the sun in them.

One of the young warriors nearby made a quiet comment, and that same coughing laughter resounded around the camp, which Tavi saw was arranged down the slope of a long, bald hill. He felt himself flush further, yet, and glanced at Fade. The slave stood beside him, no expression on his face, his eyes somewhat distant— but he put his hand on Tavi's shoulder and squeezed, as though reassuring himself that the boy was there.

Doroga stood, patiently waiting, and then nodded toward the crest of the hill. He started that way himself, clearly expecting to be followed. Tavi glanced around them at the young warriors, who watched him with studied disinterest and fingered their weapons. Tavi moved his eyes to where a couple of older Marat women were chatting to one another and piling up wood beneath a roasting spit. One of them turned to Tavi and squinted at him, holding up a weathered thumb, then compared it to the length of the spit.

Tavi swallowed and hurried up the hill after Doroga, Fade close at hand.

At the top of the hill stood a dozen huge stones the size of a small house, arranged in a loose circle, some leaning upon others. They were rounded, any rough edges filed away by the winds and rains and seasons, but had obdurately resisted the elements, with no cracks apparent in their surfaces.

At the center of the stones was a pool with seven white stones spaced around it. Upon two of the stones sat Marat.

Tavi was struck at once by the difference in their appearance. Doroga, huge and solid, paced around to one of the stones. On the way there, he passed a lean Marat woman, her pale hair shaved on the sides to leave only a long, silky mane atop her head. She, too, wore only a loincloth, though, more than her nakedness, Tavi noted an Aleran cavalry saber riding a Legion-issue belt at her hip, and three badges, tarnished silver falcons, which spangled the belt. Her skin was shades darker than most of the Marat and seemed weathered and tough, and her dark eyes were cool, appraising. As Doroga passed her, she lifted a hand, and the Chief of the Gargant Clan lightly rapped his knuckles against hers.

Doroga settled on the next rock, folded his hands, and glowered at the third Marat on the hilltop.

Tavi turned his attention to him. The man was of moderate height and lean build. His hair, though Marat-pale, grew in a wild, bristling mane that fell to his shoulders and continued to sprout from his skin down past his ears and along the lines of his jaw. His eyes were an odd shade of pale grey, almost silver, and he held himself with a slow, restless tension. The Marat caught Tavi looking at him and narrowed his eyes, baring his teeth. Tavi blinked to see huge, ripping canines, more properly called fangs, in the Marat's mouth. A snarl bubbled from his throat, and the man half-rose from his stone.

Doroga rose and spat, "Will the headman of the *Drahga-ha* defile the peace of the *horto*?"

The fang-toothed Marat glared from Tavi to Doroga. His voice came out as a bubbling growl, low, harsh, hardly understandable. *Could a wolf speak,* Tavi thought, *it would sound like this.* "The headman of the *Sabot-ha* has already defiled its sanctity with these outsiders."

Doroga smiled. "The *horto* welcomes all who come in peace." His smile widened a touch. "Though perhaps I am mistaken. Do you believe that this is the case, Skagara?"

The woman said, without rising, "I believe he thinks you mistaken, Doroga."

Skagara snarled toward the woman, his eyes flickering warily between her and Doroga. "Stay out of this, Hashat. I need neither you nor the *Kevras-ha* to tell me what I believe."

Doroga rolled a pace toward Skagara. The big Marat flexed his hands with an ominous crackling of knuckles. "This is between you and I, Wolf. Do you believe me mistaken?"

Skagara lifted his lips away from his teeth again, and there was a long and tense silence on the hill. At the end of it, he let out a spiteful growl and looked away from Doroga. "There is no need to bring this matter before The One."

"Enough, then," Doroga said. He continued staring at the other man and settled slowly back down onto his stone. Skagara mirrored him. Doroga then murmured, "We come before The One at this *horto*." He turned his face up toward the sun, eyes closing, and murmured something in his own tongue. The other two Marat did the same, speaking in a pair of distinct-sounding languages. Silence reigned on the hilltop for the space of a score of heartbeats, and then the Marat together lowered their eyes again.

"I am called Doroga, headman of the *Sabot-ha,* the Gargant Clan," Tavi's captor said in formal tones.

"I am called Hashat, headman of the *Kevras-ha,* the Horse Clan," stated the woman.

"I am called Skagara, headman of the *Drahga-ha,* the Wolf Clan." Skagara rose, impatiently. "I see no need for this *horto.* We have captive enemies among us. Let us partake of their strength and go to battle."

Doroga nodded soberly. "Yes. These are our enemies. So has spoken Atsurak of the *Sishkrak-ha.*" He turned his face to Tavi. "And none have spoken against him."

Tavi swallowed and stepped forward. His voice shook, but he forced the words out, and they rang out with clarion strength among the great stones on the hilltop.

"I am called Tavi, of Bernardholt, in the bridge valley. And I say that we are no enemies of the Marat."

There was a startled silence for the space of a breath, there at the hilltop. And then Skagara leapt to his feet with a howl of rage. From down the hill came the sudden angry shouts from dozens of throats, male and female alike, overridden by a chorus of the deep, ringing howls of direwolves.

Doroga came to his feet at the same time, eyes blazing, and though he remained silent, the sudden basso bellows of dozens of gargants rolled like thunder through the winter sky, in tandem with the more distant screams of uncounted horses.

Marat sprinted to the stones at the hilltop, though none of them stepped within their circle, pressing close, eyes wide and excited, gripping weapons, crowding to get close to see—and even so, they split themselves into three separate groups: slab-shouldered, heavily muscled Marat of Clan Gargant; Clan Wolf, silent and fang-toothed and hungry-looking; and Clan Horse, tall and lean with their hair shaved into wind-tossed white manes. The isolated hilltop transformed into the center of a seething mob, excited murmurs, brandished weapons, and threatening glances. Tension and violence rode on the air like leashed lightning, pent-up and straining for release.

Doroga moved then, standing atop his stone, and held his arms above his head. "Silence!" he roared, and his voice smothered sound atop the hill. "Silence, on the *horto*! Silence as a question is brought before The One!"

Tavi stared around him at the reaction his words had caused and discovered that he had turned and pressed his back to Fade. His limbs shook with reaction. Glancing over his shoulder, he saw that Fade had assumed that same distant expression as before, eyes focused on nothing, though he had clasped one arm across Tavi's chest, fingers gripping the opposite shoulder steadily.

"Fade," Tavi whispered. "Are you all right?"

"Quiet, Tavi," Fade whispered back. "Do not move."

Silence stretched over the hill, the sound of moaning wind the only noise. From the corner of his eye, Tavi could see Skagara, crouched before his stone, staring at Tavi with something very like hatred. Some instinct warned Tavi not to make eye contact, that it would only set the Marat into a killing rage—and that all of Clan Wolf would follow their headman, turning the ring of stones into a blood-spattered slaughterhouse.

Tavi did not move. He barely breathed.

"We-the-Marat," Doroga said, turning in a slow circle. "We are the One-and-Many people, under The One. We prepare to march against the Alerans. We go to war at the words of Atsurak of the *Sishkrak-ha*. Atsurak the Bloody." His words spat the next words, and Tavi heard the insolent contempt in them. "Atsurak the Whelpkiller."

Snarls bubbled in the throats of dozens of Marat Wolves on the hilltop, and once again came the low, harsh howls of direwolves from somewhere down the slope and out of sight.

Doroga turned to face Clan Wolf without turning away from them, no trace of fear showing in his face. "Our law gives him that right, if none step forward to call him mistaken. To call him to the Trial of Blood." His finger swung to point at Tavi. "This Aleran calls Atsurak mistaken. This Aleran says that his people are no enemy of the Clans."

"He is *not* of the Clans," Skagara snarled. "He has no voice here."

"He stands accused with his people," Doroga shot back. "And the accused have a voice at the *horto*."

"Only if the headmen of the Clans decide that they do," said Skagara. "I say he does not. You say he does." He narrowed his eyes and stared at Hashat. "What says Clan Horse?"

Hashat only then unfolded from her relaxed slouch on her stone, rising and facing Skagara without speaking for a moment, the wind tossing her mane out to the side like a banner. Then she turned, took a step into Doroga's shadow, and folded her arms. "Let the boy speak."

Excited murmurs ran through the Marat atop the hill.

"Fade," Tavi whispered. "What is happening?"

Fade shook his head. "Don't know. Careful."

Doroga turned to Tavi and said, "Speak your belief, valleyboy. Bring it out before The One."

Tavi swallowed. He glanced back at Fade and then slipped away from the slave, standing as straight as he could manage. He looked around the circle, at the Marat all staring at him with expressions of curiosity, contempt, hatred, or hope. "M-my people," he began, and choked, coughing, his stomach fluttering so nervously that he abruptly became certain he was going to sick up again.

"Hah," spat Skagara. "Look at him. Too afraid even to speak. Too afraid to bring what he believes before The One."

Doroga shot the Wolf headman a narrow-eyed glance. Then looked back at Tavi and said, "Valleyboy. If you would speak, now is the time."

Tavi nodded, swallowing a sour taste from his mouth,

and straightened again. "I am not your enemy," he said. His voice broke, and he cleared his throat. This time it came out stronger, ringing clear among the stones again. "I am not your enemy. My people have sought no quarrel with the Marat since before I was born. I don't know who this Atsurak person is—but if he says that we want to hurt your people, he's a liar."

The words rang among the stones and fell on an odd and puzzled silence. Tavi glanced over at Doroga and found the Gargant headman staring at him with his head cocked to one side. "Liar." Doroga frowned, and lowered his voice to a confidential murmur. "I do not believe Atsurak has mated with any of yours. If that is what you mean. He does not lie with Alerans."

"No," Tavi said, nervous flutters coming back into his stomach. "A liar. He's telling lies."

Doroga blinked again. Then nodded, as though in sudden comprehension. He raised his voice again and said, "You believe he speaks mistakenly."

"Yes," Tavi said. "Wait, no! No, a lie is different than a mistake—"

But Tavi's words went unheeded as a shout rose up from the Marat around the hilltop.

Skagara leapt atop his rock and raised his arms for silence. "Let him challenge! Let this Aleran whelp test his beliefs before The One! Let him face the Trial of Blood with Atsurak and end this matter!" Skagara sneered toward Tavi. "Atsurak will split his belly open before he can scream."

"Atsurak is not here," Doroga said, lifting his chin. "I am the eldest headman present. And it is thus my duty to take up the challenge to Atsurak's belief in his place."

Skagara's eyes widened. "Atsurak," he said, "would not approve."

Doroga bared his white teeth. "Atsurak," he repeated, "is not here. I will defend his belief as is proper."

Skagara growled. "As well. The strength of Doroga is well known. He will break the Aleran in the Trial of his Clan, even as Atsurak would do in a Trial of Blood."

"That would be correct," Doroga said, "if I faced the trial myself. This will not happen."

"Only you, I, or Hashat may stand for Atsurak," Skagara snarled.

"Unless," Doroga said, "I invoke the right of my heir to stand in my place in any Trial before The One."

Skagara stared at the Gargant headman in stunned silence.

"Kitai," rumbled Doroga. "Step into the *horto*."

The boy that had cut Tavi before appeared nervously at the head of the crowd—from behind the ranks of Clan Horse, Tavi noted. Doroga saw it as well and scowled. "Get in here, whelp."

Kitai hesitated at the edge of the stones, then hurried inside, steps carrying him lightly over to stand on the ground beside Doroga's stone.

Doroga put his hand on Kitai's shoulder. "In this, I ask you to stand for me. Will you?"

Kitai swallowed and nodded, without speaking.

Skagara snarled. "Then draw the circle. Bare the contestants. Let the spawn of Doroga show the strength of the sire. The Aleran is no match in a Trial of Strength, even for your whelp, Doroga."

"The trial of Clan Gargant is the Trial of Strength," Doroga said. "But Kitai is not yet Bound to a Clan. And the trial of Clan Fox, the Clan of my whelp's mother, is the Trial of Wits. Kitai may accept challenge in either. And I decree that in this the Fox Trial best serves the interest of the Marat."

Hashat frowned at Doroga, as though she didn't fully understand, but she said, "I second Doroga's opinion. Let us bring the question before The One."

"No," Skagara spat. "The Fox Clan is no more."

Doroga spun toward Skagara again and advanced a step on the other man. His hands closed into fists with a rippling crackle of popping knuckles, and his jaws bulged where he clenched them. He came to a stop, across the pool from the Wolf headman, shaking with a visible effort to restrain himself.

"I think," Hashat said, quietly, "that Doroga believes you mistaken, Skagara. I think he wishes to bring the matter before The One in the Blood Trial of the Wolf Clan."

Skagara gave one glance to Hashat and then stumbled back and off of his rock. "I will not forget this, Doroga," he said, voice strained, high. "Atsurak will know how you have perverted our laws for your purposes."

"Get out of my sight," Doroga said in a quiet, dreadful voice.

Skagara retreated, behind an uneasy wall of warriors of Clan Wolf and down off of the hilltop.

Uneasy talk broke out among the Marat watching, but Doroga turned in a circle, speaking to them. "Go back down. Hashat and I will arrange the trial. We will let The One help us decide what path we will walk."

The Marat departed then, peaceably, though there continued to be much talk among them, and though the Wolves seemed to retreat down the hill cautiously, many fangs bared, low growls warning away those who came too near.

A few moments later, Tavi and Fade stood with the three Marat alone. Doroga gave his shoulders a shake and blew out a long breath. "Very well," the Marat said. "Hashat. What do you think is an appropriate trial?"

The Horse headman shrugged her shoulders. "The usual for this *horto*."

Kitai drew in a quick breath.

Doroga grimaced. "You know what I'm trying to do."

"The Wolf is right about one thing. You challenge tradition with this, if not the law. If you stretch things too much, you will lose the support of your own Clan, and mine. Best, I think, if you stay close to tradition wherever you can now."

Doroga looked at Tavi, then at Kitai. "Are they old enough?"

Tavi stepped forward. "Wait just one second, here. I did what you said you wanted me to do, Doroga. What have I gotten myself into?"

Hashat turned to Tavi. "Aleran. You are alive, and not a meal. For that, you should give your thanks to Doroga, and be silent."

Tavi snapped, "I don't think so. This place almost exploded today. I'm being used. I think it's polite to at least tell me how. And why."

Hashat narrowed her eyes and laid a hand on the hilt of her saber, but Doroga shook his head. "No. He is correct." Doroga moved back to his stone and sat down, heavily. "Valleyboy, you have agreed to a Trial of Wits with Kitai. The victor in the trial will be considered to hold the favor of The One in the question you raised."

Tavi frowned. "You mean, if I win, then I'm right, and my people are not the enemy of the Marat."

Doroga grunted assent. "And my Clan, and Hashat's, will refuse the leadership of Atsurak, who moves against your people."

Tavi's eyes widened. "You're kidding me. Half the Marat horde just vanishes? Just like that?" He turned to look at Fade, his heart beginning to pound. "Fade, did you hear?"

"You haven't won the trial," Kitai said, spitting the words. "Nor will you."

Doroga frowned at his whelp and then said to Tavi, "It is my wish that you should win. I can take my people from this conflict. But it may not be the desire of The One."

"I know it isn't mine," Kitai said. The young Marat nodded to his father and then said to Hashat, "Is your offer still open?"

The Horse headman glanced at Doroga. Then nodded to Kitai. "Of course."

Kitai nodded at that and then stepped close to Tavi, multicolored eyes narrowed. "Wits or strength, it doesn't matter to me, Aleran. I will beat you." Then he shot Doroga an angry glance and stalked off down the hill.

Tavi blinked. "But . . . I would have thought he'd want to help you." He glanced at Doroga.

The Marat shrugged. "My whelp will try to defeat you. As it should be. It is a good trial before The One."

"But . . ." Tavi swallowed. "Trial of Wits? What is it?"

Doroga said to Hashat, "See to it that they are prepared." Then he turned and walked down the hill after his whelp.

Hashat folded her arms over her chest and eyed Tavi.

"Well?" Tavi asked. "What am I supposed to do?"

"You will leave this night, to return with the Blessing of Night from the Valley of Trees," Hashat said, simply. "Who returns with it first is the victor of the trial. Follow me." The Marat started off down the hill, lean legs taking long steps.

"Blessing of Night, Valley of Trees. Right, fine." Tavi turned to follow her, but stopped as Fade caught at his shirt. Tavi turned to the man, frowning. "What is it?"

"Tavi," Fade said. "You must not do this. Let me face the trial."

Tavi blinked. "Uh. Fade. It's a Trial of Wits, remember?"

Fade shook his head. "Valley of Trees. Remember that."

The boy frowned, turning to Fade. "What do you remember?"

"It is what the Marat call the Wax Forest." Fade looked past Tavi to the retreating Hashat, his scarred face haunted. "One of you will surely die."

᎒᎒᎒᎒CHAPTER 27

Fidelias stopped, panting, as he and Aldrick emerged from the heavily forested regions northeast of Bernardholt and reached the causeway that led down the Valley and ultimately to Garrison. His feet, though he had wrapped them in strips of his cloak and urged his furies to ease his way, had worsened. The pain alone was nearly enough to stop him, even without the fatigue from too long spent walking, casting back and forth in a fruitless effort to catch the wily Steadholder.

Fidelias sank onto a flat stone beside the causeway, while the swordsman paced restlessly out onto the road. "I don't get it," he said. "Why don't you just zoom us along like before?"

"Because we haven't been on a road," Fidelias said from between clenched teeth. "Riding an earthwave along a road is simple. Using one in the open countryside, without intimate knowledge of the local furies is suicide."

"So he can do it, but you can't."

Fidelias suppressed a sharp comment. "Yes, Aldrick."

"We're crowbait."

Fidelias shook his head. "We're not going to catch him at this rate. He left a half dozen false trails behind him and waited until we bought one of them before he raised his wave and went."

"If we had the horses—"

"We don't," Fidelias said bluntly. He lifted his foot and unwrapped some of the cloth.

Aldrick paced over to him. He stared down at his feet and swore. "Crows, old man. Can you feel them?"

"Yes."

Aldrick knelt and unwrapped a bit more of the cloth, assessing the injuries. "Getting worse. There's more swelling. If you let this go, you're going to lose them."

Fidelias grunted. "There's still time. We need to—" Fidelias looked up to see Etan dancing frantically in the nearest tree. He cast his eyes down the road west of them. "Aldrick," Fidelias said, keeping his voice low. "Two men on the road coming toward us. Legion haircuts, both armed."

Aldrick drew in a breath, closing his eyes for a moment, "All right. *Legionares?*"

"No uniforms."

"Age?"

"Young." Fidelias touched the stones of the road with one foot, reaching out for Vamma. "Using the road to help them run. Moving fast. They've got some training in warcrafting."

"How do we do it?"

"Wait for me to say," Fidelias said. "Let's find out whatever we can first." He watched the pair of young men come running toward them along the road and managed a pained smile as they approached and slowed their pace. "Morning, boys," he called. "Have you got a minute to help a couple of travelers?"

The young men slowed, and Fidelias took in the details as they came closer. Young, both of them—less than a score of years of age. Both were slender, though one was tall and already seemed to be losing his hair to a receding hairline. They shared similar long, lean features—brothers, perhaps. Both were panting, though not heavily, from their run along the road. Fidelias tried to smile again and offered them his water flask.

"Sir," panted the taller of the young men, accepting the flask. "Much obliged."

"You hurt?" asked the shorter. He leaned a bit closer, peering at Fidelias's feet. "Crows. You've really gotten them torn up."

"The storm forced us off the road last night," Fidelias said. "There was a flood, and I had to kick my shoes off to swim. Been walking without them all morning, but I had to stop."

The young man winced. "I'll bet." He accepted the flask from his brother with a nod, took a quick drink, and offered it back to Fidelias. "Sir," he said, "maybe you'd better get off the road. I'm not sure it's safe here."

Fidelias glanced at Aldrick, who nodded and made himself look busy redressing Fidelias's injured foot. "Why do you say that, son?"

The taller of the pair answered. "There's been problems in the Valley, sir. Last night there was a big uprising of furies—local furies from holders, that is. And my youngest brother spotted what he swears was a Marat scout by our steadholt—that would be Warnerholt, sir."

"A Marat?" Fidelias gave the young man a skeptical smile. "Surely your brother was having some fun at your expense."

The Warnerholter shook his head. "Regardless, there's been trouble in the Valley, sir. Me and my brothers came home to help my father with a local matter, and it got out of hand. There was a fight, almost some killings. And we saw smoke coming from out east, near Aldoholt. Put together with last night, and this sighting, we decided it would be best to put the word out."

Fidelias blinked. "My. So you're off to warn Garrison of trouble?"

The young man nodded, grimly. "Head back down the road the way we came a piece, and look for a trail to the south. It will take you to Bernardholt. We'd best not stay here, if you'll pardon us, sir. Sorry we can't help you."

"That's all right," Fidelias assured him. "We all have a duty to do, son." He frowned, staring at the younger of the two for a moment.

"Sir?" the young man asked.

"You're about my height, aren't you?"

Aldrick wiped the blood from his blade and said, "You could at least wait until he's dead."

Fidelias pulled the second boot from the shorter of the two men and sat down to pull them over his battered feet. "I don't have time."

"I'm not sure that was necessary, Fidelias," Aldrick said. "If word is out, it's out. Doesn't seem to be much sense in killing them."

"I didn't think you'd mind," Fidelias said.

"I'm good at killing. Doesn't mean I enjoy it."

"Every man enjoys doing what he's good at." Fidelias tightened the laces as much as he could, wincing in pain. "It was necessary. We have to stop anyone else from getting word to Garrison, or out the other end of the Valley, either."

"But that Steadholder has already got through."

"He's only one man, one report. The local Count won't want to commit everything based on that. It will buy us time. If we can keep anything else from getting through, we'll make sure that Garrison is off guard. Is he dead?"

Aldrick stooped over the barefooted boy for a moment. "He's gone. You want me to signal the men?"

"Yes." Fidelias stood up, testing his weight on his feet. They hurt, they hurt abominably, but the boots were a tolerable fit. They'd hold together long enough. "And we'll have to get in touch with Atsurak again. Things are falling apart. We can't afford to wait any longer."

Fidelias stepped over the bodies of the young men of Warnerholt and glanced over his shoulder at the swordsman. "I'm starting the attack now."

◇◇◇◇CHAPTER 28

Kord forced Isana to watch what they did to Odiana.

He had brought in a stool with him, and he sat behind her, within the ring of coals. He made her sit on the floor in front of him, so that they could both see, as though it was some sort of theater event.

"She's a tough one," Kord said, after a long and sickening time. "Knows what she's doing. Survivor."

Isana suppressed the sickness in her stomach, long enough to say, "Why do you say that?" Anything to take her mind from what was happening.

"She's calculated. There, see how she fights? Just enough to get a man worked up. Then goes all liquid and helpless once he's on her. She knows every man wants to think he's got that kind of power over a woman. She makes them think what she wants to—and she's barely been roughed up at all."

Isana shuddered and said nothing.

"It's tough to break someone like that. Hardened."

"She's a woman, Kord. A person. She's not an animal to be broken."

His voice carried something in it of an ugly smile. "Has she been a slave before?"

"I don't know," Isana said. "I barely know her."

"She saved your life, you know," Kord said. "When we found you by the river. I made her do it."

Isana looked back at him and tried to keep the venom from her voice. "Why, Kord?"

"Don't get me wrong, Isana. It isn't that I don't enjoy the thought of you dead. I could be happy with that." His eyes didn't waver from the scene before them, glittering with something dark, angry, alien. "But my son is dead because of you. And that mandates something more substantial."

"Dead?" Isana said. She blinked slowly. "Kord. You have got to understand. This isn't about you. It isn't about the hearing or Warner's daughter—"

"The crows it isn't," Kord said. "Because of you we had to go to Bernardholt. Because of you, we had to run out into the storm. Because of you, we had to watch and make sure no one went running to Gram for help—and sure enough, that little freak of yours did. Because of you, Bittan died." He looked down at her, showing his teeth. "Well now I'm the strong one. Now I'm the one making the rules. And I'm going to show you, Isana, how low a woman can be brought. Before I finish what the river started."

Isana turned to him. "Kord, don't you understand? We could all be in danger. Bernard saw—"

He struck her with a closed fist. The blow drove her back and to the floor, her body helplessly loose and unresponsive. After a disorienting moment, the pain started, rippling up from her mouth, her cheek. She tasted blood on her tongue, where she'd cut herself on her own teeth.

Kord leaned down and seized her hair, jerking her face up to his. "Don't speak to me like you're some kind of person. You aren't anymore. You're just meat now." He gave her head a vicious little shake. "You understand that?"

"I understand," Isana grated, "that you're a little man, Kord." She dragged in a breath, enough to make the words cut. "You can't look past yourself. Not even when something is coming to crush you. You're small. No matter what you do to me, you'll still be small. A coward who hurts slaves because he's afraid to challenge anyone stronger." She met his eyes and whispered, "You've got me because you found me helpless. You'd never be able to do anything to me if you hadn't. Because you're nothing."

Kord's eyes flashed. He snarled, a mindlessly animal sound, and hit her again, harder. Stars flew across her vision, and the dusty floor rose up to meet her.

She wasn't sure how long she lay there, pain and thirst blinding her, making her unaware of anything else. But when she came to her senses again and sat up, only Kord and his son, Aric, remained. Odiana lay in a heap on the floor, not far away, curled onto her side, her legs drawn up, her hair hiding her face.

Kord tossed a flask down beside Isana. It made a soft, slight gurgling sound, as though it held only a tiny bit of water. "Go ahead," he told her. "Nothing in that one. I want you to see what happens."

Isana took up the flask, throat burning. She didn't believe that Kord had told her the truth, but she felt faint, weak, and her throat felt as though it had been coated with salt. She pulled the cap from it and drank, almost before she realized what she was doing. Water, warm, but untainted, flowed into her mouth. Half a cup, perhaps—certainly no more. It was gone before it had done much to help her thirst, but at least it had eased the maddening ache of it. She lowered the flask, looking up at Kord.

"Aric," Kord said. "Bring me the box."

Aric turned toward the door, but hesitated. "Pa. Maybe she's right. I mean, with what Tavi said at the river and all—"

"Boy," Kord snarled, cutting him off. "You bring me that box. And keep your mouth shut. You hear?"

Aric went pale and swallowed. "Yes, Pa." He turned and vanished from the smokehouse.

Kord turned back to her. "The thing about all of this, Isana, is that you're too naive to be as afraid as you should be. I want to help you with that. I want you to know what's going to happen."

"This is useless, Kord," Isana said. "You might as well kill me."

"When I'm ready." Kord walked over to Odiana, then reached down and seized her casually by the hair. The woman whimpered and twisted her shoulders, struggling feebly to get away from him. Kord gathered her hair up, lock by lock, until he held the length of it in his fist. "See, this one here. She's a hard case. Knows what she's doing. Knows the game. How to survive it." He shook her hair, eliciting a whimper. "All the right sounds to make. Right, girl?"

With Odiana's face bowed, facing away from Kord, Isana could see her expression now. The water witch's eyes were hard, her expression cold, distant. But she kept her voice weak, shaking. "P-please," Odiana whispered. "Master. Don't hurt me. Please. I'll do anything you want."

"That's right," Kord rumbled, smiling down at the woman. "You will."

Aric opened the door and entered, carrying a long, flat box of smooth, polished wood.

"Open it," Kord told him. "Let her see."

Aric swallowed. Then he paced around, in front of where Kord held Odiana by the hair, and opened the box.

Isana saw the contents: a strip of metal, a band perhaps an inch wide, lay on the cloth within the box, dully throwing back the light of the fires.

Odiana's expression changed. The hardness vanished from her eyes, and her mouth dropped open in an expression of something close to horror. She recoiled from the box, but was brought up short by Kord's grip on her. Isana heard her let out a whimper of pain and, unmistakably, of fear. "No," she said, at once, her voice suddenly harsher, high, panicky. "No, I don't need that. You won't need it. No, don't, I promise, you won't need it, just tell me what you *want*."

"It's called a discipline collar," Kord said to Isana, in a conversational voice. "Furycrafted. They're uncommon this far north. But useful, sometimes. She knows what it is, I think."

"You don't need it," Odiana said, her voice high and desperate. "Please, oh furies, please, master, you don't need that, I don't need it, no, no, no, no—"

"Aric, put it on her." Kord jerked Odiana up, holding her weight up off the floor by her hair, forcing her chin up, the slender strength of her throat to be exposed.

Odiana's eyes, still fastened on the collar, widened, white surrounding them. She screamed. It was a horrible sound, one that welled deep in her throat and rose up through her mouth without regard for meaning, for shape, horrible and feral. She turned and struggled, even as she screamed, her hands reaching toward Kord's face with desperate speed. Her nails left bloody weals down one of his cheeks, and even as she got her feet underneath her, she kicked one bare foot at the inside of his knee.

Still holding her hair in one hand, Kord dragged her to one side, off of her feet, and with the other clutched her throat. Then, with a casual surge of power, doubtless drawn from his fury, he lifted her clear of the ground by her throat, so that her feet dangled and kicked below her torn skirts.

She fought him, even so, struggling wildly against him. She raked at his arm with her nails when she couldn't reach his face, but he held her, expression never changing. She kicked at his thigh, his ribs, but without any leverage the blows did nothing to deter the big Steadholder. She struggled, grunting, gasping, making low, animal sounds of fear.

Then her eyes rolled back in her skull and she went slowly limp.

Kord held her suspended for a moment more, before he lowered her to the floor again, and once more held her by the hair, baring her throat. "Aric."

The young man swallowed. He flicked a glance at Isana, his expression strained, difficult to read. Then he stepped forward and slipped the metal band about Odiana's throat. It settled into place with a quiet, sharp click.

She took a ragged breath and let out a little groan, a desperate sound, even as Kord released her hair with a contemptuous jerk. She fell onto her side, her eyes clutched closed, and lifted her fingers to her throat. She began pawing and jerking at the collar, desperate and clumsy.

Kord drew a knife from his belt and pricked his thumb with it, then grabbed Odiana's wrist in his huge hands and did the same to hers. Her eyes opened and saw him, and once again she went wild, letting out a little shriek and struggling against him with a confused and disoriented determination.

Kord smirked. With casual strength, he forced her bloodied thumb to the collar—and then pressed his own down beside it, scarlet marking the metal.

Odiana whimpered, "*No,*" frustration warping the word, tears making her eyes shine. Then she shuddered. Her lips moved again, but nothing intelligible came from them. She shuddered again, and her eyes lost focus. Her body relaxed, the straining against Kord's hands easing slowly away. Once more, her body shook, this time accompanying it was a low gasp.

"Bonding," Kord said, looking up at Isana. His eyes glittered. His hands roved over the woman on the ground now, casually intimate, possessive. "This will take a few minutes to set in."

Odiana gasped, arching into Kord's touch, her eyes empty, lips parted, her body moving in a slow, languid roll, all hips and back and bared throat. The collar gleamed against her skin. Kord sat over her, petting the woman like an overexcited animal. In a few moments, she was making soft, cooing sounds, curling toward him like a sleepy kitten.

"There." He stood up and said, casually, "That's a good girl."

Odiana's eyes flew open wide, then fluttered slowly closed again. She gasped, clutching her arms to her chest as though to hold something in, and for perhaps half a minute she writhed that way, letting out soft moans of unmistakable pleasure.

Kord smiled. He looked at Isana and said, quietly, "Stupid little whore."

Odiana's body convulsed, back abruptly arching into a bow. She let out another scream—this one thin, high, somehow sickened—and flung herself onto her side. She retched, violently, though there was little enough content in her stomach to come up onto the dusty floor. Her legs and arms jerked in frantic spasm, and she lifted huge, desperate eyes to Isana, her expression agonized, pleading. She reached toward the collar at her throat and spasmed again, more violently, thrashing and flailing and rolling dangerously close to the circle of coals.

Isana stared at the woman in horrified confusion for a breath, before she lurched forward, unsteady herself, and caught Odiana before she could convulse into the ring of coals. "Stop it," Isana cried. She looked back at Kord, knew that her face was pale and desperately afraid—and saw the glitter of satisfaction in his expression when she turned to him. "Stop it! You're killing her!"

"Might be kinder," Kord said. "She's been broken before." But to Odiana he said, voice smug, "Good girl. Stay here and you'll be a good girl. Do what you're told."

The frantic spasms eased out of the woman, very slowly. Isana drew her back away from the coals and kept her arms around her, her body between Odiana and Kord. The woman's eyes had lost focus again, and she shuddered in slow waves in Isana's arms.

"What did you do to her?" Isana asked quietly.

Kord turned and walked toward the door. "What you need to learn is that slaves are just animals. You train an animal by providing rewards and punishments. Rewarding good behavior. Punishing bad. That's how you turn a wild horse into an obedient mount. How you train a wolf into a hunting hound." He opened the door and said, casually, "Same with slaves. You're just more animals. To be used for labor, breeding, whatever. You just have to be trained." Kord left the smokehouse, but his words drifted back to them. "Aric. Build up the fire. Isana. You'll wear one tomorrow. Think about that."

Isana said nothing, stunned by what she had seen, by Odiana's reaction to the sight of the collar, to her condition now. Isana looked down at her and brushed some of the dark, tangled hair from her eyes. "Are you all right?"

The woman looked up at her, eyes heavy and languid, and shivered. "It's good now. It's good. I'm good now."

Isana swallowed. "He hurt you, before. When he called you . . ." She didn't say the words.

"Hurts," Odiana whispered. "Yes. Oh crows and furies, so much hurt. I'd forgotten. Forgotten how bad it was." She shivered again. "H-how good it was." She opened her eyes, and again they were wet with tears. "They can change you. You can fight and fight, but they *change* you. Make you happy to be what they want.

Make it hurt when you try to resist. You *change*, holdgirl. He can do it to you. He can make you beg him to take you. To touch you. Make you." She turned her face away, though her body was still wracked with the long, shivering shudders of pleasure, and turned her face from Isana. "Please. Please kill me before he comes back. I can't be that again. I can't go back."

"Shhhh," Isana said, rocking the woman gently. "Shhhh. Rest. You should sleep."

"Please," she whispered, but her face had already gone slack, her body begun to sag. "Please." She shuddered once more and then went completely limp, her head falling to one side.

Isana laid the woman down as gently as she could. She knelt over her, testing her pulse, putting a hand to her forehead. Her heart still beat too quickly, and her skin felt fevered, dry.

Isana looked up, to where Aric stood next to a hod for coal, watching her. When she looked up at him, he ducked his head, turning to the hod, and began to dump coals into a bucket beside it.

"She needs water," Isana said, quietly. "After all of that. She needs water, or she'll die in this heat."

Aric looked at her again. He picked up the bucket and, without speaking, walked to one side of the ring and started shaking fresh coals out of it and into the fire.

Isana ground her teeth with frustration. If she was only able to listen, she might be able to gain important insight. The boy seemed reluctant to follow his father's commands. He might be convinced to help them, if only she could find the right words to say. She felt blind, crippled.

"Aric, listen to me," Isana said. "You can't possibly think he's going to get away with this. You can't possibly think that he will escape justice for what happened tonight?"

He finished dumping out the bucket. He walked back to the hod, his voice toneless. "He's escaped it for years. What do you think happens to every slave who comes through here?"

Isana stared at him for a moment, sickened. "Crows," she whispered. "Aric, please. At least help me get this collar off." She reached down to Odiana's throat, turning the collar about and trying to find the clasp.

"Don't," Aric said, his voice quick, harsh. "Don't, you'll kill her."

Isana's fingers froze. She looked up at him.

Aric chewed on his lip. Then said, "Pa's blood is on it. He's the only one can take it off her."

"How can I help her?"

"You can't," Aric said, his voice frustrated. He turned and threw the bucket at the wall of the smokehouse. It clattered against it and fell to the floor. He leaned his hands against the wall and bowed his head. "You can't help her. The way he's left her, anyone can tell her anything and she'll keep feeling good as long as she does it. She tries to resist and she'll . . . and it will hurt her."

"That's inhuman," Isana said. "Great furies, Aric. How can you let this happen?"

"Shut up," he said. "Just you shut up." Motions stiff, angry, he pushed off the wall and recovered the bucket and started filling it with coal again.

"You were right, you know," Isana said, keeping her voice quiet. "I was telling the truth. So was Tavi, if he told you that the Valley was in danger. That the Marat may be coming again. It could happen soon. It could have begun already. Aric, please, listen to me."

He dumped more coal out onto the fires and returned to gather up more.

"You have to get word out. For your own sake, if not for ours. If the Marat come they'll kill everyone of Kordholt, too."

"You're lying," he told her, not looking at her. "You're just lying. Trying to save your hide."

"I'm not," Isana said. "Aric, you've known me your whole life. When that tree fell on you that Winterfair, I helped you. I helped everyone in the Valley who needed it, and I never asked for anything in return."

Aric added more coal to the fire.

"How can you be a part of this?" she demanded. "You aren't stupid, Aric. How can you do this to other Alerans?"

"How can I not?" Aric said, voice cold. "This is all I have. I don't have a happy steadholt where people take care of each other. I have *this*. Men who no one else would take live here. Women who no one would want to be. He's my blood. Bittan—" He broke off and swallowed. "He was my blood, too. As stupid and mean as he could be, he was my brother."

"I'm sorry," Isana said, and found that she felt it. "I never wanted anyone to get hurt. I hope you know that."

"I know," Aric said. "You heard what happened to Heddy and you wanted what was right to happen. To keep her safe, and girls like her. Crows know they need it, with Pa around like some—" He shook his head.

Isana fell silent for a long moment, staring at the young man, an understanding dawning on her. Then she said, quietly, "It wasn't Bittan that was with Heddy. It was you, Aric."

He didn't look at her. He didn't speak.

"It was you. That's why she was trying to draw her father back from *juris macto* with yours. She wasn't raped."

Aric rubbed at the back of his neck. "We . . . we liked each other. Got together when there was a Meet or a Fair. Her little brother found us. Too young to know what he saw. I got out before he seen who I was. But he went running to her father, and how could she tell him she'd been making time with one of *Kord's* sons." He spat the words with disgust. "She didn't say much, I guess, and her old man made up his own mind what happened."

"Oh, furies," Isana said, sadly. "Aric, why didn't you say anything?"

"Say what?" Aric said, flicking a hard glance at her. "Tell my father that I loved a girl and wanted to marry her. Bring her *here*?" He gestured around the smoke-house with one hand. "Or maybe I should have been all honorable and went to her father. Do you think he would have listened to me? Do you think for a second Warner wouldn't have strangled me where I stood?"

Isana rubbed a shaking hand at her eyes. "I'm sorry. Aric, I'm sorry. We've all . . . known that your father was . . . that he'd gone too far. But we didn't do anything. We didn't know things were this bad at his steadholt."

"Too late for all of that now." Aric dropped the bucket and headed for the door.

"It's not," Isana said. "Wait. Just listen to me, Aric. Please."

He stopped, his back still to her.

"You know him," she said. "He'll kill us. But if you help us get out, I'll help you, I swear by all the furies. I'll help you get away if you want to. I'll help you settle things with Warner. If you do love the girl, you might be able to be with her if you do the right thing."

"Help both of you? That woman was trying to kill you last night." He looked back at her. "Why would you help her?"

"I wouldn't leave any woman here, Aric," Isana said, voice quiet, calm. "I wouldn't leave anyone to him. Not anymore. I won't let him keep doing this."

"You can't stop him." Aric's voice was tired. "You can't. Not here. He's a Citizen."

"That's right. And so is my brother. Bernard will call him to *juris macto*. And he'll win, too. We both know that." She stood up, facing Aric, and lifted her chin. "Break the circle. Bring me water. Help us escape."

There was silence for a long moment.

"He'd kill me," Aric said then, his voice numb. "He's said so before. I believe him. Bittan was his favorite. He'd kill me, and he'd get the whole story, and he'd get Heddy, too."

"Not if we stop him. Aric, it doesn't have to be this way. Help me. Let me help you."

"I can't," he said. He looked back at her and said, quietly, "Isana, I can't. I'm sorry. I'm sorry for you and for that girl. But he's my only blood. He's a monster. But he's all I have." The young man turned and left, shutting the door to the smokehouse behind him. Isana heard several heavy bolts sliding shut on the outside. Thunder rumbled somewhere in the distance, a growling, sleepy leftover of the previous night's tempest.

Inside the smokehouse, the coals popped and simmered.

Odiana breathed slowly, quietly.

Isana bowed her head, staring at the woman, at the collar about her throat. She remembered Odiana's frantic pleas to kill her.

Isana lifted her hand to her own throat and shivered.

Then she sank back to the ground, her head bowed.

⬦⬦⬦⬦ CHAPTER 29

Amara's ankle burned and ached, and she fought to keep her labored breathing from turning into a panting gasp. Bernard, running through the ice and snow-covered trees several yards ahead of her, reached a small rise and vanished down the other side. She followed him, stumbling at the last pace, and threw herself into the ditch behind the little rise with a crunching of snow and frozen leaves.

Bernard put his hand on her back, steadying her, and lifted a hand to hold it in front of her mouth and block the wisps of vapor escaping with each exhalation. His eyes went distant, and then she felt him pull the veil over them.

Shadows shifted and changed in subtle patterns over her skin, as the trees around them sighed and rustled as though in a wind. The frozen brush did not seem to move so much as to have simply grown into a screen over them, and the sudden scent of earth and crushed plants flooded over them, veiling even that much evidence of their presence.

Only a few seconds later, they heard hoof falls in the forest behind them, and Amara moved enough to peer over the rise at the direction in which they'd come.

"Won't they see our tracks?" she whispered in a rough gasp of breath.

Bernard shook his head, his face drawn, weary. "No," he whispered. "Trees lost some leaves in some places. Grass stirred enough to move the snow in others. And it's all ice, sleet. Shadows are helping hide more."

Amara sank slowly back down behind the rise, frowning at him. "Are you all right?"

"Tired," he said, and closed his eyes. "They're Knights. Their furies are on unfamiliar ground, but they're strong. Starting to have trouble misdirecting them."

"Fidelias has pulled out all the stops if he's started a general hunt for us. That means he'll accelerate the plans for attack as well. How close are we to Garrison?"

"Few hundred yards to the edge of the trees," Bernard said. "Then half a mile of open ground. Anything at this end of the Valley will be able to see us."

"Can you earthwave us across it?"

Bernard shook his head. "Tired."

"Can we run it?"

"Not with your leg," Bernard said. "And with them mounted. They'd just ride us down and spit us."

Amara nodded and waited until the sound of the riders had drifted away from them, off in another direction. "Half a mile. If it comes to that, I might be able to carry us. Those riders are using earth furies, yes?"

Bernard nodded. "Some wood."

"Either way, we'll be away from them in the open and in the air."

"And if they have Knights Aeris with them?"

"I'll just have to be faster," Amara said. She squinted up. "I still haven't seen anyone. It would be a strain to hold position overhead with so little wind, unless they were so high in the air that the clouds were giving them cover—and that would hide us as well."

Bernard shivered and touched the ground with one hand. "Hold on." His voice had a strained note to it, and he let his breath out again a moment later with a low groan in it. "They're close. We can't stay here any longer. The earth is too hard. Difficult to hide us."

"I'm ready," Amara said.

Bernard nodded, opening his eyes, his face set in lines of grim and weary determination. They rose and headed through the woods.

It only took a few moments to get to the end of the trees and to the open ground that led up to Garrison.

The place was a fortress. There, two of the mountains that rose up all around them fell together into an enormous *V*. At the point of the Valley between them lay the grim grey walls of Garrison, stretching across the mouth of the Valley and blocking entry into it from the lands beyond with expansive, grim efficiency. The wall stretched across the mouth of the Valley from the Marat lands beyond, twenty feet high and nearly as thick, all of smooth grey stone, its walls surmounted by parapets and crenelation. The gleaming forms of armored *legionares* stood at regular posts along the wall, draped in cloaks of scarlet and gold, the colors of the High Lord of Riva.

Behind the wall stood the rest of Garrison, a blocky fortress laid out in a Legion square with ten-foot walls, a marching camp constructed of stone rather than of wood and earth. Fewer guards stood on the walls there, though they were not absent. Outbuildings had grown up around the outside of Garrison, impermanent and slapdash structures that nonetheless had somehow managed to acquire the air of solidity that accompanied a small town. The rear gates of Garrison stood open, and the causeway wound across the Valley and up to them. People drifted around, walking briskly from building to building and moving in and out of the gates to the camp proper. Children scampered around in the ice and snow, playing as they always did. Amara could see dogs, horses, a pen of sheep, and the smoke of dozens of fires.

"There's the gate," she said.

"Right," said Bernard. "We head for that. I know the men stationed out here, for the most part. We shouldn't have any trouble getting to Gram. Just remember: Be polite and respectful."

"All right," Amara said, impatient.

"I mean it," Bernard said. "Gram's got a quick temper, and he's more than capable of tossing us into holding cells until he cools off. Don't test him."

"I won't," Amara said. "Can you tell if they're getting any closer to us?"

Bernard shook his head, grimacing.

"Then we go across. Keep your eyes open, and if you

see anyone coming, we'll get into the air." Amara glanced across the plain and swept her eyes across the sky one last time, winced as she put weight on her injured ankle, and started off toward Garrison at a limping lope. Bernard shuffled along several paces behind her, his footsteps heavy.

The run seemed to take forever, and Amara nearly twisted her ankle again, more than once, as she turned her head this way and that, watching for pursuit.

But for all their fear of being ridden down in the open ground, they reached the outbuildings and then the guarded gates to Garrison itself without incident.

A pair of young *legionares* stood on guard at the gates, their expressions bored, heavy cloaks worn against the cold, spears held negligently in gloved hands. One of them was unshaven (strictly against Legion regulations, Amara knew), and the other wore a cloak that did not seem to be of standard Legion issue, either, its fabric finer, its colors unmatched.

"Hold," said the unshaven guard in a flat tone. "State your name and purpose of your visit."

Amara deferred to Bernard, glancing back at the Steadholder.

Bernard frowned at the two men. "Where is Centurion Giraldi?"

The one in the cloak gave Bernard a blank look. "Hey," he said. "Clodhopper. In case you didn't notice, we're the soldiers here—"

"And Citizens," put in the other in a surly tone.

"And Citizens," the guard in the fine cloak said. "So we'll ask the questions, if that's all right with you. State your name and the purpose of your visit."

Bernard narrowed his eyes. "I suppose you boys are new to the Valley. I am Steadholder Bernard, and I am here to see Count Gram."

Both soldiers broke out in snickers.

"Yes, well," the unshaven one said, "The Count is a busy man. He doesn't have time for visiting with every scruffy clodhopper about every little problem that comes up."

Bernard took a deep breath. "I understand that," he said. "Nonetheless, I am well within my rights to request to see him immediately on a matter of urgency to his holdings."

The unshaven guard shrugged. "You aren't a Citizen, clodhopper. You don't have any rights that I know of."

Amara's temper flashed, her patience evaporating. "We do not have time for this," she snapped. She turned to the guard in the fine cloak and said, "Garrison could be in danger of attack. We need to warn Gram about it, and let him react as he thinks fit."

The guards glanced at each other and then at Amara. "Look at that," the unshaven one drawled. "A girl. And here I thought that was just a skinny boy."

His partner leered. "I suppose we could always take off those breeches and find out."

Bernard narrowed his eyes. The Steadholder's fist lashed out, and the young *legionare* in the fine cloak landed in a senseless sprawl on the snow.

His unshaven partner blinked down at the unconscious young man and then up at Bernard. He reached for his spear, but Bernard spoke sharply, and the weapon's haft bowed, then straightened again, writhing out of the guard's reach and bounding away. The guard let out a short shriek and reached for his dagger.

Bernard stepped close to the young man and clutched his wrist, holding his hand at his belt. "Son. Don't be stupid. You'd best go get your superior officer."

"You can't do that," the guard sputtered. "I'll throw you in irons."

"I just did it," Bernard said. "And if you don't want me to do it again, you'll go get your centurion." Then he gave the young man a stiff shove, sending him clattering backward and falling into the snow at the base of the wall.

The guard swallowed and then bolted, running inside.

Amara looked from the guard in the snow to Bernard and asked, "Polite and respectful, eh?"

Bernard's face flushed. "They might be spoiled city boys, but they're Legion, by the furies. They should treat women with more respect." He rubbed at his hair. "And show more respect to a Steadholder, I suppose."

Amara smiled, but didn't say anything. Bernard flushed even brighter and coughed, looking away.

The unshaven guard emerged from the guardhouse with a half-dressed centurion, a young man little older than him. The centurion blinked stupidly at Bernard for a minute, then gave the guard a terse order, before stumbling back into the guardhouse to march off a moment later, still only half-dressed.

Several *legionares* gathered around the gate, and to Bernard's relief he recognized a few of the men from previous visits to Garrison. A few moments later, a grizzled old man dressed in a civilian tunic, but with the bearing and mien of a soldier, came walking briskly out of the gates, wisps of white hair drifting around his bald pate.

"Steadholder Bernard," he said, critically, eyeing the Steadholder. "You don't look so good." He made no particular comment about the condition of the guard lying in the snow, leaning down to rest his fingertips lightly on the young man's temples.

"Healer Harger," Bernard responded. "Did I hit him too hard?"

"Can't hit a head that thick too hard," Harger muttered. Then cackled. "Oh, he'll have a headache when he wakes up. I've been waiting for this to happen."

"New recruits?"

Harger stood up and paid little further attention to the young guard in the snow. "The better part of two whole cohorts down from Riva herself. Citizens' sons, almost all of them. Not enough sense to carry salt in a storm among the whole lot."

Bernard grimaced. "I need to get to Gram. Fast, Harger."

Harger frowned, tilting his head to one side and studying Bernard. "What's happened?"

"Get me to Gram," Bernard said.

Harger shook his head. "Gram's . . . been indisposed."

Amara blinked. "He's sick?"

Harger snorted. "Sick of rich boys who expect to be treated like invalids instead of *legionares,* maybe." He shook his head. "You'll have to talk to his truthfinder, Bernard."

"Olivia? Get her on down here."

"No," Harger said, and grimaced. "Livvie's youngest came to term, and she went back to Riva to help with the birth. Now we've got—"

"Centurion," bawled a high, nasal voice. "What's going on down here? Who is in charge of this gate? What foolishness is this?"

Harger rolled his eyes. "We've got Pluvus Pentius instead. Good luck, Bernard." Harger stooped down and scooped up the unconscious young *legionare*, tossing him over one shoulder with a grunt, and then headed back inside the fort.

Pluvus Pentius turned out to be a slight young man with watery blue eyes and a decided overbite. He wore the crimson and gold of a Rivan officer, though his uniform tended to sag around the shoulders and stretched a bit over the belly. The officer slouched toward them through the snow, squinting in disapproval.

"Now see here," Pluvus said. "I don't know who you people are, but assaulting a soldier on duty is a Realm offense." He drew a sheaf of papers from his tunic and peered at them, flipping through several pages. Then he turned and looked around him. "Yes, here it is, a Realm offense. Centurion? Arrest both of them and see them to the holding cells—"

"Excuse me," Bernard interrupted. "But there's a more important matter at hand, sir. I am Steadholder Bernard, and it is vital that I speak to Count Gram at once."

Pluvus blinked up at them. "Excuse me?"

Bernard repeated himself.

Pluvus frowned. "Highly irregular." He consulted his pages again. "No, I don't think the Count is receiving petitions today. He holds a regular court every week, and all such matters are to be presented to him then, and in writing at least three days ahead of time."

"There's no time for that," Bernard blurted. "It's vital to the safety of this valley that we speak to him at once. You are his truthfinder, aren't you? Surely you can tell that we're being honest with you."

Pluvus froze, peering up at Amara over the pages. He looked from her to Bernard and back. "Are you challenging my authority here, farmer? I assure you that I am fully qualified and can—"

Amara flashed Bernard a warning glance. "Sir, please. We just need to see Gram."

Pluvus drew himself up stiffly, his lips pressed together. "Impossible," he stated flatly. "Court is two days hence, but we have not received a written petition to be filed for that date. Therefore you will have to submit your petition to me in, let's see, no more than six days' time, in order to be received by the Count at next week's court—and that is a matter entirely separate from an assault upon a *legionare*—and a Citizen, at that! Centurion! Take them into custody."

An older soldier with several younger *legionares* behind him stepped forward toward Bernard. "Sir, under the authority vested in me by my rank and at the order of my commanding officer, I place you under arrest. Please surrender your weapons and cease and desist any current furycraftings and accompany me to the holding cells where you will be incarcerated and your case brought before the Count."

Bernard growled and set his jaw. "Fine," he said, and flexed his fists. "Have it your way. Maybe a few more broken heads will get me to see Gram that much faster."

The *legionares* came toward Bernard, but the centurion hesitated, frowning. "Steadholder," he said, carefully. "This shouldn't have to get ugly."

Pluvus rolled his eyes. "Centurion, *arrest* this man and his companion. You have no idea how much paperwork I have to do already. My time is precious."

"Bernard," Amara said, and laid a hand on his shoulder. "Wait."

Bernard faced the oncoming soldiers, his brow darkening, and the ground let out a faint tremble. The soldiers stopped in their tracks, their expressions nervous. "Come on," the big Steadholder growled. "I haven't got all day."

"Get out of my way!" thundered a voice from within the gates. Amara blinked, startled at the tone.

A man in a rumpled and wine-stained shirt thrust his way through the crowd watching the altercation. He wasn't tall, but had a barrel for a chest and a jaw that looked heavy and hard enough to break stones upon, covered by a curling beard of fiery red. His hair, shorn short, was of a similar color, though patchy with batches of grey that made his scalp look like a battleground, with troops in scarlet struggling to hold terrain against a grey-clad foe. His eyes were deep under heavy brows, bloodshot, and angry. He walked barefoot in the snow, and steam curled up from his footprints.

"What in the name of all the furies is going on here?" he demanded voice booming. "Bernard! Flame and thunder, man, what the crows do you think you're doing to my garrison!"

"Oh!" said Pluvus, his pages fluttering nervously. "Sir. I didn't know you were out of bed yet. That is, sir, I didn't know that you'd be up today. I was just taking care of this for you."

The man came to a swaying halt and planted his fists on his hips. He glared at Pluvus and then at Bernard. "Harger woke me out of a perfectly good stupor for this," he snapped. "So it had better be good."

"Yes, sir, I'm sure, that is." Pluvus waved a hand at the centurion. "Arrest them. Go on now. You heard the Count."

"I didn't say to arrest anyone," growled Count Gram, testily. He squinted at Bernard and then at Amara, his gaze sharp, penetrating, for all his bawling and staggering. "Did you get yourself another woman, Bernard? Crows it's about time. I've always said there's nothing wrong with you that a good romp or two wouldn't take care of."

Amara felt her cheeks flush with warmth. "No, sir," she said. "It's not that. The Steadholder helped to see me safely here so that I could warn you."

"Highly irregular," Pluvus stuttered to Gram, pages fluttering.

Gram irritably took the pages from Pluvus's hand and said, "Quit waving these under my nose." There was a bright flash of light and heat, and then fine, black ashes drifted away on the cool wind. Pluvus let out a little yelp of distress.

"Now then," Gram said, dusting his hands. "Warn me. Warn me about what?"

"The Marat," Bernard said. "They're on the move, sir. I think they're coming here."

Gram grunted. He jerked his chin at Amara. "And who are you?"

"Cursor Amara, sir." Amara felt herself lift her chin and met Gram's bloodshot gaze squarely, without flinching.

"Cursor," Gram muttered. He glared at Pluvus. "You were going to arrest one of the First Lord's Cursors?"

Pluvus stammered.

"One of my Steadholders?"

Pluvus stuttered.

"Bah," growled Gram. "Ninny. Bring the garrison to full alert, recall all soldiers on leave, and instruct every man to get into his armor and fighting gear, now."

Pluvus stared, but Gram had already swept back around to Bernard. "How bad are you thinking it's going to be?"

"Send word to Riva," Bernard said, quietly.

Gram clenched his jaw. "You want me to call for a full mobilization? Is that what I'm hearing?"

"Yes."

"Do you know what kind of fire is going to fall on my ears if you're wrong?"

Bernard nodded.

Gram growled, "Scouts. Deploy scouts and reconnaissance into the wilderness and make immediate contact with our watchtowers."

"Y-yes, sir," Pluvus said.

Gram stared at him for a second. Then roared, "Now!"

Pluvus jumped and then turned to the nearest soldier and started repeating versions of Gram's orders.

Gram rounded on Bernard. "Now then. I think you'd better explain what kind of idiot you are. Hitting one of *my* soldiers."

A gliding caress of cold air slid over the back of Amara's neck and made her shiver—a warning from Cirrus. She glanced behind her, out toward the blinding white of pale sunlight on snow and ice. She shaded her eyes, but saw nothing.

Cirrus stirred against her again, another warning.

Amara took a slow breath, focusing on the area behind them.

She almost didn't see through the veil.

There, perhaps no more than ten feet away, was a disturbance in the air, several feet off the ground, a rippling dance of light, like waves rising from a sun-heated stone. Her breath caught in her throat, and she sent Cirrus out toward the disturbance with a whispered command. Her fury encountered a globe of dense air, changed to bend light, much as she herself used it to view things from afar in greater clarity.

Amara took a breath and then forced Cirrus against the globe, sudden and quick.

There was a whoosh of expanding air as she dispersed the globe, and abruptly three men in armor with drawn swords appeared, hovering in the air. Amara cried out, and the men, their expressions startled, hesitated for a faltering second before acting.

One flicked himself through the air toward her, sword gleaming. Amara threw herself to one side, sweeping her hands at the man to direct Cirrus. A roar of sudden wind washed up against her attacker's flank, shoving him wide of her, guiding his course into one of Garrison's stone walls. The man tried to slow his advance, but collided hard with the wall, and dropped the blade in the impact.

The second of the men, expression cool, calm, thrust his hands forward, and a gale rose up immediately before the gates of Garrison, whirling snow and chips of ice into the air in a stinging cloud, and hurling *legionares* from their feet, driving them behind the gates for shelter.

The third took his sword in hand and shot toward Bernard's back.

Amara tried to cry out a warning, but Bernard's

fatigue, perhaps, had made him too slow. He turned and tried to dodge to one side, but snow and ice betrayed his footing, and he fell.

Gram stepped in the way. The flame-haired Count jerked the sword from the stunned Pluvus's belt and met the oncoming Knight Aeris head-on. Steel chimed on steel, and then the attacker shot on past Gram.

"Get on your feet!" Gram roared. He spat as the snow and ice clouded his vision. "Get the girl! Get inside the walls!" Gram turned his body against the icy spray and shielded his palm against his side. Amara saw sudden fire kindle there, and Gram turned toward the second of the attackers and hurled a sudden, roaring wall of flame back against the ice and snow. The attacker screamed, a horrible sound, and the gale abruptly vanished.

Something black and heavy fell smoking into the snow before the gates, and the odor of charred meat filled the air.

Amara dashed to Bernard's side, helping the Steadholder to his feet. She didn't see the man who had attacked her until it was almost too late. He rose and drew a knife from his belt, eyes focused on her. With a flick of his wrist, and a sudden pinpoint burst of air, the knife hurtled toward her, whistling with its raw speed.

Bernard saw it, too, and dragged her down, out of the path of the knife.

It hit Gram in the lower back.

Such was the force of the fury-assisted throw that Gram was hurled several paces forward into the snow. He went down at once, without so much as a cry or a gasp of pain, and lay still.

Someone on the walls cried a command, and a pair of

legionares with bows loosed at the man at the base of the wall from almost directly above him. Arrows struck him hard, one in the thigh and one in back of the neck, its bloody tip emerging from the man's throat. He, too, fell into the snow, blood staining a quickly growing scarlet pool around him.

"Where's the other one?" Amara demanded. She stood and swept her eyes over the sky. She barely saw, from the corner of her eye, another flickering of light and air, but when she focused on it, it was gone. Tentatively, she sent Cirrus out toward it, but her fury found nothing, and after questing about aimlessly for a few moments, Amara gave up the effort.

"It's no good," she whispered. "He got away."

Bernard grunted and rose to his feet, one leg held stiffly, his face twisted with pain. "Gram."

They turned to see Pluvus and several *legionares* hovering over Gram's form in the snow. The truthfinder's face was pale. "Healer!" he screamed. "Someone get the healer! The Count is hurt, get the healer!" *Legionares* stood around him, stunned, staring.

Amara let out a hiss of frustration and grabbed the nearest soldier. "You," she said. "Go get the healer, now." The man gave a nod and sprinted off.

"You," Pluvus said, his face twisted with distress, anger, and fear. "I don't know who those men were, or what is going on, but you must be in on it. You came here to hurt the Count. This is your fault."

"Are you mad?" Amara demanded. "Those men were the enemy! You have got to get this garrison ready to fight!"

"You cannot order me about like some kind of

common slave, woman!" shouted Pluvus. "Centurion," he snapped, eyes watering but with his voice ringing with authority. "You all saw what happened. Arrest these two and take them to the cells on charges of murder and treason against the Crown!"

◆◆◆◆CHAPTER 30

Despite her exhaustion, Isana could not sleep.

She spent the night holding Odiana's head in her lap, monitoring the woman's fever, with little else she could do for her. Pale light came through chinks in the walls of the smokehouse, when a grey, winter dawn rose over Kordholt. Isana could hear animals outside, men talking, crude laughter.

Despite the cold air drifting in from without, the interior of the smokehouse remained broiling, the ring of coals around the two women glowing with sullen heat. Her throat, parched before, began to simply ache, agonizing, and at times it felt as though she could not get enough air into her lungs, so that she swayed and had trouble sitting up.

Once, when Odiana tossed restlessly, Isana rose and went to the far side of the ring of coals. Her head spinning with heat and thirst, she gathered her skirts and made to step over the coals, a short leap to the far side—even though she knew the door would be locked and bolted, there might be a loose board in the wall, or something she could use as a weapon in order to make an attempt at escape.

Even as she lifted her foot, though, the ground on the far side of the coals stirred, and the swift, heavy form of Kord's fury rose up from the ground, misshapen and hideous. Isana's breath caught in her throat, and she lowered her foot again.

The malformed fury subsided and sank slowly back into the earth.

Isana clenched her fists in her skirts, frustrated, then moved back over to Odiana and took the woman's head onto her lap again. In her sleep, the collared woman whimpered and stirred languidly, her eyes rolling beneath their lids as she dreamt. Once, she let out a pathetic cry and flinched, and her hands spasmed toward the collar. Even in the woman's dreams, it appeared, Kord's collar continued its assault on her senses, her will. Isana shuddered.

The light waned, shadows shifting over the floor by infinitely slow degrees. Isana let her head fall forward, her eyes closed. Her stomach turned and twisted with worry. Tavi and Bernard and Fade. Where were they? If they were alive, why hadn't Bernard followed her here? Had the ones attacking them been too much for her brother to handle? Bernard would never allow her to remain in Kord's hands—not while he lived.

Could he be dead? Could the boy be dead as well? Surely he had escaped ahead of the flood, surely he had evaded anyone who may have pursued him even after.

Surely.

Isana shook, and gave no voice to the sobs that racked her. No tears would fall. Her body had hoarded back all the moisture it could. She longed for the freedom to weep, at least. But she did not have it. She drifted that way, head bowed, sweltering and dizzy, and thought of Bernard, and of Tavi.

The grey of twilight was in the air when the bolt at the door rattled, and Aric entered. He held a tray in his hands, and he did not lift his face toward Isana. Instead, he walked to the circle of coals and stepped over, setting the tray down.

There were two cups on the tray. Nothing more.

Isana looked steadily up at Aric. He rose and stood there for a moment, shifting his weight from foot to foot, his eyes down. Then he said, "Snow's starting up again. Heavier."

Isana stared at him, and said nothing.

He swallowed and stepped back out of the ring of coals. He went to the hod of coal and began scooping out buckets again, to spread them over the smoldering ring, fresh fuel. "How is she?" he asked.

"Dying," Isana said. "The heat is killing her."

Aric swallowed. He dumped out a bucket of coals onto the ring, spilling some out sloppily, and went for more. "The water's clean, at least. This time."

Isana watched him for a moment and then reached for one of the cups. She lifted it to her mouth and tasted, though it was all she could do not to start gulping frantically. The water was cool, pure. She had to steady herself with a deep breath and hold the cup in both shaking hands. She drank, slowly, giving each sip time to go down.

Isana only allowed herself half the cup. The rest she

gave to Odiana, half hauling the woman into a sitting position and urging her to drink, slowly, which she did with a listless obedience.

She looked up to see Aric watching her, his face pale. Isana lowered the collared woman back down and brushed a few loose strands of hair back from her neck. "What is it, Aric?"

"They're coming tonight," he said. "My father. They're going to finish the . . . Odiana and then put the collar on you."

Isana swallowed and couldn't stop the chill that went down her spine.

"After dinner," Aric said. He slopped more coals down. "It's like a celebration for him. He's handing out wine."

"Aric," Isana said. "It isn't too late to do something."

Aric pressed his lips together. "It is," he said. "There's only one thing left now." Without speaking, he finished carelessly dashing coals onto the ring of fire around them.

Kord's entrance was presaged by a low tremble in the floor of the smokehouse. Then the big Steadholder banged open the door with one fist and stepped inside, glowering. Without a word, he cuffed Aric's head, hard enough to stagger the younger man against the wall. "Where is that tar, boy?"

Aric left his head down, his body held in a crouch, as though expecting to be hit again. "I haven't got it done yet, Pa."

Kord sneered at him, placing his fists on his hips. Isana noticed the drunken sway to his balance as he did. "Then you can just get it done while the rest of us eat. And if you fall off the crows-eaten roof in the dark, that's your own affair. Don't go crying to me about a broken leg."

Aric nodded. "Yes, Pa."

Kord growled something beneath his breath and then turned to Isana. "Better get that other glass of water before my new whore figures out it's there."

Odiana let out a soft noise, curling in on herself. Kord watched her with a smirk on his face. Isana saw the ugly glitter in his eyes as he prepared to speak again, and interrupted him. "Kord. She's nearly dead as it is. Leave her be."

Kord narrowed his eyes at Isana, lips lifting away from his teeth. He took a lurching step closer to her. "Still giving orders," he murmured. "We'll see. Tonight, after I'm done with that one, we'll see what it's like. We'll see who gives the orders and who takes them."

Isana met his eyes steadily, though his words made her heart thud with dull, exhausted fear. "You're a fool, Kord," she said.

"What are you going to do about it, huh? You're nothing. No one. What are you going to do?"

"Nothing," Isana said. "I won't have to. You've already destroyed yourself. It's just a matter of time now."

Kord flushed red and took a step toward Isana, his hands clenching into fists.

"Pa," Aric said. "Pa, she's just talking. She's just try-ing to get to you. It doesn't mean anything."

Kord rounded on Aric and swept his fist at him in a clumsy swat. Aric didn't dodge the blow, so much as he let it catch his shoulder and throw him to the floor.

"You," Kord growled, chest heaving. "You don't tell me. You don't talk to me. Everything you got, you got because I gave it to you. You will not disrespect me, boy."

"No, sir," Aric said, quietly.

Kord got his breathing under control and shot Isana another glare. "Tonight," he said. "We'll see."

The ground shook again as he turned and lumbered out.

Coals sizzled in silence for a few moments. Then Isana turned to Aric and said, "Thank you."

Aric flinched at the words, more than he had from his father's blows. "Don't thank me," he said. "Don't talk to me. Please." He gathered himself to his feet and picked up the bucket. "Still have to lay out the tar. The ice didn't stick to the roof, but I have to tar it tonight or he'll feed me to the crows."

"Aric—" Isana began.

"Be *quiet*," Aric hissed. He shot a glance at the door. Then said, to Isana, "Snow's starting up again."

He left, and bolted the door behind him.

Isana frowned at him, trying to puzzle out his meaning. She took the second cup of water and took a bit more for herself, then gave the rest to the semiconscious Odiana.

Outside, the wind rose. She heard men moving around the steadholt. One of them walked past the smokehouse and banged on the walls, letting out a few crude phrases. Odiana flinched and whimpered. More raucous talk and rough laughter went up from somewhere nearby— probably the steadholt's great hall. What sounded like a fight broke out, ending in cheers and jeers, and all the while it grew darker, until only the red coals gave any light to the smokehouse's interior.

There came a bang against the wall, wood against wood. Then steps. Feet on a ladder. Someone set down a weighty object on the roof, and then hauled himself onto it.

"Aric?" Isana called quietly.

"Shhhh," said the young man. "This is the one other thing."

Isana frowned, staring up. She followed his weight as he moved from the edge of the slightly sloped roof up toward its crown, directly over the circle.

Without warning, the naked blade of a knife sprang through the shingles, dropping bits of tar-stained wood and droplets of water in. The blade twisted, left and right, opening a larger hole. Then it withdrew again.

Aric proceeded around the roof slowly, and Isana could hear him slopping tar from a bucket he must have carried down onto the roof. But every moment or so, the knife would sink in again, opening a small hole between shingles. Then it would withdraw. He repeated the action several times, and then without a word he clambered down from the roof again. His feet crunched through snow and into the night.

It only took a few moments for Isana to realize what Aric had done.

The interior of the smokehouse was smoldering hot, and its heat rose up to the roof above and warmed the materials there. No ice had stuck to the roof the night before, Aric had said, but if the roof hadn't been sealed properly, swelling of the shingles and beams would set in after they had been soaked. They would have to be sealed immediately in order to prevent leaks, especially if the construction had been slipshod to begin with. The roof would require fresh tar consistently to keep it closed against leaks.

Against water.

Droplets began to fall through the holes Aric left with his dagger. Water that pattered to the floor, first in the occasional drop and then, as the snowfall evidently increased, in a small, steady trickle.

Water.

Isana's heart suddenly thudded with excitement, with hope. She leaned forward, across the ring of coals, and caught the nearest trickle of water in one of the empty cups. It filled in perhaps a minute, and Isana lifted it to her mouth and drank, deeply, water coursing into her with a simple, animal pleasure. She filled the cup again and drank, and again, and then gave more to Odiana as well.

The collared woman stirred, at the first cup and then more at the second. Finally, she was able to whisper, "What is happening?"

"A chance," Isana said. "We've been given a chance."

Isana reached across to fill both cups again, as the trickle came down a bit more steadily. She licked her lips and looked around the circle of coals, searching for what she thought would be there. There, where Aric had slopped the coals in a particularly careless fashion. A spot where no fresh coals had landed, and only old, grey, soft-edged coals remained.

Trembling with excitement, Isana reached out and poured the water over the coals. They sizzled and spat. She refilled the glasses and did it again. And a third time. A fourth.

With a final sputtering hiss, the last of the coals went out.

Shaking, Isana caught another cupful of water, and reached out through it for her fury, for Rill.

The cup stirred and quivered, and abruptly Isana felt Rill's presence within the water, a quivering life and motion swirling within it frantically. Isana felt tears springing to her eyes, and a moment later felt Rill gently easing them back from her, felt the fury's affection and relief at being in contact with her again.

Isana looked up to Odiana, who had leaned out to catch another trickle of water in both cupped hands and who had a distant, dreamy smile upon her face. "They're talking about us," Odiana murmured. "So many cups. They're going to use me until the heat has killed me. Then it will be your turn, Isana. I think—" She broke off, suddenly, her back arching with a little gasp—then flung the water away from her, shaking her head and clapping her hands over her ears. "His voice. No, I don't want to hear him. Don't want to *hear* him."

Isana turned to her and caught her by the wrist. "Odiana," she hissed. "We have to get out of here."

The dark-eyed woman stared up at Isana, her eyes wide, and nodded. "I don't know. I don't know if I can."

"The collar?"

She nodded again. "It's hard to think of doing things that wouldn't p-please him. Don't know if I can do them. And if he speaks to me—"

Isana swallowed. Gently, she drew Odiana's hands down from her ears and then placed her own over them. "He shan't," she said, quietly. "Let me."

Odiana's face paled, but she nodded, once.

Isana reached out for Rill and sent the fury down through her touch, into Odiana's body. Rill hesitated, once within, refusing to respond. Isana had to focus with a sharp effort of will before Isana's senses pressed through and into the other woman.

Odiana's emotions nearly overwhelmed her.

Tension. Terrible fear. Rage, frantic and near mindless— all of them trapped beneath a slow and steady pleasure, a languid pulse that radiated out of the collar, threatening at any moment to reverse itself into unspeakable agony. It was like standing within the heart of a storm, emotions and needs spinning past, whirling by, nothing steady, nothing to orient upon. With a slow shudder, Isana realized that Rill had let her touch only lightly upon the water witch's emotions, on the frantic whirl and spill of them in her mind. She realized that Rill had meant to protect her from exposure to what could all too easily spill over into her own thoughts, her own heart.

Isana frantically pushed that storm of the soul away from her, struggled to focus on her purpose. Through the fury, she sought out the other woman's ears, the sensitive eardrums. With a sharp, nearly frantic effort, she altered the pressures of Odiana's body, within her ears. Distantly, Isana heard Odiana let out a pained gasp— and then the drums burst, another explosion of pain and wild emotions—glee and revulsion and impatience predominant.

Isana withdrew her presence from the watercrafter as quickly as she could, jerking her hands and her face away. Even after the contact had been broken, the wild spill of Odiana's emotions remained, flooding over her, against her, making it difficult to think, to focus on the task at hand.

Odiana's voice came to her then, very quiet, very

gentle. "You can't fight it, you know," she half-whispered. "You have to embrace it. One day, they're all going to come in, holdgirl. You have to let it have you. To do otherwise is . . . is mad."

Isana looked up to see the water witch smiling, a smile that stretched her mouth in something near a pained grimace. Isana shook her head and pressed the emotions away from her, fought to clear her thinking. Tavi. Bernard. She had to get free, to get to her family. They would need her help, or at least to know that she was all right. She hugged herself and struggled, and slowly her thoughts began to clear.

"We have to get out of here," Isana said. "I don't know how much more time we have."

Odiana frowned at her. "You've put out my ears, holdgirl. I can't hear you, can I? But if you're saying we should go, I agree."

Isana nodded toward the floor on the far side of the ring of coals. "Kord's fury. It's guarding the floor out there." She gestured and pointed at the ground.

Odiana shook her head, disagreeing. Her eyes fluttered for a moment, and she gasped in a little breath, fingertips moving to touch the collar. "I . . . I'll have all I can do just to go. I can't help you." She bowed her head and said, "Just take my hand. I'll come with you."

Isana shook her head, frustrated. Outside, a door banged open, and Kord's drunken voice bawled, "It's time, ladies!" followed by a hoarse cheer from several throats.

Panicked, Isana rose and took Odiana's hand. She reached out to Rill, sent the fury questing about the roof of the smokehouse, as the men grew closer, gathering up all the liquid water the fury could find. Isana felt it inside her, an instinctive awareness of what was there, of the water in the snow-filled air, the meltwater within the smokehouse and in the ground around it.

Isana felt it and gathered it together in one place and then, with a low cry, released it.

Water flooded down from the roof in a sudden wave that washed over the coals in a swirling ring. The coals spat and hissed furiously, and in seconds the air was filled with thick, broiling hot steam.

Without, there was a cry, and Kord's feet pounded closer. The heavy bolt to the door slid back, and it flew open.

With another flick of her hand, Isana sent the steam boiling out into Kord's face, out to the men behind him. Cries and yowls filled the yard, as men scrambled back from the door.

Isana focused on the ground before them, and at the edge of the now-guttered coals, water condensed from the steam into a shining strip of liquid as wide as a plank. She had never attempted anything like that before. Holding clear in her mind what she wanted Rill to do, Isana took a deep breath and stepped out onto the plank of liquid. There was a tension in it, wavering, but there, and it held her weight without allowing her foot to sink through to the floor.

Isana let out a low cry of triumph and stepped out onto the plank, tugging Odiana by the hand. She led her to the door of the smokehouse and leapt out onto the earth without, Odiana faltering, but staying close.

"Stop!" Kord bellowed, within the cloud of steam. "I order you to stop! Get on the ground, bitch! Get on the ground!"

Isana glanced at Odiana, but the woman's face was distant, her eyes unfocused, and she stumbled along in Isana's wake. If the collar forced a reaction to Kord's voice upon her, she gave no sign of it.

"Rill," Isana hissed. "The nearest stream!" And with an abrupt clarity, Isana felt the lay of the land about them, the subtle tilt down and away from the mountains and toward the middle of the valley, to a tributary that fed, eventually, into one of the streams that ran down through Garrison and into the Sea of Ice.

Isana turned and ran over the cold ground, now using Rill only to help her know the way to the nearest water, to keep her blood running hot through her bare feet to help them resist freezing. She could only hope that Odiana would have the presence of mind to do the same.

Behind them, Kord bellowed to his fury, and the ground to her right erupted with writhing, vicious motion, ice and frozen earth and rocks thrown into the air. Isana swerved her course to run over deeper snow, more thickly crusted ice, and prayed that she would not slip and break her leg. It was only that coating of frozen water that gave her any sort of protection at all from the wrath of Kord's earth fury.

"Kill you!" bellowed Kord's voice behind them, in the dark. "Kill you! Find them, find them and kill them! Bring the hounds!"

Her heart racing with fear, her body alight with excitement and terror, Isana fled into the night from the sounds of mounting pursuit, leading her fellow captive by the hand.

CHAPTER 31

"What do you mean, they missed?" Fidelias snapped. He gritted his teeth and folded his arms, leaning back in the seat within the litter. The Knights Aeris at the poles supported it as it sailed through low clouds and drifting snow, and the cold seemed determined to slowly remove his ears from the sides of his head.

"You really do hate flying, don't you?" Aldrick drawled.

"Just answer the question."

"Marcus reports that the ground team missed stopping the Cursor from reaching Count Gram. The air team saw a target of opportunity and took it, but they were detected before they could attack. The Cursor again. The two men with Marcus were killed in the attack, though he reports that Count Gram was wounded, probably fatally."

"It was a bungled assault from the beginning, not an opportunity. If they weren't forewarned before, they are now."

Aldrick shrugged. "Maybe not. Marcus reports that the Cursor and the Steadholder with her were subsequently arrested and hauled off in chains."

Fidelias tilted his head at Aldrick, frowning. Then, slowly, he started to smile. "Well. That makes me feel a great deal better. Gram wouldn't have arrested one of his own Steadholders without getting the whole story. His truthfinder must be in command now."

Aldrick nodded. "That's what Marcus reports. And according to our sources, the truthfinder is someone with a patron but no talent. House of Pluvus. He's young, no experience, not enough crafting to even do his job, much less to be a threat in the field."

Fidelias nodded. "Mmm."

"Lucky accident, it looks like. There was a veteran that was going to be set out with nearly two cohorts *tertius,* originally, but the paperwork got done incorrectly and they sent out a green unit instead."

"The crows it was an accident," Fidelias murmured. "It took me nearly a week to set it up."

Aldrick stared at him for a moment. "I'm impressed."

Fidelias shrugged. "I only did it to lessen the effectiveness of the garrison. I didn't think it would pay off this well." He wiped a snowflake from his cheek, irritably. "I must be living right."

"Don't get your hopes up too far," the swordsman responded. "If the Marat lose their backbones, all of this will be for nothing."

"That's why we're going out to them," Fidelias said. "Just follow my lead." He leaned forward and called to one of the Knights Aeris, "How much longer?"

The man squinted into the distance for a moment and then called back to him, "Coming down out of the cloud cover now, sir. We should be able to see the fires . . . there."

The litter swept down out of the clouds, and the abrupt return of vision made Fidelias's stomach churn uncomfortably, once he could see how far down the ground was.

And beneath them, spread out over the plains beyond the mountains that shielded the Calderon Valley, were campfires. There were campfires that spread into the night for miles.

"Hungh," Aldrick rumbled. He stared down at the fires, at the forms dimly moving around them for several moments, while they sailed over them. Then turned to Fidelias and said, "I'm not sure I can handle that many."

Fidelias felt the corner of his mouth twitch. "We'll make that the backup plan, then."

The litter glided to earth at the base of a hill that rose up out of the rolling plains. At its top stood a ring of enormous stones, each as big as a house, and within that circle of stones stood a still pool of water, somehow free of the ice that should have covered it. Torches rested between the stones, their emerald flame giving strange, heavy smoke. It gave the place a garish light. The snow on the ground gave the whole place an odd light, and the pale, nearly naked Marat could be seen keeping out of the light of the nearest torches, watching them curiously.

Fidelias alighted from the litter and asked the same Knight he'd spoken to before, "Where is Atsurak?"

The Knight nodded up the slope. "Top of the hill. They call it a *horto* but it's up there."

Fidelias rolled his ankle, frowning at the pain in his foot. "Then why didn't we land at the top of the hill?"

The Knight shrugged and said apologetically, "They told us not to, sir."

"Fine," Fidelias said, shortly. He glanced at Aldrick

and started up the hill. The swordsman fell in on his right and a step behind him. The slope made his feet hurt abominably, and he had to stop once to rest.

Aldrick frowned, watching him. "Feet?"

"Yes."

"When we wrap this up tomorrow, I'll go get Odiana. She's good at fixing things up."

Fidelias frowned. He didn't trust the water witch. Aldrick seemed to control her, but she was too clever for his liking. "Fine," he said, shortly. After a moment, he asked, "Why, Aldrick?"

The swordsman watched the night around them with neutral disinterest. "Why what?"

"You've been a wanted man for what? Twenty years?"

"Eighteen."

"And you've been a rebel the whole time. Fallen in with one group after another, and they've all been subversives."

"Freedom fighters," Aldrick said.

"Whatever," Fidelias said. "The point is that you've been a thorn in Gaius's side since you were barely more than a boy."

Aldrick shrugged.

Fidelias studied him. "Why?"

"Why do you want to know?"

"Because I like knowing the motivations of the people I work with. The witch follows you. She's besotted with you, and I have no doubt that she'd kill for you, if you asked her to."

Again, Aldrick shrugged.

"But I don't know why you're doing it. Why Aquitaine trusts you. So, why?"

"You haven't worked it out? You're supposed to be the big spy for the Crown. Haven't you figured it out yet? Analyzed my scars or poked into my diaries, something like that?"

Fidelias half-smiled. "You're honest. You're a murderer, a sellsword, a thug—but an honest one. I thought I'd ask."

Aldrick stared up the hill for a moment. Then he said, tonelessly, "I had a family. My mother and my father. My older brother and two younger sisters. Gaius Sextus destroyed them." Aldrick tapped a finger on the hilt of his sword. "I'll kill him. To do that, I have to knock him off the Throne. So I'm with Aquitaine."

"And that's all there is to it?" Fidelias asked.

"No." Aldrick didn't elaborate. After a moment of silence, he said, "How are your feet?"

"Let's go," Fidelias said. He started back up the hill again, though the pain made him wince with every step.

Perhaps ten yards short of the summit of the hill, a pair of Marat warriors, male and female, rose out of the shadows around the base of the stones at the top of the hill. They came down toward them, through the snow, the man holding an axe of Aleran manufacture, the woman, a dark dagger of chipped stone.

Fidelias stopped short of them and held up his empty hands. "Peace. I have come to speak to Atsurak."

The man stepped up close to him, his eyes narrowed. He had the dark, heavy feathers of a herdbane braided through his pale hair. "I will not permit you to speak to Atsurak, outsider, while he is at the *horto*. You will wait until—"

Fidelias's temper flashed, and it was with a flicker of

annoyance that he reached down into the earth to borrow strength from Vamma and dealt the axe-wielding warrior a blow that lifted the Marat's feet up off the ground and stretched him out senseless in the snow.

Without pausing, Fidelias stepped over the silent form of the fallen Marat. He limped up to the lean female warrior and said in exactly the same tone, "Peace. I have come to speak to Atsurak."

The Marat's amber-colored eyes flicked up and down Fidelias, bright beneath heavy, pale brows. Her lips lifted from her teeth, showing canine fangs, and she said, "I will take you to Atsurak."

Fidelias followed her up the rest of the hill and to the great stones there. The smoke from the torches, heavy and dark along the ground, held a curious odor, and Fidelias found his head feeling a bit light as he stepped into it. He glanced back at Aldrick, and the swordsman nodded, nostrils flared.

Seven stones, smooth and round, their surfaces protruding above the heavy smoke, sat around a pool of water, somehow unfrozen despite the cold. The smoke seemed to sink into it and swirl beneath its surface, leaving it shining and dull, reflecting back the light of fires and the dull night glow of snow and ice.

Scattered around the pool were perhaps a hundred other Marat, their hair plaited with herdbane feathers, or else showing the shagginess of what Fidelias assumed to be the Wolf Clan. Male and female, they ate, or drank from brightly painted gourds, or mated in the sultry, dizzying smoke with animal abandon. In the shadows stood the tall, silent shapes of the herdbane warbirds and crouched the low, swift shapes of wolves.

On one of the stones lounged Atsurak, his bruises all but gone already, the cuts bound in strips of hide and plaited grass. Aquitaine's dagger rode through a strap at his waist, the blade contained within a rawhide sheath and positioned to be clearly on display. On either side of him curled a female Marat warrior, of the heavy-browed and fanged variety. Both were naked, young, lithe.

The mouths of all three were smeared with fresh, scarlet blood. And bound over the stone beside them was the shivering form of a young Aleran woman, still wearing the shreds of a farm wife's skirts and apron, and still very much alive.

Aldrick's mouth twisted with disgust. "Savages," he murmured.

"Yes," Fidelias said. "We call them that because they're savage, Aldrick."

The swordsman growled in his throat. "They have moved too soon. There aren't any Aleran settlements on this side of the Valley."

"Obviously." Fidelias stepped forward and said, "Atsurak of Clan Herdbane. I understood that our attack was to begin two dawns from now. Was my understanding in error?"

Atsurak looked up, focusing on Fidelias, as an older woman, also showing the signs of Clan Wolf, rose from the smoke at the base of one of the stones, coated liberally in blood, and crossed to him. She folded her arms casually over his shoulders, amber eyes on Fidelias. Atsurak lifted his hand to touch the woman's, without looking at her, and said, "We celebrate our victory, Aleran." He smiled, and his teeth were stained scarlet. "Have you come to partake?"

"You celebrate a victory you do not yet have."

Atsurak waved a hand. "For many of my warriors, there will be no chance to celebrate, after."

"So you broke our agreement?" Fidelias asked. "You struck early?"

The Marat lowered his brows. "A raiding party struck first, as is our custom. We know many ways in and out of the bridge valley, Aleran. Not ways for an army, but for a scouting party, a raiding party, yes." He gestured toward the bound girl. "Her people fought well against us. Died well. Now we partake of their strength."

"You're *eating* them *alive*?" demanded Aldrick.

"Pure," corrected Atsurak. "Untouched by fire or water or blade. As they are before The One."

As he spoke, a pair of Herdbane warriors rose to their feet and moved to the prisoner. With casual, almost disinterested efficiency, they drew her up, tore the clothes from her, and bound her back down over the stone again, belly up to the stars, arms and legs spread.

Atsurak looked over at the captive and mused through bloody lips, "We take more strength in this way. I do not expect you to understand, Aleran."

The girl looked around, frantic, her eyes red with tears, body shaking in the cold, her lips blue. "Please," she gasped, toward Fidelias. "Please, sir. Please help me."

Fidelias met her eyes. Then walked over toward the stone upon which she was bound. "Matters have changed. We must change the plans to suit them."

Atsurak followed him with his eyes, expression growing wary. "What change, Aleran?"

"Sir," the girl whispered up at him, her expression desperate, ugly with tears and terror. "Sir, please."

"Shhhh," Fidelias said. He rested his hand on her hair, and she broke down into quiet, subdued sobs. "We have to move forward now. The troops at Garrison may be warned of our coming."

"Let them know," Atsurak said, lazily leaning against one of the women at his side. "We will tear out their weak bellies regardless."

"You are wrong," Fidelias said. He raised his voice, enough that all of the Marat around the pool would hear. "You are mistaken, Atsurak. We must strike at once. At dawn."

Silence fell over the hilltop, abrupt, deep, almost as though the Marat were afraid to breathe. All eyes went from Fidelias to Atsurak.

"You call me mistaken," Atsurak said, the words low, soft.

"The younger of your people listen to the elder, head-man of Clan Herdbane. Is that not true?"

"It is."

"Then you, young hordemaster, listen to me. I was there when last the Alerans fought your people. There was no glory in it. There was no honor. There was hardly any battle. The rocks rose against them, and the very grass beneath them bound their feet. Fire was laid on the ground, and fire swept over them and destroyed them. There was no contest, no trial of blood. They died like stupid animals in a trap because they grew too confident." He twisted his lips into a sneer. "Their bellies too full."

"You dishonor the memory of brave warriors—"

"Who *died* because they did not use what they had to fullest advantage," snarled Fidelias. "Lead your people to death if that is your wish, Atsurak, but I will be no party to it. I will not waste the lives of my Knights in an attempt to neutralize the Knights of a forewarned and prepared garrison."

Another Marat, a Herdbane, rose and snarled, "He speaks the words of an Aleran. The words of a coward."

"I speak the truth," Fidelias said. "If you are wise, young man, you will listen to the older."

Atsurak stared at him for several moments in silence. Then he exhaled and said, "The Alerans fight as cowards. Let us force them to the trial of blood before they can prepare their spirits to hide behind. We will attack at dawn."

Fidelias let out a slow breath and nodded. "Then this celebration is over?"

Atsurak looked at the captive, shivering beneath Fidelias's hand. "Almost."

"Please sir," the girl whispered. "Please help me."

Fidelias looked down at her and nodded, touching her mouth with his other hand.

Then he broke her neck, the sound sharp in the silence of the hilltop. Her eyes looked up at him in shock for a few seconds. Then went slowly out of focus and empty.

He let the dead girl's head fall limply back onto the stone and said, to Atsurak, "Now it is over. Be in position when the sun rises." He walked back across the circle to Aldrick, working to hide the limp.

"Aleran," snarled Atsurak, his voice heavy, bestial.

Fidelias paused, without turning around.

"I will remember this insult."

Fidelias nodded. "Just be ready in the morning." Without looking back, he walked, with Aldrick, back down the hill and toward the litter. Aldrick paced beside him, silent, scowling. Halfway down the hill, Fidelias's belly rolled violently, out of nowhere, and he had to stop and squat down, weight on his injured feet, his head bowed.

"What is it?" Aldrick asked, his voice quiet and cool.

"My feet hurt," Fidelias lied.

"Your feet hurt," Aldrick said, quietly. "Del, you killed that girl."

Fidelias's stomach fluttered. "Yes."

"And it doesn't even bother you?"

He lied again. "No."

Aldrick shook his head.

Fidelias took a breath. Then another. He forced his belly back under control and said, "She was dead already, Aldrick. Chances are, she'd just seen her family or friends eaten alive. Right there in front of her. She was next. Even if we had taken her out of there in one piece, she'd seen too much. We just would have had to remove her ourselves."

"But *you* killed her."

"It was the kindest thing I could do." Fidelias stood up again, his head clearing, slowly.

Aldrick remained quiet for a moment. Then he said, "Great furies. I've no stomach for that kind of killing."

Fidelias nodded. "Don't let it stop you from doing your duty."

Aldrick grunted. "You ready?"

"I'm ready," Fidelias said. They started back down the hill together. "At least we got the Marat moving." His feet still hurt horribly, but going back down the hill was easier than going up. "Get the men ready. We'll hit the Knights at Garrison just as we planned on the way here."

"We're down to the fighting, then," Aldrick said.

Fidelias nodded. "I don't think there are any major obstacles to the mission now."

ᚖᚖᚖᚖ CHAPTER 32

Tavi's teeth chattered together, and he hugged himself beneath his cloak, as he and Fade were shown out of the tent they had been kept in. He wasn't sure if it was the cold that made him shake, or the sense of raw excitement that filled him, made him eager to move and burn away the chill of the winter in motion.

"M-m-more snow," Tavi noted, as he crunched along behind the silent form of Doroga. Great white flakes drifted down in a calm, heavy curtain. Already, the snow had gone from a thin coating of ice on the ground, the night before, to a soft, heavy carpet as deep as Tavi's ankles. He slipped on a thin patch where the ice was barely covered, but Fade reached forward and caught his shoulder until he could regain his balance. "Great."

Doroga turned back toward them without stopping. "It is," he said. "The snow and the darkness may help more of the Keepers to sleep."

Tavi frowned at the Marat headman. "What Keepers?"

"The Keepers of the Silence," Doroga said.

"What's that?"

"You will see," Doroga said. He kept pacing through the snow, until he reached an enormous old bull gargant, placidly chewing its cud. Doroga went to the beast and gave no visible signal, but it knelt in any case and let him use the back of its leg to take a step up and seize the braided cord dangling from the saddle. Doroga swarmed up it easily, and then reached down to help Tavi and Fade up behind him.

Once they were mounted, the gargant hauled itself lazily to its feet, made a ponderous turn, and started rolling forward through the snow. For a time, they rode through the night in silence, and though the warmth of the beast and the riders on either side of him had chased the chill away, Tavi still shook. Excitement then. He felt his mouth stretch into a smile.

"So, this thing we're supposed to be getting," Tavi began.

"The Blessing of Night," Doroga said.

"What is it?"

"A plant. A mushroom. It grows in the heart of the Valley of Silence. Within the great tree."

"Uh-huh," Tavi said. "What good is it?"

Doroga blinked and looked back at him. "What good, valleyboy? It is good for everything."

"Valuable?"

Doroga shook his head. "You do not understand the meaning of the word in this," he said. "Fever. Poison. Injury. Pain. Even age. It has power over them all. To our people, there is nothing of greater value."

Tavi whistled. "Do you have any?"

Doroga hesitated. Then shook his head.

"Why not?"

"It grows only there, valleyboy. And only slowly. If we are fortunate, one person returns every year with some of the Blessing."

"Why don't you send more people?"

Doroga looked back at him for a moment, then said, "We do."

Tavi blinked, then swallowed. "So, uh. I guess something happens to the ones who don't come back?"

"The Keepers," Doroga said. "Their bite is a deadly venom. But they have a weakness."

"What weakness?"

"When one falls, the Keepers swarm the fallen. All of them. They will not pursue anyone else until that one has been devoured."

Tavi gulped.

"This is the trial of my people before The One, valleyboy. It is newly night. You will go into the Valley of Silence and return before dawn."

"What if we don't come back before dawn?" Tavi asked.

"Then you will not come back."

"The Keepers?"

Doroga nodded. "At night, they are slow. Quiet. No one escapes the Valley of Silence while The One fills the sky with light."

"Great," Tavi repeated. He took a deep breath. "So where is your son?"

Doroga blinked up at the sky and then back to Tavi. "My what?"

"Kitai. Your son."

"Ah. My whelp," Doroga said. He moved his eyes back to the ground before them, expression uncomfortable. "Hashat brings Kitai."

"He's not riding with you?"

Doroga remained silent.

"What?" Tavi asked. "Is he fighting with you? Hanging around with the Horse Clan?"

Doroga growled in his throat, and the gargant beneath them let out a rumble that shook Tavi's teeth.

"Never mind," Tavi said, quickly. "How far is it to this great tree and back?"

Doroga guided the gargant down a long slope and pointed forward. "See for yourself."

Tavi strained to look over Doroga's broad shoulders, finally resorting to planting a foot on the broad back of the gargant bull and half-standing, with Fade steadying him by his belt.

Down a long slope of land, dappled in patches of shadow next to round, ice-covered boulders, the land fell off and down as abruptly as if some enormous hand had gouged out an inverted dome from the earth. A low ridge rose all around the precipice, which was a circle that stretched so wide in the falling snow that Tavi could not see the majority of its curve or the circle's far side. A dull, greenish light licked up at the edges of the pit from below, and as the Gargant plodded closer, Tavi could see its source.

The bottom of the pit, a great bowl gouged into the earth, was covered with a valley of trees—trees the likes of which Tavi had never seen before. They rose up, their trunks twisted and gnarled, stretching many branches each high into the air, like the reaching hands of a drowning man.

Covering the trees was the source of the light. Tavi squinted and peered, and it took his eyes a moment to sort out what he was seeing. Covering the trees was some kind of growth that gave off the faint, menacing luminescence. It seemed to cover the trees as might some kind of fungus, but rather than simply existing as a light coating of some other plant, it had grown over them in a thick, gelatinous-looking mass. As the gargant drew closer to the edge of the precipice, Tavi could see that the growth had runnels and areas that looked as though bubbles of air had been trapped beneath it, and for all the world looked like melted wax had been dripped over the surfaces of the trees, but for the desperately reaching branches high up in them, layer upon layer, until the whole resembled some fantastic, bizarre work of art. As far as he could see, in the faint light of the glowing wax, those odd trees writhed and twisted, their branches and trunks hung in festoons and swirls of the waxy growth.

At the heart of the scene stood a single, ancient tree, barren trunk lifting high, dead branches mostly worn away by time. Though there was nothing to hold to scale, Tavi thought that the spire of ancient, dead wood had to be huge.

"The Wax Forest," Tavi said, quietly. "Wow. They didn't say it was so pretty."

"Danger," Fade said, quietly. "Danger, Tavi. Fade will go."

"No," Tavi said, quickly. "I'm the one who spoke. I'm the one who has to answer the trial." He glanced at Doroga. "Right?"

Doroga looked back at Tavi and then glanced at Fade. "Too heavy," he said.

Tavi tilted his head. "What?"

"Too heavy," Doroga repeated. "His weight will break the surface of the *croach*. The wax. It will alert the Keepers as soon as he steps on it. Only our whelps or a small female can enter the Valley of Silence and live."

Tavi swallowed again. "Right then," he said. "It's got to be me."

Fade frowned, but fell silent.

The gargant's slow-seeming steps covered ground quickly and carried them down to the edge of the precipice. There, Tavi saw Hashat standing beside a large, pale horse, the wind tossing their white manes off to one side, the lean Marat woman with her long legs somehow a mirror of the big grey beside her. The cool winter light gleamed on the captured eagle brooches on her sword belt.

Over to one side, seated at the edge of the precipice, near a couple of lumps in the snow, was Kitai, still dressed in his rough smock, skinny legs dangling over the edge, feet idly waving. The wind pressed his hair back from the slender, stark lines of his face, and he had his eyes narrowed to slits against the drifting flakes of snow.

Tavi scowled at the other boy, and his face stung for a moment, where he had been cut the previous morning.

Doroga nodded wordlessly to Hashat and clucked to his gargant. The great beast let out a snort and rolled to a stop before lowering itself almost daintily to the ground. Doroga tossed down the saddle strap and used one hand to steady himself with it as he slid down. Tavi followed suit, as did Fade.

"Doroga," said Hashat, coming toward them, frowning. "Are you ready?"

Doroga nodded, once.

Hashat said, "Word is abroad. The wolves were leaving, as I left to bring Kitai here. They attack with the dawn."

Tavi drew in a little breath and looked at Fade. The slave looked worried, though his eyes weren't focused on anything. He just stared out over the Wax Forest.

Doroga grunted. "Then this will decide it. If the Aleran prevails, we avoid the struggle."

"Atsurak will not be happy with you, Doroga."

The big Marat shrugged. "He may not survive the day. If he does, he does. That is yet to come."

Hashat nodded. "Then let us begin."

"Kitai," Doroga rumbled.

The figure at the edge of the precipice did not move.

Doroga scowled. "Whelp!"

Still, he did not move.

Doroga glared at Hashat. The maned Marat turned her face away a little too late to hide her smile. "Your whelp is growing up, Doroga. They always get moody before they bond. You know that."

Doroga rumbled, "You just want Kitai to be part of Horse."

Hashat shrugged her shoulders. "Speed, intelligence. Who wouldn't want that?" She lifted her chin and called, "Kitai. We are ready to begin."

Kitai stood up, idly dusted snow off of his smock, and paced toward them, his expression cool. He stopped not a pace away from Tavi, glaring at the Aleran boy.

Tavi felt a sudden fear, as his cut throbbed again, and then set his jaw stubbornly. He had never allowed a bully to frighten him. He'd been beaten often enough, but he'd never surrendered to fear. He took a step closer to

Kitai, eyes narrowed, facing the other boy's opalescent gaze with his own. Their eyes were on a level, and the other boy did not seem to be much bigger than Tavi was. Tavi folded his arms and stared at his opponent.

Kitai seemed uncertain how to react to Tavi's stance and glanced at Hashat.

Doroga growled irritably. "You both know the trial. The first to recover the Blessing of Night and return it to my hand will be the victor." He turned to Tavi. "Aleran. The Blessing is shaped as a mushroom. It has a flat head, slender stalk, and is the color of night. It is located at the base of the great tree, within its trunk."

"Black mushroom," Tavi said. "Great tree. Fine, got it."

"Kitai, you are familiar with the trial."

The other boy nodded. "Yes, sire."

Doroga turned to him and placed his huge hands on the boy's slender shoulders. He turned Kitai to face him, an effortless flexing of Doroga's shoulders. "Then be careful. Your mother would want you to be careful."

Kitai lifted his chin, though his eyes glittered bright. "My mother," he said, "would have fetched the Blessing and been back by now while you talked, sire."

Doroga's teeth showed, suddenly. "Yes," he agreed. One of his hands squeezed Kitai's shoulders, and he released the boy, to turn to Tavi. "We will lower you down and wait until dawn. Once you begin, there are no rules. The results are all that matter. You can choose not to face the trial now, if you wish, valleyboy."

"And go back to your camp and be eaten?"

Doroga nodded. "Yes. Regrettably."

Tavi let out a nervous laugh. "Yeah, well. I'll take my chances with the Keepers, I think."

"Then we begin." Doroga turned to one of the lumps in the snow and dug into it with his huge hands, uncovering a great coil of rope of a weave Tavi had never seen before. Beside him, Hashat did the same with a second coil of rope.

Tavi saw Kitai step up beside him out of the corner of his eye. The Marat boy watched the two adults uncovering the rope and testing its length. "It is rope from the *Gadrim-ha*. From the ones you call the Icemen. Made of the hairs of their females. It will not freeze or break."

Tavi nodded. He asked, "You've done this before?"

Kitai nodded. "Twice. It wasn't for a trial, before. But I have gone in twice and returned with the Blessing. I was the only one who returned."

Tavi swallowed.

"Are you afraid, Aleran?"

"Aren't you?"

"Yes," Kitai said. "Afraid to lose. Everything depends on this night, for me."

"I don't understand."

Kitai sniffed. "When I return with the Blessing before you, I will have defended my sire's honor in a trial before The One. I will be an adult and may choose where I live."

"And you want to live with Hashat," Tavi said.

Kitai blinked and looked at Tavi. "Yes."

Tavi studied the other boy. "Do you, uh . . . are you sweet on her?"

Kitai frowned, pale brows coming together. "No. But I wish to be a part of her Clan. To be free with her Clan. Not to plod around with Doroga and his stupid *Sabot*." He glanced aside, to be sure no one was close, apparently, and confided in a low voice to Tavi, "They smell."

Tavi lifted his brows, but nodded. "Yeah. I guess they do."

"Aleran," Kitai said. "My sire is right about one thing. You have courage. It will be an honor to face you in a trial. But I will defeat you. Do not think that this will end in any other way, despite whatever spirits are yours to call."

Tavi felt a scowl harden his features. Kitai's eyes narrowed, and he stepped back a half pace, one hand falling to the knife at his belt.

"I don't have any," Tavi said. "And back at my steadholt, we have a saying about counting your chickens before they've hatched."

"My people eat eggs before they've hatched," Kitai said, and stepped toward the coiled ropes. "I thought you might make it out alive, Aleran, thanks to your spirits. But we will only need to use one rope before dawn."

Tavi started to say something quick and heated back, but Fade's hand gripped his shoulder abruptly. Tavi turned to face the slave.

Fade frowned at him, his scarred face hideous and concerned. Then he said, "Be careful, Tavi." And with that, he took the pack that had been slung over his shoulder and dropped it onto Tavi's.

The boy let out a breath at the sudden weight. "Fade, uh. Maybe it would be better if I didn't take anything with me. I'll move faster without it."

"Marat stronger than Tavi," Fade said. "Faster."

"Thank you," Tavi said, testily. "I needed that kind of encouragement."

Fade's eyes glittered with something like good humor, and he ruffled Tavi's hair with one hand. "Tavi smart. There. Bag of tricks. Be smart, Tavi. Important."

Tavi tilted his head to one side, peering at the slave. "Fade?" he asked.

The glitter faded from the man's eyes, and he gave Tavi his witless grin.

"Valleyboy," Doroga called. "There is no time to waste."

Tavi said to Fade, quickly, "If I don't come back, Fade, I want you to remember to tell Aunt Isana that I love her. Uncle, too."

"Tavi," Fade nodded. "Come back."

The boy blew out a breath. Whatever spark of awareness had been in the man's eyes was gone now. "All right," he said, and walked over to Doroga. He shrugged into the pack, drawing the straps down to their smallest size, so that it would fit closely to his back.

Doroga was handling his rope. Tavi watched as the Marat worked a loop into the end of it with the skill of a sailor and drew it tight. The Marat stood, leaving the loop just touching the ground, and in a moment of understanding, Tavi stepped forward and slipped his foot into the loop, taking up the rope itself to hold it tight.

Doroga nodded his approval. To Tavi's right, Kitai had knotted the rope himself and stood at the edge of the precipice, his expression impatient. Tavi walked awkwardly to the precipice's edge and stared over it to a drop of several hundred feet down a nearly sheer surface. His head spun a bit, and his belly suddenly shook and felt light.

"Are you afraid, Aleran?" Kitai asked, and let out a low little laugh.

Tavi shot the other boy a sharp glance and then turned to Doroga, who had secured the far end of the rope to a stake driven into the earth and looped it about a second such stake, so that he could let the rope out gradually. "Let's go," Tavi said, and with that, took a step back over the precipice and swung himself down into space.

Doroga held the line steady, and after a very short moment of terror, Tavi bumped against the wall and steadied himself, holding on. Doroga began to lower the rope, but Tavi called up, "Faster! Let it out faster!"

There was a brief pause, and then the rope began to play out quickly, lowering Tavi down the face of the cliff at a rather alarming rate.

From above, there was a yelp, and Kitai swung out into space. The boy plummeted down for several yards, and Tavi got the impression that when the rope finally did tighten and catch him that Hashat had only just managed to do so. Kitai shot Tavi a bright-eyed, angry glance and called something up the cliff in another tongue. A moment later, he, too, began to descend the cliff more quickly.

Tavi used one foot and one hand to keep himself from dragging on the stone and found that it was more effort than he would have expected. He was shortly panting, but a swift glance up at Kitai told him that he had thought correctly: Doroga's huge muscles had an easier time letting out the rope at a faster, controlled rate than the more slender Hashat's did, and Tavi had gained considerable distance on the other boy as they descended.

As he came down, closer to the lambent green glow of the croach, he shot a glance up at Kitai and smiled, fiercely.

Kitai let out a sharp whistle, and the line abruptly stopped playing out.

Tavi stared up at him in confusion. Until the other

boy drew his knife, reached across to the rope that held Tavi thirty feet over the floor of the bizarre forest below and, with an answering smile, used the dark, glassy knife to begin swiftly slicing through Tavi's rope.

◇◇◇◇ CHAPTER 33

Tavi took one look at the thirty odd feet between him and the ground below, then reached a hand up, fumbling at Fade's pack. He jerked the flap open and grabbed the first thing his fingers could reach, though all the squirming made him twist and spin on the rope. He squinted up as best he could and then flung it at the Marat above him.

Kitai let out a yelp and jerked back in a dodge. A hunk of cheese smacked into the stone beside the Marat's head, clung for a moment, then dropped and fell toward the wax-covered ground below.

Kitai blinked at the cheese and then at Tavi, his face twisting into a scowl. Doroga hadn't stopped lowering the rope, and so the cut the Marat had begun had already descended out of his reach. Kitai steadied himself against the cliff face, then reached out with his knife and began slicing at the rope again. "Foolish, Aleran. Kinder if you fell, broke a leg, and had to turn back rather than be devoured by the Keepers."

Tavi scrambled in the pack and found cloth wrapped around several biscuits. He grabbed the first and hurled it at Kitai. "So I could be eaten by your people instead?"

Kitai scowled, not deterred this time. A biscuit bounced off his outstretched arm. "We would at least not eat you alive."

"Stop that!" Tavi shouted. He threw another biscuit, to no effect. A thick strand of the braided rope parted with a whining snap, and Tavi's heart lurched as the rope spun and swung from side to side. He glanced below him. Another twenty feet to ground. He'd never be able to fall that far without hurting himself, possibly too badly to continue.

Another strand parted, and Tavi swayed wildly back and forth, his heart hammering high in his throat.

Arms and legs shaking with excitement, Tavi took one last glance down (fifteen feet, or a little more?). He slipped his foot out of the loop at the bottom of the grey rope, and as quickly as he could, he slipped down the rope, gripping with his hands, and letting his legs swing below him. He reached the loop and with a gulp grasped onto it, letting his legs swing out far beneath him.

The rope parted with a snap. Tavi plummeted.

Between Doroga lowering the rope from above and the few feet he had gained by letting himself farther down the rope, the fall might have been little more than ten feet. Not much higher than the roof of the stables, and he had jumped from there several times—always into mounds of hay, true, but he had made the jump without fear. He tried to remember to keep his legs loose, to fall, roll if he possibly could.

The fall seemed to take forever, and when Tavi landed

it was a shock to his ankles, knees, thighs, hips, back, all in rapid succession as he tumbled to the earth. He landed on one side, arms flailing wildly out and slapping down with him, and his breath exploded out from him in a rush. He lay for a moment without moving, dimly aware that he was on the ground, still clutching the loop in the end of the rope in his fist.

He regained his breath in a few moments, becoming aware of a couple of incongruous facts as he did. First, there was no snow, down here in the chasm. Of course, he had seen no snow from above, but the significance of it hadn't quite registered on him until he reached the ground. It was warm. Humid. Nearly stifling. He sat up, slowly, pushing himself up with his hands.

The ground beneath him, or rather, the greenly luminous wax beneath his fingers felt pleasantly warm, and he let them rest against it for a moment, letting his chilled fingers recover from the cold wind that had frozen them on the way down from the top of the cliff. His ankles stung as though being prickled by thousands of tiny needles, but the sensation faded after a moment, leaving them feeling merely uncomfortable and sore.

Tavi gathered himself to his feet, the pack shifting about uncomfortably on his back, and squinted at his surroundings.

What was beautiful from high above was, once among it, disorienting and a little disturbing. The waxy growth, the *croach,* grew right up to the stone walls of the chasm and stopped there, but for one place he could see, where it had crept up the walls, evidently to engulf a lone and scraggly tree trying to grow from a crack in the stone. The luminous glow made shadows fall weirdly, with one engulfed tree casting several ghostly weak shadows on the glowing floor of the forest. Beneath the *croach,* the shadowy outlines of the trees themselves reminded Tavi uncomfortably of bones beneath flesh.

Tavi heard a scrabble on the wall and turned in time to see Kitai drop the last dozen feet to the floor of the forest, landing soundlessly, absorbing the shock of landing on both feet and on his arms, crouching for a moment on all fours, pale hair and opalescent eyes wild and greenish in the quiet light of the *croach.* His gaze darted left and right, wary, and his head tilted to one side, listening, focused on the lambent forest before him.

Tavi's temper flared, fear and pain quickly becoming an outraged anger that made arms shake with the sudden need to avenge himself. He rose and stalked silently toward Kitai. Tavi tapped the Marat on the shoulder, and when Kitai turned toward him, he balled up his fist and drove it into the other boy's ribs as hard as he could.

Kitai flinched, but didn't move quickly enough to evade the blow. Tavi pressed his advantage, jerking the Marat's arm away from his flank and punching him again in the same spot, as hard as he could. Kitai fumbled for his knife, and Tavi shoved him away as hard as he could, sending the other boy sprawling onto the glowing surface of the *croach.*

Kitai turned his opalescent eyes toward Tavi and pushed himself up with his hands. "Aleran," he snarled, "my sire's generosity is wasted on you. If you want a Trial of Blood, then——"

Kitai stopped abruptly, his eyes going wide.

Tavi, prepared to defend himself, blinked at the sudden change in the Marat. Gooseflesh rippled up his arms. Silent, he followed the Marat's gaze down—to his own feet.

Some of the oozing green light of the *croach* seemed to have spilled onto Tavi's boots. He frowned and peered closer. No. When he had landed, one of his heels must have driven into the *croach* and broken its surface like a crust of drying mud over a still-wet furrow. Whatever that glowing goo was within the wax, it had splashed droplets onto the leather. The droplets glowed, pale and green.

Tavi frowned and shook them off. He looked up to find Kitai still staring at him, eyes wide, his mouth open.

"What?" Tavi asked. "What is it?"

"Foolish Aleran," Kitai hissed. "You have broken the *croach*. The Keepers will come."

Tavi felt a chill roll over him. He swallowed. "Well I wouldn't have fallen if *someone* hadn't cut my rope."

"I'm not that stupid," Kitai retorted. His eyes moved past Tavi, flicking among the trees. "The *croach* beneath the ropes is very thick. That's why we chose there to enter. I once saw someone fall nearly six times the height of a man without breaking it."

Tavi licked his lips. "Oh," he said. He looked down at the forest's glowing floor. "Why did I break through it, then?"

Kitai glanced at him and then paced over to the spot where Tavi had landed, crouching down beside it. He touched the glowing fluid with his fingertips. "It's thinner, here. I don't understand. It's never been like this."

Tavi said, "Looks like they were expecting company."

Kitai turned to him, his eyes wide, body tense. "They knew where we were coming in. And now they know that we're here." The Marat boy's eyes flicked left and right, and he took several steps sideways, toward Tavi, his back to the stone of the wall.

Tavi backed toward the wall as well, emulating Kitai, and almost tripped on an incongruous lump in the smooth surface of the *croach*. Tavi glanced down and then leaned over, peering at it.

The lump was not large: perhaps the size of a chicken. It rose from the otherwise smooth floor of the forest in a hemisphere of greenish light with something dark at its core. Tavi leaned closer, peering at the shadowed lump.

It stirred and moved. Tavi hopped back from it, his breath catching in his throat.

"That," he gasped. "That's a crow. There's a crow in there. And it's alive."

"Yes, Aleran," Kitai said with scarcely veiled impatience. "The crows are sometimes foolish. They come down and peck at the *croach,* and the Keepers come for them and entomb them." Kitai cast his eyes to one side, where several other lumps, quite a bit larger, lay only a dozen long strides from the ropes at the base of the cliff. "They can live for days. Being eaten by the *croach.*"

Tavi shuddered, a cold sensation crawling down his spine like a runnel of melting snow. "You mean. If these Keepers get one of us . . ."

"A Marat can live for weeks buried in the *croach,* Aleran."

Tavi felt sick. "You don't rescue them?"

Kitai flashed him a look, his eyes hard, cool. Then, in a few silent strides, paced over to the crow. He drew his knife, reached down, and slashed the blade over the surface of the lump. With a swift, curt motion, he reached down for the crow's neck and drew it from the clinging goo of the *croach*.

Parts of the bird peeled and sloughed away, like meat from a roast that had been cooked to tender perfection in a carefully tended oven. It let out a rasping sound, but its beak never attempted to close. Its eyes blinked once and then went glassy.

"That takes only hours," Kitai said and dropped the remains back near the slit in the wax. "Do you see, Aleran?"

Tavi stared at the ground, sickened. "I . . . I see."

Kitai grimaced at him. He turned and started pacing away, following the wall of stone again. "We must move. The Keepers will come to investigate the break you made and put the rest of the crow back. We should not be here when they arrive."

"No," Tavi whispered. "I guess we sh—"

In the trees, Tavi saw something move.

It was indistinct at first. Just a lump in the wax on the trunk of the tree. But it shuddered and twitched with life. Tavi thought for a moment that a piece of the *croach* had broken from the tree trunk and would fall to earth. It had a lumpy shape and coursed with the same luminous green fluid as the rest of the wax. But as the Aleran boy watched, legs writhed free of the lump's sides. Something like a head emerged from a shell-like coating of the *croach,* pale eyes round and huge. All in all, eight knobby, many-jointed legs stretched free of the thing's body, and then, with a quiet, horrible grace, it paced down the trunk of the tree and across the floor of the forest to the break in the surface of the *croach,* where greenish glowing fluid bubbled and seethed like blood in an open wound.

A wax spider. A Keeper of Silence. Silent and strange and the size of a large dog. Tavi stared at it, his heart pounding in his chest, and felt his eyes widening.

He shot a glance to Kitai, who had also frozen and was staring at the Keeper. The creature bent down and spread wide a set of smooth mandibles at the base of its head. It scooped up pieces of the crow and using its foremost set of legs, tucked them back into the open wound in the *croach.* Then it hovered over the slash, several of its legs working back and forth over it in swift, methodical movements, sealing the wax closed over the carcass.

Tavi shot a glance back at Kitai, who motioned to Tavi and then covered his own mouth with his hand, a clear command to be silent. Tavi nodded and turned toward Kitai. The Marat's eyes widened in alarm, and he held up his hands, palms out, to tell Tavi to stop.

Tavi froze.

Behind him, the quiet rustle of the Keeper's limbs over the wax had come to a halt. From the corner of his eye, Tavi could just see it gather all its limbs beneath it again, bobbing up and down in restless agitation. It began to emit a series of high pitched chirrups, not quite like a bird's voice, or anything else Tavi had ever heard. The sound made shivers slither down the length of his body.

After a moment, the Keeper appeared to go back to its work. Kitai turned toward Tavi, his motions very, very slow, graceful. He gestured toward Tavi with his hand, every movement smooth and circular and rolling, exaggerated. Then he turned and began to walk away, silent and slow, his steps flowing almost as though in a dance.

Tavi swallowed and turned to follow Kitai, struggling to emulate the Marat boy's steps. Kitai walked before him, close to the stone wall of the chasm, and Tavi followed until they were several dozen yards away from the Keeper. Tavi felt its presence behind him, bizarre and unworldly, disturbing as the legs of a fly prickling along the nape of his neck. When they were out of its sight, he felt himself relaxing and moving closer to Kitai out of reflex—as different as the other boy might be, he was more familiar, more friendly than that buglike creature entombing the crow within the glowing wax.

Kitai looked back over his shoulder at Tavi and then past him, eyes wide. There was something in them— tightly controlled terror, Tavi thought. He thought that Kitai looked a bit relieved to see Tavi standing so close to him, and the two boys exchanged a silent nod of acknowledgment to one another. Tavi felt the understanding between them without words needing to be said: *truce.*

Kitai let out a breath, slowly. "You must be quiet," he said, whispering. "And move smoothly. They see sudden motions."

Tavi swallowed and whispered, "We're safe if we're still?"

Kitai's face grew a shade paler. He shook his head, giving the gesture a circular accent to smooth it out. "They've found even those who were still. I've seen it."

Tavi frowned. "They must have some other way of seeing. Smell, hearing, something."

Kitai rolled his head in the negative again. "I don't know. We do not stay where they are to learn of them." He looked around and shivered. "We must be careful. It called. Others will come to search. They will be slow for now. But the Keepers will come."

Tavi nodded and had to swallow and force himself to make the gesture slowly, not in nervous jerks. "What should we do?"

Kitai nodded toward the ancient tree rising from the center of the forest. "We continue the trial, Aleran."

"Uh. Maybe we shouldn't."

"I *will* continue, Aleran. If you are too afraid to go on, then stay." His lips curled in a mischievous sneer. "It is what I would expect of a child."

"I am not a child," Tavi hissed furiously. "I'm older than you. What are you, twelve years old? Thirteen?"

Kitai narrowed his eyes. "*Fifteen,*" he hissed.

Tavi stared at the other boy for a moment, then started smiling. He had to struggle not to break out into sudden laughter.

Kitai's scowl deepened. "What?"

Tavi rolled his head in a slow negative, and whispered, "Nothing. Nothing."

"Mad," Kitai said. "You people are mad." With that, he turned and glided deeper into the glowing forest.

Tavi followed close behind him, frowning, struggling to keep the irrational laughter from his lips, his steps silent. After they'd put several dozen more yards between them and the Keeper they'd seen, he reached back and unslung the pack Fade had pressed onto him from his shoulders. He opened it and rummaged inside.

The pack contained two small jars of fine lamp oil,

firestones in their two-chambered black box, a small lantern, a box of fine shavings to serve as tinder for a fire, dried meat twisted into braids in a fashion odd to Tavi, two fine, warm blankets, several slender lengths of wood that could be fitted together into a fishing pole, lines, and fine metal hooks.

And at the bottom of the pack, a cruel, curved knife, heavy and with a spiked guard that covered the knuckles. It had a blade twice the length of Tavi's entire hand. A combat weapon.

Where had Fade got something like that? Tavi wondered. Why had the slave had this pack stored with such efficiency inside his chambers, presumably ready to go at a moment's notice? He had returned with the pack so quickly that he could not possibly have packed it. It had to have been ready to go.

Tavi shook his head and almost bumped into Kitai, who had come to a sudden stop in front of him. He came to a halt, close enough to the other boy that he could feel the nearly feverish heat of the Marat's body.

"What is it?" he whispered.

Kitai shivered and moved his head almost imperceptibly.

Tavi looked to his left, moving only his eyes.

A Keeper squatted on a gnarled root that rose from the forest floor, draped in a mantle of glowing croach, not ten feet away. Tavi looked the other way, seeking the nearest means of moving away from the Keeper.

A second spider-like creature sat on a low, wax-shrouded branch, on level with Tavi's head. It let out a high-pitched chirrup, bobbing up and down on its knobby limbs.

The first Keeper answered it in a different pitch. It

too began to bob in fluid, steady motions. Other chir-rups sounded from around them, out of sight. Many of them. A great many.

Tavi shuddered. He hardly breathed as he whispered, "What do we do?"

"I . . ." Kitai shivered again, and Tavi saw that the other boy's eyes were wide, panicked. "I do not know."

Tavi's eyes flicked back to the nearest of the two Keepers. It shook its head, pale eyes peering this way and that, twitching in independent motion, a dark dot at their center the only thing that resembled a pupil. Then, as Tavi watched, something strange happened. The Keeper's eyes changed color, right there before his own: They changed from a pale shade of maggot-white to something as bright orange as a candle's flame.

In that instant, the Keeper went deathly still. Both eyes swung to orient on the boys, and it let out a pierc-ingly loud whistle, something that sounded like a mad bird's scream.

Kitai's breath caught in his throat, and the boy leapt forward.

Tavi's eyes swept left and right, and he saw what the Keepers did very clearly. The further Keeper's eyes swirled to orange as well, and oriented immediately upon Kitai's form. It too let out a shrill shrieking scream, and, mirroring the first, started after the Marat boy with a deceptively languid, deadly grace.

In that moment, Tavi saw exactly how the Keepers had detected them, and how they might be able to thwart them. "Kitai!" he shouted, and then bounded after the other boy. "Wait!"

More shrill whistles went up all around them, as Tavi

raced to catch up with Kitai. It was all but impossible. The Marat boy carried no pack and moved with the grace and speed of a terrified deer. Tavi could barely keep the Marat in sight as he ran—and all around him gathered the glowing orange eyes of the wax spiders, standing out in sharp contrast to the green glow of the *croach*.

If Kitai hadn't tripped on a sudden dip in the *croach*, perhaps where one of the wax spiders had recently raised itself up out of it, Tavi didn't think he'd have caught up to the other boy. Instead, he swooped down and hauled Kitai to his feet by the boy's wild hair.

"Ow!" Kitai hissed, eyes wild.

"Shut up!" Tavi said, his voice sharp. "Follow me."

Kitai blinked in startled surprise, and Tavi gave the boy no time to argue with him. He looked to his left and darted forward, tugging the other boy forward a few steps to get him moving, then sprinting as quickly as he could toward the rocky wall of the chasm. A Keeper suddenly appeared on the ground in front of them. Tavi stifled his fear and kept running at the creature.

The wax spider reared up onto its rear sets of legs as Tavi approached, but before he reached it, the boy began a spin, holding the heavy pack out in both arms. The pack almost pulled him off balance, but instead he took a pair of whirling steps and felt the weight of the pack slam hard into the creature. The Keeper was lighter than it looked. The blow threw it to one side and slammed it hard into the wax surrounding a tree. It crumpled into the impact, legs curling up around it.

Tavi ran on, and behind him, around them, the chirps of the Keepers grew louder, more shrill, filled with what Tavi imagined must have been a chill and alien anger.

They reached the stony cliff face, both of them panting. Tavi dropped the pack long enough to put both hands against the stone, staring up and then to either side of the face, studying the dark stone as best he could in the faint light of the glowing *croach*.

"The ropes are far from here," hissed Kitai. "There is no escape for us."

"We don't need escape," Tavi said. He pressed his mouth to the stone and touched his tongue to it briefly, then spat out the sour taste of lime. "This way," he said. He picked up his pack and continued on through the green light of the Wax Forest, the rocky wall on his left. He dug in the pack as he went.

"They are surrounding us," Kitai said, voice cool. "Boxing us in."

"We don't need to get much farther," Tavi said. He tossed back one of the jars of oil to Kitai. "Hold that."

The Marat caught the jar awkwardly, then scowled at Tavi as they both ran on. "What is this?"

"Hold it a minute," Tavi said. "I have an idea."

Orange eyes flickered on his right, and Tavi didn't see the Keeper hurtling toward him until it was already halfway there. Kitai's foot kicked at his own and sent him stumbling to the forest floor.

The spider hurtled over him, missing him by a hair. It landed on the wall, its legs clinging to the nearly vertical surface, then spun on all of its legs, whistling. Its mandibles clicked and snapped against its carapace.

Tavi watched as Kitai drew his stone knife and hurled it. The glassy blade entered the creature's head, drawing a sudden fount of greenish glowing fluid, mixed in with something dark and acrid smelling. The Keeper hurled its body out again, but unguided it simply bucked in a high arch and landed on the ground, twitching and convulsing.

Kitai hauled Tavi to his feet and said, "I hope it is a good idea, Aleran."

Tavi felt himself quivering with terror and nodded jerkily. "Yeah. Yeah, so do I." He started running again, Kitai close behind him.

The sound of trickling water came to Tavi a moment later, and he lengthened his strides, leaping over another twisted root. Before him, the rock wall had parted in a long, narrow fissure. Water trickled out of it in a slow, steady stream, meltwater from the ambient heat of the *croach*. At the base of the fissure was a long, narrow pool, an area where the *croach* had not grown over the bare earth. The pool looked hideously dark, and Tavi could not see how deep it was.

"We cannot climb this, Aleran," panted Kitai. Another shriek sounded from near at hand, and Kitai twisted in place, body crouching in tension.

"Shut up," Tavi said. "Give me the oil." He took the jar from Kitai's hand, jerked the broad cork out of its mouth. He turned to the area behind himself and Kitai and stomped hard on the ground several times, breaking the surface of the wax and drawing out more of the sludgy, glowing fluid.

More outraged, chittering shrieks rose through the glowing forest.

"What are you doing?" hissed Kitai. "You show them where we are!"

"Yes," Tavi said. "Exactly." He dumped the oil onto the *croach*, into the depression his boots had made, and took the firestone box into his hand. He opened the two separate chambers and took the firestones into his hand, kneeling beside the oil. He looked up to see the glowing orange dots of dozens of eyes closing in on him with that same weird, alien grace, knobby legs rippling across the surface of the *croach*.

"Whatever you are doing," Kitai half-shouted, "hurry!"

Tavi waited until the eyes were close. And then he reached down to the oil and struck the firestones together.

They sparked brightly, glowing motes falling down, into the spilled oil. One of them found a spot where the oil was not deep enough to drown it, and in a rush, the whole of the small pool took sudden, brilliant flame. Fire leapt up from the depression in the *croach*, as high as Tavi's chest.

The boy recoiled from the flames, grabbed Kitai by the Marat boy's one-piece smock, and hauled him toward the pool. They tumbled into the cold water together, and Tavi pulled them both down.

The water was shallow, no more than thigh deep, and viciously chill. Tavi and Kitai gasped together at the cold. Then the Aleran boy stared at the Keepers.

The wax spiders had gone mad at the kindling of the fire. Those nearest to him had fallen back and were scuttling in circles, letting out high pitched shrieks. Others, farther back, had begun to bob up and down in confusion or fear, letting out high-pitched, interrogative chirrups.

None of them seemed to see either of the boys in the pool.

"It *worked*," Tavi hissed. "Quick, here." He reached

into the pack and drew out both blankets. He shoved one at Kitai, then took his own and dipped it into the water. A moment later, he lifted it and draped it over his shoulders and head, shivering a bit with the cold. "Quick," he said. "Cover up."

Kitai stared at him. "What are you doing?" he hissed. "We should run while we have a chance."

"Quick, cover up."

"Why?"

"Their eyes," Tavi said. "When they were close to us, the color of their eyes changed. They saw you and not me."

"What do you mean?"

"They saw your heat," Tavi stammered, lips shaking with the cold. "The Marat. Your people feel like they have a fever to me. You're hotter. The spiders saw you. Then when I lit the fire—"

"You blinded them," Kitai said, eyes widening.

"So soak your blanket in the water and cover up."

"Clever," Kitai said with admiration in his voice. With a quick motion, he jerked the hem of his smock up out of the water in an effort to avoid wetting any more of it. He tugged it over his hips, then bent to dip the blanket in the water and shroud himself as Tavi had done.

Tavi stared at the Marat in sudden shock.

Kitai blinked back at Tavi. "What is it?"

"I don't believe it," Tavi said. He felt his face flush and he turned away from Kitai, drawing the soaked blanket further about his face. "Oh, crows, I don't believe it."

"Don't believe what, Aleran?" Kitai demanded in a whisper.

"You're a *girl*."

CHAPTER 34

Kitai frowned, pale brows drawing together. "I am what?"

"You're a *girl*," Tavi accused.

"No," Kitai said in a fierce whisper. "I am a whelp. Until they bond, all Marat children are whelps. After I bond to a totem—then I will be a young female. Until then, I am a whelp like any other. Your ways are not our ways, Aleran."

Tavi stared at her. "But you're a *girl*."

Kitai rolled her eyes. "Get over it, valleyboy." She started to stand and move slowly up out of the water.

"Wait," Tavi hissed. He lifted a hand to block her way.

"What?"

"Wait until they've gone. If you go out there now, they'll see you."

"But I am covered by the cold blanket."

"And if you walk in front of that fire, you'll be the only cold thing there," Tavi said. "Stay here and be still and quiet. When the fire dies down, they'll spread out to look for us again, and we'll have our chance."

Kitai frowned, but slowly settled back into the water. "Our chance to do what?"

Tavi swallowed. "To get inside. To that big tree."

"Don't be foolish," Kitai said, though there was a reluctant weight to her words. "The Keepers are roused. No one has ever gone to the tree and come out again when the Keepers had been stirred from sleep. We would die."

"You forget. *I'm* going to die anyway." He frowned. "But it might be just as well. I don't want to lead a girl into that kind of danger."

The Marat girl scowled. "As if I am any less able to defeat you now than a few moments ago."

Tavi shook his head. "No, no, it isn't that."

"Then what is it?"

He shrugged beneath the blanket. "I can't explain it. We just—we don't treat our women the same way we do our men."

"That's stupid," said Kitai. "Just as it is stupid for us to pursue the trial. If neither of us comes back with the Blessing, the trial is inconclusive. They'll wait until a new moon and hold it again. You will be Doroga's guest until then, valleyboy. You will be safe."

Tavi frowned and swallowed, thinking. Part of him had all but let out a shout of relief. He could get out of this bizarre chasm with its alien creatures and return to the world above. It wasn't a friendly one, among the Marat, but it was living, and he would at least be kept alive and unharmed until the next trial. He could survive.

But the new moon wouldn't be for weeks. The Marat would move long before then, attack Garrison and then the steadholts in the valley beyond, including his own home. For a moment, Tavi's imagination conjured up an image of returning to Bernardholt to find it deserted, thick with the stench of rotten meat and burned hair; to open one of the swinging gates and see a cloud of carrion crows hurtle into the air, leaving the bodies of people he had known his whole life ravaged and unrecognizable on the cold earth. His aunt. His uncle. Frederic, Beritte, Old Bitte, and so many others.

His legs started shaking—not with cold, but with the sudden realization that he could not turn his back on them now. If returning with that stupid mushroom meant that he would gain his family even a better chance to survive what was coming, then he could do nothing less than everything in his power to retrieve it. He couldn't back down now, he couldn't run now, even though it meant he might go into mortal danger.

He might wind up like that crow, sealed into the *croach*, devoured alive. For a moment, the pale, colored eyes of the Keepers haunted his mind. There had been so many of them. There still were, gathered all around the now-guttering fire, crawling mindlessly over one another in all directions, their long, knobby legs falling feather-light onto the surface of the *croach*. Their leathery shells made squeaking sounds as they crowded close, rubbed against one another. And they smelled. Something pungent and acrid and inexplicably alien. Even as he realized that he could smell them, Tavi felt the hairs on the back of his neck prickle up, and his shivering increased in reaction.

"I have to go," Tavi said.

"You'll die," Kitai said, simply. "It cannot be done."

She shrugged and said, "It is your life to waste. Look at you. You are shaking hard enough to rattle your teeth." But her odd, opalescent eyes stayed on him, intent, curious. She didn't speak the question, but Tavi all but heard her ask: *Why?*

He took a shuddering breath. "It doesn't matter. Doesn't matter that I'm afraid. I have to get that mushroom and get out again. It's the only thing I can do to help my family."

Kitai stared at him in silence for a long moment. Then she nodded once, an expression of comprehension coming over her features. "Now I understand, valleyboy," she said, quiet. She looked around them and said, "I do not wish to die. My family is not at stake. Freedom from my sire is useless to me if I am dead."

Tavi chewed on his lip, thinking. Then he said, "Kitai, is there any reason that we can't both get the Blessing? What happens if we both get back with it at the same time?"

Kitai frowned. "Then it will be assumed that The One tells us there is merit in either side's argument," she said. "The headman will be free to decide on his own."

"Wait," Tavi said, his heart pounding faster. "You mean that you'd get out from under your father, *and* he would be free to lead your people away from the battle with mine?"

Kitai blinked at Tavi and then smiled, slowly. "By The One, yes. That was his plan all along." She blinked her abruptly shining eyes several times and said fiercely, "The problem is that Doroga does not *seem* to be clever. No wonder my mother loved him."

"Then we work together," Tavi said. He offered the girl his hand. She glanced down at his hand, frowned at him, and then mimicked the gesture. Her hand was slim, hot, strong. Tavi shook and said, "It means we agree to work together."

"Very well," Kitai said. "What do you think we should do?"

Tavi shot a glance back to the Keepers, who were slowly, randomly dispersing again, crawling away in different directions and at different speeds.

"I have a plan."

An hour later, Tavi, covered with the soaked and chilly blanket, moved in silence over the smooth surface of the *croach*, his pace never varying. He kept count to himself as he walked, one pace per count. He was near five hundred. A Keeper walked perhaps ten feet in front of him, on a slow and steady pace toward the great tree at the center of the chasm. Tavi had followed it for several minutes without it turning to look at him or giving any indication that it sensed his presence. He had become more confident that he had determined how the things would detect him. So long as he was careful to be quiet and moved smoothly, he was effectively invisible.

The enormous tree loomed closer and closer, though the more Tavi could see of it, the less certain he was that *tree* was the right word to describe it.

Though the rest of the forest was covered in a sheath of the greenly glowing *croach*, this one tree, smooth sided, branchless, straight, was only covered to a height of ten or fifteen feet. The trunk was enormous, fully as big around as Bernardholt's walls. It didn't look like it had any bark at all—just smooth wood that reached up to a height of more than a hundred feet before ending in round, irregular edges, as though the tree had been snapped off by some giant hand, then had its rough edges smoothed by time.

At the base of the tree, there was a cavernous opening, a sloped and irregular triangle where the trunk parted, allowing entrance to the interior. Tavi paused and watched the Keeper he had been following. It paced slowly into the tree's interior, and as it passed within, another Keeper moved out on the other side of the opening, as though it were a tunnel in the causeway.

Tavi stopped for a few moments and watched. Shortly, the Keeper he'd been following or another like it came out of the tree in exactly the same place. Still another came creeping in from another direction and entered the tree in exactly the same manner as the first, emerging again a few moments later.

The Keepers must have been taking something into the tree. But what? Something small, if they were just scuttling in and out, like ants in and out of their hills. Food? Water? What did they carry?

Tavi shook his head and touched the blanket with his fingertips. Though it was still cool, it didn't feel as cold as it had a few minutes ago. The air down here in the chasm was just too warm. He had to hurry, he knew, because with each passing moment his method of concealment became less effective.

Tavi struggled to calm the pounding of his heart. What if these bugs were smarter than he thought? What if they had only allowed him to come this far because they wanted him there anyway? What if they just wanted to get him to a place where he could not escape and would then leap on him and devour him?

And what, he thought, could possibly be there inside

that tree? What would be there that the Keepers would be carrying something to? If they were like ants, existing in a colony, where some carried food, and some fought, and so on, would they have a queen, like ants did? If so, would she be inside the tree, at the heart of their domain?

A dozen more questions flicked through Tavi's mind, before he realized that he was doing nothing but wasting his time. He didn't have any answers to any of the questions, and he wouldn't get the answers standing in place—all he would get would be warmer. More vulnerable.

He kept counting in his head and reached five hundred.

Tavi all but held his breath, poised to flee if the plan went wrong, though he knew that his chances of escaping from the heart of the chasm were slim indeed. Tavi waited. And waited. Nothing happened.

He felt his heart begin to race as panic crept over him. Had Kitai abandoned him and her own part of the plan? Had something gone wrong? Had she been found and killed before the time limit was up? Could she even count to five hundred? What had gone wrong?

Tavi remained still and kept counting, deciding to give her another hundred counts before he fled.

Then the stillness and silence of the Wax Forest dissolved into a symphony of whistling shrieks. If Tavi had not seen it happening, he would never have believed that so many of the Keepers could be so close to him without his knowledge of them. They erupted from everywhere, from every surface where the *croach* glowed, ripping their way up out of the waxy forest floor, dropping from the glowing branches of the twisted trees, boiling out of the interior of the great tree trunk itself. Hundreds of them appeared, and the air itself shook with their whistles and clicks and the squeak of shell rubbing on shell.

Tavi froze, panicked. It was everything he could do to keep from bolting at the sheer speed with which they had appeared. One of the Keepers swept past him, almost close enough to brush against his soaked cloak.

They all swarmed off in the same direction—that opposite of the one that lead back to the ropes to the world above. Kitai had done her job, Tavi decided. She must have been keeping a slower count than Tavi had. She had used half of their remaining oil and the fires-tones to light a blaze that would draw the Keepers. If she was all right and had kept to the plan, she would even now be huddled beneath her blanket, moving for the ropes out.

The last of the Keepers in sight fled, vanishing into the glowing trees. All that remained was for Tavi to accomplish his part of the plan.

A lump crept up into his throat, and his knees felt like someone had simply slipped the muscles and tendons out of them. He thought that they might abruptly buckle and pitch him to the surface of the *croach* at any time, he was so afraid. He struggled to keep his breathing slow and quiet, to make sure that his trembling didn't result in any twitches that the Keepers would see as sudden, jerky movement, and stepped forward, into the trunk of the tree.

Inside, the *croach* wasn't in a smooth layer on the floor and walls—it was spilled and dumped and heaped and piled like wheat in a granary. Great swirling loops of it twirled up the walls or wound intricately through one another like the guts of some great and glowing beast. Tavi stared at them for a moment, in confusion and incomprehension. It was beautiful, in a bizarre, alien way—strange and unsettling and fascinating.

He jerked his eyes from one of the more intricate structures and moved closer to a wall, where it would be less likely for a newly entered Keeper to simply bump into him, looking around, struggling to orient himself according to Kitai's description.

He paced deeper into the eerie stillness inside the tree, around a mound of whirled *croach* that looked like an anthill and forward through a small field of lumpy *croach*, which could have contained another thousand Keepers, silent beneath the surface.

He found the mushrooms in a ring at the center of the field, just as Kitai had said. They grew at the base of a glowing mound twice the height of a man, as big around as a small house. The mound pulsed with greenish light, and Tavi thought he could see the shadow of something dark, something slender within.

He drew closer, a sensation of raw dread flowing over him like an icy bath, even worse than the soaked blanket he wore as a cloak. His knees grew weaker, and his breathing, despite his best efforts, became ragged.

Kitai was rather pretty, he thought. *Though she was a savage, there was something about her face, her eyes, that he found intriguing. If she wasn't dressed up in a ragged smock (which really was shamefully short now that he thought about it), she might look more like a girl, less wild. Of course, he had begun to see her without the smock. If he had told her to get more into the water, she might have taken it off altogether. The thought made his cheeks burn, but lingered in front of him, enticing in its exotic appeal.*

Tavi shook his head abruptly. What was the matter with him? He had to be careful and get the Blessing of Night. The dark mushrooms had some kind of spiny thorns on their undersides, Kitai had said, which had pierced her hand once and left welts that lasted for months.

He glanced up and around him, but saw no Keepers. That could be an illusion, he knew, There could be a dozen within arm's reach, But no matter how afraid he was, Tavi had to press on.

That was the history of his people, after all. The Alerans had never let fear or the odds of failure deter them from overcoming, prospering. Their oldest histories, his uncle had once told him, reached so far back into time that the hide and vellum and stone they had been scribed upon had worn away. They had come to Carna from another place, a small band of only a few thousand, and had found themselves pitched against an entire world. They had overcome the Icemen, the Children of the Sun and their stronghold in the Feverthorn Jungle, had repelled the Marat and the Canim over the centuries to claim the land of Alera as their own. They controlled the seas around their home, had walled out the Icemen in the north, overcome the Marat through sheer savage fighting. With their furies and their furycrafting, the Alerans dominated the world, and no other race or peoples could claim mastery over them.

Tavi shuddered and blinked his eyes several times. He must have stood there, his hand extended toward the first of the mushrooms for nearly a full minute, not moving. What was the matter with him?

The hairs on the back of his neck prickled up more sharply as he reached for the nearest mushrooms. He hurried, breath rasping, picking one, then another, careful to put them into the pouch at his belt.

And then he thought he saw something in the great mound in front of him *move*.

Tavi jerked his eyes up to it, flinching, and felt an immediate, hot pain in the fingers of his hand. The thorns on the next mushroom had pierced him. He jerked his hand back, and droplets of his blood flashed out and arced through the air, sprinkling the glowing mound in front of him.

Tavi stared at the mound, the droplets of his blood on it. The surface of the glowing *croach* abruptly pulsed, bulged, and then rippled beneath the droplets of his blood, moving like the skin of some hideous, enormous creature and making Tavi's own flesh crawl in response. He watched as the droplets of blood vanished into the mound, sinking into the surface of the *croach* like snowflakes into a still-melted pond.

And the shadowy shape within the mound abruptly shuddered. And moved. A slow unwinding of limbs, languid, liquid, as though from a sleeper that had, after an endless passing of seasons, finally awakened. It moved, and Tavi *felt* its movement, felt a vast, bewildering awareness that swept over him like the gaze of some ancient and horrible beast.

Terror flooded over Tavi, raw and *hot* rather than cold, terror that set his limbs on fire and burned any thought from his mind, save one: escape.

Tavi spun on his heel and, heedless of the danger in revealing himself, broke into a panicked sprint.

He would remember little of his run, later. One or two chirruping whistles, perhaps, echoed through the trees after him, but they were sparse, and he left them behind him, his steps light on the surface of the *croach,* terror lending him more speed than he would have credited to himself before that night.

He flicked one glance over his shoulder as he ran and saw something through the glowing trees, at the base of the monolith, the opening he'd fled through. He saw something tall, glistening—*alien.* It stood just within the central tree, just behind the doorway. Tavi could not quite see it, but he could *feel* it in a way both horribly intimate and beyond simple description.

The lower-pitched whistle that went out through the trees felt, to Tavi, like some sort of hideous, mocking laughter.

Tavi fled and did not look back again.

He ran over the *croach* until his legs were burning and his limbs felt as though they would be ripped apart by the demands he placed on them. He almost didn't see the strip of blanket that he had torn off and tied to a low tree branch before he left to mark his way back. He headed for it, and from that flag spotted the next, and the next, laying out his escape route back to the ropes at the base of the cliff.

"Aleran!" came a voice from before him. Kitai dropped from a tree branch ahead of him. "Do you have it?"

"Got two!" Tavi yelped. "Couldn't get any more!"

Kitai extended her hand, and Tavi shoved one of the mushrooms into it. "Run! Go, go go!"

Kitai nodded once, then stooped to the ground. Tavi hesitated behind the girl, dancing in place as he looked back over his shoulder. "Hurry," he panted. "Hurry, hurry, hurry."

Kitai drew out the firestones smoothly, her expression cool, and struck them together. Sparks fell from the stones onto the oil-soaked blanket that lay on the *croach* before them. Kitai watched the flames leap up, then moved quickly, reaching up to grab the end of the fishing line that Tavi had soaked in the icy water before he left. She jerked the line toward her, hand over hand. The other end of the line looped up over one of the higher branches of the tree, up where living leaves grew above the grasp of the *croach*, and then fell back down to where it was tied at one corner of the oil-soaked blanket. Kitai hauled the line in, and the blazing blanket rose up into the tree's branches and snagged among the living leaves.

Fire leapt up from the tree in a blaze, sudden and high, and once again, from the direction of the central spire, whistling shrieks rose up in a solid wall of terrifying sound—one underlaid, this time, by that deeper whistle, one that overrode the shrieks and continued over the silence.

Kitai stared at Tavi, her eyes suddenly wide. "What is that?"

"I don't know," Tavi said. "But, uh. I think, uh. I think I woke it up."

They looked at one another once more and, in silent accord, turned together and fled toward the ropes a few yards away, toward the safety at the top of the cliffs. To either side of him, Tavi saw the Keepers flooding toward the fire through the trees, closing on them in a carpet of glowing eyes and knobby limbs and leathery shells.

Tavi had reached the ropes and Kitai was only a few paces behind when something dropped down from one of the *croach*-shrouded trees above them, something tall and slender and horribly fast. Whatever it was, it wasn't a Keeper, because it reached out with one long limb and wrapped hard-looking, chitinous fingers around Kitai's ankle, hauling her to the ground. The girl let out a scream of sudden terror and twisted in that grip.

Tavi only saw what happened in bits and pieces. He remembered turning to see something that he thought was like some kind of hideous wasp, semitransparent wings fluttering in the glowing light of the *croach*. It bent over Kitai, weirdly humped shoulders flexing as its head whipped down, as mandibles sank into her thigh. Kitai let out a horrible scream and struck down at the thing's head with her fists, once, twice. Then her eyes rolled back in her head and her body started jerking and twisting in helpless spasm, limbs flailing. She kept trying to scream, but the sound came out broken, irregular.

The wasp-thing, covered in the glowing slime of the *croach*, lifted its head and let out a signal-whistle that echoed around the chasm like the tones of some vast bell. It shook blood from its mandibles, and Tavi caught a flash of multifaceted eyes, of some kind of yellowish fluid at the edges of Kitai's wounds.

"Valleyboy!" shouted a distant voice. Tavi looked up to see Doroga, one hand on the rope, leaning far out over the cliff, and even from so far below, Tavi could see that his face was anguished. "Aleran! You cannot save her! Come up!"

Tavi looked back and forth between Doroga and the Marat girl on the ground, the horrible thing crouched over her twitching body. Terror rose through him, a horrible taste in his mouth, and he couldn't see, couldn't seem to focus his eyes. One hand tightened on the rope in helpless frustration.

Kitai had saved his life.

She had trusted his plan to get them both out of the chasm alive.

He was the only one who could help her.

Tavi let go of the rope.

He turned and ran, not toward the thing crouched over Kitai, but past it, around several glowing trees and to the one they had set on fire. Keepers crowded in all around him. He could hear them coming through the forest toward him, shrieks and whistles resounding.

Tavi leapt up to the lowest branches of the tree, hauling himself into them and started scrambling toward the top, toward the fire. Halfway there, he hauled himself up and found himself face-to-face with a Keeper, which reared back from him in surprise, its mandibles clacking against its shell.

Tavi didn't have time to think. His hand flashed to where he'd put Fade's wickedly curved knife at his belt. He slashed it at the creature's eyes. It scuttled back from him. Tavi followed it, wriggling forward, thrusting the knife at the thing's face.

The Keeper let out a shriek and fell backward, out of the tree, its limbs flailing. It hit the ground twenty feet below with a crunch and a wet-sounding splat, and Tavi looked down to see it writhing on its back, legs flailing, its broken body trailing glowing fluids out onto the forest floor.

Tavi heard more Keepers coming. He hauled himself up higher into the tree, until he reached a branch bare of the *croach,* slender and unable to support his weight. Farther out along the branch hung the burning blanket. Fire spread along it, toward the trunk of the tree.

Tavi hacked at the branch with the knife, the steel biting into the soft wood. Then he gripped the knife in his teeth and hauled at the branch with both hands.

It swayed and then broke, peeling away from the tree. Tavi scrambled down, trailing the long branch with its flaming leaves, the oil-soaked blanket, and when he had reached the forest floor, he ran toward Kitai.

The thing crouched over her saw him coming and turned toward him with a hiss, its mandibles spreading wide, along with its chitinous arms. Though its eyes glittered and reflected the light of the fire from a thousand facets, it had a horribly slime-covered, unfinished look to it, as though it hadn't finished becoming whatever it was to be. Half-born, half-alive, the huge wasp-thing rattled its wings in a furious buzzing sound and whistled to the Keepers around them.

Tavi screamed and swung the branch in a broad, clumsy arc, fire trailing.

The thing hissed and drew back from the flames, jerking its wings back sharply.

Tavi seized on the advantage, shoving forward with the branch and driving the hissing monstrosity back from Kitai's still form. The girl lay, pale and silent, her eyes open but unmoving, her chest heaving in labored breaths. Tavi slipped an arm beneath her and, in a rush of terror, hauled her up onto his shoulder. He staggered beneath her weight, but grasped the branch and spun about, wildly swinging the blazing wood and leaves and blanket about him.

The creature leapt lightly away from him, landing on the wall several yards down from the ropes, horrible eyes focused intently on him.

Oh crows, Tavi thought. *It knows. It knows I'm going for the ropes.*

If he didn't move, he was finished. Even if the creature didn't leap on him, he would shortly be drowning in Keepers. Even his terrified strength was beginning to fade, his body to burn under all the effort. He had to get Kitai to the ropes, at least. He could tie her foot and Doroga could haul her up.

Doroga. Tavi looked up to the top of the cliff and saw Doroga's pale form there, staring down at them. Then the Gargant headman shouted, "Courage, valleyboy!" and vanished back over the lip of the cliff.

There was still a chance. Shoving the branch in front of him along the ground, he rushed toward the creature, which scuttled nimbly up the wall, a crablike sideways motion. Tavi looked above it, to an outcropping of rock. No good. He had to get it to move toward him, toward the ropes.

Tavi ground his teeth in frustration on the blade of the knife. "Oh furies, Kitai. I hope this works." Gracelessly, he dumped the girl onto the ground, then leapt toward and grabbed the nearest rope and started climbing.

The creature let out a whistle and scuttled toward him. He knew that he did not have a chance of escaping it, or of fighting it, there on the ropes, but he took the knife from his teeth and swiped it at the thing.

It paused, hesitating just out of his reach. Its horrible head tilted, as though assessing this new threat.

"Doroga!" Tavi screamed. "There it is, there it is!"

From above came a slow and tortured scream, bellowing in Doroga's basso, filled with anger and defiance.

Tavi would never have believed that a man could lift a boulder that large. But Doroga appeared at the top of the cliff again, bearing a stone the size of a coffin over his head, arms and shoulders and thighs bulging with effort. He flexed the whole of his body, a ponderous motion, and the huge stone hurtled down toward the creature.

Its head abruptly whirled on its neck, whipping around to face directly behind it. The creature moved, its wings buzzing, but it was not fast enough to wholly escape the plummeting stone. It flashed by Tavi, missing him by the breadth of a few fingers. The creature leapt away from the wall, but the stone crushed against it, sending it spinning out of the air to land on the ground many yards away. The stone itself hit the ground and shattered, chips of rock flying, glowing slime from within the *croach* hurled into the air as from a fountain.

Hot pain flashed along Tavi's leg, and he looked down to see his trousers cut by a flying piece of stone, blood on his leg. From above came Doroga's defiant howl of triumph, a bellowing roar that shook the walls of the chasm.

The creature let out another whistle, this one higher, filled with fury and, Tavi thought, with sudden fear. It staggered but could not rise and instead began dragging itself back into the trees, as the glowing eyes of dozens of Keepers began to appear behind it.

Tavi dropped the knife, slid down the rope, and ran to Kitai. He seized her and began dragging her back toward the ropes, grunting with effort but moving quickly, jerking her over the ground.

"Aleran," she whispered, opening her eyes. Her expression was pained, weary. "Aleran. Too late. Venom. My father. Tell him I was sorry."

Tavi stared down at her. "No," he whispered. "Kitai, no. We're almost out."

"It was a good plan," she said.

Her head lolled to one side, eyes rolling back.

"No," Tavi hissed, suddenly furious. "No, crows take you! You can't!" He reached into his pouch, fumbling through it as tears started to blur his vision. There must be something. She couldn't just die. She couldn't. They were so close.

Something stuck sharply into his finger, and pain flashed through him again. The crows-eaten mushroom had jabbed him with its spines. The Blessing of Night.

Fever. Poison. Injury. Pain. Even age. It has power over them all. To our people, there is nothing of greater value.

Weeping, Tavi seized the mushroom and started tearing off the spines with his fingers, heedless of the pain. Shrieks rose all around him, came closer, though the still-blazing branch seemed to have confused some of the Keepers, to have temporarily slowed their advance.

Tavi reached down and slipped an arm beneath Kitai's head, half hauling her up. He reached down to the wound over her thigh and crushed the mushroom in his hand.

Musty-scented, clear fluid leaked out from between his fingers and dribbled over the wound, mixing with blood and yellowish venom. Kitai's leg twitched as the fluid touched it, and the girl drew in a sudden breath.

Tavi lifted the rest of the mushroom to her lips and pressed it into her mouth. "Eat it," he urged her. "Eat it, you have to eat it."

Kitai's mouth twitched once, and then began to chew, automatically. She swallowed the mushroom and blinked her eyes slowly open, focusing them on Tavi.

Time stopped.

Tavi found himself staring down at the girl, suddenly aware of her, entirely aware of her in a way he never had been aware of anyone before. He could feel the texture of her skin beneath his hand and felt the abrupt compulsion to lay his fingers over her chest, to feel the beat of her heart beneath it, slowly gaining in strength. He could feel the surge of blood in her veins, the fear and regret and confusion that filled her thoughts. Those cleared as her eyes focused on him, widened, and Tavi realized that *she* had felt his own presence in the same way.

Not moving her eyes from his, Kitai reached out a hand and touched his chest in response, fingers pressed close to feel the beating of his heart.

It took Tavi a frozen, endless moment to separate the beating of his own heart, the rush of blood in his own ears, from hers. They beat together, perfectly in time. Even as he realized it, his own heartbeat began to speed, and so did hers, bringing a flush of heat to his face, one answered in her own expression. He stared at the wonder in her eyes and saw that it could only be a reflection of that in his own.

The scent of her, fresh and wild, curled up around him, through him like something alive. The shape of her eyes, her cheeks, her mouth. In that single moment, he saw in her the promise of the beauty that would come in time, the strength that had still to grow, the courage and reckless resourcefulness that matched his own and flamed wild and true in her.

The intensity of it made his eyes blur, and he blinked them, tried to clear the tears from them, only to realize that Kitai was blinking as well, her eyes filling with tears, going liquid and blurry.

When Tavi had blinked the tears away, his eyes returned to hers—only to find not opalescent swirls of subtle, shifting color, but wide pools of deep, emerald green.

Eyes as green as his own.

"Oh *no*," Kitai whispered, her voice stunned, weak. "Oh *no*." She opened her mouth, started to sit up—then shuddered once and slumped in his arms, abruptly overwhelmed with exhaustion.

The frozen moment ended.

Tavi lifted his dazed head to see the first of the Keepers edging past the blazing blanket and branch. Tavi hauled himself to his feet, lifting Kitai, and stumbled toward the ropes. He stepped into the loop at the base of one, then reached over to the other, and wrapped it around his waist, around her legs, tying her to him. Even before he was finished, Doroga had started hauling the rope up the face of the cliff. The other rope came in as well, where Hashat must have been pulling it along to keep it tight.

Tavi held on to the rope, and to Kitai, not really sure which one he held tighter. He closed his eyes, overwhelmed, and did not open them again until he and Kitai sat at the top of the cliff, in the cold, fresh, clean snow. When he opened his eyes again, he sat with his back against a stone and idly noted the fresh earth beside him, where Doroga had uprooted the boulder and hurled it down.

A moment later, he realized that Kitai lay against

his side, beneath one of his arms, warm and limp, half-conscious. He tightened his arm on her, gently, confused—but certain that he wanted her to sleep, to rest, and to be right where she was.

Tavi looked up and found Hashat staring down at them, wide-eyed, her expression bewildered and then, by slow degrees, becoming indignant. She turned to Doroga and demanded, "What are you going to do about this?"

The headman, veins still standing out on his arms and thighs, tipped his head back and poured out a rich and rolling laugh. "You know as well as I, Hashat. It's done."

The Horse headman scowled and folded her arms over her chest. "I've never heard of such a thing," she said. "This is unacceptable."

"This *is*," Doroga rumbled. "Other matters are before us now."

Hashat flipped her mane out of her eyes with a toss of her head. "I don't like it," she said, her tone resigned. "This was a trick. You tricked me."

Doroga's eyes glittered, and a smile lurked at his lips, but he said in a stern tone, "Keep your mind on why we are here, Hashat."

"The trial," the Marat woman said and turned back to Tavi. "Well, Aleran? Did you recover the Blessing?"

Tavi shivered and felt abruptly stupid. He had forgotten. In all the excitement and confusion, he had forgotten the trial. He had forgotten that he had used the mushroom he'd needed to win on Kitai. And though he may have saved the girl's life, he had lost the trial. His own life was forfeit. And the Marat, united, would ride against the people of his home.

"I . . ." Tavi said. He reached toward his pouch—and felt warm fingers inside.

Tavi looked down and saw Kitai drawing her hand back out of his pouch. Her eyes blinked open once, toward his, and he felt more than saw the silent gratitude in them, the respect for his courage.

"But it was so stupid," she whispered. Then she closed her eyes again.

Wordlessly, Tavi reached inside his pouch and found the second Blessing of Night where Kitai had left it. He drew it out on fingers already pricked and bleeding and offered it to Doroga.

Doroga knelt down on both knees in front of Tavi and accepted the Blessing, his expression grave. He looked down at the mushroom, then at Kitai's thigh, the yellowish venom drying there. His eyes widened with sudden realization, then went back to Tavi. Doroga's head tilted to one side, staring at him, and the boy felt certain that Gargant headman knew exactly what had happened in the alien valley below.

Doroga reached out and laid one huge hand on Kitai's pale hair for a moment, eyes gentle. Then he looked back at Tavi and said, "I loved her mother very much. Kitai is all I have left of her. You have courage, Aleran. You risked your life to save hers. And in doing so, you have saved not one, but two whom I love. Who are my family."

The Marat rose to his full height and reached down his hand to Tavi. "You have protected my family, my home. The One demands that I repay you for that debt, Aleran."

Tavi drew in a sharp breath and looked from Doroga to Hashat. The Horse warrior's eyes gleamed with a sudden excitement, and she drew in a breath, laying one of her hands on the hilt of her saber.

"Come, young man," Doroga said quietly. "My daughter needs to rest. And if I am to repay you, I have work to do. Will you come with me?"

Tavi took a breath, and when he spoke, his voice sounded, to him, to be deeper, more steady than he'd heard it before. For once, it didn't waver or crack. "I will come with you."

He took Doroga's hand. The huge Marat headman showed his teeth in a sudden, fierce smile and hauled Tavi to his feet.

⋄⋄⋄⋄ CHAPTER 35

Amara took off her belt in pure frustration and used the buckle to rap hard against the bars in the tiny window of the cell she'd been thrown into. "Guard!" she shouted, trying to force authority into her tone. "Guard, come down here at once!"

"Won't do any good," Bernard said, stretched out on the pallet against the far wall of the room. "They can't hear anything down here."

"It's been hours," Amara said, pacing back and forth in front of the door. "What could that idiot Pluvus be waiting for?"

Bernard rubbed at his beard with one hand. "Depends how gutless he is."

She stopped to look at him. "What do you mean?"

Bernard shrugged. "If he's ambitious, he's going to send out his own people to find out what's going on. He'll try to exploit the situation to his advantage."

"You don't think he is?"

"Not like that, no. Odds are, he's got Gram put in a bed somewhere, and he's dispatched a courier to carry word to Riva, informing them of the situation and asking for instructions."

Amara spat out an oath. "There isn't time for that. He'll have thought of it. He's got Knights Aeris around the perimeter of the Valley to intercept any airborne couriers."

"He? The man at the ford. The one who shot at Tavi." Though his tone didn't change much, Bernard's words held a note of bleak determination.

Amara folded her arms over her chest and leaned against the door, exhausted, frustrated. If it would have helped, she'd have started crying. "Yes. Fidelias." The bitter venom in her own voice surprised even her, and she repeated the name more quietly. "Fidelias."

Bernard turned his head to look at her for a long, quiet moment. "You know him."

She nodded once.

"Do you want to talk about it?"

Amara swallowed. "He is . . . he was my teacher. My *patriserus.*"

Bernard sat up, frowning. "He's a Cursor?"

"Was," Amara said. "He's thrown in with someone.

A rebel." She flushed, her face heating. "I probably shouldn't say any more, Steadholder."

"You don't have to," he assured her. "And call me Bernard. As long as we're stuck in a storage closet together, I think we can skip the titles. There won't be room for all of us."

She gave him a weak smile. "Bernard, then."

"He was your friend, this Fidelias."

She nodded, looking away from him, quiet.

"More than that?"

Amara flushed. "If he'd have let it happen. I was about thirteen when I started training with him, and he was everything. He didn't though. He didn't . . ." She let her voice trail off.

"He didn't want to take advantage of you," Bernard suggested. At Amara's flustered silence, he said, "I can appreciate that in a man."

"He's good," she said. "I mean, skilled. One of the Crown's best. He's got more missions on record than any Cursor alive, and there are rumors of many more that were never recorded. Some of the things he's done are in textbooks. He's saved the lives of thousands of people who never even knew he was there." She swallowed. "And if you'd asked me a week ago, I would never have dreamed that there could be a man more loyal to the Realm." She heard her voice grow bitter again. "A patriot."

"Maybe that's the problem," Bernard said, pensive.

Amara frowned and looked at him. "What do you mean?"

"There's two kinds of bad men in the world. I mean, there's all kinds of ways for a man to go bad, but when you get right down to it, there's only about two kinds of men who will hurt others with forethought. Premeditation. Men that don't figure there's anyone else alive who matters but them. And men who figure that there's something that matters more than anyone's life. Even their own." He shook his head. "First one is common enough. Petty, small. They're everywhere. People who just don't give a scorched crow about anyone else. Mostly, the bad they do doesn't amount to much.

"The second kind is like your *patriserus*. People who hold something dear above their own lives, above anyone else's. They'll fight to protect it and kill to protect it, and the whole time they'll be thinking to themselves that it has to be done. That it's the right thing to do." Bernard glanced up at her and said, "Dangerous those. Very dangerous."

Amara nodded. "Yes. He's dangerous."

"Who said," Bernard rumbled, eyes steady, "that I was talking about Fidelias."

Amara looked up at him sharply.

"It all comes down to people. You can't have a Realm or an ideal without people to believe in it. Support it. The Realm exists to protect people. Seems kind of backward to me to sacrifice people to protect it."

"It's just not that simple, Steadholder."

"Isn't it? Remember who taught you," Bernard said, his voice gentle, the words clear, firm. "Right now, he's out there and he probably thinks he's doing the only thing he can. Crows, he probably thinks he's doing the right thing. That he's in a position to know when others don't, and so it's his choice to make and no one else's."

She pushed her hair back from her face. "How do I know that he hasn't made the right one?"

Bernard stood up and moved toward her. He put a hand on her shoulder, eyes earnest. "Because a sound tree doesn't have bad roots, Amara. No enterprise of greatness begins with treachery, with lying to the people who trust and love you."

Tears did burn her eyes this time, and she closed them for a moment. He tugged her a bit toward him, and she leaned against his warmth for a moment, his strength. "I don't know what else to do," she told him. "I've done everything I can think of to try to avert what's coming. It hasn't been enough." And Gaius had counted on her. Had entrusted her with this mission.

"Sometimes," Bernard rumbled, "the only smart thing to do is nothing. Sometimes you just have to be still and see how events begin to unfold before you move. Be patient."

She shook her head. "There isn't time for that," she insisted. "We have to get someone down here. You have to make them listen to me or—"

Bernard put both large hands on her shoulders, gripped her lightly, and pressed her shoulders against the heavy wood of the door. Then he leaned his weight against her, trapping her there, and lowered his mouth to hers in a kiss that managed to be abrupt and relaxed all at the same time.

Amara felt her eyes widen in surprise. His mouth was soft, warm, and she felt a surge of outrage. Did he think she was some vapid, chattering child to be distracted with a kiss, like a twittering schoolgirl?

Granted, his warmth, his closeness, were very comforting. Granted, the gentle power of his hands and body was something that felt compelling, reassuring, and intimidating all at once. And granted that the scent of him, leather and the wind outdoors and something indescribably, utterly masculine, was something she felt she could take off her clothes and roll about naked in.

She lifted her hands to shove him away from her, but found her palms just resting on the heavy muscle of his chest, taking the measure of his strength, his heat, while her mouth turned farther up to his, her lips parting, pressing against his, exploring and tasting him.

He let out a small, hungry sound, pressing closer to her, his body to hers, and her heart raced. She was still annoyed with him. Of course. And she had a job to do. And regardless of how nice he might smell, or feel, or how her body responded so quickly to his—

She broke the kiss with a frustrated growl. He drew away, just a little, his eyes searching hers.

"What do you think you're doing?" she demanded. Her voice came out more quiet than she meant it to, low.

"I think I am locked in a small room with a beautiful woman," Bernard said, evenly. "And I am kissing her."

"I don't have time to kiss you," Amara said, but her eyes focused on his mouth and her own lips felt a little pang of separation.

"But you want to kiss me," Bernard said.

"No," Amara said. "I mean, this isn't the time."

"No? Where did you plan to go?" He bent his head and placed a soft kiss upon the side of her throat, mouth warm. His tongue fluttered over her skin, and lightning raced out through her limbs in response, yearning more fierce than anything she had felt before. She felt her body melt against his, though she didn't really mean for it to.

She grasped at his hair and dragged his mouth back up to hers, sudden and hungry, kissing him, pressing back against him with a kind of defiant abandon, her hands sliding over his chest, arms, shoulders. Then she shoved against the wall with her hips, pushing him away from it, her body still close to his. She kept him going, back to the pallet, until it hit the back of his knees and he dropped down onto it.

She never lifted her mouth from his, following him, settling astride his hips as he sat down. His hands settled on her waist, huge and strong, and her hunger doubled on itself, sudden irrational desire to feel those hands on her thighs, her back, her throat, everywhere.

"This is just a kiss," she whispered, against his mouth, lips too hungry to touch his to spare much time for words. "That's all. Just a kiss." She followed her urges, trailing a line of kisses down over his jaw to the softer skin of his throat, the beginning of the slope of one shoulder, biting at his skin.

"That's all," he agreed, though there was a groan hidden inside the words. His hands tightened on her waist, sliding down to her hips.

Amara drew up sharply as her hips pressed against his, focusing on his face, struggling to clear her thoughts. But it was hard—it would be so much easier to get rid of her clothing, his, naked skin between them was what she wanted. She wanted to feel his weight pinning her down, feel the hot strength of him pushing into her, to struggle and test her strength against his, and to be overcome. It was a fire inside of her, a raw and primitive *need,* something that could not be denied. With a snarl of pure, animal hunger, she started tearing at his belt.

"Wait," Bernard said. "Oh, oh *crows,* Brutus you *idiot.*" He moved beneath her, abruptly, lifting her and dropping her unceremoniously on the pallet. She landed with a thump.

Bernard took a pair of swift steps away from her and held up his hand, palm toward her, motioning her to stop. He frowned in concentration and muttered, "No. Brutus, *down.*"

And Amara abruptly found herself staring at Bernard from the pallet, cold and hungry and panting, body aching with fading need, her clothing disheveled, her hair mussed, her lips swollen from the heat and intensity of the kisses.

She lifted a hand to her temple. "Y-you . . . you crafted on me."

"I know," Bernard said, his face flushing bright red. "I didn't mean to. I'm sorry."

"You *earthcrafted* me."

"I'm sorry," Bernard said again, quickly. "Brutus is . . . my fury is a strong one, and he starts to thinking he knows what's good for me better than I do sometimes." Bernard sank down against the floor. "I'm sorry. I didn't know he was doing it, or I would have never. I mean, I—" He shook his head. After a moment he said, "It's been a long time. And Brutus just . . . wanted to make something happen."

She stared at him for a long moment, settling onto the pallet, getting her breathing, her feelings back under control. She gathered her feet up and wrapped her arms around her knees, staring down at her shoes, the slippers Isana had put on her feet at Bernardholt.

"You were married," she said, quietly.

"Ten years ago," Benard said, the words quiet, soft, as though they were burrs that would tear at his mouth if he sent them out too quickly. "She died. Blight. My daughters, too."

"And you haven't . . ." She let it hang unspoken.

He shook his head. "Been busy. Haven't really wanted to be close to anyone until—" He drew in a breath. "Until you kissed me last night. Guess it stirred up some things."

Amara couldn't keep the wry tone from her voice. "I guess it did."

Bernard flushed further and didn't lift his eyes.

She let out a tired laugh. "Bernard. It's all right. You didn't hurt me." And she'd enjoyed it. Wanted it. She had to work to keep from blushing herself. Just the memory of the molten need of that kiss was enough to make her shiver.

"Doesn't make it right." He looked up at her, his eyes worried and, she thought, exquisitely vulnerable, exposing how much he cared about what she would think. "You sure you're all right?"

She nodded. "Well. The obvious parts of being locked up aside."

"I don't think we'll have to worry about it too much longer. That's why I wanted to steal a kiss. I didn't mean that to happen, but I wanted a chance to kiss you before."

"Before what?"

Bernard tilted his head to one side. "Listen."

Dimly, outside, Amara heard a chime tolling the midnight hour.

"Change of the watch," Bernard said. "If Pluvus follows the regulations, he'll go to his bed and appoint one of his senior centurions as the watch commander."

"All right," Amara said. "What does that do for us?"

"It gets us a chance to talk to someone I know," Bernard said. He rose, head tilted as he listened, and only a moment later the heavy door at the top of the cellar stairs rattled and banged open.

Amara felt her heart race again. "Will they let us out?"

"One way to know," Bernard said, and stood by the door.

Amara came up to stand beside him. "You wanted to kiss me?"

He cleared his throat. "Yes."

"Why?"

"I like you," he said.

"You like me."

Color crept up his cheeks. "You're pretty, and you're brave as anyone I ever saw. And I like you."

She felt her mouth creep up at the edges and fought the smile. Then gave in to it, looking up at him, and rose onto her toes to plant a kiss on the roughness of his cheek.

He glanced down at her, his gaze, for just a moment, showing that heated hunger that she had felt in his kiss. "Sometime, I think I'm going to get you alone when there isn't some kind of life threatening situation to interrupt me."

Amara's tongue promptly stuck to the roof of her mouth, which had as abruptly gone dry. She tried to gather up enough of her suddenly scattered wits to respond, but the sound of heavy boots on the stairs came first, and a key rattled in the door.

The door opened, and Pluvus Pentius faced them with a vacuous expression.

Or rather, that was Amara's first impression. The truthfinder's head lolled forward on his neck, and a moment later he let out a distinct snore. The door opened farther, and Amara saw two men on either side of the snoozing truthfinder, supporting his limp weight. One she recognized, the grizzled old healer from earlier in the day. The other wore a centurion's breastplate and helmet, a round-faced man of middle years with dark, squinting eyes.

"Bernard," said Harger cheerfully. "I was just asking Pluvus here if we shouldn't let you out, and he said 'yes.'" Harger seized Pluvus's hair and vigorously rocked his head back and forth. "See? The boy can't handle his drink, I'm afraid."

"Steadholder," said the centurion, his voice tense. "This could be worth my helm."

"Giraldi." Bernard stepped forward and clasped the man's shoulder. "Good to see you. How's Rosalia?"

"Worried," Giraldi said, his squinting eyes moving from Bernard back to Amara. "Bernard, what's going on?"

"The Marat are coming. Here. And we think they have the support of a company of mercenary Knights."

Giraldi stared at Bernard, his mouth dropping open. "Bernard. That's crazy. That couldn't happen. Alerans helping the Marat?"

"I was half killed by a Marat warrior near Garados two days ago," Bernard said. "Last night, a group of crafters stronger than me tried to kill my nephew, who had also seen them."

"Tavi? Great furies, Bernard."

"There isn't any time. I told Gram, and he believed me. He ordered a full arming and mobilization, scouts to be sent out, messengers to Riva for reinforcements, before we were attacked by more of the same at the gates to Garrison. Has it been done?"

"I've ordered my full century on watch and armed, Bernard, and I've sent runners to the watchtowers to make sure the balefires will be lit if there's trouble, but that's as much as I can do on my authority."

"Then do it on Gram's," Bernard said. "Get the Knights armed and ready and the rest of your Legion armed out. Bring the local folk inside the walls and get word to Riva. Without the support of the Rivan Legions, it might not matter if we *are* ready to fight."

With an irritated growl, Giraldi shoved Pluvus's weight onto Harger, who accepted it with a grunt. "Bernard," Giraldi said, "you don't understand. Pluvus is bringing charges against you. Treason, Bernard. He says you were a part of a plot to assassinate Gram."

"That's a load of slive droppings, and you know it."

"But I'm not a Citizen," Giraldi said, his tone quiet. "And off your steadholt, neither are you. With Gram down—"

"How bad is he?"

Harger grunted. "Not good, Bernard. Unconscious. The knife got him low in the back. He's not as young as he used to be, and he'd been drinking pretty heavy the past few weeks. I've done as much as I can for him, but we sent one of our Knights Aeris to bring a healer with more skill than me. I'm a workhorse, but this is delicate. Beyond me."

"At least you've done that. Did he take any word of the attack?"

Giraldi made a frustrated sound. "Bernard. There hasn't been an attack. There hasn't been any sign of an attack."

"It's coming," Bernard snapped. "Crows and carrion, you know what Gram would do. Do it."

"I *can't*," Giraldi snarled, "Pluvus gave specific orders against a general arming at 'wild and unfounded rumor.' Unless Gram gives me orders himself, I won't be able to do any more than I already have. You don't think I want to, Bernard? I've a wife and three children here. I don't have the authority."

"Then I'll—"

Giraldi shook his head. "You don't either. There are men here who know you, but there are a lot of new ones, too. Those fools you met at the wall today."

Harger let out a nasty chuckle.

Giraldi shot the healer a hard look. "You flattened the son of a Rivan Lord, Bernard. They're insulted, and they aren't going to take any orders from you. You don't have the rank to do this."

Amara stepped forward and said, "I do."

The three men fell abruptly silent. Giraldi reached up and swept off his helmet, a polite gesture. "Excuse me, young lady. I didn't see you there. Miss, I know that you want to help, but—"

"But this is man's work?" Amara asked. "None of us have time for that, centurion. My name is Amara ex Cursori Patronus Gaius. His Majesty has seen fit to grant me the honorary rank of Countess, which I believe entitles me to the same privileges of command as Count Gram."

"Well, young lady, in theory I'm sure that—"

Amara stepped closer to the centurion. "Why are you wasting my time, centurion? You obviously believe that there is a threat, or you wouldn't have armed your men. Stop getting in my way and tell me who I have to bring to heel to get anything done around here."

Giraldi stared at her in baffled surprise. Then he looked at Bernard and said, "Is she telling the truth?"

Bernard folded his arms and eyed Giraldi.

The centurion passed a hand over his close-cropped hair. "All right, Your Ladyship. I suppose the first place to start would be Pluvus—"

Harger drawled, "Pluvus agrees with whatever the lass says, don't you sir?" He took Pluvus's hair and nodded his head back and forth. "There you have it. I'm the doctor, and in my medical opinion, this man is of sound judgment. Sounder than when he's awake, anyway."

Giraldi swallowed nervously. "Yes, and then you'd have to speak to Pirellus, Your Ladyship. He's the Knight Commander of the garrison here. If he goes with you, the other centurions will follow his lead, and their men with them."

"Pirellus? Pirellus of the Black Blade?"

"Aye, Your Ladyship. Strong metalcrafter he is. Fencer like I've rarely seen. Old blood, old family, that one. He don't care much for these puppies we got, but he don't care to be ordered about by a woman, either, Your Ladyship. He gave 'Finder Olivia headaches like you never saw."

"Wonderful," Amara said, drawing in a breath, thinking. Then she turned to Bernard. "I need my sword back."

Bernard's eyes widened. "Don't you think killing him is a little extreme? Especially since he'd cut you apart."

"It won't come to that. Get it for me." She turned to Giraldi and said, "Take me to him."

"Your Ladyship," Giraldi said hesitantly. "I don't know if you understand. He and the rest of the Knights are abed already."

"They're gambling and wenching you mean," Amara said. "I've seen it before, centurion. Take me to him."

"I'll have the sword, Countess," Bernard rumbled.

She looked back at him and flashed him a quick smile. "Thank you, Steadholder. Healer, perhaps the truthfinder needs a good bed."

"I think he does, at that," agreed Harger cheerfully. He toted Pluvus into the cell and dumped him unceremoniously on the bare palette. "The closest bed possible."

Amara had to stifle the laugh that leapt to her throat and struggled to keep her expression stern. "Centurion, lead on."

"Come on, Bernard," Harger said. "I know where they put your stuff."

Amara followed Centurion Giraldi up out of the basement of what turned out to be a storage building and into Garrison itself, laid out in the standard formation of a marching camp. "Mutiny," he muttered. "Assaulting a senior officer. Abducting a senior officer. Misrepresenting the orders of a senior officer."

"What's that, centurion?"

"I'm counting how many ways I'll be executed, Your Ladyship."

"Look at it this way," Amara said. "If you live to be hanged, we'll all be very fortunate." She nodded toward the barracks that would customarily house the Knights of a camp. Lights still glowed inside, and she heard a piper and laughter from within. "This one?"

"Yes, Lady," the centurion said.

"Fine. Get to your men. Make sure they watch the signal towers. And ready any other available defense of the walls."

The centurion drew in a breath and nodded. "All right. Do you think you'll convince him, Lady?"

"The only question is whether or not he survives it," Amara said, and her voice sounded cool to her, very certain. "One way or another, those Knights will be ready to fight, by the Crown."

Harger came panting up to them out of the dark, blowing like an old but spirited horse. He held the sword Amara had claimed from the Princeps Memorium in his hand and offered her the hilt. "There you go," the healer panted. "Hope you work quick, girlie. One of the guards thought he saw a light from the furthest tower, but it went out. Bernard took a horse out to see what's going on."

Amara's heart skipped a beat. Bernard alone in that country. The Marat that close. "How far is the tower from here?"

"Seven, eight miles," Harger said.

"Centurion. How long to move troops that far?"

"Without furycrafting? At night? That's rough country, Lady. Maybe they could be here in three hours or a little more, as a body. Light troops could do it a lot faster."

"Crows," Amara breathed. "All right. Get the rest of the troops out of bed, centurion. Assemble them and tell them that the Knight Commander will address them in a few moments."

"Uh, Lady? If he won't come—"

"Leave that to me." She slipped the sword's scabbard through her belt, holding it at her hip with her left hand and stalked toward the Knight's barracks, her heart pounding in her throat. She stopped outside the doors and took a breath to stabilize herself and clear her mind. Then she put her hand on the door and shoved it open, hard, letting it rattle against its frame.

The inside of the barracks was thick with the smell of wood smoke and wine. Furylamps burned in shades of gold and scarlet. Men played at draughts at one table, stacks of coins riding on the game, while groups threw dice at two others. Women, most of them of an age to speak of their status as camp women, draped on a man's arm here and there, carried wine, or sprawled on a sofa or in a chair, drinking or kissing. One girl, a lithe young thing in a slave's collar and little more, danced to the music of the piper before the fire, casting a slender, dark shadow there like some kind of exotic ornament.

Amara took a breath and walked to the nearest table. "Excuse me," she said, keeping her voice cool, business-like. "I'm looking for Commander Pirellus."

One of the men at the table looked up at her with a leer. "He's already had his girls for tonight, lass. Though I'd be happy to fill your . . ." His eyes wandered suggestively. ". . . time."

Amara faced the man and said, cooly, "I'm going to pretend I didn't hear that. Where is Commander Pirellus?"

The man's face darkened with drunken anger, and he straightened, picking up a knife in his fist. "What? You saying I'm not good enough for you? You some kind of snob whore that only goes for rich boy Citizens?"

Amara reached for Cirrus and borrowed of her fury's swiftness. Her arm blurred, drawing the short guardsman's blade from its scabbard at her hip. The sword leapt across the space between them before the startled soldier could react, and Amara leaned forward enough to let it dimple his throat. The room abruptly went dead silent, but for the crackle of the fire. "I am a Cursor of the First Lord himself. I'm here on business. And I have no tolerance for drunken fools. Drop the knife."

The soldier made a strangled sound, holding up one hand to her, palm out. The other, he lowered to the table and set the knife down. Amara could feel the ugly stares of the men around him focusing on her like the tips of a dozen spears about to be driven home. Her throat grew tight with fear, but she allowed none of it to be seen on her face, leaving her expression cool, calm, and merciless as an icy sea.

"Thank you," Amara said. "Now. Where is Pirellus?"

Amara heard a door open behind her, and a calm, almost languid voice said, in a lazy Parcian drawl, "He's having his bath. But he's always at the disposal of a lady."

Amara drew the sword from the throat of the soldier before her and with a glance of disdain, turned her back on him to face the speaker.

He was a man, taller than most, his skin the dark golden brown of her own. His night-black hair, worn long against Legion regulations, spilled down in a damp tangle around his shoulders. He was lean with hard, flat muscle, and bore a slender, curved sword of metal blacker than mourning velvet in his hand. He faced Amara with an expression of bland, confident amusement on his face.

He was also dripping wet and as naked as a babe.

Amara felt her cheeks start to heat and firmly kept herself from giving away her embarrassment. "You are Pirellus, Knight Commander of Garrison?"

"A Parcian girl," Pirellus said, a wide, white smile coming over his mouth. "It has been a very long time since I have sat down and entertained a Parcian girl." He inclined his head, though his sword did not change its casually ready position at his side. "I am Pirellus."

Amara arched an eyebrow at him and looked him up and down. "I'd heard so much about you."

Pirellus smiled, confident.

"I thought you'd be," she coughed delicately, letting her gaze linger significantly. "Taller."

The smile vanished. With it, Amara would hope, some of that arrogance.

"Put on some clothes, Commander," Amara said. "Garrison is about to come under attack. You will arm and prepare your men and address the members of the Legions who are assembling outside even now."

"Attack?" Pirellus drawled. "By whom, may I ask?"

"The Marat. We believe they have the support of a company of Knights. Possibly more."

"I see," he said, his tone unconcerned. "Now, let me

see. I've seen you somewhere before. I'm trying to remember where."

"The capital," Amara said. "I went to some of your matches two years ago and was in a class you lectured at the Academy."

"That's right," Pirellus said, smiling. "Though you were dressed up like a woman at that time. Now I remember—you're that little windcrafter girl who saved those children in the fires on the east side of the city. That was bravely done."

"Thank you," Amara said.

"Stupid, but brave. What are you doing here, schoolgirl?"

"I'm a Cursor now, Pirellus. I've come to warn you of an attack before you get buried in a Marat horde."

"How thoughtful of you. And you are speaking to me instead of the garrison commander, because?"

"I am speaking to you because you are the ranking capable officer. The Count is unconscious, Pluvus an idiotic politico, and the watch commander a centurion without the rank to order a general mobilization. You will order it and send to Riva for reinforcements."

Pirellus's brows shot up. "On whose authority?"

"On mine," Amara said. "Countess Amara ex Cursori Patronus Gaius of Alera."

Pirellus's expression changed again, to a scowl. "You got yourself a title for that little display, and you think you can go where you please and order around who you like?"

Amara abruptly reversed her grip on her sword and laid it, blade gleaming, on the table beside her. Then she turned to face him and walked toward him, stopping less than an arm's length away. "Pirellus," she said, keeping her voice to a low murmur. "I'd rather not be here. And I'd rather not pull rank on you. Don't force me to push this as far as I'm willing to."

His eyes met hers, hard, stubborn. "Don't threaten me, girl. You've got nothing to do it with."

In answer, Amara called upon Cirrus again and struck the man with her open hand across his cheek, a ringing blow that had landed and turned his head before he could avoid it. Pirellus stepped back from her, blade coming up to rest pointing at her heart in pure reflex.

"Don't bother," Amara told him. "If you will not do what needs to be done, I challenge you to *juris macto* here and now, for negligence of duty treasonous to the Realm." She turned from him and reclaimed the blade, turning back to face him. "Blades. I can begin when you are ready."

The commander had stopped and was staring at her intently. "You're kidding me," he said. "You've got to be joking. You could never beat me."

"No," Amara said, "but I'm enough of a blade to make you kill me to win. You'd be killing a Cursor in the execution of her duties, Commander. Whether I'm a man or woman, whether I'm right or wrong about the coming attack, you will be guilty of treason. And we both know what will happen to you." She lifted her sword and saluted him. "So. If you are willing to throw your life away, please, call the duel and let us be about it. Or get dressed and make ready to defend Garrison. But one way or another, you will *hurry*, Commander, because I have no time to coddle your ego."

She faced him across the space of a pair of long steps,

her blade held up, and did not blink at him. Her heart raced in her throat, and she felt a drop of sweat slide down her jaw to her neck. Pirellus was a master metal-crafter, one of the finest swordsmen alive. If he chose to engage in the duel, he could kill her, and there would be little she could do to stop him. And yet it was necessary. Necessary to convince him of her sincerity, necessary for him to know that she was willing to die to get him to act, that she would sooner die than fail in her duty to Alera, to Gaius. She stared at his eyes and focused on the task before her and refused to give in to her fear or to let it make the sword tremble at all.

Pirellus stared at her for a moment, his expression dark, pensive.

Amara held her breath.

The Knight straightened, slowly, from his casual slouch. He laid the fiat of his blade across his forearm, holding it in one hand, and bowed to her, the motion graceful, angrily precise. "Countess," he said, "in the interests of preserving the safety of this garrison, I will do as you command me. But I will make a note of it in my report that I do so under protest."

"So long as you do it," Amara said. Relief spun in her head, and she nearly sat down on the floor. "You'll see to the preparations, then?"

"Yes, Your Ladyship," Pirellus said, his words exqui-sitely barbed and courteous. "I think I can take care of things. Otto, let's get something into the men besides tea. Wake everyone up. Camdon, lass, fetch me my clothes and armor." One of the men at the draughts table and the collared dancer went running.

Amara withdrew from the room and out into the

town again, sheathing her sword and taking deep breaths. It was only moments later that she heard a tightly focused roar of wind and looked up to see a pair of half-dressed Knights Aeris hurtle into the night sky on different headings, bound for Riva, she had no doubt.

She had done it. Finally, Garrison was readying itself for battle. Troops started assembling in the square at the center of town. Furylights glowed. Centurians barked orders, and a drummer began playing fall in. Dogs barked, and wives and children appeared from some of the other buildings, even as other soldiers were dispatched to wake those in the outbuildings and to draw them into the protection of the town's walls.

It was in the hands of the soldiers now, Amara thought. Her part was done. She had been the eyes of the Crown, its hands, giving warning to Alera's defenders. Surely that would be enough. She found a shadow against one of the heavy walls of the town and leaned back against it, letting her head fall back against the stone. Her body sagged with sudden exhaustion, relief hitting her like a hard liquor, making her feel heavy and tired. So very tired.

She looked up at the stars, now and then visible through the pale clouds overhead, and found herself vaguely surprised that no tears fell. She was too tired to cry.

Drums rolled, and trumpets sounded out orders, different brazen tones calling to separate centuries and maniples of the Legion. Men began to line the walls, while others drew water in preparation for fighting fires. Watercrafters, both Legion Healers, like Harger, and homeskilled wives and daughters of the *legionares* made their way to the covered shelters inside the walls, where tubs of water were filled and held in preparation to receive the wounded. Firecrafters tended to blazes on the walls, while windcrafters of the Knights at Garrison took to the air above, flying in patrol to warn and ward any surprise attack from the darkened night skies. Earthcrafters manned stations at the gates and walls, their weapons nearby, but their bare hands resting on the stone of the defenses, calling on their furies to imbue them with greater obdurate strength.

The wind began to blow from the north, bringing to Amara the scent of the distant Sea of Ice and of men and of steel. For a time, as distant light began to brush against the eastern horizon, all was silent. Tense anticipation settled over those inside the walls. In one of the barracks buildings, emptied now of men and filled with the children from the outbuildings and the town, children sang a lullaby together, the sound of it sweet and gentle.

Amara pushed away from her darkened patch of wall and paced forward, toward the gates that faced out into the Marat lands beyond Garrison. The guards at the base of the walls stopped her, but Centurion Giraldi saw her and waved her past them. She mounted a ladder that led up to the battlements above the gate, where archers and firecrafters had gathered the most thickly, prepared to rain death down on anyone attempting to storm the gates of the town.

Giraldi stood beside Pirellus, now decked out in armor of gleaming steel. The Parcian swordsman glanced at her and then out at the darkness. "There's been no sign," he said. "No balefires lit by the watchtowers."

Giraldi said quietly, "One of my men saw something earlier. A scout went to look."

Amara swallowed. "Has he come back?"

"Not yet, Lady," Giraldi said, his expression worried. "Not yet."

"Quiet," said one of the *legionares* abruptly, a lanky young man with large ears. He leaned out, one hand lifting to his ear, and Cirrus stirred gently against Amara, telling her of the windcrafting the young man was working to listen.

"A horse," he said. "A horseman."

"Lights," said Pirellus, and the command echoed down the walls. One by one, furylamps, brilliant and blue and cold lit along the walls, casting a glare out onto the predawn darkness beyond.

For a long moment, nothing moved on the snow. And then they could all hear it, the sound of galloping hoofbeats. Seconds later, Bernard plunged into the light atop a hard-ridden grey, with foam on its withers and blood on its flanks, torn flaps of skin hanging from the terrified beast where something had raked at it. Even as Bernard rode closer, the horse bucked and screamed, and Amara could scarcely understand how the Steadholder kept his seat and kept the animal streaking toward Garrison.

"Open the gates!" Bernard shouted. "Let me in!"

Giraldi waited until the last possible moment before barking a command, and the gates were thrown open and then shut again behind the frantic horse, almost before it was through them. A groom came to take the animal, but it reared and screamed, panicked.

Bernard slid off the horse and swiftly away, but the frenzied animal slipped on the icy stones of the courtyard and collapsed onto its side, bleeding, wheezing. Amara could see the long rents in the beast's flesh, where knives or claws had torn at it.

"Get ready," Bernard panted, turning and swiftly mounting the ladder to the battlements above the gates. The Steadholder, his eyes wide, face pale said, "The Cursor was right. There's a horde out there. And about ten thousand of them are coming right behind me."

◇◇◇◇ CHAPTER 36

Amara swept her gaze out over the ground before the walls, stark and white and cold in the blue-white furylights, and then looked back at Bernard. "Are you all right?"

The big Steadholder held up a hand to her, his breathing still heavy, and addressed Giraldi and Pirellus. "I couldn't get close enough to tell much. Light troops, moving fast. A lot of them had bows, and I thought I saw some scaling poles."

Giraldi grimaced and nodded once. "Which clans?"

"Wolf, Herdbane," Bernard said. He leaned a shoulder against one of the battlements. Amara turned to a bucket of water hanging on a hook nearby and scooped out a drinking ladle, passing it to Bernard. He nodded to her and drank the ladle away. "Giraldi, I'll need a sword, mail, arrows if you've any to spare."

"No," Pirellus said, stepping forward. "Giraldi, you shouldn't have given this civilian a horse, much less let him be on the walls when we're expecting an attack."

Bernard squinted at the Knight Commander. "Young man, how long have you been in the Legions?"

Pirellus faced Bernard squarely. "What matters is that I am in them now, sir. You are not. It is the purpose of the Legions to protect the people of the Realm. Now get off the wall and let us do our job."

"He stays," Amara said, firmly. "Centurion, if there's any mail that might fit me, have it brought as well."

Giraldi turned and pointed a finger at one of the *legionares* on the wall. The man immediately leapt down a ladder and dashed into one of the guardhouses. Both Bernard and Pirellus turned to blink at Amara.

"No," Bernard said.

"I think not."

Both men frowned at one another.

Amara let out an impatient breath. "Commander, you have sent your Knights Aeris to bring reinforcements, and those that remain are flying patrol overhead. They're under strength and may need whatever help they can get. The Steadholder is a furycrafter of considerable strength and has military experience. He is within his rights as a Citizen to stand in defense of his steadholt."

Bernard scowled at Amara and said, "I don't like it."

Pirellus nodded. "I must agree, Countess. You presumably do not have military experience beyond personal defense. I don't like it either."

"Fortunately, I do not need either of you to like it." Amara arched an eyebrow at Bernard as the *legionare* came running back up, both shoulders draped with coats of mail, one arm loaded down with weaponry. She took the mail he offered her, a long vest of interlocking rings, and took off her cloak to shove her arms into its padded undervest, and then into the mail itself. She started fumbling with the buckles, only to have Bernard push her fingers away and start cinching the buckles tight with practiced speed.

"You shouldn't be up here," he said.

"Because I'm a woman?" Amara pulled a cloak on over her shoulders again and buckled on a belt with a clip for her sword's scabbard.

"Because you're green. Unblooded. It's got nothing to do with you being a woman."

She glanced at him, arching an eyebrow.

Bernard shrugged, tugging another buckle closed. "Almost nothing. Here, move your arms a bit, so that this will settle."

By the time she'd finished, Bernard had dumped his cloak in exchange for a mail shirt of his own and a steel cap whose flanges spread down over the back of his neck, while the metal guard pressed down over his nose. He strapped on the sword belt, while his eyes swept the ground outside the walls, then took up his bow.

"Quiet," said the big-eared *legionare* again, from down the wall. He tilted his head for a moment, then swallowed. The man looked down the wall at Pirellus and nodded. "Sir? Here they come."

Pirellus gave the man a nod, then said to Bernard and Amara, "Help if you wish, then. It's your blood. But stay out of my way." He looked up and down the wall and said, "Archers."

Amara watched as centurions repeated the command down the length of the wall on either side of her and men stepped up to the battlements, bows in hand, arrows resting on quivers beside them. They set arrows to the strings, eyes focused intently at the edge of the area lit by Garrison's furylights, and held their bows half-raised. Tension made their forms gaunt, the harsh lights behind them casting their eyes into shadow, making them faceless. Amara heard a soldier not far away take in a deep breath and blow it out, as though impatient for it all to be finished.

Her heart pounded faster, and she had to work to keep her breath from racing out of control. The mail on her shoulders had a solid, comforting weight to it, but something about the smell of the metal set her on edge and made the hairs on the back of her neck stand up. She put a hand on the hilt of the sword at her belt and felt her fingers shake. She wrapped them hard around the weapon's hilt to stop anyone from noticing.

Bernard stared thoughtfully out at the darkness, having not yet drawn an arrow to his bow. He shrugged one shoulder, as though trying to settle the mail on it more comfortably. He took a step closer to her and said, quietly, "Afraid?"

She frowned at him and shook her head. Even that gesture was too jerky. "Where are they?"

"Out there. Outside the light. They'll come into it as soon as they've massed for their charge."

"Ten thousand." She pressed her lips together. "Ten thousand."

"Don't focus on the numbers," he said, in that same low tone. "This is a simple, solid defense. We have the wall, the light, the ground in front of us. They built Garrison here because it's the best point of defense anywhere in the Valley. It gives us an enormous advantage."

Amara looked up at him again, then up and down the length of the wall. She couldn't stop her voice from shaking. "But there are so few *legionares*."

"Easy," Bernard rumbled. "That's all right. Pirellus has his most experienced troops on the walls. Career fighting men, most of them with families behind them. The compulsory terms are down in the courtyard as reserves. These troops can fight ten times their number from this position with a good chance of victory, even without the Knights here. Pirellus and his men are the ones who are really going to win this battle. The *legionares* just have to hold the horde off of them until the Knights can bring their furies to bear on the Marat. We'll bloody their noses, and as soon as we can determine who is leading them, the Knights will take him down."

"They'll kill their hordemaster," Amara said.

"It discourages new hordemasters," Bernard said. "Or that's the idea. Once enough Marat are dead and their leader is gone, and they've not managed to break our defense, they won't have the stomach for any more fighting."

She nodded, pressing her lips together. "All right. What can I do to help?"

"Look for their leader. They don't wear anything much beyond what a normal warrior does, so you just have to look for someone shouting orders near the center."

"And when I've found him?"

Bernard drew an arrow and set it to the string of his bow, finally. "Point me at him. They should come in any moment now. Good fortune, Cursor."

"And you, Steadholder."

On her other side, Pirellus leaned a hand against a merlon and leaned a bit forward. "Ready," he whispered. "Come on. We're ready."

They came without warning. The Marat surged forward, thousands of screaming throats with one voice, plunging into the cold furylight like a sudden, living tide of muscle and bone. Their battle roar washed over Amara, deafening, terrifying, more sound than she would have believed *could* happen. Before she realized what she was doing, she was screaming, too, shouting out her fear and defiance, her sword in her hand, though she didn't remember drawing it—and beside her, Pirellus, sword held high, did the same.

"Archers!" he thundered, voice stentorian on the wall. "Loose!"

And with the thrum of a hundred heavy bows, death went flying into the ranks of the charging Marat.

Amara watched as the first rank of the enemy bucked and went down, only to be crushed by those coming behind them. Twice more, Pirellus cried to the archers, and twice more arrows flickered into their ranks, sending Marat sprawling and screaming, but doing nothing to stop the tide of bodies flooding toward Garrison's walls.

"Spears!" Pirellus barked, and along the walls the archers stepped back, while *legionares* bearing heavy shields and long, wickedly pointed spears stepped forward.

Arrows driven by short, heavy Marat bows began to flicker over the tops of the walls, and Amara had to jerk her head to one side while a stone-tipped shaft flew past her face. Her heart surged with terror, and she crouched down enough to take her head from view as a prime target, while Pirellus, in his helmet, stood staring down at the oncoming Marat, ignoring the arrows that buzzed past him.

The ground shook as the Marat reached the wall, a physical trembling that traveled up through the stones to Amara's feet. She could see them, a sea of wild, inhuman eyes, teeth that stretched into animal's fangs, and wolves ran beside them, among them, like great, gaunt shadows. The Marat reached the wall, where the gate suddenly shook with the blow of a tree trunk being held by a dozen hands, used as a ram. Several long, slender poles arched up into the air, studded along their lengths with short spikes, and once they came to rest against the walls, Marat began to climb the poles, nimble and swift, their weapons held in their hands, while companions beneath them fired arrows up at the defenders on the walls.

It was too loud to be believed, screams splitting the air, making any kind of communication nearly impossible. Arrows flew thicker than raindrops in a storm, their dark heads gleaming in the furylight, shattering where they struck stone or good Aleran steel—but Amara watched as one grizzled old veteran pitched back from the wall, the dark shaft of an arrow piercing his throat, and another man dropped motionless in his tracks, six inches of haft and fletching showing from the burst socket of his eye.

"Hold!" Pirellus bellowed. "Hold!"

The *legionares* fought with ruthless efficiency. Regardless of the incredible grace of the Marat rushing up the scaling poles, they thrust home spears with deadly accuracy into Marat flesh. Pale barbarians fell from the walls, back into the savage throng beneath, drawing further cries from those below. Again and again, Legion spearmen repelled the Marat assaults, shoving the scaling poles back down, driving the warriors clambering up them back with cold steel. The *legionares* fought together, each man with his shield partner, so that while one would engage the enemy's weapon, the other would drive a spear home with a short, hard thrust at the vitals or a leg, toppling the attacker from their precarious position atop the walls. Blood stained the Aleran spears, the *legionares'* shields and armor, and spattered thick on the battlements, mute testimony to the courage of the Marat attackers.

Below Amara's feet, she could hear the steady thud and thump of the ram being driven at the gates—but suddenly found herself whirling to the walls as a savage-eyed Marat swung himself up between two merlons from a scaling pole and swept a heavy wooden club at her head.

Amara ducked the blow, dodged a second swipe that came straight down at her shoulder and whirled to whip her blade across the Marat's heavy thighs, opening the pale flesh in a sudden river of blood. The Marat screamed and toppled toward her, club flailing. Amara moved lightly to one side, thrusting her short blade at the Marat's ribs as he fell past, feeling the weapon sink home, the quivering, twisting jerk of the Marat's scream something that coursed through the metal and into her hands. Half revolted, exultant at having survived the exchange, she let out a scream and jerked the sword back, leaping back from the Marat warrior as he tumbled limply down to the courtyard beneath the wall.

She looked up, panting, to find Pirellus staring at her. He nodded, once, and then called, "Try to throw them back down the wall on the outside. We don't want clutter where our own troops are moving around." Then he turned back to his study of the ground below, almost absently frowning when a stone arrow-tip shattered against the crest of his helmet.

Amara chanced a look over the wall, out at the chaos below, and arrows whistled through the air toward her as soon as she did. She jerked her head back and down, to find Bernard crouched next to her. The Steadholder, too, took a glance over the wall, before half rising to a crouch, to lift his bow, drawing the arrow back to his cheek. He aimed for a breath, then loosed the arrow, which threaded its way between a pair of *legionares* to sink into the ribs of a Marat with a steel axe who had gained the wall over a stunned *legionare* with a dent in his helmet. The force of the arrow's impact drove the Marat back over the wall, and he vanished as he fell.

"Spotted their general yet?" Bernard called to her.

"I can't see anything!" Amara shouted. "They shoot whenever I look!"

"No helmet," Bernard said. "I'd shoot at you, too."

"That's a comfort, thanks," Amara said, wry, and the Steadholder grinned at her, before standing up to loose another arrow into the crowd below and drop back down behind the wall again.

Amara stood up to take another look—but Bernard caught her wrist. "Don't," he said. "They're getting packed in down there. Keep your head down."

"What?"

In answer, he nodded toward Pirellus. Amara turned her head to look at the man and saw him point a finger off to one side at a pair of men, standing behind heavy ceramic pots, and three armored Knights who stood behind them, with no weapons in their hands.

"Firepots?" Amara asked, and Bernard nodded. She watched, as Pirellus lifted his sword and then dropped it, a swift signal.

The two men with the firepots—earthcrafters, surely, for only they could lift the man-sized pots of coals so easily—heaved them up and over the wall, to crash down into the Marat on either side of the gate.

Pirellus signaled the three men behind them, and the Knights, as one, lifted their arms and faces to the sky, crying out over the screams and din of battle.

The fire answered them in a roar that deafened Amara and rattled her teeth against one another. Heat swept up, and sudden, brilliant light, scarlet and murderous in contrast to the cool blue furylights, a wind that roared upward, lifting Amara's hair up off her neck. A column of fire shaped like some huge winged serpent rose above the battlements, curled back down, and crashed to the earth below.

The battlements mercifully shielded her from seeing what happened to the Marat caught in the sudden storm of living flame, but in the wake of that fire, as its roar died away to echoes, she heard them screaming, men and wolves alike, screaming in terror and in pain, high and breathless. There was madness in those screams, frustration, futility, terror beyond anything that she had heard before—and there was something else: the sure and certain knowledge of death, death as a release from an agony as pure and hot as the flames that had caused it.

A smell rose from the ground before the battlements in those silent moments after, the scent of charred meat. Amara shuddered, sickened.

A silence fell, broken only by screams and moans, coming from the ground below. She rose and looked down, over the ground before the walls. The fire serpent had broken the Marat, sent them and their wolves howling away from the walls of Garrison. At a command from Pirellus, the archers stepped forward and sent arrows arching into the retreating barbarians with deadly accuracy, dropping more to the earth, clutching at the barbs piercing their flesh.

She couldn't see much of the ground immediately beneath the walls, for which she felt silently grateful. The smell of burned hair and worse nearly overwhelmed her, until she bade Cirrus to keep it from her nostrils and mouth. She leaned a hand against the battlements and stared out at the blood-soaked, scorched earth, littered with a carpet of pale-haired bodies.

"Furies," she breathed. "They're not much more than children."

Bernard stepped up beside her, his face pale, grim, eyes hidden in shadows beneath his helmet. "Young warriors," Bernard said. "Their first chance to prove themselves in battle. That was Wolf Clan. One more to go."

Amara glanced at him. "They send their youngest to fight?"

"To fight first. Then, if they survive, they can join the adult warriors in the main battle."

She looked back at the field and swallowed. "This is only a preliminary to them. It isn't over."

"Not without getting the leader," Bernard said. "Get some water in you. You don't know how much you need it. Next one won't be so easy."

And indeed, a *legionare* came around carrying a bucket, and a thong threaded through the handles of tin cups, passing water to each man on the walls. More *legionares,* younger troops from the reserves in the court-yard below, came onto the walls to help carry down the wounded and bear them back to the watercrafters work-ing at the tubs in the courtyard. As usual, those with functional and light injuries were treated first, a round of swift crafting that bound closed bleeding wounds, mended over simple broken bones, and restored a whole, if weary, fighting man to the defense of the garrison. The more seriously injured were remanded to the care of surgeons, men and women skilled in more pedantic medicinal practices, who labored to keep them alive and stable until one of the watercrafters had the time to attend to their injuries.

"Pretty much like we expected," Pirellus was saying, on the wall somewhere nearby. She focused on the con-versation, listening. "Though the ram was a new tech-nique for them. They learn fast."

Giraldi grunted. "Children. Crows, but I don't like this kind of bloodletting."

"How are the men?"

"Well enough, for not having slept a full night. Light casualties on the northern side of the wall. Only injuries on the south."

"Good," Pirellus said. "Get water to everyone and arrows to the archers. Make sure those new firepots get up here in one piece, and get some food to my firecrafters. They don't do as well on an empty belly."

"You want something for that?" Giraldi asked.

"For what?"

"You're bleeding."

"Edge of my helmet," Pirellus said. "Arrow drove it into my skin. Looks worse than it is."

"You don't want it bleeding in your eye at the wrong time. Let me get a surgeon up here."

"Let the surgeons see to the men that are hurt," Pirellus said, his tone firm. "Get yourself some water, too, centurion."

"Aye, sir."

Amara frowned, pensive, and stood up, walking a bit farther down the wall. Bernard sat there, his back against the battlements, frowning down at his hands.

"Something's occurred to me," Amara said. "This doesn't make any sense."

Bernard squinted up at her. "It's like that, your first battle."

She shook her head impatiently. "No, not like that. It doesn't make sense for the Marat to do this. To send a fraction of their force against us—and the one least experienced and capable at that. Why should they fight us piecemeal when they could bring everyone against us at once?"

"Marat don't think like we do," Bernard said. "You always get their raw recruits out in front. Sometimes they're out like velites, skirmishing in front of the larger masses of troops, and sometimes they're raiding parties that go out the night before, but they're always in front. This is just another example."

"They aren't stupid," Amara said stubbornly. "How many of their young men died just now? Hundreds? A thousand? For what? They killed half a dozen *legionares* and wounded more that will be back up on the walls in an hour at most."

Pirellus stepped down the wall, abruptly standing before Amara, arms akimbo. "You would have preferred it if they had killed more, perhaps?"

"Don't be stupid," Amara snapped. "I just think that there must be something else to what they're doing." She looked at Bernard. "Where are the Knights we saw before?"

The Steadholder frowned at her, but Pirellus spoke before he could say anything. "Indeed, Countess, where *are* they? I acknowledge that the Marat are on the move, but we have seen only one warband, thus far, with no hordemaster in evidence. You will be quite the laughing-stock if Riva brings both his Legions here only to find no Marat to face."

Amara's temper flashed, and she faced Pirellus, ready to bring the man to task. Bernard stood up, as though to get between them.

Down the wall, one of the brass horns sounded a call to arms, a clarion note that clove through the cold furylit air and brought the veteran troops on the wall to their feet, shields and weapons ready, before its notes had died away.

"Sir," snapped Giraldi, from the wall over the gates. "They're coming again."

Pirellus turned his back on Amara and leapt up to his position over the gate.

Out at the edge of the light, the Marat appeared again, rushing forward in a howling mob—but this time, their screams were punctuated not by the howling of the great, dark wolves, but by the metallic, whistling shrieks of the giant predator birds that raced beside them as the pale tide charged toward the walls.

"Archers," Pirellus called again, and once more, in three humming, whistling waves, Marat dropped to the ground, the life driven from them by Aleran shafts. "Spears!" Pirellus called, and once again, the Legions squared up to face the Marat.

But that was where the similarity to the charge of Clan Wolf ended.

There were no scaling poles this time, no ram to assault the gates. Instead, the first rank of the Marat, howling their defiance, simply hurled itself at the walls and, running at a furious pace, *leapt up to the top*.

If Amara had not seen it happen, she would never have believed it possible—but the Marat, without aid of any kind, simply hurtled into the air, grasped at the top of the fifteen-foot wall with one hand, and hauled themselves up to fight. The great birds stalking beside them leapt up, too, even higher, furiously beating at the air with their stubby wings and holding themselves aloft just long enough to rake at the defenders atop the walls with their vicious talons, driving Aleran men back long enough for the young Herdbane warriors to haul themselves onto the battlements and throw themselves forward into battle with a fearless, even mindless abandon.

Amara stared in startled horror as a Marat hauled himself onto the wall not ten feet from her, and his great bird landed beside him with a scream, its beak slashing wildly at an upraised shield. The Marat lifted his knife and leapt at her, shrieking, while behind him another scrambled atop the wall in his place.

Amara tried to dodge to one side, only to realize that there was nothing but the empty air of the courtyard beneath her. She sent out a frantic call to Cirrus, and, as the Marat rushed her, took two steps out onto the empty air, then sprang back to the stones of the wall behind him. He stared at her, stunned for a moment, even as he spun to pursue her. She thrust with the guardsman's blade, flat of the weapon parallel to the ground, and it sank home at one side of his chest, sliding between ribs and coming out again smoothly.

Something shrieked behind her, and hot pain flashed across her back. She threw herself forward and down, over the fallen Marat, and turned her head to see the great herdbane lunge toward her, dark eyes glassy and empty of anything like fear, its beak flashing toward her eyes.

She threw up her hands, willing Cirrus out before her, and the fury rushed out, sweeping up the great bird and hurling it into a merlon. It stumbled and spun to reorient on her, but even as it did, a heavyset *legionare* swept his sword at it in a powerful stroke and, with earth-born strength, swept the herdbane's head from its neck. The *legionare* flashed her a smile, then turned and hurled himself toward the newest arrival at the top of the walls.

Amara struggled to her feet again. Fighting raged all along the wall and had spilled over into the courtyard behind. The reserve troops, after a startled moment, had been ordered forward by their young officers and engaged those Marat who either leapt from the wall or followed the bounds of their warbirds down into the courtyard.

More screams, frantic and terrified and wild with battle-rage, whirled around her, disorienting, terrifying. On the other side of the gate, the Marat had taken a section of the wall and held it tenaciously, more of their number pouring in at every moment, until Pirellus himself entered the fray.

The golden-skinned Parcian drew his dark sword and started what could only be described as a deliberate stalk down the length of the wall, calling *legionares* out of his way as he went. He met the first Marat with a blow so swift that Amara never saw it begin. She only saw blood flicker out in an arc, while the Marat tumbled down to the earth below, lifeless. One of the great birds lost its talon when it raked at Pirellus, and its head followed it to the stones a breath later.

More Marat threw themselves at the master metal-crafter, both man and beast in a furious wave, but the swordsman was their match. Every motion avoided a blow or enabled him to deal out a stroke of his own—and none failed to be lethal. With a calculated precision, Pirellus swept down the occupied section of the wall, brushing away the enemy like cobwebs, and the Legions flooded back into the space, kicking bodies clear of the battlements, fighting savagely to hold the regained section of the walls.

Pirellus shook the blood from his sword, expression neutral, remote, and pointed a finger again at the men with the firepots. The earthcrafters removed the lids and prepared to hurl the pots over the battlements to the ground below. The firecrafters behind them stood with their expressions distant, mouths moving silently, calling to their furies in preparation of the hellish storm they prepared to unleash on the enemy.

And that was when Amara felt it. When she felt the currents of air thrumming with tension, heard with some part of her that she could not fully describe the rising tide of wind moving in the darkness above.

She turned her face up, only to be blinded by the furylights mounted above the battlements, veiling the skies above—but all along the wall, the winds rose, whipping wildly back and forth. Amara thought she could hear cries above, where Garrison's few Knights Aeris should have been patrolling. Something sprinkled down from above, and for a moment she thought that more rain had begun to fall. But the sensation was hot, not cold, and when Amara wiped at her cheek, she saw blood smeared upon her fingers.

"Bernard!" she shouted. "They're here!" She didn't have time to make sure she had been heard. Instead, she called to Cirrus and leapt into the air, felt the roar of wind enfold her as she hurtled up, above the battlements and into the darkened sky over the besieged fortress.

The air teemed with Knights Aeris—duelling, whirling pairs of men who swept through the skies in deadly combat, as much between furies as men, each trying to cut off the other's flow of air or to wound their opponents badly enough with their blades to shatter their concentration and send them falling. Even as she watched, one of the men in Rivan colors whirled away from a flickering blade, only to let out a sudden, terrified scream and begin to plummet from the sky like a stone. He fell past Amara and onto the ground before the walls of Garrison, the thud of impact swallowed by the tumult beneath them.

Amara swept her gaze around the sky, picking out the shapes of airborne Knights as much with Cirrus's senses as her own, and found thirty at least, three times the number of the fortress's defenders. More graceful battles played out above and around her, but their outcome was a foregone conclusion: Garrison's Knights Aeris would be driven from the skies or killed, and the enemy would control all movement above the fortress.

Amara spotted, high and at the rear of the enemy positions, what she had dreaded—several litters, borne by more Knights, litters that would carry more of the powerful furycrafters they had faced before. Even as she watched, several Knights formed an escort around three of the litters, and the whole of the group dove toward the embattled fortress.

Specifically, toward the gates where Pirellus and his Knights directed the Aleran defenses.

Amara did not take time to consider her plan. Instead, she gathered Cirrus beneath her and sent herself hurtling up toward the oncoming litters. A startled Knight turned to face her in the air, but with an almost casual gesture, she flashed past him, dealing him a blow that began a cut low on one of his legs and ran all the way up his back to his shoulder, sheering through the leather leggings he wore and even biting through some of the mail upon his back. He let out a cry and fell, his focus fluttering with his pain, dropping toward the earth like a leaf cut from a tree.

Amara hurled herself forward and used a terrific rush of air to catapult her up. Then, while her momentum still carried her toward the foe, she gathered Cirrus's presence up before her and sent the fury lashing out at those supporting one of the litters.

She wasn't strong enough to cut all four of the Knights bearing the litters from their furies, and she hadn't even tried. Instead, she had focused on the two forward Knights, intending only to cut off their wind for a few crucial seconds. She succeeded. The men let out startled cries and fell, straight down, taking the poles whose weight they supported with them.

And dumping a half-dozen screaming men inside the litter into the open air. Two of the men still wore their restraining straps and dangled precariously on the litter as the Knights bearing it struggled to right it again, but the others, evidently anticipating a quick dismount upon the walls, had already unstrapped. Those six plummeted toward the ground, and though a few of the escorting Knights plunged after them, Amara knew that they would never be able to save the men from a fall so close to the earth.

She felt dozens of eyes focus on her at once, as her momentum carried her to the peak of its energy, then let her begin to fall again. She spun in the air, faced down, and kept her limbs in close to her body, to keep from being slowed as she reached out to gather Cirrus back to her, and to reestablish her own windstream before one of the other Knights of the air cut her off.

Half a dozen windstreams converged on her at once,

and she clawed for air in frustrated terror, even as the furylights of the fortress below loomed closer. She got lucky: So many of the enemy had moved to cut her off that she was able to use their own efforts against one another, writhing the windstreams into a tangle and then altering the direction of her fall with her arms and legs. Cirrus gathered beneath her in a rush, and she gained control of her fall, just as another Knight, less reticent than the others, swept toward her, light gleaming on his drawn sword.

Amara twisted to one side, but he matched her fall, and the sword swept at her. She caught it on her own blade and pressed in close, sword-to-sword, struggling to gain control of the wind around them and turn it to her advantage. Her foe gripped her wrist, and they began to spin wildly, still falling.

Amara shot a glance down at the courtyard welling up before her eyes and looked up to her foe's face just as he did the same. There was a mute moment of concord and then both pushed away from one another, furies gathering beneath them in a roar, attempting to slow their fall.

Amara got one frantic look at Garrison beneath her and guided her fall into a stack of hay bales beside the stables. The bales, solidly packed, would have done little to break her fall without Cirrus rushing currents, both slowing the impact and scattering the bales into loose strands. Amara crashed through the topmost stack of bales and out onto the ground on the far side.

Her foe, more able than she, or less tired, landed neatly on the ground beside her and pivoted to drive his blade at her throat. She caught the thrust on her own sword, barely, parrying the blade into the bale of hay beside her, while her other hand dragged the short knife she'd stolen from Fidelias from her belt and drove it back into the windcrafter's boot.

He fell back with a yelp, then gestured with his hand, expression murderous. The wind roared, and Amara felt pressure pin her hard to the ground. She struggled to move, or to lift her sword, but the man's fury kept her from doing it. She reached for Cirrus, but she knew she had been too slow, and she could only watch as he lifted his blade again.

There was a buzzing hiss, and an arrow drove through the Knight's mail shirt where it crossed just beneath his throat. The arrow drove him back a pair of jerking steps, before he fell dead to the stones.

The pressure on Amara abruptly eased, and she could breathe again, move again. She started struggling to her feet, but, still dizzy from the fall and her efforts to control it, had only got partway there when Bernard reached her, his bow still in hand, and said, "Crows and furies, are you all right? Where are they coming in?"

"The gate," Amara gasped. "The firepots. Get them off the gate. *Hurry.*"

Bernard's face went pale, and he pelted off across the courtyard, back toward the walls. A Marat, dazed from a fall from the battlements above, lifted a stone-headed hatchet, but Bernard flicked a hand and the hatchet's wooden haft abruptly spun in its owner's grip, the back of the stone whipping into the Marat's temple, and sending him in a loose tumble to the ground.

Amara felt a dull pain in her shoulder and back, and it was too much effort to stand, but she watched as Bernard bounded up one of the ladders and onto the wall.

He took his bow in a two-handed grip and clubbed his way past a Marat fighting a pair of *legionares* and ducked past the flashing claws of a wounded herdbane that lay on its side, raking wildly with its remaining leg, to reach Pirellus's side. He gripped the Knight Commander's shoulder and shouted to him over the din.

Pirellus's face blanked with incredulity, but Bernard pointed up, and Pirellus turned in time to see the first of the other pair of litters sweeping down, mailed Knights Aeris all around it. His eyes widened, and he shouted to his men on the walls, even as a roar of wind sent men flat to the battlements and drove leaping Marat back and away from the walls.

Bernard lost his bow but stayed on his feet, drawing on the strength of his fury, Amara knew. He grabbed Pirellus and another man beside him and dragged them forward and off the wall, to fall into the courtyard beyond.

Amara's eyes swept back up to the litters, to see Fidelias in one, pointing down and calling something to one of the men in the other, a tall, thin man with pinched features. The man stood up, eyes closed, and reached out his hand.

In answer, the firepots, waiting on the walls beside the firecrafters now pinned down by the gale winds above them, exploded into blinding flame.

The firestorm swept over the walls above the gates, where Garrison's Knights were pinned down. Scattered and whipped to a dangerous fury by the wind, more of the flame nonetheless rushed out along the walls, playing havoc with *legionares*, Marat, and predator birds alike. The fire went over the walls like a scythe, sending men screaming to the ground, running from the flames, rolling frantically to put out their own burning bodies. Some even leapt off the battlements and into the savage Marat horde waiting below.

Amara watched in stunned horror as the litters swept down to the courtyard, where a half a dozen disorganized *legionares* attacked the invaders. Aldrick ex Gladius dismounted from the litter and, with the Knights Aeris with him, met them and drove them back.

Fidelias stepped from the litter and walked to the gates. As Amara watched, he glanced around him, eyes quick and hard, and then laid his bare palms against the heavy wood. For perhaps half a minute, he stood there, eyes closed. Then he withdrew, barked an order to his men, and limped back to the litter. Aldrick and the others withdrew to the litter, and the whole of the group swept up into the air again and out of sight.

Amara regained her feet, finally, and recovered her sword. She lifted her head to see what Fidelias had done to the gates.

She saw them shudder. Then she saw dust fly from one of them. And then the cruel, rending talon of one of the herdbane ripped through the heavy beams of wood as though they were paper, and tore its way back out again.

She could only watch in numbed horror as the Marat, howling like madmen, hauled the gates of Garrison to kindling before her eyes, and began to pour into the fortress.

She swallowed, her head still whirling, her hand trembling as she gripped her sword, and stepped forward to meet them.

CHAPTER 37

Amara looked left and right as she approached the gate, even as the Marat began to tear their way through it. To one side, several of the young *legionares* stood, stunned and horrified, staring as the Marat poured in. To the other, scorched bodies and badly burned men lay, scattered as they had fallen from the walls above, along with a dazed-looking Bernard and Pirellus, gathering themselves together after the explosion on the walls and the fall after.

"Form up!" Amara shouted, toward the *legionares,* but she wasn't sure the young men even heard her. She singled out one of the young men in a centurion's helmet and barked, "Centurion! Hold the gate!"

The young man in his fine cape looked from her to the gate to the shattered walls above, eyes wide, mouth trembling. "B-back!" he stammered, though it seemed that no one listened to him. "Fall b-back!"

Amara looked to the other side in desperation. "Pirellus!" she shouted. "Get up! Command the Legion!"

Pirellus, his helmet blasted from his head, the hair on one side scorched nearly to his scalp, stared at her in blank incomprehension.

The Marat tore through the last fragments of the

remaining gate, and the first, a burly young warrior wielding a stone-headed axe, shoved his way through.

There was no time for anything else. If the Marat gained control of the gates, they would be able to pour into Garrison, and nothing would stop the weight of simple numbers from smothering the Aleran defense. Though her head still spun and though the injury on her back still pained her, Amara threw herself toward the sundered gates.

She heard herself let out a shrill cry, even as the Marat warrior turned to face her and swept the axe in a great flat arc meant to shear her in half at the hips. Instead, she reached out for Cirrus and leapt, throwing herself neatly over the axe, and sweeping her blade out at eye level. The fine steel of the blade bit into the Marat's face, and he dropped to the ground with a scream, even as one of the huge warbirds tore its way through the gates.

Amara tried to dodge from its path, but the beast's beak shot out and gripped her left arm in a sudden, crushing grip. Pain flashed through her, and she knew that only the mail had kept her arm from being snipped off at the elbow. The bird shook its head violently left and right, throwing Amara about like a puppet, until she slashed desperately at the base of the bird's thick neck, eliciting a brassy shriek and causing the bird to hurl her away from it.

Another Marat came through the gates, but the wounded herdbane whipped around at the sudden motion, snapping and lashing with its brassy beak, driving the Marat back. Amara let out a cry and drove forward, thrusting with the guardsman's sword, sinking it into the bird's vitals and whipping it forth with a half-twist that sent the beast snapping and clawing its way to the ground in a welter of gore.

Amara gasped for breath as the Marat warrior came through, aiming another cut at this one. He dodged to one side, making way for a second, this one a lean young woman carrying an old Aleran saber. The Marat female thrust at Amara's face, and the young Cursor swept the blow aside—only to be hit hard in the flank and thrown to the ground by the first attacker.

She struggled and fought against him, letting out a furious, futile cry, but he had gotten inside her guard and pinned her sword arm to the ground. He lifted his fist, his face emotionless, and drove a blow into her mouth that stunned her for a moment, left her silent. Then he said something in a guttural tongue, satisfaction in the tone, as his hand gripped her hair, hard, and he turned her head slightly toward the woman, who lifted the old saber for a downward blow.

Scalping me, Amara thought. *They're taking my hair.*

There was a sudden shriek, high-pitched and panicked. The Marat warrior leapt back and off Amara, even as his companion lifted her saber and engaged the furious, reckless assault of one of the young *legionares.* The young man hacked and chopped with his Legion blade, more in elemental fury and brutality than in any coherent assault, and drove the pair away from Amara.

He turned back to the other young *legionares,* and Amara recognized the young man who had been on guard at the gates the day before from the purpling bruise on his jaw. "Come on!" he snarled, to his companions. "Are you going to stand there while a woman fights?" He turned back to his opponents with a cry of, "Riva for Alera!" and attacked again.

First one, then two, then several more *legionares* surged forward with sharp cries of fury, joining together in a shieldwall that contained the tide of Marat struggling to pour in through the shattered gates. But the young *legionares,* though they acted in concert, began to be driven back step by steady step.

Amara felt herself hauled back along the ground by one elbow and barely managed to keep hold of her sword. She looked up, dazedly, to find Healer Harger crouching over her, fingers touched lightly to her temples.

"The arm's broke," he said a second later, voice rough. "Maybe some of your teeth, too. There are broken rings in the mail over your back that are cutting into it, and something is sprained. But you'll live." He shot a glance up at the embattled gate, then gave her a quick smile and said, "Bravely done, girl. Shamed those city boys into the fight at last."

"Pirellus," Amara managed to gasp. "Other side of the gate. Stunned."

Harger's eyes widened. "Great furies, he lived through that?"

"Bernard. Pulled him off the wall."

Harger nodded, tense, and hauled her to her feet. "Show me. If anyone can do anything, it will be Pirellus."

Amara gasped with the pain and saw the Healer wince and draw in a quick breath of his own. He steadied her, and then she lead him forward, around the slow pressure of bodies and the desperate thrust and hack of weapons at the gate, to where she'd seen Bernard and Pirellus moments before.

She found them, Bernard just now starting to stagger to his feet, Pirellus still on his hands and knees. Harger went to the Knight at once, touching fingers lightly to his temples, then grunting and shaking the man roughly. Harger hauled back a hand to deliver a slap to the Knight Commander's face, but Pirellus caught the Healer's wrist as it swept toward him. He shook his head once, blinked his eyes, looked up at the gates, and then staggered to his feet to stare up at the walls.

Then he spun, looking around the courtyard, and nodded to Amara. "Countess," he said, voice haggard. "That blast will have heated the stones, but they'll cool quickly, and Marat will be coming over them even if we hold the gate."

Amara swallowed. "What do we do?"

"Move these *legionares* up to the walls," Pirellus said.

"Then who will hold the gate?"

His chin lifted a fraction. "I will."

Amara stared at him. "Alone? Who will command the Legion?"

"They won't need much commanding in this," Pirellus said. "They'll hold the walls, and I'll hold the gate, or we'll all be dead in the next few moments."

"How can they hold the walls?"

"They can't for long," he said. "You'll have to figure out something."

Amara snapped, "*What*? That's not a plan!"

"It's all I have," Pirellus said. "Countess, I hope to the furies you're clever as well as brave. If you don't find some way to get them off of us, we're dead, right here, right now." And with that, he nodded to Amara and stepped toward the melee at the gate. He paused, halfway there, to pick up a long, heavy length of wood that had been one of the drawing traces of a cart crushed by falling debris. He turned crisply and handed it to Bernard as the dazed Steadholder stood up.

"What do you want me to do?" Bernard said.

"Follow me," Pirellus said. "Keep any strays off my back. Stay out of my way." Then he turned and walked into the struggle at the gate. With a few harsh, barked phrases, he stepped up between the young *legionares* and drew his sword. Within seconds, three Marat warriors lay bleeding on the ground, and their advance halted.

Pirellus snarled orders at the young *legionares,* and after a frantic half-moment they moved, breaking into a pair of elements and heading up the stone stairs to the battlements, slopping buckets of water ahead of them to cool the heated stones as they went.

Pirellus stood in the gates alone. Amara saw him set a grim, polite little smile onto his lips. He bowed to the Marat standing just beyond the gate and then with the fingers of one hand beckoned them forward.

Bernard gripped the heavy wooden pole and swallowed, looking back at Amara. His eyes were a little wide, and he drew in an unsteady breath, but he turned back to the gate and stood perhaps ten feet behind Pirellus, standing steady.

Amara felt a scream of frustration well up in her, even as the Marat again began to come through the gate, by ones and twos. The Parcian swordsman met them, more than a match, and first one, then another, then another of the barbarians fell to the dark sword. But even Pirellus was not untouchable. A pair of warriors came through together, facing him. Pirellus neatly parried a thrusting spear and spun to thrust toward the other warrior—and suddenly hesitated, faced with a half-naked young Marat woman.

He did not pause for so long as the space of a breath before he lunged forward, driving the dark sword between her breasts, but that hesitation cost him. The Marat beside him swept the butt end of the spear at his leg, striking the side of his knee with a crunch of impact, and if Bernard had not stepped forward to drive the young warrior to the earth with an overhand sweep of the thick wooden pole, Pirellus might have been killed.

Instead, the warrior grimaced, moving with no more than a slight limp, and continued what Amara knew would ultimately be a hopeless, if heroic defense of the gates.

Harger came to her side, his eyes sunken, worried, as they traveled up to the walls, and Amara looked to see the *legionares* there engaging the enemy, heard the screams of the warbirds and of their Marat masters.

"Lady," Harger growled. "What do we do?"

Amara wanted to scream at the man out of sheer frustration and fear. Even as she watched, a young *legionare* fell from the wall, screaming and clutching at his face, blood pouring from his fingers. He fell no more than a few feet away. Bernard barely dodged a suddenly thrust spear as he swept another Marat from Pirellus's flank.

How was she to know what to do? She wasn't a military commander. The abrupt destruction of Garrison's Knights had crippled their defenses, she knew. How was she to know how to overcome that loss?

Amara drew in a sudden breath. She wasn't.

She sheathed her sword and seized Harger's sleeve. "Healer. Take me to Count Gram."

He did so at once, leading her to the center of the fortress, where a pair of senior *legionares* stood guard before the door of a heavy, practical structure of brick. Amara swept past them and into a building, up a flight of stairs, and into the Count's bedchamber.

Gram lay in his bed, his head to one side, his face grey, eyes sunken. There were flecks of some kind of white film on his lips, and his broad, capable hands lay limply on the sheets, looking frail, the skin as thin as parchment.

Amara looked at the man and swallowed. She knew that what she was about to do might kill him. She did it anyway. "Wake him up, Harger."

Harger let out a shaking breath. "Lady. I can, but it could—"

"I know it could kill him, Healer," Amara said. "But if the walls or the gate falls, he'll be dead either way. We need him. The garrison needs him. I do not think that he would wish us to let them fall when he might be able to help."

Harger looked at her for a moment and then shook his head. The old healer sagged for a moment, his face drawn. "No. I don't suppose he would."

"Get him moving," Amara said, quietly. "I'll get the guards to help carry him."

She went downstairs to the two *legionares* there, returning with them to Gram's bedchamber. She found Harger standing over the old Count, whose face was flushed with unnatural color. Gram dragged in a panting breath and opened his eyes, squinting at her. He grunted and said, "Harger says my Knights are gone. Just the green troops left."

"Yes," Amara said, her voice tight. "They're on the

walls. Pirellus is alive, but wounded, holding the gates alone. We need to get you out there—"

"No," Gram said. "Don't bother. Won't do any good."

"But, sir—"

"Fire," Gram croaked.

"The enemy used the Knight's firepots against them. Made them explode on the walls."

Gram closed his eyes. "Are they all at the gates?"

"No," Amara said. "They're up on the walls again, too. Spread all along them."

"Can't be done," Gram said, sighing. "Even if I wasn't hurt. Even if we had more firepots. Can't call up that much fire, that wide."

"There's got to be something you can do," Amara said, dropping a hand onto his.

"Nothing," Gram whispered. "Can't burn something that wide. Not strong enough."

Amara chewed on her lip. "What about another kind of crafting?"

Gram opened his eyes again. "What?"

"A firecrafting," Amara said. "The Marat can't counter it with anything."

Gram looked from Amara to Harger, then back again. "Fear," he said. "Fire."

"I don't know if they're afraid of fire—"

"No," Gram said, his expression weakly irritated. "Get fire. Get a torch. You."

Amara blinked at him. "Me? But I'm no firecrafter."

Gram waved a hand impatiently, cutting her off and fixing her with glittering eyes. "Can't walk. Someone else has to carry. Are you afraid, girl?"

She nodded, tightly, once.

He cackled. "Honest. Good. Get a torch. And get ready to be brave. Braver than you've ever been. Maybe we can do something." Gram broke off, coughing, the sound weak, his face twisting into a grimace of pain.

Amara traded a look with Harger, then nodded to one of the *legionares*. The man stepped out, returning with a torch a moment later.

"Here, girl," Gram whispered, beckoning with one hand. "Bring it close."

Amara did, kneeling down by the bed and holding the torch out to the wounded Count.

Gram closed his eyes and reached his bare palm into the flame. Amara winced, almost drawing the torch away, but Gram did not stir or flinch, and his flesh remained, it would seem, untouched by the fire.

Amara felt it inside of her first, a panicky little thrill that raced through her belly and thighs, turned her legs watery and uncertain. Her hand started to shake, and she lifted her other to hold the torch steady. Gram let out a slow, quiet sound of pain, and the sensation in her redoubled, mindless and sudden fear, so that she had to fight to keep from bolting from the room. Her heart abruptly raced, pounding frantically, the pain of her wounds seemed to increase, and she suddenly could not get a breath.

"Girl," Gram rasped, opening his eyes again. "Listen to me. Get this out to the front. Out in front of all of the Marat. Get it to where they can see it." He let out a wheezing breath, his eyes closing. "Don't drop it. And don't let the panic take you. Hurry."

Amara nodded, rising to feel her body trembling, weak with fright.

"Steady," Harger said. "Get out there. Hurry. I'm not sure how long he can hold the crafting."

Amara had to stammer twice before she managed to say, "All right." She turned and walked from the chamber, fighting to control her breathing, to keep her paces steady, even. The fear flowed through her like winter ice, cold little chips of it flowing in her blood, making her heart skip painful beats. She could barely keep her thoughts focused on the gates, on carrying the torch without dropping it—though she struggled to remember that if she dropped it, or if she surrendered to the fear and fled, that Gram's efforts would be for nothing.

She felt herself begin to sob as she walked into the courtyard, felt her body begin to weaken with the mind-numbing terror. More than anything, she wanted to turn away from the gate, to flee, to take to the air and leave their savage enemies far behind.

Instead, she kept on, toward the gates, growing weaker, less steady, by the step. Part of the way there, she swayed and fell, and her tears blinded her. But she kept moving forward, crawling on her knees and her wounded arm, clutching at the torch and keeping it from falling to the ground.

Suddenly, from right in front of her someone screamed, and she felt herself hauled to her feet with terrifying strength, facing a towering giant with blazing eyes bearing a cudgel the size of a tree in one fist.

She fought against the terror, against the sobs that choked in her throat. "Bernard," she said. "Bernard. The torch. Get me to the walls. Get me to the walls!"

The giant scowled and roared something at her that had her choking down a hysterical scream. Then he simply picked her up under one arm and carried her to the stairs and up them, to the frantic, screaming panic of the battlements. She felt herself come down on her feet again, and she staggered forward, toward the walls above the gates.

She could not think, could not control herself over the last few feet. She staggered forward, screaming and sobbing, bearing the torch aloft and certain that death was there for her, breathing softly, black wings rustling like those of the crows that waited, waited somewhere in the predawn darkness to sweep down on the eyes of the dead.

Somehow, she gained the battlements over the gate and stood above them, a sure and simple target for Marat archers, the torch held aloft.

It went up in a sudden furnace of sound and heat, an abrupt river of roaring light that shot into the sky and lit the ground for a mile in every direction. All of that terror, all of that fear in her blossomed out with the torch, poured out with the sudden, raging flames, swept out of her, magnified a thousandfold, onto the ground beneath.

There was an instant, horrible stillness, as the power of the firecrafting swept over the Marat below. And then a scream, born in one moment from thousands of throats, rose up into the air. The pressure of the Marat assault vanished, more quickly than it had arrived. The pale tide of Marat warriors abruptly flooded back from the walls of Garrison, howling in terror, joined by the whistling, panicked shrieks of the fleeing warbirds. The battered *legionares* defending the walls began to cheer, as the Marat were swept under by the firecrafting and broke and ran.

Amara saw them go, even as the terror flowed out of her, poured out together with whatever strength she had left. She staggered and nearly fell from the battlements, only to be supported by Bernard, who had appeared behind her. She leaned back against him, exhausted and barely able to keep her eyes open, while all around her Aleran warriors threw defiant cheers after the fleeing enemy.

She closed her eyes, and when she opened them again, the sky was lighter. She sat on the battlements, wrapped in Bernard's cloak. Numb, aching, she swayed to her feet and looked up and down the wall and down into the courtyard below.

The wounded, the dying, and the dead lay everywhere. Healers and surgeons alike labored with the fallen, with men burned so badly that they could hardly be recognized as human. Amara watched as one man let out a choking shriek and then stiffened, a blackened hand curled into a claw. The *legionare* with him, himself sporting a scarlet-stained bandage, drew a cloak over the man's head. Then, with the help of another *legionare,* he carried the body to a growing number of rows of corpses on the other side of the courtyard.

She turned and looked down the walls. Perhaps a dozen *legionares* stood along them, young, strained, unwounded, holding their spears at attention.

On the battlefield below the walls, the crows had come for the dead.

They swarmed over them in a croaking black carpet,

wings flapping, eyes glittering with glassy hunger, uncaring of the loyalties of the fallen. They hopped from body to body, tearing at tongues, eyes, and when Amara saw one of the bodies stir, only to be buried in the winged beasts, she felt her numb belly twist and turned away.

Bernard appeared a moment later, his face strained, and handed her a ladle of cold water. She drank.

"It's bad," she said, quietly.

"Bad," he agreed. "Even once we get the lightly wounded back on their feet, the garrison lost two-thirds. There are only three Knights still alive, counting Pirellus. The gates are broken, and there's no way to replace them—and the enemy can jump the walls in any case."

"How's Gram?"

"Harger says he isn't likely to wake up again before he dies. That last crafting took too much out of him."

"Crows," Amara swore softly. "He's a brave man."

"Yes."

"The Marat are coming back then," Amara said.

"Soon."

She closed her eyes, wearily. "What else can we do?"

Bernard said, "I don't know."

"We should get the women and children out. The men's families. Put them in wagons and send them toward Riva as fast as they can go."

"We can't. Those Knights didn't just take out the gates. Some others got into the stables and panicked the horses. It drew the attention of maybe half a dozen herdbane. There aren't any horses left."

Amara looked up at him. "Can they flee on foot?"

"I've talked to Pirellus about it, and Giraldi. Even on

the causeway, the women and children can't run faster than the Marat. Even if we hold on to Garrison for as long as possible. There just aren't enough men—and most of the families won't leave. They've decided that they'll stay and fight, rather than be killed running. Pirellus is keeping their spirits up. Telling them that reinforcements are bound to come from Riva."

"No," Amara said, numb. "I never thought they'd have so many Knights Aeris to use to cut off the Valley. I don't think anyone could have gotten through that many."

Bernard nodded, once. "We've sent out runners, on foot, to warn the steadholts. We're hoping to buy them some time. If they head for Riva right away, they might make it out of the Valley . . ." He let his voice trail off, tiredly.

Amara stood up beside him and leaned against him. He leaned back, and the two shared a long moment of silence in the predawn stillness.

"You should go," Bernard said. "You can fly out of here. You should take word to the First Lord."

"Even if I could still fly," Amara said, "my duty is to do what I can to stop what's happening here. To find out who began it. Bring those responsible to justice. I couldn't just leave."

"There's no reason for you to die here, Countess."

"There's no point in this argument, Steadholder. I can't fly. Not now. I'm too tired." She leaned her cheek against his shoulder. He felt strong and warm, and she took whatever comfort she could in that.

After a moment, she felt him move an arm around

her, and she pressed closer to him. "I'm sorry, Bernard," she said. "I'm sorry I wasn't faster. I didn't do something differently. I'm sorry about your sister, your nephew."

He swallowed. When he spoke, his voice came out rough, quiet. "Nothing to be sorry for. I just hope to the furies that they're all right."

She touched his arm, and they stood together, quiet, with the caws of the crows before them and the moans of the dying behind.

The sky lightened further, and Amara felt Bernard draw in a sudden breath. "Merciful furies."

She opened her eyes and looked out onto the plains beyond Garrison, now being lit as the sun rose over them, and shone down upon a sea of pale bodies.

The Marat.

Thousands upon thousands of Marat. They stretched from horizon to horizon, as far as the eye could see. Twenty thousand. Thirty. Fifty. She had no way to accurately estimate numbers that vast. She looked out at them as the horde poured slowly closer to Garrison over the plains. Enough to drown the defenders of the little fortress. Enough to swarm over the Calderon Valley. Enough to rampage over the unprepared lands beyond and to destroy thousands of defenseless Aleran communities.

She glanced up at Bernard and then stepped forward, away from him, to lean one hand on the battlements, watching the enemy come on.

"You'd better get Pirellus," she said, quietly. "Tell him to get ready."

Chapter 38

Though they were not cold, Isana's feet were battered and bruised by the time she dragged the shambling Odiana out of the rough undergrowth of the woodland and out onto the causeway that ran the length of the Calderon Valley. She had barely caught her breath in the predawn darkness when she heard the drumming beats of running horses coming along the road, swift and steady.

She seized Odiana's wrist and dragged her back toward the edge of the causeway, but it was too late. Riders, blazing along the furycrafted stones of the causeway, were already upon them and all but ran them down before bringing their horses, huge, plunging shapes in the darkness, rearing and fighting to a halt.

"Mistress Isana?" gasped a startled young man's voice from the darkness. "What are you doing out here?"

Isana blinked up at the riders, startled. "Frederic?"

"Yes, ma'am," the young man said. He spoke quietly to the horse and then slid from the animal's back, keeping a hand on the reins. "Furies, ma'am, but we didn't think we'd see you again. Are you all right?"

The other rider slid down, and Isana recognized Steadholder Roth from the pale white shock of hair drifting around his head. He stepped to her at once and embraced her. "Thank goodness, Isana. We feared the worst."

She leaned against the old Steadholder, suddenly feeling the exhaustion in her arms and legs, and had to have Rill's help to keep the tears from her eyes. "I'm all right. It was a near thing, but I'm all right."

"Who is this?" Roth asked, looking up past Isana to squint at where Odiana sat beside the road, looking at nothing, her expression listless.

"It's a long story. I'll take care of her. But what are you doing out here?"

"Outriding," Roth said and turned to nod back down the road.

From down the causeway came the drum of more hooves, the rattle of cart wheels strained by the pace. Isana watched as more horses, some pulling heavy farm carts, others bearing riders, came down the road toward them. Frederic let out a sharp whistle and waved his arms, and the carts began to slow to a halt as they approached.

"But what are you doing?" Isana demanded.

Roth's expression looked very tired in the dimness. "Isana. The Marat got into the Valley yesterday. Sometime last night. They attacked Aldoholt and burned it down. As far as we can tell, no one made it out."

Isana took a deep breath, shocked. She felt dizzy. "Everyone?"

Roth nodded. "We saw the fires at dawn, and Warner and his boys went to check it out. He sent them out to warn Garrison and to Riva. The two heading for Garrison were murdered. We found them cut up not two miles back. We don't know about the others."

"Oh no," Isana breathed. "Oh, furies, poor Warner."

"Then, tonight, Frederic here was out in the fields working."

Frederic nodded. "That big rock. I didn't get it before the storm, and I couldn't sleep and all, so I was back there tonight, Mistress Isana. And these two men just fell out of the sky."

"Out of the sky? Knights Aeris?"

"Yes, ma'am. And one of them was all in black, and one was in Rivan colors ma'am, and hurt, so I hit the other one on the head with my shovel." His voice had an anxious note to it, as though he wasn't sure he'd done correctly. "That wasn't wrong, was it?"

"Course not, boy," Roth snorted. "He was a messenger from Garrison, Isana, sending to Riva for reinforcements. Said a Marat horde was on its way. And someone wanted him dead pretty bad. He had an arrow in him, and they'd sent a Knight to chase him to ground. Frederic here put a dent in the murderer's noggin that won't come out for a while, or we'd have asked who sent him."

Frederic ducked his head.

The wagons halted, and a moment later Otto and Warner had both hurried up to them and each hugged Isana, Otto with warm relief, Warner with stiff, quiet determination.

"So you're heading to Garrison?" Isana asked them.

Warner nodded. "We sent messengers to Riva, through the woods, where anyone watching from the air wouldn't be able to follow them. But it will take them longer than by the air or the roads, so we're heading out to fill in the gap ourselves."

Isana looked back at the wagons, at the people filling

them. "Great furies, Warner. You must have brought half of your holders."

"A bit more," Otto said, anxious. He wrung his hands. "Everyone able or who can do some useful crafting, Isana."

"These people aren't soldiers," Isana protested.

"No," Warner said, quietly. "But all the men have done their time in the Legions. Isana, if Garrison falls, there's nothing that's going to stop a horde from doing what it did to Aldoholt to every steadholt between here and Riva. Better for us to give our help and it not be needed than the other way around."

"What about the children?"

"Some of the older ones led the youngers into the back country. Beggar's Cave and such places. They'll be safer there than in the steadholts, until this blows over."

Isana blew out a breath. "What about Tavi? My brother? Has anyone seen them?"

No one said anything, until Frederic rubbed at his hair and said, "I'm sorry, Mistress. No one's seen or heard from anyone that ran out the night of the storm. We figured you all was dead or—"

"That'll do, Frederic," Roth said, sternly. "The woman's exhausted. Isana, you and this girl get in the back of the lead wagon, there. Otto, get something warm in them and around them, and we'll get moving again."

"Right," Otto said, and took Isana's arm. He reached down for Odiana's, but the woman flinched from him and let out a high-pitched little sound.

"I'll do it," Isana told him and leaned down to touch Odiana's chin. A broiling storm of emotion flowed up her from the touch, and Isana had to work to hold it away. She lifted Odiana's face to hers and murmured, only moving her lips, "Get in the wagon."

Odiana stared blankly at her, but rose when Isana tugged on her arm, and climbed up into the wagon willingly enough, settling in a back corner, eyes flicking out from behind her tangled hair to watch the other holders in it. Isana climbed in beside her, and a moment later, the wagon began rattling down the causeway again.

Someone passed her a heavy blanket, which she draped over the both of them, and a moment later a flask of something hot. She drank, some kind of spiced wine that burned in her belly but made her limbs feel warm and less tired. She passed the flask to Odiana, who had to hold it in her hands for a long moment, as though she had to work up the courage to drink, and who curled up beneath the blanket and dropped into what seemed to be an exhausted sleep a moment after.

"You look exhausted," Otto said, from across the cart, his face sympathetic. "Try to get some rest. We'll be in Garrison soon, but try."

Isana passed him the flask and shook her head. "I'm not tired, Otto, honestly. I've too much on my mind."

But after she sat back again, she leaned her head against the back of the cart, and didn't wake up until the driver called back to Otto, "Holder! There it is!"

Isana jerked awake and sat up enough to see ahead of the cart. The morning was cold on her face and throat, and the icy coating on the ground gleamed in the pale light of a dawn that was not far away.

Smoke hung over Garrison like a funeral shroud.

Isana's heart lurched into her throat. Were they too

late? Had the fort already been attacked? She climbed up onto the driver's seat of the wagon, even as the driver, one of Otto's holders, began to cluck to the horses that pulled the wagon, slowing them from their fury-enhanced speed. Their breath steamed in the dim light.

As they approached, Isana saw a single young *legionare* on guard duty above the western gate of Garrison. A second look showed that he wore a heavy swath of bandages over his forehead and left eye, and that those bandages were so recent that they were still spotted with blood. A dark bruise discolored his cheek, though it looked a day old, at least. As the group of wagons and horses closed, the young soldier leaned out, staring at them.

Warner raised a hand to the guard. "Hello the gate! Let us in!"

The young man stammered, "Sir, you shouldn't be here. The Marat are attacking, sir. You shouldn't be bringing holders here right now."

"I know the Marat are attacking," Warner snapped. "We've come to help, and everyone here has something they can do. Let us in."

The young *legionare* hesitated, but there was a motion on the wall behind him, and a man in a dented Centurion's helmet appeared. "Holder Warner?"

"Giraldi," Warner said, with a curt nod. "We heard you were having company and thought we'd invite ourselves over to help you entertain them."

Giraldi stared down at them for a moment and then nodded. "Warner," he said. "you'd be better off turning around and heading for Riva while you still can."

His words silenced every holder on the ground below.

Isana stood up in the wagon's seat. "Good morning, Centurion. Have you seen my brother?"

Giraldi squinted down and then his eyes widened. "Isana? Oh, thank the furies. Your brother is here. He's inside at the east gate. Isana, the Count's been badly wounded, and Livia is back in Riva with her daughter. Harger and the legion crafters did what they could, but they say without more skilled help he won't live."

Isana nodded, calmly. She let her awareness slowly out toward Giraldi, gaining the sense of the man's emotions. Anger, weariness, and most of all despair hung on him like a coating of thick, cold mud, and Isana shivered. "I take it the Marat have already attacked."

"Just their vanguard," Giraldi said. "The rest of the horde will be here within the hour."

"Then we'd best stop wasting time with talk, Giraldi. Open the gates."

"I don't know if the Count would—"

"The Count has no say in this," Isana said. "And if the Marat take Garrison, they'll be able to destroy everything we have. We've the right to fight to defend our homes and families as well, Giraldi, and every man here who is of age is a Legion veteran. Open the gates."

Giraldi bowed his head and nodded to the young *legionare*. "Furies know we need the help. Do it."

The holders moved into Garrison in short order, and Isana noticed that adult men—the veterans—drove all the wagons. They pulled into the fortress as though part of the Legion on duty there, lining up their wagons in neat rows in the westernmost courtyard. Men started caring for the horses at once, unhitching them and leading them to be watered and sheltered from the winter winds. Every Legion camp was laid out identically, enabling veterans and newly transferred units to be exactly aware of the operations and layout of any camp they came to. Even as some men picketed the horses, others began forming up the veterans into files outside the armory, and Giraldi and another young *legionare* began to outfit them with shields, swords, spears, breastplates, helmets.

Isana stepped down from the wagon, holding Odiana's hand and leading the dazed woman, who kept the blanket wrapped around her like a sleepy child. "Harger," Isana called, spotting the healer supervising a number of young women, barely more than children really, who were shredding bedsheets into bandages.

The old healer turned when he saw her, a tired smile touching his face. "Help," he said. "Well, maybe we can make a fight of it after all."

She moved to him and embraced him quietly. "Are you all right?"

"Tired," he said. He looked around them and then said, "This is bad, Isana. Our wall isn't high enough, and our Knights went down in the first attack."

Isana's throat tightened. "My brother?"

"A little banged up, but well," Harger said. "Isana, we've got less than an hour. By the time the sun rises, you'll be able to walk from here to the watchtowers on Marat shoulders."

She nodded. "There, see Steadholder Otto? He's a strong crafter. Not too delicate, because he mostly crafts injured livestock rather than people, but he can mend broken bones better than anyone I've ever seen, and he can do it from dawn to dark. There are one or two other men at least as skilled as a Legion watercrafter, and many of the women are better. You have injured?"

"Plenty," Harger said, his eyes calculating. "Really? Women better than a Legion watercrafter?"

"See Otto. He'll get our healers over to help yours. You're in the eastern courtyard?"

Harger nodded, blinking his eyes a few times. Then he clasped Isana's shoulder. "Thank you. I don't know if it will do any good in the long run, but there are men dying who won't have to now."

Isana touched her hand with his and said, "Where can I find Bernard?"

"On the wall above the gate," Harger said.

Isana nodded to him and started toward the far side of the fort. She passed the commander's quarters and the officers' barracks at the center of the fort, then walked briskly past barracks after barracks. She found the first bodies at the near side of the eastern courtyard, in the stables. Dead horses lay inside, crows already darting in and out of the stable's doors, their raucous cries rising from their darkened interiors. More bodies littered the courtyard around her—Marat, and the great predator birds had been tossed into a rough heap at one side of the courtyard, where they would be out of the way of the troops moving about inside. Legion casualties were laid out in neat rows on the other, troops wrapped in their cloaks, heads covered to keep the crows from their eyes.

The rest of the courtyard was filled with the wounded and the dying. A bare scattering of *legionares* stood watch on the walls, but there seemed to be so *few* of them.

Isana walked forward, stunned at the carnage. She had

never seen anything like it. Pain pressed on her, sensed from the wounded like heat radiating out from an oven. She shivered and folded her arms. Behind her, Odiana, still following closely and holding her hand, let out a small, frightened whimper and did not lift her head.

"Isana!"

She looked up to see her brother running toward her, and she didn't fight either the tears that sprang to her eyes or the smile that touched her mouth. He embraced her, hugging hard, and lifted her up off the ground as he did it.

"Thank the furies," he rumbled. "I was so afraid for you."

She hugged him back, hard. "Tavi?" He froze for a moment, and the motion sent ice running through her. She leaned back, taking his face between her hands. "What happened?"

"After the flood, I lost him. I couldn't track him in the storm. I managed to get the Cursor girl out of the water, and then we came here."

"Was he alone?" Isana asked.

"Not entirely, if you count that Fade was still with him. I thought you'd have found him after the flood."

She shook her head. "No. I couldn't. Kord pulled me out of the river, Bernard."

Her brother's eyes went flat.

"It's all right," she assured him, though she folded her hands over a little quiver of fear in her belly at the memory of Kord's smokehouse. "His son, Aric, helped us escape. I got away from him."

"And came here?"

"Not alone," Isana said. "I had just reached the

causeway when Warner and the rest came down the road. I rode here with them."

"Warner?" Bernard said.

"Warner, Otto, Roth. They brought all their holders here. Yours too. They've come to help."

"Those *idiots*," Bernard sputtered. But his eyes glittered, and he looked back toward the wall and the shattered gates leading into the fort. A rough barricade had been shoved into place, consisting of a pair of wagons upended, barrels, and bunks. "How many did he bring?"

"Everyone," Isana said. "Nearly five hundred people."

"The women, too?"

Isana nodded. Bernard grimaced. "I guess we've got it all resting on one throw, then." His eyes went past her to Odiana. "Who's this?"

Amara swallowed. "One of Kord's slaves," she lied. "She saved my life. That's a discipline collar on her, Bernard. I couldn't leave her there."

He nodded, glancing back at the walls again, and let out a slow breath. "Might have been kinder to. It's not going to be good."

Isana frowned at him and then at the walls. "Bernard. Do you remember when we had our holdraising?"

"Of course," he said.

"Everyone in the Valley helped with that. Brought up the whole steadholt, walls, all in one day."

He blinked and turned to her, his voice suddenly excited. "You mean that we could make the walls higher."

She nodded. "If it would help. Giraldi said they weren't high enough."

"It might," Bernard said. "It might, it might." He looked

around. "There. That centurion there, he's the engineer. See the braid on his tunic? We'll need his help. You tell him, and I'm going to round up our earthcrafters."

Bernard hurried off. Isana approached the man, who glanced up, blinked at her, and then scowled at her from over a bristling grey mustache. He listened to her without speaking while she told him of her plan.

"Impossible," he said. "It can't be done, girl."

"I've forty summers, Centurion," Isana retorted. "And it must be done. My brother is bringing our earthcrafters right now."

The Centurion faced her more squarely, his face and throat flushing a deep red. "Holdfolk crafters," he said. "This isn't a barn raising. These are siege walls."

"I don't see how that matters."

The man snorted in an explosion of breath. "These walls are made of layers of interlocking strata, girl. They're hard, flexible, heavy, and can stand up to any kind of pounding you care to dish out. But you can't just make them higher once they're in place, like some pasture fence. If you go toying with the wall, you'll disrupt the foundation, and the whole thing will collapse. We won't have a wall at *all*, much less a taller one."

"As I understand it," Isana said. "You might as well not have the wall as it stands in any case."

The man blinked at her for a moment, then scowled and bowed his head, snorting from beneath his mustache.

"I understand that it might be difficult, but it's worth a try, isn't it? If it works, we might be able to hold out against them. If it doesn't . . ." Isana shivered. "If it doesn't, then I'd just as soon it didn't take too long in any case."

"No," the engineer said, finally. "If there was a chance, it might be worth the risk. But these aren't engineers. They're *holders*. They don't have the kind of strength it takes."

"You've never had to live in this valley, have you?" Isana said, her voice wry. "Not everyone with a strong fury wants to be a Knight. There are boys barely more than children in my steadholt who can tear boulders larger than a man out of the ground. And as I see it, we have nothing to lose."

The engineer eyed her. "Impossible," he said, then. "It can't be done. If I had a full corps of Legion engineers, it would still take me half a day to get that wall higher."

"Then it's a good thing we're not a corps of Legion engineers," Isana said. "Will you try?"

A new voice cut into the conversation. "He'll try."

Isana looked up to see the Cursor standing not far away, wearing her brother's too-large clothes and a borrowed tunic of mail. She wore a sword at her hip, and her left arm had been splinted. Amara looked tired and sported a bruise on throat, abrasions on her chin, but she regarded the engineer calmly. "Coordinate with the Steadholders. Make the attempt."

The engineer swallowed and then inclined his head to her in a bow. "As you wish, Countess." The man turned and hurried away.

Amara turned to face Isana, the slim girl's expression quiet, calm. Then she glanced past Isana, to where the water witch still stood, wrapped in her blanket, her expression distant, and hissed a quiet curse. She reached for her sword.

"Wait," Isana said, stepping close and putting a hand over Amara's. "Don't."

"But she's—"

"I know who she is," Isana said. "She isn't going to hurt anyone now. She saved my life—and a slaver put a discipline collar on her."

"You can't trust her," Amara insisted. "She should be locked up."

"But—"

"She's a Knight herself. A mercenary. A murderer." The Cursor's voice snapped with anger. "By all rights I should kill her right now."

"I will not allow that," Isana said, lifting her chin.

Amara faced her quietly. "I'm not sure it's your decision to make, holder."

Just then, a tall, dark-skinned man with the look of a Parcian, his armor magnificent but stained with smoke and blood, stepped over to them. "Countess," he said, calmly. "The horde is nearly here. I'd like you to stand with me. See if you can spot their hordemaster."

Amara glared at Isana and turned to the Parcian. "Do you think killing him will do us any good now, Pirellus?"

He smiled, a sudden flash of white teeth. "As I see it, it can hardly hurt. And in any case, I'd rather make sure that whatever animal is responsible for this," he gestured around vaguely, "doesn't go back home to brag about it."

Isana withdrew a pair of steps, then calmly turned and led Odiana away from the pair. "Come on," she murmured to the collared woman, though she knew that Odiana could not hear her. "They're terrified and angry.

They wouldn't treat you fairly. Let's find someplace for you to be out of sight until we can get through this."

She hurried through the courtyard to one of the large warehouse buildings at the far side. Even as she opened the door and hurried in, a group of holders, bundled up in their homemade winter cloaks but wearing Legion steel, went tramping by in neat files, heading for the gates. Another file, led by Bernard and the engineer, speaking in hushed, intent tones, went past right behind them.

Isana opened the door and led Odiana into the warehouse. The interior was dark, and she could hear the scrabble of rats somewhere inside. A rangy grey tomcat rushed past her legs and into the darkness, intent on a meal. Crates and heavy sacks stood in neat, ordered rows, their contents clearly labeled. It was too dim to see clearly, so Isana looked about until she found a furylamp and willed it to life, lifting the clear globe in her hand and looking up and down the rows.

"There," she said, and started to tug the woman forward, continuing to speak in a low, quiet tone, hoping that the deafened watercrafter would at least find some comfort in the intent of the words. "Bags of meal. It will be softer than the floor, and if you cover up, you might be able to get some sleep. You'll be out of everyone's way."

She hadn't taken a dozen steps when the door to the warehouse slammed behind her.

Isana whirled, holding the furylamp aloft, shadows dancing and spinning wildly in the room.

Kord, dressed in a dirty cloak, dropped the heavy bolt down over the reinforced door of the warehouse. He turned to Isana then, eyes gleaming, and smiled, his teeth as grimy and smudged as the Steadholder's chain about his neck.

"Now then," he said, his voice quiet, almost purring. "Where were we?"

◇◇◇◇ CHAPTER 39

Amara nodded to Pirellus. "But will they be able to raise the wall?"

Pirellus shrugged. "Again—it can't hurt. The wall isn't going to slow the Marat down as it stands in any case."

Nearby, Bernard and the engineer had led nearly a hundred men and women, ranging in age from those below Legion age to a wizened old grandmother, who doddered along with the help of a cane and the arm of a brawny, serious-looking young man Amara recognized from Bernardholt. "Are you sure it isn't a terrible risk? We held it before," Amara pointed out.

"Against Marat who had never seen a battle," Pirellus said. "Half-trained, green troops. And we were nearly destroyed as it was. Don't fool yourself. We got lucky. There are five times as many of them out there now. They're experienced, and they won't be operating in separate tribes." His fingers drummed on the hilt of his dark blade. "And remember, those Knights are still out there."

Amara shivered and abruptly looked behind her. "Exactly. Which is why, Mistress Isana, we should—" She broke off abruptly. "Where'd she go?"

Pirellus looked around behind him, then shrugged. "Don't worry about it. There's a very limited amount of trouble the woman can make in any case. That's the advantage of certain death, Cursor—it's difficult to become impressed by further risks."

Amara frowned at him. "But with this help—"

"Doomed," Pirellus said, flatly. "We'd need three times that many troops to hold, Cursor. What these holders are doing is admirable, but unless one of their messengers got through to Riva . . ." He shook his head. "Without reinforcements, without more *Knights,* we're just killing time until sunrise. See if you can spot the hordemaster, and I'll try to help them sort out the wounded and get more men back on their feet."

She started to speak to him, but Pirellus spun on his heel and walked back to the other courtyard. His knee was swollen and purpling, but he did not allow himself to limp. Another talent she envied in metalcrafters. Amara grimaced and wished she could will away the pain of her broken arm so easily.

Or the fear that still weakened her knees.

She shivered and turned to walk toward the gates, purposefully. The barricade had been hastily removed, as the earthcrafters had begun to set up for their attempt on the walls. A squad of twenty *legionares* stood outside the broken gates in formation, on guard, lest any Marat should try to slip through undetected. The possibility seemed unlikely. Even as Amara walked beneath the walls and out into the open plain beyond, stepping around the grim and silent young men, she could see the Marat horde in the slowly growing light, like some vast field of living snow, marching steadily closer, in no great hurry.

Amara walked out away from the walls by several yards, keeping her steps light and careful. She tried not to look down at the ground. The blackened remains of the Marat who had perished in the first firestorm lay underfoot and all around, grotesque and stinking. Crows flapped and squabbled everywhere, mercifully covering most of the dead. If she looked, Amara knew, she would be able to see the gaping sockets of the corpses whose eyes had already been eaten away, usually along with parts of the nose and the soft, fleshy lips, but she didn't. The air smelled of snow and blood, of burned flesh and faintly of carrion. Even through the screen Cirrus provided her sense of smell, she could smell it.

Her knees trembled harder, and she grew short of breath. She had to stop and close her eyes for a moment, before lifting them to the oncoming horde again. She lifted her unwounded arm and bade Cirrus make her vision more clear.

The fury bent the air before her, and almost at once she could see the oncoming horde as though she stood close enough to it to hear their footsteps.

Almost at once, she could see what Pirellus had meant. Though the fleeing elements of the Marat horde had rejoined it half an hour before and been absorbed into the oncoming mass, she could see the difference in the warriors now moving toward Garrison, without needing to engage them to understand part of Pirellus's fears. They were older men, heavier with muscle and simple years, but they walked with more of both confidence and caution, ferocity tempered with wisdom.

She shivered.

Women, too, walked among the horde, bearing weapons, wearing the mien of experienced soldiers, which Amara had no doubt that they were. As near as Aleran intelligence could determine, the Marat engaged in almost constant struggles against one another—small-scale conflicts that lasted only briefly and seemed to result in few lasting hostilities, almost ritual combat. Deadly enough, though. She focused on the horde grimly. The dead behind the walls of Garrison proved that.

As she watched them come on, Amara was struck by a sudden sense that she had not felt in a long time, not since, as a small child, she had first been allowed out onto the open sea with her father in his fishing boat. A sense of being *outside*, a sense of standing balanced at the precipice of a world wholly alien to her own. She glanced at the walls behind her, eyes twinging as they refocused. There stood the border of the mighty Realm of Alera, a land that had withstood its enemies for a thousand years, overcome a hostile world to build a prosperous nation.

And she stood outside it, all but naked, despite her armor. The sheer size and scope of the rolling plains that lay beyond this last bastion of Aleran strength made her feel suddenly small.

The voice that came to her whispered in the rustle of the lonely wind, low, indistinct. "Never be intimidated by size itself. I taught you better than that."

Amara stiffened, dropping the visioncrafting before her hand, glancing around. "Fidelias?"

"You always hold your legs stiffly when you're afraid,

Amara. You never learned to hide it. Oh, and I can hear you," the voice responded. "One of my men is crafting my voice to you, and listening for your replies."

"I have nothing to say to you," Amara whispered, heated. She glanced at the *legionares* too close behind her and stepped forward, away from them, so that they couldn't overhear. She lifted her hand again, focusing on the oncoming horde, searching through their ranks for one who might be their leader.

"Useless," Fidelias commented. "You can't hold the walls. And even if you do, we'll break the gate again."

"Which part of 'I have nothing to say to you' did you not understand?" She paused a moment and then added as viciously as she knew how, "Traitor."

"Then listen," Fidelias said. "I know you don't agree with me, but I want you to think about this. Gaius is going to fall. You know it. If he doesn't fall cleanly, he'll crush thousands on his way down. He might even weaken the Realm to the point that it can be destroyed."

"How can you *dare* speak to me of the safety of the Realm? Because of you, her sons and daughters lie dead behind that wall."

"We kill people," Fidelias said. "It's what we do. I have dead of my own to bury, thanks to you. If you like, I'll tell you about the families of the men you made fall to their deaths. At least the dead inside had a chance to fight for their lives. The ones you murdered didn't. Don't be too liberal with that particular brush, apprentice."

Amara abruptly remembered the men screaming, falling. She remembered the terror on their faces, though she hadn't taken much note of it at the time.

She closed her eyes. Her stomach turned over on itself.

"If you have something to say, say it and have done. I have work to do."

"I've heard dying can be quite the chore," Fidelias's voice noted. "I wanted to make you an offer."

"No," Amara said. "Stop wasting my time. I won't take it."

"Yes you will," Fidelias said. "Because you don't want the women and children behind those walls to be murdered with the rest of you."

Amara stiffened. She felt suddenly cold.

"Leave," Fidelias said. "You. Lead the women and children away. I'll have my Knights see that the Marat are delayed long enough to give you a safe lead."

"No," she whispered. "You're lying. You can't control the Marat."

"Don't be so sure," Fidelias said. "Amara, I don't like what has to be done. But you can make a difference. You can save the lives of innocent people of the Realm. You lead them. If you don't, personally, then there's no deal." There was silence for a moment, before he said, weariness in his voice, "You don't know what you're doing, girl. I don't want to see you die for it. And if I can save the lives of some noncombatants while protecting you, so much the better."

Amara closed her eyes, her head spinning. The stench of the burned corpses, of the carrion the crows had torn into, came to her again. She was a Cursor, a skilled fencer, an agent of the Crown, a decorated heroine of the Realm—but she did not want to die. It terrified her. She had seen the men the Marat had killed, and none of them had gone pleasantly. She had joked before, lightly, that she would never want to end her life in less than a viciously bloody fashion, as alive as she could possibly be, but the reality of it was different. There wasn't any consideration in it, no abstract philosophy. Just glittering, animal eyes and terror and pain.

It made sense, she reasoned. Fidelias wasn't a monster. He was a man like any other. He *had* cared about her, when they worked together. Almost more than her father had, in some ways. It was reasonable to assume that he did not want to see her die if he could avoid it.

And if she could save some more people, if she could lead those who would surely die away from the coming struggle, surely it would be worth it. Surely there would be no shame for her in fleeing, no dishonor before the Crown.

Or before Bernard's memory.

It wouldn't be wrong. Fidelias was giving her a way out. An escape.

"Amara," Fidelias's voice said, gently. "There isn't much time. You must go quickly, if you are to save them."

She abruptly saw the trap. Though she didn't understand it yet, though she wasn't sure exactly where it lay, she recognized what he had scattered out to blind her— raw emotions, fear, the desire to protect, the need to save her own pride. He had played on them, just as he had tried to put her into a raw, emotional state of terror and grief when he had betrayed her before.

"I must go quickly," she said, quietly. "*I* must go. Me. Or there's no deal." She took a breath and said, "Why would you want to make sure I was not a part of this battle, Fidelias? Why now, instead of an hour ago? Why did you make this offer only after you saw me observing the enemy?"

"Don't do this to yourself, Amara," he said. "Don't rationalize your way out of life. Don't let it *kill* those children."

She swallowed. He was right, of course. Perhaps she was being manipulated. Perhaps accepting his offer *would* mean that she had sacrificed some unknown advantage. But could she really argue against that statement? Could she make some attempt to play at maneuvers against him, here, now, when she would almost certainly die? And when it would cost the lives of *children.*

Run. Save them. Grieve with the Crown over the Valley's loss.

"Your purpose as a Cursor is to save lives, Amara. Stay true to your purpose. And let me stay true to my choice."

The crows croaked and swooped all around her. She opened her mouth to agree.

But a sudden sound stopped her. Without warning, the ground began to rumble, low, hard, rhythmic. She staggered and had to crouch to keep her balance. She looked back at the walls of Garrison.

A shout went up from the *legionares,* who immediately marched forward, away from the walls, breaking into ragged formation as the pitching of the earth made them stagger left and right. They came out to the same distance she stood at and turned to stare at the walls with her.

The walls of Garrison heaved and shuddered, like a sleeper stirring. They rippled, a slow wave rolling through the seamless grey stone. And then, with a screeching of breaking earth, they began to grow.

Amara stared at it in sudden wonder. She had never

seen any such feat done on such a scale before. The walls rolled up, higher, like a wave approaching the shore. They ground forward several paces toward the enemy, until Amara realized that they were growing thicker at the base, to support the greater height. The walls grew, and the grim grey stone began to streak with ribbons of scarlet and azure, twined within the rock, the colors of Alera proper, and then with scarlet bound with gold, the colors of the Legion's home city of Riva. The battlements grew higher, and with an abrupt shriek of stone, spikes erupted at the summit of the battlements and then sprang out all along the walls themselves, long, slender daggers of some dark stone that gleamed in the growing light. The spikes spread, as though they were tendrils sprung from some deadly vines beneath the surface of the wall, and raced out over the ground before the walls as well, rippling into place like blades of grass growing all in an instant, their gleaming tips pointing out at the oncoming horde.

The crows, dismayed, flew into the sky in a sudden storm of black wings and raucous cawing, circling around the field of battle like wreathes of panicked smoke.

The rumbling eased. The walls of Garrison stood, thirty feet high and grim, and bristled with razor-edged daggers of the same black stone, Amara could now see, that the Marat used for their own weapons. The ground itself lay ready to impale any attackers.

And, in the stunned silence, she heard Fidelias's voice whisper, "Bloody crows."

The *legionares* beside her erupted into sudden cheers, and she was barely able to hold back the shout of defiance that came to her own throat. She snapped an order to

the men, to send them back inside, and they began picking their way painfully across the field of spikes before
the wall. One of the men slipped and cut his leg, drawing, of all things, a sudden and enthusiastic discussion
about how sharp the spikes were and how well they'd cut
him. The loudest voice of praise was from the injured
man. More cheers rose up from inside the fortress, and
as Amara watched, more *legionares* crowded the wall,
and someone raised the banners of the Legion and of
Riva into position above the gates. Within, one of the
musicians began to trumpet the call to arms, and the
legionares, professional and holder alike, answered it in
a sudden roar that shook the stone of the hills framing
the fortress.

Amara spun back out to face the horde coming over
the plains and hissed, "Fight for what you want, Fidelias,
but it will not be handed to you. The future of these
men and women, children and soldier alike, is not cast in
stone. If you want the fortress, then come and take it."

There was a long and terrible silence before Fidelias
responded, and when he did, his voice was calm, even.
"Good-bye, Amara."

With the softest whisper of wind, the contact faded.

Amara turned and called to Cirrus. She stepped forward and leapt lightly over the field of spikes, thirty
yards or more, landing in the gate ahead of the *legionares*
returning from outside. Her heart pounded in swift, hot
defiance, determination.

She tried not to notice that it made her broken arm
throb as well, with pain.

Amara moved quickly into the courtyard, and the
shadows of the now-higher walls had changed the

perspective of the entire place. It took her a moment to orient herself, but she spotted Bernard sitting at the base of the new wall with a group of jubilant-faced, panting men, talking. Shields and weaponry and breastplates lay near each man, and one of the women had brought water to them. As much seemed to have been tossed over their heads as down their throats, and their tunics were splotched with water, their breath turned to steam before smiling mouths. Pirellus stood nearby Bernard and nodded to her when he saw her.

"Interesting," Pirellus said, jerking his head back toward the wall. "It's going to force them to use their scaling poles and to try to take the gate. We'll be able to make a good fight of it, at least."

"Incredible," Amara said, grinning first at Pirellus and then at Bernard. "I've never seen anything like it."

Bernard looked up with a tired smile of his own. "Always amazing what you can do when you must."

Pirellus asked, "Did you spot anything?"

"No," Amara said, "but I believe our opposition was afraid that I would." She told them, in brief, about the conversation with Fidelias.

Bernard frowned. "You know. Maybe we *should* get as many people as we can into the wagons and get them on the road again. Can we hold long enough to let them get away?"

Pirellus looked at the wall and then at the other side of the courtyard. "It's a risk worth taking. I'll see to it," he said, shortly. "There won't be enough room for everyone, but we could get the children out, at least."

"Thank you," Amara told him.

Pirellus nodded to her. "You were right last night,"

he said. "I was wrong." Then he headed out across the courtyard, steps steady despite his wounded leg.

Bernard whistled and said to Amara, "That cost him something, I think."

"Nothing he couldn't do without anyway," Amara said, her voice dry. "Bernard, those Knights are still out there, and they're going to be coming in on us again."

"I know," Bernard said. "But we don't have enough Knights Aeris to hold the sky. We don't know when or where they'll come."

Amara nodded to him. "But I think I have a good guess. Here's what I want you to do."

She laid out brief instructions for him, and he nodded, gathered up some more of the holders with him, and hurried off to carry out her plan. Amara checked in with Harger and then headed up onto the wall. The battlements were crowded with men, but she located Giraldi, standing soberly in position at the center of the wall, over the gate.

"Centurion," she greeted him.

"Countess."

"How does it look?"

He nodded out toward the oncoming Marat, hardly more than a mile away now. "They've stopped," he told her. "Out past our best bow range, even for these holder boys. They're waiting."

"For what?"

He shrugged. "Sunrise maybe. If they give it a few minutes, the sun will be in our eyes when it comes up."

"Will it hurt us much?"

He shrugged. "It won't help."

She nodded. "How long can we expect to hold them?"

"No telling with these things. If we can keep them off the walls, out of the gates, a good long while."

"Long enough to give a group of wagons a running start?"

He glanced at her. "The holders' wagons?"

Amara nodded. "We're loading them with the women and children right now."

Giraldi looked at her steadily for a moment, then nodded. "All right then. We'll hold them long enough. Excuse me." He turned and stepped back from the battlements to meet a panting *legionare* who had made his way down the wall. Amara followed him. Giraldi frowned and asked, "Where are those canteens, man?"

The *legionare* saluted. "Sorry, sir. They're in the east warehouse, and it's already been secured."

"Already been secured," Giraldi growled. "How do you know?"

"Door was locked."

Giraldi frowned at the man. "Well, find Harger and get him to—what's that on your shoes?"

"Hay, sir."

"Where did you get hay in your boots, *legionare*?"

"One of the holders threw it there, sir. They're tossing it all over the courtyard."

"*What?*"

Amara stepped in. "My orders, Centurion."

"Uh," Giraldi said. He swept off his helmet and rubbed at his shortcropped hair. "With all due respect, Your Ladyship, what kind of idiot order is that? If you put hay all over the courtyard, it'll make the prettiest fire you ever saw, and among our own, to boot. For all we know they're going to be shooting flame arrows over the wall."

"It's a calculated risk, Centurion, that I cannot explain here."

"Lady," Giraldi began to protest.

From down the wall, someone shouted, "Sir!"

Amara and Giraldi both turned to look down the wall.

A pale-faced young *legionare* jerked his chin out toward the plains beyond the fortress. "Here they come."

◁◁◁◁ CHAPTER 40

Amara rushed back to the battlements with Giraldi beside her and watched as the Marat horde, beneath the droning yawls of huge, hollowed animal horns, began a determined advance, moving forward at a steady trot, with wolves and herdbane loping along beside them.

"Crows," whispered one of the *legionares* beside Amara. She saw the man reach for his spear, fumble it, and drop it. She flinched, hand flashing out and batting the falling weapon away from her.

Giraldi caught it in one scar-knuckled hand. "Steady," he growled, eyes on Amara. He passed the spear back to the *legionare*. "Steady, lads."

The horde grew closer. The sounds of thousands

of feet hitting the ground as they ran rose like far off thunder.

"Steady," Giraldi said. He looked up and down the line and barked, "Archers! Shields!"

The *legionares* stepped up to the battlements. In each crenellation stood a man with one of the huge Legion wall shields. Behind each, another *legionare,* armed with a bow and a thick war-quiver of arrows, strung his bow and took position. Most of the archers were holders from the Valley.

The Marat grew closer, the eerie droning of their horns growing louder, more unnerving. A restless shuffle went down the line of shieldmen.

"Steady," Giraldi commanded. He glanced at the young holder in borrowed armor beside him. "You sure you lads can shoot that far?"

The holder peeked around the edge of the shield of the burly *legionare* in front of him. "Yes. They're in range."

Giraldi nodded. "Archers!" he growled. "Fire at will!"

All up and down the line, archers set arrows to their bows, their tips pointing up at the sky, standing close to their shield man. Amara watched the nearest young man half draw his bow, then bump his partner with his hip. The *legionare* knelt, lowering the shield, and the archer drew as he lowered the bow, took quick aim, and loosed at the oncoming Marat. His partner stood up again swiftly, bringing his shield back into position.

All along the wall, the archers began shooting. Each man loosed an arrow every five or six breaths, or even faster. Amara stood beside Giraldi in the one crenellation not occupied by a shieldman and watched the arrows slither through the air and into the oncoming Marat ranks. The deadly aim of the Aleran holders dropped Marat and beast alike with equal ferocity, littering the ground with fresh corpses, making the eager crows swoop and dive in a swarm over the charging horde.

But still the horde came on.

The archers had begun shooting at close to six hundred yards—an incredible distance, Amara knew. They had to have been woodcrafters of nearly a Knight's skill to manage such a feat. For perhaps a minute, there was no sound but the grunt of archers drawing bows, *legionares* kneeling and standing again, the droning blare of Marat horns, and the rumbling of thousands of feet.

But when the Marat closed to charging range of the walls, the entire horde erupted in a sudden shout that hit Amara like a wall of cold water—chilling, terrifying in its sheer intensity. At the same moment, the war birds let out a shrill, piercing shriek, terrifying from one such beast, but from the thousands below, the sound almost seemed a living thing all its own. At the same moment, the sun broke the horizon across the distant plains, a sudden harsh light that swept over the top of the battlements first, and made archers flinch and squint as they attempted their next shot.

"Steady!" Giraldi bellowed, voice barely carrying over the din. "Spears!"

The shield-bearing centurions gripped their spears, faces set in a fighting grimace.

Below, the Marat charge hit the first razor-edged defensive spikes the holders had crafted out of the earth itself. Amara watched closely, her heart in her throat. The leaders in the Marat charge began to leap and skip among the spikes, looking for all the world like children playing at hopping games. Behind them leapt their animals. Amara saw some of the Marat, with heavy, knotted cudgels, begin to strike the spikes from the sides, shattering them.

"The ones with clubs," Amara said. "Tell the archers to aim for them. The longer we can keep the spikes in place, the harder it will be for them to pressure the gate."

Giraldi grunted and relayed her order up and down the walls, and the archers, instead of firing into the enemy at random, began to pick their targets.

Scaling poles and ropes with hooks fashioned of some kind of antlers or bone began to lift toward the wall. *Legionares* thrust at the poles with the crossguards of their spears, pushing them away, and some drew their swords to hack at ropes as they came up, while the archers continued to fire on the enemy. Arrows began to flicker up from the horde below, short, heavy arrows launched from oddly shaped bows. One of the archers beside Amara lingered in aiming his shot for too long, and an arrow struck him through both cheeks in a sudden welter of blood. The holder choked, dropping.

"Surgeon!" Amara yelled, and a pair of men on the wall moved quickly to the fallen man, dragging him down before going to work on removing the arrow.

Amara stepped back to the battlements. She swept her gaze over the enemy below, but she couldn't see anything beyond a horde of Marat and their beasts, so many thousands of them that it was difficult to tell where one left off and the other began.

Giraldi abruptly seized her shoulder and dragged her back from the edge. "Not without a helmet," he growled.

"I can't tell what's happening," Amara panted. She

had to shout to make herself heard. "There are too many of them."

Giraldi squinted out at the enemy, then drew his head prudently back. "About half of their force is here. They're holding the rest back, ready to bring them in when they get an opening."

"Are we holding them?"

"The walls are doing all right," Giraldi called back, "but the gate is our weak point. They attack the walls only to keep most of our men busy up here. There are too few men at the gate. They'll force the barricade sooner or later."

"Why didn't they craft the gate closed?"

"Can't," Giraldi reported. "Engineer told me. No foundation under it for extra wall, and the interior surface is lined with metal."

From below them there came a crunching sound and a sudden chorus of mixed Aleran war cries of, "Riva for Alera!" and "Calderon for Alera!"

Giraldi glanced out over the field again. "They must have gotten part of the barricade down. The hordemaster has ordered the rest of his troops in, and they're on the move. They'll try to put pressure on the gate until the defense breaks." Giraldi grimaced. "If they don't repel this first thrust, we're done for."

Amara nodded to him. "All right. Almost time, then. I'll be back up as soon as I can." She leaned out to look down into the courtyard below. She could just make out the forms of a couple of *legionares* standing their ground almost within the gate itself, spears thrusting. There were shrieks and cries from below, and Amara's eyes caught a flash of motion, a dark blade seen for only a second as its wielder spun it out behind him. Pirellus was holding the gate once more.

Amara hurried to the nearest stairs and pelted down them to the courtyard, looking around wildly. Hay from the bales she had crashed through earlier that morning lay scattered everywhere over the courtyard. All but a few of the wounded had been pulled back to the west courtyard, and the last of them were being loaded onto stretchers. She started across the courtyard toward the stables. As she did, she saw Pluvus Pentius emerge from one of the barracks, white-faced and nervous, one hand wrapped around the hand of a little boy, whose hand stretched back behind to another child, and so on, until the truthfinder was leading half a dozen children across the courtyard.

Amara hurried to him. "Pluvus! What are these children still doing here?"

"H-hiding," Pluvus stuttered. "I found them hiding under their fathers' bunks in the barracks."

"Crows," Amara spat. "Get them to the west courtyard with the wounded. They're supposed to be fortifying one of the barracks to hold them. And *hurry*."

"Yes, right," Pluvus said, his skinny shoulders tightening. "Come on, children. Hold hands, and stay together."

Amara dashed to the stables and found Bernard sitting with his back to the wall just inside one of the doors, his eyes half-closed. "Bernard," she called. "The gate is under attack. They'll be coming."

"We're ready," Bernard mumbled. "Just say when."

Amara nodded to him and turned, focusing her attention on Cirrus, then sent him up and out into the sky, feeling for the windcrafters she knew would be carrying Fidelias's rogue Knights toward the fortress.

She felt it a moment later, a tension in the air that spoke of a coming stream of wind. Amara called Cirrus back and worked another sightcrafting, sweeping the sky, searching for the incoming troops.

She spotted them while they were still half a mile from the fortress, dark shapes against the morning sky. "There," she shouted. "They're coming in from the west. Half a minute at the most."

"All right," Bernard murmured.

Amara stepped out into the open, as the Knights Aeris with their transport litters swept down from the skies, diving for the fortress. A wedge of Knights Aeris flew before the litters, weapons ready, and the sun gleamed on the metal of their armor. They headed toward the gate in a steep dive.

"Ready!" Amara shouted, and drew her sword. "Ready!" She waited a pair of heartbeats more, until the enemy reached the valley-side wall and passed over the western courtyard then the garrison commander's building. She took a breath, willing her hands to stop shaking. "Loose!"

All around her in the courtyard, hummocks and lumps of scattered hay shook and shimmered, and a full fifty holder bowmen, covered with handfuls of hay and by the woodcrafting Bernard had worked over them, became vaguely visible. As one, they lifted their great bows and opened fire directly up at the underside of the incoming Knights.

The holders' aim proved deadly, and their attack had taken the mercenaries completely by surprise. Knights Aeris in their armor cried out in sudden shock and pain, and men began to plummet from the skies like living hailstones. The archers stood their ground, shooting, even as the stunned mercenaries began to recover. One of the Knights Aeris who had not been hit began to weave the air into a shield of turbulence, and arrows began to abruptly veer and miss. Amara focused on the man and sent Cirrus toward his windstream. The Knight let out a cry of surprise and fell like a stone.

The second and third litters listed and began to spin out of control toward the ground, while injured and surprised bearers struggled to keep them from simply dropping. The first litter, though one of its bearers had taken an arrow through the thigh, made it through the withering cloud of arrow fire, though it had to veer to one side, and dropped onto the roof of one of the barracks on the opposite side of the courtyard.

Knights Aeris began to swoop and dive toward the courtyard, attacking, and though the holders' archery had done well when the Knights had not been prepared to face it, the air shortly became a howling cloud of shrieking furies, rendering the holders' arrows all but useless.

"Fall back!" Amara shouted, and the holders began to withdraw, harried by the airborne Knights, toward the stables. The Knights gathered together for a charge, their intention evidently to take the courtyard and hold it, and rushed at the retreating archers in a swift and deadly dive. Amara hurled Cirrus at the opposing furies, and though she was able to do little more than disrupt the formation of the Knights Aeris, they broke off the charge, swooping back up into the sky above the fortress, enabling the archers to retreat into the carrion-stink of the stables.

Amara herself turned and pelted toward the *legionares* stationed outside the gate. She caught a glimpse of
the Knight Commander standing beside the makeshift
wooden barricade. The Marat had managed to find two
or three ways to crawl through it, and Pirellus danced
from one spot to the next, his blade, and the spears of
the two men backing him up, keeping the Marat at bay.
"Pirellus!" she shouted. "Pirellus!"

"A moment, Lady," he called, and whipped his sword
out in a blinding thrust. The Marat who received it died
without so much as a struggle, simply collapsing in the
gap among the various wooden objects. Pirellus took a
pair of steps back and nodded to the spearmen and to a
few of the other *legionares* standing by. The men moved
forward to hold the barricade, and Pirellus turned to
Amara. "I heard you calling. The mercenaries attacked?"

"Two of their litters went down outside the walls,"
she said, and pointed, "but a third landed on the roof of
that barracks."

Pirellus nodded once. "Very well. Stay here and—
Countess!" The black blade swept out and something
shattered with a brittle sound. Amara, who had begun to
turn, felt splinters of wood flickering against her cheek,
and the broken fletching of an arrow rebounded from
her mail. She lifted her eyes to the barracks and saw Fidelias there, calmly drawing another arrow to his stout,
short bow and taking aim, even as behind him, several
men began to clamber down from the roof. The former
Cursor's thin hair blew in the cold wind, and though
he stood in the shadow of the newly risen walls, Amara
could see his eyes on hers, calm and cool, even as he
drew back the second shaft, aimed, and loosed.

Pirellus stepped in the way of the shot, cutting it from the air with a contemptuous slap of his blade, and called to the men behind him. Fidelias's soldiers were joined by the Knights Aeris who circled back above the fortress and then dove toward the gates.

Pirellus dragged Amara back to the stables and growled, "Stay down." Even as he did, Amara could see the *legionares* form into a ragged rank that met the oncoming troops and the Knights above with an uncertain tenacity. Fidelias, on the barracks roof, climbed down to the ground, his eyes flickering over the hay scattered there. He knelt into it. There came a blurring in the air, and then he simply vanished, covered by a woodcrafting of his own.

"There!" Amara cried, grabbing at Pirellus's arm. "The one who shot me! He's covered with a woodcrafting and headed for the gates." She pointed at a flickering over at one side of the courtyard, hardly visible behind the struggling *legionares* with their backs to the gate.

"I see him," Pirellus replied. He glanced down at Amara and said, "The Steadholder exhausted himself with that woodcrafting. Good luck." Then he rose and stalked out into din and whirl and scream of the fight in the courtyard.

Amara looked behind her to find Bernard sitting where she had left him, his eyes open but not focused, his chest heaving with labored breaths. She went to his side and took her canteen from her belt, pressing it against his hands. "Here, Bernard. Drink."

He obeyed, numbly, and she remained beside him, turning to watch the fight. The *legionares* were having a hard time of it. Even as she watched, a giant of a swordsman, Aldrick ex Gladius, closed in on the shield-wall, swept one blade aside, danced past another, and killed a man in the center of the line with a sweeping cut that sheered through his helmet and skull, dropping him to the ground on immediately senseless legs. Without pausing, he engaged the two men on either side of the first. One of the men moved quickly and got away with no more than a crippling thrust to his biceps. The other lifted his shield too high in a parry, and Aldrick spun, sweeping his leg off at the knee. The man screamed and toppled, and the mercenaries surged forward hard against the shields.

Pirellus appeared among the Legion ranks, his black blade flickering. One of the Knights Aeris, his dive too low, clutched at his belly with a sudden scream, and tumbled to the courtyard. One of the mercenaries on the ground, wielding a forty-pound maul in one hand as though it weighed no more than a willow switch, swung his huge weapon at Pirellus. The Knight commander slipped to one side with a deceptively lazy motion, and his return blow struck off the man's hand at the wrist. The maul fell heavily to the ground. A third mercenary darted his blade at Pirellus, only to be parried and almost casually disarmed, the sword tumbling end over end to rattle against the wall of the stable not far from Amara.

"Fall back to the gate!" came Aldrick's bellow. "Fall back!" The mercenaries retreated, quickly, dragging their wounded with them, but a similar shout from Pirellus caused the Legion troops to halt their advance as well. Neither Aldrick nor Pirellus retreated, leaving the two men standing a pair of long steps apart.

Pirellus extended his blade toward Aldrick and then

swept it up before his face in a gliding salute, which Aldrick mirrored. Then the two men dropped into a relaxed on guard position.

"Aldrick ex Gladius," Pirellus said. "I've heard about you. The Crown has a pretty bounty on your head."

"I'll be sure to check the wanted posters next time I go through a town," Aldrick responded. "Do you want to settle this, or do you need me to go through another few dozen of your *legionares*?"

"My name is Pirellus of the Black Blade," Pirellus said. "And I'm the man who will end your career."

Aldrick shrugged. "Never heard of you, kid. You're not Araris."

Pirellus scowled and moved, a sudden liquid blur of muscle and steel. Aldrick parried the Parcian's first thrust in a sudden shower of silver sparks, countered with one of his own that proved to be a feint, and whirled in circle, blade lashing out. Pirellus ducked under it, though the blow struck sparks from his helmet and clove away part of its crest, to lie glowing and smoldering on the straw-strewn ground.

The two men faced one another again, and Pirellus smiled. "Fast for an old man," he said. "But you missed."

Aldrick said nothing. A heartbeat later, a slow trickle of blood dribbled down from beneath the rim of Pirellus's helmet, and toward his eye.

The swordsman must have driven the helmet's rim into the cut Pirellus had taken earlier, Amara reasoned, opening it again.

Now Aldrick smiled. Pirellus's face had gone sallow beneath his brown skin. He lifted his lips at Aldrick and came forward, sword lashing out in swift blows, high, low, high again, Aldrick parried him in showers of silver sparks. The swordsman shifted onto the offensive himself, blade sweeping in short, hard cuts at the smaller warrior. Pirellus's black blade intercepted each blow, sparks of a purple so dark as to hardly be visible exploding at each point of impact. The blows drove the Parcian back a number of steps, and Aldrick pressed forward ruthlessly.

As Amara watched, Pirellus almost took down the swordsman. He slipped beneath a cut, slammed the swordsman's arm aside with his open hand, and drove his blade at Aldrick's belly. Aldrick twisted aside, and the Parcian's blade struck more dark sparks from Aldrick's armor, cutting through it like paper. The thrust missed, though it drew blood in a long scarlet line across Aldrick's belly. Aldrick recovered, parrying another thrust, and another, while Pirellus followed him up with determined strokes.

The swordsman seemed, to Amara, to be waiting for something. It became apparent what, in the next few seconds. Blood, running over Pirellus's eye, forced him to blink it closed, and he snapped his head to one side in an effort to clear it.

In that moment, the swordsman moved. Aldrick slipped inside the Parcian's slow thrust and lashed out with his foot in a short, hard kick, a simple stomp, as though he'd been driving a spade into the earth. But it wasn't a spade his boot hit. It was Pirellus's already wounded knee. The bones broke with a clean, sharp crack, and Aldrick drove his shoulder into Pirellus's, throwing him to one side.

The Knight Commander's face showed nothing but

determination, but as he stumbled, he put weight on his knee, and it simply could not support his body any longer. He crumpled to the ground, turning for another cut at Aldrick as the swordsman stepped toward him.

Aldrick parried the blow aside with casual power, more indigo sparks erupting.

Then, with a step to one side and a swift cut, he took Pirellus's head from his shoulders.

Blood spurted in an arch as the Knight Commander's body fell to the stones of the courtyard. His head rolled to a stop several yards away. His body lay twitching, his sword arm, even in death, slashing left and right.

Amara stared at the fallen Knight in horror, as her instincts screamed at her, forced her to remember that Fidelias was still on the move and had not been stopped. She rose, uncertain what she could do to stop what was happening in the courtyard. Aldrick turned on a heel and, without even pausing, began to stalk, alone, toward the *legionares* guarding the gates.

Before he could reach them, the wood of the barricade groaned, let out a tortured scream, and began to warp and writhe. Splinters and shards of wood exploded out, sending *legionares* reeling back from them in stunned horror. Then the wood itself began to writhe and move, the legs of tables twisting and clutching, planks shattering, the wagon letting out a tortured scream and then collapsing upon itself.

The Marat, on the other side, began to shove hard against the barricade, and without the hastily constructed stability of the various pieces, the barricade itself began to wobble and crumble in.

Fidelias appeared, not far from Aldrick, and then

turned to signal one of the Knights in the air. The man
swept down and grabbed Fidelias beneath the arms, lifting him back to the roof of the barracks, and Aldrick ex
Gladius stepped over Pirellus's fallen corpse to lead the
other handful of mercenaries after them.

The *legionares* at the gate formed up to face the incoming Marat, but the invaders leapt on them with an unyield-
ing savagery and began to drive the men near the gates
back step by slow step.

Amara rose and rushed into the stable to shout to the
archers, "Take up a shield and sword! Hold the gate!"
Men rushed about in the stable's interior, taking up weapons and rushing outside to join the defense at the gate.

When Amara returned to Bernard, he had regained
his feet. "What's happening?"

"Their Knights came in. We bloodied them, but they
managed to weaken the barricade. Pirellus is dead." She
looked at him. "I'm not a soldier. What do we do?"

"Giraldi," Bernard said. "Get to Giraldi. He'll send
more men to reinforce the gates. Go, I'm not up to running yet."

Amara nodded, and fled, sprinting across the courtyard and up the steps to the wall. The fighting there was
more hectic, and she stepped over the body of a Marat,
proof that they had gained purchase on the wall at least
once.

"Giraldi!" she shouted, when she reached the command area over the gates. "Where are you?"

A grim Legion shieldman, his face half-masked in
blood turned to her. It was Giraldi, his eyes calm despite
the bloodied sword in his hands. "Countess? You said

you were looking for the hordemaster. And there he is, finally," grunted Giraldi. "There, see?"

"It doesn't matter," Amara said, her voice numb. "Pirellus is dead."

"Crows," Giraldi said, but his voice was too tired for it to be much of an oath. "Just seems like someone should pay him back for this."

Amara lifted her head, something hot and hard and terrible pulsing in her belly. The fear, she realized, had vanished. She was too tired to be afraid, too *afraid* to be afraid anymore. There was a sort of relaxation that came with inevitability, she realized, a sort of mad, silent strength. "Which one is he?"

"There," Giraldi said, pointing. An arrow shattered on his shield, and he didn't flinch, as though he was too tired to let it bother him. "See, the tall one with the birds all around him and the Aleran spear."

Amara focused on him and saw the Marat hordemaster for the first time. He was marching steadily through the ranks of Marat hurling themselves against the walls, his chin lifted, an arrogant smirk on his mouth. Black feathers had been braided into his pale hair, and several of the herdbane stalked behind him like some deadly guard of honor. Other troops went before, chanting.

The hordemaster's troops began to part for him, crying out in a steady chant as they did. "Atsurak! Atsurak! Atsurak!"

Amara brought up Cirrus in a visioncrafting, determined to learn this man's features, to find him and at all costs to kill him for leading the horde against them this day. She memorized the shape of his nose and cruel mouth, the steady breadth of his shoulders beneath a thanadent-hide cowl, the—

Amara caught her breath, staring, and willed Cirrus to bring her vision even closer to the hordemaster.

Riding at his hip, through a thin braided twist of cord he used as a belt, was the signet dagger of an Aleran High Lord, its gold and silver hilt gleaming in the morning sun. Even as Amara stared, Cirrus let her see the dagger's hilt, the crest wrought in steel upon it: Aquitaine's falcon.

"Furies," she breathed. Aquitaine. Aquitaine himself. No one more powerful in the Realm save the First Lord. Aquitaine's Knights, then, Aquitaine who subverted Fidelias, Aquitaine who had attempted to gain knowledge of the palace from her, in order to—

In order to kill Gaius. He means to take the throne for himself.

Amara swallowed. She had to recover that dagger at any cost. To bring such a damning piece of evidence before the Senate would finish Aquitaine and terrify anyone working with him into loyalty again. She could prove who the true culprit behind today's vicious deaths had been, and though she had thought she hated the hordemaster now striding toward the buckling defenses of Garrison's gates, she felt a sudden and furious rage against the man whose ambitions had engineered the events of the past several days.

But could she do it? Could she recover the dagger?

She had to try. She now realized why Fidelias had wanted her out of the fortress. He had wanted to hide this very thing from her, knowing full well that only she and perhaps two or three other people in the fortress would recognize the signet dagger for what it was.

She shook her head, forcing her thoughts to focus, to take one thing at a time. "Giraldi! We need reinforcements," she stammered. "The gate is about to fall!"

Giraldi grimaced, and as she watched, his face fell, the lines in it deepening, making him look as though he had aged years in the space of a breath. "Doesn't matter," he said, and jerked his chin toward the field below the fortress. "Look."

Amara looked, and when she did, the strength went out of her legs. She leaned hard against the battlements, her head swimming, her heart pounding in light, irregular beats.

"No," she breathed. "No. It's not fair."

Out on the plain, beyond the savage horde of Marat below, there had come another horde, every bit as large as the first. This one included elements of cavalry, though she could make out little beyond that. Cavalry, useless for taking a fortified position, but the ideal troops for raiding into an enemy's lands. Fast, deadly, destructive. The sheer numbers of the newly arrived enemy had, she knew, abruptly changed the fight from a desperate battle to a hopeless one. She looked up at Giraldi and saw it in his eyes.

"We can't win," she said. "We can't hold."

"Against *that*?" He shook his head. He took his helmet off and wiped sweat from his brow, replacing it as arrows buzzed through the air.

She bowed her head, her shoulders shaking. The tears were hot and bitter. A stone-headed arrow shattered on the merlon above her, but she didn't care.

Amara looked up at the Marat, at Atsurak about to take the gates, at the enormous number of Marat still fresh and unbloodied, now moving quickly over the plains toward the fortress. "Hold," she told Giraldi. "Hold as long as you can. Send someone to make sure the Civilians have started running. Tell the wounded to arm themselves to fight as best they can. Tell them—" She swallowed. "Tell them it looks bad."

"Yes, Countess," Giraldi said, his voice numb. "Heh. I always figured my last order would be 'pass me another slice of roast.'" He gave her a grim smile, turned to swing his sword at a climbing Marat almost absently, and headed off to follow her commands.

Amara climbed back down off the wall, taking absent note of the courtyard. Fidelias and his men were nowhere in sight, probably gone again, safely lofted up by their Knights Aeris. At the barricade, more Marat had pushed through, and though they had trouble advancing over the corpses fallen on the ground, yet they came on, despite the desperate cries of the Alerans pitted against them.

She drew her sword, the sword from the fallen guardsman in the Princeps Memorium, and stared at its workmanship. Then she looked up, at the Marat pushing through the gates, sure that in time she would see their hordemaster, here to claim the fortress for himself.

Bernard stepped up beside her, still looking tired, but holding a double bladed woodsman's axe in his broad hands. "Do we have a plan?"

"The hordemaster, I saw him. I want to take him down." She told him about the dagger at his waist, the second horde coming on.

Bernard nodded, slowly. "If we get to him," he said, "I'm going to try a woodcrafting on you. Take the knife and run. Get it back to the First Lord, if you can."

"You're exhausted. If you try to work another crafting it could k—" She stopped herself and took a slow breath.

"Pirellus was right," Bernard commented. "The good part of being doomed is that you have nothing left to lose."

Then he turned to her, slipping an arm around her waist, and kissed her on the mouth, with no hesitation, no self-consciousness, nothing but a raw hunger tempered with a kind of exquisite gentleness. Amara let out a soft sound and threw herself into the kiss, suddenly frantic, and felt tears threaten her eyes again.

She drew back from the kiss far too soon, looking up at him. Bernard smiled at her and said, "I didn't want to leave that undone."

She felt a tired smile on her own mouth, and she turned from him to face the gates.

Outside, there came a blaring of horns, deeper, somehow more violent, more angry than the first ones had been. The ground began to shake once again, and shouts and rumbles outside the walls rose into a tidal wave of sound that pounded at her ears, her throat, her chest. She thought she could feel her cheeks vibrating from the sheer volume.

The final defense at the gate began to crumble. The Marat began to force their way into the courtyard, their eyes wild, weapons bloodied, pale hair and skin speckled with scarlet. One armed holder went down before a pair of enormous wolves and a Marat fighting with nothing but his own teeth. A great herdbane pinned a crawling Aleran to the ground and with a birdlike bob of its head seized the Aleran's neck and broke it with a quick shake.

The Marat poured in, and there was sudden bedlam in the courtyard, lines disintegrating into dozens of separate smaller battles, pure chaos.

"There," Amara said, and jabbed her finger forward. "Coming through the gate right now."

Atsurak strode through the gates, his beasts all around him. With a casual motion of his captured Aleran spear, he thrust it through the back of a fighting *legionare* and then, without watching the man die, withdrew the spear to test its edge against his thumb. Several Alerans rushed him. One was torn to shreds by one of the huge birds. Another dropped to the earth before he got close to Atsurak, black-feathered Marat arrows sprouting from both eyes. No one got within striking distance of the hordemaster.

Bernard growled, "I'm going in first. Get their attention. You come right behind me."

"All right," Amara said, and put her hand on his shoulder.

Bernard gripped the axe and tensed to move forward.

Sudden thunder shook the air in a roar that made what came before sound like nothing more than the rumbling of an empty belly. Screams, frantic, howling cries, rose in a symphony. The walls *themselves* shook, just beside the gates. They shook again, beneath a thunderous impact, and a web of cracks spread out through them. Again, the thunder rammed against the outer walls, and with a roar an entire section gave in. Alerans on the battlements had to scramble to either side, stone tumbling down in huge and uneven sections, dust flooding out, light from the newly risen sun pouring through the dust in a sudden flood of terrible golden splendor.

Through the sudden gap in the walls came a thunderous bellow, and the vast shape of a black-coated gargant, a gargant bigger than any such beast Amara had ever seen. Bloodied, painted in wild and garish colors, the beast seemed something out of a madman's nightmare. It lifted its head and let out another bellowing roar and tore down another ten feet of wall with its vast digging claws. The gargant bellowed again and shouldered its way through the wall and into the courtyard itself.

A Marat warrior sat upon the gargant's back, pale of hair and dark of eye, with shoulders so broad and chest so deep not even the largest breastplate could have fit him. He bore a long-handled cudgel in his hand, and with an almost casual sweep he leaned to one side and smote it down onto the head of a Wolf Clan warrior strangling a downed Aleran, dropping the Marat to the earth with a broken skull.

"ATSURAK!" bellowed the Marat on the back of the maddened gargant. His voice, deep, rich, furious, shook the stones of the courtyard. "ATSURAK OF HERD-BANE! DOROGA OF GARGANT CALLS YOU MISTAKEN BEFORE WE-THE-MARAT! COME OUT, YOU MURDEROUS DOG! COME AND FACE ME BEFORE THE ONE!"

Whirling with insane grace, the gargant spun to one side, great forelegs rising together. The beast brought his clawed feet down on top of a charging Herdbane Clan warrior, simply smashing him flat against the courtyard's stones. At that, though the din outside the walls continued to rise, the battle in the courtyard fell into a sudden, shocked silence.

As the great beast turned, letting out another defiant

bellow, Amara saw, in the golden light pouring through the breached walls, the boy Tavi clinging to Doroga's back, behind him on the great gargant, and behind the boy sat the scarred slave, clutching at him and gibbering.

Tavi looked wildly around the courtyard, and when his gaze flicked toward them, his face lit with a ferocious smile. "Uncle Bernard! Uncle Bernard!" he shouted, pointing at Doroga. "He followed me home! Can we keep him?"

◇◇◇◇ CHAPTER 41

Isana took a pair of quick steps back, pressing Odiana along behind her, and lifted her chin. "I've always thought you a pig, Kord, but never an idiot. Do you think you'll get away with a killing, right here in Garrison?"

Kord laughed, a rough sound. "In case you didn't notice, they've got bigger fish to fry. I just walked right on in like all those other fools who came to die here."

"It doesn't mean you can escape, Kord. Assuming that one of us doesn't get to you when you try it."

Kord laughed again, the sound of it dry, rasping. "One of you. Which one would that be? Come here, bitch."

Isana faced him evenly and did not move.

Kord's face flushed red and dangerous. "I said come here."

"She can't hear you, Kord. I saw to that."

"Did you?" His eyes moved from Isana to the huddling woman behind and beside her. Odiana flinched, even at the glance, haunted eyes widening.

"No," Isana said, though she knew the words were useless. "Don't look."

But Odiana glanced up at Kord. The murderous expression on his face, a finger he jabbed at the ground in front of him, were apparently enough to activate the discipline collar. Odiana let out a sudden breathless shriek and fell to the ground, clawing at the collar. Even as she did, she struggled against her own convulsing body to crawl closer to Kord, to obey the command he'd given her. Isana reached down to hold her back, but the sudden wave of terror and unbearable anguish that washed up through that touch nearly blinded her, and she stumbled back and away.

Kord let out a harsh laugh and took a step forward, taking the woman's face in his hands. "That's better," he said. "You be a good girl. I'm going to break your pretty neck and then put that collar on Isana. Hold still."

Odiana whimpered, body still twitching, and did not struggle against him.

"Kord, no!" Isana shouted.

The door suddenly rattled on its frame. There was a hesitation, and then it rattled again, as though someone was trying to get in and hadn't expected to find it bolted. Kord whirled to face it.

Desperate, Isana cast the globe of the furylamp in her hand at Kord. It struck the Steadholder in the back of the head. The furylamp shattered, the spark imp inside it flashing into brilliant light for a moment, and then gone.

The interior of the warehouse sank into darkness, and Kord began to curse viciously.

Isana swallowed her terror and hurried forward, through the darkness. There was a horrible, frantic moment of feeling in the dark, listening for Odiana's whimpers and Kord's heavy, snarling breathing. Her fingers found Odiana's hair first, and she dragged the slave woman against her. She got the woman to her feet and started dragging her farther back into the warehouse, hoping that she moved in the right direction. Odiana began to whimper, and Isana clapped one hand firmly over the woman's mouth.

"Don't do this, Isana," growled Kord's voice, from somewhere in the dark, back toward the door. "You're just drawing things out. We both know how this is going to end."

Isana felt a ripple in the ground beneath the wooden floorboards, but knew that Kord's fury would have difficulty locating them through the wood, just as it had through the ice. She continued to draw Odiana deeper back into the warehouse, until she bumped against the back wall. She felt her way with her hands, and though the predawn light was showing through cracks in the wall, there still was not enough light to see. She pressed the woman down into the dubious shelter between two crates, then lifted Odiana's own hands and pressed them over the woman's mouth. The slave shook almost violently, but managed to nod. Isana drew her hands away from the woman and turned to face the darkness.

"Come on, Isana," Kord said, his voice more distant. "The collar's not so bad. Once you put it on, you won't have any more doubts. You can see the good part of it, too. I'll do that for you."

Isana swallowed, revolted, and debated her options. Simplest was to shout for help. There were hundreds of people within Garrison. Surely some would hear her.

Surely. But at the same time, she would be giving her position away to Kord. She did not know how long it might take help to break down the barred warehouse door, but it surely would not take Kord long to break her neck. Though it made her seethe with frustration, she could do little but remain silent and try to find a way to escape the warehouse or to deal with Kord directly. She crouched in the darkness and struggled to think of other options.

The ground rumbled and shook for perhaps a minute, and then there was a sudden round of cheers and blowing horns from outside. Useless. She didn't know what had happened, but she would never be heard over that din. She had to find out where Kord was and either circle out to open the door or attack him herself—and that would be mad. Even if she could find him, he was far stronger than she. She could loose Rill on him, but what if she wasn't fast enough? No, such a confrontation was a last desperate resort.

A calculated risk, then. She took a breath and tried to keep her voice monotone, droning, to better conceal the direction. "You think that will make me happy, Kord?"

His reply came from much nearer to her, perhaps down the same row of crates. "Once I get that on you, whatever I want makes you happy."

"I suppose a man like you needs something like that,"

she said, moving back, trying to circle around to another row to slip past him.

"Keep talking. Just going to make it sweeter when I get my hands on you." His voice was on the move as well.

From outside, there was a series of shouts, a trembling in the ground, as of thousands of feet striking it. Horns blew the signals to engage, and Isana knew that the Garrison was under attack.

Kord spoke again, and his voice came from not ten feet away from her, in the darkness, so close that she could suddenly feel the cloud of rage and lust around him like a hot, stinking mist. "See there? Bigger fish to fry. Leaves me all alone with you."

She didn't dare reply. Instead, keeping her movements as quiet as she could, she moved across the row to the far side, to press against the crates there. If she strained, she could hear Kord moving slowly down the row of crates, within a long arm's reach, now, but even more, she could sense him against her, the churning muck of his ugly emotions. It drew even with her, and she held her breath as it crept on past, the pressure on her senses slowly changing, as though something warm and moist brushed over her left cheek, then her mouth, then her right cheek, as Kord crept past.

But he hesitated there, and Isana held her own position. Had he sensed her, somehow? Did he know she was there?

"Smell you," Kord murmured, his voice very close. "Smell you. Smells good. Makes me hungry."

Isana held her breath.

He moved, sudden and fast, the sense of him flashing across her cheek, mouth, cheek again, as he moved back toward the door. She lost him after only a second. He had moved beyond the range of what her crafting could feel.

But it came to her, suddenly, that she had a weapon he did not. His fury might be able to lend him tremendous strength, but he would not be able to use it to see. His power could reach no farther than his own fingers. But she could use her own crafting to locate him, even in the total darkness, if her reach had been longer. How could she extend it?

By provoking him, she realized. By stoking his emotions to a brighter blaze, he would radiate them more strongly, make himself more easy to sense. Dangerous plan, indeed. But if she could pinpoint where he was, she could slip past him to the door and go for help.

She moved, first, back to the far end of the rows, picking another at random, before she started down it and lifted her voice again. "Do you know how we escaped, Kord?"

Kord let out a growling sound, now several yards away. "Some damn fool didn't patch the roof right."

"Were you too drunk to remember?" Isana taunted, gently. "You sent Aric to patch that roof."

"No," Kord growled. "Wouldn't do that."

"You did. You hit his face right there in front of me and made him."

Kord's voice answered, harsher, panting, moving closer. "Happens. It happens. I get mad. He understands."

"No he doesn't, Kord," Isana said, even more quietly. "He helped us escape. He made holes in the roof so that meltwater would run in and give us our crafting back."

"Lying bitch!" Kord snarled. His fist lashed out against one of the crates, and the solid wooden staves of its side broke with a heavy crunch. At the same time, fighting erupted from very nearby, somewhere just outside the warehouse, in the courtyard itself.

"He hates you, Kord. Did he come with you? Is he here helping you? You've got no sons, now, Kord. Nothing to come after you. Bittan is dead, and Aric despises you."

"Shut up," howled Kord. "Shut up before I break your lying head!"

And the sense of his anger, his mad, blazing rage, abruptly washed through the warehouse. Isana pleaded silently with Rill to leave her even more open than usual to the emotions.

She felt him. Exactly where that rage was. Ten feet away, on the next row of crates, and pacing swiftly toward her. Isana moved silently, trying to get past him and back to the door, but as she came even with him one row over, his steps stopped and he started reversing them toward the door.

"Oh no," he growled. "No, that's a trick. Make me mad and make me come chase you, then you run while I find that slave bitch and break her bitch neck and you get away. No, no. You aren't smarter than me."

Isana paced him silently, frustrated, unsure of how near she had to be to make him remain within the circle of her senses. She kept the row of crates between them, until they came to the end.

Kord stopped, and she felt the surge of hope and lust in him as well, as he inhaled through his nose. "Smell you, Isana. Smell your sweat. You're scared." She heard his knuckles crack. He stood opposite her, standing while she crouched. She reached out her hand and felt the stack of crates that was between them, one, two, three, four high, at least.

"Smell you," Kord purred. "You're close. Where are you?"

Isana made up her mind in a flash. She turned to the top crate, leaned against it, and pushed with all her strength. It felt like it took forever for the crate to tilt and then to fall, carrying the two beneath with it, but it could only have been a second. The crates fell, Kord let out a short, sharp cry, and there was a shockingly loud crushing, crunching sound of impact.

Isana scrambled back to the door of the warehouse, fumbling in the dark. She found the bolt and threw it back, then opened the door, letting in pale morning light, though the warehouse remained in the shadow of the walls. She turned and looked back inside.

Kord lay on his belly on the ground, the wooden crates over him. One of them had struck him between the shoulder blades, and still lay half on him, unbroken. The other had to have clipped his head, because there was blood on his face. It lay over to one side.

The last had landed on his lower back, buttocks, and thighs. It had broken open, revealing the cracked and broken forms of heavy slate tiles used on the roofs of the buildings in the garrison. Isana drew in a breath. The tiles were each made of a heavy fired ceramic, and each of the crates had to have weighed close to three hundred pounds.

She watched as Kord tried to move, straining. He snarled and muttered something, and the earth beneath him stirred weakly. He tried again, but could not get out from under the crates. He subsided to the floor again, panting, whimpering beneath his breath.

Isana walked over to him and stood looking down

at him. She knelt and touched a fingertip to his temple, willing Rill to impress his condition upon her.

"Your legs are broken," she said, tonelessly. "So is your hip. So is your back." She felt a moment more. "And you're exhausted. You must have been drawing on your fury to pursue us." She drew her hand away. "You aren't going anywhere, Kord."

"Bitch," he snarled, the sound weak. "Finish it. Get it over with."

"Were you in my place, you would break my head open." She picked up one of the heavy tiles, and ran a finger over its squared edge. Held up lengthwise and driven down, it could indeed break a skull. "Maybe with one of these. Crush my skull and kill me."

"I had you beat," he growled. "When I die, I'm going to be thinking of it. You in that circle scared out of your head. You just remember that."

She stood up and dropped the slate. Then she walked down one of the rows.

"What are you doing?" he growled. "When I get out of here—"

Isana went to Odiana and took the woman's hand. She lifted the woman to her feet, then covered her eyes with her hands. Odiana nodded, weakly, and hid her eyes in her own hands. Isana led her out, stepping wide around Kord, who struggled to grab at her ankles and failed.

"You aren't getting out of here," Isana said. "I only know of one person, offhand, who could treat your injuries in time to heal you, Kord. She isn't inclined."

Isana stopped and looked down at him, then stooped down. He clutched at her ankle, and she kicked his hand away with a contemptuous, "Stop that." She grabbed his Steadholder chain and tore it off over his head. Then hit him with it, hard, across the mouth.

Kord stared up at her, the pain stunning him, robbing him of speech.

She spoke to him in a detached, clinical tone. "You don't feel your injuries Kord. But you'll never walk again. You'll have to have someone clean you like an infant. I'm not sure you'll be able to sit up without help."

She turned and began to walk toward the entrance, leading Odiana with her. "But you *will* be able to face trial. Like that. Helpless. Stinking of your own waste. You'll go to trial before the Count, and everyone in the Valley will see what you *are*. I'll see to that. And then they'll kill you for what you've done."

Outside, deeper, louder horns began to blare, almost drowning out Kord's sudden, vicious, pathetic sobs. "Isana! You stupid bitch, you can't do this. You can't do this!"

She swung shut the door behind them and said, "I can't hear you, Kord."

Then the battle swept over her, desperation and agony and wild exultation all blended together. She struggled to merely remain standing, and Odiana clung to her, helped her to keep her balance. The two watercrafters could barely manage to hobble from the warehouse to the quiet spot between one of the barracks. Isana's newly opened senses that had served her so well in the darkness now incapacitated her, and she sank to the ground, to her knees, curling her arms up over her head while she tried to tune down some of the emotions that pounded in her. Dimly, she felt the ground shake again, heard the bellowing of some enormous beast, an equally enormous voice roaring a challenge.

By the time she lifted her head, Odiana was gone. Isana looked up to see one dirty foot vanishing up onto the roof of the barracks building. She shook her head, still dazed, and moved until she could see the wild chaos of the courtyard, and the gargant with its ferocious rider as it turned to flatten a Marat warrior beneath its feet in a sudden rush of fierce anger and swiftly fading pain.

"Oh, no," she whispered, her eyes opening wider, lifting up to the gargant's rider again, and his passengers. "Oh, child, what have you gotten yourself into. My Tavi."

◁◁◁◁ CHAPTER 42

Tavi swallowed, his hands tightening on Doroga's belt. The gargant beneath them stirred restlessly, but other than that, the courtyard was nearly silent.

Bodies lay everywhere. Tavi tried not to look at them, but it seemed that everywhere he moved his eyes, someone had died. It was horrible. The bodies didn't look like people should. They looked misshapen and wrong, as though some careless child had been playing with his wooden soldiers and idly thrown them away after breaking them. There was blood, and that made his belly shake, but more than that, there was a horrible sadness in seeing the torn and broken forms, Marat and Aleran, man and beast alike.

It seemed such a waste.

The courtyard had grown almost quiet. In the gate and spread in a loose half-circle around it were Atsurak and his Marat. Loosely grouped around the stables were the Aleran defenders, among them Amara and his uncle.

Atsurak stared at Doroga, and the big Marat's eyes were flat with cool hatred.

Doroga faced Atsurak steadily. "Well, murderer?" Doroga demanded. "Will you face me in the Trial of Blood, or will you turn and lead your clan back to your lands?"

Atsurak lifted his chin once. "Come die then."

Doroga's teeth showed in a fierce smile. He turned back to Tavi behind him and rumbled, "Get down, young warrior. Be sure you tell your people what I said."

Tavi looked up at Doroga and nodded. "I can't believe you're doing this."

Doroga blinked at him. "I said that I would help you protect your family." He shrugged. "A horde stands in the way. I did what is necessary to finish what I began. Climb down."

Tavi nodded, and Doroga shook out the saddle cord. Fade swung down from the gargant's broad back first and all but hovered beneath Tavi as the boy came down. Doroga barely used the strap, but landed lightly on the courtyard and stretched, tendons creaking. He spun the long-handled cudgel in his fingers and stepped toward Atsurak.

Tavi led Fade around Doroga's gargant, stepping wide

around its front legs and the wet splatter on the stones there. Tavi's belly heaved about restlessly, and he swallowed, hurrying across the stones to his uncle.

"Tavi," Bernard said, and enfolded the boy in a rib-creaking embrace. "Furies but I feared for you. And Fade, good man. You're all right?"

Fade hooted in the affirmative. There was the sound of running footsteps, light on the stones, and Tavi felt his aunt Isana, unmistakably his aunt, even if he did not see her, wrap her arms around him and hug him tight to her. "Tavi," she said. "Oh, Tavi. You're all right."

Tavi pressed up against his aunt and uncle for a moment and felt the tears in his eyes. He leaned against them and hugged them back. "I'm all right," he heard himself saying. "It's all right. I'm all right."

Isana laughed and kissed his hair, his cheek. "Fade," she said. "Thank the furies. You're all right."

After a moment, Amara said, "Bernard, they're not looking. If we rush the hordemaster now, we can get to the knife."

"No!" Tavi said, hurriedly. He freed himself from the embrace, looking at the Cursor. "No, you can't. Doroga explained this to me. It's a duel. You have to let him have it."

Amara looked at him sharply. "What duel?"

"What knife?"

Amara frowned. "The knife proves one of the High Lords is behind this attack. We can catch him, if we recover it, and keep him from doing something like this again. What *duel*?"

Tavi tried to explain. "Doroga and Atsurak are both headman of their clans. They're equals. Atsurak can't order another clan to follow him as long as their head-man stands up to him in a Trial of Blood—a duel, but no one had the courage to stand up to him before now. Doroga has challenged Atsurak's decision to attack us, before all of the rest of the Marat. If he defeats him in the trial, then it breaks Atsurak's power, and the Marat leave."

"Just like that?" Amara demanded.

"Well, yes," Tavi said, defensively. "If Doroga wins, it means that the Marat will understand that The One supports him and not Atsurak."

"The one what?"

"The One," Tavi said. "I think they think it's some kind of fury that lives in the sun. When they have a big decision, they have a trial before The One. They believe in it completely."

He felt his aunt's hand on his shoulder, and he turned to find her looking down at him earnestly. Her head tilted to one side. "What happened to you?"

"A lot, Auntie."

She smiled, though there was a weary edge to it. "It shows. Are you sure you know what you're saying?"

"Yes ma'am," Tavi said. "I know."

Isana looked at Bernard, who looked at Amara. The Cursor drew in a slow breath, her eyes in turn moving to Tavi. "Tavi," she said, keeping her voice quiet. "Why did Doroga choose now to challenge this Atsurak?"

Tavi swallowed. "Um. Well, it's kind of a long story. I'm not really sure I understand everything that happened myself. Doesn't really matter, does it? If he's here?"

Outside, there were high-pitched whistles sounding,

and the frantic howls of the Marat and their beasts had subsided to a low rumble.

"Giraldi?" Amara called up to the battlements. "What's happening?"

"Crows take me," called a panting voice back from the walls above the gates. "The Marat were fighting one another, then they all started blowing whistles and falling back from the fighting. They're drawing into tribes it looks like."

"Thank you, Centurion."

"Countess? Orders?"

"Hold the walls," Amara responded, but her eyes went back to Tavi. "Do not attack unless first attacked."

Tavi nodded to Amara. "This is what Doroga told me would happen. The Marat tribes fight all the time. They're used to it. The whistles are to call a halt to fighting and let the headmen talk."

Bernard blew out a breath and looked at Amara. "What do you think?"

The Cursor reached a hand up and pushed a few loose strands of hair back from her eyes, staring at Tavi. "I think your nephew, here, has managed to learn more about the Marat than the Crown's intelligence service, Steadholder."

Tavi nodded. "They, uh, eat their enemies. And anyone who shows up without permission is considered to be one." He coughed. "It probably makes it sort of difficult to learn about them."

Amara shook her head. "If we get out of this, I want to know how you managed to not get eaten and wind up leading a Marat horde of your own to save this valley."

Fade let out a low, apprehensive hoot of warning. Tavi

looked at the slave and found him staring intently at the walls.

In the ragged hole in the fortress's walls, shapes stirred. Several riders on horseback, tall Horse Clan Marat, rode in. Tavi recognized Hashat at once, her pale mane flowing, though fresh blood spattered her hair, upper body, and saber arm. Tavi identified her to Amara and his uncle.

"Headman?" Bernard demanded, something in his tone offended. "She's a woman. And she's not wearing a shirt."

Amara let out a low whistle. "Those eagles on her belt are from Royal Guardsman. If they're genuine, she must have been part of the horde that killed Princeps Septimus."

"She's nice enough," Tavi said. "She won't confront Atsurak herself, but she'll follow Doroga's lead. I think they're friends."

At the gate, the Marat stirred and parted to let the Wolf headman in with a pair of rangy direwolves beside him. A long, clean cut marred the pale skin of his chest, clotted with dark red. The man looked around the courtyard and bared his teeth, showing the long canines of his clan. "Skagara," Tavi supplied. "Wolf Clan headman. He's a bully."

Hashat dismounted and stalked over to stand beside Skagara. She faced him the whole way with a danger-ous little smile on her mouth. Skagara took a step back from her when she reached him. Hashat's teeth showed, and she made a point of examining the cut on his chest. Then she turned to face Atsurak and Doroga, folding her arms, one bloodied hand remaining near her saber. Skagara gave her a sullen scowl, then did the same.

Doroga leaned on his cudgel, staring at the ground. Atsurak stood patiently, spear loosely gripped in one hand. Silence and mounting tension reigned for several moments. Only the crows made any noise, a low and steady cawing in the background outside the walls.

"What are they waiting for?" Amara asked Tavi.

"The sun," Tavi said. "Doroga said they always wait for the sun to rise on the results of a trial." He glanced up at the walls, the angle of the shadows there. "I guess they don't think the fight will take very long."

The morning light swept across the courtyard, as the sun rose higher. The line of shadow described by the still-intact walls swept from west to east, toward the two Marat headmen.

Doroga looked up, after a time, to the sunlight where it had barely come to rest on the head of his staff. He nodded, lowered the weapon with a grunt, and advanced on Atsurak.

The Herdbane headman whirled his spear in a loose circle, shrugged his shoulders, and stalked toward Doroga on cat-light feet. He moved swiftly, his spear's tip blurring, as he thrust it at the other Marat, but Doroga parried the blow to one side with the thick shaft of the cudgel, then swept it in a short thrust at Atsurak's head.

Atsurak avoided the blow and whipped the spear's tip toward Doroga's leg. The Gargant headman dodged, but not quickly enough, and a line of bright scarlet appeared on his thigh.

The Marat in the courtyard let out a low murmur. Someone among the Herdbane said something in a grinding tongue, and the warriors let out a rough laugh. A low chatter began between the Herdbane and Wolf present.

"Are they betting on the fight?" Amara asked, incredulous.

Tavi nodded. "Yeah, they do that. Doroga won his daughter betting on me."

"What?"

"Shhhh."

Doroga drew back from the exchange with a grimace and glanced down at his leg. He tried to put his weight on it, but faltered, and he had to swing the staff of the cudgel down to help support him. Atsurak smiled at that and spun his spear around again. He began a slow, deliberate stalk toward Doroga, circling the Gargant headman, forcing him to turn to face his enemy, putting pressure on his wounded leg. Doroga's face twisted with a grimace of pain.

"Tavi," Amara breathed. "What happens if Doroga loses?"

Tavi swallowed, his heart pounding. "Then The One has said that Doroga was wrong. And the rest of the clans follow Atsurak like they would have before."

"Oh," Amara breathed. "Can he do it?"

"Five silver bulls on Doroga," Tavi responded.

"You're on."

Atsurak rushed Doroga abruptly. The Gargant headman whipped up his weapon and parried the spear aside, but his return stroke was clumsy and drew him off balance. Atsurak dodged and immediately leapt in again. Once more, Doroga barely deflected the incoming stroke, and this time it cost him his balance. He fell to the stones of the courtyard.

Atsurak pressed in for the kill, but Doroga swung the long-handled cudgel at the hordemaster's feet, forcing him to skip back to avoid it. Atsurak scowled and spat some harsh-sounding word, then lifted the spear, circled, and darted in at Doroga with deadly purpose.

The Gargant headman had been waiting for Atsurak's charge. With an easy grace, he swept the spear aside with one hand, jabbing the tip into the stone, then gripped the shaft in one huge fist. He drove it back toward Atsurak with almost casual power, the spear's butt striking the hordemaster in the belly and stopping him in his tracks.

Doroga jerked the spear from his opponent's grasp. Atsurak backed warily away, sucking for his breath. Doroga stood up with a casual grace. Then he lifted his wounded leg and snapped the haft of the Aleran spear, tossing its bits to one side.

"He tricked him!" Tavi said, gleefully.

"Hush," Amara said.

"He's got him now," Bernard said.

Doroga tossed the huge cudgel to one side. It landed on the stones with a dull thump.

"I remember the Fox," he said, his voice very quiet. Then he spread his hands wide, and with that same flat, hard-eyed smile, he came toward the smaller Marat.

Atsurak paled, but spread his own hands, circling Doroga. He moved abruptly, a darting motion reminiscent of one of the predator birds, leaping and kicking high on Doroga's chest.

Doroga took the kick full on, though it stopped him in his tracks and rocked him back a step, but his hands flashed up to Atsurak's ankle and caught his foot before the other could draw it away. Atsurak began to fall, and Doroga's shoulders knotted, his hands twisting.

Something in Atsurak's leg broke with an ugly pop.

The hordemaster gasped and fell, but kicked with his good leg at Doroga's ankle. The Gargant chief's foot went out from under him, and he fell, grappling with his foe.

Tavi watched, but could see that Atsurak was at a disadvantage too serious to overcome. Overwhelmed by sheer physical power, too hurt to get away, it would only be a matter of time. Doroga's hands lifted and locked around the hordemaster's throat. Atsurak locked his hands onto Doroga's, but Tavi could see that it would be a hopeless effort.

Tavi stared, unable to look away—but something drew his attention, a faint motion in the background. He glanced up and saw the Marat all focused on the contest, stepping closer, eyes bright. Hashat was all but panting, her eyes open too wide as she watched Doroga's struggle.

Beside Hashat, though, Tavi saw that Skagara, the Wolf headman, had taken a step back, behind her vision. He reached a hand back behind him, and Tavi saw one of the Wolf warriors touch a stone-tipped arrow into a small clay jar, then pass it to Skagara, together with one of the short Marat bows. Moving quickly, the Wolf headman drew the poisoned arrow, and lifted the bow.

"Doroga!" Tavi shouted. "Look out!"

Doroga's head snapped up, at Tavi and then over at Skagara. Doroga rolled, and wrenched Atsurak's form between himself and the would-be assassin.

Tavi saw Atsurak draw the Aleran dagger with its gold hilt from his belt and slash wildly at Doroga's hand. The Gargant headman cried out and fell back, and Atsurak rolled free of his grip.

"Kill them!" shouted the hordemaster, his eyes blazing. "Kill them as we did the Fox! Kill them all!"

Doroga roared and rose to his feet, charging toward Atsurak.

Without a breath of hesitation, Skagara loosed the poisoned arrow. Tavi saw it flicker across the brief distance between them and vanish into Doroga's arm with a meaty crack. The Gargant headman went down.

Hashat spun, her saber flashing in the sun as she drew it, and cut through Skagara's bow and the Wolf headman's throat in the same slash, sending him to the ground in a sudden wash of blood.

The courtyard erupted into chaos. The great Herdbane birds near Atsurak screamed as he turned to them and flicked a hand at Doroga. They charged the fallen Gargant headman. At the same time, Doroga's gargant bellowed and rolled forward to his defense. Outside the walls, what had been hushed silence erupted once more into tumult and cacophony. Hashat's clan charged forward, toward the fallen Doroga, and Atsurak's warriors did the same.

Fade let out a wail and clutched hard at Tavi's shirt.

"The knife!" he heard Amara yell. "Get the dagger!" The Cursor started forward, only to be stopped by the sudden press of Marat warriors, spears glittering with the same dark deadliness as the eyes of the herdbanes beside them. The Aleran troops fell into lines, even as Bernard grabbed at his sister's arm, and Amara's, and dragged them both back behind the shields of the troops.

Fade let out a screech of fear and turned to follow Bernard, mindlessly dragging Tavi along.

"Fade!" Tavi protested.

"The knife!" screamed Amara. "Without the dagger, it's all for nothing!"

Tavi didn't stop to think. He just dropped his weight, lifting his arms up and slipping out of the too-big tunic. He rolled to his feet, looked around the courtyard wildly, and then ran toward the downed Atsurak. The hordemaster's warriors now either engaged the Alerans or faced Doroga's furious gargant and were far too occupied to notice the fleeting form of one rather small boy.

Atsurak watched the melee around Doroga's gargant. The great beast had rumbled forward and crouched over Doroga's fallen form, swinging its huge head, clawing, kicking, and bellowing at anyone who came close. Tavi licked his lips and saw Doroga's fallen cudgel. He picked it up, though it was a strain, prepared to give it one good swing at Atsurak's head, grab the knife, and run back to his uncle.

Instead, there was a sudden rush of wind that threw up hay (what was hay doing all over the courtyard?) and dust and blinded him, all but throwing him down. Tavi shielded his eyes, looking up to see several men in black tunics and armor, wielding weapons of steel, hovering over the courtyard. One of them had his hand extended toward Atsurak and must have been controlling the winds that buffeted the courtyard.

Another Knight Aeris swept down and dropped the same innocuous-looking, balding man Tavi had seen before onto the stones of the courtyard. The man stepped forward to the blinded Atsurak, and with a casual jerk on the man's hair and a short knife, cut the hordemaster's throat.

The hordemaster jerked and twisted wildly, and the

dagger flew from his hand, skittering over the stones of the courtyard and landing in a clump of hay not far from Tavi.

"The dagger!" barked the man with the bloodied knife. "Get the dagger!"

Tavi stared at the man standing over Atsurak's jerking, twitching form. He had no doubt that this man would kill him just as quickly. But he also knew that the man was not loyal to the Crown, that he had been pursuing Amara and Tavi, and that he had tried to hurt his aunt and uncle.

Two days ago, Tavi thought, he might have let the man recover the dagger. He might have turned and run. He might have found someplace to hide until all of this was over.

"Two days ago," Tavi breathed, "I had a lot more sense."

Then he darted forward, seized the dagger where it lay, and began to run.

"There!" Tavi heard the man yell. "He's got the dagger! Kill that boy!"

ᴏᴏᴏᴏ CHAPTER 43

Tavi ran for his life.

The courtyard was a mass of confusion and motion, but he knew the one direction he *had* to go: away from the man who had killed Atsurak. Tavi spun, dashed around a pair of struggling Marat warriors, and fled toward the other side of the fort. He heard a roar of wind above him, and then a sudden burst of it sent him tumbling along the ground. Tavi yelped and tried to make sure that he didn't stab himself to death with the knife in his hand, rolling and bumping along the stones of the courtyard.

When he came to a stop, he looked up to see a Knight Aeris in full armor diving toward him, the spear in his hand held extended. Tavi clawed at his pockets. Even as the Knight came on, Tavi hurled a handful of rock salt he had taken from Bernardholt's smokehouse at the oncoming Knight, and then dove frantically to one side.

The Knight let out a sudden shout, clawing at the air—but he dropped to the ground, moving too fast, skipped along for a pair of desperate steps, and began to tumble end over end on the unforgiving stones. Tavi heard one of his limbs hit with a sharp crack of impact, and the Knight shrieked.

Tavi regained his feet, looking around him wildly. More Knights Aeris had risen above the courtyard, looking for him. On the other side of a struggling knot of *legionares,* the huge swordsman Tavi had seen in the stable at Bernardholt spotted him and came toward him, sword lifting to clean any opposition out of his way. The man who had killed Atsurak was nowhere to be seen.

Tavi ran away from the swordsman and down the length of the stables, toward the center of the fort and the far gate. Surely there would be someone there who wasn't already hips-deep in Marat by now, or a safe building that he could hide in.

Tavi reached the end of the stables at the same time a bulky figure, dressed in a half-buckled breastplate and a helmet that hung down over his eyes, plunged out of the doors of the stables, shouting, "I'm coming, I'm coming!"

Tavi slammed into the young man, and both went to the ground. The man's shield tumbled away wildly, though he managed to keep a grip on the well-worn handle of a spade. The man pushed his helmet back, then gripped the spade in both hands, raising it.

Tavi shielded his head with his arms. "Frederic!" he shouted. "Fred, it's me!"

Frederic lowered the spade and stared. "Tavi? You're alive?"

"Not for long!" he panted, struggling to his feet. "They're trying to kill me, Fred!"

Frederic blinked. His helmet fell over his eyes.

Tavi reached up to push it away, and saw the next Knight Aeris swooping down at him as he did. He reached into his pocket for more salt, but in his haste he had turned the pocket inside out, when he had drawn out salt before. It had all fallen out as he ran.

"Tavi," Fred said. "The Steadholder says I'm not to take that helmet off—"

"Look out!" Tavi said, and bulled into his friend, overbalancing the larger boy and taking him down. The Knight flashed past, his sword reaching down, and Tavi felt a sudden, hot sting on one arm.

Frederic blinked at Tavi and at the Knight flying on past, circling around again. "Tavi," he said, stunned, looking at the boy's arm. "He cut you." Fred looked up at Tavi, eyes widening. "They're trying to kill you!"

"I can't tell you how glad I am that you're here to tell me that," Tavi said, wincing at the sudden flash of pain. Blood had stained his shirt, but he could move his arm. "It isn't bad. Help me up."

Frederic did, his face showing his fear and confusion. "Who are they?"

"I don't know," Tavi said. "But he's coming again!"

Tavi turned to duck into the building—only to see, at the far end of the stables, the unmistakable outline of the swordsman against the doors on the far side, blade in hand.

"Can't get out that way," Tavi breathed. He looked back around behind him. The Knight Aeris had been joined by one of his companions, and they had lined up for another charge. "Fred, we need Thumper."

"What? But Thumper doesn't know how to fight!"

"Salt, Fred. We need salt to throw at those windcrafters, a *lot* of it!"

"But—"

"*Hurry, Fred!*"

The Knights Aeris hurtled toward them in a screaming torrent of wind.

Tavi gripped at his knife and looked around wildly, but there was no place to run.

Frederic stepped forward, in front of Tavi, his spade gripped in both hands. He let out a yell that grew into a deep-throated roar and drew back the spade. When he brought it around again, it came straight over his head and down in a great swooshing arc that met the leading Knight just before his sword could reach Tavi's friend.

The blow crumpled the Knight as though he had been made of straw, slapped him out of the air and to the ground in a single short, violent motion. Tavi had no doubt at all that Frederic had crushed the life from him.

Frederic lifted his spade and swung wildly at the next Knight, as the man swerved to avoid him. Frederic missed, but even as he swung, Tavi saw the light glittering on something shining on the blade of the spade, hard white lumps—crystals of salt. The salt swept through the Knight Aeris's windstream, and the man let out a yelp, tumbling to the ground and rolling with bone-breaking violence into the wall of one of the barracks.

Fred stared at the two men, his eyes wide, panting. He turned to Tavi and stammered, "I already had my spade salted. After I hit that first one, when I was working on that boulder." He blinked at the spade, and then at Tavi. "Are you all right?"

Tavi swallowed and looked back over his shoulder at the interior of the stable. Inside, someone had leapt out of the shadows at the swordsman. There was a confused blur of outlines, a short cry—and then the swordsman continued toward them.

Frederic swallowed, gripping his spade. "Tavi? What do we do?"

"Give me a minute," Tavi stammered. "I'm thinking."

Without warning, a Marat warrior hurled himself at Tavi, plowing into his side and lifting him, carrying him to slam painfully against the wall of the stable. Tavi let out a croaking shout and swung his knife weakly at the Marat warrior, a blood-smeared member of Clan Wolf, but the knife glanced off, barely breaking the Marat's skin.

The warrior tore at Tavi with his fangs, drawing back just enough to slam him against the wall, once, and then again, driving the breath from his lungs and stars into his vision.

Fred loomed up behind the warrior, shoved one brawny arm beneath his chin, and wrenched the Marat back from Tavi, hauling the Marat off of his feet and eliciting a strangled scream of protest. "Tavi!" Fred shouted. "Run!"

Tavi landed on the ground, woozily, and pushed himself to his hands and knees. He looked up to see the swordsman still coming for him and turned, the gold-handled dagger still clutched in his fist, and started moving again, staggering off into the wild melee of the courtyard.

Tavi ducked the butt of a *legionare*'s spear, slipped on a dark wetness he did not take the time to look at, and scrambled forward. A bloodied holder Tavi recognized from Rothholt turned toward him and lifted his sword, but recognized Tavi before striking and yelled something at him through the tumult and din.

Wind roared over the courtyard once more, and Tavi looked back to see another Knight Aeris hovering, eyes searching over the courtyard. His gaze swept to Tavi and stopped. The man's eyes widened, and he dived down toward him.

Somewhere close, Tavi heard the scream of a horse, and Tavi turned toward it, his eyes widening. He slipped past a stout old holder hauling a wounded *legionare* back out of the main knot of combat in the courtyard's center, to find a knot of horses, riders wielding spear and blade and forcing their way across the courtyard.

"Hashat!" Tavi shouted.

The Marat's head whipped around, white mane flying, and she flashed Tavi a fierce smile. "Aleran!" she called, her voice merry. Her eyes snapped into place above him, and she hissed, tightening her legs on the back of her horse. The beast plunged forward, all but bowling Tavi over, then reared. Tavi looked up in time to see the Knight Aeris that had been coming for him slash at Hashat and miss, only to have the Marat's saber whip across his face. The man shouted, clawing at his eyes, but he managed to thrust himself up higher into the air, bobbing drunkenly away from the courtyard. One of the other warriors spun with one of the heavily curved Marat short bows in his hands, and loosed an arrow that felled the Knight from the sky.

"Bah!" Hashat shouted at the archer. The man only grinned at her, drawing another arrow. She lifted the bloodied saber to her teeth and extended a hand to Tavi. "Up, Aleran!"

Tavi took her hand and was startled by the slender woman's strength. She hauled Tavi up to the light cushion of a saddle the Marat used, wrapped one of his arms around her waist, and shouted to the warriors near her in a tongue he could not understand. Together, the horses turned and plunged toward the outer wall, forcing their way through the crowd of screaming beasts and men.

"What is happening?" Tavi shouted.

"Your people have been forced back onto their wall!" Hashat shouted. She shrugged, and Tavi saw a number of loops of black cloth over her shoulder—the dark sashes worn by the enemy Knights. "Wolf and Herdbane were closest to the walls. Our people are fighting their way here through them, but it might take time. We are helping your people get onto the wall or to fall back to the other courtyard!"

As Tavi watched, the butt end of a spear scythed through the air and took one of the mounted warriors of the Horse Clan from his saddle, dropping him into a knot of Herdbane warriors. One of them plunged a glass knife into his throat, and then as blood fountained from him, grasped his pale mane and cut it from his head together with the scalp.

Hashat, seeing this, let out a piercing scream of pure rage, her horse rearing and plunging its hooves at the chest of the fallen Herdbane warrior. The man dropped, screaming, one side of his chest warped oddly. One of the other Marat raised his spear, but Hashat lifted a hand, spitting a command. The spearman nodded and whipped the spear down at the Marat, its tip leaving a long cut over the Marat's ribs. He slashed again, into an X, and then the horses surged on.

"What was that?" Tavi asked.

"He took Ishava's scalp," Hashat snarled. "Attempted to destroy his strength. That is different than killing, Aleran."

"Why didn't you kill him?"

"Because we will not lose Ishava's strength. We marked him. After the fight, Aleran, we will partake of that Herdbane and let Ishava rest."

Tavi blinked and stared at Hashat. The Horse headman's dark eyes gleamed with something hard and savage, and she only smiled when someone hurled another spear at her, and she had to raise up on her stirrups to cut it out of the air with her saber.

They reached the wall, but the press of the combat

had forced them to the northwest corner of the courtyard, where part of the wall had collapsed when Doroga's
gargant had come charging through it.

"Doroga!" Tavi shouted. "Where is Doroga?"

"Out!" Hashat responded. "We got him onto his
gargant and sent him back to his people." She looked
around the courtyard and shook her head. "We cannot
remain here long, Aleran. The Wolves and Herdbane are
being forced inside your walls by our people."

"My friend!" Tavi said. "Fred! Tall boy carrying a
spade! He's back by the stables! You have to help him!"

Hashat looked back at Tavi, expression dark. Then
flashed him a brilliant smile. "I will help him. Now,
Aleran. Stand up. Hold on to my shoulders."

Hashat rode close to the crumbled section of the wall
and looked up into the sun to see figures moving up there.
One of them dropped a rope down. Tavi stood up, his arm
throbbing where he had been cut, his feet on the Marat
saddle, his hand on Hashat's slender, strong shoulders.
He shoved the gold-handled dagger through his belt and
grabbed on to the rope. Hashat glanced up at him, then
kicked her horse into motion, leaving him swinging in the
air, as whoever was up above began pulling the rope up.

"Fade!" Tavi exclaimed.

Fade let out a happy hoot and hauled Tavi up onto
the broken section of the wall. The slave's scarred face
twisted into a grotesque smile, as he grasped Tavi's shoulders and then hurried him up onto the battlements, away
from the edge of the broken walls.

At the top, several *legionares* crouched upon the battlements, panting and exhausted. None were unwounded.
They crouched with their backs against the crenellation,

their shields held between them and the courtyard below. Bernard crouched there, too, but rose to come to Tavi and clutched at his arm fiercely. "Tavi!"

"Uncle! Where's Aunt Isana?"

Bernard shook his head, his face pale. "We got separated." He took the boy's shoulders and guided him up against the crenellation, pressing him to crouch against the stone, and kneeling with his own body between Tavi and the courtyard. Tavi looked out at the battlefield outside the fortress, awed. He had never seen so many people, much less so many people struggling to kill one another. The battlefield outside was as confusing a jumble as the one in the courtyard, but on a far grander scale. Gargants screamed and bellowed in the distance, plowing a slow but steady path toward the walls, while wheeling groups of mounted Horse Clan dashed and feinted everywhere, engaging packs of Wolf warriors or disorganized bands of Herdbane with their uncontrollable warbirds.

"Great furies," Tavi breathed.

"Get your head down," Bernard rumbled. He picked up a heavy Legion shield and held it across his body, facing the courtyard. "Someone still stops to shoot an arrow once in a while."

"What about Aunt Isana?"

Bernard grunted, as something struck the metal shield with a hollow, heavy thump. "We're doing all we can, boy. Stay down!"

Fade let out an alarmed cry from behind his shield, and Tavi looked back in time to see someone make a running leap from the other side of the gap in the wall. Amara landed on the battlements beside Fade with a rush of wind and a grunt of effort and wormed her way behind Fade's shield at once, panting.

"Tavi?" she said, her eyes widening. "I never thought you'd make it out of that."

"I had help."

"Do you have it?"

"Yes," Tavi said. He turned the knife's handle toward her and passed it over. Amara took the dagger, paling, and shook her head. "I have to get this to the First Lord."

Bernard grimaced. "What's Giraldi have to say?"

"We're cut off," Amara said. She wiped sweat from her brow, and Tavi saw that her hand was shaking. "Horse and Gargant are pushing the other Marat into Garrison. They hold the west courtyard except for the wall. East courtyard has pulled all its people back into buildings for defense. Giraldi thinks that Doroga's people will drive a wedge between Herdbane and Wolf within the hour and they'll have to quit the field."

Bernard blew out a breath. "An hour." Something else slammed against his shield, shoving his shoulder into Tavi's. "We aren't going to last that long. My sister?"

"She's in one of the barracks in the east courtyard, with Gram. Giraldi said that he saw her go in with him."

"Good," Bernard rumbled. "Good."

Down the wall, one of the *legionares* cried out. Tavi looked up and saw an arrow protruding from the man's upper shoulder. It didn't look like a life-threatening wound, but within a few seconds, the man's head rolled on his neck and he fell quietly to his side.

Bernard grabbed Tavi's arm and crab walked down the battlements behind his shield, keeping it over both of them. He checked the man's throat and grimaced. "Must have hit the artery. He's gone." Then he frowned and leaned closer. "This isn't a Marat arrow."

The next *legionare* on the wall abruptly jerked. His head snapped back, where a few scant inches of his helmet showed over his shield. He blinked, a few times, and then blood ran down between his eyes and over one temple. His eyes unfocused, and then he toppled to his side as well, the arrow piercing his helmet.

Amara dragged Fade down the wall and flicked a glance around his shield. "It's *him*," she hissed.

The third man crouched behind his shield, tucking everything in close—too close. The next arrow slammed into the shield itself, pierced it, and went on into the man's chest, at his ribs. He let out a wheezing cry, blood suddenly a froth on his mouth.

Tavi stared in horror at the *legionares* dying on the wall beside him. It had happened so *fast*. It hadn't taken half a minute for the unseen archer to kill three men.

"We have to get out of here," the last of the *legionares* stammered. He started to rise. "We can't stay here."

"Stay down, you fool," Bernard shouted.

But the *legionare* turned to run down the wall, toward the rope that lay coiled by the gap. As soon as he rose, he cried out, and Tavi saw a thick black arrow impaling the man's leg. He fell to the ground with a shout, landing on top of his shield.

The next arrow struck square against his ear. The man folded quietly down, as though going to sleep, and didn't move again.

"Damn you, Fidelias!" Amara shouted, her voice raw.

Tavi looked up and down the wall. Behind him,

the battlements abruptly ended at the gap Doroga had crushed into the wall. Before him, the battlements ran steadily along until they reached a wall of solid rock. The builders of Garrison had used the old granite bones of the hills on either side of the fortress to serve as its north and south walls, and they were little more than a sharply sloped face of rock. "Can we climb that? Can we get out that way?"

"With all those Knights Aeris?" Amara shook her head. "We wouldn't stand a chance."

The courtyard itself, Tavi could hear, seethed with the cries of Marat and their beasts, the occasional scream of a horse, the snarling of wolves, the whistling shrieks of herdbane. Even if they did climb down the rope, they would only be falling from the frying pan and into the fire.

"We're trapped," Tavi breathed.

Another arrow slammed into Bernard's shield, its steel tip bursting through the metal lining and wood of the shield, sharp point emerging for the width of several fingers and barely falling short of his temple. Bernard went white, but his expression didn't change, and he covered himself and Tavi with the shield resolutely.

Wind howled at the gap in the wall, and Tavi looked back to see the man who had ordered the Knights Aeris earlier being dropped off on the battlements by one of the airborne Knights. A moment later, the huge swordsman landed next to him.

Amara drew in a breath, her face pale. "Get away from here, Fidelias."

The innocuous-looking man regarded those crouching on the walls with a flat, neutral gaze. "Give me the dagger."

"It isn't yours."

"Give me the dagger, Amara."

For an answer, Amara rose, and drew the sword from her side. She took the dagger from her belt and tossed it onto the stones behind her. "Come take it, if you can. I'm surprised you didn't kill everyone while you had the chance."

"I ran out of arrows," the man said. "Aldrick. Kill them."

The swordsman drew his blade and began walking down the wall.

Amara licked her lips and held her guardsman's blade low, parallel to her thigh. Tavi could see her hand trembling.

Beside him, he heard his uncle growl. Bernard jerked at the straps of the shield and loosened it from his arm. Then he handed the straps to Tavi and said, "Hold on to this." Bernard rose, taking up the double-bitted axe, and moved down the wall to stand beside Amara.

Tavi swallowed, staring.

Aldrick paused several feet away, abruptly becoming absolutely still.

Bernard shrugged one of his shoulders and then let out a shout and rolled forward, axe sweeping across his body in a vicious arc at the swordsman's head. Aldrick ducked beneath the blow, and the axe bit into the stones of one of the merlons, shattering it into flying bits of rock and powder. Bernard spun, using the momentum, and brought the axe sweeping down in a blow meant to split the swordsman's body in two.

Aldrick waited until the very last second to move and then hardly seemed to move at all. He twisted his hips to one side, drawing the line of his body away from the descending axe, so that it whipped past his chest by the breadth of a hair.

As he did, his sword rose. The tip plunged into Bernard's flank, just above the belt of his trousers. Bernard stiffened, his eyes widening. He let out a short, harsh groan, and his fingers loosened from the handle of the axe. It fell to the battlements with a thump.

Tavi stared in horror. Aldrick twisted the blade as he tore it back out of Bernard's flank, then casually let him fall from the battlements, toward the chaos of the courtyard below.

"Uncle!" Tavi screamed.

Amara reached out a hand toward him as he fell. "Bernard!"

Fade let out a shriek, dropping his shield, and ran back to Tavi, clutching to the boy and gibbering incoherently.

Aldrick flicked his weapon to one side, and droplets of blood, of his *uncle's* blood, splattered against the stones of the battlements.

Amara's face set into a sudden mask of cold disdain. "Crows take you, Fidelias," she said in a cool, quiet voice. "Crows take you all."

Tavi didn't see her strike, so much as he saw a blur of color the same shade as the cloak the Cursor wore. She moved toward the swordsman with her guardsman's blade, and the sword made the air whistle as it darted at Aldrick.

The swordsman took a pair of quick steps back, no surprise on his face, no emotion. He lifted his blade, and caught Amara's blow on it. Three more blows followed, so fast that they chimed in what almost seemed a single tone, but the swordsman stopped them all, despite Amara's sheer speed, his blade close to his body, his movements very short, quick.

Tavi crawled forward, tears blurring his eyes, lugging the huge shield and the sobbing Fade with him. He recovered the dropped dagger and shoved it through his belt again, watching the battle, helpless and terrified.

Amara whirled and crouched and whirled again, her blade whipping at Aldrick's throat, knees, and throat again. The swordsman blocked each strike and then with a sudden, hard smile, his blade lashed out. Amara hissed, and the sword tumbled from her hands, falling to the stones near Tavi.

Aldrick whipped his blade in a horizontal line, and Amara let out a harsh cry, staggering against the battlements, her hair fallen around her face. Tavi could see blood on the mail around her belly. Amara turned toward Aldrick, unsteady on her feet and swung her arm at him in a strike. The swordsman slapped her hand aside, and his foot lashed out at her knee. Amara gasped and fell to the stone. She struggled to rise again.

Aldrick shook his head, as though disgusted, and slammed one heavy boot down onto Amara's splinted arm. She let out a cry and jerked. She looked up at Tavi, her eyes not focused, her face bedsheet-white.

Aldrick did not pause. He drew back his blade, crouching, and with two hands swung it toward the paralyzed Cursor.

Tavi didn't stop to think. He seized the fallen sword in his left hand and lunged forward from his knees, toward the swordsman. The guardsman's blade flicked out and found the gap between the swordsman's mail and the tops of his boots, drawing an insignificant cut across the skin. But it was enough to make Aldrick divert the blow aimed for Amara's neck, to parry Tavi's clumsy thrust aside.

Aldrick snarled, his face suddenly suffused with scarlet anger, making an old scar stand out white against his cheek. He slammed his weapon against Tavi's. Tavi felt the jolt of it in his shoulders and chest, and his arm went numb in a tingling wash of sensation, from fingertip to elbow. The sword flew off somewhere behind him.

He rolled back and tried to lift the shield to cover himself, but the swordsman kicked it aside, and it tumbled out of Tavi's grasp and into the courtyard below.

"Stupid boy," Aldrick said, eyes cold. "Give me the dagger."

Tavi clutched his hand on the dagger's hilt and started worming his way back along the wall. "You killed him," Tavi shouted, his voice hoarse. "You killed my uncle!"

"And what happened to my Odiana is your fault. I should kill you right here," Aldrick growled. "Give up. You can't win."

"Go to the crows! If I don't beat you, someone else will!"

"Have it your way," the swordsman said. He whirled the sword in his fingers and closed toward Tavi, lifting the blade, eyes cold. "If Araris Valerian himself was here, he couldn't beat me. And you aren't Araris."

The swordsman brought both hands to the hilt of the sword and struck. Tavi saw the cold, bloodied metal of the blade falling toward him and knew that he was about to die. He screamed and lifted a hand, knowing full well that it would do him no good, but he was unable to do anything else.

The sword came down in the death stroke.

And met steel in a cold, clear chime, like a bell. A cloud of silver sparks rained down where Aldrick's blade had met the steel of the guardsman's sword.

Fade stood over Tavi, both hands on the hilt of the short blade, his legs spread out wide, knees bent, his body relaxed. The swordsman bore down on his weapon, but Fade seemed able to hold it away from Tavi with little effort, and after a scant pair of heartbeats, Fade twisted his body. Aldrick's blade slid to one side, and he skipped back from a counterstroke—but not fast enough. Fade's sword whipped toward Aldrick's face, and split the white scar there open anew, blood flowing.

Aldrick dropped back into a guard position, watching Fade, his eyes wide, his reddened face going pale. "No," he said. "No."

Fade took a step forward and stood between Tavi and the other two men on the wall. His voice came out quiet, low, steady. "Stay behind me, Tavi."

Tavi stared in shock. He clutched the dagger and scooted back from the two men.

"You aren't," Aldrick snarled. "You can't be. You're dead."

Fade said, "You talk too much."

Then he spun forward, deftly stepping over Amara's unmoving form, his sword gliding toward the swordsman. Aldrick parried in a shower of scarlet sparks, slid a thrust to his belly aside, and cut at the slave's head. Fade dropped to a crouch, and the blow struck cleanly through two feet of furycrafted battlement stone. A chunk of stone the size of a big washtub slid down the wall and fell into the battle outside the fortress.

Fade rose, blade dancing, and pressed the swordsman back, down the battlements, his ragged and unkempt hair flying about his head, his scarred face set in an expression of cool detachment. When his sword struck Aldrick's, scarlet fire rained down, and when he caught one of the swordsman's strikes, clouds of silver-white motes flew forth in a flash.

Tavi saw Aldrick begin to panic, his movements becoming jerkier, faster, less elegant. He retreated step by step, and Fade pressed him relentlessly. The slave swept one blow at Aldrick that missed altogether, throwing up another shower of sparks as the blade cut through the stone near Aldrick's feet, but the slave seemed to recover rapidly, and he began to push Aldrick down the wall once again.

Tavi had never seen anything so graceful, so terrifying, as the two men clashing together. Though Aldrick was the larger of the pair, Fade seemed more nimble, his movements more fluid, again and again blocking blows that might have killed him to miss by the barest margin. He leapt over one strike, ducked under another, and thrust at Aldrick's belly once more. The swordsman parried him aside, spinning on his feet to reverse positions with Fade on the narrow battlements, so that he now stood with his back to Tavi.

Aldrick rained a pair of heavy blows down on Fade, who danced aside from one and slid the other off the guardsman's blade. Fade countered with a volley of cuts and thrusts too swift for Tavi to follow, and Aldrick once again backed down the wall, defending himself.

Fade's blade whipped at Aldrick's foot and missed, slashing stone. Aldrick kicked the slave in the face with one heavy boot, and Fade's face snapped to one side. He turned the motion into an upward slash, but that blow too missed Aldrick altogether, instead slashing through the massive merlon beside him.

Aldrick's sword darted down to Fade's wrist, a swift cut that drew blood and threw the sword from the slave's hands and down into the courtyard below. Fade cried out and fell to his knees, clutching the hand to his chest.

Aldrick stood over Fade, panting, white around the eyes, and drew his sword slowly up behind him. "Over," he said. "Finally over. You lose."

Fade said, "Look where you're standing."

Tavi looked down at Aldrick's feet, at the deep slashes in the battlements where Fade's sword had cut through the stone.

Aldrick looked down, and his face went white.

The merlon beside him slid to one side along the upward-sweeping line Fade had cut in it, the stone falling with a ponderous grace to the weakened floor of the battlement. It struck, and the two slashes Fade had made in the stone became a sudden myriad of crumbling cracks. Aldrick tried to step back, but the stone beneath his feet gave way like a rotten board, and with a howl Aldrick ex Gladius and a thousand pounds of stone went crashing down to the courtyard below.

Fade closed his eyes for a moment, panting, then looked up at Tavi.

The boy stared at him. "How?"

Fade moved one shoulder in a shrug. "Aldrick has always thought in lines. So I thought in curves."

Tavi saw a movement behind Fade and shouted, "Fade! Look out!"

The slave whirled, but not before Fidelias, holding the rope they had used to climb to the wall, had tossed a loop of it over Fade's head. Fidelias jerked on the rope, and it tightened. Then the man planted his feet and hauled.

Fade struggled, but he had no leverage. The rope hauled him off the battlement. Fidelias let go of the rope, and Fade fell out of sight. The end of the rope had been tied off to one of the crenellations, and the rope tightened with a sudden, snapping jerk.

"No," Tavi breathed.

Fidelias turned toward Tavi.

"No!" The boy rose to his feet and threw himself at the man on the wall, brandishing the dagger. He leapt at Fidelias, knife extended.

Fidelias caught Tavi by his shirt, and without any effort spun him around and threw him to the stones of the battlement. Tavi felt the rock hit his back with an impact that stole his breath and turned the steady, hot sting of his wounded arm into a raging fire.

He let out a weak sound of pain and tried to struggle away from Fidelias, but within a few inches he felt the crumbling edge of the shattered battlement behind him. He looked back and down on a drop into the hard, jagged rubble of the fallen section of wall, where Marat and beasts fought in savage efficiency, killing.

He turned back to Fidelias, clutching the dagger.

"Give me the knife," Fidelias said, his voice quiet, his eyes dead. "Give me the knife, or I'll kill you."

"No," Tavi wheezed.

"You don't have to die, boy."

Tavi swallowed. He squirmed out as far as he could on the broken battlements and heard the stones begin to crackle and groan beneath him. "Stay away from me."

Fidelias's face twisted in anger, and he jerked his hand in a sudden gesture. The stone *rippled*, as if it had been a sheet snapped by a holdwife, and threw Tavi a few feet toward Fidelias, stunning the boy.

Fidelias reached for the knife. Tavi swept it at him in a desperate cut. Fidelias clutched the boy's throat, and Tavi felt his breath cut off with a sudden jerk.

"Just as well," Fidelias said. "No witnesses."

Tavi's vision began to dim. He felt his grip on the dagger begin to loosen.

Fidelias shook his head, and the pressure on Tavi's throat began to increase. "You should have given me the knife."

Tavi struggled uselessly, until his arms and legs seemed to forget how to move. He stared up into Fidelias's hard eyes and felt his body going limp.

And so it was that he saw Amara weakly stir and lift her head. He saw her writhe, lifting one knee beneath her, and reaching back to draw a short, small knife from her boot. She clenched her jaw and shoved her broken arm beneath her, her forearm across the floor, lifting her body.

Then, in one motion, she drew back the knife and flicked it at Fidelias's back. A sudden jet of wind propelled the knife toward him.

Tavi saw the man jerk suddenly, startled surprise on

his features. He stiffened, fingers loosening from Tavi's throat, and reached a hand up toward his back, his expression twisting with sudden agony.

"You wanted a knife, Fidelias," Amara hissed. "There's the one I took from you."

Fidelias, his face blank, frightened, turned back to Tavi and clutched at his hand, at the dagger.

There was a frantic moment of scrambling, and Fidelias let out a gasping cry of pain. Tavi felt a hand around his wrist, a sudden pressure, heard the crack of breaking bones. Agony roared over him, and he saw his hand dangle uselessly.

Fidelias reached for the dagger and grabbed its hilt.

Tavi seized Fidelias's belt and hauled with all of his strength and weight.

Fidelias overbalanced, let out a harsh croak and fell from the battlements, to the sharp-edged rubble of the gap in the wall. Tavi turned and looked down, saw the man land on the stones, with his feet under him. Tavi thought he heard bones break.

Fidelias fell to the ground, and a tide of Marat washed over him.

Tavi stared, panting, exhausted, in more pain than he thought could exist in the entire world. Uncle Bernard. Fade. The tears welled up, and he couldn't stop them, couldn't stop himself from sobbing, letting out ugly, harsh little sounds. He laid his cheek down on the stone and cried.

He felt Amara crawl to him a few moments later. The Cursor dragged a shield with her. She lay down beside Tavi and used the shield to cover them both.

He couldn't stop sobbing. He felt her hand pat

clumsily at his back. "It's all right, Tavi. It's all right." She leaned her cheek against his hair. "Shhhh. You're going to be all right. It's over."

Over.

Tavi cried quietly, until the darkness swallowed him.

◦◦◦◦ CHAPTER 44

Isana watched the battle on the shattered battlements with her heart in her teeth, trapped on the second floor of a barracks building in the east courtyard, and helpless to do anything to influence its outcome.

She saw her brother fall from the walls and, through a haze of tears, saw the Cursor dropped to the battlements as well. She screamed when Tavi took up the fallen sword and faced the enormous swordsman, and again when Fade took up the old weapon and fought the man up and down the battlements. She watched, careless of the occasional buzz of a flying arrow, as Fade was hanged and thrown off the walls, as Tavi fought for the dagger, and as the traitor Cursor fell from sight.

She watched as Tavi collapsed and as the wounded Amara dragged her shield over both of them—then went still.

"Tavi," she heard herself say. "Tavi, no. Oh, furies." She turned and ran out of the room, down the stairs to the first level of the barracks, a common room for the soldiers living there. Heavy iron shutters had been closed over the window, but the iron bars that could be fastened shut over the door had been torn away from their hinges only moments before, along with the heavy wooden door, and now the doorway had been blocked with a pair of heavy tables, leaving the upper half of the doorway open.

Frederic stood in the doorway, a Legion shield strapped onto his left arm, his dented spade clutched in his right hand. One of the women of Garrison stood with him, a stout, stern-looking matron with bare feet and a bloodied spear gripped in her hands. The young gargant herder's hair hung around his face, damp with sweat, and he bore a cut that would leave a long white scar leading from his jawline to his ear, but his eyes were determined, hard.

As Isana came down the stairs, another Marat threw himself at the barricade, stone-headed hatchets in either hand. The Marat swung the first at Frederic, but the herder lifted his shield and the head of the hatchet shattered upon it. The woman standing with him drove her spear viciously into the Marat's thigh, and the warrior dropped his second hatchet in a blow aimed at the spear's haft.

Frederic shouted and thrust his spade at the Marat, the steel blade of the tool gouging roughly into the Marat's chest. Frederic jerked the spade back to him and with a roar leaned back and kicked the stunned Marat in the belly. The warrior went flying away from the fury-assisted blow, landing in a heap upon the stones of the embattled courtyard.

Isana rushed to the doorway. "Frederic. I've seen Tavi and Bernard. They're hurt, and I've got to help them."

Frederic turned to her, panting, his handsome face speckled with droplets of blood, "But Mistress Isana! There's Marat running around everywhere out there."

"And they're lying wounded in it. I need you to help me carry them out of the fight."

The woman with the spear nodded to Isana. "Go on. We can hold the door for a while."

Frederic frowned, his expression torn. "You're sure?"

"Thank you," Isana said, and clasped the woman's arm. Then she grabbed Frederic's. "They're near the gate, on the broken section of wall."

Frederic swallowed and nodded. "So we just go to the other courtyard, right?"

"Yes."

Frederic settled his grip on his spade's handle and nodded. "All right, then."

Isana clutched tightly to Frederic's shoulder, as he leaned forward, took a quick look around the courtyard, and padded swiftly toward the other side of Garrison, keeping near to the wall. The carnage in the courtyard was like some kind of nightmarish slaughterhouse. The Marat roamed everywhere, attacking buildings, fighting with one another and with the Aleran defenders.

A shrill scream cut across the courtyard, terror filled. In the doorway of the barracks building across the court-yard from them, a pair of herdbanes appeared. They dragged a wounded *legionare* out into the courtyard, one on either arm, and tossed him to the ground between them.

Even as Isana watched, the *legionare*'s helmet tumbled

off, revealing Warner's bald head and exhausted face beneath.

"Warner!" Isana cried.

Warner looked up, his face ashen, and tried to sweep his sword at the nearest bird, but the movement was listless, as though he barely had the strength to move. The terrible birds began to wrench the Steadholder apart, shrieking. Two Marat, their hair bedecked with dark herdbane feathers, watched until Warner had been savaged and lay still upon the earth. Then one of them stepped forward with a knife in hand and, after a moment's consideration, removed the Steadholder's ears. He said something to his companion that drew a rough laugh, and then as the birds continued worrying the corpse, the pair of them rose and walked into the barracks Warner had been defending.

The cries within Garrison were joined by others—the screams of terrified children.

"Someone's going to help them," Frederic breathed. "Right, Mistress Isana? Someone's going to go help, aren't they?"

Isana looked between the far courtyard and the barracks, while children screamed. She came to her decision in the space of a breath. For while Tavi might be hurt, he at least had a chance of survival. If she did nothing, those children would have none.

"We are," she said. "Let's go."

Frederic swallowed and nodded. He shook her hand off of his shoulder and stalked forward, sweeping his spade nervously in his hand. Isana followed him.

Neither of the herdbanes took note of them until Frederic swept his spade in a broad arc that ended at the neck of the larger one, which broke with a brittle snap. The bird went down immediately, while the second turned toward Frederic and lunged, snapping at the gargant herder's face. Frederic shuffled back, and the bird followed him.

Inside the barracks, the children continued screaming. Isana waited until the remaining herdbane had stalked another few paces away from the door and then she darted inside.

"Mistress Isana!" Frederic called. "Wait!"

Isana slipped inside the barracks to find the two Marat facing a dozen children who hid behind several trunks and bunks knocked over and formed into a crude barricade. Some of the older children carried Legion spears and thrust them viciously at the Marat whenever they came close. The Marat spoke to one another in low voices, evidently deciding how best to dig the children out from behind their barricade.

Isana moved silently to the nearest Marat, reached out, and touched his neck, calling to Rill as she did.

The Marat jerked and let out a hoarse scream that wound down into a gurgle, as water frothed from his nose, his mouth. The second Marat spun, one hard-knuckled fist lashing out as he did. Isana felt it hit her high on the cheekbone and throw her to the ground.

She tried to scramble away, but the Marat caught her by the ankle and dragged her back. She kicked at him, but the warrior slashed at her leg with his knife, a sudden line of screaming fire across her calf. She felt him move, felt his weight come down atop her, and a rough hand tangled in her hair, jerking her head back. Out of the corner of her eye, she saw the glitter of a glossy stone dagger, diving toward her throat.

She lifted an arm, gasping, and blocked the Marat's forearm with her own, halting the blade a scant inch from her throat. The Marat grunted and bore down, and she felt her arm forced to give way under the warrior's greater strength.

Isana twisted, gasping, calling for Rill once again, hoping that the first Marat would remain incapacitated when she called Rill from him. Her fury came flowing into her, and Isana drew Rill in, even as she sank the nails of her free hand into the Marat's forearm. Blood welled from the tears in the pale skin, and Isana sent Rill flowing through those rents.

The Marat gasped, shuddering, and the power of his arms began to wane. He jerked and twisted and abruptly released both Isana and the knife. His body bucked, and he fell back from Isana, back arched into a bow, clutching at his chest.

Isana shuddered and tried to shield herself from the sudden terror and panic in the Marat, but she did not release him from Rill's grip. The Marat heaved in breaths like a fish out of water, but Isana knew it would do him no good. The fury had stopped the blood in his veins, stopped the beating of his heart.

It was over in a minute. Isana found herself staring at a dozen frightened, wide-eyed children over the corpses of the Marat warriors she had killed.

Frederic appeared in the doorway, panting, a moment later. The young holder had discarded his shield, and instead carried a slender and half-dressed girl wearing a slave's collar and a dancer's silks. The girl's leg had been bloodied, and she leaned on Frederic, her face buried against his shoulder, weeping.

"Mistress Isana," Frederic gasped. "You're all right?"

"For now," Isana said. She moved to Frederic's side and helped him draw the girl over to the little barricade. "Frederic, you must stay here and protect the children. Hold this building. All right?"

He looked up at her, his face concerned. "But what about you?"

"I'll manage," Isana said. For a moment, the terror and pain and panic of those around her seemed to rise up in a wave that threatened to drown her. The corpses of the Marat lay on the floor, twisted and stiffening, their expressions agonized. She heard herself letting out a low, unsteady laugh. "I'll manage. I have to get to him."

Frederic swallowed and nodded. "Yes, Mistress."

She fought to take a deep breath, to control the emotions coursing through her. "Hold the door, Frederic. Keep them safe." Then she walked out the door of the barracks as quickly as she could and started toward the far courtyard again.

The battle, it seemed, was winding down. Corpses and the wounded lay everywhere. She watched as a Herdbane Marat came pelting around a corner, only to be ridden down by a pair of Marat on horses, spears run through his back as he fled. A blood-maddened direwolf threw itself at one of the horses, fangs ripping at one of its hind legs, bringing the beast to ground, while its rider leapt from its back and spun, spear in hand, to face the wolf.

Isana pressed on, past the command building, where a grim, grizzled *legionare* shouted to her to get inside. She ignored him and pressed on into the easternmost courtyard.

Here, the fighting had been worst, and the carnage

was greatest. Not only had the dead been laid out here earlier in the day, but now hundreds more bodies lay on the ground, mostly Marat, though here and there the red and gold of a Rivan *legionare's* tunic stood out from among the pale barbarian bodies. She could have walked to the far side of the courtyard without setting a foot on its stones.

She began to pick her way across the courtyard, twice dodging aside as Marat fled past her, heading for the broken gates, eyes wild and panicked. She stayed out of their way and let them pass. Once, several Marat riding horses thundered through the corpses, hooves crushing indiscriminately, riding out the gate. Here and there, the wounded stirred, dragged themselves along, or waited quietly to die. The place was thick with the smell of blood, with the septic stink of ruptured bellies, and Isana's head was swimming by the time she reached the broken section of wall, where she had last seen Tavi.

She had to crawl over a mound of rubble to reach the far side, steeling herself for what she was afraid she would see: her brother, dead on the stones. Fade, hanging at the end of a rope, strangled, or his neck broken. Tavi above, bled to death.

Instead, she found Bernard laying quietly against the base of the wall. His mail shirt had been unbelted and rolled away from where the mercenary's sword had pierced him, and the skin there was pink and smooth— newly crafted whole. She stumbled across the stones to her brother's side, reaching for his throat. She found his pulse, slow and steady and strong.

Tears blurred her eyes, even as she heard movement

and looked up, to see Fade rising from his seat not far away. His throat was raw and abraded, his sleeve stained with blood, but the cut upon it had been crafted closed, pink skin clean and almost glowing.

"Fade," Isana breathed. "How?"

The slave turned his face up toward the battlements. "Tavi," he said, voice thick with tension. "They're with him up there."

Gravel pattered down around her, making Isana look up.

Odiana stood upon the wall, staring down, her expression detached, dark eyes somehow empty, hollow. She moved one bare foot, kicking at a coil of knotted rope beside her, and it unwound, falling down to bump against the wall beside Isana's head.

"Come up," Odiana said.

"What have you done with him?" Isana demanded.

"You know I can't hear you," the water witch replied. "Come up." She vanished from the edge of the battlements.

Isana looked at Fade and reached for the rope. The slave stepped closer, his expression serious, and put his hands on her waist, lifting her as she began to climb.

Isana reached the top of the wall to find Odiana standing over the unmoving forms of Tavi and Amara. Both were pale, still, but breathing steadily. Isana went to Tavi's side at once, reaching down to touch his face, to brush an errant curl back from his eyes. She felt herself sob in relief, felt some easing in the terror and the fear of the past several days that demanded tears to fill the void. She didn't bother to craft them away.

"Happily reunited," Odiana murmured. "There." The woman turned to walk toward the rope, evidently in preparation to climb back down it.

"Why?" Isana asked, her voice choked. She looked up at the water witch. "You saved them. Why?"

Odiana tilted her head to one side, eyes focused on Isana's mouth. "Why? Why, indeed." She shook her head. "You could have killed me at Kordholt. Or simply left me behind. You did neither. You could have given me to the Cursor girl. You did not. It deserved a reply. This is mine."

"I don't understand."

"Saving your life would have been a small grace, I think. Saving the lives of your blood is another matter. You love the boy as a son. You love him so much it hurts my eyes. The Steadholder. Even the slave. They are important to you. So I give you their lives. Our scale is balanced. Do not expect it again."

Isana nodded. "What about the girl?"

Odiana sighed. "I was hoping she would die, out of general principles, but she'll live. I neither helped nor hurt her. Take that as you would."

"Thank you."

The water witch shrugged and murmured with something like genuine warmth in her tone, "I hope that I never see you again, Isana."

And with that, she descended the rope, and once at the bottom walked briskly across the courtyard, deeper into Garrison, eyes wary.

Isana turned her back on the departing mercenary and knelt down to touch Tavi's forehead, to send Rill gently into the boy, to assure her of his health. She sensed that he was in pain and that he would need a more thorough crafting to put him to right, but that the water witch had ensured that he would live to be treated.

There was a scraping of leather on stone behind her, and Fade hauled himself up the rope, glowering at it reproachfully after. "Tavi?"

"He's all right," Isana whispered. "He's going to be all right."

Fade put a hand on Isana's shoulder, silently. "He is brave. Like his father."

Isana glanced up at Fade and smiled, wearily. "The battle? Is it over?"

Fade nodded, looking down over the courtyard, the gates. "It is over."

"Then help me," Isana said. "We need to get them into a bed so that we can see to them."

"What then?" Fade asked.

"Then . . ." Isana closed her eyes. "Then we go home."

CHAPTER 45

Fidelias woke in somewhere dark, cool. He ached everywhere. He opened his eyes.

"Good," Odiana purred. "You're awake." She leaned over him to rest fingertips lightly on his temples. The cool, pale metal of a discipline collar gleamed at her throat. "No more bleeding."

"What happened?" Fidelias asked.

She watched his mouth very closely as he spoke, then answered, "I found my Aldrick, and then I found you. We're not out yet. We need you to help us."

"Where are we?"

"In a warehouse in Garrison. My love is running an errand, and then we'll go."

"The dagger?"

"In your hand. You wouldn't let it go."

Fidelias lifted his hand and saw the dagger there. "Where are the men?"

"Already gone."

The door to the warehouse creaked open, and Aldrick, wearing the tunic of a Rivan *legionare*, entered. "There isn't much time," he said, voice tense. He limped to Odiana and tossed down several bloody scraps of flesh attached to sweeping manes of fine white hair. Scalps. "The Marat are sweeping the buildings for any stragglers."

"There's one more circle to close," Odiana said, smiling, and lifted the scalps. She began to hum to herself and walked over toward a pile of fallen crates and spilled junk in the dimness of the warehouse.

Fidelias rose and wavered on his feet, gasping. He looked down to find himself wearing a Rivan tunic as well.

Aldrick caught him, though the swordsman himself seemed none too steady. "Easy. You were hurt pretty badly. Odiana stabilized you, but you're going to need some serious attention."

Fidelias nodded. He tucked Aquitaine's dagger into his pouch and tied it shut. "All right," he said, "how do we get out of here?"

"Everything's still in chaos out there," Aldrick said. "The Alerans are confused, there are many wounded, and some of the buildings are on fire. The Wolves fled and left the Herdbanes to rot. Most of them fought to the death, and they're still flushing them out of attics and basements."

Fidelias nodded. "The men?"

"Banged up pretty well. We're going to be paying off a lot of death benefits. If we can get out of Garrison, we should be able to rendevous with them. Can you stand?"

"Yes." Fidelias squinted over toward Odiana and limped toward her.

She crouched beside the nearly still form of a huge, grimy holder. Broken crates lay all over him, along with spilled slate shingles. The man was obviously crippled, and he was not conscious.

Odiana was touching his hair with gentle fingers and smiled at Aldrick as he and Fidelias approached. Then she leaned forward and touched the man's head. "Wake up, Master Kord."

Kord shivered, and his eyelids fluttered open. After a moment, he shivered and focused on them. Fear touched his features.

Odiana leaned down, smiling, and kissed his forehead.

Aldrick rested the tip of his sword lightly against Kord's cheek. "Take off the collar," he said. "Now."

Kord licked his lips and whispered, "Why should I?"

Aldrick pressed the tip of the sword into Kord's skin. The man cringed away. "All right. All right." He reached up and fumbled at the collar. Odiana shivered as it came free, holding it and staring at it.

"We should go," Fidelias said.

Odiana murmured, "One thing more, Master. I have a gift for you before I leave."

"Wait," Kord stammered. "I did what you said. I took the collar off."

Odiana leaned down to look into Kord's eyes and murmured, "Isana is too kind a person to kill you, Kord. She's too good a person to kill you. And, you poor thing." She kissed his forehead again. "So am I."

She took the scalps Aldrick had brought, and draped one of them over Kord's arm. Then tucked one through his belt and left the third wrapped about his wrist. "These are scalps of the Horse Clan," Odiana said. "They take scalping very seriously. And they're emptying the buildings one by one, looking for enemies. They should be here any moment, poor Master. They're going to tear the heart from your chest and eat it while it still beats. You'll get to see part of it." She let out a sigh and turned to Aldrick. "But we won't?"

He shook his head. "But it's a pretty morning at least. Time to go, love."

Odiana watched his mouth, then thrust out her lower lip, but stepped to Aldrick's side and rested her hand on his arm.

Fidelias grimaced, glancing down at the scalp-draped Steadholder. Then he turned to walk away.

Kord clutched at his ankle. "Wait. Please. Don't leave me here. Don't leave me here for those animals."

Fidelias paused long enough to grind his heel down on the man's fingers and then walked away, wearily pulling up the woodcrafting that would shelter him,

Aldrick, and Odiana from view while they slipped out of the battle-ravaged fortress.

They left the warehouse and saw a half dozen of the Horse Clan dart inside, weapons in hand. In less than a minute, Kord began to scream. Long, drawn out, agonized, terrified, horrible screams.

Odiana leaned her head against Aldrick's shoulder and murmured, "You're right, my lord. It is a lovely morning."

ᴏᴏᴏᴏ CHAPTER 46

Tavi woke up in bed, in a room in Bernardholt used mostly when there were extra guests at hand. He felt tired, thirsty, but except for a mild ache, he did not hurt. He moved his legs and felt some kind of short breeches on them.

"I don't know why," his uncle's voice rumbled from a bed nearby. "She bent over me and I thought she was going to cut my throat. Then she crafted the wound shut instead. Said she didn't want me to bleed to death."

Amara's voice held a frown. "Did she say anything?"

"Yes. To tell Isana that they were even."

Tavi sat up and looked around. His uncle sat in the bed beside him, white bandages wrapped around him from where his belly showed at the edge of the sheets to under his arms. He looked pale, and bruises marred his shoulders and half of his face, but he smiled when he saw Tavi. "Well, well. We thought you'd sleep forever."

Tavi let out a glad cry and threw himself across the space of beds at his uncle, hugging him tightly.

Bernard laughed. "Careful, careful. I'm delicate." His arms folded around Tavi and hugged him back. "Good to see you, boy."

Amara, dressed in a blouse and skirts of rich brown, smiled at him. "Hello, Tavi."

He flashed the Cursor a smile and looked back at Bernard. "But how?" Tavi asked. "How did you live?"

"Odiana," Bernard said. "That water witch that attacked you in the river. Your aunt saved her from being killed by Kord. She was hiding among the corpses at the base of the wall. She saved me. Fade, too."

Tavi shook his head. "I don't care who did it, as long as you're all right."

Bernard laughed again. "What I am," he said, "is hungry. You?"

Tavi's stomach grew queasy. "Not yet, Uncle."

Amara turned to a pitcher nearby and poured water into a cup for Tavi, handing it to him. "Drink up. Once you get liquid back in you, you'll be hungry, right enough."

Tavi nodded his thanks to her and drank. His hand, the one that had been broken, felt a little weak, and he switched the cup to the other. "You're all right, too?"

She smiled, a wan expression. "Alive. Some scars. I'll be all right."

"I'm sorry," Tavi said. "I lost the dagger."

Amara shook her head. "You've nothing to be sorry

for, Tavi. You stood against two men who have killed more people between them than anyone I know of. It was very brave. You shouldn't feel ashamed for not getting the dagger."

"But without it, Aquitaine gets away with it. You can't prove he's guilty, right?"

Amara frowned. "I'd be careful what I said, if I were you, Tavi. If someone overhears you, you may face prosecution yourself for slander."

"But it's the truth!"

She half-smiled. "Not without the dagger. Without that, it's just a suspicion."

Tavi frowned. "That's stupid."

Amara laughed, a sudden, bright sound. "Yes," she agreed. "But look at it this way. You saved the Valley and who knows how many steadholts beyond it. You're a hero."

Tavi blinked. "Uh. I am?"

Amara nodded, her expression grave. "I filed my report yesterday. The First Lord himself is coming out tomorrow to present several people with rewards for their courage."

Tavi shook his head. "I'm not very courageous. I don't feel like a hero."

Amara's eyes sparkled. "Perhaps you will, later."

Isana walked briskly into the room, wearing fresh clothing and a crisp apron. "Tavi," she said, her tone brisk. "Get back into bed this instant."

Tavi leapt for the covers.

Isana frowned at Bernard. "And you. Bernard, you *know* I told you to make the boy stay in bed."

He grinned, sheepishly. "Oh, right."

Isana stepped over to her brother and touched his temples. "Hmph. Well you're not going to cause chaos in here any longer. Get your lazy bones out of bed and go eat."

Bernard grinned and leaned forward, giving Isana a kiss on the forehead. "Whatever the watercrafter orders."

"Bah. Amara, are you still feeling well? No fever, no nausea?"

Amara shook her head, smiling, and turned her back tactfully when Bernard rose to pull on his trousers and a loose tunic, moving stiffly. "I'm fine, Mistress Isana. You did a wonderful job."

"Good. Now get out. The boy needs to rest."

Bernard smiled and ruffled Tavi's hair. Then he stepped up beside Amara and took her hand. The Cursor blinked and looked down at his hand, then back up at his face. She smiled, and her cheeks flushed with color.

"Oh go on," Isana said, and slapped Bernard's shoulder. He grinned, and the two walked out of the room. They weren't walking very quickly, Tavi noticed. And they walked very close together.

Isana turned to Tavi and put her fingers on his temples, then smiled at him. "How are you feeling?"

"Thirsty, ma'am."

She smiled and refilled his cup. "I was so worried. Tavi, I'm so proud of what you have done. Everyone in the Valley thinks you're quite the young hero."

Tavi blinked at her and sipped at his drink. "Do I . . . you know. Have to do anything? Learn to make speeches or something?"

She laughed and kissed his forehead. "Just rest. You're a brave person, Tavi, and you think about others more than yourself, when hard times come. Always remember who you are." She rose. "There are some visitors coming, but I don't want you to talk to them for very long. Drink your water and then get some more sleep. I'll bring up some food later this evening, when you're ready."

"Yes, ma'am," Tavi said. He watched her walk toward the door, and just before she left, he asked her, "Aunt Isana? Who is Araris Valerian?"

Isana stopped in the doorway, frowning. She drew a breath. "He . . . he was one of the royal guardsmen. One of Princeps Septimus's personal bodyguards. A famous swordsman."

"Did he die with the Princeps?"

She turned to face him and said, very quietly, very firmly, "Yes, Tavi. He died. Fifteen years ago. Do you understand?"

"But—"

"Tavi." Isana sighed. "I need you to trust me. Please, Tavi. Just for a little while."

He swallowed and nodded. "Yes, ma'am."

Isana smiled at him, wearily. "Here are your visitors. Remember, don't talk for too long."

She slipped out. A moment later, Doroga ducked his head to slip beneath the doorway and strode into the room. The huge Marat headman was dressed in his loincloth, together with a cloak with a mantle of thanadent feathers and a garish, pale red tunic. Aleran boots dangled in his belt, though his own feet were bare, and rings decorated every finger. His left arm was in a sling, swollen and discolored, but he seemed in good spirits and smiled at Tavi, moving to his bed and crushing his hand in a friendly, monstrous grip.

Behind him walked Kitai, scowling, dressed in a loin-cloth and wearing an Aleran tunic carelessly stained with food and dirt. Her long, pale hair had been pulled back into a neat braid, revealing the delicate curves of her cheekbones and neck.

"Well, young warrior," Doroga said. "I have paid you back for saving my whelp—"

"Daughter," Kitai interjected. "I am not a whelp any-more, father."

"Daughter," Doroga rumbled, with an expansive smile. "You saved my daughter, and I paid you back for it. But then you saved me as well. I find myself still in your debt."

"I didn't do anything," Tavi said.

"You shouted a warning to me, Tavi," Doroga said. "Without it, I would have died." He squeezed Tavi's shoulders, and Tavi briefly thought something was going to break again. "Thank you."

"But what I did was small. You're the one who did all the big things. You led a horde against another horde, sir. A horde of your own people."

"I set out to repay my debt to you," Doroga said. "Finish what you set out to do. It is part of being a man." Doroga smiled at him and rose. "Kitai."

Kitai scowled.

Doroga frowned at her.

Kitai rolled her eyes and snapped, to Tavi, "Thank you. For saving my life."

Tavi blinked mildly at her. "Um. Sure."

She narrowed her eyes. "Don't think I'm going to forget it, either."

Tavi thought that it sounded a great deal more like a threat than a promise. "Uh. No. I don't think that."

Kitai's scowl deepened, though something around her eyes softened at the words. "I am going to learn to ride a horse," she stated. "If it is all right with you."

"Uh. Sure, whatever. Good, that's great, Kitai." Tavi glanced at Doroga, hopefully.

Doroga rolled his eyes and sighed. Then said, "We should go. Your headman wants to thank me tomorrow, and Kitai should wash her tunic."

Kitai snapped, "Whelps wear tunics. It is foolish to make me wear this one. I don't like it, I don't want it. Why shouldn't I wear what the rest of the Marat women wear?"

"You want to walk around here naked like that?" Tavi demanded. "Are you crazy? Dress like a normal person while you're here."

Doroga abruptly smiled at Tavi, his face stretching into a broad grin. "Good. That is good."

Kitai folded her arms and shot Tavi a look that could have crumbled stones to dust. Tavi sank a bit under the sheets. Kitai made a sound of disgust and stalked out of the room.

Doroga broke into a rumbling laugh and ruffled Tavi's hair in a gesture peculiarly like Uncle Bernard's. "Doomed, young warrior. Doomed. But her mother and I started off that way."

Tavi blinked. "What?"

"We will see one another again." Doroga turned to go.

"*What?*" Tavi said again. "Her mother *what*? Doroga, wait!"

Doroga didn't slow, rumbling out a low laugh as he left the room. "Remember what I said, Tavi. We will speak again."

Tavi settled back on the bed, scowling, folding his arms, pensive. He had the definite impression that he had gotten in over his head, somewhere along the way.

Tavi frowned, pondering. "Finish what I started."

There was a gentle knock at the doorway, and Tavi looked up to see Fade's scarred, homely face smiling in at him from the hall. "Tavi," Fade said, his tone happy.

Tavi smiled. "Hello, Fade. Come in?"

Fade shuffled inside, eyes vacant, carrying a long package of red cloth.

"What's this?" Tavi asked.

"Present," Fade said. "Present, Tavi." He offered the cloth bundle to him.

Tavi reached out to take it and found it heavier than he expected. He lay it on his lap and unwrapped the cloth from around it. The cloth turned out to be one of the scarlet capes from the Princeps' Memorium, and wrapped within it, in an old and travel worn scabbard, was the battered old blade Amara had carried from the Memorium, and that Fade had used upon the wall.

Tavi looked up at Fade, who smiled witlessly at him. "For you."

Tavi frowned. "You don't have to keep up the act, Fade," he said quietly.

For a moment, something glittered in Fade's eyes, above the coward's brand on his cheek. He regarded Tavi in silence for a moment and then gave him a deliberate wink. "For you," he repeated in that same voice, and then turned to go.

Tavi looked up to see a man standing in the doorway. He was tall, broad of shoulder and long of limb. His face did not look much older than his uncle's, but there was something about his faded green eyes that spoke of more years than were evident. Silver streaked his hair, and a heavy cloak of plain, grey fabric covered him except for what his hood revealed of his face.

Fade drew in a sharp breath.

"A princely gift," the man murmured. "Are you sure it is yours to give, slave?"

Fade lifted his chin, and Tavi saw the slave's shoulders straighten. "For Tavi."

The man in the doorway narrowed his eyes, then shrugged his shoulders. "Leave us. I would speak to him alone."

Fade glanced warily back at Tavi and then nodded his head deeply to the stranger. He shuffled out the door after giving Tavi another witless smile, and vanished into the hall.

The stranger shut the door quietly behind Fade and moved to sit down on the bed beside Tavi's, his green eyes never leaving the boy. "Do you know me?"

Tavi shook his head.

The stranger smiled. "My name is Gaius Sextus."

Tavi felt his mouth drop open. He sat up straight, stammering. "Oh. Sir. Sire, I didn't recognize you, I'm sorry."

Gaius held up a gloved hand in a soothing gesture. "No, stay in bed. You need your rest."

"I thought you were coming tomorrow, sire."

"Yes. But I came here incognito this evening."

"Why?"

"I wanted to speak with you, Tavi. It would seem that I am in your debt."

Tavi swallowed. "I was just trying to get my sheep home, sir. That's all I meant to happen, I mean. After that, everything just sort of . . ."

"Got complicated?" Gaius suggested.

Tavi flushed and nodded. "Exactly."

"That's how these things happen. I don't want to keep you up long, so I'll come to the point. I owe you. Name your reward, and you'll have it."

Tavi blinked at the First Lord, his mouth falling open again. "Anything?" he asked.

"Within reason."

"Then I want you to help the holders who got hurt, and the families of those who were killed. Winter's coming on, and it's going to be hard for all of us."

Gaius lifted both eyebrows and tilted his head to one side. "Truly? Given anything to choose from, that is your choice of rewards?"

Tavi felt his jaw set, stubbornly. He met Gaius's eyes with his own, and nodded.

Gaius murmured, "Amazing." The First Lord shook his head. "Very well. I'll have Crown aid dispensed to those who suffered loss on a case-by-case basis by the local Count. Fair enough?"

"Yes, sire. Thank you."

"Let me add one thing more to that, Tavi. My Cursor tells me that you wish to attend the Academy."

Tavi's heart thudded abruptly in his chest. "Yes, sire. More than anything."

"It might be difficult for someone with your . . .

limitations, shall we say? You will be in the company of the sons and daughters of merchants and nobles and wealthy houses from all over Alera. Many of them strong crafters. It may provide you with a great many challenges."

"I don't care," Tavi blurted. "I don't care about that, sire. I can handle myself."

Gaius regarded him for a moment, then nodded. "I believe you can. Then if you will accept it, it will be done. I will give you patronage for your attendance at the Academy and assist you in choosing your fields of study. You will be Academ Tavi Patronus Gaius. Go to the capital. The Academy. See what you can make of your life given a chance, hmm?"

Tavi's head spun, and he felt his eyes fill with tears. He blinked them many times, trying to hide the tears. "Sire. Sire, you don't know what it means to me. Thank you."

Gaius smiled, and the skin at the corners of his eyes crinkled up as he did. "Rest, then. Tomorrow will be all ceremony and display. But please know that you have my gratitude, young man. And my respect."

"Thank you, sire."

Gaius rose and inclined his head. "Thank you, Academ. I'll see you tomorrow."

He left the room, leaving Tavi feeling a little dizzy. The boy lay down on his pillow, staring up at the ceiling, his heart racing. The capital. The Academy. Everything he had wanted. He started to cry and to laugh at the same time, and he hugged himself tightly, because he felt as though if he didn't he might burst.

The First Lord of all Alera had told him thank you. That he would see him tomorrow.

Tavi stilled for a moment, mulling over what had been said to him that day.

"No," he murmured. "There's something I need to do first. Need to finish what I've begun."

◇◇◇◇ CHAPTER 47

Fidelias sank into the warm bath in aching relief, his eyes closing. Nearby, Lady Aquitaine, dressed only in a robe of pale silk, placed Aquitaine's signet dagger into a coffer on her dresser, and shut and locked it.

"And my men?" Fidelias asked.

"All being cared for," she assured him. "I repaired your watercrafter's hearing, and she and her man went to their suite." She half smiled. "They deserve the time, I think."

"I failed," Fidelias said.

"Not entirely," murmured Lady Aquitaine. She tested the temperature of the water, and then lay her fingers on Fidelias's temples. "Without the dagger, Gaius has nothing but suspicions."

"But he knows," Fidelias said. He felt briefly dizzy as a slow wave of warmth pulsed over him. His aches began to vanish into a molten cloud of blessed relief. "He knows. Aquitaine isn't working in secret any longer."

Lady Aquitaine smiled. Then she stepped around the tub and let the silk robe slip from her shoulders. She slid into the water with Fidelias and wrapped her arms around the man's shoulders. "You worry too much."

Fidelias shifted uncomfortably. "Lady. Perhaps I should go. Your husband—"

"Is busy," Lady Aquitaine purred. She gestured, and in the water shapes rose, solid outlines as though dolls upon a tiny stage. There were two figures there, on a great bed in a well-appointed chamber, writhing together in sensual completion, then kissing, slow, heavy kisses.

"There, sweet lady," Aquitaine's voice, tinny and distant murmured. "Are you feeling better?"

"Attis," a young woman's voice whispered, lazily contented. "So strong." She shivered and began to sit up. "I should go."

"Nonsense," Lord Aquitaine said. "He'll be handing out rewards for hours yet. You and I have time for more."

"No," she murmured, "I shouldn't." But Fidelias could hear the excitement in her voice.

"You should," Aquitaine murmured. "There. That's better."

"Such a lover," the woman sighed. "And soon, we can be together like this whenever you desire."

"That's right," Aquitaine said.

"And Lady Aquitaine?" the woman asked.

Lady Aquitaine's lips split in a cool little smile.

"She won't be a problem," Lord Aquitaine said. "No more talking."

Fidelias watched as Gaius Caria, First Lady of Alera,

wrapped her arms around Lord Aquitaine and drew him closer to her.

"You see," Lady Aquitaine purred, letting the images slide away into the water again. "We have more than one knife at his back." She turned to Fidelias, her lips at his ear, and he felt himself begin to respond with slow, ardent hunger. "The story is not yet done."

Gaius Sextus, First Lord of Alera, descended to the Calderon Valley upon a winged steed of pure fire. Around him flew a full Legion of Knights Aeris, five thousand strong, and the Royal Guard in their scarlet capes, Knights Ferro and Ignus, Knights Aqua and Terra and Knights Fauna, all of them of ancient high blood. Trumpets announced their arrival, and despite the vast numbers of men aloft, the air hardly seemed to stir. The First Lord descended on Bernardholt with a full Legion in his train, and the people of the Calderon Valley turned out to meet him.

Amara stood foremost before the crowds, and Gaius dismounted, the stallion of flame vanishing to a wisp of smoke as he did. Amara knelt as he approached her, but he took her hand and raised her to her feet, embracing her with gentle arms. He wore the scarlet and azure of Alera, a blade at his side, and carried himself with pride and strength, though there seemed to be more lines of care worn into the corners of his eyes.

He stood up and looked down at her eyes, smiling. "Amara. Well done."

Amara felt the tears touch her eyes, and she straightened with pride. "Thank you, sire."

The Legion settled behind them like hundreds of

gleaming, deadly dragonflies, and Amara stood a little straighter in her borrowed gown. "Sire, I'll present them to you in the order I discussed in my report?"

Gaius nodded. "Yes. Do. I'm eager to meet them."

Amara called out, "Let Frederic of Bernardholt approach the Crown."

There was a startled gulp from the crowd, and someone pushed the tall, brawny youth up out of the crowd to the general laughter of the holders. Frederic looked around, folding his hands nervously, then sighed and walked forward to Amara and the First Lord. He began to bow, then knelt, then changed his mind and stood up to bow again.

Gaius laughed and took the young man's hand and shook it firmly. "I am given to understand, young man, that you bested not one but two of the mercenary Knights in single combat, armed with only a shovel."

"Spade, sir," Frederic corrected him. Then flushed. "That is, uh. I hit them, yes sire."

"And I am told that in the battle, you defended a door of a building in the east courtyard, protecting the children inside from harm at the hands of the Marat."

"Yes. With my spade, sir. Sire. Sorry."

"Kneel, young man."

Frederic swallowed and did. Gaius drew his sword, and it gleamed in the sun. "For courage, loyalty, and resourcefulness in the face of enemies of the Realm, Frederic of Bernardholt, I do hearby dub thee a Knight of the Realm, with all the responsibility and privileges therein. You are, from this day, a Citizen of the Realm, and let no man dispute your devotion. Rise, Sir Frederic."

Frederic stood up, stunned. "But . . . but all I know

is herding gargants, sir. I don't know about that fighting and whatnot. Sire, sorry."

"Sir Frederic," Gaius intoned, "I wish all of my Knights knew a skill so useful." He smiled and said, "We will discuss, in time, your duties here."

Frederic bowed, clumsily. "Yes, sir. Thank you, sir. Sire. Sir."

Gaius gestured, and Frederic took a few dazed steps to one side.

Amara called, "Let Bernard of Bernardholt come forth."

Bernard, dressed in rich fabrics of brown and woodland green, stepped forward from the crowd and dropped to one knee before Gaius, bowing his head.

Gaius took Bernard's hand and raised him. "I understand you helped take over matters when Gram was injured."

"I only helped, sire," Bernard said. "I did what anyone would have."

"You did what anyone *should* have," Gaius said. "There is a difference. A broad difference. Steadholder, your courage in the face of such overwhelming danger is not overlooked."

Once again, Gaius tapped his sword to either shoulder. "By the authority of the Crown, I do hereby dub thee Bernard, Count of Calderon."

Bernard's head snapped up, and he blinked.

Gaius smiled. "With all the responsibility and privileges therein, and so on. Rise, good Count."

Bernard stood up, staring at Gaius. "But Gram is the Count here."

"Gram is now a Lord, I'm afraid, your Excellency."

Gaius lowered his voice with a glance around. "He has a comfortable assignment in the Amaranth Vale now, while he recovers from his injuries. I need someone who the local people respect and who I can trust to take over for him. Also someone who the Marat will respect. You're it."

Bernard's face slowly spread into a smile. "Thank you, sire. I'll . . . do my best not to disappoint you."

"You won't," Gaius said. "We'll need to keep in close touch at first." The First Lord glanced aside at Amara and said, "I will have to appoint a special courier to be our go-between. I'll see if I can find someone willing to come all the way out here."

Bernard flushed, and Amara felt her own face heating at the same time.

"Thank you, sire," Bernard said, more quietly.

Gaius winked. He gestured, and Count Bernard stepped to his left side, to stand with Sir Frederic.

Amara smiled and said, "Doroga, of the Gargant Clan of the Marat. Step forward."

The crowd parted for the giant of a man, and Doroga strode over to Gaius, decked in gewgaws and rich clothing, which holders and *legionares* had given to him. He put his fists on his hips and looked Gaius up and down, then declared, "You aren't old enough to be a headman."

Gaius laughed, the sound rich and rolling. "I look young for my age."

Doroga nodded wisely. "Ah. Perhaps that is it."

"I am here to thank you, Headman Doroga, for what you did for my Realm."

"I didn't do it for your Realm," Doroga said. "I did it

for the young warrior. And would do it again." Doroga lifted a finger and poked it lightly at Gaius's chest. "You be good to him. Or you and I will have words."

Amara stared at the barbarian, appalled, but Gaius oniy tilted his head to one side, his lips quivering with the effort to restrain laughter. Then he took a step back and bowed to Doroga, to a sudden murmur from the Legion and the holders. "I will do so. Name me a boon, and if it is within my power, I will grant it to you."

"I owe favors to enough people already." Doroga sighed. "We done?"

"I think so, yes."

"Good." Doroga turned and let out a piercing whistle, and from around the hill came a sullen young Marat girl on an enormous black bull gargant. Doroga walked over to her, swung up onto the great beast's back, and nodded to Gaius before turning to ride away.

"Colorful," Gaius commented.

"I'm sorry, sire. I didn't know that he would—"

"Oh, no, Cursor. It's perfectly all right. Who is next?"

They ran through a number of *legionares* and holders who had performed bravely during the incident, including a stammering Pluvus Pentius, who had saved a handful of children from a wounded herdbane by clubbing it to death with his accounts ledger.

"Isana of Bernardholt," Amara called, finally. "Please step forward."

Isana came forward in a gown of dark grey, her dark hair pulled back into a severe braid, her chin lifted. She walked forward and stopped before Gaius for a long moment before performing a deep and graceful curtsy to him, without lowering her eyes. Amara saw something cold there, something defiant, and she blinked at the hold woman.

Gaius remained silent for a long moment, studying Isana. Finally he said, in a very quiet voice, "I understand that your courage and bravery saved a great many lives."

"There was only one I was truly concerned with, sire."

Gaius drew in a slow breath and nodded. "The boy. Your—"

"Nephew, sire."

"Nephew. Of course." Gaius glanced aside, at Amara. "And I am told you have ownership of a slave who likewise performed above and beyond anything expected of him."

Isana inclined her head again.

"I will purchase this slave from you."

Isana looked up at Gaius, her expression strained. "I'm sure he isn't what you think, sire."

"Let me be the judge of that. In the meanwhile, Isana, please kneel."

Isana did, her expression puzzled. Gaius once more drew his blade. "I dub thee Steadholder Isana, with all the responsibilities and privileges therein."

There was a second's silence, and then a shocked murmur from the crowd of holders and from the legions behind Gaius.

Gaius murmured, "The first appointed female Steadholder. Isanaholt. It has a nice ring to it, doesn't it?"

Isana flushed. "It does, sire."

"And your brother is going to be busy with his new duties. Someone needs to assume control. I see no reason anyone could object to you. Rise, Steadholder."

Amara smiled, as Isana stepped aside. "Tavi of Bernardholt, please step forward."

There was an eager murmur from the crowd.

But no one stepped forward.

Amara frowned. "Tavi of Bernardholt. Please step forward."

Still, no one did. Gaius arched an eyebrow, and Amara shot a helpless look at Isana. Isana closed her eyes and sighed. "That boy."

Gaius said, "Are you sure he wanted this reward, Cursor?"

"Yes, sire," Amara said. "He told me he was trying to return some sheep, so that he could use them to help him save some money for a semester at the Academy. That's why he stumbled onto things to begin with."

"I'm not offering him a semester. I'm offering him patronage. He should be here."

Isana blinked at Gaius. "Patronage? To the Academy? My Tavi?"

"The finest center of learning in all of Carna," Gaius said. "He can study there. Grow. Learn all that he needs to lead a successful life."

Isana said, "He doesn't need the Academy for that."

"Yet that is his wish, Steadholder Isana. And that is his reward. He will be Tavi Patronus Gaius and be trained at the Academy."

Isana nodded and said, "Yes, sire," but her expression was worried.

Bernard frowned, looking around for a moment. Then pointed and said, "Sire. There he is."

Everyone turned to look to the north of Bernardholt.

After a moment's silence, Gaius asked, "That is this Fade, with him?"

Amara nodded. "Yes, sire."

Gaius frowned. "I see. Cursor, why wasn't the boy here?"

"He, um. He seems to be rather independently minded, sire."

"I see. And why is he doing that, instead of accepting his reward."

Amara fought to keep a smile off of her lips. "Sire. He's a shepherd's apprentice. I suppose he's doing that because it's what he set out to do."

And so the First Lord of Alera, surrounded by subjects, Citizens, and Knights of the Realm watched in silence while Tavi drove home Dodger's little flock of ewes and lambs, the shaggy-haired Fade loping along behind him.

THE DRESDEN FILES

Wizards are cool.

I mean, come on. When it comes to fantasy, you can't swing a cat without hitting a wizard somewhere, striding through the shadows and wars of epic battles of light and darkness, uncovering lost knowledge, protecting, inspiring, and guiding others toward the future. Merlin, Gandalf, Allannon, Dalben, Belgarath, Raistlin, Goblin, and One-Eye—and their darker counterparts like Morgana, Arawn, Soulcatcher, and Saruman. Wizards wield secrets as warriors do swords, driven by a vision that lets them see and know more than mere mortals, gifted with a power that makes them treasured allies—and terrifying foes. Throughout fantasy fiction, when the need is most dire it is the wizard who stands to face balrogs and dragons, dark spirits and fearsome beasts, natural catastrophes and dark gods.

Harry Blackstone Copperfield Dresden, wizard for hire, is happy if he manages to pay the rent for another month. He's in the Chicago Yellow Pages, under "Wizards." He's the only entry there. Most people think he is some kind of harmless nutball at best, and a charlatan-psychic at worst.

But then, most people haven't seen what Harry's seen. Most people don't know the truth: that the supernatural is perfectly real, existing quietly side by side with most of humanity's perceptions of reality. Trolls lurk under bridges, and faeries swoop down to kidnap children. Vampires prowl the shadows by night, restless ghosts rise up from the darkness of the grave, and demons and monsters to boggle the mind lurk in the shadows, ready to devour, maim, and destroy.

A few people know the truth, of course. Wizards such as Harry know. So do a few of the cops, like Lt. Karrin Murphy, head of Chicago P.D.'s Special Investigations division, who knows the touch of the supernatural when she sees it, and who hires Chicago's only professional wizard to come in as a consultant when an investigation begins to look like an episode of *The X-Files*.

And other people learn the truth the hard way, when something out of a bad dream shows up at the front door. For those poor mortals, the supernatural becomes a sudden, impossible, terrifying nightmare come true—a nightmare no one can help them wake up from.

No one but Harry Dresden, that is. Hauntings, disappearances, missing persons, murders, curses, monsters— you name it, and Harry knows something about it. More than that, he shares the convictions of his literary ancestors—a deep and genuine commitment to use his power to protect those who cannot protect themselves, to stand between the darkest beings of the supernatural and his fellow man.

When the need is most dire, when the night is most

deadly, when no one else can help you, give Harry Dresden a call.

He's in the book.

**Jim Butcher's newest Harry Dresden novel,
Changes, is now available in paperback from Roc.**

Stay tuned for a special look at

BURNING ALIVE
BOOK ONE OF THE SENTINEL WARS

by Shannon K. Butcher

Available now from Onyx!

Helen's front window blasted into the living room. A splinter of glass sliced across her cheek, but she barely noticed. Her attention was fixed on the monster standing in the middle of her living room. It was vaguely wolflike, but twice as big. Its muzzle was all wrong, though. It had the wide jaw of a shark and was filled with rows of serrated teeth. Where its eyes should have been were empty black holes surrounded by singed flesh, as if they'd been burned out of its head with a hot poker. Rust-colored fur covered its body and it shook off bits of broken glass like a dog did raindrops.

Blood trickled down her cheek and the thing swiveled its head around and stared at her with those empty black holes. Even without eyes, she was sure it could see her.

Helen screamed.

She was still standing partly in the hall and saw Thomas rush by from the kitchen with a gleaming sword in his hands. His big body blocked her from the monster's sight, giving her a chance to pull herself together.

"Out of the way!" shouted Drake from behind her, and she pressed herself against the wall to allow him and Logan room to pass.

Drake also wielded a sword—a big heavy one that

had to have been longer than her arm. He leapt past her just as a second monster jumped in through the shattered window. Drake stepped to his right so that he was between it and her. The thing stared past him, looking right at her with empty sockets. It bared its shark teeth and let out a rattling hiss that froze her in place.

"Time to go," ordered Logan. He grabbed her arm and started tugging her down the stairs toward the front door.

"Miss Mabel! We can't leave her behind."

Helen jerked away from his grasp and saw Miss Mabel rising unsteadily from a kitchen chair. She ran to the older woman's side to help her up. There was a door leading out to the deck, but it was a whole flight of stairs down to the backyard. Miss Mabel would never make it in time and Helen wasn't strong enough to carry her.

Before she could yell for help, another monster slammed into the glass of the back door, trying to break it, and it no longer mattered. They were trapped.

Logan was there by her side again. "I'll get her. You get yourself out of here."

Helen nodded. Logan lifted Miss Mabel into his arms, surprising her with his strength. He was too thin to lift her that easily, but Helen wasn't complaining.

The monster flung its body against the glass again, and this time the frame around the door splintered. The door banged open and the monster stepped inside on silent paws.

"Go. Now!" shouted Logan.

Helen picked up one of the nearby fire extinguishers and pulled the pin. "You first."

"Like hell," said Logan. "Drake! Kitchen!" he bellowed.

The monster sniffed the air, and once again she was on the receiving end of an eyeless stare. It was only eight feet away and looked like it wanted to come closer.

Helen aimed the fire extinguisher and pulled the trigger. Yellow powder spewed out, hitting the thing right in the face. It let out a roar of pain, opening its shark mouth wide.

Drake ran into the kitchen and she saw something oily and black dripping down the blade of his sword. He stepped in front of them, facing the monster. His shoulders were wide, the muscles in his back and arms coiled and ready to strike. He wasn't frightened or breathing hard like she was. In fact, he looked like this was just another normal day for him. Get up. Go to work. Kill some monsters. Go home. No big thing.

The monster prowled forward but Drake held his ground. "Get her out of here."

Logan had no free hands to grab her, but Miss Mabel did. She clutched the strap of Helen's tank top in her bony hand and didn't let go so that Helen had to either follow along or risk hurting Miss Mabel. Logan headed for the front door, but through the narrow sidelight windows, Helen could see at least three more of the monsters sniffing around, looking for a way in.

They weren't going to make it out of here. No way.

"We'll go out through the garage," Logan told her. "My van is just outside and the keys are in the ignition. If you can get out, don't wait for the rest of us. Just go."

"I won't leave you all behind." Helen grabbed her purse from the table by the door.

"We know how to take care of ourselves. If you stay, you'll just get in the way."

Before she had a chance to respond, the wooden door that led into her garage shuddered under the weight of an assault. They weren't getting out this way, either.

"Any more exits?" asked Logan.

"Just through the bedroom windows."

"How far up are they?"

"Eight or ten feet, maybe."

Logan glanced down at Miss Mabel. "That's not going to work."

"Don't you dare stay behind for me," said Miss Mabel. "I've had a good run. Just give me one of those fire extinguishers and I'll hold them off so you can get out."

Helen's heart broke a little in the face of Miss Mabel's selfless courage. She thought that because she was old, her life was of less value than the others'. For all Helen knew, Miss Mabel had a lot more years to live than she did. "Not going to happen," replied Helen. "We're all going to get out of here."

"New plan," said Logan. "You two will hole up in the bathroom until we can clear a path."

There were no windows in her hall bathroom—no way for the monsters to get in except for the door. It sounded like a good idea to her. Helen nodded, slung her purse strap over her neck, and picked up a fire extinguisher.

As they passed by the front door, one of the monsters lunged into it. The thin metal sheath around the insulating core buckled, leaving a lump in the door about waist high. Helen yelped and scrambled up the stairs, nearly running into Thomas, who was holding off one of the beasts.

Three furry bodies lay crumpled on her carpet, leaking black blood. A fourth monster leapt for Thomas's throat and he sliced at it with his heavy blade. He scored a thin line along its chest, but the thing kept coming. Drake had killed another two monsters in the kitchen and a third one scrambled over the pile of his fallen brothers in order to swipe a claw at Drake's face.

Helen's throat closed down on a scream and her body went tight. *Please, God, don't let him get hurt.*

Drake dodged the strike, his sword flashed, and the monster's severed paw hit the kitchen wall, bouncing off. Oily blood sprayed across Helen's oak cabinets and it was all she could do not to vomit. She would never be able to cook in this kitchen again. Hell, she'd never be able to walk into this house again. Assuming she was able to get out of it alive.

The monster Drake had maimed let out a scream that sounded almost human. Chills raced over her limbs and her body froze in place. Which was probably for the best because at that moment Thomas took a long step back. He ducked below a furry body, shoved his sword into its belly, and stood up, hurling it over her head and down the hall with a massive burst of strength. He came only inches from knocking her over.

The monster lay sprawled in the hall, unmoving, soaking the carpet with its blood and . . . something else leaking out of its wounded abdomen.

Now all five of them were gathered at the top of the stairs where the hall, living room, and kitchen all met. There were monsters pounding at the front door, nearly through it, and more were climbing in the broken back door and front window, crawling over the dead bodies.

"We need an exit," said Logan in a calm, even tone.

"Working on it," said Thomas.

Drake kept his eyes on the approaching monster who was struggling to climb over the slippery bodies of the dead. "We've got maybe two minutes until the Handlers show up. Then things are going to get ugly."

Get ugly? She didn't know what he was looking at, but from where she was standing, surrounded by dead monsters leaking black blood all over her carpet and kitchen, she'd never seen anything uglier. She didn't even want to think about something uglier.

She felt panic start to set in now that she wasn't moving, and she had to fight it down with a force of will. She couldn't afford to lose it until she got Miss Mabel away safely.

"Van's in front," said Logan. "We won't make it out on foot with humans along."

"Thomas?" asked Drake.

"I'm on it," replied Thomas.

"How long do you need?" asked Drake.

Helen had no idea what they were talking about, but she didn't stop them to ask questions. The metal sheet on the inside of the front door was ripping open a little more with every thud. She could see a wide set of furry jaws snapping at her through the crack. No way was she going to distract them from making sure those shark teeth didn't get to her and Miss Mabel.

Thomas stepped forward to meet the monster that had just made it over the pile, hissing and pawing at the furry bodies. "Sixty seconds," was the answer to Drake's question.

"You got them." With that, Drake and Thomas both whirled into action, their powerful bodies making quick work of the remaining monsters. She'd never seen anything so beautiful, so deadly, as the two of them wielding their swords.

With one hand, Drake lifted Helen's kitchen table over the pile of dead bodies and used it to cover the hole where the back door used to be. He braced his left hand against it, holding it in place while he kept his sword in his right hand, ready to strike. He looked at Helen and gave her a reassuring smile and a wink. "Follow Logan out. He'll get you to the van."

"I don't want to leave you."

"You're not. I'll be right behind you. Now go!"

Helen felt a tug on her shirt—Miss Mabel's fingers around the strap of her tank top again—and followed along behind Logan. Thomas had gone berserk and was slashing through monster after monster as if he were cutting down wheat. As soon as one came scrambling through the window, he sliced it open or sent it flying. Sweat darkened his hair and made his shirt cling to his back.

Logan led her over the dead bodies and she tried not to think about the feel of the fur on her bare leg or the squish of blood under her feet. Thomas was through the front window and Helen briefly wondered whether her neighbors were watching this whole show. Not that she cared. As long as they all got out of this alive, she'd figure out something to tell them. Attack by wild dogs, maybe. She wasn't going to continue to live here, anyway. Not after tonight. Let the neighbors think what they want.

Logan cleared the remaining shards of glass away from the window frame with his booted foot and hopped down. She wasn't sure how Thomas did it, but he managed to keep his sword between them and every monster that came after them. And there were a lot. She didn't stop to count, but Thomas had already killed a bunch and there were at least four more coming for them. They'd abandoned the idea of getting in the front door as soon as they'd seen Thomas jump out into the front yard. For a big guy, he was fast and he used that bulk to push forward, clearing them a path to the van sitting in her driveway.

Miss Mabel had lost her hold on Helen's shirt somewhere along the way and she and Logan were a few feet in front of her. Helen jumped out of the window and looked over her shoulder, hoping to see Drake right behind her. Instead, she saw his body fly out of the kitchen, followed closely by her kitchen table. He hit the railing at the top of the stairs, nearly spilling over it. His body crumpled to the floor and the kitchen table slammed into him, pinning him there. Then nothing moved. He didn't get up.

Frantic, Helen lifted herself back up into the window, feeling a bit of glass slice into her palms, and scrambled over the bodies to reach him. He was big, but she could drag him out. It was only a few feet. She could do it.

Helen shoved the table off him and he let out a groan. His eyes fluttered open and he shook his head as if to clear it. It only took a couple of seconds for him to become coherent again, and when he did, he looked pissed.

He opened his mouth to say something to her, but then his gaze slid past her and Helen turned her head to see what he was looking at.

It was tall, easily seven feet tall. It walked upright like a human, but it wasn't even close to being human. The thing's head was too large, missing a nose and lips to cover the openings in its skull. Pointed teeth gleamed and dripped saliva. Its legs bent the wrong way. Its skin was snow white, completely hairless, and for clothing, it wore a cloak made out of the rust-colored fur of the monsters. In one hand it held a whip made from fine chain links and in the other it held a red-hot metal rod three feet long. Little wisps of flames danced up from the tip of the rod.

Fire. *Oh God, no.*

She felt her muscles lock up with terror. The thing stepped forward on oddly jointed legs, appearing to be in no hurry.

Drake shifted his grip on his sword and pushed himself to his knees. She heard him stifle a gasp of pain and wanted to reach out to him, but couldn't. She couldn't move. Couldn't think.

The thing cracked the whip, hitting the railing next to Drake's shoulder. The wood burst into flames and even from three feet away, Helen could still feel the deadly heat. The railing needed no time to catch fire; it just went up in a blaze, spreading faster than normal fire ever could. But then, this was not normal.

Drake was still trying to gain his feet. The thigh of his jeans was soaked with blood and she could see a sharp spike of bone sticking partially through the tough fabric. His leg was badly broken. There was no way he was going to be able to stand on it, much less fight.

She wanted to tell him that, but her throat was closed tight—too tight to speak, too tight to breathe.

The thing lifted the glowing rod and pointed it toward Helen.

"No!" shouted Drake. Somewhere, he found the

strength to jump to his feet and lunge at the thing. His sword sliced high, taking off the arm that held the rod.

Fire erupted from the place where its arm used to be. Drake threw his body over hers, knocking her to the ground beneath him.

Helen felt a blast of heat and sound, but could see nothing. Her face was buried in the greasy fur of one of the dead monsters and the heavy animal stench of it made her sick. She could feel the cold squish of blood under her knees and Drake's heavy weight atop her.

Drake's body stiffened and he let out a deep groan of pain that got louder and louder until it turned into a scream. Then he fell silent and limp atop her.

The heat abated and Drake's weight disappeared. Helen pushed herself up to scramble to her feet. All she wanted was to shove her shoulder under Drake's and help him get out of here, broken leg or not.

But it was too late.

Logan had been the one who picked him up off her, and now she could see the burns running down the right side of Drake's body. His hair and some of his clothes had been burned away, revealing blistered flesh beneath. Some beyond blistered to blackened.

Logan's too-pretty face became a mask of grief and pain, and Helen knew then that even if Drake was alive, he wouldn't be for long.

Drake had used his body to shield her from that fire and now he was going to die.

Logan had to get Helen out of here before another Handler showed up or before the fire near the stairway started burning out of control. Drake had killed the

Handler, though Logan had no idea how he'd gotten close enough to manage that. Handlers were frail, but they rarely got closer than they needed to strike out with their whip. That was usually close enough for them to kill something. Even if it wasn't, the fire their bodies bled when injured burned hot enough and fast enough to take down anything unlucky enough to be in its path.

Thomas made sure the Handler was dead while Logan pulled Drake off Helen. He didn't like leaving Miss Mabel in the van unprotected, but Helen was the one who was important here. He had to figure out how she'd been able to absorb Drake's power. It could be the key to stopping the slow death of all the Sentinel races. The key to winning the Synestryn war.

Logan took in Drake's injuries in a sweeping glance. The broken leg and ribs were no problem, but the burns . . . Drake wasn't going to make it, not even if Logan put every ounce of his dwindling reserves into healing the Theronai. He just didn't have the strength. He'd fed tonight, but the bloodline had been weak and it hadn't even managed to ease his gnawing hunger, much less fuel his magic. Walking Helen's and Drake's memories had taken enough out of him that it was as if he hadn't fed at all.

It was so fucking unfair that Logan wanted to howl. To have the ability to heal his ally but not the strength made him furious—made him want to lash out and drain every blooded human he could find. Take their power and leave their corpses to rot. Why should he even care anymore what happened to the humans?

Thomas's wide shoulders blocked out the overhead light, forcing Logan to look up. This was the part he hated most—admitting his weakness, crushing Drake's friends with the weight of grief. Living with that weight himself.

"How bad is it?" asked Thomas, his deep voice thick with rage.

Logan just shook his head. "I can ease his pain. It won't last long."

"No," said Helen. Her voice was thin and high and breathless. Almost panicked. "He's not going to die."

Denial. It always happened and Logan hated every fucking second of it. "I'm sorry, Helen."

"You don't understand. He can't die. He has to watch *me* die."

Logan had no idea what she was talking about, but something in her words tugged at a memory.

"We don't have time for this now," said Thomas. "We have to get out of here."

Logan picked up Drake's heavy body, being careful to avoid getting cut by Drake's sword. The flames had seared his fist closed, locking the weapon in his grip. Thomas took Helen by the arm. Behind them, Helen's house was swiftly being engulfed by flames. Thankfully, she was too worried over Drake to really notice. A small favor.

Sirens screamed in the distance. The human authorities were coming. It was time to go.

They laid Drake in the back of the van on a clean white blanket. He didn't even groan. The stench of burning flesh stung Logan's nose and made his empty stomach twist with nausea.

Helen scrambled in behind him and reached for

Drake, but Logan stopped her. "Don't touch him. He has enough pain as it is."

Helen swallowed hard and nodded. Tears welled up and slid down her dirty cheeks.

THE CODEX ALERA SERIES BY
JIM BUTCHER
**#1 *New York Times* Bestselling Author
of the Dresden Files Novels**

"Sharp, fast moving, full of deadly
dangers and double-dealing."
—Simon R. Green, *New York Times* bestselling author

"Few writers balance military realism and cinematic
swashbuckling with so much skill or wit."
—*Publishers Weekly*

Book One: Furies of Calderon

Book Two: Academ's Fury

Book Three: Cursor's Fury

Book Four: Captain's Fury

Book Five: Princeps' Fury

Book Six: First Lord's Fury

M319AS0709

THE DRESDEN FILES

The #1 *New York Times* bestselling series

by Jim Butcher

"Think *Buffy the Vampire Slayer* starring Philip Marlowe." —*Entertainment Weekly*

STORM FRONT

FOOL MOON

GRAVE PERIL

SUMMER KNIGHT

DEATH MASKS

BLOOD RITES

DEAD BEAT

PROVEN GUILTY

WHITE NIGHT

SMALL FAVOR

TURN COAT

Available wherever books are sold or at penguin.com

M329JV0709